£1

The Ships of Merior

By the same author

Janny Wurts

THE SHIPS OF MERIOR

The Wars of Light and Shadows:
VOLUME 2

HarperCollins*Publishers*

HarperCollins*Publishers*
77–85 Fulham Palace Road
Hammersmith, London W6 8JB

Published by HarperCollins*Publishers* 1994
1 3 5 7 9 8 6 4 2

A catalogue record for this book
is available from the British Library

ISBN 0 00 224078 5

Photoset in Linotron Trump Mediaeval by
Rowland Phototypesetting Ltd, Bury St Edmunds, Suffolk

Printed in Great Britain by
HarperCollinsManufacturing Glasgow

Acknowledgments

Thanks go to Mike Floerkey, Suzanne Parnell, Peita Pentram:
for early warning on missed plot points;
and to David Bell, Mickey Zucker Reichert, Mike Freeman,
Perry Lee, and Steve and Martha Mollet:
for practical angles on some research that went beyond mere books;
Deanne Miller, for back-up support;
Jeffrey Watson, for scanning the old glossary;
And for my longsuffering editors, for letting the project take
its own path:
Jane Johnson, John Silbersack, Christopher Schelling.

Athera
Continent of Paravia

Age of the Mistwraithe

North Ward
Grimwood
Fallowmere
East Ward
ain of Araithe
Perlorin
Riverpoint
Crescent Isle
Sterra
Valleygap
athain
Durhling
Minderl Bay
Earl Rocks
Ithilt
amon
Eastwall
Shand Mountains
Minderl Ruin
Minderl Strait
Severnir River
Ithanon
Highscarp
Saint's Point
East Gate
Adhir Ruins
arrens
Shelseng
Vaelot
Vaststrait
Rockfell
Bay of Eltair
Northstor
sport
Tharidor
Whitehold
Farsee
Varens
Eastair
Tirans
Perdith
Atwood
Tirans Ruins
Ailain
East Halla
idhatla
Alestron
Kalesh
Mountains
Adruin
iac
Mirthlvain Swamp
Orvandir
Durn
Methisle
Methlas Lake
Ishlir
Ganish
Six Towers
Eissine
Shand
Archer
Asland
Telzen
Scimlade Tip
Merior
River Ippash
Selkwood
Sickle Bay
Sheddorn
rton
Forthmark
Southshire
Innish
Desert of Sanpashir
lidhatla
Ishish
Ruins
Sanshevas

Cildein Ocean

Los Lier

South Sea

Scale in Leagues
0 10 25 50 100

KEY	
Sorcerers' Preserve	
Cities	
Second Age ruins	
City that did not fall in uprising	
Worldsend Gates	
Standing Stones	
Kingdom Borders	
Rivers	
Forests	
Marshes or Mires	
Wastelands	
Second Age Roads	
Trade Roads	
Mountains	

© 1989 Janny Wurts

N

To my husband,
Don Maitz,
with all my love;
for understanding of desperate, long deadlines
above and beyond the call of duty.
This one's for you.

Contents

Two princes, dark and fair
Cursed by the Mistwraith, Desh-thiere
Hate bound them
Blood crowned them
'Til cold death, war must hound them:
Vie for the shadows and the light
Die blind in shadows, burned in light
Cry, 'Down the shadows, hail the light!'

verse from a children's game
Fourth Age 1220

I. MISCREANT

On the morning the Fellowship sorcerer who had crowned the King at Ostermere fared northward on the old disused road, the five years of peace precariously re-established since the carnage that followed the Mistwraith's defeat as yet showed no sign of breaking.

The moment seemed unlikely for happenstance to intrude and shape a spiralling succession of events to upend loyalties and kingdoms. Havish's coastal landscape with its jagged, shady valleys wore the mottled greens of late spring. Dew still spangled the leaf-tips, touched brilliant by early sunlight. Asandir rode in his shirtsleeves, the dark, silver-banded mantle lately worn for the royal coronation folded inside his saddle pack. Hair of the same fine silver blew uncovered in the gusts that whipped off the sea; that tossed the clumped bracken on the hill crests and fanned gorse against lichened outcrops of quartz rock. The black stud who bore him strode hock-deep in grass, alone beneath cloudless sky. Wildflowers thrashed by its passage sweetened the air with perfume and the jagging flight of disturbed bees.

For the first time in centuries of service, Asandir was solitary, and on an errand of no pressing urgency. The ruthless war, the upsets to rule and to trade that had savaged the north in the wake of the Mistwraith's imprisonment had settled, if not into the well-governed order secured for Havish, then at least into patterns that confined latent hatreds to the avenues of statecraft and politics. Better than most, Asandir knew the respite was fated not to last. His memories were bitter and hurtful, of the great curse cast by the Mistwraith to set both its captors at odds; the land's restoration to clear sky bought at a cost of two mortal destinies and the land's lasting peace.

Unless the Fellowship sorcerers could find means to break Desh-thiere's geas of hatred against the royal half-brothers whose gifts

1

brought its bane, the freed sunlight that warmed the growing earth could yet be paid for in blood. With the restored throne of Havish firmly under its crowned heir, Asandir at last rode to join his colleagues in their effort to unbind the Mistwraith's two victims from the vicious throes of its vengeance.

Relaxed in rare contentment, too recently delivered from centuries of sunless damp to take the hale spring earth for granted, he let his spirit soar with the winds. The road he had chosen was years overgrown, little more than a crease that meandered through thorn and brushbrake to re-emerge where the growth was browsed close by deer. Despite the banished mists, the townsmen still held uneasy fears of open spaces, once the sites of forgotten mysteries. Northbound travellers innately preferred to book their passage by ship.

Untroubled by the after-presence of Paravian spirits, not at all disturbed by the foundations of ancient ruins that underlay the hammocks of wild roses, the sorcerer rode with his reins looped. He followed the way without misstep, guided by memories that predated the most weathered, broken wall. His appearance of reverie was deceptive. At each turn, his mage-heightened senses resonated with the natural energies that surrounded him. The sun on his shoulders became a benediction, both counterpoint and celebration to the ringing reverberation that was light striking shadow off edges of wild stone.

When a dissonance snagged in the weave, reflex and habit snapped Asandir's complaisance. His powers of perception tightened to trace the immediate cause.

Whatever bad news approached from the south, his mount's wary senses caught no sign. The stallion snorted, shook out his mane, and let Asandir rein him over to the verge of the trail. Long minutes later, a drum roll of galloping hooves startled the larks to songless flight. When the messenger on his labouring mount hove into view, the sorcerer sat his saddle, frowning; while the stud, bored with waiting, cropped grass.

The courier wore royal colours, the distinctive scarlet tabard and gold hawk blazon of the king's personal service snapped into creases against the breeze. No common message bearer, he owned the carriage of a champion fighter. But the battle-brash courage that graced his reputation was missing as he hauled his horse to a prancing, head-shaking halt.

The man was a fool, who eagerly brought trouble to the ear of a Fellowship sorcerer.

Briskly annoyed, Asandir spoke before the king's rider could master his uncertainty. 'I know you were sent by your liege. If my spellbinder Dakar is cause and root of some problem, I say now, as I told his Majesty and the realm's steward on my departure: there is no possible difficulty that might stem from an apprentice's misdeeds that your High King's justice cannot handle.'

The messenger nursed lathered reins to divert his eye-rolling mount from her sidewards crabsteps through the bracken. 'Begging pardon, Sorcerer. But Dakar got himself drunk. There was a fight.' Sweating pale before Asandir's displeasure, he finished in a crisp rush. 'Your spellbinder's got himself knifed and King Eldir's healers say he'll bleed to death.'

'Oh, indeed?' The words bit the quiet like sheared metal. Asandir's brows cocked up. Features laced over with creases showed a moment of fierce surprise. Then he started his black up from a mouthful of grass and spun him thundering back toward the city.

Alone in the derelict roadway on a sidling, race-bred horse, the royal courier had no mind to linger. He was not clan kindred, to feel at ease in the wild places where the old stones lay carved with uncanny patterns to snag and bewitch a man's thoughts. The instant his over-strung mare quit her tussle with the bit, he nursed her along at a trot, relieved to be spared the company of a sorcerer any right-thinking mortal knew better than to presume not to fear.

The city known as the jewel of the southwest coast flung an ungainly sprawl of battlements across the crown of a cove. Built over warrens of limestone caves once used as a smuggler's haven, the architecture reflected twelve centuries of changing tastes, battered as much by storms as by war, and bearing like layers in sediment the mismatched masonry of refortifications and repairs. Sea trade provided the marrow of Ostermere's wealth. Walls of tawny brick abutted bulwarks of native limestone, scabrous with moss and smothered in lee-facing crannies by salt-stunted runners of wild ivy. The whole overlooked a series of weathered ledges that commanded a west-facing inlet, each tier crusted with half-timber shops and slate-roofed mansions still gay with bunting and gold streamers from celebration of the king's accession. If the merchant galleys docked along the seaside gates no longer flew banners at their mastheads, if the guards by the harbourmaster's office had shed ceremonial accoutrements for boiled leather hauberks and plain steel, a charge of excitement yet lingered.

In all the realm, this city had been honoured as the royal seat until the walls at Telmandir could be raised out of ruin and restored to the splendours of years past. An alertness like frost clung to the men hand-picked for the royal guard. Out of pride for their youthful sovereign, they had the unused north postern winched open and the shanty market that encroached upon its bailey cleared of beggars and squatters' stalls when Asandir's stallion clattered through.

In a courtyard still gloomy under overhanging tenements, the sorcerer dismounted. He tossed his reins to a barefoot boy groom grown familiar with the stud through the months of change as town governance had been replaced by sovereign monarchy. Without pause for greeting,

Asandir strode off, scattering geese and a loose pig from the puddled run-off by the wash house. He dodged through men in sweaty tunics who unloaded tuns from an ale dray, avoided a bucket-bearing scullion and crossed without mishap through the tumbling brown melee of a deer-hound bitch's cavorting pups.

Just arrived, all but brushed aside with the same brisk lack of ceremony, the captain of Ostermere's garrison pumped on fat legs to join the sorcerer. A capricious gust snatched his unbelted surcoat. Clutching scarlet broadcloth with both hands to escape getting muffled by his clothing, he relayed facts with a directness at odds with his untidy turnout.

'It was a damnfool accident, the Mad Prophet so drunken he could barely stand upright. He'd visited the kitchens to meet a maid he claimed he'd an assignation with. Muddled as he was, he kissed the wrong doxy. Her husband came in at just the right time to lose his temper.' The city captain gave a one-handed shrug, his brows beetled over his beefy nose. 'The knife was handy on the butcher's block, and the wound—'

Asandir cut him off. 'The details won't matter.' He reached the servants' postern, flung it open fast enough to whistle air, and added, 'Your gate guards are missing their gold buttons.'

Ostermere's ranking captain swore. An unlikely, swordsman's agility allowed him to nip through the fast-closing panel. 'The meatbrains got themselves fleeced at dice. Not a man of them will own up, but since you ask, there were bystanders who fingered Dakar as the instigator.'

'I thought so.' Light through an ancient arrow-slit sliced across Asandir's shoulders as he traversed the corridor behind the pantries and began in long strides to climb stairs. Instructions trailed echoing behind him. 'Inform your royal liege I'm here. Ask if he'll please attend me at once in Dakar's bedchamber.'

Dismissed with one foot raised to mount an empty landing, the city captain spun about. 'Ask my liege, indeed! I know a command when I hear one. And I'd beg on my knees for Dharkaron Avenger's own judgement before I'd shift places with Dakar.'

From far above, Asandir's voice cracked back in crisp reverberation. 'For the Mad Prophet's transgressions this time, Dharkaron's judgement would be too merciful.'

High-browed, intelligent, and shrewdly even-tempered for a lad of eighteen years, King Eldir arrived in a state of disarray as striking as his ranking captain's. Swiping back tousled brown hair, sweat-damp from a running ascent of several flights of tower stairs, he heaved off cloak, sash and tabard, and shed a gold-trimmed load of state velvets without apology onto a bench in a lover's nook. In just dread of Asandir's inquiry, he jerked down the tails of an undertunic threadbare enough to have belonged to an apprentice labourer and mouthed exasperated excuses to himself. 'I'm sorry. But the drawers the tailors' guild sent had enough ties and eyelets to corset a whore, and too much lace makes me itch.'

Eldir broke off, embarrassed. The sorcerer he hastened to meet was not attending his injured charge, but standing stone-still in the hallway, one shoulder braced against the doorjamb and his face bent into shadow.

The young king paled in dismay. 'Ath's mercy! We reached you too late to help.'

Asandir glanced up, eyes bright. 'Certainly not.' He inclined his head toward the door. Muffled voices issued from the other side, one male and laboured, another one female, bewailing misfortune in lisping sympathy.

Eldir's interest quickened. Even in extremis, it appeared the infamous Mad Prophet had pursued his ill-starred assignation. Then, practical enough to restrain his wild thoughts, Havish's sovereign sighed in disappointment. 'You've healed him already, I see.'

The sorcerer shook his head. Dire as oncoming storm, he spun in the corridor, tripped the latch without noise and barged into Dakar's bedchamber.

The panel opened to reveal a pleasant, sunwashed alcove, cushioned chairs carved with grape clusters, and a feather mattress piled with quilts. The casement admitted a flood of ocean air lightly tainted by the tar the chandlers sold to black rigging. Swathed like a sausage in eiderdown, a chubby man lay with a face wan as bread dough and a beard like the curled fringe on a water-spaniel. Caught leaning over to kiss him, the pretty blonde kitchen maid with the knife-wielding husband murmured into his ear, 'I will grieve for you and pray to Ath to preserve your undying memory.'

'Which won't be the least bit necessary!' Asandir cracked from his planted stance by the doorway.

At his shoulder, Eldir started.

The maid snapped erect with a squeal and the quilts jerked, the victim beneath galvanized to a fish-flop start of surprise. A fondling hand recoiled from under a froth of lace petticoats as Dakar swivelled cinnamon eyes, widened now to rolling rings of white.

The tableau endured a frozen moment. Already pale, the sorcerer's wounded apprentice gasped a bitten-off curse, then to outward appearance fell comatose.

'Out!' Asandir jerked his chin toward the girl, who cast aside dignity, gathered her skirts above her knees and fled trailing unlaced furbelows.

As her footsteps dwindled down the corridor, the sorcerer kicked the door closed. A paralysed stillness descended, against which the rumble of ale tuns over cobbles seemed to thunder off the courtyard walls outside. Beyond the opened shutter, the call of the changing watch drifted off the wall walks, mingled with the bellow of the baker's oaths as he collared a laggard scullion. The yap of gambolling puppies, the grind of wagons across Ostermere market and the screeling cries of scavenging gulls seemed unreal, even dreamlike, before the stark tension in the room.

Asandir first addressed the king, who waited, frowning thoughtfully. 'Although I ask that the secrets of mages be kept from common knowledge in your court, I would have you understand just how far my apprentice has misled you.' He stepped to Dakar's bedside and with no shred of solicitude, ripped away quilting and sheets.

Dakar bit his lip, poker stiff, while his master yanked off the sodden dressing that swaddled the side the baking girl's husband had punctured.

The linen came free, gory as any bandage might be if pulled untimely from a mortal wound. Except the flesh beneath was unmarked.

King Eldir gaped in surprise.

'Dakar,' Asandir informed, 'is this day five hundred and eighty-seven years old. He has longevity training. As you see, the suffering of wounds and illness is entirely within his powers to mend.'

'He was in no danger,' Eldir stated in rising, incredulous fury. He folded his arms, head tipped sidewards, while skin smudged with the first shaved trace of a beard deepened to a violent, fresh flush. That moment, he needed no crown to lend him majesty. 'For whim, the realm's champion was sent out and told to run my fastest mare to death to fetch your master?'

Naked and pink and far too corpulent to cower into a feather mattress, Dakar shoved stubby hands in the hair at his temples. He licked dry lips, flinched from Asandir and squirmed. 'I'm sorry.' His shrug was less charming than desperate.

'Were you my subject, I'd have your life.' Eldir flicked a glance at the sorcerer, whose eyes were like butcher's steel fresh from the whetstone. 'Since you're not my feal man, regretfully, I can't offer that kindness.'

Sweat rolled through Dakar's fingers and snaked across his plump wrists. His breathing came now in jerks, while lard at his knees jumped and quivered.

Eldir inclined his head toward Asandir. 'Perhaps I should wait for you without?' Mindful of his dignity, he side-stepped toward the door.

Alone and defenceless before his master, Dakar covered his face. Through his palms, he said, 'Ath! If it's to be tracing mazes through sand grains again, for mercy, get on with your traps and be done with me.'

'That wasn't what I had in mind.' Asandir advanced to the bedside. He said something almost too soft to hear, cut by a wild, ragged cry from Dakar that trailed off to snivelling, then silence.

Eldir rushed his step to shut the door. But the panel was caught short before it slammed, and Asandir stepped through. He set the latch with steady fingers, turned around to regard the King of Havish, and said succinctly, 'Nightmares. They should occupy the Mad Prophet at least until sundown. He'll emerge hungry, and I sadly fear, not in the least bit chastened.' Between one breath and the next, the sorcerer recovered his humour. 'Do I owe you for more than your guardsmen's allotment of gold buttons?'

'Not me.' Eldir sighed, strain and uncertainty returned to pull at the corners of his mouth. 'The oldest son of the town seneschal staked his mother's jewellery on bad cards, and I'm not sure exactly who started the dare. But the cook's fattened hog escaped its pen. The creature wound up in a warehouse and spoiled the raw wool consigned for the dyers at Narms. Truth to tell, the guild master's council of Ostermere is howling for Dakar's blood. My guard captain held orders to clap him in chains when the fight broke out in the kitchen.'

'I leave my apprentice to protect you for one day and find you exhausted by a hard lesson in diplomacy.' Asandir's grin flashed like a burst of sudden sunlight. He laid a steering hand on the royal shoulder and started off down the corridor. 'From this moment, consider my apprentice removed from the realm's concerns. Your steward Machiel should be able to guard your safety well enough, since you've managed to hold Havish secure through Dakar's irresponsible worst. I've decided exactly what I shall do with our errant prophet and I doubt he takes it well.'

'You'd punish him further?' The habits of an unassuming boyhood still with him, Eldir paused by the windowseat to gather his discarded state finery. 'What could be worse than harrowing the man with uninterrupted bad dreams?'

'Very little.' Asandir's eyes gleamed with sharp irony. 'When Dakar awakens, you will send him from court on a travelling allowance I'll leave for his reassignment. Tell him his task is to keep Prince Arithon of Rathain from getting murdered by Etarra's new division of field troops.'

Eldir stopped cold in the corridor. After five years, accounts were still repeated of the bloody war that had slaughtered two thirds of Etarra's garrison and left the northern clansmen feal to Arithon nearly decimated in the cause of defending his life. Motivated by a feud between half-brothers embroiled in bitter enmity; lent deadly stakes by the same powers of sorcery that had once defeated the Mistwraith; and fanned hotter by age-old friction still standing elsewhere between clanborn and townsman, the conflict had since brought the unified opposition of every merchant city in Rathain. The prince with blood-right to rule there was a marked and hunted man. Every trade guild within his own borders was eager to skewer him in cold blood.

Havish's emphatically neutral sovereign made a sound between a cough and a grunt as he considered Dakar's penchant for trouble appended to the man called Master of Shadow, that half of the north wanted dead. 'I shouldn't presume to advise, but isn't that fairly begging fate to get Rathain a killed prince?'

'So one might think,' Asandir mused, not in the least bit concerned. 'Except Arithon s'Ffalenn needs none of Dakar's help just now. On the

7

contrary, he's perhaps the one man alive who may be capable of holding the Mad Prophet to heel. The match should prove engagingly fascinating. Each man holds the other in the utmost of scorn and contempt.'

Petition

The next event in the widening chain of happenstance provoked by the Mistwraith's bane arose at full summer, when visitors from Rathain's clan survivors sought audience with another high chieftain in the neighbouring realm to the west. Hailed as she knelt on damp pine needles in the midst of dressing out a deer, Lady Maenalle bent a hawk-sharp gaze on the breathless messenger.

'Fatemaster's justice, why now?' Bloodied to the wrists, her knife poised over a welter of steaming entrails, the woman who also shouldered the power of Tysan's regency shoved up from her knees with a quickness that belied her sixty years. Feet straddled over the half-gutted carcass, the man's leathers she preferred for daily wear belted to a waist still whipcord trim, Maenalle pushed back close-cropped hair with the back of her least sticky wrist. She said to the boy who had jogged up a mountainside to fetch her, 'Speak clearly. These aren't the usual clan spokesmen we've received from Rathain before?'

'Lady, not this time.' Sure her displeasure boded ill for the scouts, whose advance word now seemed negligently scant on facts, the boy answered fast. 'The company numbers fifteen, led by a tall man named Red-beard. His war captain Caolle travels with him.'

'*Jieret* Red-beard? The young s'Valerient heir?' Grim in dismay, Maenalle cast a bothered glance over her gore-spattered leathers. 'But he's Deshir's chieftain, and Earl of the North!'

A state delegation from across the water, no less; and led by Prince Arithon's blood-pacted liegeman, who happened also to be *caithdein*, or 'shadow behind the throne', hereditary warden of Rathain. Maenalle let fly a blistering oath.

Then, infected by spurious, private triumph, for she despised formality and skirts, she burst into deep-throated laughter. 'Well, they'll just have to take me as I am,' she ended with a lift of dark eyebrows. 'I've got time to find a stream to sluice off? Good. The hunting party's off down the gorge. Somebody ought to go after them and let my grandson know what's afoot.' She bit her lip, recalled to the deer, too sorely needed to abandon for scavengers to pick.

The young messenger offered to take the knife in her stead. 'Lady, I can finish up the butchering.'

Maenalle smiled. 'Good lad. I thought so, but really, this should be Maien's problem.'

Her moods were fair-minded enough to let the boy relax. 'Lady, if you both meet Prince Arithon's delegation reeking of offal, s'Gannley might be called out for insult.'

'Imp.' Maenalle relinquished her fouled blade and took a swipe at the child's ear, which he ducked before he got blood-smeared. 'Titles aside, Rathain's warden is very little older than you are. If he cries insult, I'll ask his war captain to cut down a birch switch and thrash him.'

Which words seemed a fine and suitable retort, until Maenalle's descent from the forested plateau forced an interval for sober thought. Chilled by the premature twilight of an afternoon cut off from sunlight, she entered the hidden ravine that held her clans' summer refuge. In silence, she numbered the years that had slipped past, all unnoticed. Red-beard was not a childish nickname. Jieret s'Valerient in sober fact was but one season older than Maien; no boy any more, if not yet fully a man.

Small wonder the young scout had stifled his smile at her mention of birch canes and thrashing.

Hatefully tired of acting the querulous ruler, and greeting nobody she passed, Maenalle crossed the dusty compound with its stinks of sun-curing hide. She barged into the comfortless hut that served as her quarters, flicked up cuffs still dripping from her stream-side ablutions and slammed back the lid of her clothes trunk.

Her hand hesitated over the folded finery inside, then snatched in sharp resolve: not the indigo regent's tabard with its glittering gold star blazon. Instead Maenalle shook out a plain black overtunic, expensively cut, and worn but once since its making. She would don the *caithdein*'s sable, by tradition the symbol of power deferred in the presence of her true-born sovereign.

If she still held the regency in Tysan, the office was not hers by choice; the s'Ilessid scion forepromised by prophecy had returned to claim his royal title. But the Mistwraith he had lent his gift of light to help subdue had avenged itself and cursed Prince Lysaer of Tysan to undying enmity against Arithon, Master of Shadow. For that, the Fellowship sorcerers entitled to crown him had withheld their sanction for his inheritance. Grieved beyond heartbreak for the betrayals which had forced their judgement, the realm's lady steward tugged the dark garment over her dampened leathers. She belted on her sword, firm in this one defiance. Let black cloth remind the envoy sent by Arithon of Rathain that the final call on clan loyalty in Tysan was not fully hers to command, however desperate the cause they surely came here to plead.

A brisk knock jostled her doorpanel. Maenalle raked quick fingers through hair cropped close as a fighting man's, then straightened in time to seem composed as Lord Tashan poked his white head inside.

'Your visitors have passed the last check-point.' The rotten old fox was smiling. As age-worn as she through long years of shared hardship, he would guess she was flustered; and in hindsight, the blighted black cloth was a mistake that would accent any pallor born of nervousness.

Tartly, Maenalle attacked first. 'I could go and maybe lend a semblance of decorum if you'd make way and let me pass.'

Before Tashan could move, she brushed by, still shrugging to settle the tunic over her shoulders. Canny enough not to query her forceful choice of wardrobe, the old lord hurried his limp to flank her, while dogs barked and dust flew, and sun-browned children in scuffed deerhides ran in a game of hunters and wolves through the stream-threaded shade of the defile. Built under cover on either side, the rows of ramshackle cabins sagged with the wear of storms and weather. If unglazed windows and walls laddered green under vines seemed uncivilized, Maenalle held no bitterness. Here, surrounded by inhospitable terrain; abutments of knife-edged rock and slide-scarred crags where loose shale and boulders could give way and break legs, the persecuted descendants of Tysan's deposed liegemen kept a grim measure of safety. Even the most fanatical town enemies were deterred from ranging too zealously for fugitives. Poor as her people were, at least the mountains allowed them the security to raise children under timber roofs and to keep horses in limited herds.

The old blood clans elsewhere had far less in the centuries since the merchant guilds had overset kingdom rule, and headhunters rode to claim bounties.

None of Arithon's envoy travelled mounted, which explained the scout's misleading first report. Maenalle reached the palings that served as the outpost's main gate just as the arrivals from Rathain filed through. Except for the eastern inflection as one commented, 'Ath, will you look? This place could pass for a village,' the party might have blended with one of her patrols. Jieret's band were weather-worn, observant to the point of edged wariness, and dressed in leathers lacking any dyes or bright ornaments. Their weapons had seen hard use, and every last man carried scars.

The rangy, tangle-haired red-head who stepped out to present his courtesies was no exception. Near to her grandson's age he might be, yet when he arose from his bow and towered over her, Maenalle revised her assessment. The eyes that met hers were chilly and wide, the mouth amid a gingery bristle of beard, fixed and straight. This was no green youth, but a man of seventeen years who had seen his sisters and parents die in the service of his liege. Grief and premature responsibilities left their mark: a boy of twelve had grown up with the burden of safeguarding the north against the wave of vengeance-bent aggression that had dogged his people ever since the year the Mistwraith's malice had overset Rathain's peace.

In Tysan, where the feud between townborn and clan burned hotly enough without impetus from geas-cursed princes, Lady Maenalle shrank to imagine what extremity might bring this man to leave his native glens, to abandon his people and risk an overland journey through hostile territory to seek her.

'My Lord Earl,' she murmured. 'Forgive the lacklustre welcome, but surely you bring us bad news?' She accepted his kiss on her cheek and stepped back, unwilling to test her dignity too long against the younger man's frightening sense of presence.

Jieret bent upon Tysan's lady steward the unsettling intuition inherited from his late mother. 'We've surprised you.' The blood on her boots did not escape him, nor the reserve behind her *caithdein*'s black. 'Let me ease your mind. We didn't call you back from the joys of the summer hunt to beg armed support for the sake of my liege lord, Arithon.'

'Not hers to give, if you had,' grumbled Tashan.

The comment fell through a misfortunate lull in the racket made by curious children. Stung into movement like a bothered bear, a grizzled, fifty-ish war captain with inimical black eyes elbowed past his young chieftain's shoulder.

'Don't flatter yourselves for restraint.' Caolle loosed a clipped laugh. 'His Grace of Rathain's quite vicious enough on points of pride without anybody's outside help. He'd spurn even gold that fell at his feet, did it come to him struck with his name on it.'

Unsettled to learn the prince himself had not backed this surprise delegation, Maenalle forestalled the airing of issues more wisely discussed in private. 'Your war captain sounds like a traveller sorely in need of a beer.'

'Well, beer won't help,' Caolle groused. 'Just a fair chance at gutting that blond-haired *prandey* who lounges in silk, and sends every trained sword in Etarra and beyond thrashing the countryside to harrow us.'

The trail scouts who guided the visitors stiffened, and a youngster close enough to overhear shouted, 'Hey! That man called our lord prince the Shandian word for a gelded pleasure bo—'

Maenalle spun swiftly and grabbed the child by the shoulder. 'Don't say such filth. Your mother would thrash you. And you shouldn't be concerned with your elders' speech when to my knowledge you aren't on my council.'

The miscreant gasped an apology, darted an enraged glance at Caolle, then sidled away as his lady chieftain released him. To the red-bearded *caithdein* and his grinning, insolent war captain, the steward of the Kingdom of Tysan finished in flat exasperation, 'By Ath, this visit of yours had better justify the aggravation.'

To which Earl Jieret s'Valerient said nothing. That the two gifted men who had restored Athera's sunlight were entrapped in an enmity which bent their bright and deadly talents against each other was a havoc too heartsore for reason.

Neither was he inclined to dwell on ceremony. Minutes later, seated by an untouched glass of wine across the planks of the outpost's scarred council table, he pulled a letter from the breast of his tunic. The dispatch was speckled with bloodstains. Since affairs between clans were never committed to writing, Maenalle's eyes flicked at once to discern which town seal impressed the broken wax.

Deshir's youthful earl saw her interest. 'The seal was royal, and Tysan's.' A reluctant pause, then his quick movement as he offered the missive across the trestle. 'This was captured from a guild courier riding the Mathorn Road under heavy escort. A state copy, you'll see, bound for official record with the trade guilds at Erdane. Clan lives were lost to intercept it. We must presume the original reached its destination.'

Maenalle accepted the folded parchment, its ribbons and gilded capitols done in the ornate style of Etarran scribes. She verified her kingdom's star blazon in its couch of indigo wax. Her glance at the flamboyant heading raised a flash-fire rush of antagonism. 'But our prince was disbarred from royal privilege! Why should he presume to write under Tysan's crown seal importuning the Mayor Elect of Korias?'

'Read,' growled Caolle.

White in dismay, Maenalle scanned down the lines, growing tenser and angrier, until even Lord Tashan's dry-witted tolerance snapped. 'What's in that?'

'A petition.' Jieret all but spat on the beaten earth floor. 'From a prince denied right of sovereignty demanding title and grant to lands and city. By claim of birth, Lysaer s'Ilessid seeks leave to restore Tysan's capitol at Avenor.'

'He'll never get it,' Tashan said, halfway to his feet in indignation. 'Never mind that the merchant guilds won't stand a royal presence, the palace is ruins, now. Not one stone stands upright on a foundation since the rebellion wrecked the old order. Past fears will prevail. Not a town-born mason would set foot there, haunted as they believe the site to be. And no clan in this kingdom can endorse a s'Ilessid claim without lawful sanction from the Fellowship.'

'But that's half the point,' Jieret said, too emphatically calm for a man under twenty years of age. 'The trade guilds in West End have nothing to lose. If the old land routes are rejoined with the Camris roads, they'll gain profits. The Mayor Elect in Korias will draw up the documents just for the chance to slight royalty. He's isolated enough not to know your deposed prince has the finesse to create the impossible. Daelion as my witness, in just five years Lysaer's reconciled Etarra's stew of rival factions. He's got guild ministers and town councilmen kissing like brothers, and every independent city garrison in the Kingdom of Rathain conniving to exterminate my clansmen. If Lysaer can whip up armies to challenge a shadow master and a sorcerer, do you think he can't get walls and barbicans built around the shades of a few thousand ghosts?'

'Royal sanction or not, your prince won't lack funds for his enterprise,' broke in Caolle. 'The towns are bothered to panic. To curry favour with the man whose gift of light offers protection against wild fears of Arithon's shadows, every trade guild owing notes to Etarra has offered their gold to fund armies. What townsman would pause to sort the difference between Arithon's feal liegemen and clanborn everywhere else?' Caolle slammed opened hands on the table, causing the thick planks to jump. 'Fiends! They're not so damned stupid, citybred fools though they be. If his Grace of Rathain turned up in any clan haven asking guest right, what chieftain would refuse him hospitality?'

'Havish's, under High King Eldir, would be wise to.' Maenalle shut her eyes, her fist with the letter bunched hard at her temple, and her free hand nerveless on the tabletop.

Unless and until the Fellowship sorcerers unriddled a way to break the blood feud engendered by Desh-thiere's revenge, the perils were too dire to deny.

These men at her table had seen the forefront of the war unleashed between the cursed princes. Even heard at second hand, the ruthless scale of the conflict was enough to bring cold sweats. When Prince Lysaer had raised the Etarran garrison to cut down Rathain's royal heir, one battle had seen two thirds of Deshir's clansmen fight to the death, despite the unstinting protections of sorcery and shadows lent by the liege lord they defended. Losses to the attackers had been more devastating. Fears of further retaliation by magecraft had drawn Lysaer to stay on in Rathain to unite its merchant guilds and quarrelsome, independent city governments. Against the rifts of old politics, he had seen stunning success. Every summer, headhunters rode out in greater force to hunt down and slaughter clan fugitives in their search for the Master of Shadow.

For centuries, townsmen had killed clansmen on sight; the stakes now were never more dangerous. The beguiling inspiration of the Prince of the West lent city mayors powerful impetus to pool resources and systematically exterminate enemies already driven deep into hiding.

Having met Lysaer s'Ilessid only briefly, Maenalle still sighed in regret for a gifted statesman's skills twisted awry by Desh-thiere's curse. Through the course of just one past visit, her most reticent scouts had warmed to their prince enough to sorrow rather than rage over his treacherous alliance with town enemies. As for Arithon of Rathain, he was mage-trained: secretive, powerfully clever, and too fiendishly innovative to crumple before whatever odds Lysaer would raise against him.

'Where is your liege?' Maenalle asked. 'Does Arithon know his adversary now looks to claim ancestral lands in Tysan?'

Because her eyes were averted, only Tashan saw the exasperated look that flashed between the earl and his war captain. To Jieret's staunch credit, he found courage to answer her directly. 'We came to give warning. Of Arithon's intent, we've no clue. When he left us, he made his will plain. He would not have his presence become a target to encourage the geas that drives him and Lysaer to war.'

Still bluntly irked over a clash of wills fully five years gone, Caolle knotted ham fists on the trestle top. 'We haven't seen or heard from our liege since the rite sung over our war dead. Ath knows where he is. His Grace himself won't deign to send word.'

Which explained the hardness behind Jieret's focused maturity, Maenalle concluded in silent pain. To him alone had fallen the task of guarding his people from Etarra's seasonal purge by headhunters. The woman in her ached for her grandson, who might come to taste the same griefs.

If Lysaer won title to Avenor, the rift engendered by Desh-thiere's ills, that had sundered Rathain and sparked old hates to furious bloodshed, must inevitably sweep into Tysan.

'Our clans will prepare for the worst,' Maenalle concluded in bitterness. She arose, let the wrung parchment fall on the tabletop, then offered the beleaguered young earl the courtesy due to an equal; for whether he had gained the privilege of swearing fealty to a lawfully sanctioned prince, like her, he was *caithdein* to a realm without a king. His liege lord did not back him; by himself, Jieret had shouldered the risk, had left Rathain's shores with the fourteen companions who were his last surviving peers to bring word of Lysaer's false intent.

For all her sixty years, Maenalle felt tired and disheartened; beaten down with sorrow enough to contemplate what this red-bearded stripling would not, even for grief since the slaughter of his family: break down and give way to hatred, abandon himself to vindictive killing.

'You don't resent your prince for going,' she found herself saying in unabashed awe. Tashan turned around to stare at her, while Caolle looked on, nonplussed.

Their reactions passed unheeded as Jieret gave her the first true smile she had seen. 'I admire Arithon, much as my father did, though my line's gift of Sight warned us both that my family would die in royal service.'

'I met your liege once,' Maenalle admitted. 'Though I never saw him work shadows or magecraft, Ath grant me grace, I wish never to cross wits with him again.'

Rueful in grim understanding, Jieret said, 'Never mind Ath. If my liege has his way, you probably won't. I believe he finds contentment in obscurity.'

Neither cynical Caolle nor Tysan's lady steward wasted breath to belabour the obvious: that Prince Lysaer's public presence and insidious charisma must eventually come to prevail. Arithon of Rathain would awaken one day, else be battered from his complaisance.

Grant

Talith, sister to Etarra's Lord Commander of the Guard, could recall when early autumn had filled the city with the smell of ripe apples. Hauled in on the farm-wains that toiled up the winding roads through the passes, the fruit had been unloaded in piles on burlap in the raucous expanse of the markets. In imitation of the pranks of older gallants, bored, rich young boys once delighted in upsetting the stacks to the detriment of passing traffic. Birds squabbled over the cidery crush milled under by the cart-wheels, and winds whisked their burden of scraping, flying leaves, sharpened by frost off the peaks.

But if the sunlight restored since the Mistwraith's captivity had increased the orchards' bounty, Etarra held widespread change.

Spurred to fears of attack by shadows and sorcery, and through promise to aid armed resource with the powers over light that alone could protect and counterward, the brilliant statesmanship of one man had annealed strained politics into alliance. Due to Lysaer s'Ilessid's dedication, the disparate city governments inside Rathain's borders now stood united in common cause. The miracle of their accord brought unprecedented co-operation. Against the barbarian clans who had harboured the fugitive Master of Shadow, every garrison in the north levied troops to support Etarra's campaign.

Apples were now stacked in barrels to discourage pilfering, and the season's turn jammed streets built wide enough to accommodate the heaviest caravans with shipments of provisions and arms for the bursars. Arranged like a hub in the Mathorn Pass, the wealthiest trade centre on the continent spent its treasury to house and maintain a war camp through the winter. The hayfields nearest to the walls sprouted a muddy, trampled maze of officer's shacks, supply tents and barracks, each block marked off like street signs by standards with sun-faded banners. Grown yearly more familiar, the taint of coal from the armourers'-fires wrapped the rooftops in haze that deepened with dusk to blue mist.

Lady Talith disdained to share in the commotion of the returning army. She disliked loud-voiced men and salons packed with women nervously desperate for news. That the royal-born sorcerer Etarra's new field host was intended to annihilate had so far refused to reappear did nothing to blunt the unease in the streets: his spells and his shadows had bought seven thousand deaths five years past in Deshir. The grief and the terror remained, never to be forgotten. The garrison that endured sustained its festered rage by bloodying what remained of Arithon's allies, clan barbarians systematically pursued and ferreted out of the wilds. For deeply personal reasons, Talith hated the boastful stories of ambush and campaign, the reminiscences of past seasons. And so she disdained the invitations and the crush, and stood with her chin pillowed on furred cuffs to gaze over the square brick embrasure that faced the mountains.

When the troops first marched in, she had heard what mattered from Diegan: the crack divisions deployed into Halwythwood's deep glens had returned with markedly poor success. No barbarian camps at all had been found to be put to the sword.

Again, the brigands under Caolle and Jieret Red-beard had made sport of the headhunters' efforts. Except for one isolated incident, their bands of clan scouts had escaped, despite repeated complaints of raiding and couriers brazenly killed or waylaid as near as the Mathorn road.

Lysaer s'Ilessid had warned that the barbarians would organize; that Arithon's ongoing disappearance presaged more devious plans. Having met the Master of Shadow just once, Talith shared his unrest.

A light voice cut across her thoughts. 'I thought I should find you here.'

The postern door had opened silently and the step that approached was dancer-light. Talith did not turn, though the hair pinned in coils by her gold-wired pearls trapped heat at the base of her neck. Haughtily still in her wrappings of tawny velvet, lined by the flicker of the lamplighter's torch as he shuffled on his eventide route down the wall, she loosed an invisible sigh.

The man most sought after and admired in all the rich halls of Etarra, Lysaer s'Ilessid, called Prince of the West and saviour of the city, perched with poised grace at her elbow. A pause developed as he examined her; a man would be dead, not to suck a rushed breath for her beauty.

Torchlight caught his sapphires like splintered ice as he added, 'At long last, I've had word.'

Talith raked her teeth over her lower lip to redden and brighten her pout. 'You've located your bane? The Master of Shadow has been found?'

His stark and stubborn silence informed her that he had not.

From behind, glass chinked as the arthritic old servant fumbled to unlatch the postern lamp's cover. Lysaer pushed off the crenellation, gave a casual flick of his hand. A spark jumped from his finger across empty air and snapped the wick into flame behind the smudged panes.

The lampsman gave a violent start and spun around. Made aware of just who stood with the lady, he gulped in pale awe and knelt. 'Your royal Grace.'

'Ath bless, you need not bow.' Lysaer gave the man a grin and a silent, conspirator's gesture to hurry along on his rounds. Never one to flaunt his gifted powers, this night, the prince was jealous of his privacy.

'Ah,' sighed the lampsman, recovering. He returned a wink and hurried off, trailing the oily reek of torch smoke around the bend by the gatehouse. Inside the ward room, a guard lost his dice throw and cursed, his epithets obscured as a wagon rumbled down the thoroughfare below.

Persistent despite interruptions, Talith said, 'What word could move you but the wish of your heart, to find out where Arithon's hiding? Ath knows, you've searched every cranny in Rathain.'

The prince who had helped wrest the sun clear of mist was never an easy man to nettle. 'If I'd unmasked that sorcerer's whereabouts, beloved, your brother's troops would be marching, winter ice or not.' Unlike the fashion of the dandies, Lysaer wore no scent. He required none. The closeness of him seemed to burn Talith through to the skin. She needed to shed the clinging weight of her mantle, but dared not.

He touched her arm and gently turned her. Even after five years, the beauty of him stole her breath. The flare of new lantern light fired his gold hair, gilded perfect cheekbones and sculpted chin and a bearing instinctively royal. As earnestly as the city gallants strove to emulate such carriage, inherent majesty eluded them. Then, forthright as no man born Etarran would ever be, the prince cupped her face and kissed her.

Passion flurried and tangled Talith's thinking.

He was excited by something. His hands trembled and his eyes drank in the sight of her with scarcely veiled anticipation.

Piqued enough by his secrecy to use looks that could bring men to their knees, Talith drew back and struck him lightly on the jewelled sleeve of his doublet. 'What have you learned?'

Lysaer laughed, a flash of perfect teeth. 'The best news. Never mind the Master and his shadows.' Eagerness let him speak of his nemesis without his usual brooding frown. 'The Mayor of Korias has finally set seal to my claim. Avenor and its lands are to be mine.' He caught her waist and spun her, while around them, the flutter of night insects battered hot glass in their fatal, blind swoop to the light. 'We can officially formalize our engagement. That's if you can find heart to marry a prince who has title, but no subjects, and fields gone to briar and wilderness.'

Talith looked into deep sapphire eyes and shivered. 'Everywhere you go you have subjects,' she said. 'Not least that decrepit old lampblack. He'll brag to his grandchildren until he dies, for your tricks. Never say it was I who insisted on meaningless propriety.'

19

He reached, brushed back the loose curl at her temple, then began with abandon to pluck out jewelled pins. Neither of them noticed the dicers' revealing silence in the gate house as a cataract of wheat-gold hair unreeled over his ringed knuckles. Lysaer touched her brow with his lips. 'I could accept no estate as a gift from Lord Diegan.' His mouth trailed down her cheek, caressing. 'Not when I'm the one laying claim to his sole, magnificent sister.' He reached the left corner of her mouth. As her lips parted to receive him, he held back for one last rejoinder. 'I shall plunder this city, nonetheless. The jewel of Avenor's restoration shall be your hand. My word as prince, your beauty and your children will become the crown treasures of Tysan, and the ones most munificently cherished.'

At long last he tasted her fully.

Down the battlement, the wide-eyed watch clapped and raised rough cheers. Lysaer inclined his head their way in courtly salute, then turned his shoulder and rearranged tawny velvet to shield the face of his beloved from their chaffing.

Talith melted into his embrace, every nerve in her stretched to match the bent of his desire. She could wish her heart was not cruelly held captive; she could ache with the hard female knowledge this marriage to come must eventually consume and destroy her. Like the moths, she could not steer away and save herself from the blinding.

The man in her arms was too much for her. Foremost a prince, he was the selfless instrument of others dependent on his protection. His daunting gifts already bound him to commitments far stronger than love. The hands that tenderly cradled her, that had casually sparked flame to a recalcitrant lamp, could as easily raise power with the virulence of summer lightning. Against the deceit of Arithon s'Ffalenn, and the scars of a city that had survived a war fuelled with the selfsame shadows that had beaten back the Mistwraith, this man's defence had been dedicated.

Exalted and imprisoned by shameless happiness, Lady Talith blinked back rising tears. What was Avenor to become, if rebuilt, but a broader base of support for wider campaigns and more armies? She understood with a rage that drove her to hate the more fiercely. Lysaer s'Ilessid would never have peace. Nor would he become fully hers until the day the Master of Shadow was found and run down, to be finally, safely put to death.

Evasions

Taxed to aching exhaustion by another joint effort at scrying, the First Enchantress to the Koriani Prime retorts in ragged exasperation: 'We've swept the lanes through five kingdoms, exhausted every clan haven in Rathain, and set tag spells and trigger traps along trails and roads and taverns for half a decade! If the Master of Shadow had died, or fallen off the face of Athera, we should have recovered *some* trace of him . . .'

Far to the east, in a city bounded by the waters of Eltair Bay, a sweating, obsequious millwright stammers frightened excuses to an official in black and gold robes emblazoned with the lion of mayoral authority, 'But of course, my word of honour, the errors in design shall be corrected. The crown moulding for his lordship's lady wife shall be redone and delivered to the city inside the next fortnight . . .'

As autumn days shorten toward solstice and the stunted firs of high altitude moan to the batter of cold winds, Dakar the Mad Prophet begs a ride to the next town; and the charge laid on him the past spring, to find and safeguard the most hunted man on the continent, remains cheerfully ignored for the pleasures of beer and loose women . . .

II. *VAGRANT*

Dakar the Mad Prophet opened his eyes to a view of the steamed-over glass in some backwater tavern's dingy casement. Rain spiked with ice chapped against rondels filmed over with smoke soot. The boards under his cheek were rudely cut, sticky with rancid layers of grease and spilled ale. His mouth tasted as if it had hosted a convocation of snails. Clued by the ache in his back that he had probably slept where he sat, and familiar enough with his excesses to know when the wrong move could hurt, he groaned.

No female rushed to soothe him; the slight noise instead spurred an explosive pain in his head. He stirred, eyes squeezed shut, and pressed chilled hands to his temples. His ankles were also ice cold, result of having parked nightlong in a draught with his feet still encased in wet socks. Both boots appeared to be missing.

The Mad Prophet moaned in self pity, but softly. With caution he managed to straighten up. His eyes refused to focus, a common problem; he had been born near-sighted. The point became moot, that Asandir's tutelage had schooled him to correct the deficiency, as well as the torment of bad hangovers. To reverse any bodily failing, he needed to be sober and clear-minded, neither one a state to be desired. Dakar fumbled through a succession of capacious pockets in quest of a coin to buy beer.

Across the tavern's cramped common room, somebody screamed. Drilled through the ears by the sound, Dakar shot bolt upright and banged his knees against the trestle. He aimed a bleary glare at a mule drover who howled still, apparently over a winning throw at darts. The tanner with the frizzled moustache stood up as his opponent doled out the stake, while a half-toothless roisterer on the sidelines shouted, 'Where's your courage man? Try another game!'

Dakar winced and groped tenderly through another pocket. As the barmaid whisked past bearing ale to the victor, he dredged up a hopeful smile.

Blonde and fast-tongued and inaccessible, she noticed his search through his clothing. 'Your pockets are empty as your purse. And no, you weren't robbed while you slept.'

The Mad Prophet absorbed this, lamenting that she moved too briskly for him to land an effective pinch. He stared owlishly as the flagon was carried on to the victor. Soon enough, the renewed thwacks of a fresh game's thrown darts pierced through the complaints of the loser.

About then it dawned with awful force that his pockets contained only lint. He found himself destitute on the edge of winter in a sheep farming village in the Skyshiels. Dakar's yell rivalled the mule drover's, and the barmaid, incensed, hurried over and clanged her tray of emptied crockery by his elbow.

While Dakar cringed back from the din, she ran on, 'I *said*, nobody robbed you. What coppers you had barely paid for last night's ale.' To Dakar's softly bleared gaze, annoyance stole nothing from her charm. 'I see you don't remember? That's odd. You put away fifteen rounds.'

Probably truth, Dakar reflected muddily; the state of his bladder was killing him. He braced chubby hands on the trestle, prepared to arise and embark for the privy.

Warmed now to her tirade, the barmaid unkindly refused him passage. 'The only reason you weren't thrown out is because the landlord took pity for the weather.'

Since Dakar had yet to raise concern over what the day looked like outdoors, he surveyed the room to fix his bearings. The tavern was of typical backlands construction: two storeyed, with the ceiling beams that supported the second floor set low enough to bother a tall man's posture. The single lantern hissed and sputtered, fuelled by a reeking tallow dip that smoked far worse than the hearth. In a dimness tinged luridly orange, darts flurried between support posts into a shaggy straw target. The mule drover cursed a wide throw, which prompted a laugh from the tanner. A gnarled old cooper in the corner muttered slurred lines of doggerel, and sniggers erupted like the feeding squeals of a hog's farrow. Dakar, brimming and uncomfortable, rolled long-suffering eyes. When the bar wench failed to move, he succumbed to temptation and shoved a hand down her bulging blouse.

No matter how unsteady he was on his feet, his fingers knew their way about a woman.

The wench hissed in affront. Her shove plonked the Mad Prophet backward on the unpadded timber of the bench. The air left his lungs in a whistle. Tediously, he started the effort of dragging himself upright all over again.

'Slip on the ice,' snapped the serving maid. She snatched up her tray to an indignant rattle of cheap crockery. 'The door will be barred when you come back, and I hope your bollocks freeze solid.'

Suffering too much for rejoinder, Dakar pried his gut from behind the trestle and carved a staggering course toward the doorway. As he bypassed the party at the fireside, a dart flew to another barrage of shouts. The mule drover had hit another bull's-eye.

'Damn me to Sithaer,' cried the tanner in beet-faced irritation. 'You cheat like the Shadow Master himself!'

Dakar tacked sharply and caught himself a bump against the doorpost. 'Hardly,' he volunteered to whoever was wise enough to listen. 'Yon one's no man for harmless games. His sort of tricks infuriate and kill and make enemies.'

But the Mad Prophet's slurred advice was pre-empted by warning from another bystander. 'Don't speak that name here! Would you draw him, and the winds of ill luck? Sorcerers hear their names spoken. There's a burned patch, I've heard, in Deshir where the soldier's bones lie that will never again grow green trees.'

Dakar half-turned to denounce this, but lost his chance as the latch let go under his hand. The doorpanel he leaned on suddenly swung wide and spilled him outside in a stumble. He yowled his injured shock as grey slush soaked both feet to the ankles; no boots, he remembered belatedly. The struggle to go back in and search for them entailed too much effort, his hose being already sodden.

The inn yard wore ice in sheets unsliced by the ruts of any cartwheels. Unless there were east-running storms, travellers on the Eltair road were unlikely to choose the byway through the foothills. Beleaguered by gusts that cut straight off the summits of the Skyshiels to rattle the signboard of the cooper's shack, stung by an unkindly fall of sleet, Dakar yawed and slipped on his errand. He collided with the firewood hovel, a hitching rack and a water trough, and cursed in dark conclusion that mountain villages were an uncivilized place to suffer the virulent effects of brewed hops.

Returned an interval just short of frostbite, with his points tangled and his hair screwed to ringlets by the damp, he blundered back to the tavern door. He had sheltered in the privy until the cold came near to killing him, and was ready primed with pleas in case the barmaid was still piqued. But the panel was not locked against him. Intensely relieved, Dakar hauled his mushy socks into the taproom as furtively as his shivering would allow.

Nobody noticed him.

The door had stayed unbarred in the bustle created by a new arrival, a slender, aged gentleman even now being solicitously ushered to the fire-side. The landlord had personally stirred from his parlour for this service, and even the sour-tempered bar wench had brightened in her haste to cheer the gloom with rushlights.

Probably some rich man stranded in the passes by a wrong turn in the storm, Dakar supposed; until he noticed the dart players standing stalled in mute awe with their coins abandoned on the table.

'Fiends plague me, I never thought to live as witness,' the mule drover said in a powerful whisper. 'The Masterbard himself, come to visit our village?'

Dakar blinked in astonishment. Halliron, *here?*

Beyond the smoke-grimed support beams, the newcomer tossed back his sleet-crusted hood. Shoulder-length hanks of white hair tumbled free, caught with sparkles of unmelted ice. Then, striking and clear as a signature, a mellowed voice addressed the landlord. 'What a storm. The passes are awful. We have silver if you've got quarters for extra lodgers.'

'Oh, no!' protested the innkeeper. 'That is, I have rooms. All tidy. Cleanest linen on the coast side of Highscarp. But your coin stays in your purse. Every penny. Your presence will draw customers just for the news, even if you don't care to sing.'

'Your commons won't go tuneless, for your kindness,' Halliron promised. Erect despite more than eight decades of age, he had a prominent, aristocratic nose, and spaced front teeth that flashed in a smile. 'We'll need two beds. My apprentice will be in as soon as he's stabled the pony.'

Crouched down to build up the fire, the landlord straightened up, horrified. 'My boy, didn't he meet you in the yard? Why, that laggard, no-good –'

The door latch tripped amid the tirade. Wind-driven sleet slashed in on the draught that breathed chill through the fug from the fire as a figure muffled in wet woollens entered, moving fast. Dakar's parked bulk was side-stepped and a new voice cut in, declaiming, 'Your anger's misplaced. Your groom is hard at work. The harness was wet and needed oiling, and Halliron's pony hates boys. My master would have told you, I usually tend him myself.'

Impatient with his headache and his relapsed eyesight, Dakar squinted at the latest arrival. Layered as he was in tatty mufflers and a cape-shouldered, nondescript mantle, there seemed more wool to him than man. A path cleared before him to the hearthside. Caked ice cracked from his clothing as he undid fastenings to disgorge a long, tapered bundle laced in oilskins. This he deposited carefully out of reach of the fire's leaping heat. A pair of wet gloves flew off after, to land smartly on top of the settle.

Then movement at the corner of his vision caused the stranger swiftly to spin. 'No,' he said firmly. 'Let me.'

And Halliron, who had reached to unfasten his cloak brooch, found his wrists gently caught and restrained.

'You must spare those fingers,' chided the Masterbard's apprentice. All unwittingly, he had managed to draw every eye in the room.

Too congenial to be embarrassed by public attention, the aged bard gave a hampered shrug. While younger hands worked to shed his weight of sodden mantles, the innkeeper's spaniel-eyed sympathy raised his humour. 'Never get old. It's a ridiculously uncomfortable process Ath Creator should be made to find a cure for.'

Remiss for his neglected hospitality, the innkeeper barked at his barmaid. 'Mulled wine, girl, and hot soup. And if the wife is still dallying about the kitchen, tell her to cut the fresh bread.'

While the wench hustled off, a thoughtful Dakar propped his swaying balance against the nearest trestle. As unabashed as the dart players, he stared while the bard's apprentice left off attending his master and turned to peel off his own heavy cloak. The man revealed underneath proved to be an indeterminate age in his twenties, compactly built to the point of slenderness. Nondescript ash brown hair fell lankly over thin cheekbones, and his eyes were a muddy grey hazel.

He was nobody Dakar knew.

While the visitors settled themselves, the landlord retired behind the bar to industriously buff water spots off the few tankards he owned that had glazing. Over the flow of resumed conversation as the dart players renewed their dropped game, the high-pitched exclamations of the tavern mistress rang from the depths of a pantry closet, followed by a banging of pots and hurried footsteps. A drudge appeared with bristle brush and bucket to scour the grime from the boards, while Dakar took himself off to an unobtrusive window nook, brightened by his upturn in prospects. Penniless still, sober enough to be plagued by the granddame of all headaches, he barely winced as other steps thumped the boards over his head: some servant, dispatched no doubt to ensure the linens lived up to the innkeeper's boasts. The back door banged. Outside, through the whirl of grey sleet, one of the innkeeper's mop-headed children dashed to spread word that the Masterbard of Athera had taken up residence for the night.

Soon enough, the stable boy came in with the bard's bundles of baggage. The apprentice accepted the burden and was shown upstairs to their lodgings, while the Masterbard sat by the settle to drink hot spiced wine and share news with the early arrivals. He had come down the cape coast, not through Eastwall, he told the shepherd eager to know the latest price of wool at the inland markets. When somebody else inquired if Minderl's trade galleys had safely put in for the winter, a silence developed. Halliron admitted he had bypassed the main road and shortcut across the old, ruined trail that ran wound its way west from the cape.

'And no,' he said quickly, before someone asked, 'I saw no Paravian ghosts. Just old marker stones covered with lichen and acres of bracken bent with rain. The old routes are shunned for no reason under sky I can see.'

'Sorcerers use them,' the mule drover muttered. 'And travellers see strange lights on them at night.'

Since the subject left folk uneasy, the serving wench was sent off in a flounce of skirts to bring back a fresh round of tankards. Dakar, who held small aversion to the hauntings of ruins and unused roads, trained crafty attention toward the bar. In the interval while the girl made rounds with her tray, and the self-important innkeeper held station in the Masterbard's circle, the beer keg stood unattended.

Something Halliron said raised a round of knee-slapping laughter. The Mad Prophet stood, and sidled, and in a move that bespoke long practice, worked his bulk between the countertop and the broached barrel. His eyes turned innocently elsewhere, he trawled through the suds in the washtub, hooked up a tankard, and positioned it upright for filling. No one looked his way, even through the ticklish task of twisting the spigot behind his back.

Dakar darted a glance toward the fireside. Aware to a hair's-breadth of the interval needed for a large-sized tankard to brim over, and ready with a vacuous smile, he rolled furtive eyes to make sure of the passage to the kitchens.

A shadow loomed at his flank: the bard's hazel-eyed apprentice, arrived without sound, and all but standing on top of him. The Mad Prophet gave a violent start that slopped foam in cold runnels down his backside. 'I don't think we've been introduced,' he assayed, caught up meanwhile in a disastrous grab to stem the copious gush of the beer. He fumbled the twist. Brew rose hissing over the tankard brim and pattered over the frayed heels of his socks.

The apprentice minstrel gave a wicked grin, leaned across, and deftly turned off the spigot. 'I'm called Medlir. And I suggest you're mistaken. I'm very certain I know you.'

'From some bad line in a ballad, maybe,' Dakar said, plaintively concerned with rescuing a soap-slicked tankard from upset as he juggled it from his backside to his front. That small victory achieved, he looked the bard's apprentice in the eye and began pouring beer down his gullet. When the tankard was three quarters empty, it belatedly dawned that the odd little man was going to keep quiet about his theft. Dakar stopped swallowing to catch his breath. His sodden hose squelched in puddled beer as he pressed forward, intent now on making his escape.

Medlir side-stepped and blocked him. 'Don't be a fool.' He tipped his head a surreptitious fraction to show the barmaid, shoving toward them in outraged determination.

The Mad Prophet's dismay darkened to a glare shared equally between the girl and Halliron's obstructive apprentice. 'Ah, damn!' He prepared in martyred pain to scuttle his purloined brew into the washtub.

'Not so fast.' Medlir stopped the move with long, slender fingers and flipped a silver with clanging accuracy into the bowl on the bar wench's tray. 'Drink to my health,' he invited Dakar. 'The change should pay for the spill on the floor, and keep your throat wet through this evening.'

Startled speechless, the Mad Prophet let himself be ushered away and seated with a squish of wet clothing at a trestle off to one side. Oddly uneasy with the way his luck had turned, he sucked a long pull from his tankard, licked foam from his moustache, and grimaced at the lye taste of soap. 'Surely a ballad?' he ventured obliquely.

Medlir sat very still, his lank hair now dry and fallen in fronds against his temples. 'Actually not. I met your master.'

A nasty, tingling chill started in Dakar's middle and ended in raised hair on his neck. '*Asandir? Where?*' He twisted on his bench, his eyes edged white like oyster buttons. Then, in stinging suspicion, he said, 'But of course! You travel with Halliron. The Masterbard's friendly with the Fellowship.'

'Should that trouble you?' Medlir signalled across a slat of shadow to draw the attention of the barmaid.

'Oh no,' Dakar said quickly. The girl arrived, annoyed to a hip-switch of skirts that extended to grudging service in replenishing the now emptied tankard. The Mad Prophet grinned at her, raised his drink to Medlir, and added, 'To your health.'

The door banged open to admit yet another knot of villagers, men in boots stained dark from the byre and cloaks that in dampness exuded an aroma of wet sheep. Matrons carried baskets of dyed fleece for carding, or distaffs and spindles and tablet looms, or nubby old socks to be darned. The unmarried young came dressed to dance. The village's cramped little tavern quickly became crowded, and the laughter and chat by the fireside mounted to a roar of jocular noise.

Aware that the trestles were filling, Medlir arose in clear-eyed regret. 'I'm needed. Perhaps later, we can find time to talk.'

Ever and always agreeable to the man who would keep him in beer, the Mad Prophet grinned lopsidedly back. 'Here's to later,' he said; and he drank.

Day progressed into evening. Half sotted, still in his stockings, and wedged like a partridge between a swarthy little gem-cutter with a squint, and a fresh-faced miner's wife, Dakar roared out a final, bawdy chorus in excruciating, tuneless exuberance. Overcome by wine and good spirits, the woman beside him flung an arm around his shoulders and kissed him. Dakar, beatific, alternately sampled her lips and his tankard, by now refilled enough times that it no longer tasted of washing suds.

The common room had grown from close to stifling, every available table and chair crammed beyond sane capacity. Planks sagged and swayed to the weight of packed bodies. The floor bricks glistened with slopped spirits. The air smelled of sweaty wool and hung thick enough to cut, and the clientele, either standing, sitting, or comatose in its half-unlaced linens, no longer bothered with decorum. Halliron had not played, but his apprentice was skilled, and possessed of an energy that made the trestle planks bounce to the beat of their stamping.

Which should not have surprised, Dakar thought, in a passing break between reels. Halliron had auditioned candidates for apprenticeship life-long. This man he had chosen in his twilight years had been the sole applicant to match his exacting standards. Medlir applied himself with abandon to the lyranthe, spinning for sheer pleasure the ditties, the drinking songs and the dances that an upland village starved for entertainment in an ice storm could serve him in bottomless demand.

Midnight came and passed. Two casks had been emptied to the dregs, with a third one drained nearly dry. The innkeeper out of clemency finally elbowed to the fore and pressed a plate of stew on the musician. Medlir flashed him a fast smile, bent aside in consultation with his master, and at a nod from the old man, surrendered the lyranthe to Halliron.

The hum of appreciation dropped to sudden, awed silence.

Halliron Masterbard arose and regarded his audience in wry delight. 'By Ath, you had better make some noise,' he said, his voice pitched for the sleepy child who slumped in a young matron's lap. 'Too much quiet, and the folks near at hand will notice my knuckle joints crack.'

Medlir arranged the stool and the Masterbard sat. He adjusted the lyranthe in blue-veined hands, and tested the strings for tuning. The pitch was perfect; Medlir knew his trade. But the old man fussed at the peg-heads out of performer's habit.

The stillness swelled and deepened. From the rear of the tavern, a reveller called out, 'Master singer! Folk passing out of Etarra speak of a battle fought in Deshir some years back against that sorcerer prince who shifts shadows. Do you know aught of that?'

Halliron's hand snapped off a run, distinct as a volley of arrows. 'Yes.' He locked eyes for a second with Medlir, who set aside his meal and said something contrite about forgetting to check on the pony. To the rough-clad miner's request the Masterbard replied, 'I can play that ballad. No one better. For in fact, I was there.'

A stir swept the room, loud with murmurs. Folk resettled in their seats, while Halliron damped his strings, bent his head, and veiled in a fall of white hair, sat through a motionless moment. He then made the lyranthe his voice. His fingers sighed across strings to spill a falling minor arpeggio, from which melody emerged, close-woven and transparent as a spell. Notes climbed, and spiralled, and blended, drawing the listeners into a fabric of shared tension.

'You won't feel too drunk when he reaches the ending of this one,' Medlir said to Dakar as he passed on his way to the door.

The Mad Prophet was too besotted to respond beyond a grunt, but the gem-cutter beside him ventured comment. 'How so? Won't we be stirred by the war's young hero, that blond-haired prince from the west?'

Medlir's lips thinned to tightness. 'What is any war but a massacre?' Through the drawing beat of the secondary chords, he shrugged off introspective impatience. 'Even without lyrics or story, Halliron's melody by itself could wring tears from a statue.'

The balding gem-cutter looked dubious; while Medlir melted into the crowd to resume his course for the stables, Dakar tangled fingers in his beard, fuddled by thought that the eyes of Halliron's apprentice should be some other colour than grey-hazel.

Then the spangled brilliance of the Masterbard's instrument was joined by his beautiful voice, haunting and rich and clear-toned; in its thrall every listener was transported to a morning in spring when the mists had lifted over the marshes of the river Tal Quorin. The odds in their favour ten to one, a town garrison had marched on the forest bred clansmen who dared shelter Arithon s'Ffalenn, the renegade Prince of Rathain also called Master of Shadow.

> 'What law has sanctioned a war for one life,
> when no bloodshed was sought at Etarra?
> Shadow fell in defence, for no man died
> by command of the prince to be harrowed.'

There came an uneasy shifting of feet, of creaking boards, and flurried whispers that Halliron's art skilfully reined back short of outrage. For this ballad's course commemorated no beloved saviour in glittering gold and sapphires, avenging with righteous bolts of light. This spare, driving, tragic account held no bright hero at the ending, but only men ruinously possessed by their hatreds to grasp the first reason to strike down longstanding enemies.

> 'Who shall weep, Lord Steiven, Earl of the North,
> for the refuge that failed to spare your clan?
> The prince in your care once begged to fare forth,
> then stayed; his liegemen were fate-cursed to stand.'

Notes struck the air now like mallet-blows. No one spoke. None moved as the ballad unfolded, each stanza in pitiless stark cadence unveiling fresh atrocity. There were no heroics, but only desperation in a Shadow Master's talents bent to confuse and detain; in unspeakable measures undertaken in a defence without hope, when the dammed-back waters of Tal Quorin were unleashed in reaving torrents to scythe down Etarra's trapped garrison. Nor did there follow any salve of vengeance, but only bitter brutality, when a band of headhunter survivors lashed back in a frustrated foray of slaughter against the encampment that concealed the clan women and their children. The spree of rapine intended to draw their defenders into open ground for final reckoning had seen abrupt and terrible ending.

> *'Deshir's butcher and Prince Arithon's bane,*
> *Lysaer s'Ilessid loosed his gifted light*
> *Sixty score innocents writhed in white flame*
> *for miscalled mercy, blind justice, and right.'*

Halliron's tones dipped and quavered, searing the pent air with images of horror and tragedy. His lyranthe in an unrelenting, lyrical sorrow bespoke senseless waste and destruction. In Deshir, by design of the Mistwraith, the extraordinary talents of two princes had collided to devastating losses, with nothing either proven or gained.

> *'This day, under sky unthreatened by dark,*
> *the Etarran ranks march to kindle strife.*
> *Headhunters search the wide woodlands to mark*
> *one fugitive who owns no wish to fight.'*

The last, slashing jangle of chords rang and dwindled in dissonance.

For a suspended moment, nothing stirred. Only when Halliron arose and made his bow, then bent to wrap his fine instrument did the shock of his weaving fall away. Listeners paralysed in unabashed tears cracked into an explosion of talk.

'Ath's own mercy! What a skill! The lyranthe herself was made to weep.' A belated fall of silvers clanged across the boards by Halliron's stool, mingled with a few muted bravos. The Masterbard had not played for an encore; no one held doubts that this ballad had been his last performance for the evening. Though one maudlin fieldhand shouted for the bar wench to bring out spirits, the rest of the patrons arose and pressed, murmuring, toward the tavern door. As the room emptied, a woman's tones pierced through the crush. 'Had I not lost my jewels to those murdering clan scoundrels in Taernond, I could almost feel sorry for the Deshans.'

Dakar simply sat, eyes round as coins fixed morosely on the hands that cradled a tankard of stale beer. In time, some minutes after Halliron had retired upstairs to his room, Medlir arrived, and sat down, and unstoppered a cut-glass decanter. He produced two goblets of turned maple and poured out three fingers of peach brandy, the rich smell piquantly sharp in the heated sea of used air.

One the bard's apprentice pressed upon the Mad Prophet; the other, he nursed for himself.

In companionable sympathy for a well-timed escape to the stables, Dakar sighed, 'These folk will go home tonight and maybe think. By tomorrow, over sore heads, they'll say the Masterbard must have exaggerated. Deshir's barbarians are best off dead, they'll insist, and shrug off what they heard entirely when the next Etarran wool factor passes through. What did your master hope to gain?'

Medlir swirled his brandy, his face without expression and his eyes veiled under soot-thick, down-turned lashes. 'Why care?'

Dakar bestowed a shrill hiccup into a pudgy, cupped palm. 'You met my Fellowship master, so you said.'

Strong brandy could make anybody patient. Medlir waited. Presently Dakar tucked up his stockinged feet and propped his bearded chin on one fist. 'Well, you'll know Asandir's not the sort to be lenient when he's crossed.'

'No wonder you're driven to drink.' Medlir hooked the flask from between his knees and refilled Dakar's goblet. 'What have you done?'

'Nothing,' Dakar said. 'That's my problem. That bastard of a sorcerer, the one the Deshans fought for? I was sent off to find him, and save him being mauled by his enemies. But let me tell you, Halliron's ballad aside, if you'd met him, you'd cheer Etarra's garrison.'

Medlir took a sip from his goblet, leaned back against the trestle, and closed his eyes. 'Why so?'

'He's crafty,' Dakar said, fixed on the sway of the bar wench's hips as she made rounds to darken the lanterns. 'Secretive. He doesn't at all take to company that's apt to meddle in his business.'

'And what would his business be, do you think?' Medlir asked from the darkness.

Dakar stuck out his lower lip and choked through a spray of fine spirits. 'The Fatemaster himself only knows! But Arithon's a vindictive bastard with self-righteous aversions to liquor and ladies and comforts. I'd sooner take Dharkaron Avenger to be my drinking companion.'

'Ah,' said Medlir. He raised his lids and smiled, his eyes caught like a cat's in the dying gleam from the fire. 'If you fear Asandir might catch up with you, why not share the road with us? We're headed into the low country, then southward to Shand in easy stages.' He arose, stretched, then set the half-emptied flask companionably by Dakar's left knee. 'Halliron's fingers get sore in the cold and lengthy hours of performance tax his strength. We seldom play long at one tavern. As our guest, you'd have free beer and most of the comforts you could wish.'

'Oh, bliss.' Dakar laughed, drained his goblet and licked the sweet dregs from his moustache. 'I've just been kissed on the lips by lady fortune.' He hefted the decanter with slurred thanks, and savoured the brandy by himself until he passed out in a heap beneath the bench.

The Mad Prophet awakened thick headed and tasting a tongue that felt packed in old fur. If lady fortune blessed him with her kiss the night before, she had stomped on his head the next morning. Peach brandy dealt a hangover to rival the most horrible torments of Sithaer. He could hardly have felt less miserable if somebody had sunk a pair of fleecing shears up to their handles in both eyes.

His discomfort was not improved by the fact he sat wedged between bundles of baggage in a jostling, low-slung conveyance that just now was rolling downhill. Small stones and gravel cracked and pinged under iron-rimmed wheels that made as much noise as a gristmill. Poked in the ribs by something hard, buffeted to sorry chills by winds that smelled of spruce and fresh ice, Dakar groaned.

'Oh, your acquisition is alive, I see,' somebody observed with jilting humour. 'Should we stop and offer him breakfast? Or no. Better ask first if he needs to piddle.'

Dakar cracked open gummed eyes. Granted a retreating view of a switched-back road edged with evergreen, he groaned and rolled back his head, only to be gouged in the nape by a flat griddle. He was in the Masterbard's pony cart, inveigled there by Medlir's sweet tongue and imprudent consumption of alcohol. Being stranded and broke in a back-country tavern in hindsight began to show merits.

The brandy had spun him wicked dreams.

Badgered through his sleep by a quick-tongued man with green eyes, black hair, and the sharp-planed features of s'Ffalenn royalty, the Mad Prophet wondered what prompted his mind to play tricks and prod him with memories of the Shadow Master.

Then the cart jerked to a stop, which taxed his thought to a stand-still. A shadow fell over him. Somebody not much larger than his nemesis in build, but with intentions infinitely kinder said, '*Do* you have to pee?'

Dakar rubbed crust from his lashes. Medlir leaned on the cart side and watched him with eyes of muddied hazel. His smile was sympathetic. 'I don't imagine you feel hale. Who'd have thought you the hero, to drain that flask to the dregs?'

'If there'd been another just like it, I could've emptied that one as well. You would too, if you knew the man I'm supposed to be protecting.' Dakar added with thick urgency, 'Since you asked, the bushes are a very good idea.'

Medlir let down the tailgate, whose fastening pins and boards and battered hinges combined to make a terrible racket. Holding his head, Dakar levered himself up and out from his nest amid the camp gear. He staggered into the roadway, not to relieve himself, but to find himself a cranny in which to crouch and be sick. He managed to reach the ditch by the roadside. There Medlir's thoughtful grip was all that kept him from pitching head-down into puddles scummed over in ice and stitched with brambles.

That wretchedness finished, back upright on unsteady legs, Dakar real-ized his feet were no longer unshod. Somebody had kindly, if carelessly, restored his mislaid boots. The beer-damp stockings inside had crumpled in a way sure to chafe him a wicked set of blisters.

Still, Dakar concluded as he hauled himself back to the wagon, he would perish of a million wasting hangovers before he would bend to Asandir's will concerning the Master of Shadow. 'If my life wasn't bothered by sorcerers, maybe then I could stop drinking,' he confided as he moled his way under a carriage rug.

Halliron unbraced the brake and clucked to the shaggy buckskin between the shafts. The cart rattled south down the Eltair road, that ran like a track of unreeled string, pinched between the black rock shores of the bay and the snow-bearded range of the Skyshiels. Cold winds scoured with salt off the water parted the pony's rough coat. Halliron drove with his hands layered in mittens, while Medlir walked, his stride loose and long, and his mind preoccupied with recitation of ballads, or some lilted line of melody to which his master would often contribute comment.

A bard's apprenticeship involved rigorous study, as Dakar came to appreciate in the hours while his hangover lifted. Although Halliron wore his age well, his years numbered eighty-seven. The damp bothered more than his hands, and although he seldom complained of his aches, he was engaged in a desperate race to train his successor before vigour failed him.

In an afternoon stop at a post station, where a room was engaged to allow the old man to rest, Medlir admitted to Dakar that the trip to Shand was for sentiment. 'The Masterbard was born at Innish on the southcoast, where River Ippash meets the sea. He would see his home before he dies and have his ashes laid by the canals near his family.'

'He has family?' Dakar said, surprised. As many years as he had known Halliron, he had never heard mention of roots.

'A daughter, I think.' Medlir picked at a plate of sausage and bread, too considerate for unrestrained gossip. 'The mother preferred not to travel.'

Thoroughly familiar with every road in the continent, Dakar weighed distances and miles. 'You could make the south coast by the summer.'

'Well, yes.' Medlir smiled. 'We hope to. If every tavern in between can stop flinging us blandishments to tarry.'

The common room was nearly empty, the last relay of messengers from Highscarp being mounted outside in the yard. Flushed from the morning's raw winds, or maybe the heat of the fire, Medlir appeared not to mind the way Dakar surveyed him relentlessly: from slim, musician's fingers that tapped whistle tunes on the edges of the crockery, to the unique way he chose to style his shirts, with sleeves full and long to the forearm, the cuffs tight-laced over the wrists to end at the heel of his hands.

In the hour of the Mistwraith's curse, Arithon had once fielded a strike from a light-bolt that left him welted from right palm to elbow, Dakar remembered. The unbidden association made him frown. He stared all the closer at Halliron's apprentice, who leaned back to stretch in the sunlight that sloped through the casement.

His hands proved unscarred on both sides.

Dakar stifled an oath of self-disgust. Paranoia was making him foolish. The Master of Shadow was mage-trained. To another eye schooled to know talent, his aura should have blazed with unshed power against the darkened panelling of this room. By now sobered up enough to use Asandir's teaching, Dakar squinted and peered, but detected nothing beyond the life-force that should halo the form of an ordinary man in prime health. He relaxed and started to sit back, then swore beneath his breath as he realized: such a detail could be masked with shadow.

'What?' Medlir regarded him inquiringly. 'You seem bothered. Are you certain you won't share my meal?'

The Mad Prophet looked into the man's guileless face, then on impulse raised his hands and summoned power until his fingers streamed trailers of mage-fire.

Grey eyes ticked with mustard flecks watched him back, neither dazzled nor curious. Not a lash or a lid quivered at Dakar's display; the minstrel apprentice's pupils, widened in the dimness, failed to narrow so much as a hair's-breadth.

'Forgive me,' Medlir said. 'I wasn't thinking, of course. You must still be feeling quite shaky.' He pushed aside his plate, leaned on his elbows, and peeled a flaked callus from a fingertip well thickened from fret board and lyranthe string. 'We probably won't be moving on today, anyway. Halliron slept poorly last night. Since he'll do best if he rests until tomorrow, I will play in the common room to satisfy the landlord. You can have a bed and hot soup.'

Now Dakar grinned slyly back. 'Actually, I'd rather hear you sing me the ballad of the Cat and the Mead.'

'Which version?' Medlir reached across the bench, lifted Halliron's instrument, and began with enthusiasm to untie wrappings. 'There's the one that's suitable for little children, and the one fit for nowhere but the bawdy house, and a half dozen variations that fall in the range in between.'

'Oh, try the one that's obscene,' Dakar said, his plump chin propped on folded knuckles and his cheeks dimpled in contentment over his scraggle of red beard.

'The one with eighty eight verses and that awful repetitive chorus?' Medlir tucked the lyranthe on his lap, made swift adjustment of the strings, and caught Dakar's nod as he dashed off a run in E major to test his tuning. 'Well,' he said with a long-suffering patience that Arithon s'Ffalenn had never owned, 'About verse fifty, please remember, you were the one who insisted.'

Tribulation

When Halliron took a chill that left him unfit to travel for two days, Medlir accepted the setback in stride. In no haste himself to reach Shand, he regarded his requisite nightly performance in the posthouse taproom as time well spent in extra practice.

Confounded by his good nature, for the apprentice bard spent both mornings and afternoons put to task under his master's critical ear, Dakar warmed his feet by the hearth and his belly with flagons of ale. He listened to Medlir's stock of drinking songs, ready to pounce if the repertoire suffered repeats. When the minstrel's inventiveness did not falter, he snatched sleep in catnaps and escaped any dreams of vengeful sorcerers.

Their last night at the posthouse was made rowdy by a passing company of mercenaries, ten men under a surly, sword-scarred captain who demolished a platter of roast turkey in the best corner and smoked a pipe until the air around his head blued to fug. Still in their mail and rust-stained tunics, his fighting company drank and gambled, enthusiastically abetted by Dakar.

Between the jingle of gear and rattling dice, the bitten curses and sarcastic slurs and rounds of big-bellied laughter, there came the inevitable exchange of news.

'You come from northwards,' the captain bellowed across the taproom to Medlir. He paused to pick gristle from his teeth. 'What've you heard? We're bound that way into Etarra. Ship's Port was thick with rumour that the Prince of the West is hiring on swords to build a retinue.'

Medlir companionably shrugged, his hands in idle play upon his strings. 'Why should he? The city council keeps him in comfort. Last I heard, he hadn't yet tired of the garrison commander's pretty sister.'

The mercenary captain hunched forward like a bear. Through the incisors clamped on toothpick and pipe stem, he said, 'Well, the recruiter sent out by the headhunters' league claimed Prince Lysaer's been deeded Avenor's lands. The grant came from the Mayor Elect of Korias.'

The silvery spill of notes changed character, became thinner, brighter, more brittle. 'If so, the charter's hardly legal.'

Nobody took umbrage; the comment was scarcely out of turn, Athera's Masterbard being a keeper of traditions often consulted to clarify rules of precedence. As Halliron's probable successor, Medlir would be trained for the day the supreme title might fall to him.

'Huh. Swords, and not paper, will settle that issue.' The mercenary captain tossed away his toothpick and removed his pipe, which had stubbornly smouldered and gone out. 'If there's pay being offered for a winter position, we'd be fools not to go have a look. At worst, we'd weather till spring in Etarra, then sign with Pesquil's headhunters when the new campaign season starts.'

'Well, fortune to you,' said Medlir, laughing softly. 'Avenor's a ruin. One of the old sites that folk won't go near for the hauntings. There might be pay, if you fancy the chance to lay bricks.'

'You've been there?' The mercenary captain stared at the minstrel through the curling flame of his spill.

'No.' Medlir launched off a sprightly jig, foot tapping, and a gleam to his eyes at strange odds with his earlier humour. 'Ath grant I never live to see the place.'

The following morning dawned to grey, misty rain and a clammy east wind off the bay. In the tidewater region of the coast, winter's hold settled lightly. The mild airs drawn north by ocean currents could brew the occasional warm day. Above Jaelot, the road lay softened to muck, through which cartwheels sucked and splattered to the fitful grate of flint-bearing gravel. Medlir strode at the buckskin's head to steady the bridle as the pony skated and slid through league upon league of soupy footing. Swathed in faded quilts on the driver's board, Halliron sat looking tired.

'I've no wish at all to stop in Jaelot,' he insisted, unusually quarrelsome. 'The town's a cesspit of bad taste. I won't have you wasting your talents there.'

'Well, at least that's a first.' Medlir steered the pony cart toward the verge to allow a packtrain bearing southern spices and silk bales to make its laboured way past. Over the yips of the drovers, he said, 'Not long back, I recall your phrasing the matter quite the other way about, that my fingering was too clumsy to inflict on a tinker, never mind any public audience.'

'Well, that was then.' Halliron blotted his dripping nose and sniffed. 'You still have a great deal to learn.'

Through the jingle of gear and harness, and the whip-snaps as carters forced their ox teams from drifting to scent the horses as they passed, Medlir kept a weather eye on Dakar, perched like a woodchuck on a bony chestnut gelding won over dice with the mercenaries. More accustomed to pack straps hung with cooking pots than to bearing saddle and rider, the creature had wall-eyes and knock-knees and a tail stripped of hair like a rat's. The buckskin pony shied well clear. More a shambling liability than a source of reliable transport, the chestnut changed nature like a weathercock, friendly and fiendish by turns.

Dakar's indifferent horsemanship was hampered further by short thighs that stretched like a wrestler's to straddle his mount's width of barrel. Watching the pair careen through the pack beasts and drays, reins flying loose and heels drumming to indignant slaps of the silly, naked tail, Medlir was hard pressed not to chuckle.

Halliron looked in danger of swallowing his lips, until he resorted to muffling his whoops behind quilts.

The last laden mule in the cavalcade passed, with the gelding spinning left, and then right, in some doubt of its proper orientation. Dakar thwacked its goose rump with his rein ends and hauled, to no good effect. The narrow, bony head on a great pole of ewe neck swivelled back to stare where the leather had stung, its expression determinedly flummoxed.

Medlir shut brimming eyes.

'What's so funny?' howled Dakar. He stabbed the gelding in its cavernous ribs with his heels and flapped elbows until it ambled in a sequence of steps by no means definable as a gait.

After one prolonged gasp against the buckskin's wet mane, Medlir tucked his chin in his mufflers and stared without focus straight forward. 'Ah!' He made a manful effort, clutched his ribs, and said, 'No one's laughing. Halliron has a terrible cough. I could be suffering the same.'

Dakar's reply unravelled into oaths as the gelding's racketing shy sallied the width of the roadway. A stiff-featured Medlir applied himself to guiding the pony cart from its parking place amid the burdock, while Halliron wheezed and wiped rheumy eyes and murmured, 'Ath, now my stomach is aching.'

Their journey resumed under mists spun to gold under late-breaking sunlight. Flocking gulls rose and wheeled in the sea-breeze off the tide flats. To the right, at each turn in the road, steep-sided valleys of evergreens yawned into gorges, some threaded with falls that spilled like frayed floss, and others with deep, narrow lakes lying polished as moonstones.

The country was beautiful, but wild, the foothills scarred by old rockfalls and too steeply pitched to grow fodder. Under sky like lucid aquamarine, the storms seemed remote, that could lash without warning off the bay and hurl salt spume against the mountains. The trees and the moss bore the scars in broken branches, and rock abutments burned clean of lichens. An equinox gale could wreck a steading in a night, with the buildings rebuilt again out of the splintered rubble, or ship's planks, washed in by the tide. Hostels and posthouses were widely spaced and nowhere inside a day's ride of a walled town.

When the sun swung behind the peaks and purpled shadow hardened the road in the grip of early cold, Halliron began to shiver with chills. His nose was buffed red, and his eyes shone too bright, and his thickest quilts lent no comfort.

Medlir said nothing, but watched his master in concern through the pause as they watered the horses.

Embarrassed at last by his own misery, Halliron capitulated. 'Oh, all right. We'll shelter in Jaelot, to spare you the bother of tending an invalid in the open.'

'What bother?' Medlir redistributed the mud-flecked blankets over the Masterbard's knees. 'If these townsmen have execrable taste, I could always try those ballads we heard in the sailor's dives at Werpoint.'

Halliron returned a choked cough, whatever he had in mind undone by Dakar's antics as he fell off the same stone twice trying to remount the brown gelding.

'You'll break your neck getting on that way!' Medlir called, his fingers busy taking the pony's surcingle up a hole.

Puffing, beet-faced, in no mood for criticism from a man who understood nothing about the trials of being fat, Dakar clambered back up the rock. 'Since when do you know so much about horses?'

'Maybe my parents were drifters,' Medlir said.

'Hah!' The Mad Prophet achieved precarious balance on one foot. 'Foxes, more like. You say crafty little about yourself.'

A shallow smile touched Medlir's features, accompanied by ingenuously raised brows. 'Foxes bite.'

'Well, I *know* I'm prying.' Dakar poised himself, leaped, and grabbed, while his steed staggered into a clattering half-passe. The Mad Prophet landed astride through a miracle, both fists balled in mane-hanks to arrest a pitch over the saddle's far side. As his mount was coerced to cease milling, he added, 'Faery-toes makes better company.'

'Faery-toes? That?' Halliron poked his nose out of his blankets and fixed dubious eyes on hooves that were round and fluted as meat platters.

'Well of course,' said Dakar, offended. 'The name suits him fine, don't you think?'

The party moved on, into shadows that lengthened to grey dusk, swallowed early by fog off the bay.

Darkness had fallen as they rounded the bend before Jaelot's wide gates. Situated on a beak-head of land that jutted out into the bay, the town was walled with black rock. Torches in iron baskets burned from the keeps, which were octagonal, with slate roofs buttressed by gargoyles that loomed and leered and lolled obscene tongues over gate-turrets chis-elled from white quartz. These were emblazoned with rampant lions, each bearing a snake in its mouth.

'Ugly.' By now querulously tired, Halliron regarded the carvings with distaste while the tarnished strips of tin hung as ward talismans jangled and clinked in thin dissonance. 'The Paravian gates torn down from this site were said to be fashioned of agate, and counter-weighted to swing at a hand's touch.'

'This was a Second Age fortress?' Medlir asked. 'How surprising to find it inhabited.' He soothed the cross-grained buckskin to a halt as the gate watch called down gruff challenge. He had to answer without hearing his master's return comment. 'We're wayfarers, two minstrels and a com-panion. We shouldn't be stopping here at all, except the old man needs shelter.'

'Pull aside then.' The watch captain lounged in his niche, his breath plumed in flamelight. 'The post courier's overdue from Tharidor, and the gates'll be opened when he's in.'

'There's courtesy for you,' Halliron said between sneezes. 'I knew we should have made camp. If the courier hasn't come to grief in the dark, we'll have our choice of three inns, all of them cavernously dim and dirty, and not a one of them honest.'

'Which has the best ale?' asked Dakar.

'Who knows?' The Masterbard sighed. 'In Jaelot, they cut the brew with water.'

By chance, their wait became shortened. While Medlir fussed over his master, and Dakar communed with his mount, a barrel-chested wagonmaster in sheepskins rolled in, swearing at his team and unhappy to be missing his dinner. He brandished his whip at the gate house, while his sweated horses sidled and stamped and struck blue-edged sparks from the pavement. 'It's that thrice-cursed shipment from the mill I'm carry-ing, the one with the mayor's seal on it.'

The gates were opened very swiftly indeed, while something clicked in the brain of Dakar's camel-necked chestnut that said stable, and com-fort, and oats. It pinned back rabbity ears and lunged to harry the wagon team through.

The lead pair were blinkered. The first the near one knew of Faery-toes' attentions was a nip of yellow teeth at its flanks.

It veered to a bounding grind of singletrees, while Dakar, howling mightily, sawed nerveless mouth with both reins and fell off. He had the aplomb to roll clear, while the carter whipcracked and cursed.

The lash caught the gelding on the nose. He windmilled sideways on splayed feet, rat-tail flailing. Eyes rolled white, his nostrils expanded into a snort that blew steam, he half-reared and reversed to a thunderous clatter of hooves. His gaunt rump jammed the wheel horse in the shoul-der. It staggered, squealing. The rest of the team careened sideways and

41

jack-knifed the dray between the gate turrets with Faery-toes folded amidst them like a misguided log in a torrent.

Oaths became lost in the crack of shod hooves as a brief show of stamping coalesced to a five horse brawl amid the traces.

The carter clung to his swaying box like a man on a half-foundered vessel, plying his lash and a poisonous stream of threats upon his scuffling team to no avail. Leather parted; terrets burst from collar stuffing to a scream of splintering wood. Unnoticed atop the swaying wagon bed, lashings creaked and shifted loose. A springy bundle of cypress teetered, then tipped like an unfolding set of shears and swan-dived onto the pavement.

The splintering crack of impact raised stinging reverberations under the confines of the gate arch. The wheel pair parted sideways in a violent shy and the carter threw down his whip, crying murder, as eighty board feet of rare moulding custom-carved to please the mayor's wife became milled to pale slivers beneath his wheels.

Through a small, stunned second, the torches dimmed in a swooping gust of wind. Under their demonic flicker, the carter turned red and tore at his sideburns with his fists. The draught team milled, netted in slackened traces and flighty as shoaling fish; while the mis-shapen cause of the disaster stood nonplussed, conversing in great sucking gusts with the wheel horses.

'Curse of a fiend!' The carter unfurled from his box in a frog-leap that landed him beside the russet-brown bundle that was Dakar. 'What in Sithaer will you do about that misbegotten insult of a horse?'

'Misbegotten? Insult?' Dakar inspected the burly antagonist planted over him, fists cocked for mayhem, and his hair screwed free of an oiled felt cap like tufts of snarled wool on a shuttlecock. 'You're pretty ugly yourself, you know.' Through the half-breath while the carter was stunned speechless, the Mad Prophet pushed past, retrieved trailing reins, and hauled Faery-toes out backwards from the tangle of shafts and shredded harness.

While Halliron and Medlir watched amazed, a safe distance removed in the pony cart, Dakar came back, towing horse. He poised before the irate carter, oblivious to the pounding from the adjacent gate houses, as the watch on duty pelted downstairs in armed readiness to forestall an altercation.

'I suggest you forgive the old boy.' When the nag butted a congenial head against the carter's shoulder and knocked him a half-step back, Dakar added, 'How could you not? He likes you.'

The carter purpled and swung. The suet-round face of his target vanished as Dakar ducked and fled beneath the saddle girth. Bunched knuckles smacked against the barrel-sprung ribs of the horse, who responded from both ends with a grunt and a fart like an explosion.

'Oh my,' cried Dakar, stifling a chortle. 'Your wife's nose must look like a pudding if that's your reaction to her kisses.'

The carter dove under the gelding's neck in a fit of killing fury while the horse, ears flat, parted gaunt jowls and snapped.

Teeth closed over greasy fleece, and the breeches of the carter burst a critical seam. The Mad Prophet side-stepped around the chestnut's churning quarters, blithe in rebuke as he passed, 'Leave him alone, Faery-toes. Your affection's a wee bit misplaced. You know this fellow you're undressing's about as nice as a hawk-pecked snake.'

Arrived in a rush that packed the postern, Jaelot's guardsmen cracked into laughter.

Faery-toes switched its nubby tail just as the carter began his rush. Caught a dizzying lash in the face, and howling falsetto invective, the man lunged with full intent to mangle just as the horse lost its poise. Its knurled spine humped. Enormous hooves battered for purchase as its hind end heaved up and cleared the ground. One hind leg hooked out in a cow-kick that demolished the front wheel of the dray. A descant of splintering spokes sounded above the crash as the hub hammered into the cobbles.

Set dancing in nervy refrain, the unattended team hit their collars. The crippled vehicle dragged in their wake with a blistering screech that harrowed up six yards of paving. Some fast-witted bystander caught their bits and muscled them to a standstill, all unnoticed in the ongoing tumult beneath the archway.

The carter expended one last volley of monosyllabic epithets. Fairytoes, carried away in a careening sidle, lost the last of his questionable footing. He dropped belly-down in a splay-legged heap to a whistling grunt of astonishment.

Felled by peals of mirth, Dakar buckled to his knees not far off. With both eyes squeezed shut and leaking helpless tears, he failed to notice when the officer of the watch stopped sniggering. Jaelot's men at arms snapped to in dutiful propriety as a four-in-hand hitch and black lacquered coach thundered up the thoroughfare. Gilded, lion-blazoned doors sparked in the torchlight as the vehicle slowed and pulled up before the obstruction that clogged the city gate.

Stiffened as pokers, watch gate captain's men saluted as boy grooms in velvet livery leapt down to catch the bridles of the lead horses, which were also black, and matched like images in mirror glass with smart blazes and white stockings. A footman dispatched from the driver's box strolled over to the carter, even yet hopping back to escape the gelding's thrashing first effort to rise.

'There is some difficulty?' the footman opened coldly. The gold braid and blazon of the authority he represented glittered through the smoke of the torches.

Speechless, the carter stabbed a skinned finger at the gelding, which gathered its fantastic assemblage of joints and surged, snorting, to its feet.

A woman's voice called from the carriage. The footman nodded deference, then turned his chin stiffly over his pearl-buttoned collar and inquired, 'May I ask, in the name of my Lord Mayor, what you have done with the new crown moulding?'

The carter straightened his ripped britches, sweat sliding slick down his temples. 'I? Vengeance of Dharkaron, that horse!'

Faery-toes curled an insouciant lip and shook like a dog amid a tempest of flapping reins and stirrups. The footman's regard turned sceptical before he swung back to the carter. 'I doubt if that bundle of incompetence is able to move four feet in consecutive order.'

'Well, that says it all in a nutshell,' cried the carter in exasperation.

'Who owns the beast?' The glance of the mayor's footman ranged loftily over the bystanders, flickered past the pony cart and its pair of frozen figures, then lowered inexorably to the last, still wheezing on the pavement. 'Who?'

Dakar's disordered features snapped sober. 'I just donated him to the city almshouse.'

The carriage door opened and slammed. The footman gave way before a robed secretary with overbred hands. Mincing like a rooster with hackles raised for combat, the official bore down upon the unkempt fat man who, like his horse, belatedly scrambled upright.

'You will be chained and held in custody until tomorrow, when this matter will be settled in the court hall of Jaelot to my Lord Mayor's satisfaction. I suggest until then that somebody competent puts that creature away. At least have it removed from the streets before it can cause further mischief.' To the carter, he added without sympathy, 'The guard will help clear your debris. If you wish to claim settlement for damages, attend the hearing and make your plea to the mayor's justice.'

While the watch captain's men closed in armed force to take the Mad Prophet into custody, and the retinue of the Jaelot's mayor retired back to the carriage and whisked off on gilded wheels, Halliron pressed mittened hands over streaming eyes and groaned through the muffling fur. 'Ath, I knew, I just *knew!* We should never have come into Jaelot.'

Trial

His Lordship the Mayor of Jaelot was not disposed to rise early. In his courts of law, appointments by hour were unheard of; the city alderman sent his list daily to the watch captain, who detailed men at arms to the dungeons. The accused were fetched out without breakfast and escorted to the annex chamber, a windowless, black-panelled vault with groined ceilings built into a cellar beneath the council hall. There, cuffed in manacles that made it difficult to scratch accumulated flea bites, Dakar the Mad Prophet was obliged to wait with two other men and a woman, whose crimes ranged from public brawling to theft and bloody murder.

Through the course of an uncomfortable night, he had cursed his careless learning. A brass lock or latch, he could have opened with spells; and had, many times, in egress from the bedchambers of willing wives whose husbands had come home untimely. But the fetters and bars of Jaelot's dungeons were never fashioned for decor in castings of soft, refined metals. Chilled yet from lying huddled on dank straw, Dakar ground his teeth over dilatory habits that had let him drift through his centuries of Fellowship apprenticeship without fully mastering the contrary properties of alloys bearing cold iron.

The dilemma bequeathed him by Faery-toes had long since ceased to seem funny.

In the beleaguered light shed by one candle, the mayor's dais and desk loomed over the prisoner's dock, a marble edifice of gothic carvings and fluted supports and grotesque, hunch-backed caryatids, whose suffering poses were painted in shadows like scenes from Sithaer's bleak pits. The air smelled of wax, of parchment, of the dried citrus peel and Shandian spices used to overpower the stink of condemned men kept chained in straw acidified with rat urine. Behind the prisoners' enclosure, board benches lined the rear wall. On these gathered complainants in clean shirts and scrubbed boots; also the wives, the relations and the long-suffering friends of the day's accused, to wait in fidgeting silence. The curious came too, but unobtrusively. In Jaelot, a loquacious jailer told Dakar, a beggar who had taken illicit shelter in the Mayor's courtroom had lost all his fingers as punishment.

In this chamber, a merciful sentence might be a swift beheading; a severe one, a dismemberment, or breaking on the wheel before burning. Dakar shifted from foot to foot in an attempt to ease the drag of the chain; the unending bite of fetters whose steel, to one of mage-trained sensitivity, scoured the awareness with the tang of past misery and old blood.

Self-contained in his distress, he noted little beyond the glowering arrival of the millwork's wronged carter; still, the benches were not empty of friends.

Halliron Masterbard had come, dressed in all the splendour of his rank. From the depths of the gloom, his neat cloak and slashed doublet of black watered silk lined in saffron shimmered like flame with caught light. Topaz studs and gold ribbon sparked and flashed in wry and stabbing satire, perhaps, that the mayor's state colours were the same. Stationed at his side, Medlir wore brown broadcloth, a modest brooch at his collar.

The carillons that signalled the hour boomed faintly down from the bell tower. Aching and irritable, Dakar endured the arrival of Jaelot's Lord Mayor with a dawning sense of the absurd. He had seen a high king's ceremonial open with less pomp.

The hall doors boomed back, held by bowing servants in sable livery. Halberdiers in black armour marched in double files, followed by page-boys who unreeled gold-edged carpet, emblazoned each yard with Jaelot's snake-bearing lions. A girl in a hooped farthingale fringed with jingling bullion chains strewed hothouse roses from a basket. She was trailed by two braces of secretaries in wool robes cuffed with marten, then their serving boys, bearing satchels and writing papers furled in yellow ribbon. Next, the judiciary, robed in black velvet and white ermine, and wearing a mitred felt cap edged with moth-eaten braid; the city alderman, burdened down like a moulting crane in layers of brocade and ruffled cuffs. After these, soft as pudding, the city's vaunted mayor, who swayed at each step, his voluminous robe billowing off his padded shoulders like sails let free of their sheetlines.

Forced to duck as a rose struck his face, Dakar stared in amazement as the processional ended. Like trained bears, the players arrayed themselves on the dais. There should have been music, he thought, as the flower maid emptied her basket in the precinct of the mayor's chair, and the boys unpacked the scribes' satchels as if laying a cloth for a picnic. The halberdiers dressed weapons with a clang of gold gauntlets, and the tubby mayor berthed himself in his overstuffed throne of state.

Beaked as a vulture beneath his tatty hat, the judiciary rattled a triangle and pronounced, 'The Jaelot City Court is in session.'

The alderman unrolled a list on parchment and called out Dakar's name.

'Well, thank Ath, we're first,' the Mad Prophet cracked in dry relief.

Two unamused men at arms who did not wear costly gauntlets caught him under the armpits, hauled him forward and threw him face-down before the dais.

There he was held by two booted feet pressed solidly into his shoulderblades. The alderman cleared his throat, pushed a spidery set of spectacles up his nose, and recited the list of offences: disruption of the city peace; obstruction of the public thoroughfare; wilful damage to the mayor's property; interference with commerce; negligent handling of horseflesh; and lastly, insolence to officers while in custody.

'What do you plead?' The judiciary peered over his spiked and scented beard at the accused crushed prone on the floor.

His jaw jammed against cold granite, Dakar tugged a breath into compressed lungs and swore.

'Impertinence while in court,' the alderman droned. Like synchronized vultures, four near-sighted secretaries dipped quills and scribbled the addition to their documents.

'Fiends and Dharkaron's vengeance!' Dakar pealed. 'What wilful damage? *You* saw my horse. Did Faery-toes look at all like the sort to attack passing drays out of hand? Ath's own patience, you'd kick something yourself, if some lout hauled off and rammed his fist in your ribs!'

On the benches, the carter gritted sturdy teeth and restrained himself from springing to his feet to cry protest. Caught up in its rut of due process, the court continued with the prisoner.

'Insolence to superiors,' said the alderman, displaying an unfortunate lisp, while the pens of the secretaries twitched and scratched.

The mayor stifled a yawn and eased the silver-tipped laces on his waistcoat. 'I never saw your beast.' In tones of boredom marred by faint shortness of breath, he admitted, 'My wife was the one out in the carriage. The moulding was cut to satisfy her whim. Its destruction has left her indisposed. As the horse's owner, you are responsible for its unprovoked fit. Since the question of innocence does not arise on that charge, your punishment must recompense the lady's losses.'

The carter could no longer contain himself. 'Does my team and dray count for nothing? Two of my horses are lame, and wheelwright's services are dear!'

'Be still.' The judiciary looked up from adjusting his rings. 'City justice must be satisfied before any appeal for compensation can be opened.'

Hot and fuming in his town clothes, the carter sat down. Halliron looked deadpan, a sign of irritation; Medlir's bemusement masked disgust.

Pressed still to the floor, his face twisted sideways and his hair rucked up like a snarl of wind-twisted bracken, Dakar rolled his eyes at the crick that plagued his neck. Heartily tired of embracing clammy stone, he followed the proceedings with difficulty.

An exchange between the city alderman and the prim-faced judiciary again roused the pens of the secretaries. Nibs scritched across parchment like the scurry of roaches, and a pageboy jangled the triangle to some unseen administrative cue.

'Guilty on all counts.' The judiciary produced a flannel handkerchief and honked to clear his nose. Then he adjusted his hat and tipped his undershot chin toward the alderman.

'A fine and six months on the labour gang,' that official pronounced, then followed with a sum a prince would be beggared to pay.

'You already confiscated my saddle bags!' Dakar yelped in outrage. 'You'll know I don't carry any coin.'

'You're not lacking friends.' The mayor swivelled porcine eyes toward the elegant figure of the Masterbard. 'They may balance the debt for you, should they be so inclined. It is to them you must now beg for clemency.'

'They have nothing to do with me,' Dakar insisted between frog-flop attempts to wiggle free.

The Lord Mayor raised his eyebrows. 'Then what brings them to Jaelot?'

'You speak of Halliron Masterbard and his apprentice.' Dakar stopped struggling, appalled to unwonted seriousness. 'They ask nothing more than license to practise their art. There's not a town anywhere that wouldn't welcome their presence.'

The alderman's fishy eyes completed their inventory of glittering silk and cut topaz. 'Is this true?'

Halliron swept to his feet. In a voice burred rough by his cough, but modulated to lyrical acidity, he said, 'What's true is that no man alive owns the sum Jaelot's court of *justice* sees fit to demand.' The barbed threat of satire behind his inflection rang without echo into silence.

The Lord Mayor fluttered a hand in capitulation. 'Well then. We'll mediate the sentence, naturally. Since my lady was the party offended, it's fitting that she gain compensation. The spoiled moulding cost four hundred royals, true-silver. The carter's list of damages will be compiled and paid off to the penny. The city's fine I will waive on this condition: that Halliron Masterbard entertain my lady's guests at the feast upon mid-summer solstice.' A glistening, toothy smile parted the mayor's lips. 'License to practise your art, if you will, before this city's finest. If your playing matches your reputation, no doubt, folk of pedigree will shower their gold at your feet. You might even earn a tidy profit.'

Medlir's lightning surge to arise was stopped by a feather touch from the bard.

From the floor, Dakar gagged in strangled outrage. 'That's rank insult.'

48

The secretaries' nibs scraped through a poisonous silence. Halliron, white hair thrown back, light eyes fixed on a point midway between ceiling groins and dais, said nothing. Medlir's poised stillness showed tension more appropriate to a swordsman than a singer, while the halberdiers who were not one whit ceremonial shifted their balance to readiness.

Strangely desperate, Dakar said, 'Don't answer. I don't require it.'

'What bargains you strike between yourselves are entirely your personal affair.' The mayor parked his hands amid the foamy lace of his waistcoat. 'The city's terms will stand: either pay the fine or render performance, with enforced restriction to remain inside city walls until the terms of the sentence are met. You have seven days in which to give your decision.'

At the edge of the candle's pooled light, the judiciary's smirk flashed like the teeth of a feeding shark. 'Set the record.' His attention brushed Halliron, then bent dismissively to share his amusement with the alderman. 'It's a convenient arrangement, since the offender's stint at forced labour will expire near the same date.' To the bard, he added gently, 'Of course you could decline the option. Your companion would then languish in prison till he dies, or his debt to Jaelot is paid.'

On the dais, a striker flared in a scribe's veined hand. The scent of heated wax curled through the smell of roses, the tang of stale citrus and the unwashed heat of despair that clung to the prisoners uneasily awaiting their turn at trial. The secretaries raised sharp knives and busily resharpened their pens, while the alderman brandished the city seal and impressed Jaelot's lions on four documents.

'Case dismissed,' intoned the judiciary.

The carter pressed forward to cite his damages, while before the marble dais, the men at arms hoisted Dakar upright by his manacles and towed his bulk from the hall. Stumbling and wordless, the insouciance of yesterday bled out of him, he never once turned his head in appeal; while Halliron and Medlir made swift departure through the crooked stair that led upward into the daylight.

Later, in a dingy garret room where winter winds tore at loose slates, and draughts flowed and creaked through the gaps in warped shutters, Medlir sat over a mug of spiced wine, his flattened hands tapping a jig tune on the chipped and dingy porcelain. 'Will you let him off?'

'Was there ever any question?' Four hundred and sixty royals of their store of coin had already been dispatched to the lumber mill and the wheelwright's coffers. Halliron sat on the pallet opposite, swathed in quilts and coach rugs taken from the pony cart's baggage. The inn's bedclothes had been banished into care of the laundress; if this establishment maintained any servant to fill the post. Scraping an idle fingernail through the grime on the bed boards, Halliron was inclined to think not. 'Your obligation to Asandir must take precedence.'

Medlir jerked his chin up. 'It does not.' The fluttering tallow dip underlit his face, lending baleful emphasis to his anger. 'The Fellowship sorcerers would agree. Your business is in Shand, not in mending the Mad Prophet's excesses.'

Halliron tisked gently. His slow grin unveiled gapped front teeth. 'I can teach you as readily here as in the south. Shand can wait.'

'If six months in Jaelot doesn't contrive to ruin us both.' Medlir's veneer of irritation dissolved as he arose to add billets to the ill-vented hearth, burned down to a smouldering, sullen bed of coals that belched smoke at each breath of wind. As the new wood caught, he sighed. 'All of this concerns my life before I accepted your apprenticeship. I'd rather you weren't burdened.'

'You're more to me, now, than an apprentice.' Fresh flame curled up, laying a bronze patina over the spider-tracks of wrinkles that scored the bard's skin, and gilding age-chiselled face-bones still windburned from the open road. 'And anyway, you're the one most inconvenienced. I shouldn't care to stand in your shoes when the Mad Prophet discovers you've deceived him.'

His back turned, Medlir shrugged. 'Forced labour won't give him much chance.'

Eyes clear as sky studied the tension in the younger man's shoulders; noted the absorbed, almost desperate focus he bent upon the slate apron beneath his boots. As if his eyes could see into soot-dusted, grainy layers of stone, and perceive the dance and spark of primal energies that laced its matter into being; as indeed, Halliron knew, they once had, before raw abuse of such powers in Deshir's defence had raised barriers. A mage once trained to know the mysteries was unlikely to forget the awesome, wild winds of destruction a binding of unmaking could unleash. Backlash and scarring had rendered the spirit blind and mute.

With a gentleness roughened by the congestion in his chest, the bard said, 'Be patient. The sight will come back to you. Nature offers more than one path to perception, and your musical gifts may grow to compensate.'

The one who named himself Medlir raised hands to cover his face, the beaded ends of unstrung laces swinging and tapping against his knees. He crouched so for a long moment, then gathered himself, stood up, and turned toward his master an expression of unspeakable pain. 'I've felt the power stir in snatches, an echo here and there between notes.' His frustration revealed his difficulty, that he could not accustom himself to the change. The energies he had studied as pure spirit light felt indecipherably strange, transliterated to vibration and sound.

Halliron's smile held bedrock firmness. 'Well, work at it. Six months in Jaelot will certainly leave you the time.'

The Masterbard's apprentice returned a clipped sigh and bent to unwrap the lyranthe. He extended a foot in a swordsman's move and hooked the chamber's one stool. Its broken brace scarcely troubled his poise as he perched on the rat-chewed rush seat.

'Give me the Ballad of Taerlin Waters,' Halliron said. 'Mind you don't slur the runs in the third bar, or the grace notes that lead into the chorus.'

Medlir flicked back the untied gusset of his cuffs to free his fingers for tuning; here, where disguise was not needed, firelight caught raw and red on a scar that grooved the flesh in a half-twist from right palm to elbow. The hair that fronded his cheek as he bent to the sweet ring of strings was no longer the bland, ash brown Dakar knew, but glossy black as chipped coal.

His eyes, when he finally raised them to sing, were as penetrating a green as the royal ancestor whose natural looks he had inherited.

Links

Before the spring winds thaw the Mathorn Pass, Lysaer s'Ilessid, Prince of the West, rides out at the head of a cavalcade bound for ruined Avenor, his fair betrothed at his side; with him, under heavy escort of Etarran men at arms and ex-mercenaries sworn to feal service, travel a hundred wains bearing funds for his city's restoration, and tapestries, chests, fine furnishings and the jewels apportioned as his lady's dowry . . .

The journey of the royal retinue is marked by covert bands of scouts who relay word through messengers to the borders of Rathain and beyond; until news of Lysaer's movement is shared by clansmen who muster in deep, hidden glens against the day that Prince Arithon may have need of them . . .

On the east facing-wall of Jaelot, whipped by cold airs off the bay, the man who is prince and fugitive, Master of Shadow and Masterbard's apprentice, sends a request intended for Sethvir, Fellowship sorcerer and Warden of Althain Tower; and his missive is not scribed on parchment, but in his own blood upon a flake of slate that he dries over live flame, then tosses into the heaving breakers at high tide . . .

III. *FIRST INFAMY*

Committed as an impulsive donation by Etarra's Governor Supreme to the ruined city Prince Lysaer undertook to restore, Lord Diegan, ex-commander of the garrison, sat his glossy bay warhorse and glared through the pennons that cracked at the head of the unwieldy column bound for Avenor. The gusts off the Mathorn's high slopes still bit like midwinter; as unforgiving were Lord Diegan's eyes, bleak and flat as black ice.

He wore the trappings of an Etarran dandy; intrigue still drove him as naturally as each drawn breath, but five summers spent in the wilds on campaign against forest barbarians had tempered him. He knew when boldness would not serve him. Yet masterfully as a man could contain himself, last night's argument had flared too hotly to be masked behind banality. Lord Diegan found himself glaring once again at the blond-haired prince who rode to his left.

Clad for travel in blue-dyed suede and a cloak of oiled wool, his hair like combed flax under the gold-stitched velvet of his hat, Lysaer s'Ilessid adjusted his reins in gloved hands and suddenly, generously smiled. Still looking forward, as if the roadway behind were not packed with a chaos of groaning, creaking wagons and the whip snaps and epithets of bored carters, he said, 'Still angry? At least that way you'll keep warm.'

Too raw not to rise to provocation, Diegan felt his horse startle and jig. Annoyed to have dug in a thoughtless spur, he snapped, 'I still can't believe you're dragging my sister Talith into this.'

Lysaer turned his head. Eyes as brilliant as glacial ice touched Diegan, then flicked away. 'Be careful. Don't let me think you believe I take her so lightly as to cast her into needless danger.'

Had Diegan not needed both hands to settle his sidling mount, he could have struck the prince in exasperation. 'Ah, Ath, why won't you listen?'

No need to repeat those facts already thrashed through: that town mayors in the kingdom of Tysan had never seen the horrors of the Shadow Master's powers; to them the massacre that broke an army in Strakewood forest was history told at second hand. Of more immediate concern were the fragmented archives which survived the ancient uprising that first overthrew Athera's high kings. If few guilds and merchants recalled the truth, that the same barbarian clans who plundered their trade goods once had ruled their cities, Erdane's mayor was not among them. Scathing letters from his barristers on the subject outlined the ramifications: s'Ilessid blood made Lysaer the last legitimate royal heir and no city in Tysan cared to risk a return to crown rule.

Heated now beyond restraint, Diegan burst out, 'You know you'll be arrested and condemned as a dissenter? In Isaer, likely as not, they'll throw you to the headhunters' mastiffs. Sithaer's Furies, man, just for some mouldy historical right to lay claim to clan fealty, you're the living embodiment of these peoples' fear of insurrection. I don't care to see two hundred Etarran soldiers give up their lives to keep you from being savaged by a dog pack!'

'Well then,' Lysaer said equably. 'The Etarran division will be sent home before any political misperception can arise to start any bloodshed.' In maddening, single-minded majesty, he looked straight ahead as he added, 'Diegan, this issue is greater than me, more important than Tysan's disorders. Somewhere in hiding, the Master of Shadow weaves plots. Sitting secure in Etarra flushing out barbarian encampments is never going to make him show his hand.'

To which Lord Diegan could do nothing but clench his jaw, wheel his courser out of line, and pound off at a canter to review the order of his troops. Speechless in frustration, he wished he had a lance in his hand and a living target to skewer. For it was never Lysaer's dedication to the cause of killing Arithon s'Ffalenn that had been under contention; only the folly of allowing the Lady Talith to believe herself secure amid the troop who rode out to renew s'Ilessid claim to Avenor's charter.

Prince Lysaer's cavalcade travelled westward at a pace its seasoned war captains concurred was better suited to the staging of an invalid's retinue. Those mercenaries with prior experience of moving troops complained mightily to their superiors, then arranged rough drills in the open camps to keep their cohorts smart. Unused to being fresh and idle, their men at arms diced and got fractious with each pause. Settlements and towns along the Mathorn road were favourably disposed toward Lysaer's retainers, since the barbarian raids out of Halwythwood that distressed their trade had eased through Etarra's campaigns. Lord Diegan grew accustomed to state dinners followed by exhaustive mornings of fielding grievances.

For the royal cavalcade grew longer, more massive, more weighed down with gifts with every city it passed. If the Prince of the West journeyed into his ancestral kingdom to win allies against the Master of Shadow, each mayor and guild left inside Rathain's borders set themselves to ingratiate. However they might disparage royalty, they needed Lysaer's goodwill lest the dreaded sorcerer think to turn on them with impunity once the prince who had defended Etarra was gone. The aftermath became familiar unto habit. Diegan sat in some draughty tent with a lap-desk, grim-faced as he battled the breezes that snatched at his lading lists and tiresome tallies of wagons. From Narms, they had five loads of carpets and woven silk, sumptuously coloured; from Morvain, downcoast, wool bales profitably traded for crystal from the famed glassworks at Falgaire. They had lanterns in wrought brass, barrels of rare wines and brandies, and from some beneficent farmer, foundation stock for a pig herd.

Lord Diegan came to wince at the creatures' squeals, much as he did when the camp followers shrieked obscenities at cheating customers. Whatever Lysaer believed, a war camp was no place for anybody's pedigree sister.

Since the baggage train made transport by water impractical, the prince's retinue crept by road around the shoreline of Instrell Bay. Caught by a late-breaking ice storm, they crawled over the low pass at East Bransing, which parted the weathered summits of the Storlains from the furze-cloaked hills that northward gave rise to the loftier spur of the Thaldeins.

Despite Lord Diegan's forebodings and a hostile letter of warning delivered by mounted courier from Erdane's reigning mayor, the caval-cade crossed with the thaws into the realm of Tysan, past seat of the s'Ilessid high kings.

Camped in pastures, quartered in hay byres, they bought wood, milk and early greens from red-cheeked country matrons. To Diegan's everlast-ing uneasiness, the company blatantly proclaimed itself to the eyes of every passing shepherd. The bellying, bullion-fringed standard with its brilliant blue cloth bore a sigil not seen for five centuries: the royal twelve-pointed star of pale gold. The curious came out to stare in droves. Whatever the sentiments held by city governments and their mettlesome packs of trade guilds, the crofters of Tysan lent tacit trust once assured the prince's captains would pay for provender. Young boys watched the marching men in their helms, shining mail, and the bright, sharp steel of their longswords, and dreamed; or else turned up in holed boots and motley tunics, reeking of cow dung from the tilling and begging to be taken on for training.

Lysaer s'Ilessid turned none of them away.

'Why leave them on the farms where their families must struggle to feed them?' Oblivious to the squalor, he sat by the hearthside cracking nuts for Lady Talith in a peasant's croft near Dyshent. Crickets chirruped in the smoke-grimed shadows of the corners and round-eyed children peered through the boards of the cattle stalls, where the matron had locked them for safety. Outside, amid a glitter of campfires, the fighting force sprawled at their ease in the mild night, while the off-duty watch laughed and cast bets, and the day's new recruits dug pits for latrines behind the thorn fence of a sheepfold. Attentive to the timbre of the officer's calls that wafted through opened shutters, Lysaer added, 'These boys' skills will be sorely needed later. Any unsuited for our fighting force will be given land of their own to husband, once Avenor's rebuilt.'

'If we ever get there,' Lord Diegan grumbled acidly. Dark where his sister was leonine, he dug his knuckles into eyes gritted raw from the dust thrown up by his prince's ridiculous train of wagons, columns of light horse and pack-mules. The rains ended earlier since the banishment of Desh-thiere's mists; if the past plagues of bloodsucking insects were lessened, the air hung as close as new summer. 'We'll need to cut tents out of carpets, at this pace. Next winter's frost will catch us before we can raise a roof to keep the rust from our weapons stores.'

'Spend the cold season in Erdane with Talith, then,' Lysaer said, and grinned in suave provocation. He wore neither doublet nor shirt. Since his offer to sling yoke buckets in from the dairy, the matron had carped until he stripped off his fine silk. Afterward, nobody remarked that his lack of finesse in the farmyard had left him bespattered with milk. Unjustly magnificent in fitted breeches of blue suede embroidered with seedpearls, he leaned down and scooped another nut from the poke by his ankles.

Across the cottage, the farmwife's daughter thumped her churn, her gaze never leaving the beautiful prince, except to stab in envy at the tawny-haired lady who curled like a cat at his knee.

'Or else go back to your Lord Governor in Etarra,' Lysaer resumed, well aware of his captain's coiled tension as he flipped up and fielded a nut-meat. 'The Etarran division will return as I promised, once we reach the crossroad to Camris.'

'You can't be serious about that!' Lord Diegan's sharp movement rucked the braided hearth-rug and upset the little sack, and nuts cascaded into the embers. 'You're carrying the endowment to found a city, and –'

'And what?' Lysaer stretched and pecked a kiss on Talith's cheek, letting her retire before the debate could encompass the Master of Shadow. Left to the censure of her brother, the prince stayed unmoved. 'This is Tysan. My ancestors ruled here.'

'For which Erdane's mayor sent an edict to draw and quarter you!' Hot in his velvets, Lord Diegan endured discomfort rather than let the dairy girl make unflattering comparisons. 'The fanatics on his council will have troops out to slaughter your bodyguard before you'll gain passage through his town.'

Lysaer looked back in reproach. 'These are my people, Diegan. However I have to win my way past Erdane, whether my troops come to shelter under carpets or wind-breaks cut from our best murray silk, I won't cross this land in such haste that I cannot understand the land's needs.'

'Sithaer take your royal principles, I'd do better arguing with a half-wit!' Lord Diegan stood, the jingle of his spurs cut by the crunch of scattered nuts as he stalked past the fire and escaped to nurse his pique outside.

The cavalcade pressed on at its snail's crawl upcoast to Dyshent, over roads rutted deep by the passage of the season's last lumber sledges. While the chip fires used to season beech blocks skeined dusky smoke above the houses, the prince's guard troop quartered in yards piled with bark for the tanner's, or between their own laden wagons, parked amid stacks of green planks. In complete disregard for the craftsmen who spat in the path of his retinue, Lysaer visited the guild halls and the town ministry. Gold saw his officers billeted in the sheds used to season rare woods, and his lordly good manners won over the councilmen's wives.

Diegan waited, edgy as the captains who lost sleep to stop their men from making trouble; but the deep-seated resentments toward Tysan's royal blood failed to spark into contention.

Lysaer took leave of Dyshent's council and rode out in proud form before his cavalcade.

Unappeased, Lord Diegan forced his mount to pace Lysaer's. 'This isn't Isaer, or Erdane, where a few costly gifts can turn heads.'

The peaked roofs of the city's mills were by then lost to sight. Ahead stretched league upon league of wild downs. Rounded, scrub-clothed hills cradled the stones of a Second Age ruin, and chipped old arches lay throttled under greening trailers of bitter vine. There, where wispy marsh-lights flocked the fogs on dank nights and the spirits of long-dead Paravians were rumoured to wander abroad, no town-bred company cared to linger. Astride his steaming, mud-spattered courser, Lysaer drew firm rein, while behind, in a welter of belatedly shouted orders, his massive column blundered to a stop.

Straight-shouldered in a hooded cloak pinned with a sapphire, the prince waited, while the mists licked through the air between. 'Are you for me, or against?' he asked softly.

Lord Diegan ignored the chill that grazed the length of his spine. He strove to stay angry, to outmatch that worldly gaze which caught and pierced him to the heart. But like an onset of sudden pain, emotion wrung the truth from him. 'I fear for you, friend. You're the only man we have whose gift of light can match the Shadow Master's sorceries.'

'Then give me your trust,' Lysaer said. 'Worry does nothing, after all, but undermine morale and abet the cause of an enemy ruthlessly prepared to exploit every one of our weaknesses.'

*   *   *

The next day, they reached the crossing of the Great West Road. Against every reasonable inclination, Lord Diegan presided over commands shouted through a misery of rainfall as the crack Etarran divisions he had personally selected to protect his prince were split off and turned back to Rathain.

Afterward, with the downpour a fringe of silver off his mantle, Lord Diegan huffed through the runnels that channelled through his moustache. 'By Ath, I'll trust you have a plan. Would it strain your royal pride too much to share it?'

'You couldn't guess?' As sodden as the house staff and officers who attended him in gloomy huddles, but oddly outside of their misery, Lysaer shook back wet hair and laughed. 'My Lord, your Etarrans are too loyal. All filled with brash courage and intent to ruin Arithon, which is just what we'll do on a battlefield. But since their numbers are too small to flush out the Shadow Master, just now their sentiments could cause problems. For our safety and theirs, they can't be risked.'

The long-faced secretary intended for the post of Avenor's seneschal looked ready enough to offer protest had the prince not spurred his mount to a trot. Any mercenaries who groused over his dispersion of troops found themselves reassigned drover's work. In rainfall and mud, the caravan slogged its way westward under half its original armed escort.

The trouble Lord Diegan expected found them soon after the Etarran cohorts had passed from sight. A body of lancers swept down on Lysaer's company in fast moving formation from the north. Through trailing curtains of rain, the men set as watch scouts squinted to make out their banner; the wet rendered everything colourless, except for the axe-blade sigil done in silver, and encircled by a linked wheel of chain.

'That's a headhunter company out of Isaer!' identified an inbound rider. 'Here under orders to spill the guts of a royal pretender, I shouldn't doubt.'

The doleful secretary spun in agitation to the prince. 'Fiends plague your Grace's stubbornness, your captain at arms tried to warn you. The bounty offered for s'Ilessid blood won't have changed for the past five centuries.'

Silent and whitely bitter, Lord Diegan spurred his horse to try against weather and odds to assemble a defensive deployment from mercenary captains now scattered throughout the caravan.

But Lysaer's fist on the bridle rein jerked the Lord Commander's move short. 'No, Diegan. Stay. Have your officers hold their position. You'll start a pitched battle if our troops draw their weapons and I don't want anybody killed. Not when I'd hoped to be asked to pay respect to his Lordship, the Mayor of Isaer.'

Then the moment for organized defence was lost as the headhunter lancers thundered down and swarmed like bad-tempered hornets around the liveried horsemen and banners that surrounded Prince Lysaer.

'We've come for the upstart who styles himself heir to s'Ilessid!' The captain who shouted was bald, had a torn ear, and wore chainmail and bracers set with wrist spikes. The huge grey gelding who bore him was ugly, but unscarred, and taken by a sudden, poisonous aversion to standing still. The beast backed and sidled in half circles, gouging up spatters of soaked turf. Its rider sawed reins and cursed, while the younger of Lysaer's liveried page boys approached and bowed, then announced in his clear child's treble that his Grace the prince was pleased to accept invitation to call on the Lord Mayor of Isaer.'

'Invitation!' The captain hammered his mount's neck with a fist, then hauled its nose around to his stirrup to forestall a bucketing rear. 'What gall! There's been no invitation!' His ire found no other outlet; underneath him, his warhorse went berserk.

Ears flattened to streaming neck, it bit the air, crow-hopped and danced sideways on bunched hindquarters. The headhunter captain stayed astride by dint of determined fury, while the neat ranks of his riders were bashed out of formation by the unravelling temper of his mount. Lances dipped, wavered and cracked into a cursing tangle of men and disgruntled horseflesh.

Too cynical for surprise, Lord Diegan glanced aside to find Lysaer watching the affray, his unruffled, wide-eyed dignity at odds with innocent intentions. The older page half-hidden by his horse cloths was deviously engaged with a handful of smooth pebbles and what looked like a rawhide bird sling.

A lifetime of Etarran politics lent Diegan the presence to mask astonishment. He was prepared and listening for the low-voiced string of orders from his prince. 'The headhunter captain's horse is shortly going to bolt. Before it does, I'll need an honour guard assembled, a delegation from our guild representatives and city officers, and the wagon bearing Lady Talith and her servants. This will be a state visit to Isaer, I shall make it so. But warn the men: on pain of punishment, and despite the most grievous provocation, they must hold their tongues and their tempers.'

No fool, Lord Diegan did as he was bidden; and so he missed the moment when the headhunter's huge grey at last tore free of restraint and exploded kicking and snorting into a tail-streaming run. Somebody dispatched an equerry at speed to chase after the luckless captain. Before the sergeant left as second in command could restore the wrecked order of the troop, Lysaer rode forward to meet him.

'Never mind the formalities,' the prince opened, magnanimously forgiving, and sure enough in stature to shake the confidence of a struck bronze monument. He followed with a phrase that caused several lancers to break into laughter. While the sergeant was torn between outrage, uncertainty, and an explosive attack of pure mirth, Lysaer managed with light-hearted, lordly arrogance to make several sensible suggestions.

The headhunter lancers sorted themselves back into order, to find themselves seamlessly joined by the prince's personal honour guard, a wagon bearing a woman beautiful enough to leave a man staring and silly, and a dozen trade dignitaries who were fed up with rain, and expressing thanks for the Mayor of Isaer's timely consideration.

At the sergeant's stirrup rode Lysaer, at patent length and diffidence inquiring what sort of silk would compliment his Lord Mayor's colouring; the other gifts, he added hastily, were less personal. Unless the mayor's lady wife had the misfortune to disdain Falgaire crystal?

Thoughtful, bemused, not entirely without sympathy for the sergeant who stammered answers to the royal inquiries under Talith's distracting regard, Lord Diegan rode silent through the rain. In a humour that was piquantly Etarran, he watched Lysaer's masterful diplomacy take the city of Isaer by storm.

There followed six days of formal dinners and protracted hours spent touring guild sheds where last year's flax harvest lay hackled for bleaching. Lord Diegan followed the talk as he once had ravished the courtesans he seduced from the beds of wealthy patrons.

Yet even under close scrutiny, these discussions pursued the same topics as others in cities to the south, once Isaer's mayor recovered from the flustered irritation of being hazed into guesting the very same prince he had dispatched his headhunters to set shackles on. The city's guild ministers in circuitous politeness inquired whether Lysaer intended to launch from Avenor the same campaign he had spearheaded at Etarra: raise a garrison to meld forces with the headhunters' leagues to clear Tysan's wilds of barbarians. Trade with Camris, they said, suffered unduly from raids in the Thaldein passes.

Lysaer heard their woes in rapt sympathy. When the banquet was finished and the fine brandies poured, he graciously ventured opinion. 'The clans of Rathain were stamped out by Etarra because they fell to ill usage by the Shadow Master.' A frown marred his brows. The glitter of his hair and his jewels hung still in the lamplight as he paused in disturbed reminiscence. 'Your difficulties in the passes of Orlan must be approached carefully.' In the face of poisoned fear – that as scion of s'Ilessid he might lay claim to clan loyalty and upset rule in the towns – he said outright, 'If a way can be found to avoid outright slaughter, I would seek that before war.'

Silence fell, tensioned with threat.

While inimical stares from the councilmen sharpened around the table, and the Mayor of Isaer whispered something to a servant that brought guardsmen in full mail to block the doorway, Lord Diegan groped to draw the hidden dagger in his sleeve.

The prince acknowledged none of this, but centred upon a careworn alderman who fluttered his napkin in dismay. 'You can't suggest a treaty with the clanborn! Ath! There's no way to reason with such, uncouth as they are. Like animals.' While the mayor's fat steward retreated without refilling the wine goblets, he added with whispered distaste, ' 'Tis said of Maenalle s'Gannley that she wears uncured animal skins.'

For a moment Lysaer looked blandly mystified. Then he roused and said in forbearance, 'Forgive me. I can't support such hasty thinking.' Under the table, his hand clamped hard on Diegan's arm, locking the little knife in its sheath. 'What would an armed campaign accomplish except to drive Tysan's clans to share grievance with their brethren in Rathain? No. Blood-hunts are too dangerous an option, and Arithon s'Ffalenn too wily an adversary to risk driving allies to his cause. Of all things, I dare not draw his interests to your land to threaten the industry of your cities.'

With a deftness that seemed natural chance, the discussion was deflected to threats of shadow and sorcery; Lord Diegan swept into passionate description of the heinous slaughter that occurred on the banks of Tal Quorin, when a grisly chain of traps had savaged Etarra's proud garrison.

The telling set him in a cold sweat. Deshir's clansmen had always been killers; allied with Arithon s'Ffalenn and his demonic touch at spellcraft, they had narrowly been stopped from threatening civilized Rathain. Hands clenched on his cutlery, Lord Diegan spoke; as if the roar of Tal Quorin's flood still battered his ears, and the screams of those troops swept away. Sucked back into memory like nightmare, he heard the crack of arrows striking through foliage and flesh; the ripping of timber and earth as concealed spring traps and deadfalls left his lancers gutted and bleeding out their lives in whimpering agony. Death did not account for all the losses. Some men were permanently deranged by the maze wards and shadows Arithon had used to bind them into confusion; others had been broken in spirit, prone to fits and raving when relivings wrenched them from sleep.

By itself, the account of the battle the Shadow Master had launched in Strakewood was enough to inspire terror. Isaer's council ministers departed mollified; by direct command of their mayor, the men at arms tactfully dispersed.

Later, lighted by perfumed candles in a tapestried upper chamber, Lord Diegan chose his moment and cornered Lysaer before the prince called his valet to retire. 'What are you playing at? I thought we agreed at Etarra that barbarian havens anywhere were too ready a tool for the Master's use and design!'

'You're worried?' The brandy had been particularly fine; yet an edge of irritation burned through the prince's flush as he crossed the guest suite's floral patterned carpet. Contained as smoothed marble, he said, 'Then rest content, the raids in the passes will be ended. One way or another. By armed force as a last resort.'

Lord Diegan met and held those blue eyes, that could seem inhumanly assured in their candour. 'Pretty manners and slick language might disarm the mistrust in Isaer. But tonight's talk at supper would get you bloody and dead on the other side of the passes. Don't fool yourself. Erdane's mayor won't be stood off with sweet talk and gifts.'

A frown knitted Lysaer's brows. 'I thought as much.' He sighed and stifled a yawn behind a blaze of sapphire rings. 'It's inconvenient, I admit, but we're going to need every city's loyalty against Arithon. We'll just have to find something else to ease the Lord Mayor of Erdane's antipathy.'

To which Diegan could say nothing, but only turn on his heel and retire to a bed where sleep did not ease him.

The following morning, the royal retinue left Isaer to rejoin its abandoned caravan, now moved thirty laboured leagues to the west. After the escorting honour guard trailed four ox-wains crammed full of pottery, patterned linen and dyed feathers. The mules bearing the last crates of Falgaire crystal took a dislike to the ox teams, which occasioned much swearing from the drovers.

Surrounded by confusion that stirred a third of the cavalcade into a brew of bawling animals and stopped wagons, Talith's suave brother screamed orders until his teeth grated from inhaling airborne grit. He ignored the ragged crofters who had paused at their sowing to stare. If he also missed the hoofbeats that approached through the din made by children beating clappers to scare flocking sparrows from the seed grain, Diegan obstinately faced forward as the rider arrived and fell in alongside.

'Stop sulking.' Lysaer laughed to his uncommunicative future brother-in-law. 'When the snow comes, we can haul the fancy feathers out for mattress stuffing.'

'Did you look in those sacks?' Diegan reined around his dust-caked mount, his calf gloves fringed with hanging threads where use had torn off the beadwork. 'They hold goose quills. Stiff ones, for pen nibs. If you can coax my sister to sleep on those, I'll pick you nettles to plump your pillows.'

Caught on a hill crest against sky, his gold hair wind-ruffled against racing fleeces of spring clouds, Lysaer regarded the riled profile of Avenor's Lord Commander at Arms. He said in teasing merriment, 'That merchant's vixen daughter refused you, I see.' Which comment got him shoved from his saddle into dung-spread furrows in just and indecorous vengeance.

From astride his snorting charger, Lord Diegan glared down at his prince, who accepted his demise without rancour for mud-spoiled velvets.

'In Erdane, the headhunters' league is lawfully sanctioned to torture clanborn captives for public amusement. As a prince in line for the succession, they'd hold a festival over your ripped carcass.' Hurting in his affection as if his liege were an endangered brother, Diegan finished, 'Will nothing I say dissuade you?'

Lysaer picked himself up, dusted loose earth from his breeches and cloak, then ascertained that one of his pages had recaptured his cantering horse. His eyes still pinned into distance, he said, 'Wherever the Master of Shadow lies hidden, whatever his current machination, he's unlikely to be exposed without risks. I set out to bring these lands protection from his sorceries.' Wide as sky, the blue eyes lifted to regard Avenor's captain at arms. 'Diegan, don't ask me to reject a whole city just because its governor is petty, and terrified, and convinced royal blood can harm his position. We will ride through Erdane. Should I come to die there, then Tysan will require no prince. A townborn man like yourself will go forward to rebuild Avenor and unify this kingdom in my name.'

The last time Lysaer crossed the Thaldeins by way of the Orlan Pass, the mountains had been mantled in mist and blizzard. Hastened then in the company of a Fellowship sorcerer, he recalled no landmarks beyond drifts and treacherous abutments of seamed rock. With the visible sky a ribbon of blue overhead, the scarp traversed today under knives of morning sunlight looked savage and strange, a tableau of hanging slate overhangs, wind-chiselled ridges, and stands of gnarled evergreen slashed and skewed with the boulder-strewn scars of old slides. The road wound and jagged between buttressed peaks, a mere lip in places over vast, windy chasms of cold air. The forested valleys unfolded below like creases in a painted silk fan, delicately blued in haze and criss-crossed by the gliding flight of hawks.

Here, a raffish band of barbarian scouts had once dangled Arithon s'Ffalenn upside down from a rope over a precipice. Lent abrasive reminder of a deceit that had once beguiled his trust and friendship, Lysaer gazed down a cliff wall bared of snow and jumbled with bone-grey, splintered timber and stone shards. He could wish now that the knots in the noose had failed.

Had the Shadow Master fallen to his death on that day, seven thousand Etarrans would still be alive with their families.

Over the bends and the rises, the wagons rattled and groaned, their hubs scraping rocks scarred by a thousand such impacts, while the opposite wheel rims flicked gravel in clattering spurts over the sheared edge of the verge. On the approach to the high pass, the carter's quips echoed through the narrowing way, until Diegan sent outriders ahead to clear the road. Once committed, the drays could neither turn nor manoeuvre; caught between their lumbering bulk, horses and mules could not pass, should wayfarers meet them head on.

Merchants who hauled goods through the pass of Orlan for that reason eschewed use of carts. Informed of the risks, Lysaer had ignored all advice. Mounted, exposed in the vanguard, he looked least surprised when three riders positioned abreast approached and blocked off the trail.

Their mounts were a matched set of bays in gold-beaded bridles; silken manes and tails, and caparisons of loomed wool fluttered and tugged in the wind. Annoyed to see his advance guard had lapsed in their duty to detain so small a party until the prince's retinue cleared the narrows, Lord Diegan flicked his boot with his crop and began to swear.

His imprecations trailed tamely into silence as he noticed the leader of the trio was mounted sidesaddle. A woman; a boy in his late teens and an elderly man her sole escort, she carried straight shoulders impertinently mantled in a tabard bearing Tysan's royal blazon. The habit underneath was of flowing black silk, her grey hair, close-cropped as any campaign-bound mercenary's. Slung at a practised angle beneath her belt lay a baldric and a gleaming sword.

'Fiends plague us all,' Diegan said crossly. 'Who in Sithaer is she?'

Lysaer raised a hand to halt his column in the roadway. 'The lady is Maenalle s'Gannley, chieftain of the clans of Camris, and if her records can be trusted for accuracy, empowered Steward of Tysan.' Then, his lips curved in welcome, he spurred his gelding forward to greet her. 'To judge by the hang of her blade, I'd hazard a guess it's the living hides of Isaer's merchant's she hunts to furnish her wardrobe. I've been expecting her most of the morning.'

'You know her? You've met her before this?' Belatedly pressed to neaten his wind-crumpled mantle, Lord Diegan expelled a breathless laugh. 'You do have a plan!' Lost to confounded delight, he urged his horse into step.

Fifteen paces beyond his honour guard, Lysaer drew rein. Uncrowned beyond the majesty of his sunlit gold hair, he seized royal prerogative and spoke first. 'Lady Maenalle, well met.' His nod acknowledged the elder, whom he recalled as her seniormost peer, Lord Tashan; his friendly smile was for the youngster, now grown, who had attended him as page-boy through his past brief visit, before he had joined his gift of light with an enemy's shadows to banish Desh-thiere's mists from the sky. In brisk invitation, Lysaer addressed the lady chieftain who had impressed him with her iron-willed fairness. 'I go to raise Avenor out of ruin and hope you take joy in my tidings. Will you come, and bring your clans out of hiding to join in rebuilding the sovereign city of old Tysan?'

'Alliance!' Shocked to white-faced incredulity, Lord Diegan rounded upon the prince. 'Are you mad? The realm's mayors will never condone this!'

In the clan chief's party, the grizzled aristocrat looked incensed. The young man seemed torn by a longing that drove his gaze sidewards and away; while the lady resplendent in Tysan's state colours held her emotions so savagely in check that the sun-caught gold in her tabard flashed only once and fell still.

Lysaer inclined his head toward his outraged commander at arms. 'Why waste the resource to retrain our new garrison to fight and manoeuvre like headhunters?' He added in compelling reason, 'The clansmen these delegates represent are masters at wilderness tactics already.'

Maenalle's mount recoiled as her hand snapped taut on the rein. Amber-pale eyes centred in black like a hawk's never left the features of the prince. Unlike the young grandson who wore his heart in plain view, and despite an unsettled royal bodyguard forestalled by the interposed body their own liege from stringing short bows to take her down, she showed neither nerves nor defiance. 'There has been no oath of fealty sworn here, nor any sanction for crown sovereignty given by the Fellowship of Seven.' The fine-grained lines on her face stayed unsoftened. 'How dare you speak of annexing my clans as a fighting force? We have no cause to support your wars.'

'Do you not?' The significance of her dress, with the colours of kingdom authority overlying the *caithdein*'s plain black, had not escaped Lysaer's notice. Diminished a little by sadness, he crossed his hands on his saddle pommel and sighed. 'Let me pray, then, that you haven't been beguiled into giving your loyalty elsewhere. That would grieve me. The clans of northern Rathain were all but wiped out for abetting the Master of Shadow.'

'They defended their sanctioned prince,' Maenalle corrected.

'With children sent out to stab men in the back who were down and wounded,' Lysaer shot back in bitter truth. 'With sorceries and traps that slaughtered seven thousand souls in a day. The scion of Rathain is a trickster without morals, a sorcerer who preys on the innocent.'

'That's not how the Fellowship phrased it.' Unflinching as swordsteel, Maenalle never glanced at her grandson, white-faced and stiff at her side. 'Nor Jieret s'Valerient, Steiven's heir, whose parents and sisters all died because of Etarra's invasion.'

'Who were these people but deluded allies?' Lysaer's attentiveness shifted to the boy. 'If you doubt me, my Lady, look to your own, who is of the right age to be influenced.'

The young man raised his chin. Silent, near to weeping from betrayal, he touched his mount with his heels. Hooves cracked like a shout against silence as his horse obediently turned, presenting the straight back of its rider to the man who once promised just sovereignty.

'Oh, but Maien was influenced,' Maenalle said, as drawn now as the grandson at her side, who held his station, trembling and flushed. 'But not by Arithon of Rathain. The boy's loyalty was yours, and his love, until Desh-thiere's curse wrecked the peace. Let us not confuse our issues and deny the sad facts of this feud. You seek to kill a man who is your half-brother, who has these last six years made no effort to outfit a war host against you. My clansmen cannot support your towns against him. Nor may we acknowledge false claim to Avenor. Our allegiance is to be held in reserve for the one of your heirs that the Fellowship endorses to be crowned.'

A cat's paw of breeze fluttered the sigil on Maenalle's tabard. Fresh with ice-scent and evergreen, the air seemed too sharp to breathe. Locked separate by nothing beyond glacial cold and state etiquette, Lysaer and the lady steward regarded each other through a charged and measuring silence.

'We're to be enemies then?' the prince said finally. 'I'm sorry. That outcome isn't what I'd have chosen. Let me be clear, for your clans' sake: you are free at any time to change your mind.' Magnanimously regal, Lysaer finished, 'If that happens, send me word. And until then, may Ath show you mercy.'

Maenalle's bold laugh sheared in flat echoes off the rocks. 'The Creator need not concern himself. As a guest who swore oath at my table, you will be allowed to leave this place without being stripped of your horse and arms. The same can't be said for your escort.'

'That's insolence.' Prepared to add more, Lord Diegan lost the chance as the wizened old clansman snapped off a hand signal.

The rock abutments by the roadside sprouted movement, followed by a hissed thrum of sound. The draught team harnessed to the lead wagon abruptly slacked backward in their traces and collapsed with a whistling, surprised grunt of air. The drover at their lines took a moment to start shouting; then every man within earshot shared his anger, that each fallen horse lay spiked through its crest with the feathered shaft of a barbarian broadhead. Creased by flawless marksmanship, the animals died in quivering spasms that sent small pebbles clattering off the brink.

Erect and exposed in his saddle, provoked to lordly affront, Lysaer raised his hands.

He would engage his given gift of light, Diegan saw, dazzled by the lightning flare of power summoned at his prince's fingertips. One blanketing discharge, and the crannies that sheltered clan archers could be scorched by immolating fires. Prepared to seize the initiative, Lord Diegan drew his blade in a scream of steel. He called swift commands to his mercenaries. Prompt action could see Lady Maenalle and her party taken hostage; Erdane's mayor would pay a rich bounty for their trial and execution.

But before the Prince of the West unleashed his annihilating burst, a second flight of arrows sang down. The barbarian volley chipped stone in splintering explosion under the belly of his mount. The powerful horse shied back on bunched haunches. Forced to nurse the reins and jab in spurs to curb a rear which threatened to toss him over the ledge, his royal rider lost concentration. The light-bolts he shaped dispersed in flat sheets that threw off a harmless burn of heat.

Above the scrambling batter of hooves, Lady Maenalle voiced her ultimatum. 'Don't think to try killing with your powers, Lysaer s'Ilessid. Tell your men who draw steel to stand down. Or a next round will fly and take every life in your company.'

'Isn't that what you planned?' Diegan shouted, his rage torn through strangling mortification. Fighting the horse that shied under him, he snatched a glimpse down the switch-back. The trailing wagon in the column had wrenched crooked, its ox-team folded at the knees, as cleanly arrow-shot as the horses. The prince's brash cavalcade was hemmed in from both ends and trapped at the mercy of barbarians. In a cry that rebounded through the winds above the valleys, Diegan cried, 'What are you, woman, but the pawn of the Shadow Master, after all?'

'I am sworn only to Tysan,' Maenalle said, her calm like snap-frozen ice. 'As appointed steward of the realm, my duty upholds the crown's justice until such day as the Fellowship sorcerers declare a lawful successor.'

Lord Diegan whipped his horse straight. 'Where's the equity in robbery and murder?'

'Don't resist and no lives will be taken.' Maenalle tipped her chin at the elder, who dismounted and passed his reins to the boy. Still vigorous despite his weathered looks, he took charge, while scouts in dust-grazed leathers deployed in fierce order to plunder. Their lady commander ended in brevity that rang like a sentence after trial: 'Only weapons will be confiscated, and those goods offered as bribes by town mayors. Be assured, any gold that might be used to outfit an army for persecution of clan settlements will be turned to a worthier cause.'

Blade clenched in hand, Diegan dug in his spurs. His horse belted sidewards in a crab-step, frustrated and dragged offstride by a rough-looking girl with scarred hands who had managed to dart in and snatch its bridle. She jerked her head for him to dismount, while someone else with painful force laid hands on his person to disarm him.

'Try a dagger in my ribs, you'll die with me,' Diegan gasped, struggling.

'Don't be a fool, Lord Commander,' the prince said in glass-edged urgency. 'I need you alive!'

The commander at arms cast a smoking glare at Maenalle. Unable to speak as the muscles in his jaw spasmed taut, barely able to breathe for the blow to his pride, he swung from his saddle. The last, grinding irony hurt the most, that the horses and the mules could not be manoeuvred past either one of the disabled wagons. Even had he wished to risk engagement, his men at arms could not bolt over sheer cliffs to find cover. While scouts poured like rats from the ridge top and divested him of jewels and purse, he hurled back insults in sweating, savage bursts. They ripped off his cloak and took the beautiful, chased belt knife bought to match his confiscated sword. Down-trail, the venomous oaths of the mercenaries marked the loss of weapons well proven in battle. The more seasoned officers curbed combative tempers before excuse could be found for barbarian arrows to make bloody end to dissent.

Maenalle's scouts were thorough, immune as wild goats to steep rocks and bad footing. At masterful speed, Lysaer's disabled caravan and fighting company found itself weaponless and wagonless, then abandoned afoot in the rim walled gorges that led through the ford of the river Valendale. Bitterness replaced their purloined baggage. Although no man suffered harm, and Maenalle's matchless discipline had prevented anything worse than wisecracks and whistles to befall Lady Talith, no one inclined toward forgiveness.

The wainloads of goods that had been cursed every league across Atainia now became cause for mortal affront.

Pacing at Lord Diegan's side, his affianced lady astride the one mount that guest oath had held sacrosanct, Lysaer stayed withdrawn. In boots not fashioned for hiking, he blistered his feet with the rest on the wretched, frost-cracked stone. That he carried the only sword among two hundred seasoned fighting men seemed not to concern him unduly. While the shadows swallowed the cliff walls and the day eased to cobalt twilight, Diegan chafed at the silence. His worried glance at his prince was met and matched by a sidelong flicker of mirth.

In no mood for jokes, he spun with such force that a fir branch switched him in the cheek. 'Fiends and Sithaer's fury, your Grace, whatever are you thinking?'

'You've got evergreen needles in your velvets,' Lysaer observed. He broke into a shocking, sunny smile. 'Do you miss your horse all that much?'

Avenor's weaponless commander at arms stared, stupefied. His spurs jangled as he kicked at a moss-coated rock, then recouped sufficient dignity to glare at the prince to whom Etarra's lord mayor had so highhandedly awarded his service. When Lysaer absorbed his pique in brazen merriment, he frowned. 'Ath! I've seen you blast trees to charcoal at the merest flick of a thought.'

Lysaer said nothing.

Jabbed to suspicion, Diegan added, 'You pulled your strike against those archers on the slope! You planned this *whole thing*, didn't you?'

A dying thread of sunlight bloodied sparkles in gold hair as Lysaer gave back the barest shrug. 'Not precisely.' His levity vanished and his eyes went suddenly hooded. 'You might say I expected things might happen as they have. If I tried for a happier outcome, the end result isn't setback. No one can say, now, that Tysan's clans weren't fairly offered their chance to lay due claim to s'Ilessid loyalty.'

But the issue went deeper than that, Lord Diegan saw in awed respect. As the impoverished victim of a clan raid, Lysaer s'Ilessid had bought footing for condolence. Bound on to Erdane as a charity case, not even the city's irascible mayor might question his need to raise troops. Far from feeling threatened by the muster, his guilds would be moved to endorse it: the prince's cause would win aid out of congenial commiseration and sympathy. Etarran enough to appreciate a master turn of statecraft, Lord Diegan laughed in the teeth of the wind.

'By Ath,' he said in exultant admiration. 'You'll have your kingship of this realm, then your army to harry out the Shadow Master. After the scale of today's losses, the guilds and the town councils will fall over themselves to lend you their funds to raise a garrison.'

Messenger

Four days after the raid that beggared Prince Lysaer in the Pass of Orlan, a messenger was dispatched at speed from the clansmen's mountain outpost. No matter that the hooves of his horse were dampened by late-season snow; the muffled vibration of his passage was heard and tracked by a mind a hundred leagues distant.

Through the five centuries since the Paravian races had vanished from the continent, wardenship of the tower built to guard their artefacts and culture had fallen to a Fellowship sorcerer. Most days he could be found in a black-beamed chamber that creaked in the unquiet winds, elbows braced on a library table heaped as a gull's nest with parchments and opened books. Scrolls stuffed the niches in between, trailing moth-eaten ties, or else weighted flat at the corners by oddments of tea-stained crockery and tinted glass inkwells missing corks. Ensconced amid his clutter like a packrat, Sethvir sat with his ankles hooked on a stool. While his hair grew in untidy tufts, and his maroon robe gathered dust and loose threads, he kept and catalogued records, and tracked world events as they happened.

As long as Athera had lain fogbound, he had followed the phases of the moon through the pull of the tides. He felt the daily tramp of Etarra's drilling armies shake the earth alongside prints in dry dust traced by fieldmice. A missive scribed in blood that had passed through flame, then rinsed off in brine from the face of a thrown bit of slate, touched him in fourfold vibration; amid the voices of a billion dropped stones, that one he noted and marked apart. He sensed the grand music of the planet's twelve power lanes, and the warp through weft lacework of energies still channelled over land and air by the residual dance of Paravian mystery.

So long had Sethvir's mage-sense been twined with the thunderous

70

chord of world life-force, that his thoughts took on the patterned aspects of stone, with but tenuous hold on the present.

When at length the clang of a sword hilt against the portcullis nine storeys down echoed through the bowels of his sanctuary, Sethvir already knew the name and the errand of the courier; had been aware of both since the moment Tysan's lady steward had dispatched her rider to his tower.

Limned in the gloom of failing day, the Warden of Althain finished a line of spidery handwriting. He leaned sidewards, rinsed his quill in the tepid dregs of a teacup, then raised eyes of pale turquoise that looked vacuous as sky; but in fact, held a relentless train of review as the interstices of this moment's event unreeled to bear on the future.

Below him, marring the crystalline cry of first starlight, the swordsman continued to hammer. To Sethvir's ear, the metallic din bespoke forge-fire, and hill steel, and centuries of unrequited bloodshed. 'I'm coming,' he grumbled in a tone as tart as an old hinge. He stood up. Dust and bits of scribbled paper settled on a floor already littered with outworn quill pens and the dropped caps of inkwells. The sorcerer sneezed, peered down as if touched to unwitting delight by the faded weave of the carpet, then stumped in his over-sized fur buskins to the casement, which had been unlatched for days, banging and creaking in the gritty north gusts off the desert.

The bulwarks of Althain Tower were fashioned of granite, stark and grey, the rough-chiselled grooves of a desperate need softened under green seals of lichen. Sethvir crossed his arms on the sill, took absent notice of a hole chewed by moths in his sleeve, then leaned through the casement and peered down.

'I'm not at all deaf,' he chided gently.

Below him, lent an ant's perspective, a shaggy bush pony stood with its hip cocked, its reins looped through the elbow of a man in the undyed leathers of a clansman. The shoulders energetically working flinched and stopped. The visitor glanced up, sheepish, from the tower's locked entry and hurriedly sheathed his sword. While the reverberations from his pounding subsided to a rumble, then a whisper, he called, 'I beg your pardon. Sethvir of Althain?'

Outlined against dusk by a halo of blowing white hair, the sorcerer grinned like a pixie. 'Your lady wishes me to bear a message to Arithon, Prince of Rathain. No, don't speak. I know the contents. What makes you think I'll deliver it?'

Hotly flustered, Maenalle's courier said, 'The *caithdein* of Tysan asks. She said you were the only spirit in Athera who would know where to seek the Shadow Master.'

Sethvir hooked an ink-stained knuckle through his beard. For a moment he appeared to forget himself, as well as the anxious emissary down below. His gaze encompassed the deepening arch of the heavens

71

as if the answers to unwritten riddles could be read in the white ice of cirrus clouds.

Deferential to the ways of great mages, the courier waited, while his pony dropped its head and cropped the weeds that grew wild over the tower's sole door sill.

Presently, Sethvir answered. 'I'll commit the Lady Maenalle's message to a parchment inscribed to Arithon s'Ffalenn. But tell her: the scroll will be delivered at the time of my choosing.'

The courier eased in relief. 'She will be satisfied.' He gathered up his pony's reins, prepared to mount and ride immediately.

Sethvir's eyebrows arched at the lapse implied in his hospitality. 'No need to rush off. I have oats for your horse in the barn. It's a very long road back to Camris, and tomorrow will be wretched with rain. You'd do better to weather the storm here. Have a bath, and a bed, and whatever you can scrounge from my larder. Certainly there's plenty of good tea.'

While the clanborn courier hung poised between uncertainty and blind courage, Sethvir withdrew from the casement, his voice a diminishing echo from the unlighted cavern of the library. 'Bide there. I'll be down to unfasten the gates.'

He moved on at sharp speed that belied his dreamer's appearance; take the stairs too slowly, and the courier would be mounted and gone at a pace his road-weary pony did not deserve. The company of a Fellowship sorcerer had harmed no man; but legend told of many who had emerged changed from the experience. Whether Maenalle's appointed courier would prove exempt from fate's handling was a fine point Sethvir was loath to promise.

Eviction

After the confiscated brown gelding, Faery-toes, kicked his stall doors to slivers, bit every groom within reach and knocked the head ostler off his feet, the alderman of Jaelot's under-secretary at last seized the initiative to set seal to a writ to dispatch the beast to the knacker's. He grumbled as he waited for the wax to harden. Horse hide, glue and dogmeat were not in high demand; the proceeds from the slaughter of one swaybacked head of stock could scarcely defray all the damages.

The head ostler narrowed his eyes and nursed his bruises. 'Keep the beast, then, and rack up more costs in wrecked boards.'

The writ was slapped into his hands with the official seal still warm, while in the next room, voices of higher authority heated and flared into argument. The difficulties posed by the horse's last owner, the fat prisoner consigned by city justice to suffer forced labour until solstice, were never as simply arranged. While the ostler retreated with the horse's death warrant, invective assailed the secretary's headache through the shut panels of the doorway, as it had without cease for a week: Dakar took ill in the draughty shacks where the convicts were housed. Poor food made him sick unto misery. His feet swelled from chilblains until he could not arise in the mornings without loud-voiced, piteous complaint.

His fellow inmates used their fists to stop his whining. His moans and his mewling as he languished from their beating disturbed what little sleep they could scrounge after days of backbreaking labour in the mason's yard, dressing stone blocks for the sea walls that storms crumbled down every spring. With both eyes puffed shut with bruises, Dakar could not see to swing his mallet. Stone chips flew on wild tangents. A guardsman was home with a badly gashed face and an overseer limped on smashed toes.

Packed off to solitary confinement, Dakar passed his hours of punishment with singing. Even cold sober, he had no ear for pitch. The yawling echoes created by his ballads made the prison sentries grit their teeth, then brawl among themselves in driven fits of frustration. A gag was attempted. Dakar somehow ingested the cloth. The coarse fibres gave him a bellyache, but otherwise seemed not to faze him.

The healer dispatched to examine him emerged from the depths of Jaelot's dungeon, his tongue clicking in amazement behind the scented kerchief he carried to mask the stench. 'The man's crazed,' he said in a nasal twang. He removed the linen and spat into it. After eyeing the sputum with the reflexive habit of his profession, he treated the head warden's sallow complexion to the same disconcerting regard. 'Thinks he's immortal, your prisoner. Insisted he could survive a straight draught of deadly nightshade, and then offered to show me, the mad fool. Keep him chained on a diet of herb broth. Then if you take my advice, send him on to the crazy house run by the Brothers of Ath's Initiates.'

Cocooned in fur vests to ease a chest cold, the head warder shrugged his exasperation. 'That would be a frank relief, to be rid of him. But the judiciary's adamant. It's the work team for Dakar till the advent of summer, and naught short of death will shift the sentence.'

'Well, let him lie,' the healer said, repacking his satchel in sour humour. 'He might get pox, or perish of rat bite. At least, by Daelion's justice, he should catch your cough and lose his voice. Does your wife brew cailcallow tea?'

The glum warden shook his head. 'No wife.'

'Ah, too bad.' The healer departed, whistling; and whatever sort of ills beset Dakar's jailers, the prisoner proved maddeningly immune. He carolled himself hoarse in the darkness, then rasped on in a blithe and froggy baritone, while his guardsmen wore mufflers tied about their ears in an effort to dampen the dissonance.

At mid-spring, with the hemp cloth smock worn by the condemned sagged like empty sacking over his depleted belly, and skin turned mushroom pale, the Mad Prophet informed the man sent down to fetch him that he had never stayed sober for more than a fortnight, even as a babe at his mother's knee. Three months was a lifetime record, Dakar insisted, as if astounded to still be alive.

Nobody succoured him with beer. He was prodded from his lair in the pits of Jaelot's dungeon. The blocks shaped at the mason's throughout the winter were now being loaded onto flat ox-wains and rolled in slow rounds to the headland. There, a team of men at arms in leather brigandines raised their bull voices to harry on a wretched line of workers. Scoured by salt-spray and the white-laced surge of high tide, bleeding from barnacle grazes and stone cuts, Jaelot's convict labour team bent their backs to restore the torn bulkheads and jetty.

Their work was cruel and dangerous; where currents had undercut the sea wall, the granite might shift and slide. A man could break his hands or his legs, caught in an unlucky place. Incoming waves could crest and slam down without warning, and a seething froth of brine would tumble the huge blocks like knucklebones stewed in a cauldron. Men died pinched like insects, or dragged under to drown in the weight of their fetters and chain.

Dakar had no wish to end ground in shreds to be picked by the bay's hordes of scavenger crabs.

While the wains were pulled up for unloading, he stole a moment while the watch was diverted, and behind the move of blowing on chapped hands, cast a sharp eye across the waves. His month in the dungeon had left him more time than he liked for uninterrupted concentration; his eyesight was clear as a sailor's.

A gruff voice shouted behind him, 'You!' A pikestaff hit Dakar across the shoulders. 'Back to work! And hurry on about it.'

The Mad Prophet stumbled forward, caught short of a trip as he ploughed shoulder down into the stone block in process of being jockeyed from the wagon bed onto log rollers for transport. Men swayed. The wagon creaked. The dressed mass of granite shifted, grating, then spun off-balance and dived. Those poles not instantly milled to slivers lumbered out of alignment, while men jumped clear and swore, the slowest ones nursing whacked shins.

'It's the fat idiot, again!' screeched the pikeman appointed to attend the wain's unloading.

Wide-eyed in affront, Dakar regarded flat folds where once he had sported a paunch. 'Fat?'

A mailed fist fetched him a ringing thump on the jaw. 'No talk. Just work. Or ye'll see yourself pressed to parchment under yon mother of a rock.'

Dakar staggered on rubbery knees and fell spectacularly flat on his fundament. Prods from the pike failed to raise him.

'Fiends plague us!' The watch captain arrived, the higher-pitched clink of his accoutrements clear over the deeper tones of shackle chains. 'Drag the lout into the spray! Cold water should rouse him soon enough.'

Two convicts were waved over to manhandle Dakar clear of the work crew. He lay sprawled at the edge of the sea wall, a crumpled heap in stained rags, bruised and apparently dazed; except that his face stayed raptly turned toward the surf that pounded below. At length, he stirred, not due to the needling spray that sheeted over him, but because he finally sighted the sign he sought amid the moiling whitecaps.

There were fiends in truth, out amid the breakers, riding the incoming tide to replenish themselves. Energy sprites native to Athera that drew fuel from the tumble of the waters, invisible to the eye except as crests that rose and broke, then subsided, unnaturally splashless, into the current of the bay. What the Paravian tongue named iyats, or tricksters, for their tireless penchant to make mischief.

Dakar's lip curled in an evil smile through split and bleeding contusions. He moaned for effect, rolled over and propped himself on his forearms. Then, eyes clenched shut in a feigned fit of queasiness, he mustered his skills as a spellbinder and inwardly massed a tight, spinning core of focused energy. Sloppily, as a novice might, he let the force bleed into his aura. The miscast conjury was imperceptible, even harmless, little worse than the flash of static discharge that might jump and ground to metal in a dry freeze. But as Dakar well knew from experience, the slightest mismanagement of mage-force was irresistible fare to the appetite of an unsated fiend.

Often enough in the past he had suffered, when negligent handling of his lessons had attracted the sprites to plague him. As much as Asandir tried to castigate him, Dakar's ways stayed incorrigible. Ever and always he remained an insatiable magnet for fiends.

He felt a shiver thrill the air as they sensed his beckoning presence. The splashless fall of the wavecrests unravelled, spouting into joyous, wild spray as the creatures arrowed from their sport and fastened upon his signature of strayed power. Never before had he revelled in the itches and small tingles that played over his skin as they spun, drinking the energy-spill off his aura. Where one came, more followed. Iyats liked travelling in packs. Prickled and lightly burned through the tuned perception of his mage-sense, Dakar judged to the second when the fiends blithely gathered to feed from his handout became charged and engorged beyond their simple needs. He groaned and groped and stood upright with just enough show to draw the eye of the watching overseer.

For once in league with shouted oaths and harsh orders, the Mad Prophet let the guardsmen prod him. Chivvied, cursed, and shoved on by impatient pike butts, he let himself be hazed into the thick of the work crew, no longer unloading carts, but labouring and groaning to lever the heavy blocks into place on the broken sea wall. The smells of salt-damp wool and sweat combined with the squeak of ropes through blocks and tackle; the grind of stone over stone. Pressed amid the heat of straining bodies, made to shoulder his share of the weight, Dakar licked crusted blood from his teeth and cut off his trickle of leaked energy.

The invisible fiends knit about him in spirals of distorted breezes. They buffeted and pinched and tweaked at his hair in signal fits of irritation. When he refused to give in and fuel their wants further, they lent themselves in their madcap way to tease, to frustrate, to annoy, that they might sip what stray spurts of emotion they could wring from whatever victims were available.

In an eyeblink, the work on the jetty erupted into chaos.

Stone chips and rocks sprang up and whirled airborne, clanging off the helms of the officers and unmercifully pelting the conscripts. Bruised and screaming in wild surprise, men heaved off the encumbrance of their loads. The massive dressed blocks misaligned and jarred awry, then dropped with a thud to quake the sea wall. Granite rasped against granite, grinding off falls of small pebbles that ripped aloft to sting flesh. Men coughed out curses and spat grit while the older blocks already mauled by storms and ice loosened, cracked, and gave way, to fall with thunderous, geysering spray into white petticoats of surf.

A waterspout kicked up where no breath of wind was in evidence. It shrieked and snarled and snaked itself a passage like a whip through mild air. The lead ox teams scrabbled back, whuffing. Pounds of solid muscle strained against the constraints of leather and shafts, while the stout cart behind struck a wall of rock and compressed. The wagon bed groaned and burst in a wreckage of timber. The next dray in line jounced and jammed two wheels in cracked paving, its hubs wrenched off to a squeal of sheared linchpins.

Yards away, three stolid drovers appeared to entangle themselves in their ox goads and fall flat.

'Ath spare us!' yelled the captain in charge. He ducked too late to miss the sliced foam off a wave top that poured itself down his back. Red-faced, dripping, ready to murder for sheer fury, he hopped from one leg to the other. 'We're caught in a damned plague of fiends!' The pikestaff in his hands came alive with the urge to bang down and hammer at his insteps.

Bleeding now from a dozen minor gashes, men at arms threw aside polearms to slap at the hail of small pebbles. While the oxen bucketed against their yokes, and bedevilled carters strove to quiet them, iyats possessed the very reins in their hands and exuberantly undid the buckles. The dropped leather twined snake-fashion and laced around ankles and fetlocks. While the animals bawled and the convicts thrashed in their shackles, the beleaguered guardsmen unsheathed their daggers. They bent to hack themselves free, then stamped and slapped at cut bits of leather that groped up their calves like maggots.

'Men, get the prisoners to form ranks!' shouted the harried captain.

While his troop pushed, punched, staggered, and shoved the distraught work team into ragged columns, a sizeable stretch of the sea wall began in bounding starts to unravel. Rocks flew and cracked, whistling the air like slingshot.

'Back!' screamed the officer of the watch. 'Inside the gatehouse! The talismans there will fend off the fiends.'

Braced on planted feet just shy of the crumbling jetty, the Mad Prophet laughed through his reddish frizzle of beard. If the little tin fetishes that dangled from the gatehouse had once held power to ward, time and attrition had drained the spells. The residue that lingered might deflect one fiend; never a full pack bent on a spree of wild mischief. Against common belief, the jangle and chime raised by wind-tossed strips of tin caused no warding vibrations. Their sound was good for nothing but warning and the iyats would pass them unscathed. Dakar knew from bleak experience: having tasted the heady discharge of spell-force on his person, the sprites were apt to dog his tracks for days.

As unrepentant instigator, he set his jaw against the throttling tug of his prison smock, that a smaller iyat seemed bent on unravelling into a garrotte. He marched in his shackles through splintered carts and the steaming heaps of dung littered by the terrified ox teams, and felt inordinately cheerful. Singing bawdy ditties in confinement was vastly preferable to hard labour that might see a man's bones ground for fish food; worth even the torment of a plague-storm of fiends to regain a safe state of idleness.

Four days later, engrossed in a target shoot against Jaelot's second captain of archers, the Masterbard's apprentice Medlir poised at the butts in the practice yard to tally the score of his arrows.

An off-duty guardsman hailed him from the gate across the field. 'Hey, minstrel! Did you hear? That fat man your master must play to redeem was let off his term of forced labour!'

Wrapped in a faded dun cloak, lashed about the ankles by the wind-crumpled stands of spring grass that had finally pushed through the mud, Medlir flicked back his hood. Eyes as changeably flecked as the lichen tinged wall behind his shoulder widened under up-turned brows. 'You speak of Dakar? What's to hear?'

His shooting companions clustered around, sand piggins empty, their shafts still jammed in straw targets. The silver they stood to lose if the count was completed left them amiably open to diversion.

Now able to laugh at the afternoon's pestering annoyance, the guard just off watch in the dungeons strode over, his conical helm tucked beneath his arm. 'Fool bailiff had to release him. No choice. Besides being crazy, the fat man's a breathing, walking lure for stray fiends. Brings them on like a lodestone draws iron, and not a blighted talisman in the city seems to hold power for protection.' Arrived at the butts, and soldier enough to count and weigh odds at a glance, he slapped Medlir on the shoulder. 'You're winning? With *that*? Against longbows?'

'I was.' The minstrel gave a crooked smile. Long, supple fingers unstrung the horn recurve, then surrendered the weapon to a page boy for return to common stores in the armoury. 'You didn't tell Dakar the name of the inn where we're quartering?'

The guardsman's brisk humour turned wicked. 'The city dungeon won't keep him. Who's left? I hope you've got patience for waking up with your bootlaces snarled into knots.'

'Well, I don't.' Energetically merry, Medlir laughed.

He kept to himself the piquant truth that a masterbard's art included chords arranged in particular harmonic resonance to repel fiends. Halliron had forbidden his apprentice to perform any music in public; for himself, the old man avowed to make no appearance until the moment he was compelled by the terms of the judiciary's bargain. If Jaelot was pestilent with iyats due to Dakar's incarceration, the Masterbard and his singer in training would retreat to their attic and share rich appreciation of the havoc.

Spirit Tracks

Touched across distance by a prompt from the Warden in Althain Tower, a raven flaps and rouses a Fellowship mage, who ignores the stiffness of old wounds to arise, don his threadbare black cloak, and journey eastward across Radmoore Downs toward the spell-guarded stronghold on the edge of the dread mires of Mirthlvain . . .

In western lands, the same call is heard and declined by another spirit mage who stands watch over an enclave of enchantresses; in particular one initiate with dark auburn hair and a guarded heart, entrapped in the web of greater intrigue that surrounds the Master of Shadow . . .

Far removed from Athera's spinning orb and the sphere of Sethvir's provenance, the discorporate awareness of a sorcerer departs from a world bound in ice and shackled under brooding bands of fog; and as his conscious presence arrows on through the emptiness that freezes the space between stars, he fears the next place he seeks to unlock the Mistwraith's secrets may prove as lifelessly desolate as the last . . .

IV. CONVOCATION

Some days after the clanborn courier had taken leave of his tower eyrie, Sethvir, Warden of Althain laid out a fresh square of parchment. With one elbow braced against a tome on celestial mechanics whose listed orbs and planetary bodies lay nowhere near his present world of inhabitancy, he pondered; his hands out of fussy habit trimmed pen nibs the way a duellist might whet fine steel. Then, his left hand curled around a tea mug, the sorcerer penned out the message Tysan's lady steward had asked him to send on to Arithon s'Ffalenn. Moved by purposeful afterthought, he added an inventory that filled twelve close-spaced pages. The items he catalogued had been on Maenalle's mind, too lengthy for a courier to memorize. Willing servant to her intent, Sethvir let the breeze dry the ink. Then he rummaged through a cupboard, salvaged a battered seal from a tin full of oddments, and secured the document under the device of the ancient princes of Camris, from whom the lady traced descent.

The waning night beyond the casements was the eve of the vernal equinox, by custom a time for the Fellowship sorcerers to gather in convocation.

Althain's Warden tucked the finished letter into a satchel already packed for the occasion and descended to his equally cluttered living quarters. There he replaced his threadbare robe with another only slightly less ink-stained. Outside, the sky lightened to dusky pearl. Bright-eyed despite not having slept for several days, Sethvir continued down the stairwell.

No cressets brightened the black iron wall sconces. The commemorative statues of Paravians housed on Althain's ground floor wore a gloom only fitfully broken as the gleam that leaked through the arrowloops jinked across gold braid and trappings.

Sethvir required no torch to see his way past the ranks of marble unicorns; the horned majesty of centaurs that loomed above his head; the waist-high maple pedestals that elevated the diminutive bronzes of Sun Children. If concern for the future burdened his thoughts, here, the past weighed unquiet as well. Through mage-sense, Sethvir felt the vibrational echoes left by the steps of former visitors. In winnowed air currents like moving chiaroscuro, he could trace the tides of old magics, ones wrought by Paravians in subliminal harmonics; and others more recent, of Fellowship craft, that feathered the skin like a tonic. Surrounding all, enduring as bedrock, lurked the guardspells that sealed Althain Tower from the world and its troubles outside.

The sorcerer bypassed the gold-chased panels, built to mask the massive, geared chains and windlass that worked the tower's grand portal. His satchel slung like a knapsack, he knelt by an inset trapdoor and paused, apparently overcome by reverie; in fact, his mind sharpened in search and coursed outward, beyond Athera's cloud layer and into deep vacuum through which the stars drifted like lamps.

But the far distant spirit of the colleague who journeyed to study the Mistwraith's origin returned no response; nor had for an uneasy score of months.

With Lysaer extending his influence into Tysan, the peace could scarcely last. Time to reclaim the cursed princes from the Mistwraith's geas was growing sorrowfully short.

Raked by a shiver, Sethvir aroused, recalled to those troubles close at hand. A ring-pull lifted to his touch; defence wards dissolved and the heavy stone rose to a stir of moving counterweights. The chamber's miasma of aged cedar and wool gave way to the draught that welled up, spiked like a storm-breeze with ozone. A stair shaft cut downward into cold dark, limned like dust on ebony by the silver-blue glimmer of the power focus set into the dungeon below.

Sethvir secured the trapdoor behind him and descended. Daybreak was nigh, its song plain to read in the soft, bursting static of the earth lane's magnetic signature. Althain's Warden stepped off the landing. He crossed a concave depression paved with lightless black onyx, then the focus itself, of concentric circles over-scribed in Paravian runes, mapped out in pearlescent phosphor. Tingled by the unshielded play of elemental forces, he positioned himself at the pattern's centre. His feet rested on the apex of a looping star interlace that met in a nexus of five lines.

He closed his eyes, gripped his satchel and waited.

Outside the tower, sunrise touched light through the mists.

A flux of wild energy crested along the lane, and the focus in the cellar floor responded, crackling to incandescent white. The moment sang into a chord of suspension, laced about with dire powers.

Then the dawn sun-surge peaked and passed. The rune circles shimmered to quiescence, and the Warden of Althain was gone. Air displaced by his departure eddied over gargoyle cornices and sighed to final stillness through attrition.

Relocated three hundred and eighty leagues to the south-east, Sethvir opened his eyes. Through a lingering shudder of reaction, he sucked in a breath dank as fog off a retting pond with the taint of mildew and mould. He wrinkled his nose. 'I'd forgotten how Meth Isle smelled.'

'That's possible?' His host, the master spellbinder Verrain, stood in straight quiet like a cat-tail, furled against the damp in a mud-splashed, brown frieze cloak. 'I wasn't sure, I've been here so long.' Full lips that once had wrung sighs from Daenfal's fairest maidens crooked in humourless irony. 'Welcome to the bogs of Mirthlvain.'

Sethvir gave his spinning senses a moment more to settle, then stepped off the lichened patterns of a lane focus centuries older than the one at Althain Tower. Gilded with flickers from the rushlight by the doorway, he gripped the wrists of the apprentice mage, who had stood guard over the dread spawn of Mirthlvain for more years than any soul deserved.

'You have tea?' asked the Fellowship sorcerer.

His anxious note caused Verrain to grin. 'My cupboards are stocked.' He led off up a brick stair, hollowed by moisture and footfalls. 'The others await you above.'

The pair climbed in darkness alive with the tick and splash of condensation. From some bleak chamber down a corridor, a caged thing chittered and screeled; the echoes cut at the nerves, caused the hair of warm-blooded listeners to prickle and stab erect.

'Karth-eels?' Sethvir asked.

'A breeding pair.' Verrain unbarred an upper doorway to a squeal of rusted hinges. He retrieved a staff of grey ash, while the spill of filtered daylight traced over knuckles left scarred by bites, and claws, and fell scratchings. 'A new mutation, I fear.'

'Hardly fresh,' Sethvir murmured, 'if these ones you've caught are amphibious, with fangs and webbed feet as well as the usual venomed spines.'

Verrain glanced aside in surprise, his eyes so bleak they looked lightless. 'You've seen footed spawnings before this?'

'Actually, yes. But not for five thousand years.' In disquiet thought, the sorcerer hitched at the strap of his satchel. 'Certainly none since the hate-wraiths who caused the aberrations were prisoned in Rockfell pit.'

'The records in the library don't list those.' Verrain ducked to traverse the peculiar, low arches of a connecting hall. One of Meth Isle fortress's many cats streaked past as he flung back the door to another stairway. 'No. They wouldn't.' Moved to an airy shift of subject, Sethvir said, 'There's a most urgent reason why we chose to meet here for the equinox.'

The light strengthened with the climb, warmed to buttery, cloud-hazed sunshine. This far east, the morning was already several hours gone. Windows battened under diamond-meshed grilles opened onto Meth Isle fortress's vista of slate roofs and terracotta chimneys, tufted under yellow moss and fungus. Tiled gutters with gargoyle spouts loured over a lakeshore scummed with lily pads and beyond them, darker, deeper waters rippled and scaled silver with wind. Mirthlvain's landscape of steaming mires loomed in the distance, an imprinted silhouette of marsh maple and cypress cobwebbed with trailing, tattered moss.

But the inside air now carried welcoming heat and a perfume of clean burning birch. An orange tabby bounded across the landing to weave against Verrain's shins. He crossed a marble antechamber inhabited by beetles in lichened corners and led into the grand hall beyond.

Past the braced doors, lofty hammerbeamed ceilings hung splotched acid green from the damp. A black iron cauldron steamed on the hob, and there Sethvir's host gestured with the flick of a dimple on each cheek. 'Your tea water. Sufficient to last out the day, I should hope.'

The sorcerer returned a pleased grin, then hastened on to greet the two colleagues who waited, already seated. Other carved chairs with upholstery felted with cat hair sat empty before the stone gryphons that fashioned the table's massive pedestal.

A white and tortoiseshell tom poured itself from Asandir's lap as he arose. 'Sethvir! Come sit. How long has it been since you remembered to eat?' Tall, windburned, worn lean from travel, he made room for Althain's Warden, in the process displacing a sleepy kitten.

The black-clad sorcerer opposite hunched over a plate of smoked fish and scones, his mouth too full for speech. But the raven perched on his shoulder swivelled beady jet eyes and croaked.

'Hello to you too, little brother.' Sethvir dumped his satchel on the floor and sat, his diffuse gaze no longer bemused, but trained in sharp inquiry upon the quieter of his two colleagues.

Traithe stayed riveted on his food. His wide-brimmed black hat with its tarnished silver band hung from the knurl on his chair arm. The caped sable mantle he still wore failed to mask the tender movements left over from crippling injuries; in the hour of the Mistwraith's first invasion, Traithe had made tragic sacrifice to unbind the spells on the South Gate portal and cut off the creatures' point of entry.

When his raven clipped him a peck on the ear, he looked up, his brown eyes dark with affront. 'Yes,' he snapped as though to an unwanted inquiry. 'My scars ache today. But since meeting was called for at Mirthlvain, I presume we save our strengths for something more pressing than small healing.'

Above a twist of frosty hair the raven had tousled, Asandir and Sethvir locked glances. Had Traithe still possessed his full faculties, no one need say that Mirthlvain's ills were quiescent.

'Actually,' the Warden of Althain admitted, 'this is the closest active focus to Alestron, where one of us needs to pay a visit. A copy of Magyre's papers has apparently survived and fallen into the hands of the duke's scholars.'

'Black powder again?' asked Verrain, arrived with a stalker's silence to settle on Traithe's other side. He had shed his frieze cloak. Lank blond hair tied by velvet ribbons feathered through the ruffles of a dandy's collar several centuries out of fashion.

Sethvir sighed. 'The very same old tired story.' He looked askance at Asandir, who had forgotten to pass on the scones. 'It's scarcely on your way, but you'll need to visit the city before going north to Rockfell to check on the Mistwraith's confinement.'

Then, mindful the cruellest of Traithe's distress would not stem from old injuries, Sethvir tucked his hands in his sleeve cuffs. Carefully, aloud, he said, 'No, I have yet to hear word.'

His inference was to Kharadmon, their discorporate colleague dispatched across the gulf to resurvey the paired worlds left severed by the closure of South Gate. There, for a purpose beyond comprehension, the abomination wrought of mists and trapped human spirits first became amalgamated into the Mistwraith that endangered Athera.

Worries abounded. The icy, lifeless void between stars was inhospitable, even to the bodiless spirit; worse, the alienated worlds presumably harboured the wraith's greater portion, still at large and potently malevolent. The calamity that resulted from the creature's confinement here had unveiled frightening truths: for the mist's bound spirits were intelligent, able to wrest the key to grand conjury from another mind trained to mastery. They had even proved capable of movement and planning across the threshold of time.

Best of any, the Fellowship sorcerers understood the ugly details. The curse they undertook to unravel to reconcile two princes was daunting in scope, and ranged about with perils that lay outside of all augury.

Kharadmon's journey had been launched at unmentionable risk. If he suffered mishap and failed to return, far more than the hope of the royal heirs' reconciliation would be lost. The Fellowship itself might never be restored to its original circle of seven sorcerers.

Amid bitter silence, and stalked by the interest of three cats, the raven spread glossy primaries and dived in to peck at the scones. Traithe beat it back to a flurry of wings, snatched the butter crock away, then hissed until the bird retreated to fluff indignant feathers on his chair back. Since mention of one discorporate colleague brought the other to mind, he said, 'Luhaine has no plans to join us?'

'Sadly not.' Sethvir rescued a scone the bird had mauled and dipped up a creamy scoop of butter. 'The Koriani witches have renewed their efforts to find Arithon.' He bit down and chewed with absent relish. 'For equinox, they've planned a grand scrying. A circle of twenty-one seniors, to be matrixed through the Skyron crystal. Luhaine's needed to try and scatter their energies everywhere else but toward Jaelot, a touchy task. We'd rather his influence wasn't noticed.'

'*Jaelot?*' Verrain's expostulation re-echoed off the vaults of the ceiling. 'That cesspit of snobbery and bad taste? Why Jaelot?'

Asandir sighed, the broad line of his shoulders looking tired. 'The affair involves an exploit of Dakar's that's too idiotic to mention. But to redeem the Mad Prophet's foolishness, Halliron is confined there till solstice. His apprentice naturally won't leave him.' The sorcerer hooked his chin on steepled fingers, not needing to add that a stay of such length left Arithon's identity as Medlir vulnerable, and not just to auguries done on the balance point of equinox. Since the secret of the Shadow Master's alias was the fragile linchpin that frustrated the directive of Desh-thiere's curse, Luhaine was bound to be misleading enchantresses for some while yet to come.

'Well,' murmured Traithe in dry conclusion. 'This isn't so much a convocation as a gossip list of our weaknesses.'

'From which we can certainly spare a moment for minor healing,' Sethvir interjected with a glance of prankish triumph toward his colleague. 'For the task that lies ahead of us tonight, we can't do without your sense of humour.'

A flick of amusement rekindled the laugh lines at the corners of Traithe's spaniel eyes. 'What's amiss that's any worse than the monsters mewed up in these mires?'

Turned blankly vague, Sethvir fiddled pastry crumbs out of the folds of his cuffs. 'The Koriani Council's pursuit of Arithon s'Ffalenn. But let that bide for a little.'

His wistful glance toward the cauldron moved Verrain to arise and fetch mugs, and steep a pot of bracing tea.

When eventide dimmed the Mirthlvain marshes, the peepings and shrills, the skreels and the croaks of its nocturnal denizens racketed across the shallows of Methlas Lake. The mists had not yet arisen, to lure out the will o' the wisps and the seeping flares of the marshlights. Unquiet waters lay black as a facet of obsidian, stippled by the light-prints of stars, and one anomaly: a thread of reflection sculled on the shore's dying currents, cast out into darkness by a firelit casement high up in Meth Isle fortress.

There, around the stone table in a hall dimmed to cavernous shadow, three Fellowship sorcerers hunched in conference. They concluded their survey of far-reaching responsibilities, for they alone had been left as guardians of Athera's ancient mysteries since the old races' inexplicable disappearance. Wards of protection that confined creatures dangerous in malice had been checked over world gates and preserves. As always, defences had weakened; four months of difficult travels lay ahead for Traithe and Asandir. The demands on them both were relentless, with their discorporate colleagues committed elsewhere. Of two other sorcerers outside tonight's active circle, none spoke: the shade of Davien the Betrayer remained banished in seclusion since the hour of the high kings' fall; Ciladis the Lost, still gone beyond reach, on his failed quest to find the Paravians.

The sole augury that forecast the Seven's reunity, the last hope to accomplish the old races' return: all remained jeopardized by the Mistwraith's curse, and two princes shackled into enmity. Brought at last to that point, and the reason for gathering at Meth Isle, Sethvir peered into his empty mug. The tea leaves scummed in the dregs deceptively appeared to absorb him, while his eyes mapped the sonorous currents of the earth, and the fine, singing tracks of distant stars. 'It is time.'

Gaunt and silent, Asandir arose. He collected the used crockery, Verrain's chipped pot with its sprung wicker handle, and the moth-eaten quills filched from the library. With hands that moved much more freely, Traithe rolled up a marked map. He slipped the parchment into its case and across the cleared table, spread the black cloth of his cloak.

Sethvir stooped by his chair to rummage something from his satchel. While the cats piled next to Verrain's ankles scampered off, and the one in his lap stretched and left, the Guardian of Mirthlvain out of habit used mage-sense to tag the cause of their unrest. But this time no aberrated creature from the swamps had strayed inside to be hunted. Verrain's query touched the edge of a cold ward, a boundary field laid down to contain a flux of refined vibration. He realized, alarmed, that the Fellowship meant to cast strands. The augury they could wring out of still air and power would be exactingly accurate, and undertaken only at grave need. More disturbing still, the Warden of Althain straightened up and offered him a tin canister and stone pipe.

Verrain need not unseal the container. The pungency that seeped from the dried herb inside charged his senses with dreadful remembrance of its poisons. Shaken, he said quickly, 'I shouldn't need tienelle to follow the progression of a strand pattern.'

Sethvir did not back down, but cradled the master spellbinder's hands within his own tepid palms. 'Tonight, we're not sounding the future.' Fallen into shadow as Asandir made a spell to darken the glow of the fire, the Warden looked oddly wizened; momentarily no sorcerer at all, but an old man rubbed spiritless and thin by a lifetime's uncountable sorrows. 'You weren't told earlier. But the Mistwraith's curse that sets Lysaer and Arithon into conflict is far worse than a geas of fixation. The knowledge which might shed light on their condition lies two ages back in the past.'

A creeping shudder harrowed Verrain's nerves. 'You wish to tune the strands to examine the *methuri* that created the abominations here at Mirthlvain?'

'Desh-thiere's binding over the princes is not far removed from the corruptions effected by the hate-wraiths.' Asandir folded his lean length and sat with his usual economy of movement. 'Both arose from the meddling of spirit entities. Both were imprinted into living flesh, with bonds of compulsion that can't be undone without losing the victim in death.'

As Sethvir's touch slipped away, Verrain flicked open the little tin, his dimples erased by trepidation as he cleaned and packed the stubby pipe. The biting smell of the tienelle enveloped him, fierce enough to make him cough. Just how a strand casting could be ranged across time, he desperately wished not to learn.

Sethvir unkindly answered his thought all the same. 'Time's riddle is only opaque to those senses attuned through the flesh.'

Verrain's horrified start shot the canister lid in a clanging arc to the floor. 'Ath forfend! Can't we ask Luhaine to handle this?'

But already Asandir had slipped beyond hearing. His tall, dark-robed form lay slumped across the table, his cheek cradled on folded arms. His flesh was a vessel emptied of spirit, with Traithe already set in anguished silence by his shoulder to stand ward and guard.

The plain fact could not be forgotten, that just such a perilous scrying had stripped Kharadmon to discorporate status. Verrain snapped a flame off a finger tip that trembled and ignited the herb in his pipe. As drug-laden smoke twined in ghostly step to the dance of some aimless air current, he called on six centuries of discipline to wrest his uncertainty aside. Then he drew on the stem and gasped as the tienelle's drug whirled through his senses like wildfire.

Vertigo upended him in a savage, exhilarant rush. There followed a glass-sharp awareness that scoured his dross of flesh, until the stillness of the room compressed his ears like cotton and his eyesight gained hurtful clarity. The lofty, crystalline expansion of awareness overturned him like a plunge from great height. He clung to his chair in desperation to stay anchored, while around him the floor lost its semblance of solidity. Changed perception showed him the layers of dizzy energies that bound its cool stone into matter.

Verrain fought to master the reeling hyperbole that savaged him. As Sethvir's expectancy jabbed through his trance, he recalled his place and purpose: for the knowledge to redeem Athera's cursed princes, Asandir now twisted the flow of time. The thread of his existence hung poised in suspension on the threshold between life and death.

The spellfield the sorcerer laid out above the black cloth on the tabletop had limits; its influence encompassed little more than the span of one cubic yard. But the resonance where its edges grazed up against the present raised a whine past the limit of hearing, and a flesh-stripping ache that made human bone marrow shiver and jump like kicked mercury. Hazed by indescribable discomfort, his blond hair strung limp with sweat, Verrain cobbled a grip on his frayed consciousness and spun out three filaments of light.

Sethvir raised power and spoke. An answering resonance of mage-force tingled outward as his words parted drug-heightened senses like razors, touched the strands hanging poised against darkness, and set over them a signature that gave Name.

Ruled in parallel with the life-currents that endowed Ath's creation, the filaments quickened, interleaved into patterns the trained mind could unriddle at a glance. Verrain called forth another strand, and another, while through some unseen linkage with the time-pocket carved out by Asandir, Sethvir spoke Names upon them that recreated constructs of *this* stone, and *that* mud-pool, then seeded them with plants, insects, salamanders and trees in their individual, teeming thousands. Here lay like pen strokes the growth and death of moss. There, in skeined interlace, the play of breezes through reed beds, ringed with black water scribed by stitched curves that marked the life-dance of fishes. In glowing, intricate splendour against a dark like layered velvet, a mile square portion Mirthlvain's mire became replicated in a linear analogue of patterns.

Transfixed by awe, and a harmony that wrung him breathless, Verrain wept as he realized: the bogland he viewed was still governed by nature. The creatures there had yet to be enslaved, corrupted and cross-bred to birth the monstrous perversions induced by the hate-wraiths' possession.

Softly out of shadow, Sethvir said, 'Commence.'

Verrain felt the hair stir at his nape as channelled power sparked through the strands.

A pent sense of danger prevailed, like the quaver of a note too long sustained, or the chill of sharp steel masked in cloth. Now, any misplayed distinction between the quick force of life and the raw burn of elemental energy might sunder the time-ward's fragile balance and rip Asandir spirit from flesh. Verrain trembled in his battle to keep the herb's explosive prescience tied in to geometric augury as Sethvir alone called forth the final strand, then shaped it to the Name of the *methuri*.

The matrix mapped an origin Verrain had studied only in ancient text: here, in spikes and jagged angles, he *experienced* the leaked bit of storm charge that had displaced half-formed beings from the thought-shaped, nether-realm of drake-dreams. In twists and snagged knotwork, he saw anomalies that to this world were half demon, half monster, change vibration and emerge to rampage and slay. The original *methurien* were creatures deranged by pain, animate consciousness torn into breathing life from an existence of shadowy apparition. Their bodily deaths on Paravian weapons had served only to release their twisted essence as free wraiths.

His centuries of handling the cross-bred abominations left behind as their legacy could not prepare Mirthlvain's Guardian for the concentrated, driving hatred the *methuri* had embodied. Needled breathless by passions bent and whetted for destruction, Verrain felt his consciousness twist to escape. The drugs in the tienelle gave no quarter, but held his awareness channelled open through the shivering flinch of full contact.

'Steady. Hold steady,' Sethvir cautioned.

Verrain's fingernails split under the force of his grip on the table as the first wraith ensnared a live victim. The moment of its possession was terrible to witness: clean-edged lines that delineated a mouse unique unto itself in Ath's creation flickered and spiked into a chaotic jumble that, even two ages later, seemed to shock the night air with scream upon scream of torment. Verrain stung as though every nerve in his body had been sieved out and scorched in hot acid.

Locked into step with the strands' unfolding sequence, he watched the signature pattern of the mouse blur, coil, then fix in a flare of cold fire into something wholly wrong, in mind and matter remoulded to a parasitic hybrid that was irrationally, unthinkably *other*. What moved and breathed in the heart of the strands' reflection was a thing outside the Major Balance, the warp and weft of its birthright wrenched contrary to natural law.

Revolted to spasms of dry nausea, the spellbinder clamped hands to his lips until the blood felt squeezed from his fingers. He compelled himself to abide as Sethvir broadened his study: and snakes, insects, otters and frogs all suffered possession in turn. The moment of change in each case was sliced free of time and dissected; line for line, contortion for mauled contortion, the maligned detail of the hate-wraiths' workings wrung out in white pain from their victims. Life-force itself became impressed and internally warped until only the husk of the body remained, to spawn its altered, aberrant offspring. The warped things birthed from such breedings in turn became subservient to the whim of the host.

Drenched in a cold sweat, Verrain tracked Sethvir's analysis of the past as *methuri* abominations insinuated a rift in earthly order, to knot a linkage through the breathing essence of spirit and the energy coils that underpinned fleshly matter. The conclusion in the strands was most clear. Not only would separation trigger the dissolution of bodily substance, but the wraith in possession could unkey the quickened flesh and impose wilful change with impunity.

Aghast, Verrain whispered, 'You think Desh-thiere's curse upon the princes may work in a similar way?'

Sethvir looked up, the strand-wrought, desecrated patterns imprinted in frosty reflection upon his emotionless eyes. 'That's what we're here to determine.' He succumbed to a shudder, as if his detachment gave way and the horrors reeled off in cold augury overcame him in one slamming wave. Then he blotted damp palms on his sleeve cuffs and spoke a single clipped syllable. The knit mesh of forces that energized the strands bled off in a crackle of sparks.

Asandir drew a racking breath and stirred, while Traithe stepped aside and dropped into a chair as though his knees had failed him.

For an interval spanning several minutes, nobody cared to try speech.

Verrain finally pushed upright and made his unsteady way to the hearth to unshield the fire and brew tea. The toxins in the tienelle had left him dehydrated and queasy; spurious starts of vision still snatched through his senses like flares. Tired to his bones, his hyper-sensitized awareness cringing even from the rub of the grey tom just returned to bask by the settle, the spellbinder struggled for the self-command to weather the withdrawal and transmute the herb's fatal poisons.

Behind him discussion continued, Fellowship voices mazed in grim echoes as comparisons were drawn from their study of the *methuri*, and the Mistwraith's curse on the princes. Verrain rubbed stinging eyes, unable to quell his ripping shudders as true-sight relived the hideous aberrations the strands had etched into memory. The hissing splatter of boiled over water yanked back his straying thoughts. Cold and sick unto lassitude, he bent to mind the cauldron. He could never regard the monstrosities of Mirthlvain in quite the same fashion again; dangerous as they were, and vicious, still, they deserved his full measure of pity.

The chance that two sons of Athera's royal lines might suffer a similar disfigurement offered horror beyond sane belief.

Braced by hot tea and determination, Verrain reclaimed his chair. He realized with renewed disquiet that the Fellowship prepared another scrying. Though this next divination was simple and harmless, an image drawn from straight recall, Asandir looked hollow-eyed. His craggy profile jutted into hot light as his large-knuckled hands attended the task of striking fresh flame to a candlewick. The wrist Traithe raised to put aside his raven trembled in apprehension.

Even Sethvir seemed on edge. Mantled in tawdry burgundy velvet, his collar caught with hair like snagged fish line, he raised eyes touched to fevered brilliance and regarded each of his colleagues. 'We're caught in a critical moment.' To Asandir, whose part was to draw the scrying, he said obliquely, 'Will the reliving in depth be too much?'

'Ath have mercy, it will become so, if uncertainty leads me to procrastinate.' Asandir's distress was noticed by the cats, who streaked from dim corners to crowd his lap, lace through his ankles, and vie for the chance to offer comfort. His strong hands moved, returning their attentions in rueful, saddened irony. 'Little brothers, I'm truly grateful. But our night's work isn't through yet.'

The sorcerer's words reached triangular pairs of ears and imparted uncanny understanding. As clear in their disdain of spell currents as a chance-met douse in cold water, the cats dashed off in a twitching flinch of back fur, a shaking of paws and scything jerks of offended tails.

Verrain might have chuckled at their haughtiness had the moment been less distressed. Whatever troublesome development was afoot, the sorcerers gave no explanation. Asandir set aside the rusted striker and poised in concerned stillness. While his fierce eyes closed, that alone had witnessed the moment when Desh-thiere's curse claimed its victims, the oddity recurred: this same exhaustive search had been accomplished years since, in the hour the disaster had befallen.

The spellbinder's puzzlement became crushed aside by a rising wave of bright force. Power coalesced, great enough to melt rock or ignite metal like a twig of dry tinder. Over the dusky weave of Traithe's cloak, carved out by will and clean conjury, Asandir's augury reformed the sphere of the candle's fire, to recreate an event six years past when Etarra's teeming thousands had turned out to celebrate the crowning of Rathain's sanctioned prince . . .

Spring sun flooded over the royal banners, streamered in Rathain's colours of silver and green. On a gallery overhanging the city's wide square, above the surge of a multitude, one man's gold hair and fine jewellery flared in caught light as he raised his arms in sudden violence. His words scribed no sound in the window of Asandir's re-conjuring; the instant Desh-thiere's fragmented wraith enacted its possession over Lysaer s'Ilessid, he raised his gift in a lightning-bolt attack against an enemy singled out . . .

Despite knowledge that the Mistwraith's vengeance had exploited Lysaer; that its meddling distortion of the justice a benevolent past conjury had grafted into the s'Ilessid royal line had lent it the leverage to wreak ill, nothing could prepare for the naked, wasting passion launched against the Master of Shadow. Racked by a spasm of visceral revulsion, Verrain watched, riveted, as the moment continued to unfold.

The light-bolt sheared on, a fateful, white arc of fire that tore a scream from roiled air. The black-haired victim who was its sure target thrashed to escape, while two terrified, burly merchants held him pinioned at wrists and knees. The sword he might have turned to cut his way free as well had not been in his hand. He ignored his captors' efforts to wrest the blade away. To Arithon s'Ffalenn, all else lost meaning before the attack set against him by his half-brother.

Pinned like a moth to a card by a needle of sick fascination, Verrain saw the crystalline flicker that sheeted through the burn of Lysaer's assault: an unexpected, warning blaze of Paravian spellcraft released by Arithon's heirloom sword. Then the weapon was wrenched away, to fall in mute motion to the pavement.

As Rathain's disarmed prince raised his hand to shape shadow, Sethvir interrupted like the slap of a whip striking flesh, 'Stop it there.'

In control that disallowed pity, Asandir locked the scrying. Like a reflection cold frozen in a mirror; or a jewel spiked through a ravelled plane of darkness, he held a fragment excised out of time.

The result felt as rendingly ghastly as a dying man's drawn out scream. Again, Verrain wondered why the Fellowship sorcerers should distress themselves to launch this irrelevant review.

Arithon s'Ffalenn had tipped his face skyward. Eyes widened to a tourmaline blaze of anguish, he tracked a raven that arrowed in flight above the mob etched motionless in the square. The hand cocked back in the first blooming burst of cast shadow showed his fingers flexed in concentration. The directive to guide the spell's homing was set for Traithe's bird, dispatched at need to find Sethvir. A heartbeat shy of disaster, the prince's concern lay unmasked, not for himself, but for a wasp's nest of ramifications: that if the Fellowship sorcerers went unwarned of this crisis, far more than his own life and destiny were going to fall forfeit in consequence . . .

'The farsight of s'Ahelas!' Verrain looked up, shocked by the evidence before him. 'No one told me Rathain's prince had inherited the marked gift of his mother's line along with s'Ffalenn compassion.'

'To his sorrow and that of his half-brother also,' Sethvir affirmed in quiet grief. 'Both carry the attributes of two royal families.'

Across the table, embattled by raw recriminations, Traithe sucked a fast breath and shut his eyes. 'Ath's blessed mercy, I should never have lent him my raven.'

'The bird's guidance changed nothing,' Asandir disagreed in jarring firmness. Distanced from emotion by the fearful discipline he needed to stabilize the scrying, he added, 'You'll see as much once the vibration is refined to show a clear imprint of the aura.'

Unhappiness dwelled like a sore point, that such redefinition was required only to match the shortfalls of Verrain and Traithe; or else for some larger, interconnected reason that remained too elusive place.

Then Sethvir cut in with an adamance to end Verrain's laboured speculation. 'Dare we overlook a single facet? The Mistwraith and its malice are unprecedented. We might need every angle at hand to unkey the riddle of the curse.'

Asandir bowed his head and realigned the augury. Still mazed under influence of the tienelle, Verrain flinched as the image shimmered into a delicate, prismatic fire of patterns. These displayed the character and emotions of Rathain's prince through the unshielded vibrations of his life-force. The outrage of the merchants showed also, a rinsed flare of ruby that fringed the peripheral edges. But their coarse-textured hatred became discarded like noise before the tight-meshed imprint that was Arithon.

Verrain shuddered, confounded by a warring urge to weep and hold his breath.

The aura of the s'Ffalenn prince sang through the vision in spare and forceful irony, even as Lysaer's must have done through the hour of crisis when Sethvir and Asandir between them had disentangled him from the possession of the wraith that had sealed Desh-thiere's vengeance.

Distaste like sand in his gut, Verrain pushed past grief to see more: through passage to Athera by way of the Red Desert, this prince had acquired the matrix imparted by the Five Centuries Fountain, a structure of riddles and spells built and abandoned by Davien the Betrayer in the years before he raised the insurrection to overturn kingdom rule.

'Fatemaster's mercy.' Verrain expelled a sharp exhalation. '*Both* half-brothers came here by way of the Worldsend Gate. Are they equally marked by the Betrayer's enforced longevity? If so, this geas of Desh-thiere's could upset the whole continent through the course of five hundred years!'

Sethvir's hand dropped, warm and steady on the spellbinder's shoulder. 'Save thought for more than despair. Davien's gift of added lifespan might equally lend us grace to achieve the princes' salvation.' But in comfortless fact, his platitude held no certainty.

That moment, driven to straight urgency by some unseen cue, Althain's Warden cried, '*Now!* Jump ahead to the moment of the curse.'

The image in the candle-flame unlocked to kaleidoscopic change; and Verrain felt as a man sent to dam back a cataclysm with only a wish and bare hands.

Lysaer's bolt struck.

A scintillant flash bisected the sphere of the vision. Seared from palm to right elbow, Arithon recoiled from worse than scorched flesh. Jabbed and enveloped through the crux of half-formed defences, he opened his mouth to scream as he tasted the measure of his downfall.

And peril incarnate closed over him. Lysaer's killing band of light shimmered and exploded, to unveil the Mistwraith's covert conjury: the bane-ward of the curse, transferred inside an attack no schooled mind had ever thought to suspect.

'Slow the sequence,' Sethvir commanded in a sharp-etched whisper.

Verrain jammed his fists against his temples as the brilliance shed away to unveil the stripped armature of the geas, a serried mesh ugly as flung blood, but never random. The spellbinder who shared its ruthless symmetry could wish his own tears could scald and blind him.

'Dharkaron witness,' he managed on a rasped catch of breath. 'The creature baited its binding with Arithon's personal imprint.'

'Lock and key.' Sethvir's affirmation came oddly muffled by distance. 'The bystanders were safe, had we known it.'

Traithe had no comment to offer; and Verrain could only ponder a third time why this scrying should be rewrought in such depth. One glance was enough to establish plain fact: Desh-thiere's curse and the signature pattern which comprised the extinct *methuri* held only chance similarity. As the Fellowship certainly realized, no further help for their princes could be garnered from Mirthlvain mire's dark history.

The present scrying edged forward. In a hideous play of stopped motion, the spell coils netted their victim. Barbed tendrils flung out like grapples and snagged, to shed pervasive currents throughout the s'Ffalenn prince's being.

His torment, physical and mental, shivered, shocked, and rebounded in a voiceless play of light. Through pain enough to cripple thought, Arithon fought back: in starbursts of mage-fire; in sigils and counterwards knotted and thrashed in harried ink-twists of shadow.

Yet Desh-thiere's malice had been configured to outflank and countermand every turn of his desperate strength.

Verrain saw the clean bars of will wrapped and smothered, the brilliance of purpose starkly crushed. Through the heartbeat while Arithon's self-awareness lay slapped back and stunned, the curse spun insidious transformation.

'Odd, don't you think, that the creature made its incursion a static one,' the spellbinder ventured. 'How much simpler to go the next step and force a degenerative erosion of the spirit.'

Sethvir's mouth thinned amid a bracketing bristle of beard. His uneasiness stayed unvoiced, that he feared such restraint held a purpose. The Mistwraith *had set the princes against each other;* it had not overtly destroyed them.

That its works could have done so was plain as the vision unreeled.

Verrain combed through the locked snarl of energies, overwhelmed by the evidence that this geas held no opening for reprieve. Leaving the s'Ffalenn personality symmetrical and intact, the bane-spell had meddled in cruel selectivity. Like a spider staked out in a web, it insinuated itself where hurt would be greatest: across will, emotion, and integrity. It waited, a dread vortex that consumed in cumulative subtlety, even as it pressed the incessant urge to battle its chosen nemesis: to kill Lysaer, and no other, a compulsion harnessed in step with life and spirit and consciousness.

The last coil sliced into place. Scarlet trailers bound close as wire, to vanish without trace in the quicksilver haze of the aura. Conclusion shaped only despair: the curse which shackled the half-brothers was a mirror-image construct that choked envenomed tendrils *around every nuance of the victim's being*. To cut or disturb the least jointure would trip a flashfire backlash of dissolution.

Flesh would die and spirit be instantly annihilated. The enslavement at face value might seem less damaging, but its depths were more insidious than any distortion inflicted by *methuri* possession. Limp as old rags from a helplessness the Fellowship must have gauged in advance, Verrain masked his face in his palms. Five centuries was not enough, he thought sadly, to solve a quandary of such reaching proportion.

'Well the curse won't pass to the next generation,' Sethvir offered to ease the spellbinder's despondency. 'Should either prince engender offspring, their heirs will be born unsullied.'

'Small comfort,' Traithe allowed, as he gathered his cloak from the tabletop. His resignation showed divided thoughts; whether to bless the mage training that gave Arithon limited means to resist the bane-spell's directive, or to curse the added peril his schooled talent could present as the conflict renewed, at stakes inevitably more dire.

Made aware by the bound of a cat into his lap that the candle now burned clean of conjury, Verrain welcomed the animal's small warmth against the chills of withdrawal and grief.

Dawn shed a leaden glimmer through the casement. Dulled as wind-beaten linen in its light, Asandir stretched, his move to arise cut short by Sethvir, who exchanged a weighted glance, then bent to recover his satchel.

'You're headed north,' the Warden of Althain said, settled erect with his hands full. 'I'd be obliged if you could deliver this to Arithon when his apprenticeship with the Masterbard ends.'

Asandir's eyes snapped up, keen-edged as steel raised to guardpoint. 'Not so soon!' he exclaimed. Then in brittle capitulation, he reached across the table and relieved Sethvir of the satchel. Once his grip closed over the ties, he knew the list of its contents. 'Nautical charts and Anithael's navigational instruments? Why?'

'Arithon asked for them,' Sethvir replied in painful, unsmiling directness. 'He hoped to hasten Halliron's passage to Shand. But the sea may have to answer a more urgent need, and the letter Lady Maenalle sent as well.'

The grievous implication hung through suspended quiet, that the six years of peace Arithon had bought since the massacre at Strakewood forest, that he had wrested from his fate by denying his half-brother any viable target to strike at, might be threatened well before any means lay at hand to challenge the Mistwraith's fell binding.

Unless and until Kharadmon came back successful from his quest, the hands of the Fellowship remained tied.

Traithe jammed on his hat to mask trepidation.

Afflicted by more personal ties to the princes, Asandir pushed back his chair and strode out with a speed that shed draughts and snuffed the spent flicker of the candle.

Verrain could only clench his knuckles in cat fur, his throat closed against questions too fearful to ask, and his eyes flooded from what he hoped was flung smoke from the wick that glowed briefly and blinked out.

Disclosure

The irksome price of rushing passage across the continent by means of tapping a power lane was the wrenching disorientation that lingered after arrival. Restored to his tower in Atainia with trouble enough on his mind to threaten a thunderous headache, the Warden of Althain paced. Each step squelched across the scarlet carpet in his bedchamber, soaked since a squall had dumped rain through the casement left ajar in his absence. His thick, furry buskins wicked up the wet and added a smell like damp dog to the mustiness already in the room.

'You know,' a disembodied voice admonished in reedy bass, 'There are quite a lot of books in this tower that are going to flock and mould if you don't amend your poor housekeeping.'

Sethvir stopped short amid puddles and sundry furnishings burdened like a fair stall with clutter. 'Luhaine? You wouldn't leave the Koriani witches unguarded for the simple pleasure of berating me.'

The query raised a slow spin of air in one corner, which rocked a sagged wicker hamper crammed to bursting with cast-off socks. Several woolly toes lolled over the brim, unravelled beyond help of darning; but Sethvir's drifty attentiveness reflected no shame for his negligence.

A moment passed in suspension.

Then, typically sulky, the elusive voice proffered reply. 'After last night's exertions, what need to guard? Just now, the Koriani Senior Circle lie tucked up in quilts, comatose as buds in a hard frost.'

Undaunted by Luhaine's penchant for evasions in flowery language, Sethvir sighed. 'Don't say our ruse went for nothing. Asandir's temper is touchy as if he'd swallowed pins, and though we needed our master spellbinder's help for scrying dead *methurien*, Verrain need not have been aggrieved by what else transpired last night.'

'Well, the choice of decoy was never my idea, if you care to recall!'

Disturbed draughts huffed across the chamber, riffling the pages of a dozen opened books. 'And ruse? Dharkaron Avenger! What a blundering understatement.'

Since the Koriani had powered their rites at equinox from the fifth lane's heightened energies, and Asandir at the appropriate moment had raised a facsimile of Arithon's aura pattern in the tower above Meth Isle's focus with all the force and subtlety of a thunderclap, the conclusion was shatteringly self evident. 'Ath Creator could not have stopped your projection from entangling the Koriani scrying to perdition,' Luhaine snapped.

The Koriani probe cast out to seek the Shadow Master had been drawn to its match like a homing signal, and stuck there like nails in old oak. If their Senior Circle had been powerless to separate the energies in further search for the living man, the discorporate sorcerer's testiness was just. The unavoidable sidebar had lent them unwise insight into Arithon's character and potential. Predictably, the enchantresses had seized full advantage.

'So, how much did they learn?' Sethvir asked on a grainy note of laughter.

The request engaged a shadowy blur that defined itself into the corpulent image of the bodiless being he addressed. Robed in scholar's grey belted at the waist with a doubled band of leather that buckled suspiciously like a harness girth, Luhaine stalked soundlessly forward. Frowning over full cheeks and a wheat-shock bristle of whiskers, he stabbed a stumpy finger in accusation. 'Considering Dakar's ploys in Jaelot? By rights his plague of fiends should have drawn Koriani interest like flies to dead meat to peddle talismans against that iyat bane. I suppose we should count ourselves fortunate the enchantresses let that slip past.'

Sethvir raised bushy eyebrows.

The spirit who glided over the moist carpet seldom cursed, but his agitation showed signs of turning stormy. His rejoinder was not delivered in words, but in a cobbled scrap of memory hurled like a slap at his colleague.

For a second, Sethvir shared the tight and detailed vision of a wasted crone in violet veils bent over an ebon table. Around her like flesh-eating vultures in hoods the silky sheen of black grapes, a circle of women followed her interest as she said, 'Ah, but his endowments are to be envied.'

The subject under discussion was a shimmering web of light captured by determined scrying: the life-print of Arithon s'Ffalenn as unveiled the past night over Meth Isle's focus. As avidly as spiders might suck the juices from a trapped insect, the enchantresses analysed his attributes. They dissected the spiralled framework of his power, both latent and schooled: of a mage's chained discipline and a shadow master's wild talent linked through the blaze of a visionary mind. The cherished potential of his musician's talents were picked out in all their ethereal shadings, a silver-lace braid wound through a will stamped in flesh like bright wire. Here, the beacon symmetry of s'Ahelas farvision tangled razor-point edges with the nettle and gossamer tendrils of undying s'Ffalenn compassion. There, the enchantresses read the sorrow and despair in the moment of Desh-thiere's conquest: Arithon's self-awareness like the fixed sting of thorns, that hope and effort could buy him no better than failure.

Sethvir shrugged the burdensome image away with long-suffering patience. 'The Koriani Prime and her First Senior learned nearly as much from a spying foray six years ago. Although Arithon's personal Name pattern is now shared in common with the Prime Circle, Morriel is little more enlightened.'

Luhaine sniffed, his bodiless bulk passing without mishap between a side table stacked with gutted tea canisters and a clothes tree festooned with worn bridles, 'Well, she certainly didn't know that Arithon and Lysaer had drunk from the Five Centuries Fountain.'

Sethvir stilled. His eyes turned a dreamy, vacuous blue as he engaged direct power to sample the consternation bought on the heels of that revelation. When he found the Prime Circle scurrying in agitation like an ant hill pounded by a hailstorm, he chuckled outright. 'The news should keep them busy for a little. Why trouble? The only ramification I can see beyond hysterics, is one especially deserving young initiate will gain a course of training she would otherwise be forbidden to merit.'

Luhaine's lugubrious mood failed to brighten.

The Warden of Althain sighed. As if conceding some unseen point, he sat upon a cot he never slept in, folded veined hands on his knees, and absorbed himself in muttering a cantrip that would banish the damp from his rug. When the binding was complete and the musty smell dispersed along with the dregs of the water, he fidgeted gently and peered at the vortex that comprised his discorporate guest. 'Luhaine?'

The portly apparition spun about in a noiseless whirl of grey. 'You can't say I haven't witnessed more than my share of the Koriathain's grand councils. They've fixed on the ironies of Arithon's nature and see nothing beyond surface paradox. That, they've concluded, creates an explosive potential for instability. Once their Senior Circle divines the Shadow Master's chosen course and location, they're not going to allow him free will. He's the last of his line, and Morriel's ancient with spite. You know they're very likely to launch on a quest to see him dead.'

Sethvir seemed to hold to concentration with an effort. 'They don't know Arithon's mage powers were left impaired since the battle at Strakewood. Given that aura to study in depth, do you think they're going to plunge in and meddle without caution? We're speaking of Torbrand's descendant, after all. By Ath, at that, they'd be entitled to suffer due consequences!'

But the immediacy of the Shadow Master's peril could not be so lightly dismissed.

'I don't care how nasty a temper Rathain's prince has inherited. If he gets himself compromised by enchantresses and we make an open move to intervene, we're going to gain a whole world of trouble.' Luhaine's image bulked ominously dark against the lit square of the casement. 'Tell me now,' he insisted in point blank demand much against his stolid nature. 'How much time have we bought before the Koriathain try again? They're bound to bring still more power to bear and we can't use the same ploy twice. How long before they have their way and unriddle Arithon's disguise?'

'The outlook isn't good,' Sethvir allowed in vague discomfort. As Luhaine's black eyes glared through him, he relented in a gritty snap of grief. 'At my outside guess, three months.'

'Midsummer solstice,' Luhaine murmured. 'Daelion show us all mercy, we don't even know if Kharadmon will survive, much less return before then.'

Crisis could fall well before the Fellowship was prepared to match their powers against the Mistwraith's bane-spell. This time, when no answer was forthcoming, Luhaine lacked the will to badger Sethvir from his silence.

Disruption

The sparrows who scrapped over the breadcrusts on the windowsill stopped pecking after crumbs and flurried away on startled wings.

Their shadows flitted across the work table, cluttered with its melee of opened herb jars, powdered roots, and tied bundles of dried flowers that burdened the air with thick scents. Determined to ignore whatever spurred their panicked flight, Elaira, initiate Koriani enchantress, continued to brew the poultice paste she hoped might treat the lame shepherd; one whose leg had mended awry from a fall through a rockslide, and whom the hospice healers had tried to turn off because his need was not urgent. Though his fused joints made him limp, he could walk enough to manage, if never to scale steep slopes of Vastmark shale to drive his flocks to summer pasture.

No stranger to poverty, Elaira often shouldered illogical causes. Confirmed as a misfit, she was left by her peers to pursue her studies in a niche between the stills and the herb stores. There, in solitary, contented untidiness, she fed songbirds on crusts that were not mouldy, and concocted obscure remedies as she pleased. A loosened coil of auburn hair licked a cheek streaked yellow with powdered groundsel. Steadily swearing in gutter dialect, pale eyes level in concentration, Elaira strove to balance the conjury laid like ghostly embroidery across the heated air above her crucible.

The delicate forces flickered and twined, scorched thin at the edges as crux points strained to spin awry. To reshape a mangled bone and contracted knots of scar tissue took more than astringents configured with seals of forced growth. Renewal of any deformity required a death-spell tempered with runes of rebirth, contrary and difficult fluxes for the most gifted healer to balance; an energy binding Elaira knew better than to try while her mind was tormented to distraction.

She bit her lip, pressed by a reasonless urge to throw a glass flask just for the need to hear it shatter. The alternative was to break inside; to turn to face whoever had raised her door latch and scattered the timid songbirds. Elaira shut her lips in fierce denial, while the filigreed energies she had wrought through the course of an unspeakable morning collapsed in tangles and bled away.

She could bury herself in the pages of musty herbals and brew tisanes until she rotted away into dotage without lifting a jot of her misery. Her arcane sensitivity to water made the sea tides ring in her blood. Awareness of the spring equinox was ingrained in her being, alongside the scrying twenty-one enchantresses had undertaken on last night's lane surge, to hunt down and locate one man.

Merciful Ath, Elaira begged silently, let the Koriani Senior Council not have found Arithon s'Ffalenn.

Her plea with fate went unanswered.

'The Prime Enchantress requests your immediate presence,' the intruder in the doorway announced in a clear-edged child's treble.

No such summons would come to her if Arithon's position was not compromised. Elaira moved, stood, acknowledged the blond pageboy who looked young for his eight years in the order's quilted violet livery. 'Lead me to the matriarch.' Through a miracle, her voice came out steady.

Since the ill-starred battle at Strakewood, she had endured the years as best she could, hedged and dogged by the surety that Arithon's anonymity could not last; not when the Koriani council had named his wild talents a latent threat to society and her knowledge was their bridge to understand him.

Elaira stepped into the corridor on the heels of the page, vexed with her superiors enough to pity his adult composure. On impulse, she said, 'Let's take the short cut through the service vaults.'

'You want to?' The child grinned around missing front teeth, then raced ahead and nipped through a dingy, arched postern.

The ancient hospice abandoned to Koriani use by the initiates of Ath's brotherhood was an ungainly, rambling edifice, drilled like a battered honeycomb into the limestone scarps south of Forthmark. Its crumbling warren of storerooms harboured perpetual, clammy humidity, fed by damp, porous rock that seeped from the flow of underground hot springs. The spacious outer chambers used to house the sick were less oppressive, spared by the beat of clean sunlight through south-facing casements. There the pervasive must of mildew was scoured off by boy wards wielding buckets and holystones to earn their keep.

Elaira's mood better suited the cavernous back staircases and circuitous, low-ceilinged tunnels that twined through rootcellars and storage cells. Cobwebs streamed in the draughts, glistening like shot silk in the glow of widely spaced torches. The air reeked of tallow smoke and corroded metal, and the walls wore patinas of old soot.

Elaira hurried. Her step made no noise, despite hard-soled boots and a stone floor that threw back sharp echoes. Orphan of a street whore, raised from infancy by beggars until an unlucky brush with the law had bound her into Koriani fosterage, she kept the sly habits of her childhood. Yet no matter how unobtrusively she passed, the silver-blond fairness and amethyst silk tunic of Morriel's personal pageboy drew notice from every peer and scullion dispatched on errands to the cellars.

Ones who did not merit summons before their Prime, and who were the happier for it.

Elaira shrugged off the speculative whispers that hissed in the wake of her steps. Already marked apart for a worldly entanglement she was helpless to alter or break, she took perverse pleasure in watching the Prime's pageboy spoil his formal grooming. Past the steam-choked laundry, where red-cheeked junior novices gossiped across their washtubs, through a chattering procession of boy wards who hauled in wood for the kitchen, Elaira's cavorting escort was remarked. Aware to a fine point of the Prime Circle's use for her flaws, she dared to ignore the huffy senior taking inventory, who brandished her tally slates and scolded.

In breathless vindication, Elaira grabbed the child's hand and tugged him to refuge in a pantry. A hidden door at the back opened through the annex by the wine stores, to the boy's smothered gasp of delight.

'Didn't know about this byway, did you?' Elaira grinned, scraped cobwebs from her hair, and cupped the crystal that hung from the chain at her neck. 'You'll like it. The floorboards are infested with cockroaches.' As the power she focused brightened through her hands, she said, 'Go on. Catch a few if you want. Just don't let me find you tweaking off any legs or wings. You can horrify your dorm mistress all you like. But if the insects take any harm from your pranks, I'll blister your tail with a spell.'

The page stifled a whoop and fell to, dirtying the knees of his hose as he scavenged beneath an old grape press. Elaira watched his deviltry in sad silence. The male children selected as Morriel's pages led proscribed lives, chosen tools of Koriani higher purpose. But unlike her, whose vows constrained for life service, the boys regained freedom at puberty.

She helpfully offered her handkerchief to net and secure the live contraband, then doused her spell and hustled up the timber stair with its rickety rope and tackle, originally strung to lower filled vats, before Koriani tenure had uprooted the vineyards to grow herbs.

Elaira opened the stairwell portal. Someone had smeared lard on the hinges, probably a scullion sneaking off for assignation with a milkmaid. The enchantress shut her eyes, swept by unbidden association: of long, musician's fingers flicking dry stems of hay from her hair. Whether the tenderness in that memory had arisen from instinctive s'Ffalenn compassion, or some deeper need that touched the heart, she might never determine. Her order's inflexible codes of conduct disbarred her from amorous pursuits. Elaira shook off forbidden thoughts, while the page reassumed his lapsed duty. He preceded her down the corridor to the columned atrium Ath's initiates had originally used for their devotions.

Before the casements had been paned with stout glass, the chamber had been a terrace garden open to the sweep of mountain breezes. Marble toned like fine, blue-veined flesh had lain under snow through winter's freezes. In the hot, amber days of Shandian summer, flowering vines had laddered the pillars, shedding sweet fragrance and petals. Now, the cracked stone planters were planked over as tables, or else spell-sealed as vault space to preserve rare scrolls on arcane practice. The fountains and pools were all mortared in, their scars masked under purple carpets sewn in silver with Koriani seals of ward and guard.

Older sigils carved in the walls and the roof groins channelled more potent powers still: a captured resonance of earth song, or the clear, high vibrations spiralled in sympathy with the constellations along the ecliptic. Except for a poignancy instilled by time and death that marked its brotherhood creators as mortal, the currents ran similar to the ghostly, faded harmonies left imprinted upon the land by the mysteries of the vanished Paravians.

But no past solace imparted by Ath's initiates could bring comfort to the future. Elaira pressed leadenly forward, into sunlight and space.

Unchanged by the grand turn of centuries, a ceremonial fire burned in the squat bronze brazier set in the chamber's centre. Nested in the cushioned chair behind, the Prime Enchantress of the Koriani order awaited audience. She was old, emaciated as a dry stick. The scrappily withered features above her winged collar seemed fused with the porcelain bone beneath. Morriel wore her cloudy hair netted in diamond pins. The lavender and purple mantle of high office enveloped her torso like a calyx, and fine knuckles reduced like storm-stripped twigs rested loose in her lap.

'I heard you clearly,' she was saying, her voice the reedy scrape of dead leaves against granite. 'Your point does not signify in this case.'

The tall, graceful Senior she addressed raised her chin. Eyes of tigerish, tawny brown flashed under the silver-wired band of a high initiate's cowl. 'The girl is weak and unsuited. Dare we entrust such responsibility to a vessel twice proven to be flawed?'

Morriel Prime gave a breathy scrape of laughter. 'Are you befitted to judge?' She folded clawed hands, then restlessly laid them separate since neither position eased their pain. 'Take heed and look inward, First Senior. Your view could well be as muddled. For a fact, your speech is unwarrantedly careless.'

Quick instinct made Elaira break habit and allow her next footfall to grate.

First Senior Lirenda whirled at the noise. 'You!' A flush stained her aristocratic cheekbones, vivid above the pleated robe that yoked her trim shoulders. Her ebony hair was sleeked back in combs, no single strand out of place. 'Given the nature of your origins, I should expect you would lurk your way here through the cellars.'

'It's quicker,' Elaira provoked in the street drawl of her girlhood. Unrepentant, she hurried her curtsey of obeisance to the Prime. 'Your will, Matriarch.'

The crone watched her arise with eyes black and colourless as rubbed glass. She did not speak, but studied, ruthlessly practised in the Koriani arts of subtle observation and analysis. Elaira bore up, the more fiercely determined since street-wise bravado could never face down Morriel's weight of years and experience. As if her very thoughts were stamped into live flesh, the Koriani matriarch could read the question that grieved her; would measure the assault against pride, that eventually must crumple before need to ask outright for the results of last night's scrying.

Stiff to her toes before the urge to bolt outright, strained to her limits before a truth that held infinite capacity to wound her, Elaira scarcely heard the words Lirenda used to scold the page. Powerless, now, to assume the blame for the grime on his livery, the young enchantress endured while the hidden handkerchief was discovered and shaken out, to the First Senior's redoubled annoyance as its six-legged cargo scuttled to shelter under her skirts.

A glint too cold to be humour touched the depths of Morriel's eyes. 'But our scrying was unsuccessful, girl. We haven't yet managed to discover the refuge of Rathain's last prince.'

Elaira could not quite stifle her shuddering sigh of relief. 'You summoned. How must I serve?'

'Sit.' Morriel accompanied the command with a gesture clipped short by exhausted tolerance and sore joints. 'Our efforts were bent awry by chance interference from the Fellowship. The timing in fact lent us insight and our order has gained in the counterplay.'

Past the edge of the carpet, First Enchantress Lirenda pulped a last fleeing insect beneath her heel. Intuitively sure the creature's swift demise was impelled by more than harmless mischief, Elaira clasped her hands in sweating dread.

'Show her,' Morriel commanded.

Lirenda dismissed the chastised page. Lips compressed in capitulation that marred her air of hauteur, she stalked across the carpet. The sun at her back scythed her shadow over figured argent sigils and quenched their surface glitter as she knelt in a crisp sweep of skirts before the burning brazier.

Where Elaira's elemental affinities predisposed her to conjure through water, Lirenda used fire for alignment. At one with the will of her Prime, she closed her eyes and settled into a light trance.

As the matriarch's successor in training, her powers were impressively tempered. Grazed by a thrum of current across her nerves, Elaira struggled to quell her apprehension. Too soon, the red gold blaze of the embers changed character, became charged to cold blue that threw neither light nor warmth. Across the fire's altered energy, ethereal at first as the spell-thread stitched into the rugs, a pattern formed, fused, and blazed into a fixed configuration. Revealed in clear focus through Lirenda's consciousness, Elaira viewed a mesh of visionary artistry, then ironies complex enough to storm through will and reflex, and arrest her heart between beats. She recognized the strand pattern analogue of Arithon s'Ffalenn's living aura, exposed in the fullness of Fellowship perception.

She gasped. In uncompromising lines, the man's hidden self lay mapped out in a nuance that damned. As never before, she saw how vision and compassion, power and sensitivity, strength and pity lay paired beyond compatibility. Morriel's fear was real, that the added burden of Desh-thiere's curse might anneal the whole into a laceration of spirit with tragic potential to seed madness.

Since the order's responsibility had never condoned power with any latent bent toward destruction, the Prime would act before threat became reality. Elaira's rooted faith, that the Master of Shadow was resilient enough to retain his grip on self-command, became exposed as baseless conviction, too likely the blind offshoot of personal feelings held against the wisdom of her seniors.

'Dharkaron Avenger!' Elaira blinked through a rising well of tears. 'How could any man support such a tangle for more than a natural life-span? Or am I mistaken? Isn't that arc and counter-seal an imposed pattern for longevity?'

'Your insight runs true.' Morriel snapped dry fingers, signal for Lirenda to relax her discipline. 'The development caught us off-guard, but shouldn't have. Both Lysaer and Arithon came to this land by way of the Red Desert's World Gate. Our natural assumption should have followed, that they drank from the Five Centuries Fountain and succumbed to Davien's geas.'

'That's why you've summoned me,' Elaira said, relieved as the pattern's cruel quandary erased at last from the embers.

She blotted streaming cheeks on her sleeve, and so missed Lirenda's transition from trance to waking consciousness. A jealous, unguarded expression crossed the First Senior's face, and a glare like distilled venom drilled through the younger woman's back.

The Prime watched with hooded eyes as her chosen successor masked the lapse. Grim as steel, she held to her purpose. 'You were called to serve, initiate Elaira. Since we now know the conflict seeded by the Mistwraith will afflict more than one generation, you are asked to submit your crystal for enhancement. You won't be forced. Consider carefully. The fate of outliving your peers is not always happy or desirable.'

Lirenda maintained an elegant, stiff silence. Only the hands pinched in fists beneath her sleeves expressed her depths of resentment, that a privilege reserved for proven seniors was being offered to a girl who flaunted propriety.

Rough-edged as a hoyden by comparison, Elaira confronted the emaciated crone in her bulwark of robes and the ice-point shimmer of her diamonds. Morriel's life had extended well past a thousand years; centuries reckoned for in joints worn eggshell thin, and flesh racked and drawn to a husk of brittle fibres by powerful spells of preservation. Unlike the Fellowship of Seven, whose direct grasp of grand conjury could engender lengthened life in concert with physical law, Koriani methods were limited to energy resonance enhanced by a power crystal's lattice.

'There is pain, at first,' Morriel continued, 'but only until the body reaches primary equilibrium with the stay-spells. After the first six months, degenerative ageing is reversed until well past seven hundred years. Since Davien's mark holds influence for only five centuries, you need not live on to endure the afflictions of secondary interference.'

Surrounded by the chipped majesty of the initiates' ancient carvings, never so aware of the fall of clear sunlight, or the chirp of nesting martens in the cornices outside, Elaira hugged her arms across her breast. The warning of her Prime and the antipathy behind Lirenda's cool facade lost all impact before trepidation from another source.

Once in dusk by the seaside, a Fellowship sorcerer had offered her counsel in secret. *'I was sent to you,'* Traithe had said, *'because an augury showed the Warden of Althain that, for good or ill, you're the one spirit alive in this world who will come to know Arithon best. Should your Master of Shadow fail you, or you fail him, the outcome will call down disaster.'*

There was no decision to be made, Elaira understood in bitter calm; and so her voice did not shake as she said, 'I accept the bidding of my Prime.'

Silk rustled. A breath of eddied lavender twined on the air as Morriel inclined her head. 'So be it. Surrender your jewel for attunement.' A wrist like bundled withies lifted from her lap, its claw-skinny hand cupped to grasp.

Elaira freed a clear quartz pendant strung on braided chain like a teardrop frozen in mid-fall. Small-boned and light-footed and trained to dissemble as a pick-pocket, she displayed a courage that embarrassed as the jewel changed grasp. A charged understanding passed between the crone and the young woman who consented to a fate that might ruin her.

Then Elaira's lips bent into an insolent smile. 'I wish this course of change, as well.'

'The more fool you,' snapped the Prime. 'You have virtues, but wisdom isn't one of them.' She snatched the relinquished chain and jewel to her chest and said in querulous, point blank demand, 'Tell me. Where do you suppose the Shadow Master is hiding?'

Shocked and stonily defensive, Elaira had no choice but to answer. 'Where is Lysaer?'

Lirenda bridled in affront.

But Morriel judged the query was not impertinence. 'Tysan's prince is marching for Erdane to claim his right to Avenor's charter.'

Elaira's stillness turned brittle. In that same forbidden meeting, Traithe had assured her that obedience to her Prime would cause no additional threat to Arithon. Against her deepest inclination, but bound by the perilous nature of her Koriani vows, she answered, 'Then look for the Shadow Master in any town that borders the eastern sea. He'll be found, I should guess, as far from Avenor as the confines of dry land will allow.'

'A sensible deduction. At solstice, we shall scry the seventh lane and test the truth of your theory.' Worn from the interview, Morriel flicked a terse finger in dismissal.

'You too,' the Prime rapped to Lirenda, who lingered, poised to argue further over Elaira's longevity privileges. Distressed by an emerging flaw in her First Senior's character no longer too slight to ignore, Morriel tugged her robes around the thin knobs of her knees. 'I would meditate for an hour undisturbed.'

Lirenda curtseyed and swept out on Elaira's heels, the swish of her silk sending draughts shimmering across the brazier's live coals.

Alone with disgruntled thoughts, the Koriani Prime tightened pallid lips. She lacked the time to wait for a more qualified heir; if the current First Senior had flaws needing discipline, she possessed an extraordinary talent. In truth, Morriel conceded, the temptation in this case was not slight. Stamped bright in recall, she held every angle and line and counter-swept curve that configured the s'Ffalenn prince's aura pattern.

The strength in the man was frightening.

Were she not old, and aching, and daily yearning the release of natural death, she might have wept as Elaira had.

Instead her frail fingers clenched over the spell crystal surrendered to her in forced trust. Her eyes gleamed baleful as arctic night as she muttered, 'Curse you, son of s'Ffalenn.'

If by his mere existence Arithon of Rathain came to corrupt more than Elaira's impulsive heart; if his character upset the discipline of the First Senior chosen to be groomed as prime successor, Morriel vowed by the cold fire in her joints that she would see him suffer in full measure for her misery.

Should Lirenda fall short in her training, should she fail to survive the trials of Koriani primacy, the added century Morriel must cling to breathing life to select and mould another candidate yawned frightfully cruel and dark.

Farings

While the trees unfold lush canopies of leaves, Lysaer s'Ilessid makes his penniless entrance into the city of Erdane; and as the city's reigning mayor jettisons fixed policy to host a guest of royal birth, Lord Diegan is the sole party unsurprised to learn that although the weaponless mercenaries in the prince's train have gone three weeks without pay, their loyalty remains unshaken . . .

In the burgeoning warmth of southern latitude, a hand-picked circle of Koriani Seniors leaves Forthmark on an overland journey; by command of Morriel Prime, who rides with them swathed under quilts in her palanquin, their intent bends toward the solstice yet to come, when another scrying will seek yet again to unmask the elusive Master of Shadow . . .

Seated in the heart of Alestron's inner citadel, the Fellowship sorcerer Asandir weighs the claim of the duke's distraught seneschal, that the lord of the city and his brothers are absent to arrange a betrothal; and though a sweep of the grounds reveals no trace of foundries, nor proscribed treatises on black powder, the official is hedging around the hard fact that the armoury walls bear recent traces of an earth witch's marks of concealment . . .

V. MASQUE

The door to Halliron's attic chamber slammed with a gusto that rattled frame and hinges, but failed to disrupt the dancing play of arpeggios through an exercise in descending sevenths. The notes a seamless cascade beneath his fingers, Medlir raised his eyebrows at Dakar, tempestuously returned from the public baths with his nose buffed apple red. His clothing still hung half-unlaced, his hair was a wet, draggled fringe, and a virulent reek of attar of roses trailed from the bristles of his beard.

'I didn't know we'd given you coin for perfume,' Medlir said.

Peevish for being limited to an allowance too small to keep himself drunk, Dakar shoved aside a bundle of Halliron's correspondence and flopped onto a hassock. Since his liberty relied on the personal bond of the Masterbard, he managed a civil reply. 'The stink's a kissing present from a doxy.'

'Ah.' The scale chords never faltered in their falling, melodic progression. 'You've brought new gossip?'

Dakar fiddled to extricate his shirt cuffs, wadded inside the ribboned sleeve of an orange and green doublet he had scavenged from some back-street used-clothing stall. 'Well the city alderman's wife's giddy with another affair. Dull news, really, since she throws out a lover every month.' Defeated by a knotted lacing, the Mad Prophet resumed. 'Better, you know that fat-assed proprietress at Madame Havrita's? Well, she got herself a bloody eye. Caught the brunt of a scratching battle after insulting that spinster dressmaker on Threadneedle Street. Both claim their shop's more overworked than their rival's, and each one insists their designs will set the fashion for the ladies at the solstice feast.'

The door latch clicked. Dakar swivelled in time to catch the arrival of Halliron Masterbard, back from a shopping excursion with a packet tucked through one elbow. 'You know,' the Mad Prophet volunteered through the trill of Medlir's practice, 'This fete the mayor's brewing around your appearance is causing catfights in the ladies' parlours.'

'They can choke on their ribbons and pearls,' Halliron grumbled uncharitably.

Critical of Medlir's touch on the lyranthe strings, he tipped his head. Even his exacting ear could not be other than satisfied. The months cooped up in the inn's cramped garret had set the finishing edge on Medlir's style. Drawn in by the liquid transition of sevenths to fifths, the Masterbard felt a shiver thrill through him. He had always suspected his chosen successor might be gifted enough to outmatch him. But actually to hear the notes of repetitive practice raised to a lyric emotion his best technique could not equal stirred him to speechless delight. All he had left to desire in the world was reunion with his estranged wife and daughter.

Seven days remained until solstice. Then at last he would be free to resume his stalled journey to Shand.

'Look,' groused Dakar. 'If it's sausage I smell in that package, are we going to eat? Leave meals to you, and we'd die of starvation to arpeggios in all eight keys.'

Dragged back to mundane matters, Halliron wended a path through the garret's clutter of tin whistles, spools of silver wire and little clamps used to wind lyranthe strings, the faded scrolls Medlir bought from the salvager's bins, and dog-eared leaves of rice paper with their scribbled variations of old ballads. He elbowed aside an awl and an ink-pot, and dropped his package on the tabletop, nailed together from scrap boards on the day the tea upset once too often. The inn's original rickety trestle had ended up feeding the hearth fire. If his apprentice's hand at joinery showed a style more suited to a ship's deck, the result at least was stable. Nothing spilled or fell off through Dakar's vociferous pounce to be first to lay hand on the food.

Halliron settled on the hassock left vacant and gave the musician's labours their due. 'You aren't needing my instruction any longer.'

Medlir rounded off a last arpeggio and deftly damped the strings. 'I'm not yet willing to do without it.' His look held more than humour as he added, 'There's one ballad left you haven't taught me.'

'You guessed that?' Halliron bent his attention to stretching his fingers to keep them supple. 'What a pity Jaelot's mayor won't have you play in my stead.' He flicked his apprentice a piercing glance, then shrugged. Even on the edge of summer, stiff breeze off the bay made the streets salt-damp and chilly; the climate went ill with his joints. 'What's the rumour in the barracks?'

Leather scraped a plaintive whine from tensioned strings as Medlir slipped wrappings over the priceless instrument. 'A scandal's afoot over coin for the soldier's pay.'

'No!' Halliron slapped his knees in evil pleasure and whistled a fragmented melody. 'Don't say! The town bursar's an embezzler?'

'Better.' Medlir set the lyranthe safely down in a corner and grinned. 'Word goes he's sold his sister-in-law's ruby bracelets to hire a herb witch to hide how taxes from the town treasury found their way into the coffers of Gadsley's pleasure house.'

'The one that peddles little boys? That's rich.' Halliron spun around in time to snatch a slice of bread away from Dakar. 'I heard the mayor's shrew of a wife intends a surprise announcement. Her feast's to have a festival theme. The page who serves her table told me she intends to cut out any couple who can't afford to buy a mask.'

Medlir's eyes lit. 'Dakar! There's a secret you can leak to your doxy. How awkward, if the back-quarter courtesans had the hat shops engaged, and respectable ladies had to settle for second shrift.'

'Maybe Havrita's other eye will get scratched,' the Mad Prophet said through a cheek crammed with sausage. He tore off another chunk of bread, quiet as Medlir joined him at the table and exchanged easy banter with the Masterbard. As long and as hard as Dakar listened, he had yet to trace any regional accent in the younger man's speech. Although a musician with a well-trained ear might be adept enough to change his intonation, the fact that Medlir's relaxed moments betrayed no distinguishing trait preyed on Dakar's nerves. Almost as much as the oddity that, throughout an entire year, even since provoking a plague of fiends thick enough to draw reprimand from Althain, Asandir had yet to pursue him. Despite blatant disregard of orders to seek out and protect the Shadow Master, no Fellowship sorcerer had appeared to call down his misconduct.

Drunk, Dakar wouldn't have troubled to lay one question alongside of the other; sober, he mentally thrashed himself to cold sweats in paranoia the anomalies might be connected. How demeaning, if Arithon s'Ffalenn turned out to be holed up in Shand, with himself all unwittingly being drawn there.

With the eve of summer solstice just five days away, preparations for the mayor's masked feast reached a hysterical pitch. Artisans laboured and swore over tubs of wet plaster, mixed to make moulded figurines, while the gilder's apprentices lined up to adorn them perched idle on their paint pots and called jibes. The confectioners' shops were plunged into frenzy, and the thoroughfare through the southern gate was jammed into turmoil by the entrance of yet another mule train bearing cut flowers and myrtle. Footmen wore out boot soles delivering invitations; or else they stole kisses from the serving girls as they carried up parcels of ribbons, or jewellery ordered new for the occasion. Lamps burned in the dressmakers' all night, as women changed their fancy or their shape. The mayor's oldest daughter lost herself to excitement and ate enough comfits to spoil her waistline.

Havrita snatched at opportunity like a barracuda and won the commission to sew her new ball-gowns. 'A lot of teeth gnashing on Threadneedle street,' Dakar reported, back from an assignation with a shop girl. 'But no more bloodied eyes.'

Between the Mad Prophet's excursions from baths to brothels, and Medlir's acquaintances among the city guard, all rumours reached the attic, where Halliron spent increasing hours closeted in private with his lyranthe. He was disturbed just once, by two liveried footmen, who knocked with a small trunk of clothing furnished by the mayor for use on the night of the feast.

All but trampled by the pair's flying haste to depart, Medlir stepped into the garret to find the Masterbard cursing in unmatched couplets, his rare and red-faced fervour focused to a frightening bent of rage.

When the old man's tantrum at last succumbed to breathlessness, Medlir caught his wrists and sat him down. 'Care to say what's happened?'

Halliron shot back up the instant his apprentice loosed his grip. Pacing, distraught, his collar laces swinging undone and the hair at his temples hooked to snarls by the rake of his vehement fingers, he gestured toward the window that faced the inn's muddy courtyard. 'Never have I stayed to play for a man who insults me not once, but repeatedly!'

Medlir set his shoulders against the door post to keep from stepping back as the topaz eyes swivelled toward him, wide and snapping with fury. Quiet, he folded his arms.

'Well, the nerve of Jaelot's mayor, to dare to suggest what I should wear in the presence of his ridiculous wife!' Halliron whirled, kicked the low cot to an explosion of dust from the ticking, and staggered a hopping half-step to end bent double in a sneeze. The paroxysm effectively sobered him. He regarded his knotted fists, and the wry twist to his lips unravelled in a burst of sudden laughter. 'Dharkaron have mercy! Could you see me wearing some dandy's tight-assed hose? In *pink*, no less, against a doublet with chartreuse shoulder ruffles?'

Medlir choked back a smile. 'Imagination fails me. Did his lordship send a mask as well?'

'Ath. A lamb's head. You can picture that!' The Masterbard collapsed on his mattress, loose-limbed as a puppet whose midriff had suddenly lost its stuffing. 'I'll be deliriously happy to be quit of this town.'

Far from disarmed by the subject change, Medlir clicked the door shut with his heel. 'You didn't say what Jaelot's mayor sent for me to wear.'

'No, I didn't,' Halliron cracked back in caustic, protective sharpness. 'You at least will stay out of this.'

'Well, there we disagree.' The flexible humour Dakar could never shake disappeared. Suddenly more killer than singer, his stance radiating leashed force, the man in the doorway shook out his right sleeve and used his teeth to yank more tension in his cuff ties. 'I'm going. Don't pretend you won't need me.'

The Masterbard locked eyes with the musician he had apprenticed, and the whetted determination he encountered threw him back six years to the memory of a prince's oath swearing in a woodland dell. 'I'm no match for Torbrand's temper,' he said quickly. 'But if you make this your duty, and harm comes to you, I'll go to my grave without forgiveness.'

'Oh Ath,' Medlir said on a queer note of change. 'If you're worried only for me, then surely there's hope left for both of us.'

The sunset on summer solstice blazed over a city fragrant with fresh-split birch and cut flowers. Long since finished with his dressing, Halliron leaned on the sill of the opened casement, kneading the joints of his fingers. 'Sithaer take it, we have a visitor.'

Caught while threading his points, Medlir said sharply, 'Another servant of the mayor's? After today, I wouldn't expect such a one would dare to show his face here.'

'You still believe there's a man in this town who was born with any sense of shame?' At the thump of footsteps on the landing, Halliron wrenched the door open in the face of the startled arrival and demanded, 'Where's Dakar? Or is it true that armed guardsman snatched him off the streets in the middle of Beckburn market?'

The mayor's footman tugged down his waistcoat, ridden up over the dome of his belly in his puffing ascent of the stairs. Taken aback by the tall elder in his black silk doublet, he fell back a step and ventured, 'You speak of the mayor's prisoner?'

'I speak of a man who carries my personal word as bond on his civil behaviour.' Halliron did not look aside as Medlir snatched his belt and stepped to his shoulder to back him.

The footman cleared his throat. 'I wouldn't know anything about that.'

'But you do know where Dakar is,' Medlir cut in. 'Stop hedging.'

Dusk had fallen. Uncertain light from the chamber's single candle played into the gloom of the hall and raised hard sparkles from the trim on Halliron's dress clothes. A dimmer gleam of sweat sheened the footman's pink forehead as he fluttered his hands in ruffled cuffs. 'Well, I'm not to blame,' he began, then flinched back, though no one moved forward to threaten him. 'Your prophet's set in chains in the banquet hall. My Lord Mayor decreed his fetters shall be struck only after the Masterbard has delivered his promised performance.'

From the street three storeys below, a carriage rumbled by, the harness bells on the team a sweet trill behind a woman's airy laughter. A dog barked, and a scullion banged the door to the midden as life in the precinct of the innyard ran its indifferent course: in contrast, confined, unspeaking tension gripped the close little garret.

115

Then Halliron spun on his heel to a near soundless whisper of rich silk. None of his temper showed, nor did his words reflect rancour as he said in terse quiet to his apprentice, 'Ath forgive me, you were right. In every sense, I will need you.'

Unobtrusive in his tunic of dove-grey linen, Medlir had no words. The silver-tipped laces of his shirt sleeves tapped and chimed as he hooked the last studs on his bootcuffs. He fetched his master's wrapped lyranthe from its corner peg behind the bed, and wondered in silent and venomous fury whether any other ruler in Athera's history had grossly flaunted such ignorance, to repudiate a masterbard's given word before his very face.

'Come on now.' The footman edged toward the stairwell. 'My Lord Mayor has a carriage ready outside to collect you.'

Another insult: by ancient custom, a masterbard came and went at no man's pleasure. Halliron said stiffly, 'Tell your mayor I would break all my fingers before I accepted the ride.'

The brass buttons on the footman's waistcoat flashed to his protesting breath. 'But –'

'The weather is fine. We will walk.' Anchored against rage by the guiding touch of Medlir's hand on his shoulder, the Masterbard of Athera swept the mayor's cringing servant aside.

He left behind a garret picked clean of belongings and a paid up account with the landlord. The pony cart also waited, packed to roll at a moment's notice, in the post stable nearest to the gate.

'Dawn,' Medlir murmured. 'It can't come soon enough.'

Master and apprentice reached the base of the stairs and by unspoken agreement turned down the service corridor that let into the alley beyond the kitchen. Behind, the tavern bulked massive and dark, its high, gabled roofline like folded black paper against a sky pricked with midsummer stars. The sea breeze reeked of salt and the fish offal spread to dry for fertilizer. Birch smoke drifted from the festival fires alight in the markets by Dagrien Court. The thready, wild notes of a fiddle spun through the dark, clipped by the slap of harness leather and the grinding turn of wheels as the mayor's carriage team was shaken up and reined around to leave the stableyard, its conveyance empty of passengers.

Halliron set a brisk pace. The palace lay in the fashionable quarter across from the council hall, a distance made difficult by crooked streets and cobblestone byways that rose and fell with the terrain, or zigzagged unexpectedly into staircases cut into the ribs of the headland. After six months, Medlir knew every short-cut; given the gifts of his mastery, darkness held no impediment.

Tempered back to reason by the anonymity of the night, Halliron gave a rueful sigh. 'I should have worried more about footpads.'

'Why? Because of your jewels and gold chains?' Medlir grinned and turned his shoulder to guard the wrapped bulk of the lyranthe as he passed through a narrow archway. 'Take a closer look at yourself, my friend.'

The Masterbard glanced down, rocked by a start to see his glittering court finery masked to featureless black. 'Ath! Your shadows? I should have guessed.'

'Pray the thieves won't,' Medlir said. 'There's little risk to use my power here. No one knows my reputation well enough to send an informer to Etarra. And anyway, if you'd set foot in that carriage, I would have broken the mayor's head. I still might. Do your joints hurt?'

'Not so much.' Halliron glanced at the prosperous tall-fronted houses limned in the bronze glow of torches. A high-wheeled phaeton rattled by, driven by a dandy bedecked in peacock plumes. 'Where are we?'

'Spicer's Row,' Medlir said around a small cough. The last female to share the phaeton's upholstery had bequeathed enough perfume to shed a cloud of patchouli in the wake of the vehicle's passage. 'But never mind if you can't smell the cinnamon. Turn here.'

They crossed a formal courtyard, where Medlir out of mischief flushed an amorous tom cat from yowling serenade beneath a rose bush. A shutter cracked open overhead, and a toothless matron emerged, shouting invective.

Laughing as he ducked through an arbour of flowering vines, Medlir unlatched a side gate that let into the gutter behind the court house. 'Mind the horse piss.'

'Or not,' Halliron commented. 'If I stink enough to turn heads, do you guess the mayor's wife would throw me out?'

'She'd doubtless roast Dakar for the lapse, then sidestep sensibility by giving you a replacement pair of shoes, fancy ones with satin ruffles.' Medlir offered an arm to steady his master across the puddle. Through his thin sleeve, the old man trembled shockingly. 'It's not much further. We can cut through the guards' barracks.'

'That's not necessary.' Halliron squared trim shoulders. 'I need the walk to cool my temper.'

Companionably silent, the pair passed sights grown unwontedly familiar through the course of their enforced stay in Jaelot: the scarred stalls of the butcher's sheds, and fishmonger's baskets stacked like nested eggs in the starlit gloom of the alley. Halliron broke step to fling silver into a beggar's bowl. The mournful, deep bells in the guard tower chimed the hour, rousting up a flapping flock of pigeons. The birds wheeled above the city's muddled skyline, smudged into soot from coal fires lit to cut the sea damp.

'It's hard to believe this place was once the site of Paravian mysteries,' Halliron commented over the clop of horses and the grind of gilt-striped carriage wheels. Foot traffic crowded the road, couples cloaked and masked and laughing as they hurried to dance at the festival fires in light-hearted contrast with hawkers trudging homeward with handcarts of unsold pastries. 'The sixth lane resonance once channelled through this headland. At solstice, you'd think I'd feel the pulse of the earth's song through my very boots. Everywhere else the unicorns danced, at least a ghost echo lingers.'

Medlir shook his head, what sensitivity he had once possessed struck mute by forces less forgivable than Jaelot's tasteless arrogance. Smells of jasmine and lavender warred with the mess some lady's lapdog had excreted in the gutter. In some cranny beyond reach of lamplight, a rat chittered through the patter of a street waif's running footsteps. Farther off, the surf from the bay boomed in tireless refrain against the breakwater.

From the corner of Broadwalk Way, wreaths of climbing roses strewed a litter of leaves and petals that the wind chivvied across the pavement. The pillared façade of the mayor's palace loomed at the end of the cul-de-sac like some layered, white-iced confection, the rondeled mullions of its bow windows spangled in reflected candleflame.

'With luck, we'll have missed the silly dinner.' Halliron mounted the stair like a man about to face his executioner. His steps sank soundless into the black and gold carpet runner spread for the occasion, each riser bearing like soldiers on parade an array of bronze urns crammed with peonies.

One of the footmen on duty by the door reached to take the lyranthe. Medlir sidestepped the offer as though a viper had struck at him, to the servant's acrimonious displeasure. A chubby, bald butler scurried out to quell the disturbance. He nearly bowled over the Masterbard, who topped him by a head, and who waited to the right of the threshold in the unveiled elegance of his topaz studs and roped chains.

'Ath, it's yourself,' the butler snapped. 'My Lord Mayor's vexed. Come inside. Quickly, quickly! Most awkward you've arrived so late, they're nearly finished with dessert.'

Medlir and Halliron suffered the man's proprietary prodding across a vestibule banked with cut flowers, and on through the doubled doors into the grand hall. From the bowl of a recessed mosaic floor to the spans of its vaulted ceiling, the enormous chamber lay rinsed in dazzling brilliance. Wax candles and overdressed bodies pressed the air to steaming warmth. The reek of rich meats, fine sauces and expensively perfumed humanity stifled the senses in a wave.

Halliron ran a jaundiced glance over fake kiosks of gilded pillars, streamered in ribbon and decorated with cast-plaster orchids that dripped in swagged archways over tables packed to sagging capacity. The drone of too many voices stewed into punishing roulades of echoed noise.

Divested of feathered masks for their feasting, the aristocrats of Jaelot lounged on cushions, arguing stylishly, or exchanging sharp-witted jokes. Gilt cosmetics and jewels stung the eye in spattered flecks of light. The tinselled ruffles of discarded finery lay rowed like a milliner's wares under silk and paper arbours crammed with sprites, whose rosy cheeks and blush-tinted bare buttocks were presented on display with the same artless candour.

A statement of brute contrast, a cleared space in the centre of the floor held a scaffold transfixed by a post. There, the miserable figure of Dakar languished, chained hand and foot in his laddered, striped hose and soiled shirtsleeves. The scuffle to retake him into custody had apparently cost him his garish orange garment sleeved with ribbon.

'Well, the doublet's gone, I'm glad to see. Somewhere in Jaelot, there's a guardsman with a natural sense of elegance.' Halliron's dry sarcasm gave way to outrage as he added, 'The chains are an offence beyond forgiveness.' He never once glanced at the painted stool, waiting in vacant anticipation before the dais that raised the head table.

Behind him, moved by unsettled instinct, his apprentice loosed the lyranthe's wrappings and softly started tuning silver strings. Since Medlir's adroit placement in the doorway forestalled the butler's entrance, no one announced their arrival. The still form of the Masterbard in his stark black and gold raised no stir, until, cued by the whispers of a table servant, a guest in the back rows pointed. Conversation in her presence flurried and flagged, and stillness fanned outward like ring ripples cast by a flung stone into a trout pool.

The Mayor of Jaelot froze with a bite of confection halfway into parted lips. Elbowed by his wife, whose dark, painted eyes acknowledged Halliron's presence over her pink-feathered fan, he lowered his spoon and rearranged himself to begin a pompous speech.

The Masterbard seized his moment, lifted the unsheathed gleam of his instrument from Medlir, and outmatched the mayor's blustering introduction. 'I play nothing for your guests until the bonds are struck from the man I've pledged to redeem.'

Satiated diners stirred to languid interest as he bade his apprentice to wait, then descended the inner stair. His steps were marked by stifled whispers, while several ladies the worse for fine wine tittered behind hands laced with rings. Halliron paid no notice. Bare-headed, his silver hair combed in waves over his gold-bordered collar, he advanced through the gallery of plaster arches and presented himself before the dais.

The Mayor of Jaelot smiled at him. 'The prisoner will be freed when your word is made good. I don't indulge impertinence in my hall, or before my lady wife and her guests. Have a care for propriety. Oath-breakers by law can be executed.' He signalled with one finger.

Liveried halberdiers advanced from behind the plaster kiosks. Others joined them from the side doors and vestibule. Poised at the stair head, Medlir found himself flanked by the ungentle prick of bare weapons. He turned not a hair in response. His attention stayed riveted on his master, while the leather and cord wrappings lately stripped from the lyranthe wrung and twisted into knots between his hands.

Halliron wasted no voice in pointless argument, but spun on his heel to a fire-caught flash of topaz. He set his boot on the cushioned stool, cradled a lyranthe the last of its kind in five kingdoms, and snapped off a run to test the pitch. His apprentice's touch at tuning was never less than perfect; reft by circumstance from his customary love of theatrics, Halliron clapped down his palm, silenced his strings, and flung back his head in vivacious challenge.

Melody erupted under his hands. The notes were fast-paced, keyed to major, and led off in tripping, drunken joy through the brash lilt of a dance tune. Guests grown torpid with rich food turned jaded faces in surprise. Whatever they had expected, this spree of cheerful melody fell incongruous as a slap dealt in anger with a feather.

In sheer, provocative genius, Halliron Masterbard drew them in. The happy jinking melody stroked air and grabbed heartstrings and softened the best blood of Jaelot to smile and neglect fashion and tap their feet.

Stone-still between the shafts of two halberds, Medlir shut his eyes against anguish. Alone in awareness, consumed by crawling dread, he knew this was the ballad written for Jaelot that Halliron had refused to let him hear.

A chord pattered out, and another, soaring and quick as a swallow's flight. Somebody began to clap in rhythm. The Lord Mayor was smiling fatuously. His wife's purse-string lips hung open behind laced fingers, while her fan drooped like a wing-broken bird over the rim of her cake plate. Another moment, and decorum would give way to dancing; except that Halliron tipped back his chin and opened his throat in song.

The words were all nonsense, syllables strung together for their resonance and rhythm. Against the superlative weave of the lyranthe, the counterplay of consonant and vowel sparked like gems in a tapestry. The heart leaped in step for pure wonder. Ladies laced tight in quilted bodices began to sway in their seats like tavernmaids. Husbands by their sides whooped and stamped and applauded, while the song unreeled in merry measures that had even the mayor's guardsmen tapping weapon butts in time against the tile.

The change came with such masterful subtlety, Medlir alone could name the moment when senseless strings of syllables converged into order and meaning. Carried on exuberant melody, three stanzas passed before any guest of the mayor's noticed the first prick of satire; another appalled interval before they connected the tales in the balladry to familiar names and faces. Distilled from six months of gleaned rumour, Halliron's art exposed with rib-tearing viciousness the secrets of boudoir and council chamber, affairs of the heart and affairs of ambition that flaunted the rank lust and incompetence that riddled the channels of city government.

The foot stamping faltered and quieted. Husbands glared at unfaithful wives, or elbowed each other aside to glower and curse at rivals who had made them dupes and cuckolds. Society listened, transfixed by the sick fascination of seeing their neighbours reviled; and breathless in dread lest their own reputations become next in line to be sullied. For the corruption exposed within his precinct, and for his laughably faithless marriage, the city alderman squirmed as if he sat nude on live coals. Paralysed, silent, held spellbound by the song's provocative suspense, the best blood of Jaelot hung on each verse while one after another, their best-respected families were raked over by Halliron's gilded tongue.

A masterbard's enmity could call down an unkind legacy. For a city that ignored codes of justice, for the slights and denigration of his station, Halliron laid bare explosive internal hatreds that would either heal themselves swiftly by cautery, or else linger on, to malign and poison lives and factions unto generations yet unborn.

The last ecstatic measures laced the air to shimmering harmony and trailed away into quiet. The bard dropped his leg from the cushion. He swept down his instrument, stepped smoothly forward and bowed. The chatter of chair legs as the Jaelot's Lord Mayor sprang upright stuttered like a rip across silence.

'How dare you,' he gasped in strangled outrage. 'How dare you dishonour my guests so!'

'You've had a song to epitomize your city's hospitality,' said Halliron, his beautiful voice harshly dry. He held his dignity and his ground as the mayor slammed his fists on the trestle, and pink-ribboned tablecloths ruffled by the force jolted platters and clinked with slipped crystal. 'My art is no coin to be coerced and exposed to public ridicule. I have matched to the letter the measure of your demands.'

His statement snapped away the song's last veil of poisoned, hypnotic fascination. Citizens stabbed raw in the throes of betrayal shoved from their seats, gesticulating and fired to angry talk.

Spurred by the temper of their fury, hampered from action by two halberds, Medlir cursed in despair from the stair head. Any use of his shadow mastery to extricate Halliron would force full exposure of his identity. Constrained by horror, unwilling to seed broadscale bloodshed by letting his name draw Lysaer's armies, he snapped the leather and cord he had twisted like a whip across the eyes of the left-hand guardsman. The man fell back. Medlir side-stepped the blind thrust of his weapon. The other halberdier assigned to hold him had been a friend he had sparred with; aware he was unarmed, that one dropped his polearm, rushed, and locked arms in a vice-grip to pin him.

The savagery of their scuffle passed unnoticed as the men at arms near the mayor converged to seize the Masterbard. Before they could close, their heavyset captain dealt a brute-fisted swing launched solidly out of his shoulder.

Halliron twisted by reflex to shield his priceless lyranthe. The blow struck him behind the temple, flung him staggering backward. Tripped by the stool, he overbalanced and fell. The crack as his frame smashed through split rungs entangled with Medlir's wordless cry.

Splintered wood spun across tiles, for the suspended span of a heartbeat the only motion in the room. Then the packed ranks of guests erupted into noise and pandemonium; except for Halliron, who lay stunned and still, his jewels like flecks of dropped flame. A streak of scarlet meandered through his silver hair, while the lyranthe his fragile flesh had shielded nested unharmed in the silk-clad hollow of his shoulder.

Blanched and distraught in his chains, Dakar alone held an untrammelled view as Medlir pitched free of the guardsman. He arrowed through the pack of outraged bystanders, jabbing knuckles, elbows and knees into velvet-padded flesh with a viciousness jarringly out of character. More than one dandy sprawled moaning in his wake; weeping ladies nursed bruised arms or wrists.

Bent to his knees beside his master barely seconds after the injury, Medlir unpinned Halliron's ribboned collar and probed with shaking hands for a pulse. 'Hurry. Send a man for a healer and a litter.'

Instead he received the bite of armoured hands as the mayor's halberdiers caught him up on both sides and hauled him headlong to his feet.

From the dais, the Mayor of Jaelot met his shouted protest with narrowed, furious eyes. 'I'll have entertainment that befits my wife and guests. You will play in your master's stead. Carol for us sweetly as a lark, or else get no litter, and no healer. Just the executioner's sword for the lot of you.'

Breathing in terrible, deep gasps, his eyes distended in an expression no man could read, Medlir snapped hard against the guards' hold.

The mayor's captain slapped him. 'Be sensible, lad. What's a night's performance worth? Surely less than the lives of your mentor and friend.'

On the scaffold, his fists dragged white-knuckled against his fetters, Dakar watched in sick anger as the shoulders under grey linen shivered still beneath the gauntlets of the guardsmen. Medlir's face was turned away; given the man's oblique nature, the Mad Prophet had no means to measure his response to threats outside mercy or decency. Since Halliron's satire had broken no promise, grounds for further trust were now forfeit. Ill-tempered as a cornered mastiff in the public throes of stung pride, the Mayor of Jaelot would see bloodshed before he backed down and embraced either reason or compromise.

Arrested in sadistic curiosity, onlookers edged reluctantly aside to admit the servants who converged to sweep up the stool's scattered fragments. One hardly more than a boy disentangled the lyranthe from Halliron's slackened grasp, while a sandy-haired coachman fetched from outside bent to the chore of shifting the old man from the hall.

The sight of his master being hefted like a slab of skinned beef, and the further provocation of a cherished, rare instrument at the mercy of a stranger's inept handling at last unlocked Medlir's voice. 'For the Masterbard's life, and the prisoner's, I will play.'

The Mayor of Jaelot stroked his fat belly and smiled.

Head turned to track the brute who shouldered his unconscious master, Medlir did nothing to acknowledge his liberty as the guardsmen's restraint fell away. Controlled beyond emotion, or else simply dazed, he held his sight on the side door until the burdened coachman vanished. Then he surveyed the breadth of the hall. Sea-cold and lightless, his gaze brushed past his flushed and vindictive audience: the men in their shimmering dazzle of jewels; ladies who wetted lips with pink tongues, their feathered trains and ostentatious finery jostled awry in the press. Defined by an incandescence of candle light, the mayor's guests crowded and whispered among themselves, thrilled by the prospect of a spectacle.

Murmured comments tracked Medlir's smallest move. Exposed through a private and merciless anguish, the slight-boned minstrel weathered the inimical regard of Jaelot's bluest-blooded society. In a shirt oddly tailored and tight-laced at the wrists, his simple dress like dull mould against the flower-petal brilliance of silks and velvets and brocades, he reclaimed the lyranthe from the mayor's servant. Then he backed four steps and perched his hip against the rough-cut boards of the prisoner's scaffold. As if he were the only one breathing in the room, he set his hands to silver strings and nervelessly restored them to pitch.

The sweet-struck vibrancy of his tuning cracked the queer limbo of tension. 'He's trying to stop his hand from shaking,' a heckler ventured from the sidelines.

The joke raised high-strung laughter.

More jibes, some voices shrill with the tight, high ring of damped hysteria. 'No, look, he's checking to see that his fingers haven't jammed from stage fright.'

Medlir adjusted a peghead, patient as tide, deliberate as formed ice in a frost crystal. Like his master before him, he launched into song without any pause for introduction.

The lyranthe strings whispered, sighed, then rippled into melody like the plangent tap of autumn rain. The musician did not choose satire for vengeance. His free-running arpeggios sparked through sniggers and barbed sarcasm like pearls flung off a snapped string. Notes round and perfectly spaced and wholly without sting or anger framed a statement so powerfully at odds with the antipathy of his listeners that its overture became an act of daring.

Dakar, who was nearest, was first to feel the tingling thrill of true magic raised through a masterbard's art. The tune thrummed in waves through his bones, its siren pull too sweet to deny. Reft beyond will and deprived of his anger, he bent his head to chained wrists and shed defeated tears against the post. Medlir did not play in rancour. In bruised and demented compassion, he spun cadence to settle and heal; and then, when he had commanded attention by the sheer depth and majesty of his pity, he struck silver strings a glancing, sliding stroke and racked sound through a sharp change in key.

Like the curl of a breaker against rock, the blend of chord and notes framed a statement that forced the doors of the mind. Between the wolf-pack animosity and blood-lust; over the sour human drive to belittle and mock to hide smallness, the music cast a glittering net. In lifting, soaring, unfolding purity, Medlir flung out like jewels before beggars his eulogy for Halliron.

A masterbard's gift could encompass a spirit, weave its essence in a tapestry of sound. So the lyranthe could be used to heal, to ease a stricken consciousness into death, or to summon back life and awareness for a week, or an hour; or to shape final tribute in grief. Medlir possessed as inexorable a perception. He used his talent now as Dakar had never heard him, his harmonies set in moving counterpoint as stark as clean sunlight over snow. In complex and awesome exactness, he unveiled before the citizens of Jaelot the nature of the bard they had tormented. He made them see Halliron through his own eyes, as a generous spirit of moral courage who had sacrificed his heart to humanity through his song, at the cost of love and hearthstone for himself.

Shame cut Jaelot's perpetrators sharper than satire, deeper than their most visceral fear. *Mourn with me*, the notes cried; *weep for what may have been destroyed.* Then tears did fall, thick enough to blind, hot enough to scald, fast enough to fleck bright silk and velvet with a diamond spatter of pure sorrow.

The lyranthe rang with a power to wound and to bind, but did neither; its strains became a gift that turned to scourge breathing flesh in exultation. Pressed shaking against the oak post, Dakar felt the vibration of each fresh stanza ring through the steel of his chains. What mage-sense he owned showed the answering resonance Medlir's gift carved from the earth and the air. The very candle flames danced and dipped in their sconces in tribute to Halliron Masterbard; and still the song poured out, the minstrel lost in the throes of his art like a man drowned senseless by revelation.

Bent over flying fingers and the shimmering leap of silver strings, open body and spirit to a music that packaged his grief in bright sound, Medlir played. Half-unhinged from his senses, he more than struck notes. He *became* the chord, the spun line of melody shaped between hands and heart. He heard, like a ripple through darkness, the jarring stew of pain that was Jaelot; and beneath that dissonance, another measure reawakened by his playing: a time-lost whisper of smothered melody that neglect had nearly cancelled out.

The fragment's poignancy tugged at his sensitized nerves. Since the part of him that was s'Ffalenn prince and Shadow Master feared to end the song which was all that stayed him from violence, he plunged on to embrace the thready remnant. His fingers as willing servant reclothed its hidden measures in new sound.

The dawning emergence of changed theme raised the elements to primal awareness. Snatched into unexpected rapture by the harmonics called from substance and flesh, Medlir experienced a flash-fire bolt of inspiration. He yielded in consent before its riptide of insight: and the song that lurked dormant in the stones of old Jaelot quickened in rebirth and possessed him.

Chained by steel that chimed and warmed in shared resonance, Dakar experienced a chest-bursting joy that tore a cry of sheer wonder from his throat. He looked up, startled to awed disbelief; for the strains that thrummed from Medlir's strings in a golden-white bloom of roused power were bitterly, fearfully uncanny. Somehow the bard's talent had tapped the lost measures the Paravians had danced in past celebration of the solstice.

Like a reed plucked to sound by a squall wind, the musician added voice to his instrument; and at the centre of the mayor's palace, in a blistering sudden flare of mage-light, the spirit forms of Riathan Paravians resolved to retread the old patterns. No mortal present failed to see them. Pale in form as spun gossamer, clothed in the glimmering coils of earth-force that spindled into focus to frame them, unicorns wheeled in ethereal splendour through the spell-caught weave of the music. The spectacle was one to steal thought and stop the breath; to cauterize sight in grace and beauty. Ecstasy like reunion came paired with fierce heartbreak, a grinding, insufferable grief of recognition, that amid all the kingdoms of Athera, no living marvel existed to match these creatures whose ghost presence mirrored perfect purity.

'Ath, oh Ath, let them go,' Dakar pleaded.

His hurt was shared by every man, woman and child in the feast hall; from petty-minded, mollified old gossips to the most grizzled captain at arms; from the richest of merchants to the meanest scullion, no one was exempt. The guardsman who had struck down Halliron wept on his knees in appalled disgrace. Pride vanquished, the Lord Mayor of Jaelot clung sobbing and bereft in the arms of his sorrowfully humbled wife.

Consumed by a rapture too deep for mortal flesh, the musician who was instrument and kindling for a reconfigured invocation of the mysteries noticed none of his oppressor's punctured vanity. Long since, he had surrendered self-awareness to the consuming demand of true song. His playing framed the air and the earth, shocked out surging vibrations.

Dakar sagged appalled against his fetters. Wiser than Jaelot's enthralled citizens, he knew the solstice rite once held by Paravians served a purpose beyond celebration. As a boy before Desh-thiere's conquest, he had witnessed the ritual that husbanded magnetic power into arrows of turned force, to flow diverted from their lane-beds and channel across latitude and enrich the green-growing hills. Arrays of stone monuments, live trees, and natural landmarks had guided the energy's current, a balanced network of markers that Jaelot's trammelled heritage had long since defaced or paved over.

In dismay akin to terror, the Mad Prophet felt the nexus summoned back by Medlir's playing swell to an ascendance of poised force. The mystery would answer the song's call and reclaim its seasonal passage without regard for mortal folly and the structures raised through ignorance in its path.

'No,' Dakar shouted. 'Medlir, damp your strings!'

His warning went unheard.

The only man blind to the grace of the spirit-forms, the only one tone rendered deaf, the musician bent still to his playing, his being now locked in alignment with the intricate lilt of the dance. While the key changed register to impel the litany's consummation, the Mad Prophet looked down in desperation. He saw in an awesome, gut-twist of dread that Medlir's brown hair had transformed to raven's-wing black.

False identity had seared off like wax before the unalloyed blaze of pure energies. In shocked recognition, the Mad Prophet beheld the spirit's unveiled form.

Then impotent rage rammed him hard against his chains and he screamed the name of Arithon s'Ffalenn.

Around him, the song reached crescendo. The surge of primal forces burgeoned into climax with no trained hand to turn or guide them; not, Dakar agonized, as a thousandfold layers of intonation pealed showers of clear sound from the elements, that the act of mage or man could now stifle that mighty flux to silence.

The axis of the song unfurled power in streaming vectors that ploughed up a fountainhead of floor tiles. Ribbon streamers flagged and snapped. Columns and kiosks swayed; the gaudy, painted ornaments and cherub-studded arches crashed over in puffed dust and smashed plaster. Fanned by warped air, pummelled by chaos as feast tables overset and fine crystal chimed and shattered, Dakar cowered against the humming fibres of an oak post that impossibly quickened and sprouted leaves. Sieved through by the bone-hurting chord of grand harmony, he barely heard the screams as panic overwhelmed the mayor's company. Guests and servants shoved, clawed, and knocked each other down in mindless stampede to reach the doorway. Their flight mowed through puddled wine and spilled food, and trampled the gems and crumpled feathers of cast-off masks. Neither were the honoured officials at the head table spared as they scrambled back in shrieking terror from a dais whirled into sudden flame.

Over the stink of smeared meats and the angry orange glare of slagged glassware ripped winds as untamed as a squall line; and yet unutterably kinder: every breath drawn in panic enriched living flesh like a tonic. The stone walls that shocked into cracks and the tapestries that unravelled in burst threads did not unbind in destruction, but yielded before the surge of renewed life-force that yearly called flowers from frost, and sprouts from the germ of quickened seed.

Somewhere between cursing Arithon and shivering with the exultation of the elements, Dakar divined the reason for the backlash: underneath the mosaic in the recessed expanse of floor, the mayor's grand ballroom held the masked-over heart of the ancient, sixth lane power focus. Its rune rings captured the rising earth force and burned through the veneer of grout and masonry. Long-buried patterns reconfigured in lines of smoking char. To touch the ash over such sigils bare-handed would bring no sensation of heat. But terrified citizens dared not halt in mid-flight to examine what seemed like black sorcery. In shrieking, unstrung fear, they poured through the vestibule, into town streets that offered no haven.

The power streamed on its course like flung phosphor. Its passage hazed torches and lamps, and roused families in alarm from their beds. Women wept, and infants laughed outright. Men rushed in their night robes to grab weapons. Festival fires flared up in conflagration, scattering circles of dancers; while everywhere along the old energy paths, the roof-trees of shops and houses groaned and flexed and erupted into growing twigs and buds. Pulverized slates and chimney bricks kicked aloft in whining fragments. Every tower and wall and stone building built counter to natural alignments rang out in bell tones, then caved into collapse as the resurgence of a ritual denied for six centuries reclaimed its interrupted conduit.

Ruinous though the backlash became to human property, life and limb caught haplessly in its path took small harm beyond bruises and abrasions. A few who were elderly or worn with mortal sickness died with smiles on their lips; and miracles happened along the flux lines. A blind little girl was restored back to sight. Two cripples tried their legs and walked. A demented woman wept for sanity restored, while an accountant fell into wailing madness as he obdurately tried to reason through events outside the pale of mortal logic. Swept into the majesty of the solstice surge, no spirit in Jaelot passed untouched.

While walls and breakwaters and cottars' sheds tumbled to dust and smashed fragments, people gave way to joy and panic, and every shade of passion in between. The reawakened chord of mystery fanned outward, to blaze in renewal across the continent. In the damaged palace, amid the wreckage of the feast hall, the musician at last stilled his strings. He sat, slumped and drained, his forehead pillowed on the warm wood of a masterbard's instrument and his slack fingers dangling as the forge-fire heat of inspiration dwindled to thunderous silence.

The only individual still present to observe was the prophet chained fast on the scaffold. The wood that fastened his fetters rustled half-reborn into greenery, or else whittled wholesale into slivers. Dakar wrestled in a racked breath and said through his chattering teeth, 'Daelion Fatemaster witness! This city will burn you for a sorcerer. That's if Koriani witches don't descend on you first and rip your flesh like bloodsucking harpies.'

Limp at the feet of his accuser, the Crown Prince of Rathain stirred; straightened. He turned the dry fabric of his sleeve cuff to wipe the sheen of oil from his lyranthe strings. Very slowly he stood up. The inimical eyes at his back could have speared holes in his dampened shirt as, in an edged and dangerous weariness, he said, 'Then it would be best, don't you think, if we left?'

For answer, Dakar slammed down his wrists to a murderous clang of solid chain.

Arithon s'Ffalenn cringed from the sound. 'Please don't,' the whisper a plea, or a threat; given the nature of his bloodline, telling which could be hazardously troublesome. Black hair fronded across his collar, he tipped his head and whistled a sharp, fluting note charged still with the arts of a masterbard.

A resonance coursed through gleaming metal, and the locks that fastened the cuffs to Dakar's limbs snicked in sharp succession and snapped open. 'You might have done that earlier, damn you.'

'I couldn't,' Arithon said faintly through the rasping dissonance of fallen steel. 'The power was beyond me until a moment ago.'

Dakar stopped in the act of rubbing chafed wrists, shot out a rough hand, and spun the smaller man to face him. The prince swayed, loose-limbed and graceless as a scarecrow. Amid the severe planes of s'Ffalenn features, deep-set eyes caught the light in flat reflection, unfocused as tinted green glass.

The Mad Prophet saw, and swore mightily. 'Dharkaron's black Chariot and Spear! A lifetime spent mage-wise, and look at you! Wrecked to your boot soles, and played clean out of talent like a fish. You're going to be sick from this later.' He gestured at the scorched pattern that demarked the unmasked lane focus. 'You raised the old mysteries on spiteful purpose, didn't you?'

Arithon's brows twitched into a difficult frown. 'Halliron's eulogy was my idea. The rest was intuition. I'm certainly not about to be sorry.' Self-effacing in his disregard, that a lesser man might have been destroyed by the powers he had thoughtlessly channelled, he cradled his borrowed lyranthe against his shoulder while the sweat sprang at his temples and trickled in drops down his jaw. 'And I can't be sick. Not until we've pulled Halliron out of here. Since you're sober enough to try scrying, can you stay your grudges long enough to find him?'

'Not if I have to carry you,' Dakar replied in bitten fury. Afraid less for his own skin than for the sure retribution he would earn from his master should Arithon come to any harm, he smacked his thighs with his fists. 'Fiends eat my liver! How Asandir must be laughing!' Then, as Arithon shuddered, he was forced to grab him wrist and shoulder in a support he found abhorrent. 'Come on. The servants took the Masterbard to a servant's pallet near the pantry. If we're lucky, they'll have run off and left him.'

Unmasking

By the pull of the sea tides in her blood, Elaira knew before she opened her eyes that moonless, indigo night still deepened the arched casements of the Koriani hospice. This was not one of the bad times, waking up. The smells of herbal soap and the familiar astringency of a cailcallow tisane gently told her she lay in the wards with the sick. Three months past, she had busied herself brewing such potions. Now, in unpleasant irony, she was the invalid being dosed; crystal-resonance realignment for longevity was no course for the faint-hearted.

Elaira gingerly shifted position. The sheets clung sweat-damp to flesh that weighed like an unfamiliar burden. Her head ached, and her veins felt as if their delicate insides had been systematically reamed and scalded.

Morriel Prime might forewarn of the pain, but no one had mentioned the secondary effect of the dreams.

A breeze wafted in, perfumed by frangipani and the fruity bouquet of flowering vines that laced the old hospice's south façade. Goat-bells tinkled somewhere outside; fainter and farther off trailed the notes of a flute played by the flock's child herder.

Elaira clung to basic awareness, of smells and sounds, and the fierce, blazing tapestry of midsummer constellations.

On nights such as this, she even dwelled on raw pain to maintain her grip upon wakefulness. Any means at hand to serve as anchor against the ripping shoals of nightmare that stole upon her unawares; dreams which sucked her down into suffocating horror, then left her, shaking and sobbing and bereft of any memory to name what fear had overwhelmed her. At other times she relived the sordid terrors of her girlhood, driven to heart-pounding flight from the constable's watch through the dingy brick alleys of Morvain. The beggars and thieves who had befriended or betrayed her loomed more real than the immediate present.

Afterwards she aroused to find herself a stranger locked in a grown woman's body, dissociated from identity, cast adrift from mind and self by the alignment effects of her spell-crystal. When such transition caught her alone, for sweating, tortured minutes, she might gasp in confusion, desperate to recapture the scattered threads of an unstrung self-awareness.

If the process failed to kill her, the longevity attunement undertaken at the Prime's command would be complete in another three months. Elaira vowed then to rediscover how to laugh; she would live on to a despicable old age and hound First Senior Lirenda to twitching fits of irritation.

Such fancy tugged forth a battered half-smile, quickly stifled since even that slight movement raised a tingle like a stabbing of small needles down her nerves. The urge to shut her eyes against discomfort overpowered her, and her mind spiralled downward into sleep.

A vivid dream arose to claim her, unlike any other known before . . .

She walked on a spit of silvered sands. Spent waves lapped foam like wet lace around her ankles and stars wheeled in their summer courses above her wind-tossed hair. The polestar rode at a higher angle, and the pull of flood tide bespoke a northern latitude in the hour approaching midnight. Through the grit of each separate sand grain, in the tang of salt-braced air, Elaira felt, like an oncoming storm, the advent of midsummer solstice.

Tugged by an augury of danger; stalked by some unseen threat, she faced inland.

Nothing sinister seemed to be in evidence.

Above the curved sills of the dunes, an ancient ruin fronted the surf, half-razed towers and storm beaten bulwarks thrust like crumbled sculpture against sky. A lingering, haunted harmony of line identified the site as Paravian. By the forces that arrowed through the soil, Elaira sensed a power focus there: stone eons old, laid down in patterns; mantled now in clumps of black moss and pried at by invading sedges. The resonance bespoke the seventh lane's vibration, but an intrusive, dissonant irregularity purled through its magnetic play of static.

There; the nagging, creeping uneasiness intensified to a shiver. Elaira cupped her temples to tighten her concentration and trace the uneasy sense of wrongness.

This power was neither dead nor forgotten, but the glittering, interlocked links of fresh conjury raised by twenty-four enchantresses sealed in a spell-circle at Athir.

A distant voice shimmered through her dream. 'You must be aware, an outside spirit has tracked us.'

Elaira had no chance to be afraid. The sands on which she walked overturned and dissolved, while her isolate awareness reeled through a well of hazeless dark. Power snatched down like the nip of steel pincers, then clamped, and closed and held her pinned. When light came again, she beheld an upward view through the blue-tinged facets of a prism. A ring of female faces veiled in gauze regarded her downward in return.

'It's the initiate Elaira,' someone identified in frosty, disdainful consonants.

No sleep-induced dream brought her here, but the perilous vision of clairvoyance. A jolt of pure terror sheared her viscera as she overheard Morriel's reply to the dismayed senior who had spoken; whose safe-wards her disjointed consciousness had all too unwittingly blundered through.

'The intrusion is scarcely a surprise. The Skyron jewel was used to align Elaira's crystal for longevity. Since the stones are still paired in resonance, and our solstice scrying is tuned for the Master of the Shadow, her infatuation would naturally draw her into sympathy.'

Another voice ventured in brassy disapproval, 'A ward must be set to block her, then.'

'Let her bide,' Morriel contradicted. 'I rather think her presence may help turn the search in our favour.'

Shackled like waking nightmare by her tie to the master crystal, Elaira raged that her empathy for Arithon s'Ffalenn should be forced into usage to break his guarded privacy. She could do nothing but endure in despair as the quartz stone that altered the live tissues of her body blended with the pulse of the greater jewel held in resonance above the seventh lane focus, a thousand leagues north and west.

Power licked through joint consciousness, as twenty-four Koriani Seniors shaped their geas of compulsive summoning. Methodically dispassionate, they first recreated the personal pattern that mapped the character of Arithon s'Ffalenn.

To this, they keyed layers interlocked like ring-ripples, spell overlaid upon seal in sticky webs of attraction: entrapments as natural as the drawing force between iron and magnet; the pull between sun, moon and tide, or the honey that beckoned live bees to a flower. The Prime laced darker themes in counterpoint, as relentless as insane obsession, or the mindless craving of drug addiction, that could marry flesh with substance in drawn-out physical torment.

Heart-tied in compassion for Arithon, Elaira could feel the weaving's cruel pull. On her cot in the hospice at Forthmark, her body thrashed and whimpered, as the Koriani Circle hooked out from Athir and plucked up the core of her deepest shame. Their callous theft left her violated, soiled, as they drew from a love unasked and unwanted, and intermeshed its innocent essence to enhance their poisoned noose.

Clear as a chimed note, the moment of solstice midnight swept the lane to the east.

The power focus at Athir flared like a crucible with the vibrancy of captured earth power. More than waves and old stone drank its current.

Even across vast distance, Elaira could not escape the awful moment when the Koriani scrying meshed into the lane's swelling surge. The freed construct coursed outward, pitched to seek union with its counterpart in blind and pitiless potency.

Hide, Elaira begged the memory of a black-haired prince whose spirit had banefully marked her. *Stay still; make no move to draw notice.*

Better, surely, had she died before her fateful past encounter with the Master of Shadow. Whatever haven Arithon had found to evade the draw of Desh-thiere's curse, with his personal signature from the Fellowship linked in tandem with forced power, no shelter under earth or sky could withstand the probe of this summoning.

Tears of misery and betrayal welled up, to spill down Elaira's temples. Grief consumed her, and futile anger, while under layers of rucked bandaging, the sliver of crystal conjoined to her being rang in helpless concert with the geas channelled outward to seek Arithon. The scrying's unconscionable demand blazed through her, remorseless in its passage as a sunbeam shot to focus by a lens.

Even her pain lent no respite. Fuelled by the sweep of earth's solstice, fanned down the conduit of the seventh lane, the geas pattern combed and sieved through farmsteads and cities and village settlements. Elaira shivered in revulsion as a thousand hapless lives were encountered and winnowed aside like the toss of so much dry chaff. The scrying allowed no quarter. Broadcast outward as a mindless set of urges, raised like a damned thing to measure its need against all life in its path, it keened in insatiable demand of its match.

In a second compressed to the detail of hours, the summoning embraced the wind-raked scarps at Northstor, then cascaded through the chain of port cities set along the crescent coastline that edged the Cildein Ocean.

Elaira lay limp with exhaustion before the tingling rush of solstice midnight passed, and the lane surge sank and subsided. The Koriani summoning slackened with the ebb, until, in the sleepy fishers' shacks of Merior, it eddied back on itself in a snarl of unrequited symmetry.

Its siren call to the Master of Shadow remained miraculously unanswered.

Amid the dank and shadowed mazes of Athir's ruined walls, the Koriani Circle broke off, confounded. One by one, the order's most accomplished enchantresses stirred from the throes of deep trance. They pushed back gauze veils, bewildered, stunned; while the energies of their failed scrying frayed around them like so many wisps of torn floss.

Elaira could have laughed at the thwarted defeat on their faces. Her intuition had played them false. Ceded a victory that pierced for its sweetness, she revelled in giddy relief. Wherever the wily s'Ffalenn prince was sequestered, he was no place along the seventh lane.

The enchantresses regrouped in disgruntled frustration. Governed by discipline, they engaged rituals to disperse their bands of power; but seared through their silence while the spell seals were isolated and banished through strictly set counterwards, the unspoken fact remained: Arithon s'Ffalenn had slipped through their net once again.

Only one rebellious spirit was lapped in the sphere of the Skyron crystal's influence: Elaira alone favoured the cause of their quarry. She was left defencelessly exposed as the vindictive suspicion of several Seniors burgeoned into open accusation.

'Desist!' cried the Prime in flat rebuke. 'No charge can be called against Elaira. No mere initiate could have sheltered Rathain's prince from the draw of a grand scrying.'

'What sorry pass have we come to?' seconded another caustic peer. 'Had we not misplaced the Great Waystone, we could have had Rathain's prince crawling belly-down to find *us*!'

'Silence!' Morriel cracked back. 'Our efforts are wasted in groundless blame or misplayed regrets for what's lost. Either the Fellowship itself maligns our work, or the Teir's'Ffalenn turns his guile in a direction we never thought to search. Whichever reason has balked us, no more can be accomplished tonight.'

Crumpled in abject weariness, Elaira overheard the order for the Skyron crystal to be locked away in its coffer. But even as the appointed Senior moved to gather up the great focus stone, the inexorable turn of time carried the progression of solstice midnight westward. As the moment crossed the sixth lane, the massive aquamarine revitalized in a sudden, unbidden burst of power.

Elaira shared the shock of recoil.

Then all thoughts, all fears, were cancelled by a rolling charge of harmony that surged through the jewel's unshielded lattice. At one with Morriel's circle of Seniors, she reeled, blind and dazed, as the sensitized planes of the aquamarine erupted and blazed, incandescent in song-struck vibration. In Athir, the power focus under its tangled wrack of weeds also magnified that resonance. Its coils blazed to sudden life in a captured peal of joy so pure it kissed earth like the union of desire and perfect fulfilment.

Swept up through the link to her spell crystal, Elaira endured, along with twenty-three senior initiates slammed to witless exultation, as the life-force of forgotten Paravian mystery tolled its wakened chord across the continent.

Morriel alone retained her sense of self-command. 'Ath's grace, where is this coming from? We dare not languish in blank ignorance.'

The Skyron aquamarine was not as the Great Waystone, vanished in the chaos of the rebellion; its lesser capacity could not channel several tasks without one purpose bleeding into another. And so as cold power was retuned into alignment, Elaira shared the vision that emerged, as the flow of the night's uncanny vortex was traced down to its source. Along with Morriel's seniors, she tracked walls and stonework torn apart and scattered like straw chaff; chimney bricks rammed askew from rafters, and roof-beams clothed green in budded leaves. She heard the wails of Jaelot's terrified populace, that had seen half their town come unhinged. There at the core of destruction, exposed amid smoking mosaic and the overset tables of a feast hall, the hands that had unleashed the wild mystery: the mortal singer who had keyed the release of an earth force held mute through five centuries.

He proved a man slight in stature. A disarranged swathe of black hair could not quite mask green eyes, or the steep, angled features that marked the royal bloodline of s'Ffalenn.

'Ath preserve us all!' Morriel Prime's appalled outrage cut like glass through the Skyron link. 'A city has been all but destroyed! Innocent people have suffered! How much unconscionable meddling shall this prince be free to inflict upon our world before the Fellowship sorcerers deign to admit their mistake?' Harsh as scaled iron, she added, 'Last of his line or not, Arithon s'Ffalenn shall be curbed. Dharkaron as my witness and be damned to the Seven, who would in blind folly preserve such dangerous stock.'

That moment, with scarcely a flicker of warning, the Athir contact cut off.

Released to the scent of summer flowers, and the night quiet of her bed in the hospice, Elaira stifled a shuddering sob against the heel of her hand. The terrible wait was over; her peace irrevocably fled. The Master of Shadow was betrayed, not by her, but worse, by his passionate love for the music he held dearest to his heart.

Awed and shaken and concerned for him, Elaira turned her face to bury her misery in her pillow, and froze, her skin pricked to shivers by a draught.

Her room was no longer empty.

A figure poised by her bedside: not the initiate healer who brought her tisanes for the pain, but the uncanny presence of a broad, bearded man too ghostly still for breathing flesh. His florid features held a frown of thunderous proportions. He stood, fists planted on a belt like an ox collar, his eyes trained upon her as lightless as new sable velvet.

Elaira blinked. The creature she confronted could be nothing less than the wraith of a Fellowship sorcerer.

'The diligence of your senior enchantresses has been rewarded,' Luhaine opened, the shyness he held for outsiders girded behind unimpeachable ceremony. 'Arithon has been found in Jaelot.'

The sorcerer's portly form looked somehow tired, standing. Elaira started to slide over on her pallet to allow him the space to sit down, then recalled; a disembodied spirit would retain no need for such comfort. 'Why are you here?'

Wind from the casement brushed through Luhaine's image without stirring his wiry beard. 'To warn and to help.'

'I can already guess how Morriel plans to use me.' Elaira was careful to muffle her voice. To be caught in conversation with a Fellowship sorcerer would call down the direst consequences. 'How are you minded to help?'

Had Luhaine still been enfleshed, he would have rubbed the pink knob of his nose. 'Well,' he said, abashed to evasion. 'Sethvir said you were direct.'

'I'm afraid,' Elaira admitted. 'If the duty-watch chances to see you, I could be broken for treason.' Her initiate's ties to the Koriani Order went beyond fleshly obedience; should Morriel exercise the extreme penalty, the vow Elaira had sworn over crystal could be turned to reduce her to a mindless husk.

'Whoever should glance through this doorway will assume you talk in your sleep,' Luhaine said, deeply miffed. 'I was never sent to endanger you.'

'That's scarcely flattering, and I'm not reassured.' The logic seemed sound, that without trouble pending, no sorcerer at all would have visited. Elaira regarded Luhaine's scowl, her care for the Shadow Master's safety too burdensome to contain. 'I think you should worry for your fugitive.'

His lecturer's condescension back in force, Luhaine stirred an impatient half-step that raised no echo from stone walls. 'Lysaer's still amassing his army. Unless your sisterhood informs him, he won't know Arithon's been unmasked.'

A pitifully small consolation; Elaira shuddered through a spasm of discomfort, penalty of the crystal's reattunement. 'Don't tell me anything more about either half-brother.' She averted her face, ashamed as she admitted, 'Morriel will use every asset I have, no matter who comes to be hurt.'

'Not quite,' Luhaine rebuked softly. 'Some things you'll keep for yourself.' His image never stirred against starlight. But the unseen power he engaged in gentle pity folded the enchantress on the pallet into a painless sleep without dreams.

Elaira gave way to his mastery with a whispered sigh of release. The strain that pinched her eyes and mouth settled and slowly relaxed. Entangled amid a sweep of auburn hair, a nose and chin too angular to be delicate smoothed over like fine-polished ivory. When she was not frowning, Luhaine thought, her allure was mischievous and innocent, touched as though from within by the promise of lyric passion. Determination lent her the illusion of ruggedness; and the burden of betrayal that Koriani service set in conflict with her empathic link with Arithon.

Against the sworn obedience that ruled this woman, Luhaine could do nothing. But the longevity realignment she had undertaken for the sake of Sethvir's augury: that was another matter. Fellowship intervention had set stakes on the attraction that tied her to Arithon's fate. For that she would not be left to suffer; nor would his Fellowship colleagues sanction the surrender of her spirit to a second life binding to a Koriani spell crystal.

Elaira was not conscious to feel the warm swell of power that licked beneath her bandaged wrist. Closed eyes could not track the lacework intricacy of the spellcraft Luhaine wrought in her behalf. She would wake in the morning and feel refreshed, and even Morriel would never discern that the crystal's unnatural attunement had been arrested, then erased, its forced effect of lengthened lifespan realigned to a kinder patterning sourced by the laws of grand conjury.

She would live the same years as Arithon, but suffer no ill effects. If the hour came that conflicted interests broke her faith with the Koriani Order, the Prime who presided in judgement would gain no further power through the white quartz matrix of Elaira's personal crystal. Her vows of initiation upon the Skyron jewel alone would hold influence against her.

'Serve your Prime matriarch as you must,' Luhaine murmured in words that arrowed across the veils of sleep. 'But for the sake of your care for the last Teir's'Ffalenn, the Fellowship may sometimes intercede.'

A second later the apparition left her side, faded with as little ceremony as a star in the grey chill of dawn.

Nightmare

Lysaer s'Ilessid snapped awake with a coarse, ripping gasp. Bathed in sweat and shivering violently, he thrashed off the bedclothes that constricted his legs and chest. Driven nerves and instinct shot him halfway to his feet, one fist ablaze with a halo of light he had not consciously called his gift to raise. The darkness that threatened to suffocate him shattered, and with it, the last, vicious remnant of the dream that had torn him headlong from sleep.

Scalding glare bit flashes of reflection off gilt moulding and from the garish enamels of the cloisonné washbasin his valet had left by the window-bay. Lush woollen tapestries muffled the cries of the sentries, alarmed from their posts on the walls outside by the fiery glare through the casement. Lysaer squeezed his eyes shut. The appointments of the state guest chamber loaned by the Mayor of Erdane mocked him in undisturbed quiet. Subsided to his knees on the mattress, the light still cupped in his hands, he loosened locked jaws and forced in a deep, calming breath.

Memory of his black-haired nemesis hovered still in his mind, secretive, elusive, and maddeningly removed beyond reach. 'Dharkaron as my witness,' he swore to the empty room. 'By your shadows and fell sorceries, you can't evade justice forever!'

An instant later, the latch clicked.

Lysaer started sharply. The light in his hands scalded into actinic brilliance before he caught back raw reflex and curbed his fury to a force less likely to ignite the bedclothes. The whipcord tension in him relented a mere fraction as Lord Diegan rushed into the room, his dark hair tousled from his pillow, and his body half-clothed in last night's crumpled hose and shirt.

One glance at Lysaer, and he snatched an unlit candle from a wall

138

sconce, crossed the carpeted floor, and tipped the wick into the flash-point corona that yet burned between the prince's palms.

Over the hiss of hot wax as the candle flared into flame, the commander of a cityless garrison said in caustic care, 'If you dreamed of the Master of Shadow again, that makes the third time this week.'

'I don't need you to remind me.' Lysaer parted his hands, and the light shredded asunder and quenched like a beacon fire doused before an enemy. Surrounded now by soft dark that did nothing but exacerbate his edginess, he launched off the bed and strode to lean out the opened casement.

To the guardsmen clustered in agitation on the embrasure below, he called, 'Naught's amiss. Feel free to resume your patrols.'

While they dispersed, Lysaer remained at the window, no longer shivering, but chilled to the bone none the less. He tried to ignore the brisk footfalls as Diegan spiked the candle in a holder on the carved oak table, laid over with the drawings and maps that outlined his new city of Avenor. The flick of wool cloth passed unacknowledged as a cloak was unfurled over his nakedness.

At his shoulder, Diegan said, 'If the strain's been too much, at least take Talith to your bed. Your handfasting's lasted for years. As her brother, I won't stand on ceremony now if you decide not to wait for the wedding.'

'She's to be Avenor's queen, not my courtesan.' Distraught enough that it showed, Lysaer scrubbed his knuckles over his stiff face. 'She'll have a state ceremony in my rebuilt capital. No vagary of the Shadow Master's will drive me to consider any less.'

Diegan reached across, caught the frame of the casement, and pulled closed and latched the mullioned panes. 'If you're going to talk sedition over mayoral authority in Tysan, at least try not to be overheard.'

'I won't need to supplant any trade city's governance.' Lysaer straightened tense fingers and blotted icy sweat on the gold-edged weave of his cloak. 'Once the Prince of Rathain makes his move, his sorceries will drive town loyalty into my hands by itself. I alone will command the resource and the light to combat him.'

Diegan sought out a cushioned chair and wearily folded himself into it. 'Ath, he's been hidden for *six years*. If I hadn't been at hand to witness the slaughter he effected in Deshir, I'd wonder, as your new mercenaries do, whether Maenalle of Tysan was right in her claim that Arithon had no wish for war at all. Man, you can't gather crack troops, then sit them idle indefinitely!'

'We've been quartered in Erdane far too long,' Lysaer agreed. He chose not to mention the balance of his fear, nor the dream-image that moved in locked step with remembrance of his enemy's secretive ways. His thoughts were harrowed in equal measure by the blood that had soaked Tal Quorin's river banks in the first battle fought against the Shadow Master.

Thousands had died. For the sake of those lives thrown away through irresponsible haste, he must hold fast to his plan.

Arithon was ruthless, a sorcerer.

No matter how eager the troops were to fight, their commanders must never again be left at liberty to underestimate the foe they raised arms to destroy.

Lysaer snapped away from the window to pace the carpet. Beyond the shut casement, a homeward bound drunkard riled the headhunters' tracking dogs. The kennelled pack erupted into sharp, excited barks, answered by every alley-strayed mongrel, and the shriller yaps of a lapdog cooped up by a merchant's wife. As frustrated by his own inactivity, vexed still by overplayed nerves, the prince caught up a dozen fresh candles and lit them one by one. Rinsed in patterns of moving flamelight, he brooded over certainties he could not put into words: that the needling, insatiable drive that ate at him day and night, to seek out the Shadow Master and see him dead, was not a force to heed reason.

He controlled the urge by iron force of will, his every act bent to serve the people whose safety was his pledged responsibility. If he weakened before the drive of antipathy, if he gave way to the exhortations of Etarra's Lord Mayor and allowed the combined eastern garrison to march too quickly, many more lives might be ruined.

Even still, the need to wait for new gold to be levied through Rathain to fund his endeavour in Tysan chafed raw holes in his patience. The passage of solstice had spurred a restlessness in him that mounted now to a screaming ache. He started under sunlight at ordinary shadows. He sweated each minute in directionless certainty that *some* new development was afoot.

The letter just delivered by west-bound courier, that affirmed the dearth of rumour concerning any sorcerer who matched the Master's description, did nothing to ease his conviction. Despite the unified support of Rathain's cities, Pesquil's headhunters had routed out no barbarian camps through the past three summers' campaigns. Their scarcity compounded his certainty that the clans had organized as well.

Lysaer beat down his angry passion. The lesson instilled by Tal Quorin's massacre was his charge and his personal burden. The lack of any target to strike at was a frustration his allies must be cajoled to abide. Against the Master of Shadow, any weakness in them would be turned to grievous liability. The campaign that succeeded must have no such flaw to exploit.

Lysaer well respected the two-edged, deadly game the Teir's'Ffalenn was wont to play.

Restored back to regal equilibrium, he caught the cloak's rich fabric about his damp flesh. A small smile turned his lips as he reviewed the engineer's drawings of Avenor's proposed fortifications. However well-intentioned, his commander at arms was mistaken. A woman in his bed could never blunt his ardour to see Rathain's prince bleed on his sword. Yet by Ath, if he had to set the example of restraint, a gesture was needed in counterbalance.

'I shall send a rider west to Karfael tomorrow,' Lysaer resolved. 'Let my writ be given to the merchants' guilds, that a thousand royals in gold will reward any man who brings back confirmed news of any unnatural event. Arithon of Rathain is a sorcerer. Sooner or later, he must make a mistake, or be forced by circumstance to show his hand. The Mayor of Etarra will send out additional couriers. Our troops can train here while Avenor's rebuilt.'

Made aware by the stillness that his frustrated humour had transferred like contagion to his commander at arms, Lysaer tossed back gold hair and laughed. 'Don't you see, Diegan? We'll twist even time to our advantage. The longer Arithon hides, the further he runs, the larger the army we'll have ready on the field to slaughter him.'

'I don't know where you find your tolerance.' Diegan arose in one nettled movement, jerked open a cupboard, and hooked out the flagon of wine he needed in sudden desperation. He scrounged up two goblets and poured. 'But no doubt that's the only way we'll have a net strong and wide enough, that a conniving sorcerer can't slip through.'

Lysaer accepted the glass he was offered. Candleflame burned hot reflections in his eyes and bloodied the depths of the wine as he touched unsmiling lips to the rim and swallowed. 'Depend on that, Diegan. Let's both drink a pledge to that end.'

Cross-currents

Diverted from his course to check on the Mistwraith's prison at Rockfell Peak, Asandir drives his black stud at urgent speed through grey dawn, over the long unused southern pass through the Skyshiels toward the lowland road that skirts Eltair Bay . . .

Lee-rail awash against whipping morning winds, a trim brig under command of a laughing captain threads in dancing flight between the shoals that whiten the channel through Vaststrait, while three galleys packed with armed men and bearing official requisitions for boarding and confiscation of contraband thrash to windward in futile pursuit . . .

Under summer noon on the arch above Erdane's west wall, Lady Talith watches her betrothed and a picked guard of troops begin their march to the ruins of Avenor; and though her finger bears the diamonds and royal sapphires as token of Lysaer's pledge, she twists the jewelled ring in stiff outrage, that his will to keep her safely sheltered has compelled her to stay behind . . .

VI. *CRUX*

Armed guards swept house to house through Jaelot. The shaking pound of their boots up loft stairways, and the mailed assault of fists on wooden planking disturbed sleepers, as they banged open root-cellar doors and riffled through dusty attics in search of last night's fugitives. Their fervour suffered frenetic confusion as city officers in charge of the hunt embroiled themselves into vociferous, fist-waving arguments. By daybreak, in cold reason, no two groups could be reconciled over the physical appearance of Halliron Masterbard's apprentice.

The criminal fact remained that his sorcery had dismembered half their city.

Eyewitnesses from the mayor's feast hall only convulsed the quarrel to fresh hostility, a complication that provoked disgruntled shop owners; ones whose wares had been spared from the vortex of the lane surge, only to be ransacked and turned upside-down to satisfy the suspicions of furious officials.

The prime suspect stayed undiscovered, along with Halliron and the stout convict for whom his Masterbard's word had sworn surety.

Half the morning passed before the meaty-faced ostler who ran the livery stables by the gatehouse was shaken awake to be questioned. Twitching straw from the clothes he had slept in, and belligerently cross from a headache, he worked his stubbled jaw around a yawn and frowned at the captain who pressured him. 'Pony cart? Yes, one was quartered here last night. A dark man came for it, very late. A fat man was with him.'

'Dark?' yelped the beribboned secretary of the alderman. He bounced on his toes and flapped his hat behind a stifling press of bystanders. Since no one gave way to admit him, he jettisoned dignity and burrowed like a mole through the ranks of gawping grooms and nerve-jumpy men at arms. 'How do you mean, dark?'

The ostler hawked, spat on the cobbles, and squinted as though at an imbecile. 'Black hair. Do I look blind?'

'You're sure?' the secretary pestered. 'It was night. You aren't mistaken? His colour could have been brown?'

'Dharkaron! Do I look stupid too?' The ostler jabbed off an obscene gesture. 'The man was dark as coal soot. Green eyed, he was, and quick with his tongue as a flayer's knife. Lordly bad tempered, not to be denied, and no, he didn't say where he planned to be going!'

'Sorcerer's likely past the gates by now,' yelled a drayman perched on his load of corn sacks. 'You want him, why not chase him down?'

But none of the guardsmen on gate watch had seen any fugitives escape. Sweating over this setback in the breezeless haze of noontide, the commander of Jaelot's garrison cleared his throat and diffidently tried to shift the blame: the minstrel and his party must have slipped out of Jaelot by boat.

Turmoil transferred to the dockside as fishing smacks were commandeered to sweep the coves and the bay. To placate the sloop captains who grumbled in disagreement, mounted patrols fanned out to scour the coastal road.

The cart and its widely-sought occupants by then lay well south, pulled up in the sticks of a hazel copse to evade the headhunter teams who rode in hot hopes of a bounty. Freckled with sun-dolloped shade and fuming biliously, Dakar the Mad Prophet straddled the driver's seat, the lines hooked over his raised knee. Never a spirit to hold a grudge quietly, he cursed fate that relentless pursuit out of Jaelot should befoul his raw urge to pick a fight.

'You asked for cold water?' Sullen as a bear with a canker, he tipped his chin over his shoulder. 'There's a glacial stream down that gully.'

The royal personage he addressed unfurled from a tortured crouch in the wagon bed. Arithon surveyed the surrounding thicket through sweat-plastered strands of black hair. Taxed by the effort to raise himself, he climbed over the pony cart's tailboard. The Mad Prophet observed in viperish satisfaction as he made his way downhill, ill-balanced as a man with a gut wound. The backlash he suffered was doubly well deserved, Dakar thought; the earth power wantonly channelled through Jaelot was enough to scour sanity and leave any mortal deathly sick.

Galled past forgiveness for the trick which had played him straight into Asandir's design, the Mad Prophet curbed his impulse to bash his fist on his leg. 'Bastard,' he mouthed after the form that lurched down the stream bed.

A slurred objection arose from the blankets nested in the wagonbed. 'How unoriginal. If you're minded to try insults with Arithon, you'll need something better than a truth he's likely bored with hearing.'

'Halliron?' Diverted from his angst, Dakar twisted further to find the Masterbard wakened and regarding him.

The old man looked unwell, his complexion sickly grey except where a spreading, mottled bruise blackened his cheekbone and temple. Since the appalling blow that had felled him, he lapsed often into unconsciousness. The muscles on the battered side of his face sagged in paralysis; the opposite eye, tenuously open, was black and unnaturally dilated.

Aware such symptoms boded ill, Dakar vented his heartsick frustration against Arithon. 'You're an outright fool to defend him. And twice the fool, for last night. You shouldn't have let him talk you into travelling.'

Halliron's lips twitched in lopsided resignation. 'Better to be uncomfortable than dead. Which we would be, make no mistake, had we tried taking cover in Jaelot. I never liked their mayor's penchant for burning accomplices to sorcery alive on a pile of oiled faggots.' Palsied fingers fluttered and plucked at the blankets that springtime's moths had pricked holes in; gravely, the Masterbard added, 'I heard what Arithon played. All of it. His art crossed the bounds of unconsciousness. There's a greatness in him now that even you must appreciate.'

'By force, and in wretched sobriety,' Dakar answered, his eyes upturned and venomous, and glazed in reflection with a sun-caught matting of summer leaves. 'There you have my troubles in a nutshell.' He would have capped with epithets, had the passage of more mounted lancers not precluded the wisdom of retorts.

'You're not inclined to go back either, I see,' the Masterbard observed dryly.

Dakar lapsed into glowering silence until the object of his spite returned to nettle him. Back from the gully, stripped down to shirtsleeves and hose, Arithon held in shaking hands the tunic he had just soaked in stream water. Braced against the wagon side, he forced the concentration to fold the garment into a compress.

As he bound its wet cold to ease the Masterbard's ugly swelling, the old man made an effort, but failed to damp the shudder of pain that recoiled through his frail body. 'It's poor thanks you're getting, for winning us passage out of Jaelot.'

'I beg your pardon.' Pale himself as torn parchment, and scruffy from strain and lack of sleep, Arithon dredged up a smile. 'Dakar has shown astounding generosity. He's made six offers to abandon me, and I have accepted each one.'

'Just wait until we reach Tharidor!' the Mad Prophet snapped in choked fury. 'Then I promise, you'll see me keep my word.'

With that maddening, false complaisance which had marked his alias as Medlir, Arithon raised his head. 'Well if that's true, you can help by watering the pony.' No change of stance offered warning; he shot a hand into the stores box, hooked out the leather bucket, and in pure s'Ffalenn temper pitched it at Dakar's middle.

The Mad Prophet fumbled the catch. Smacked hard in the gut, he whooshed out a gusty belch of air that cost him the breath for rejoinder. As he stalked off in stick-snapping pique, the Master of Shadow resumed with unbroken mildness, 'How are you feeling?'

Halliron closed his functional eye. Denied its vibrancy, his seamed skin draped like wet paper over his nose and cheekbones. His eyebrows sketched a pale smear above sockets sunken into his skull. 'My bones don't take kindly to knocking about,' he admitted on a near-soundless breath.

Arithon swallowed. Sorrow overcame his spent strength. He shored up his weight on clenched fists; and for long-drawn, agonized minutes, only the fluting calls of thrushes plinked through the gurgle of brook water. Yet another company of mounted lancers thundered past the bend in the road, while below the bank of the gully, Dakar cursed and blundered to a chorus of thrashed bracken and turned stones.

'Arithon,' Halliron said with sudden force, the more wrenching as numbed lips slurred his speech from its trained and mellifluous clarity. 'You must inherit my lyranthe. My left hand has lost feeling. The fingers won't move. Let the last song I leave to Athera be the musical tradition you continue.'

The knuckles clenched against the wagon boards flexed once in soundless protest. Beyond that, Arithon never moved. His answer came simple and steady. 'I'd be honoured.'

Released as if cut from a wire, the Masterbard relaxed beneath the blankets. 'Bless your directness.' A half-smile tugged his seamed cheek. 'You shall be great. I'm not wrong. Your skill shall surpass my best talent, perhaps restore the grace of the Paravians our troubled kingdoms have forgotten.'

'You speak of dreams,' Arithon interrupted. While the buckskin gelding in the traces flicked its tail and twitched off flies, he twisted aside to mask an anguish grown suddenly too fierce to stamp down.

'No dream.' Halliron freed his arm and clasped the wrist of his successor in a reassurance undercut by icy weakness. 'One day the old races shall return. The Fellowship has never lost hope.'

His truncated smile stretched wider. 'I shall live to see the sun shine over the river delta at Innish.' The one, lightless eye flicked up briefly and enlivened pinched flesh with wry amusement. 'I had that much of Dakar.' As if the admission stole vitality, the Masterbard's hand slid down, limp. His unswollen lid drooped closed again. 'So you see, I really didn't mind playing the fool to win the Mad Prophet's freedom, nor to give that horrid mayor his come-uppance. There's only home left ahead, now. I want to die reconciled with my family . . .'

Arithon stirred, straightened, and with the rags of his unstrung dignity, smoothed down the rucked blankets. 'Rest easy. Sleep if you can. The moment it's safe, I'll find you a bed and a healer.'

Yet when twilight settled over the roadway and mantled wooded hill-sides under felted layers of dark, the pony cart bearing the Masterbard laboured scarcely three leagues further to the south. Twice more, Dakar pulled aside into hiding, with Arithon forced to spin shadow to mislead determined headhunters. Resolved not to quit empty-handed, the returning trackers and riders dispersed in formation to sweep the cobalt gloom of every spruce thicket they passed.

Clouds rolled in after sunset and sifted down veils of fine drizzle. Dakar hunched in hostile silence; slack reins left the pony free to pick its own course through the ruts, while the cart's painted wheels splashed and serried the pewter gleam of shallow, scattered puddles. Tucked dry under spread canvas, Halliron rested unmoving.

By the tailgate, damp to the skin, his arms folded over drawn-up knees to contain the cramps that knifed through him, Arithon endured the ongoing physical reaction to his past night's performance with scarcely a whimper of expelled breath. The Mad Prophet knew magecraft well enough to guess how each jolting bump fed his suffering. Since misery to his deceiver would just gratify his passion to retaliate, Arithon clenched his jaw and managed not to plead for respite. The cart must stop shortly for Halliron's sake. A camp would be chosen in the open on a site that allowed for immediate flight.

Except for the wet, the weather stayed mild. High summer tasselled the verges in groundsel and vetch, and feathered the grasses in seed heads. Too long constrained by town walls, Arithon savoured the rain-drenched scent of meadow flowers, spiked by the pitchy bite of evergreen. Now and again the east wind's breath wafted salt-scoured taint off the bay. Attuned to the dance of the seasons in sound, where his mage-sight had deserted him, he bent thought to pick out the chord of the earth through the racketing creak of the wheels; in notes subtly echoed in the warning pipe of killdeer, and between the nighthawks' thrumming, madcap flight. With closed eyes, by ear alone, he could delineate the junction of horizon and sky, while the high, sweet harmonics of stars beyond cloud chimed just outside his wakened perception.

At that moment, Dakar snapped erect and ripped out a venomous oath.

Rein leather hissed through the terrets. The buckskin snapped up its rain dripping head and the pony cart jerked to a stop. Yanked back to the stresses of overplayed nerves, Arithon raised his head in alarm from the wrists crossed and draped on his knees.

But the patrol he presumed had overtaken them seemed nowhere in evidence. There arose no thunder of spurred horses, nor the shouts of exultant guardsmen. Blurred through the drizzle, the way stretched empty ahead, alive with the rasping trill of tree frogs, and the swish and drip of breezes that riffled across soaked leaves. Nothing appeared to be amiss. Except the buckskin pony stood with raised neck, black-tipped ears pricked through his sodden swag of mane.

'Fiends plague me for a mush-brained idiot,' Dakar carped. 'I should've expected no less.' He snapped the driving lines across his palm, then cursed the more fiercely for the sting the wet leather delivered.

Arithon blinked water from his lashes and saw, stamped in the gloom above the puddles, the blacker form of a horseman, cloaked and waiting with a statue's nerveless patience across the road in their path. The pony whickered greeting through moist drifts of steam. It fretted the bit against Dakar's hold, then stamped to a silver spray of runoff.

The black ahead never flicked a muscle. He could have been a phantom's horse, he stood so still; until his rider's crisp speech dispelled illusion. 'Bring the cart on. There's a dry cave nearby with a fire lit where the smoke is unlikely to raise notice.'

The voice was Asandir's.

Arithon shut his eyes in relief, while in dire trepidation, Dakar swallowed complaint and eased his deathgrip on the pony.

The sorcerer led the way off the road to an overhang chiselled into a hillside. Some long-dry flow of spring water had etched the floor into hollows, quilted now by the musty detritus of last year's fallen leaves. The slope of the hill and the cart parked outside broke the brunt of the wind. Asandir tended a small birch fire beneath a seam that formed a natural chimney. Beside its sweet burning warmth, Halliron rested in blankets. Throughout the labour of unloading supplies, Dakar kept the scowl that had ridden his features since Jaelot, his lips pulled into a down-turned bow as if crimped by an over-taut stitch. Too brusque to humour his grudges, Asandir summarily ordered him out to mind the horses.

Without more delay, the sorcerer shed his dark mantle and knelt at the Masterbard's shoulder. As his light touch explored the bruised flesh and hot swelling beneath the limp fronds of white hair, he said to Arithon, 'Forgive me. Your own discomfort must wait.'

Seated on Halliron's other side with his knees drawn up and his chin cupped, Arithon scarcely stirred an eyelash. 'Don't you think I'd help you if I could?'

The unalloyed shame in the words gave Asandir pause. Then his hands resumed their review, while firelight played disappearing games with the creases scribed on his craggy face. Night sealed the cave in misty dark. Summer moths blundered in erratic circles through the updraughts raised by the smoke. Scorched out of flight, a delicate blue and mauve one snagged in Asandir's robe. There it battered a dying tattoo and powdered dusky crescents against the weave of the wool.

Outside, the carol of a late-singing mockingbird entangled with Dakar's snarl at the buckskin to hold still; dampness had swollen the harness leather and jammed the tongues in the buckles. In methodical, quiet contrast, Asandir finished his examination. He touched a hand to Halliron's injured temple, and the other, fingers spread, across a forehead bruised like a plum. His gaze trained on the face of his charge as he addressed the cause behind Arithon's statement.

'I gather that when Etarra's army attacked the clans of Strakewood, you engaged a spell of unbinding that has left your mage talents crippled.' A log settled and spat off hellish sparks. For a second the sorcerer was limned with red glare, a still figure poised in cold patience who held power to forgive or condemn. Then the shadows settled back and gentled him. Just as deceptively he seemed an old man, as worn by life's turns as Halliron. 'Just a little spell against a crossbow bolt, true enough, but your knowledge of grand conjury was abused. The consequence of that is most grave. Would you care to tell me the details?'

Arithon muffled a sound against the tight-shuttered palms of his hands, then raised a bloodlessly white face. 'Daelion forgive me, I've been over and over the memory. I relive the moment in nightmare and despise myself. But I can't think what other choice I had. Young Jieret survived. That's all that seemed to matter at the time.'

'Guilt,' Asandir said dispassionately. 'There's part of it, yes.' His next line stung like flung gravel. 'So, prince, are you guilty?'

Balled in a knot to quell his shaking, Arithon lashed back in desperation. 'Dharkaron Avenger only knows!'

'Then leave it there and be done with it!' His rebuke at sharp odds with his unhurried manner, Asandir moved a hand, traced a symbol on Halliron's chest, then transferred his touch to probe underneath the faded blankets. Aware that Dakar might blunder in at any moment, he added, 'As your maternal grandfather was remiss not to teach, you have only the present in your power.'

'Oh, but I don't,' Arithon said in gritty truth. 'Let me once encounter my half-brother and I'll kill him. Certainly he's kept himself busy, training new armies to stalk me. Desh-thiere's curse wasn't cast to be selective. Or is it better I'm stripped of my mage talent? When we fight, I can't misuse such gifts to slaughter every misled wretch sent against me.'

Behind this, the other grief sawed like dull wire: he should never have allowed his passion for music to slip his judgement in Jaelot. Had he not been overset by fury at the mayor's petty arrogance, had he not succumbed to the beguiling resonance instilled in Paravian mystery, the Mistwraith's curse might still be defanged, its geas of obsessive hatred denied any tangible target.

But Asandir gave that fallacy short shrift. 'Since Lysaer's resolve to restore Avenor, you knew you'd soon be forced from anonymity. Sethvir saw the same. He chose to grant most of your request.' A clipped gesture indicated the satchel tucked beside the stallion's heaped saddle packs. 'Those items sent from Althain may help. Have a look. I'll see to your health the moment Halliron is comfortable.'

While Arithon mustered his self-command to move and examine the bundle, and rain fell, and Dakar's bitten epithets shifted target to malign the black stud, Asandir raised his hands from the bard's body and traced a sigil of peace upon the air. 'How are you faring, Halliron, son of Al'Duine?'

Eased by the sorcerer's ministrations, the bard stirred and awakened. 'I do well enough, for a cripple.' In flamelight, his wide, opened eye appeared brighter, its pupil no longer distended; a faint blush of rose suffused the sills of his cheekbones.

Asandir traced his fingertips down the line of jawbone, neck and shoulder. Then, very gentle, he raised and massaged the numbed arm. His gaze all the while stayed locked with the old man's, now rekindled to a frenetic spark of life. The sorcerer said with meticulous care, 'The Mayor of Jaelot will end his life badly, in pain of his own devising.'

Halliron's slurred syllables refound their rhythm and came back in ringing sincerity. 'I'm sorry, then.'

'You would be.' Asandir's tension broke before a fresh smile. 'You're content?'

Neither one glanced aside as Arithon freed the last knot in the satchel and started to survey its wrapped contents.

'Should I not be?' Halliron managed a one-shouldered shrug that somehow missed seeming awkward. 'Dakar promised. I'll live to see Innish. That's the last of my desires.'

'The Mad Prophet claimed that?' Asandir's working fingers kept on, but his gaze assumed a jarring glint of iron. 'He's gifted with truesight. He wouldn't dare lie for your happiness.'

'Well then,' Halliron said peacefully. 'I'm more than content. My lyranthe passes to Arithon.'

Asandir glanced across the cleft in query.

Engrossed, the Master of Shadow still knelt with the lists that companioned Maenalle's letter. The set of brass instruments pulled from Sethvir's emptied satchel sliced out scintillant reflections as the sorcerer cut through his thought.

'You're fully aware of the implications, Teir's'Ffalenn?'

At the unwelcome use of that title, Arithon started and looked up. 'Forgive me, implications of what?'

'That Halliron leaves you his lyranthe.' Asandir never broke rhythm as he massaged the nerves in the bard's deadened wrist; but his eyes, fixed on Arithon, were metallically bleak and bright.

'Our Masterbard kindly offered as much.' Arithon creased the parchment into folds between wildly trembling fingers. 'I accepted as a formality, since I hoped Sethvir might send me the instrument I lost when the coronation went wrong at Etarra. She isn't here with the charts and the cross staff.'

Asandir spoke fast to deflect the inevitable question. 'No, your own instrument is not safe in storage at Althain.' Braced to mete out a cruel test, he added, 'She was smashed in pieces, at Lysaer's hand, by instigation of Desh-thiere's wraith.'

In one coiling move, Arithon shot to his feet.

'*Lysaer!*' The hatred behind his shocked outburst tore through and possessed him in an explosion all the more hideous for being mute. For a racking, volatile moment, exposed to a cruel glow of flamelight, the Shadow Master *became* the instrument of the Mistwraith's geas: a living, breathing weapon charged and driven to achieve his half-brother's death.

Still stressed to sickness from overplayed nerves, every snarling tic naked on his face, Arithon advanced three stalking steps. By the fire's edge, he checked sharply. A quiver wrung through him. His very heart seemed to stop. The fists at his hips uncurled into shaking as he expelled his pent breath in a rasping succession of gasps.

In still, fraught silence, Asandir measured the extreme act of will, as the Shadow Master fought his way back to sanity and coherence.

Arithon turned his face aside, then, his first shaken words for Halliron. 'Forgive me. I'd hoped you would change your bequest once you learned I held an instrument of similar quality. My word to you was made in that belief.'

Halliron dredged up his one-sided smile. 'Be at peace. The lyranthe I carry by tradition accompanies Athera's masterbard. Don't say you didn't feel the change in Jaelot. True music has tuned you to empathy. The power now flows through your hands, and the title is unequivocally yours.'

Arithon's shift into torment was sharp as a fast breaking stick. 'Ah, Ath, what have you given me if not another weapon for this feud?'

Aware of his grief, wise enough to stop protest, Halliron pushed half-erect and achieved the timbre and inflection he once commanded to arrest men's minds in mid-sentence. 'Yes. And you will make me no promises, not to use to the fullest what you've earned.' Steadied by Asandir's quiet grasp, unfazed by the threat of s'Ffalenn fury, the bard added, 'You forget. I have lived to see the sun's re-emergence, and your part in the Mist-wraith's defeat. If a masterbard's music can one day spare your life, or that of your loyal defenders, you will use it so, and without any binding ties to conscience.'

Arithon spun away in trapped pain. 'And if I twist that power to inflict more bloodshed and murder?'

Halliron pursued in fatherly forbearance. 'The gift was never given, but claimed.'

A widening pause ensued, while Arithon stood and grappled with the concept through tortured, horrified reassessment. As the fire sighed and crumbled in a vermilion fall of embers, the bard gently added, 'So it was with me, and every one of my predecessors back to Paravian times. I was wrong, perhaps, not to tell you in advance. I was not wrong to nurture your talent. That is my legacy to Athera.'

Eased back to rest by Asandir, the elderly singer closed his eyes. 'Abide this success. I'll have no oath from you. And, your royal word as given, you will accept the lyranthe that is your due.'

Arithon jerked around. Robbed of all grace, he stumbled past the fire. As if every tendon in his knees let go, he folded beside Halliron's blankets, bent his head and embraced the musician's withered shoulders. 'You have my gratitude, always, for everything. The joy you have given can't be measured.'

He withdrew his touch quickly, unable to master his grief, while Asandir used swift and subtle spellcraft to banish Halliron's suffering into the settled peace of sleep.

As the bard's laboured breathing steadied and deepened, the eyes of the Fellowship sorcerer and Athera's new Masterbard met and locked. 'He's dying, isn't he?' Arithon said.

The large-knuckled hands draped on Asandir's knees looked uncharacteristically helpless. 'Dakar has promised his return to Innish.'

Arithon pressed, 'Was that his guilt speaking, or true prophecy?' In response to the sorcerer's glance toward the invalid, he did not resist the tactful grip that raised him by the wrist and guided him away from the fire.

'Dakar's promise will need all my help to carry out. But that quandary must bide for the moment.' Firm that the admission was not to be dwelled on, Asandir bent, unbuckled a supply sack, and tugged out another blanket. 'Yours can't.'

Before the musty wool could be unfurled across his shoulders, Arithon snatched its folds, stepped back, and assumed the burden of his own infirmity. He sat on the studded chest that held Halliron's court clothing, and the gesture almost looked natural enough to hide that his strength had given out.

A corner of Asandir's mouth twitched, the reflex of a smile suppressed. 'Every s'Ffalenn prince since Torbrand preferred his dignity over comfort.' He stepped behind the little coffer and laid hands as light as air over Arithon's muffled collarbones.

'Leave me the indignity and discomfort. Spare me the burdens of my ancestry.' A rapid, sweeping shudder coiled through the flesh under the sorcerer's touch.

Asandir shifted, trailed his thumbs up the sides of Arithon's neck, then resettled precisely spread fingertips. Under the damp coils of black hair, the scalp he probed burned as if wasted by fever. Over the snap of the embers and the runnels of rain over rock, he said, 'The vibrations that endow the earth mysteries are very finely attuned. Like the source that fuels grand conjury, too much exposure too fast can strike an imbalance between spirit and flesh. The rite you channelled through music in Jaelot was meant to be loosed under wards. Always in the past, the raw outflow was controlled by a circle of Paravian singers.'

Relaxed by a tingling influx of healing that settled and then gently eased him, Arithon bent his head and sighed. Sudden sweat sparkled on his temples and painted gilt tracks across the downturned slant of his cheekbones. In a catch of breath too quick to allow hope, he said, 'Dakar warned I'd be sick. It's simple over-extension, then?'

'Hardly simple.' Asandir flattened his hands over the crown of the Shadow Master's head and pressed down. 'But had you lost the inherent source of your mage talent, I can promise you would be dead, as any other untrained mortal would be, who bridged the path for such powers.'

To mask the sharp tremor that ripped him, Arithon said, 'But if that's true, I have no access. The acts I committed in Strakewood have left me blank and blind.'

'The channels that transfer the higher vibrations are still intact,' Asandir admitted, dispassionate. 'The spells of unbinding you meddled in brought their own measure of damage. The magnetic flow of your aura suffered some misalignment. Given time, you have full potential to heal. But first your spirit must win self-forgiveness past the tenets of your own s'Ffalenn conscience.'

Arithon recoiled as though scalded. 'Ath! Not that. I am cursed. Where are the sureties? You know when Lysaer's armies find me, Desh-thiere's geas will just drive me to repeat the very same atrocities.'

Asandir's hands reclaimed their grip and clamped down like unmerciful shackles. 'You wanted the truth. If you mend, you must find your own path back to balance.' Then, sorrowfully aware that the shudders under his hands were no longer due to cramping, but to a silent, bitter struggle against despair even weeping could not ease, the sorcerer engaged his power with stunning force, and felled Rathain's prince into sleep.

Once the blankets were rearranged, and slack limbs laid straight and made comfortable, he looked up to find the Mad Prophet poised against the tinselled fall of rain, arms clenched through bundled loops of harness.

'Dakar? Did you think I didn't notice you were listening?'

The brass chime of buckles accompanied a shame-faced step forward, and a terret caught light, round and gold as a wyvern's eye. 'Arithon's blinded his mage-sight?'

The sorcerer arose from his crouch in a spill of disturbed air. 'Did you think I assigned him your protection for mere whim?'

'Why am I last to be informed?' Dakar tossed his load in a clashing slither beside the unloaded gear from the pony cart. 'Great Ath, I've served you both as plaything since the wintertime.'

'I *sent* Rathain's prince to collect you,' Asandir corrected acidly. 'If he chose to keep you outside his confidence, that was his privilege. Should you wish his trust, you're going to have to earn it.'

Affronted past speech, Dakar slung off his dripping cloak. He stamped to the fire to warm his hands, the back of stooped shoulders presented toward his Fellowship master.

But Asandir was nowhere near finished. 'Whatever anger you may feel, however sorely you take the fact that your faults make you easy to manipulate, nothing under Ath's sky can justify the promise you have groundlessly made to Halliron.'

Dakar cringed, eyes darting rapidly sidewards in vain search for excuse to escape. 'I only said –'

Asandir cut him off, ruthless. 'The old Masterbard will not make Innish in his current state of mind.'

Trapped, the Mad Prophet continued, 'But I thought –'

'No power inside the Major Balance can heal against the will of the spirit,' Asandir interrupted again.

Chastened to nervous habit, Dakar caught up a branch and stirred the embers. Sparks flared, brightening his sweaty flush. 'But Halliron has reason to live! With all his heart, he longs to rejoin his family.'

'A man's destiny is not ruled by desires alone, though to judge by your loose habits, you might mistakenly think so.' Sorrowful beneath his clipped tone, Asandir said, 'Mortal fate is more often subject to deeply buried human fears.'

Obstinate with guilt and confusion, Dakar parked his bulk on the woodpile. Outside, an owl hooted. Two spell-wrapped figures slept easy under blankets, while the rain fell and sluiced down the gully toward the hollow where the stream ran. Rasped to stripped nerves by the prick of the sorcerer's regard, Dakar jerked a birch log out from under his knee and hurled it into the fire. As draught-caught bits of ash winnowed and flared, harried upward by spiralling eddies, he said, 'Bother and fiends! Do me the kindness just once of telling me plainly where my fault lies.'

'The music that called Halliron to leave his family is now secure in the hands of a successor.' Inscrutable behind a billowed haze of birch smoke, Asandir sat down on an outcrop near the abandoned array of navigational instruments and rolled sea charts. 'His need to reconcile with his daughter and wife is undermined by dread. Halliron worries they will blame and reject him. On that point, I could give no reassurance. The wife is deeply bitter after so unkind an absence. The daughter was a child when her father left, too young to shape a firm opinion of his character.'

Reduced to cowering misery, Dakar said, 'Can anything be done?'

Asandir regarded him, merciless through a span of rippled air. 'Are you asking my help to mend your thoughtless pride? Or do you truly care for Halliron's sake?'

'Dharkaron's black Chariot!' Dakar exclaimed, shocked at last. 'What pride do I have? Had I never stepped whistling into Jaelot, the Masterbard would be hale, and by now reunited with his family!' He gulped a fast breath, jammed his knuckles in his beard, and finished in shattering defiance. 'I don't like Arithon. Punish me for that. But for what Halliron has sacrificed for me, and for my failures in his behalf, I beg you to lend him every consolation within reach of Fellowship powers.'

'You ask a very great deal.' Dim in silhouette against the seamed grain of shale, the sorcerer weighed and prefaced his decision. 'There's only one possible option. I can defer my review of the Mistwraith's prison and drive Halliron back to Jaelot in the pony cart. From the reactivated power focus there, I can spell-transfer us both to the waste of Sanpashir, forty leagues south-east of Innish.' The last facts were listed, in dispassion as pitiless as Ath's avenging angel. 'Halliron might not survive the transfer. He could die while crossing the desert. Or he might live to have an hour in the company of his wife and his daughter.'

The Mad Prophet made his choked plea. 'If there's hope of that much, then do it.'

'Blind haste got you into this quandary,' Asandir cautioned. 'I cannot engage grand conjury in the middle of the mayor's palace without upsetting Jaelot's citizens. The blame for the disturbance will certainly fall to Arithon. You are his assigned protector. When the call for your service comes due, are you prepared to share the price that he must inevitably come to shoulder?'

'If I must!' Twisty as a cornered rat, Dakar glared at his tormentor. 'But you ask the wrong man. What in five kingdoms would Arithon not give for the Masterbard's fulfilment?'

Asandir's sudden laugh rang unpleasant as pumice scraped on steel. 'That's the first time you've judged this prince fairly.' He knelt and started bundling the scrolls and instruments sent at Arithon's request from Althain Tower. 'Very well, Dakar. At dawn, I shall leave to convey Halliron to Shand. You will stand by the Master of Shadow, and woe betide you if you fail him.'

Preoccupied with easing off the sticks and nubs of kindling that had unkindly jabbed dents in his backside, Dakar took belated notice of the items in the sorcerer's hands. He shot to his feet amid a clattering fall of billets. 'I don't believe it!' he cried, rebounded with unmollified speed from whipped recrimination to curiosity. 'Those are Leinthal Anithael's charts.'

'His cross staff and compass, also.' As if the instruments that had belonged to the legendary Paravian navigator were of no particular significance, Asandir tied off the fabric of each packet. 'What did you think? That Sethvir keeps his storage shelves stocked like a commonplace chandler?'

'Never.' Dakar kicked clear of the miring faggots. 'You aren't giving those to the Shadow Master.'

When the only reply he received was the whickering snap of the birch fire, he wisely abandoned the subject. Much later, brooding and awake in damp blankets, he saw the answer was self-evident after all.

Begotten by a seafaring pirate prince on the splinter world of Dascen Elur, Arithon would naturally incline toward blue water. Since Athera's arts of offshore navigation had been lost with the Mistwraith's invasion, on shipboard he could steal the advantage. The armies his enemy amassed on dry land could scarcely cross trackless water to harry him.

After midnight, a freshening wind splattered droplets across Dakar's face. He awakened and barely in time, bit back a reflexive string of expletives. Flat on his back, eyes rolled upward in prayer, he listened.

Nothing stirred beyond crickets, scraping musically in the rock clefts. The embers of last night's fire picked out the arched bridge of Halliron's nose, the jut of one snowy eyebrow a chalked curve against pillowing wool. His left hand trailed free of the blankets, skilled fingers that would never again grace a fretboard fanned out in loose-knuckled sleep.

Dakar clenched his jaw. Determined not to dwell on a sorrow beyond his means to remedy, he peered through the gloom. The cloak-wrapped forms which reclined beyond the bard seemed equally quiet and oblivious. To the rear of the cleft, the seep of a spring plinked an erratic melody. Through the reedy draw of the coals and the rhythm of steady breathing, the Mad Prophet judged Arithon and the sorcerer were asleep.

He wormed forward on his elbows and tensed, stock-still. When his movement aroused no disturbance, a crafty smile split his beard. He slipped out of his bedroll, fumbled in the dark for a cloak damply redolent of horse, and groped after his boots.

Adept enough at sneaking from his countless nightly escapades with paramours, he stole to his feet. Wishing for carpets in place of mouldered leaves, and for predictable furnishings instead of heaped crates haphazardly unloaded from the pony cart, he eased his way ahead in furtive care.

Harness leather looped his leading ankle and roused a staccato chink of brass. Dakar paused, eyes widened as he mouthed a soundless epithet.

Nothing happened.

Only silence abraded his nerves. Convinced good fortune was still with him, he bypassed the obstruction and crept to the mouth of the cave. Mist grey-lit by moon-glow coiled past his silhouette, framed in a backward glance of apprehension with his footgear tucked under his elbow.

He reached the ravine undetected, jig-stepped a stride in relief, and scarcely minded as mud and bits of gravel sieved through the weave of his socks. To a slither of loose shale, he blundered through a sink hole, found a convenient rock, and sat down to don his boots.

He fussed a long time with the laces. Breeze lightly spiced with green balsam brushed his hair; above the ridge, an owl hooted. Lifted to giddy high spirits, Dakar thrust upright and pursed his lips to whistle.

A shadow barred his path: one cloaked in midnight blue and silver, that even the wind treated gently.

Dakar's ditty wailed wildly off key and died in a sucking gasp of breath.

'Avoiding nightmares?' Asandir asked in silken politeness.

'Actually, no.' A bit too shrill, the Mad Prophet shrugged. 'I drank too much water before I slept. Could you step aside? I need to –'

Still conversational, the sorcerer said, 'You took the money bag with you for *that*?'

Through an eloquent, frustrated stillness, Dakar shut his teeth with a click. 'Merciful Ath, I *hate* boats! You know how I suffer from sea-sickness.'

Asandir sighed over the skein of the wind through damp foliage. 'This time, you broke more than just my bidding. Your word *as given*, my errant prophet. You will render the service you promised.'

Overhead, the clouds parted. Shafts of white moonlight lit the mist beneath the pine boughs and blackened the shadows into velvet. The sorcerer's spread hand seemed pale and poised as the censure of an apparition. The soundless, lightless burst of conjury that followed harrowed Dakar clean through to the pith of his bones.

He blinked and stumbled back, struck to wordless outcry. But spellcraft speared through him and passed without pain. In suspicion, he assessed, but nothing seemed changed in him at all.

'What have you done to me?' Plaintive and shaken, he clenched his arms to contain the dread that yawned a sudden hollow in his chest.

The sorcerer's reply came frigidly precise. 'Nothing, unless you break your oath of loyalty.'

Excuses died. Dissolved to bleak honesty, Dakar stopped his hand-wringing affectations. 'You have no mercy and no heart. Why in the breadth of creation could you not see fit to assign me to Prince Lysaer's retinue? He at least was my friend!' At the sorcerer's fixed silence, the Mad Prophet ranted on. 'Arithon's a cheat and a trickster. He sent *young children* out to kill with Deshir's clansmen. You know this! How can you sanction the works and the cause of such a man?'

'I sanction nothing.' Asandir caught Dakar's shoulder in a vice-grip and shoved him back up the ravine. 'You have only to keep your charge alive.'

Long-strided, even over rocks in total darkness, the sorcerer made no allowance for the foot-dragging clumsiness of his apprentice. Behind his stony silence lay wider obligations the Mad Prophet rejected in blind obstinacy; laughably ironic, that Dakar himself had been the seer to shape the prophecy which held all their fates in its coils.

If the last living scion of the s'Ffalenn royal line chose to fare seaward to stall the compulsions of an unnatural geas, the tactic might stave off another war; might with just a little help buy the time for Kharadmon to complete their knowledge of the Mistwraith's origins. The least upset in unstable chains of event offered quandaries too dire to contemplate:

on Arithon's life and future rested the Fellowship's reunity back to Seven, and the key to the augury that balanced Athera's course and restored the lost presence of the Paravians.

Apparition

Jaelot's south towers speared through cobwebs of ground mist, and torches adjacent to the guard posts threw a muted snag of orange against predawn gloom like black pearl. Poised on a rise not far off, Asandir stood in studied stillness. One hand gripped the bridle of Halliron's buckskin gelding; the other fretted knots from its sweat-damp mane, while farm vehicles gathered and milled in the road for the horn call to signal the gate's opening. Exposed to plain view on the verge though he was, no one glanced Asandir's way.

The air hung dense with sea salt, fragrantly sweetened by summer-cut hay hauled in to stock the lofts above the carriage sheds. The plod of draught beasts and the creak of battered vegetable crates wove through the imprecations of a goodwife who nagged at her spendthrift husband. Not two yards distant from the sorcerer, a courier with the mayor's lion blazon on his saddlecloth reined in his foam-flecked mount.

The pony cart might as well not have been there, for all the notice it drew. While Halliron slept under blankets, Asandir measured the timbre of his breathing and swept the sky with anxious eyes. Night was waning too swiftly. The beacon light by the quay shed a sullen, smothered halo, while the dirge-deep toll of the fog bell slammed the air with vibrations. The pony gently lipped the sorcerer's sleeve, then for no apparent reason, jerked his head sharply and snorted.

The next instant, an icy lick of breeze showered the dew from the grasses.

It flattened Asandir's tunic to gaunt shoulders and flicked the ends of his hair against the weathered hollow of his cheek. Roused in mild query, he asked, 'Luhaine?'

'Sethvir had a notion you might need me.' A blot in the dimness resolved into the rotund image of his discorporate Fellowship colleague.

159

Luhaine interlaced plump fingers and reviewed the press before the gate-house. 'I gather you're wanting a concealment ward and probably a diversion for these countryfolk? A spell of misdirection?' Petulant as a librarian with a clutched load of books, the discorporate mage peered down his nose. 'Never mind that such arts of trickery are much better suited to Kharadmon's profligate style.'

'I regret to offend your principles,' Asandir said agreeably. 'But Kharadmon isn't here.'

'No.' Luhaine affected a sniff. 'Well then. You can't very easily attend Halliron's needs and engage a major power focus while every lout in Jaelot stands as witness. Though truthfully, I shouldn't mourn the tiniest bit if society here perished from the shock.'

Confounded by his colleague's quirky penchant for lofty language and lectures, Asandir ran out of tact. 'Daybreak is all but upon us.'

'You always did like to rush,' Luhaine grumbled. 'If I still lived enfleshed, I should much rather drive Halliron's gelding than play pranks and spells on armed guardsmen.'

For answer, Asandir climbed back behind the buckboard, flicked the reins, and rolled the pony cart into the roadway amid its jostling trains of oxen; its high-bred, liveried couriers; and packs of cross-gartered, sunburned farmers who ruminated over summer rains and crop blight.

Luhaine's image unravelled into a swirl of cold that caused draught beasts to blow and shy against their traces. The farmers at their lines needed full attention to control their jostling teams. Wives and field-hands brought along as helpers became engrossed in grabbing baskets of onions and vegetables that threatened to topple, or hogs that squealed and suddenly shouldered to burst enraged from their crates. Luhaine's craft was seamless enough that even little children on their mothers' knees never blinked as the bard's painted cart passed them by.

'I suppose you also expect me to contrive something to prod the watch to raise the gates.' Without Kharadmon's jibes to divert him, Luhaine liked to complain. 'That's a great deal to ask, at brief notice.'

But then, the grand conjury required to transport Halliron to Shand would become vexingly more difficult without assistance from the dawn-tide surge across the ancient power focus. Resigned to an exasperated eddy, the discorporate sorcerer departed. A moment later, movement harried through the guardsmen on the gate turret. Their captain at arms shouted something querulous up the stairwell, his phrase bent by Luhaine into unintelligible echoes. The misinterpretation did not happen by chance; the horn call for daybreak winded its mournful note with the sky still grey as smoked quartz.

Over the consternation that convulsed the duty watch to argument, Asandir murmured words that no other living ears overheard. A puff of miffed breeze, Luhaine flicked by in acknowledgement. As the windlass in the gatehouse groaned and turned and Jaelot's grand portals cracked open, a scowling churl with a cartload of chickens discovered a spurious reason to divert his team and trade gossip with a sheep drover. The sorcerer steered the cart smartly through the gap and trotted the pony through the arch.

The hanging tin talismans that had failed to repulse iyats jangled sour protest as the draft that was Luhaine trailed after him. Never loquacious, Asandir shot a scathing glance toward the space his colleague now occupied.

'Well, certainly you needed none of my assistance with the gate guards,' Luhaine admitted. A ribby mongrel scavenging garbage amid the wreckage of a cook shop raised brindled hackles and growled in his direction. A pebble dropped out of nowhere. Lightly rapped on the nose, the cur tucked tail and bolted, while Luhaine resumed, a touch sulky. 'Let's say it's a matter of subtlety. I know what you've done to ease Halliron. Don't pretend that buckskin pony drew this vehicle nightlong without your arcane intervention. Such needs have taxed you, I should think, without the added burden of Jaelot's hysterical fear of sorcery.'

Asandir's lips turned down in chiselled disgust. Above, the sky had brightened. Limned in shaded grey, the thoroughfare ahead lay jammed with flung wreckage where the earth's heightened energies had surged in exultation on the solstice. Roofs shorn of shingles and planking lifted skyward in spindly silhouette. For the follies of masons grown deaf to the mysteries, for the human obstinacy of blind greed, Asandir loosed a soft sigh. The little cart rattled bravely around a mangled stoop and past a brick mansion with all of its shutters torn off. Where the street cobbles were not ploughed up wholesale, the wheels grated over smashed flowerpots, and crushed stalks of festival poppies whose leaves, against nature, had not wilted. A hacked signpost leaned beside a lilac tree frothed in unseasonal bloom. The perfume thickened the sea air, underhung by rotted offal from the markets.

'Folk here are unlikely to forgive or forget the way Arithon spoiled their holiday,' Asandir allowed finally.

He guided the pony down Broadwalk Way, strewn still with petals and scorched garlands, the buckled slabs of flagstone paving stitched through by improbable grass. A lampblack who sauntered through a side alley turned his head at the ring of hooves and wheels. When his searching glance encountered nothing solid to partner the sounds that approached, he dropped his satchel and fled in wild panic. Then just as suddenly he stopped, his fear rearranged to blank puzzlement as Luhaine's concealing ward touched him. While the byway fell behind, the sorcerers overheard him, scratching his beard and musing on the perils of strong drink as he retrieved his tools from the gutter.

The cart reached the head of the grand boulevard, masked by a freezing ring of spells. At Asandir's urging, the pony arched its neck, threw its chest against the collar, and hauled its painted burden up the shallow marble stairway before the entry to the mayor's palace.

Glass from burst rows of bow windows gleamed in the growing light. Between skewed columns and pilasters spider-webbed with cracks, the doors gaped apart, wrung half off their hinges and trailing the shreds of blistered paint. The buckskin snorted to a jangle of bit rings, then clattered over the lip of the upper landing. There Asandir steadied the reins. The grate of iron wheels across satin-finished stonework whispered to a stop in the foyer.

A flare of grease torches burned in the cavernous chamber beyond. Unaware of any visitors, a weary band of drudges laboured with baskets and shovels to clear debris and slagged tiles from the mayor's devastated banquet hall.

The icy vortex that was Luhaine poised above their heads, an arc of disturbance only Asandir could see. 'Now you perceive why Sethvir deemed my presence might be needful. Unless your wish includes transport for twelve local servants to the desert flats of Sanpashir?'

'Confound every one of them to Sithaer!' Vexed by the jostling Halliron had taken in the course of ascending the stair, Asandir raised his brows. 'They're about to be treated to the scare of their lives in any case. At least in the middle of a wasteland, more ignorant talk couldn't cast further doubt on the character of Rathain's prince.'

'A most telling point.' The discorporate mage winnowed his way to the floor through a gloom mazed in smoke, now steeped in growing blue by the east-facing casements. 'But do please remember your earlier insistence, that sunrise won't wait for debate.'

Already moving, Asandir looped the reins and stepped down from the buckboard. He bent to Halliron, touched the bard's slackened limbs through the blankets, and measured the ebbing signature of life-force. Where the current snarled or faltered, he trailed gentle lines of power and coaxed the flow even and straight. He set healer's sigils to stabilize and runes to preserve. His delicate work left trailers like sparks, that faded softly through the wool and revitalized the flesh underneath.

Presently, Halliron opened his one eye. Above him, etched in sharp clarity against a meaningless background, he beheld the Fellowship sorcerer, Asandir, who regarded him closely in return. 'Kingmaker,' he addressed, the title taken from the lines of an ancient ballad. Pained by a voice gone gritted and slurred, he drew breath to clear his throat and was stopped by the barest pressure of spread fingers against his chest.

'Don't waste your speech,' said the sorcerer, his eyes as fathomless as silvering on a new mirror. 'I'm taking you homeward, to Innish. The passage ahead will be rough. Before we go, is there any word you would have me say to your family?'

Halliron blinked. He showed no distress at the inference that the spell-ridden journey might stress his frailty beyond salvage. 'I wrote a song for my wife and daughter that I am too ruined to perform. Arithon knows it. Let him sing my words for me, when he can. If he plays just once for my family, they will hear of my love. His art will gain their understanding, that he is my legacy to Athera.'

Asandir gathered the cold, limp fingers of the hand left nerve-dead from injury. 'Cherish my hope, master minstrel. You'll be there to sing for yourself.'

'You sacrifice too much on my behalf,' Halliron whispered, suddenly adrift in spinning weariness.

The sorcerer cradled the bard's temple in one steady hand. 'For the deep happiness you have lent the Prince of Rathain, and for your years of unstinting service, our Fellowship would grant you sky and earth.'

The touch warmed like gentle fire through an aching pressure of cold mist. Halliron let the air spin out of his throat. His eye drifted closed. Asleep or unconscious, he never felt the scalding lattice of mage-force that Asandir raised to ward the wagon that cradled him.

When the sorcerer finished, nothing inside could be seen through the unshielded glare of raw spells.

Beyond the low stair, two laggard servants departed in haste through a side door; Asandir stifled a grin for the geas Luhaine had chosen, which harried them to leave in a pressing false need that their bladders required relief.

Then his levity faded. 'There's a problem I've had to leave unfinished.' Aware of Luhaine's attention like a quill prick against exposed skin, Asandir qualified. 'The Duke of Alestron and his brothers were absent when I visited to see if they meddled in forbidden armament. I agree with Sethvir: their evasion hides purpose. Would you mind looking in on them?'

Then, too pressed to wait while Luhaine assembled his usual lugubrious reply, Asandir stepped to the pony's bridle and guided its skittery, nervous progress down tiled risers left scoured and trenched with cold scorch-marks. Behind him, the iron-rimmed cartwheels banged and slammed, and chipped parallel grooves of fresh cracks. The vehicle jounced onto level floor and scrunched across fragmented flooring.

Luhaine admonished on a surly nip of frost, 'No doubt you want the wardings checked on Desh-thiere's prison at Rockfell Peak beforehand?'

'Well sunrise won't wait,' Asandir threw back, insouciant.

Overhead, muted light slit the high, lancet windows miraculously still paned in filmed glass. Asandir reached the ash-blackened edge that traced the near rim of the power focus. He stroked the pony's nose, murmured into its ear, then straightened. He spoke his next incantation in Paravian, each lilted cadence and musical vowel cut and measured to stamp the air into arcane seals like edged foil.

Power answered.

Too mighty a flux for concealment, the force rocked a tremor through the building. Now each consonant snapped out and hammered into echoes that sifted falls of plaster from the ceiling groins. Ozone tanged the hazed spill of dust. Then stillness locked down, fixed as light trapped in glass, and the pattern underfoot flared alive.

A silver-blue shimmer raced through the old runes. The cart rolled over their heatless light, and the pony loosed a gusty, frightened snort. Its hooves jinked and rattled over glassy chips of tile as it sidled, uneasy in the traces.

Asandir soothed a hand over sweating buckskin hide, his touch now all he could spare to calm the pony's frayed nerves. For need, he attuned his awareness through his boot soles to gauge the flow of forces in the focus. The static of the lane-pulse jagged in white bursts, sparked by the advent of sunrise. Careful to sound its resonance lest the pattern's function had been impaired or corrupted by time, the sorcerer quickened step. He crossed the two inner circles, then positioned the cart on the interstice at the centre where the axis of all lines converged.

Brightening glare lined his chin with hard light as he braced in preparation. 'Luhaine.'

On that spoken signal, he ceded the powers he had awakened to the control of his discorporate colleague. All ties to sensation left him. The sole thread that grounded his consciousness to flesh became his gentling hand on the pony. The nexus of his will bent into a craft honed through thousands of years of experience. Nothing else mattered. Nerve and bone would unravel before he lost hold on his wards to shield Halliron from the wrenching flux of spell-transfer.

Daybreak charged the lane.

Power whined and crested. The pattern flared, then shattered past visible light into a pealing vibration. Luhaine's deft mastery trapped the enabled current, then directed an unruly dance of forces to turn, mesh, and ignite wild power into an orchestrated explosion.

A crack ripped the unshielded air. Winds blasted. The torn seams of tapestries whipped to frayed threads, and every glass flask and window-pane left whole in the mayor's palace burst to sugared powder and blew outward. For an awful, time-rending instant the confines of the feast hall lay scoured in primal glare.

Then normality reasserted. Eddies of mauled air spun and died. Tile fragments raked into crannies, then skittered and chinked back to rest. The spellcraft raised through the focus pattern pulsed and dimmed, and slowly died. The sorcerer, the cart and its occupant were gone, delivered to a ruins in Sanpashir's desert. The place they had occupied in Jaelot held only a smoking curl of dust and a pile of steaming manure.

For that; for the crazed marks of wheels and the crescent-shaped dents that the pony's shod hoofs had gouged in the marble stairway, a second sorcerer whose spirit was discorporate had no polite means to fix. Luhaine departed, a drifting wisp of cold, as drudges, servants and blue-blooded residents gave way to hysterical screaming.

A blind fool could guess that Halliron's apprentice sorcerer had revisited, to terrorize the city with more spells.

In due course, dishevelled officials raised in haste from their beds converged to assess the fresh damage. They called guardsmen to set chains on the perpetrators; except there were none to be found.

The Mayor of Jaelot's smashed feast hall lay uncannily empty. The roster was changed, the day's patrols recalled from the gate house, while his lordship fumed and paced. The lyranthe-playing sorcerer his judiciary wanted burned had escaped through thin air, beyond all reach of due process.

Hallucination

Dakar awakened late to the cinders of a burned-out fire. Halliron, the sorcerer, and the pony cart bearing them had departed before first light, with a note left behind in explanation. The black stud remained, pawing restlessly by the tree that tethered its headstall. Grumpy and sore from scanty sleep, Dakar stumbled out of his blankets to root for a snack amid the cache of supplies.

Nearby, damp-haired from a wash at the stream, Arithon crouched over the sorcerer's saddle packs, immersed in thoughtful study as he fingered a heavy gold coin. Clearly recovered from the past night's distress, he looked up at Dakar's blundering. His expression seemed as affable as the manner he had affected in disguise as a masterbard's apprentice.

Curdled to distrust, Dakar stared until he tracked the elusive discrepancy: a striking, indefinable tension infused the Shadow Master's presence. Stripped of the shadows he had used to veil his features, his poise reminded of a wildcat set to stalk.

'This coin is riddled with spell-wards,' he opened, his flexible voice inquiring. 'I hear them. But without more experience, I couldn't unravel the purpose behind their harmonics.'

Dakar squatted, rifled the nearest canvas bundle and fished out a wrapped loaf of bread. Guardedly wary, he settled on his hams and broke the crust. 'If Asandir left that to pay the black's stabling, it's rotten with mage-craft, sure enough.' Through a bulging mouthful, he qualified. 'You'll see that bit of gold get passed from hand to hand, from ostler to horse trader, and the stud, whether sold or rented to post riders, will find his way back to his master. He'll be where Asandir next has need of him, glossy and fit, and have not a whip mark on him.'

Arithon's interest turned rueful. 'My worry was wasted, I see.'

The sailing instruments; Dakar kicked himself for lapsed wits. With

Arithon bound seaward, a horse would be useless as tits on a fish. Disgusted to find the bread as unpalatably stale as the ship's biscuit he heartily detested, the Mad Prophet stamped off to the stream to wash down the crumbs and relieve himself.

Arithon used the interval to pack the small camp and scatter the dead embers of the fire. When Dakar puffed back uphill, he was waiting, the black stallion's bridle reins looped through one hand. Spattered green-gold in new sunlight, his black hair thrown back from angled cheekbones, the prince who was Master of Shadow appeared absorbed by the trill of the woodlarks that flitted through the boughs overhead; except the eyes he turned upon Dakar stayed emerald-hard and measuring as a trap cocked and baited to draw blood.

The Mad Prophet stopped. Determined to stay nonchalant, he hitched chubby fingers in his belt. 'You plan to ride.'

'To Ship's Port, I think.' The invitation casual, Arithon added, 'We'll take turns in the saddle, if you wish.'

The rage rose thick and hot, until Dakar felt he might strangle. 'Do as you please. I'm not going.'

'I'd thought not.' Arithon slipped a thong at the saddlebow; a canvas packet slithered loose. He flicked a neat wrist and tossed it.

Slammed in the chest by the bundle, Dakar staggered backward, gasping into the smoke-tainted cloth reflexively clutched in his arms.

'That's your share of our stores.' Over his shoulder as he vaulted astride the tall stallion, Arithon finished, 'Don't waste the coin on cheap doxies.'

'Bastard! You planned that I wouldn't be coming.' The last imprecation flurried the woodlarks away on scared wings. 'You insufferable son of a bitch!'

'Yes, to the first, who denies it?' Touched to a wicked edge of laughter, the Shadow Master raised his eyebrows. 'But the last? Dakar! How unfortunate for Lysaer.' The black stud snorted and shouldered ahead at the brush of his rider's heels. 'We did after all share a mother.'

Jostled aside, then dealt a buffeting sting by the whisk of the black's departing tail, Dakar kicked a log and howled insults until his ears rang. The fit gained him no satisfaction.

Sometimes fate seemed to dog him like the fury of an unpaid whore. Never mind the small blessing that the rain had dried up; from the moment the Mad Prophet set off hiking, the day grew perversely less pleasant.

South of Jaelot, the coast road jagged inland, to the east hemmed by rock-slashed ravines capped in fir, ruched and ruffled like a widow's collar around the stripped peaks of the Skyshiels. To the west, in summers when storms stayed mild, rolling meadowland quilted the hills in a sun drenched patchwork of hayfields. Between pocketed hollows where the farmers' crofts clustered, blooming larkspur twined sprays of indigo amid daisies, and yarrow splashed in drifts like white foam. Under wide, cloudless sky; across broad, wind-combed acres, any spirit escaped from an onerous duty might revel in new-found freedom.

Yet Dakar took no joy from leagues of magnificent scenery. By noon, his eyes itched and his nose ran; country air had never agreed with him. Each step he took reminded him how much he detested travel on foot.

The nap he snatched to refresh himself became spoiled by the diabolical placement of an ants' nest. Scratching and twitching and shaking out his clothing, he sought second refuge by a streamlet. There he fell asleep in comfort, only to discover as twilight came on that foraging muskrats had ripped open his pack and devoured every crumb of his food.

Too lazy to regret the ward-spells he might have set to protect himself, Dakar flagged a ride with a merchant's drover bearing candles and bees-wax. Since the heat of full day would damage the wares, the wagon travelled to market by night. The Mad Prophet tucked into a niche behind the buckboard, contentedly primed to share gossip.

At midnight, beaten down by judicious wheedling, the drover shared his meal of barley bread and ham. Dakar cheerfully stuffed his belly, only to waken shortly afterward, doubled over and moaning with cramps.

The meat had likely been spoiled. Far too crafty to voice such suspicion, the Mad Prophet rocked and clutched his belly. 'That stream water must have been tainted.'

The drover met the excuse with the same sappy nonsense he used to soothe his draught mules. Self-absorbed in a misery that spiked like white fire through his groin, Dakar missed the moment when his benefactor's sympathy changed to shouted imprecations.

His next clear sensation was the dry jab of weed stalks prickling into his cheek. A pungency of road dust and pepper grass made him sneeze, a detail which forced recognition: the uncharitable drover had pitched him out on the verge. Dakar sweated through the bothered conclusion. He might languish of bellyache until crows came to peck out his eyes; not precisely the plan he had intended to escape his obligation to Asandir.

Too wrung by discomfort to care, the Mad Prophet closed his eyes. Small use to dwell on dying when he could dream more pleasantly of hot, lusty tavern girls and foaming tankards of ale.

He got instead a disruptive intervention by brisk hands that first rolled him over, then latched his armpits in a grip like torture and peeled him up from the ground. Sunlight hit his face and his eyes like a slap, while the world upended and spun.

After disjointed thoughts, he unriddled the indignity that he dangled face down over somebody's saddlebow. The shoulder of the horse that bore him was sweat sheened and black; the girth unfocused inches from his nose had been stitched with sigil patterns to discourage wear.

After centuries of being collected comatose from binges, Dakar knew precisely where he was. He groaned at the gouge of the pommel in his gut until unconsciousness mercifully reclaimed him.

The most vile hangover he had ever suffered hounded him back to awareness. He sensed darkness and a fire. A demon rode his skull, one that wore spurs a half an inch long and delightedly stabbed heels through his eye sockets. Clear-minded enough to bemoan the unfairness, since no drop of spirits had passed his gullet, he clamped sweaty hands to his temples. 'Gaaah,' he grated through parched tissues. 'I feel all ground into ruts by the wheels of Dharkaron's filthy Chariot. Where in Sithaer am I?'

A rapid-fire shower of lyranthe notes drilled like bodkins through his ears.

'It appears we came to share the saddle after all,' observed Arithon from some unseen place beyond the embers. 'Since you asked, you are currently sprawled on dry oak leaves, halfway down the road to Tharidor.'

The Mad Prophet ripped out a scatological epithet, then winced at the sting of his own vehemence.

'It could be worse.' Athera's new Masterbard dampened his instrument, careless of the string that sawed out a sullen buzz against the white-gold setting of his signet ring. Amused by Dakar's flinch, he added, 'You might still be lying in a ditch, abandoned to the crows and the insects. Do you get migraines often? The wax merchant's drover decided you had plague. He carried on about pestilence until you're lucky the northbound couriers didn't overhear. They'd have rousted the watch back out of Jaelot with faggots to burn your diseased carcass.'

'Never migraines.' Dakar sniffed in corrosive irritation. 'I got indisposed from eating spoiled ham.'

He covered his ears, whimpering and uncommunicative. Though his sour stomach relented by morning, he maintained an offended silence throughout three days of hard travel. Since the man was a fool who risked the temper of any s'Ffalenn prince, Dakar sneaked away by night and begged passage into Tharidor on the slats of a salt merchant's cart.

By noon, a whistle on his lips, he kicked open the door of the city's most commodious tavern. Blinking through the fusty murk of pipe smoke, he breathed in the smells of acid oak casks, unperfumed humanity, and thicker odours of hot grease and chicken meat roasting on spits in the kitchen.

The inevitable pack of idlers clustered by the hearth. Dakar nodded greeting and chose a bench between a group of whispering merchants, fastidious in their summer silks and lace, and a foursome of sun-cured deckhands. 'Beer,' he demanded to the bar wench who scoured the stones by the hob. 'The best brew the house has to offer, and also, a plate of spiced chicken.'

The deckhands renewed their squabble over a dice throw made by a cheater, while Dakar's order arrived. He licked his lips as the head foamed over clean glassware, then raised the tankard to catch the thick stream in his mouth, eyes closed in beatific anticipation.

The taste hit his tongue, bitter enough to scour the linings of his sinuses. He huffed and slammed backward in recoil that rattled the floorboards. His eyes bulged. Tears streamed down the flushed apple curves of both cheeks and he choked through a spray of expelled droplets.

'Fiends alive!' snapped the sailor across the trestle. 'If you're minded to sprinkle, do it elsewhere, matey. Or else, understand, I'll see your stinking lard carved up and stewed into lamp oil.'

Through a half-strangled fit of pure rage, Dakar spat into his tankard. Too husky to shout, he beckoned to the barmaid. 'Look here, what's this? The drink you serve is *vile*. Pure lye.' His tirade gained volume as the pucker in his throat began to loosen. 'Do you habitually try to poison customers?'

Drawn from the kitchen by the commotion, the landlord appeared, a meat spit clamped in hand like a battle mace. 'I won't have this!' He strode past the flabbergasted merchants and shook his iron implement at Dakar. 'My establishment serves the finest fare in Tharidor.'

'Oh?' Dakar folded his arms in mulish challenge. 'Then standards hereabouts must need a boost to lick the belly of a snake.'

The spit banged into the trestle and stuck there quivering, a hair's-breadth from Dakar's planted elbow. The landlord loomed over him and bristled with both fists cocked on his hips. 'You've no cause to sling lies and insults. If you can't handle a man's brew, go back to drinking fresh cider.'

Wide eyes averted from the metal that skewered the table, Dakar coughed into his cuff. 'Well, look, you try this.' He gave the tankard a shove with his forearm. 'I'll be fair and admit to poor manners if what slops inside doesn't scald your mouth to perdition.'

The sailhands' dice clicked and stopped in suspended stillness. By the hearth, the greybeard idlers leaned forward in fascination as the landlord scooped up the glass. The merchants looked on, more discreet in curiosity, as he quaffed the contents in one draught. Then he sighed, his features hard with animosity as he licked the foam from bearded lips and thumped the drained vessel rim downward beside the upright meat fork. 'You have a lively imagination, the sort that makes trouble I don't like.'

A jerk of his chin called two enormous thugs from the one dim cranny Dakar had neglected to watch. These grasped his elbows in bruising, cruel fingers and forcibly pitched him out.

Hours later, parked on his rump in the gutter with three knuckles skinned and one side throbbing to the ache of bruised ribs, the Mad Prophet ran tender fingers over a swelling black eye and conceded to woebegone defeat. He had sampled beer vats and wine shops the breadth of Tharidor and found not a potable drop. The town tosspots making their evening rounds singled him out for ridicule, until the last tavern he visited paid heed to rumour and as firmly as though he was afflicted or insane, turned him away at the door.

The meat from the sausage stall he visited as consolation caused his belly to churn and rebel. Wary by now of offended proprietors, Dakar stilled his complaint. As his sensitized innards clenched into fierce cramps, he squeezed back tears of aggravation, paid for his scarcely touched meal, and turned his back on the puzzled vendor to sit by the gutter to regroup.

In dark thought and vile temper, the Mad Prophet weighed the temptation to ease his troubles between scented sheets in a bawdy house. But even the thought of a paid doxy's comforts shot an unpleasant, warning tingle through his crotch.

Bearded chin propped morosely on the knuckles folded over his knees, his hair stuck like crimped yarn to his brow by the stifling, seaside humidity, Dakar began serious cogitation. While elegant, lacquered carriages and dusty drays rolled to whip cracks and jingling harness past his perch, his stumbling thought met enlightenment.

'Ath!' His burst caused an alley cat to streak behind a stack of barrel hoops. A street-child clad in motley stopped scavenging hand outs to regard him with startled eyes. Dakar paid neither any mind. 'Fiends plague that interfering sorcerer, what I really need is a herb witch!'

The street-child sidled nearer and gave him a winsome smile. 'Master, I know such a person. For a half-silver, I'll take you to her cottage.'

Dakar glowered at the waif, whose bare feet and rags masked a disingenuous, well-fed frame. 'Miserable robber.' But hunger and thirst overcame his will to haggle, and he grudgingly doled out the coin.

The herb witch brazen enough to practise her craft in Tharidor kept a squalid shack in the alley behind the tanner's yard. Shown to her sagging entry by the street-waif, who bolted immediately afterward, Dakar pinched his nose with sweaty fingers and regretted his need to continue breathing. The reek that drifted from the tanner's was overpowering, even without the witch's rain barrel, heaped under in desiccated entrails and alive beneath a sun-caught swirl of flies. The eyes of scavenging rats gleamed from the shadow under the footings, then flashed in darting retreat at his irritable rap on the door.

The warped, unpainted planks cracked to a squeal of tin hinges. Fingers curled around the edge, the nails ragged and rimmed with dried blood. 'Who calls?' came a scabrous whisper.

Gagged beyond speech from the stench, Dakar jingled his wallet.

His name and his origins now a moot point, the herb witch opened her door.

Daylight struck through into clutter and darkness, and roused a dusky rustle of wings. A sleepy rooster crowed, answered by a second, while a stinging billow of herbal smoke and incense swirled out into the street. The woman who straddled the sill peered outward with red-rimmed eyes. Her hair was a nest of pale, unwashed hair, stuck with thyme sprigs and a white fluff of breast feathers that looked to have drifted and caught there. She wore deerhide painted with sigils and food stains, and her skin was blue with ingrained soot.

'What're you wantin'? A love-knot? A health philtre?' She stabbed a knotty forefinger at the bulge of her visitor's gut. 'Must be a philtre, yes? Woman left you for someone more strapping, is it? Acting shy won't change the truth.'

Dakar blinked and coughed out bad air in affront. 'Actually, I need to have a geas lifted.'

The crone cackled as coarsely as her hinges. 'Some girl's put the come-hither on you, then? Ach, that's a pretty enough lie. You expect me to believe it?'

'This has nothing to do with problems concerning a woman!' Dakar snapped. 'Besides, if you have to slit open chickens to work an unbinding, I've certainly picked the wrong party.'

He spun to leave, but a pale hand shot out and clamped the wrist holding the money bag. 'Such hasty thinking, foolish man.' A breathy exhalation cracked into another wheezing laugh. 'And as for slitting chickens, some clients expect it, which is all to the good if they pay. But one does tire of stewed fowl for supper.'

Too late for trepidation, Dakar was jerked face-about and dragged inside by a grip like steel pincers.

The herb witch pushed him down on a chicken crate, and kicked her rickety door shut with the back of a bare, bony heel. She then bent her elbows and drummed skinny fingers on her hips, while surveying her newest client through a twining maze of incense smoke.

The reek of tanner's vats and offal crept undaunted through the musk of perfume. Breathing in tortured, shallow gulps, Dakar realized that, except for the chicken coop he sat on, the cramped little cottage was clean, if oddly furnished. Crates and cages for pigeons and barnyard fowl supported a trestle table, and a cot bright with woven shepherds' blankets. Bundles of herbs dangled from the rafters, their thrown shadows entangled with talismans sewn of felt and glass beads, and the dried, yellow claws of mummified birds' feet.

'My wares,' the crone admitted in brittle amusement. She bent, scrounged up a cloisonné tin of incense, and lit a fresh stick with a snap of her nail and a cantrip ripped out in burred consonants. Then she blew on the tip to fan the ember and fluttered her fingers toward the artifacts. 'Mostly charms to ward drowning for sailors. Waste not, want not, I should say, and the hens' feet add a nice touch of mystery.' She shrugged. 'Tharidor's fashionable types aren't big on spending for spellcraft.'

Pecked on the buttocks by the birds cooped up behind the slats where he perched, Dakar fidgeted. He looked everywhere else but at the woman, who shuttled and wove around his person, muttering and tracing odd, red symbols with her incense. Smoke trailed from the ember like demon writing, distorted and erased on the draughts. The gloom clearly outlined to mage-sight the haloes of warped spells entangled in each gruesome little charm bundle. The witch worked her craft in blood-magnetism and the deep, earthy mystery that sang through the roots of eldritch plants. The draw of the moon infused the wards over her shack and less clean things, which made the knotted seals that Koriani enchantresses amplified through crystal seem clear and straightforward by comparison.

Pressed by rising uneasiness, Dakar sought excuses to escape. 'I'm not at all sure you can help me.'

The crone snapped erect, rustily cursing. Her eyes flashed baleful as the rats' as she stubbed out the stick in a brass tray cupped inside a bird skull. 'Certain it is that I cannot!' She jabbed splayed fingers through the last spent embroidery of smoke. 'That's Fellowship magecraft laid on you! How dare you set me at risk, asking to break a geas of Asandir's making? Well, I don't meddle with that sort of binding, set as it is over your own given word.'

Chickens flapped and squawked as Dakar twisted to face her. *'That's impossible.* I never –' He stopped in remembrance and caught his full lower lip between his teeth.

The crone peered at his crestfallen expression through her maniacal tangle of hair. 'So,' she concluded. 'You are trapped. Well and truly bound, and with only your fool self to blame.' Her knees creaked under her deerskins as she leaned aside, scooped a pouch from a coffer and spilled out a painted set of knuckle bones. She spat once to dampen them, rolled them in her palm, and cast them skittering across the floor.

The last one whispered to rest against the toe of Dakar's boot. Beaked heads tilted behind the crate slats as the chickens fluffed and dropped guano in suspicious scrutiny.

'I can offer you only an augury, prophet,' the herb witch resumed in a rasp like rust across velvet. 'The man you must attend can be found two days hence, at sundown, in the shrine of Ath Creator by Ship's Port.'

Dakar crashed his fists on the bird coop and cried protest over the cackle of distressed fowl. 'And if I refuse to rejoin him?'

The herb witch lifted thin shoulders. 'Then, as you have seen, the geas of your Fellowship master will react in force and sour every pleasure of the flesh, even to the food and drink your body requires to survive.'

Dakar cursed in a mixture of languages and dialects. When he ran out of breath for his viciousness, a crafty look crossed his face. 'This geas. It ties me to the living presence of a man I consider an enemy. Is that where its limits lie?'

The herb witch nodded.

'Living presence?' Dakar prodded.

The flick of a dirty nail gave affirmation.

'Then I'll kill him,' he promised, the rage embedded in his heart like gravel pressure-forced into glacial ice.' If that's what it takes to win free of his company, Dharkaron as my witness, I'll see the last Prince of Rathain well and thoroughly dead.' The Mad Prophet shoved to his feet, fumbling after his silver.

But the crone snapped her chin aside and refused payment. 'Save yourself, sorry man. To reach Ship's Port in time for a rendezvous, you'll need all your coin to rent post horses.'

Journeys

Shadowed under gold-edged dunes in Sanpashir, while the ceaseless winds worry the carved ruts of cart tracks, a Fellowship sorcerer bows his head in mourning, then stirs and veils the face of the departed, who breathed through the glory of one last southern sunrise, but not long enough to know the coral walls and spindled towers of his native Innish . . .

Eventide dims the sea mists to lavender, and softens the jagged walls and shattered drum towers of Tysan's abandoned city of Avenor; above the ruin, on a hillock clothed in myrtle, the s'Ilessid prince just arrived laughs in the teeth of ancient fears, and assures the uneasy retainers at his back, 'Here will I raise walls and a family, and the armies that will march to claim victory over the Master of Shadow . . .'

While a lone rider on a black stud fares south-east, the Koriani First Senior reports of his journey to her Prime: 'Arithon is making for Ship's Port, surely bound for the open sea. He's escaped us before on dry land. Over water, how shall we track him?' And Morriel's reply, 'By means as old as time. Elaira shall be sent after him at my directive, to insinuate herself as his mistress . . .'

VII. *SHIP'S PORT*

The shrine to honour Ath Creator lay well outside the walled harbour of Ship's Port. No ceremonial building marked the site, nor ever had; the old beliefs took after Paravian ways, that an edifice of man's design need not glorify the prime power that had made and Named all Creation. Only a worn, dusty path indented across the grey cliffs above the bay gave evidence of any activity beyond the swoop of gulls and nesting ospreys. Shadows striped the grasses as Dakar slid stiffly off the back of his lathered mount. He looped the reins over a weathered deadfall, too worn to care if the hack shied back and tore the bridle.

Exchanging horses in relays, he had been in the saddle two days. Sores galled his backside and knees like fresh vengeance; mere pittance beside the rancour that griped him due to Asandir's geas. Riled as a smoke-hazed hornet, the lowering sunlight a flood of heat at his back, Dakar stalked down the narrow, stony defile toward the site of the shrine.

No voice disturbed the sour calls of fishing birds. The sussuration of surf funnelled up from the strand seemed the last sound in the world. The solitary trace of human presence was a musk of sublimated wax unreeling on the drafts between the crags. Dakar used the stone to brace his balance. Light-headed as wind itself from days of thirst and hunger, even the thin fumes of candles turned his senses.

The cliff path plunged in descent. Ahead and to the left loomed a grotto, cut off from sound and sunlight. Cherished by no priest or attendant, water welled melodiously from the dark earth, to twine in splashing rungs toward the tide flats. Above the spring's seeping brim, niches stepped into the natural rock cradled a sediment of congealed wax, dingy with trapped carbon and grained in lichens and moss.

Amid the remains of uncounted offerings left to celebrate Ath's mystery, fresh beeswax dips shone ivory and gold, flames fluttered in the humid sea air. Limned in their crawling halos, Arithon, Master of Shadow, stood in the shrine exactly as the herb witch in Tharidor had foretold.

He would have died in that moment, had Dakar carried a knife. Bereft of any weapon; pained enough that his gorge rose for the fact his knowledge fell shy of bane-spells or riddles of unbinding, the Mad Prophet stopped in helpless hatred.

If the enemy he passionately wished to throttle heard the scraped steps of intrusion, he never turned, but sparked flame to a final candle, then spiked the light on the ledge alongside hundreds of others. Minutes passed. The sky beyond the grotto purpled and sank into indigo, while inside, the uncertain fires hissed and dwindled, to drown one by one in puddled wax.

Still, Arithon did not turn. Left no channel for his anger, Dakar fumed until reason intruded to argue why a man might burn candles alone in Ath's shrine at dusk.

'He isn't gone!' the Mad Prophet burst out. 'Daelion Fatemaster grant me one prayer. Tell me Halliron didn't die before Asandir got him home to Innish.'

Arithon bowed his head. 'He passed the Wheel this morning. Just after sunrise.' Whisper-quiet and level, he added, 'Sethvir informed a soothsayer, who sought me out to bring word.'

Dakar swallowed awkwardly. 'I'm sorry. Ath, I'm so sorry.'

Immersed in grief and self-pity, he fumbled to a spur of rock, and sat, and lost to his impulse to weep. In respect for the departed bard's dignity, he found the restraint to keep silent until the final candle consumed itself in a spitting flare of wax; one drowned flame among thousands, an honour lit for a master singer talented beyond reach of millions.

Night by then had netted the last of the light. A movement in darkness, Dakar blotted streaked cheeks on his cuffs. He raised his head, shoved sticky hair from his temples, and discovered the shrine's niche left vacant.

A moment's search revealed Arithon standing outside, nervelessly still in a gloom that, for him, held no obstacle. Lined by the pale cream of surf, his black breeches and full sleeves fitted and neat, he faced Dakar with his head tilted an intent fraction to one side, much as he had in the past while he unriddled some melodic nuance of Halliron Masterbard's teaching.

Antagonized by a mannerism drawn from his former, false identity as Medlir, Dakar stiffened. 'You knew! You heard the resonance of the geas Asandir laid upon me and never bothered to warn.'

'I did ask about the coin, if you recall,' Arithon stated. 'The harmonic pitch set about your person has strikingly similar overtones.'

Dakar fired back a filthy epithet, but got no reaction for his trouble. Riled all the more since Arithon's patience could outlast him, he blurted, 'Well, what do you intend to do now?'

'I'm overdue to visit a certain tavern on Harbour Street.' The Master of Shadow pushed away from the rocks. 'You look as if you need a beer.'

'Ath, no,' Dakar cut back. 'Not again. That ploy won't serve any more to keep me pliant and drunk.' To thwart Asandir's geas and compromise the Shadow Master, he would need subtle planning and clear thought. 'Now that I know it's your company I keep, you won't catch me muddling my wits.'

A stir of white shirt in the gloom, Arithon shrugged. 'As you wish. The truth is, *I* could do with a beer.'

'Daelion's pity!' Dakar bristled in disgust. 'Where's your respect? The bard who loved you enough to share a master's training lies dead! Is this how you honour his memory? By running straight off to get sotted?'

No expression on his face, Arithon murmured a line in liquid Paravian lost to hearing through the thrash of the surf. Surprised not to suffer the expected scalding retort, the Mad Prophet was caught flat-footed as the subject of his rebuke shouldered past. Compelled to scramble after, the fat prophet tripped and stubbed toes all the way back up the cliff path.

From sundown till dawn, the harbourside quarter of Ship's Port brewed up a teeming moil of racket and crowds. Here, where tricksters juggled flaming torches, and the pawn stalls stayed open all night for sailors to trade trinkets for coin, the raucous parade of whores and the reeling celebration of deckhands on leave packed into kaleidoscopic hubbub. If the alleys overlooked by the gable-roofed shops seemed thronged as a holiday fair, the taverns were jammed to bursting. Over-dressed or half-clothed, a stew of sweating humanity gathered in the frenzied determination of sailors to cram nine months of pleasure into their first night ashore. Most rampaged and caroused until their coin ran out, then stumbled to the purser of an outbound trader to sign for another voyage.

The taproom of the Kittiwake Inn claimed distinction as the wildest dive on Harbour Street. Since it lay nearest to the wharves, deckhands still rolling on sea legs swayed in for their first drink and often passed no further. Smugglers' crews gathered there, sober and wary, ready for swift orders from their captains, that illicitly-laden ships might slip hawsers ahead of the harbourmaster's officers for flight to a hidden cove.

At the Kittiwake, if a newcomer wanted beer or a table, he was likely to need bribes for the privilege.

Helplessly tied by Asandir's geas, Dakar forwent his urge to complain. His resolve to stay sober in the cause of bloody murder now enforced by a shortage of coin, he cursed and jabbed elbows to plough aside revellers in his need to keep pace with Arithon.

Small and unfairly quick on his feet, the s'Ffalenn prince could shoulder through crowds like an eel. He already had the ear of the landlord, a tower of a man with red-veined cheeks and an ingrained stoop left over from service as a ship's cook. The pair engaged in a conversation that Dakar was of two minds about overhearing, torn as he was between nosy habit and new-found, poisonous animosity.

Never mind that drunken song and laughter and the squealing shrieks of pinched barmaids would naturally defeat his best effort. The height of summer in a seaport was an unhealthy season in which to sample taverns. The Kittiwake's stone and plaster walls dammed in a suffocating, sweat-humid heat, and the knife-scarred beams that braced the ceilings thumped to more racket upstairs. Resigned to claustrophobia and sour boredom, Dakar unstrung every one of his shirt laces, jerked open his collar and cuffs, and stowed his bulk against a post. He endured in dripping impatience, deaf to the jeers thrown his way over the unravelled state of his clothing; apparently the herb witch's chickens had picked his seat to hanging threads. That misfortune should hardly matter, Dakar sulked, since salt air and mouldy ships would rot the breeks off a man anyway.

Something Arithon said caused the landlord to nod in enlightenment. His booming reply could not be missed. 'Captain Dhirken? From the *Black Drake*? Ship's crew's here, sure enough. Her master likes the table in the corner where the air's fresh.'

A coin changed hands and Arithon backed up, fast reflexes alone averting collision with a prostitute's overflowing bodice. He grinned at her disappointment, dropped a half-silver down the maw of her cleavage, and cheerfully bypassed temptation. 'You heard?' he called to Dakar. 'Well, come on, then.'

As he nipped on between two contentious stevedores, the Mad Prophet made determined effort to follow. But the gap proved too tight to admit his fat girth. Cut off, jostled by tar-stinking celebrants, he cursed, craned his neck, and located the window in question, placed between the weather-checked tits of a wooden mermaid and a party of caulker's lads who linked arms in rollicking song. The panes in the worn sash casement were filmed with grease, and cracked open because the tired frame had stuck that way.

'Fresh air,' the Mad Prophet grumbled under his breath. 'Didn't know this port had any that didn't reek of ship's bilge and fish.'

Arithon by then had ploughed the last yard to the table. A luck nothing short of miraculous allowed him an empty stool. He settled across the boards from a doxie with a waist-length black plait and immediately started to talk.

By now parched enough to regret his resolve not to drink, Dakar glowered, but failed to recapture the Shadow Master's attention. If the confounded prince chose to flirt on the eve of Halliron's death, that weakness might as well lend advantage; in particular since the vessel he hoped to charter was a matter of public record.

Dakar's beard hid a smile rowed with teeth like a barracuda. He measured the Kittiwake's bawling crush of patrons, chose his mark, and launched himself toward a pigtailed pack of gamers in vindictive intent to cause mayhem.

His sally bowled aside a rat-thin pickpocket and fetched him with a thump against a bench where a bald brute with notched ears and tar-blackened knuckles dealt out a quicksilver stream of cards.

Dakar hiccuped through a contrite smile.

''Scuse,' he slurred on an approximate note of apology. Graceless enough to seem intoxicated, he affected a reeling stagger, stumbled, and hooked an ankle between one rickety leg and its cross-brace. The bench upset. Dingy cards, dice, and silver cascaded in all directions. Only a seaman's fast reflex let the bald lout regain his feet.

'You there!' he screamed in indignation, jostled and poked as enterprising bystanders dropped in a seething crush to snatch and scrabble after coins.

Before the offended gambler could ram through to defend his scattered cache, Dakar raised an ear-splitting shout. 'Are you Captain Dhirken's scumbag lackey?'

The surrounding celebrants dropped into electrified silence. Swarthy bodies pressed into a close ring.

Cut off from the happy din at the fringes, red-eyed in a hellish play of lamplight, the bald brute licked broken teeth. 'What if I am?' He flexed his fists. Sun-browned, hairy forearms bulged with sliding knots of muscle.

A broad-hipped serving girl burdened with a tray saw trouble brewing and wisely changed course.

'What quarrel have you got with Dhirken?' someone screamed from the sidelines.

Dakar backstepped and rolled his eyes. Cramped by hostile shoves from slit-eyed, tattooed sailors, he jabbed his thumbs in his belt. 'Nothing, nothing.' On the tail of a disarming smile, he shrugged. 'Or nearly nothing, surely. I simply heard about a rumour . . .'

'What rumour?' The bald man kicked aside the upset bench to a forlorn flutter of disturbed cards. He sauntered closer. 'Better speak. Or believe this, I'll pound your front teeth clean down through your bladder.'

Dakar edged from foot to foot, his round face blanched suet-white. '*Are* you one of Dhirken's men?'

'Aye, so I am. The *Black Drake*'s first mate, in hard fact.' A curl of a thickened lip, a glower hot enough to sear, and a last brisk step brought the mate within range to strike. 'State yer piece, you snivelling piggin of fish bait.'

'Ah,' Dakar swallowed and contrived to look pathetic. 'Well, in the square by the harbourmaster's, somebody mentioned that Dhirken's crew were slow as tar in a hard frost. A man I know wants to hire the *Drake*. Well, he shouldn't, if this is the truth.'

'You believe that?' the bald giant shouted.

Quiet had spread like flung poison to the farthest corners of the room. Every ear awaited Dakar's answer; every eye measured his unease. The hiss of oil lamps blended with the whisper of heavy breathing, against which Dhirken's mate cracked his knuckles, the pop of each gristled joint distinct as the snap of flung gravel. He spat on both palms and dried them on the tar-stained thighs of his slops.

'Oh,' declaimed the Mad Prophet, his bulging eyes fastened on the fists cocked and ready to fight. 'I only came here to ask. But really, if the *Drake*'s a slack ship, you've shown me no proof to the contrary.'

From behind, a raw-boned sailor chuckled deeply. 'Matey, here's facts, if you want to hear straight. Dhirken's a mincing girlie a man could knock flat with a whistle, and the crew o' the *Drake*? They're a pack o' lisping sissies that my lame little brother could whip spitless!'

'You think so?' An erstwhile card-player scrambled erect, brass earrings flashing. The knuckles of both hands were packed with coin winnings, now cheerfully brandished as cudgels.

In beet-faced, maniacal belligerence, the *Drake*'s bald mate replied with a battering fast fist.

Adroit enough when it counted, Dakar dropped flat upon the floor. Knuckles whistled just over his frizzled head and smacked with dull impact into the bystander just behind. One whose lame little brother proved agile as a snake, and nastily gifted at knife-play.

Further conniving was unnecessary. This was Ship's Port's dockside, where brawling was akin to breathing reflex. The mixed crowd hemming the instigators heaved, roared, and dived joyously into the fight. Patrons caught in the crossfire scuttled like an upset basket of crabs, the timid to leap behind trestles and barricade themselves into shelter. The most hardy broke their beer mugs into jagged edged weapons and pitched howling into the fracas.

Between one breath and the next, the Kittiwake's overcrowded taproom erupted into bedlam with the wholesale abandon of a fiend storm. Whores snatched up skirts and petticoats and pulled out concealed bludgeons, or thin-bladed, pearl-handled daggers. Plates sailed and crashed against the walls; bodies flew airborne and hammered into chairs, and anything not tied down got snatched and brandished as bludgeons. Drawn by the bellows of their mate, *Black Drake*'s insulted sail-hands rallied into a knot bent on bloodshed and murder. Fisticuffs and grunts and raucous bouts of shouting dismembered civilized conversation, while Dakar scrabbled to safety on hands and knees, an overweening smile on his face.

Let Arithon try now to hire Captain Dhirken, he would justly get his liver diced for crab snacks.

By the streetside window, spattered with meat shreds and stew broth, the stoic mermaid figurehead looked on with paintless eyes as the Kittiwake's landlord rammed shoulder-down to confront someone seated at the table. While shrill questions erupted into argument, Arithon watched, cat-still and poised, his face a mask of straight-lipped irony.

Even from his vantage on the floorboards, that expression moved Dakar to a pin stab of dread. The surge of the fight now behind him, he regained his feet, ducked a flying bottle, and side-stepped a wrack of splintered chairs. Somebody had drawn a cutlass; above the belling clang of parries, and a woman's spitfire obscenities, he cocked his ear to track the altercation.

The landlord demanded payment for his damages, the sum he named exorbitant enough to redecorate a high-class brothel.

'Come now,' Arithon said, his singer's tone liltingly amused. 'You're no stranger to the habits of sailors. This tavern's weathered a hundred such frolics. Any man with eyes can see every trestle in the place is still seeping green sap from the mill wright's.'

Behind the landlord's planted stance, a pigtailed topman nipped into the rafters with his rigging knife. He screamed epithets at somebody else down below. Invective floated upward in reply. The chandelier swayed, cut loose from its mooring, and whooshed down. The spectacular crash as it struck the top of the bar made an end to further insults. Bottles toppled, fell; sloshed spirits sprayed through the wicks of rolling candles. Nobody stirred to run for water; the Kittiwake's floors were fired brick. As the puddles spat into curls of blue flame, the fighting near at hand jammed on its course like a hiccup. Pugilists and bystanders dodged and fell flat in a sliding crush to escape, while leaping tongues of fire blistered and licked at ankles and buttocks and casualties.

Intent on the brawl's fresh developments as a tax collector calculating tithes, the landlord wrung his hands in chin-thrusting refusal to be placated. 'The *Drake*'s crew are trouble. Always have been. On your word of surety, I let them in here. Well, now I've lived to be sorry. Any pack of scoundrels with a captain who's a –'

'Don't say it,' snapped a silken alto voice.

The landlord squeaked, blinked, and ceased speaking, his widened eyes turned downward to track the naked cutlass that indented the belly of his waistcoat.

'Don't,' repeated the woman with the glossy, black braid, her consonants frigidly emphatic. She uncoiled to her feet, neatly compact, every inch of her primed for a stop-thrust. 'Presume again to say how my men should be handled, and I'll spit your guts just for joy. The Kittiwake's damages will be squared to *my* satisfaction; but only after my crew gets done with mending the slight to their competence.'

Dakar stiffened in his tracks. Slack-jawed, he looked askance at Arithon. 'Captain Dhirken?' he mouthed, shaken silly by the concept that she had been female all along.

The corners of Arithon's lips twitched. 'No other. You should have noticed. Whores don't generally dress in sea boots.'

Dakar fumbled behind his back, hooked a fallen stool, set it upright and sat down. 'A woman,' he mouthed again. Then, plaintive and much louder, 'Ah, fiends! What stakes in Sithaer's chaos are you playing for?'

But the Shadow Master's focus had already shifted beyond him to survey the taproom, and a turmoil whose direction was far from random. The raw-boned man and most of his fellow dicers were heaped prone and passed out cold, while shoulder to shoulder like brothers, the *Drake*'s crew were acting in ferocious concert to level those combatants left standing.

Recovered from his terror of the cutlass, the landlord had begun to natter on again.

Dakar was past listening. Incensed by his victim's nerveless patience; well aware the saucy captain would seize due revenge for every separate provocation, he indulged his vicious urge to crack the s'Ffalenn equilibrium. 'Why so hot a bother, miss? Your crew seems to like their recreation.'

Dhirken whirled on him, her face a slim, tanned oval scattered across nose and cheeks with freckles like fine sienna ink. 'You!' Her cutlass whistled and changed target. 'Haven't I enough problems on me without your baiting my mate for sheer fun? Take your meddlesome self elsewhere before I slit your gizzard to oil the *Black Drake*'s brightwork.'

'Lady,' Arithon said, softly laughing. 'Desist, please. That one's on our side.'

Caught at a loss, too dignified to gape, Captain Dhirken spiked an exasperated glance toward the pair of them. She shrugged, finally, helpless to stay angry before Arithon's infectious bent of humour.

'Sithaer's damned, a conspiracy?' She loosened strong fingers and sheathed her blade with a hiss of whetted steel. 'If you wanted my attention, you have it. But by Dharkaron's hairy bollocks, your business had stinking well better make me rich!'

Arithon gestured toward the table, pulled out a bench, and settled to a quiet round of bargaining. Outfaced and excluded from the conversation, the landlord stalked off to tally every coinweight of his losses. Dakar stood in flat-footed amazement, forgotten as a useless piece of furniture. Disgruntled, sullen, stinging from every scrape collected through his hands and knees scuttle across the bricks, he dragged up his stool and parked his elbows on the trestle to rethink the failure of his strategy.

A tavernmaid ventured out to bring whiskey. No mugs being available, she left an opened crock, which Arithon and Dhirken passed between them, the latter with her sea boots propped crossed in front of her. She braced her back against the opened window sash, and through placid, half-lidded eyes, gauged the ongoing progress of the fight.

Over a volley of fresh shouting and a soprano spray of breaking glass, she said, 'If my mate winds up crippled or killed, I'll press-gang you both as common seamen.' She swallowed, passed the crock, and waited while Arithon drank in turn.

Dakar could not choke down his sarcasm. 'Last I saw, your precious first mate was tearing the face off some ugly brute who went at him with a butcher's cleaver. At best, your worries are misplaced.'

Captain Dhirken took back the jug. Her hands were large-knuckled, callused; no stranger at all to a whiskey crock. She downed her draughts straight, and softened into a dreamy, full-lipped smile that somehow fell short of reassurance. 'Well, that's my mate's style, sure enough. Got his ears notched by a bully when he was ten. Steel's made him jumpy ever since. Almost killed my cook, in one of his sick bouts of nerves. Remember that. He slit a man's belly while sleepwalking, once.'

Unfazed by the grotesque, Dakar scavenged a plate of roast chicken lying abandoned on a windowsill. Beyond the split trestles, over the snapped struts of downed benches, he could see the remaining roisterers were part of *Drake*'s infamous crew, or else hapless onlookers fallen by chance onto the winning side. The Kittiwake was settling. A drudge with a broom and a basket sallied out to sweep up splinters and smashed crockery. Here and there in the corners, survivors gathered, to exchange boasts and nurse cuts and compare bruises.

The landlord rounded up his barmaids, shrewd enough to judge that good custom would be lost if beer and spirits were not available.

Then, too crafty to indulge herself in drunkenness, Dhirken banged down the crock and pushed loose sleeves back to her elbows. Over an end of gnawed bone, Dakar sighed in disappointment: whether the captain's wrists were delicate or mannish, no connoisseur's eye could to tell. She wore leather bracers studded with brass and laced on with wrapped silver wire.

'You set the stage,' she said in tart opening. 'My men performed. Meet their damage fee and I'll hear out your offer. But first you must let me clear them out of here.'

Arithon gave a nod and tipped a clanging spill of coins across the trestle.

'That's too much,' snapped the lady captain. Brass studs scraped the table as she leaned toward him. 'Since I don't like bribes, what's the show for?'

'Rum, to celebrate the *Black Drake*'s triumph at the Kittiwake.' Possessed of a bard's charm when it suited him, Arithon grinned. 'Piggin, firkin, or by the whole barrel, whichever vessel gives your heart pleasure.'

Dhirken regarded the glimmering wealth with jaundiced disdain. 'Not for my pleasure, matey. That of my men, more likely, and for them, it's me who speaks. Let it be a piggin apiece, since it's my intent to have them wakeful to sail on the ebb tide at midnight.'

'As you wish.' Arithon masked his disappointment, that the bulk of his sweetening offer remained on the table. The captain shoved off to collar her rollicking crewmen and awarded him not one glance back.

Dakar worked a shred of gristle out from behind a rear molar. 'Are you possessed, or simply in love?'

'It's too early to tell, don't you think?' Too cold-nerved to be baited, Arithon stretched. 'I wanted the boldest captain to ply Eltair Bay. Dhirken fits that requirement. She handles the men well.'

A true observation, Dakar allowed, while across the littered taproom, her crew of ruffians gathered mollified around her, blotting cuts and split lips and jostling in back-slapping high spirits. The last few still engrossed in combat broke off at the first direct order from their captain. Whatever she said in her lecture did not carry; but return phrases struck through with 'insulted' and 'provoked' carried over the rising stew of voices as the tavern's battered patrons resumed their rowdy entertainments.

His last wing now stripped of its cartilage, Dakar crooked a finger at a bar wench and ordered another plate of food. 'Anyway, how did she come by her ship?'

'Brig,' Arithon corrected. 'The story goes that *Black Drake* was her father's. He died of fever while at sea. The first mate tried to seize command. That version holds that she cut out his heart with a cutlass and named herself master, and nobody else cared to argue.'

Dakar blotted grease on his sleeve. 'And the other version?'

Arithon hitched his shoulders into a tight little shrug. 'That she was the original captain's lover and cut out *his* heart with a cutlass, and nobody else –'

'I believe the second tale,' Dakar cut in, his gaze torn between searching out his coming meal, and the female captain in her fitted scarlet breeches and loose, seaman's tunic that spilled in uninformative folds over what he could see of her chest. In sullen and contrary conclusion, he added unthinkingly aloud, 'Probably binds her dugs flat, if in fact she has any.'

'You think you'll pinch her to find out? Don't whine to me when she gelds you.' Arithon tipped back the rum jug, lit to merciless merriness. 'Since I plan to buy up her services, you're just going to have to get along.'

'Fatal starvation on the dockside might be preferable,' Dakar flared back. When the barmaid arrived with a plate of thick bread, batter-fried vegetables, and a bowl of fish stew, he chose in scowling forethought to amend his three days of starvation. Enough silver lay strewn on the table-top; Arithon could well afford to pay.

Except for bruised and battered faces, and the occasional set of bloodied knuckles, the fight might as well not have happened. The least pummelled patrons in the Kittiwake righted trestles and resumed their disrupted pleasures; the wounded consoled themselves with doxies or strong drink, and the noise level swelled, as newcomers stepped over the prone and the unconscious to vie for their chance at the whores.

Black Drake's crew were not among them. Their high-hearted cheers as Captain Dhirken announced a rum ration could not obviate her final warning. 'Keep yourselves in hand! I'll hear no excuses for layabouts. *Black Drake* sails with the tide. My business here won't take long. I want my gig smart and waiting, and any man who's swilled too much to handle himself in the rigging gets pitched on the shoals for the sharks.'

Dismissed back to shipboard, the men dispersed in grumbling, happy knots and steered through the crush toward the doorway. Dhirken returned to the table, the lift of her hip as she sat less a flaunt of her sex than practical allowance for the hang of her brute-sized sabre.

Immersed in his meal, Dakar let discussion flow across him as captain and Shadow Master settled to haggle over terms. Arithon's list of requirements caused the woman to narrow dark eyes.

'Say again?' She leaned on crossed arms, the fingers hooked into her coarse linen sleeves tensed to a sudden, stark white. 'You want the *Drake*, for time unspecified, to sail to a destination, also unspecified, with added contract, that your judgement overrules mine in unfamiliar waters? Lunacy. What about cargo? My holds are filled. Or are your very bodies the contraband?'

Only Dakar caught the fleeting, bitter irony that prefaced Arithon's smile. 'I only have cargo for pick-up, and it's held in another harbour. Outbound, I don't care what you carry. The return run's all that concerns me.'

Dhirken blinked. 'Lunacy,' she repeated. 'You've wasted my time and gained an unkindly debt, through your friend's stupid meddling with my crew.'

Her phrasing raised a sudden, queasy thrill that flattened Dakar's appetite. He ceased chewing, a half-gnawed fin dangled in one hand and grease glistening in his beard. For the Shadow Master across from him did nothing, ever, without thought; he had embraced a hostile try at insurrection without a ripple of annoyance. Yet whatever tangled wiles coiled behind his mild calm, his expression stayed guileless and shuttered.

'Think about this,' he said to Dhirken, a little amused, but not patronizing. '*Black Drake* would become the fastest, richest ship to ply the ports of the continent.'

'Hah!' Dhirken straightened, hooked the flask, and banged it to a strident clash of coins between Arithon's hands, which lay relaxed on the table; soft next to hers. Not horned in callus like a sailor's, but with fingers long and fine as the musician he was, under his deep layers of subterfuge. With a scorn that presumed him inept with a sword, she gave him her sneering refusal. 'Drink, fool, and dream. My brig is already fast enough to outrun the patrols in the strait. I don't need to risk her planks to a ham-fingered idiot who would likely see her smashed on a shoal.'

The pair locked eyes, Arithon unwilling to rise to provocation, and Dhirken, cross enough to knife him. As if drawn by their dissent, the Kittiwake's owner strode back to claim his due for damages.

By chance, Dakar saw, his final accounting matched the quantity of the silver on the table. Not without forethought, the landlord was accompanied by two brute-thewed giants armed with cudgels.

'Pay my reckoning,' he demanded. Confident the loom of his heavies would leave the slighter man cowed, he bent to scoop up the coins.

Snake-quick, Arithon moved. The landlord's grab entangled with the brandy jug. One thrown silver glittered spinning through gloom, caught before it landed by a street waif half-hidden in the cranny behind the wooden mermaid.

Dirty, ragged, grinning through missing front teeth, the creature tugged a bundle from the depths of his niche, and said, 'Master, here is your instrument.'

Arithon stood. He accepted the wrapped bulk of the lyranthe, his amity toward the landlord turned baleful. 'You'll have your coin, I gave my word. What made you think you'd need force to claim my debt?'

'Fiends! You're a bard?' The landlord chewed his lip, less apologetic than uncertain. The last musician to show his face in the Kittiwake had left with his lyranthe in splinters. Flanked by Dhirken's cynical regard, and the dull-witted interest of his thugs, he hesitated just long enough to note the gleam of fine metal and jewels as Arithon unveiled the priceless instrument bequeathed him by a master now dead.

Then the last veiling leather fell away. Arithon braced his hip on the trestle edge, scattered off a run like white sparks, and tenderly nursed the abalone and ebony pegs that tuned fourteen silver-wound strings. Bright sound sheared across the Kittiwake's din. By the time he had finished, conversation had lapsed. Heads turned, and fraught silence webbed the close air to the dimmest alcove in the room.

For an instant the musician paused, head tilted that familiar fraction to one side, fingers poised above fret and string as he measured the temper of the crowd. They offered no easy, willing audience. Their wants were varied as their roughest tastes and trades: the tar-stained sail-hands with wenches like gaudy birds in their laps; the cordwainers from the ship-yards, shirtless, their muscled arms glistening hot sweat; the knife-scarred, off-duty garrison soldiers grouped in tight knots over a battered pair of dice.

Before that suspended opening could pass, Arithon reeled off through a dance tune. He played saucy and fast, in heartfelt, glorious tribute to Halliron's best style. And the Kittiwake's riff-raff roared back an approval that rattled the crockery on the shelves.

The landlord backed off, stupefied. Past the first, stiff moment of surprise, Dhirken laid her elbows in spilled spirits and coins, her chin cupped in her palms to listen.

The measures spun faster, and faster still, alive as the crackle of summer lightning. A few of the doxies sprang up to dance a jig, and soon the floor planks were shaking. In minutes the whole Kittiwake rocked in celebration, while more customers packed in from the street. By then,

Arithon had bent his head to his soundboard. Black hair veiled his expression, wholly; even Dakar, who was closest, never noticed the flash of the tears that splashed and wet his flying knuckles.

Halliron Masterbard was dead; gone. In a headlong, passionate harmony of celebration, the man proven fit to succeed him made the most coarse-mannered dive in Ship's Port reel with ruffians who stamped and clapped and shrieked. As if by whipping up joy to bring catharsis, he could fill the bereft void in his heart.

Dakar aroused from the thick dark of sleep at the gouge of stiff fingers in his ribs.

He groaned, stirred, and scrubbed bleary eyelids with his fists. The unheard-of surprise that he was not hungover shocked him enough to sit up. In a dimness red-lit by the flicker of a last, failing oil lamp, he squinted to assess his surroundings.

Against a backdrop of wildly sprawled bodies, he made out the slight form of Arithon, standing impatient with the lyranthe furled up and slung from a strap at his shoulder.

'Tide's turning,' said the Shadow Master in a low, urgent whisper. 'If you're sailing with me, I leave now.'

Dakar blinked, still turgid from sleep. He cradled pained hands over his distended belly and none too softly, belched up the aftertaste of cod. 'You spell-touched the whole house into sleep with your masterbard's gift, you unprincipled bastard.'

'You ate too much,' said Arithon in rejoinder.

'What about them?' Dakar's groggy gesture encompassed the patrons heaped and snoring over trestles and bricks.

'Brandy or beer, does it matter? The *Drake* will be ready to weigh anchor. Are you coming or staying?'

'Coming.' Dakar heaved to his feet. 'For nothing else, just to see you hurt for this.'

A soft thread of laughter mocked him back. 'Don't trouble. Dhirken's crew will likely be at my throat before your wits have had time to wake up.' Arithon flicked an airy, tight-cuffed wrist. 'Do you want to lend a hand?'

Dakar peered, made out in wavering flame light the slumped form of Dhirken's shoulders. Her hands with their blunt, close-trimmed nails, her tanned cheek, and the wind-wisped, flamboyant plait trailed through puddled brandy and wet coins. 'Dharkaron! You do ask for trouble. How'd you convince her to take your contract?'

'I didn't.' Efficient without seeming hurried, Arithon reached out, caught a wrist as lean-boned as a belaying pin, and tugged the lady captain upright on the bench. Her body lolled backward against his chest and the taut cloth of her tunic pressed the round swell of small breasts.

'Well, there's one question answered without you risking your bollocks,' Arithon said.

He flashed a fast grin, unstrapped the heavy cutlass, and thrust baldric, weapon, and the unslung weight of his lyranthe into Dakar's arms. Then he bent and hefted the woman in a seaman's carry across his shoulders. Her weight made him stagger a half-step. Wrist and feet dangling, her hips folded close against his nape, she was easily larger than he was, a limp body difficult to balance. He shrugged her bulk to ease a pressure point, and even that slight change in his stance raised a sweet-chinking clangour of metal.

The floor around the table lay spangled with silver, coins struck by the foundries of a dozen different port towns: the tribute of the Kittiwake's revellers to a masterbard whose night's entertainment had pleased them. As though embarrassed by their generosity, Arithon gave another hitch to his load. 'Well, I've settled my debt to the tavern. The landlord should be satisfied, don't you think?'

Dakar looked at him, eyes round as an adder's and his brows pinched in unaccustomed thought. 'Dhirken,' he said. 'If you wanted her service, why not spare the bother and just lie to her?'

'Because I happen to need her trust.' Green eyes reflected the expectant, curbed patience a hale man might show a blind half-wit, until the silence stretched too long. 'Oh, Dakar,' the Master of Shadow said finally, his words drenched in irony that jabbed.

'*Trust you!* Dharkaron's Black Spear and Chariot!' Dakar sucked in a breath, hot to launch into a tirade, then stopped. 'Her men,' he ventured through a pregnant pause. 'For *this*, you had to be rid of them.'

Arithon waited, quietly subtle as slow poison.

'Oh, you bastard,' gasped Dakar, slammed sick by the recognition that his rage had been teased and then used, himself a dumb pawn strategically advanced to further his enemy's design. The brawl in the Kittiwake had offered no setback at all, but played straight into Arithon's hand.

The wrapped, fragile instrument in Dakar's arms became all that stayed him from violence. His hatred soared to fresh dimensions, directed as much at himself for falling prey to a ploy so smooth he had never thought to guard. Speechless, breathless, thwarted enough to kick his own shin from sheer fury, he barged ahead. Through the Kittiwake's common room, stumbling over slack and snoring bodies, blundering around benches, he slammed at last through the doorway to reach the night air in the street. On his heels in uncanny quiet for a man with a burden, Arithon bore Captain Dhirken.

'A woman,' Dakar groused, his beard hairs caught and tweaked by a tangle of baldric straps and studs. In case he might just be dreaming, or sick, he twisted to recheck his bearings. But the pair that emerged from the Kittiwake's torpid gloom were solidly, dishearteningly real. 'Your neck's going to stiffen if you lug her like that,' he stated in unhelpful satisfaction.

Arithon bore him no rancour. 'I'll be lucky if that's the worst that befalls me.' As Dakar ploughed on toward the quayside, he tipped his chin a hampered fraction sideways. 'No, turn left. I've things to retrieve from my lodgings.'

Pulled up short in the gloom by the gate to the harbourmaster's office, Dakar threw back a blank glare.

'Navigational instruments,' Arithon prodded gently. 'Charts. How could you forget? They're the point of this whole sordid exercise.'

Which was unlikely to be the innocent truth, Dakar knew; not when the perpetrator was Arithon s'Ffalenn, whose motives ran to mazes of trickery the Fatemaster himself would be pained to unravel.

Black Drake

Captain Dhirken awakened thick-headed. Before she opened gummed eyelids, she knew by the slap and rush of the wake that her brig was well under way. The creak of burdened canvas laid the *Black Drake* over on port tack. Since the captain's elbow and hip were not jammed alee in her berth, she judged the weather was mild. The gusts that wafted through the overhead hatch grating smelled dry and unlikely to freshen. A kick of white spray off the rudder and a thrummed note of strain in the cordage meant staysails and topsails were set aloft. Attuned to her vessel as other women were to their lovers, she knew the square main should be braced around slightly more to starboard to balance the trim of the jibs.

Moved by habit, Dhirken rolled to arise, when a male voice dispatched crisp orders. Her mate acknowledged. Feet thumped on deck as sail hands moved to obey, followed by the squeal of lines through the mainsheet blocks. *Drake* rocked and settled, docile as a stroked maiden, into harmony with wind and heading.

Odd, mused Dhirken, still drowsy as her feet met cold planking. Her mate's skill at the helm had never been so deft. She braced against a bulkhead, unsettled to find she had slept in her clothes; never a habit of hers, unless a storm was brewing. The bracers she chose for her forays ashore had gouged her side into dimples, and the hair wisped loose from yesterday's braid held a clinging, smoky reek of used tobacco.

The voice on the quarterdeck called another order, and awareness woke late that its timbre matched none of *Drake*'s officers.

Dhirken ripped into an explosive, whispered fit of swearing. Impelled by sheer rage, she dredged up the memory of a sticky table in the Kitti-wake, and the blandishments offered by a green-eyed, sliver-tongued bard. His jug of strong spirits had not turned her wits. She recalled every meandering thread of his conversation, and a proposal too brash for any right-minded captain to endorse; which apparently had not stopped the scheming dog from believing he could force her will by trickery.

Balanced like a dancer as her brig rollicked over a swell, knuckles braced against a deck beam, Dhirken made a blind snatch toward the hook by the unlighted lantern. The brass-strapped scabbard of her cutlass slapped into her groping palm.

Relieved to find her weapon hung in its proper place; reassured that her ship's boy at least still minded his duty, Dhirken steadied enough to rein in the raw worst of her fury. 'Lad?' she called through the gloom.

Every boy to sign with the *Drake* answered to the same address; they earned names when they mastered the skills of deepwater sailors, and outgrew any instinct that tempted her to tousle their hair like lost little brothers.

This particular brat was a sluggard. 'Lad!' Dhirken repeated in a stabbing whisper. 'Roust out! Now! I need you.' She poked with the sheathed tip of her cutlass and entangled the mesh of an empty hammock.

A scrape at the companionway made her crouch and whirl around.

'Cap'n?' A boy's lisp accompanied a rustled movement, and a narrow face lifted in the gloom. 'Is it wash-water you're wanting?'

'No.' Dhirken flicked her blade free and beckoned the child closer. 'Not yet.' Through the roll as *Drake* mounted a crest and sloughed through, she weighed the groaning creak of her working vessel. Nothing seemed amiss or unfamiliar: not the thickened smells of hemp cordage and tar, nor the musk of sea-swollen planking made pungent by coal smoke from the galley fire. Past the stern windows, foam ruffled off the wake, flurried over in a scatter of sparks as a crewman trimmed the wick in the deck lantern. Though the dark was not close or foggy, neither stars nor moon scribed their reflections on the swells. No distant sparkle of watch beacons lined the coast to guide the course of night sailing traders. Gripped by a primal urge to yank her steel screaming from its sheath, Dhirken tipped her crown against the bulkhead.

Gritty as scraped rust, she asked, 'Lad, last night when I was brought back on board, who came with me?'

'A fat man. And the other captain, who's steering now. The one who said *Black Drake*'s going to be the fastest, richest brig ever to plough the deeps of the Cildein.' In a child's unvarnished curiosity, Lad finished, 'They said you were pleased over that. How much rum did you drink?'

Dhirken clamped a forearm across her belly to lock back an oath like a mastiff's snarl. 'Not enough to save their miserable hides. The fat man, where is he now?'

Lad snickered. 'Bent over the leeside rail. Ever since we weighed anchor, he's been belly-down and heaving.'

'Well, here are my orders.' Dhirken spoke fast and low, then gave Lad a brisk push. The hinges on her bulkhead door were superbly kept; the boy, well trained, moved as silently. In the interval after he slipped out, the captain picked out her plait, used her tortoiseshell comb, and retied her dark hair for hard action.

No crewman lasted on a smuggler's brig if he failed to attend orders without noise. Dhirken whipped the last knot in her thong when the door latch ticked up. Her barefoot, rangy topman and *Drake*'s slab-thewed cook padded in on a breath of salt air.

Between them, white and moist as a shelled oyster, they bundled Dakar the Mad Prophet. A dish-sponge crammed in his mouth stayed his outcry, and both plump wrists were creased by lashings his desperate struggles could not slip.

'Well done!' Dhirken grinned, a flash of bared teeth in the gloom. 'Dump him on my close stool. We'll see how he likes to talk.'

Plonked down with less ceremony than a biscuit sack, Dakar collapsed in a jelly-legged heap. The instant the cook yanked the sponge from his mouth, he moaned and bent double into dry heaves. The edge of Dhirken's blade against his bared nape could scarcely make him sweat faster, wringing wet as he already was from sick misery and the salt spray that doused off the bow.

'Who is that dark-haired upstart, and what does he want with the *Drake*?' Dhirken pressed him.

'Ah, captain, 'twas a dismal poor effort, I know.' Wrenched breathless by another spasm, Dakar rolled his eyes. 'But in my own fashion, I tried very hard to turn your crew from the Master of Shadow.'

Astonishment whetted Dhirken to fresh anger. 'Master? Shadow! You refer to the mad prince who slaughtered Etarra's army? Do I look the fool, to swallow such rubbish?' Her steel niggled down another fraction. 'That meddling little string-plucker who's commandeered my brig is anything but royal and a sorcerer.'

'I beg your pardon.' Dakar cringed away until his forehead ground into his cramped knees. He said in muffled injury to his trousers, 'I lie well enough when I have to. Never, ever about that man.' Despite the hands lashed behind his back, he managed a soulful shrug. 'His string-plucking lulled you unconscious, a bard's spell few could equal. That's hardly the worst. Look outside. It's black, though true night is past. Arithon has spun clever shadows to make you think you see a shoreline. But where are the signs of solid land?'

The first, creeping chill ruffled Dhirken's composure, while the cook made a sign to avert evil. Unnerved enough to venture opinion, *Drake*'s most fearless topman said, 'Captain, something *is* queer, I said so earlier. Damn me, I couldn't finger what. But now it's mentioned, the wind carries all the wrong smell.'

Dhirken feathered her cutlass against the creased fat beneath her victim's earlobe. 'I should cut you dead here and be damned to the mess. You've caused me a packet of trouble.'

'Kill Arithon instead,' Dakar suggested, reamed already by cramps that made beheading seem merciful by comparison. 'It's a fair bet I hate him more than you do.'

'I don't bet,' Dhirken answered, clipped.

Amid the Kittiwake's raucous turmoil, she had seemed staunchly determined; here, in cramped quarters kept so ascetically neat they scarcely felt inhabited, her presence loomed volatile as a touch match dropped head-down on dry lint. Dakar shivered in the throes of his nausea, helpless to guess which way female fury might turn her.

Then, with a move that slapped air, the *Drake*'s captain lifted her weapon. Habit drove her to finger an old scar that extended past the end of her bracer. 'Depend on this,' she finished with an edge that caused her seamen to shrink where they stood. 'I will wrest back my command.'

At her gesture, the cook jammed Dakar back upright. The topman stuffed the sponge back into the prisoner's mouth and twisted it tight with his tar-stained shirt. A discreet tap sounded against the boards beneath the Dhirken's berth. A mercuric arc of reflection marked the changed angle of her cutlass as she peeled aside ticking and blankets and pried up a concealed hatch beneath.

Lad's tow head and angular body emerged amid a gush of sour air from the bilges. 'Your men on deck say they're ready, captain.'

On a predatory flash of teeth, Dhirken slipped out of her cabin. The ship's cook and the topman padded like mismatched shadows on her heels.

Lad stayed, the galley's best flensing knife clenched in his hand, with instructions to fillet the prisoner if he sought to raise the alarm.

An idiotic and unfair precaution, Dakar sulked, his pouched eyes squeezed shut as he retched in balked spasms against his gag. A knife in the gizzard was no sort of thanks for information given in good faith; and even had illness lent respite for the purpose, he would cheerfully choose strangulation before he gave warning to spare the confounded Prince of Rathain.

Outside the swinging halo of her running lamp, *Drake* lay shrouded in darkness. Pricked in salt rime, shrouds and rigging angled upward from the spooled rail and lost form against a featureless sky. The bearing creak of filled canvas and the chafing squeal of trusses reduced hidden masts and tackle to a ghost presence overhead. If any shoreline bounded the horizon, neither light nor beacon tower showed. Dhirken tightened grip on her cutlass. She smelled neither shingle or sheep cot; no fragrance of green growing fields. The air held only clean scoured salt, and the tarry bite of blacked cordage. Her brig settled easy over fair-weather swells, not a sail in her rig set amiss.

Master of Shadow or master singer, the man at the helm knew his seamanship.

Which competence brought no forgiveness; Dhirken tapped the wrists of her topman and cook to signal her intent. Then, wraith-still by the aft companionway, she gestured, and other crewmen rousted by Lad to lie in wait for her order moved ahead. Movement answered from the darkness. In grumbling pairs, laden with buckets and holystones, they filed from the forecastle and invaded the quarterdeck. There, amid cheerful oaths and grousing, they industriously knelt to swab planks.

The black-haired upstart stationed at the helm voiced a mild query.

A hulking mass at his shoulder, *Drake*'s first mate waved the seamen on about their business. 'Our captain keeps a trim vessel,' he assured. 'Any land dirt left on her ship's decks by dawn, and she'll roust up our bosun to flog backs.'

'Land dirt,' mouthed Dhirken, convulsed by a soundless chuckle. 'How perfectly apt.' She flicked her sleeves clear of her bracers, jerked her chin for the cook and second mate to back her only as needed, then swung alone up the ladder to the quarterdeck.

Limned in orange by the stern lantern, the conniving little bard who had played the Kittiwake's scum to a standstill stood in still grace before the binnacle. He still wore his oddly-tailored shirt. Silver-pointed cuff ties chimed at the wrist held negligently crooked around a wheel spoke. His pose of inattention was deceptive; the brig kept her heading like a gannet. Languid as poured honey, Dhirken stepped up to meet her adversary. He did not loom dangerous enough for a sorcerer, she thought; he lacked the grand majesty of a prince. Beyond hands too slim for their office, he could have been a ship's boy with wind-ruffled black hair, bare feet braced against the heeled deck.

Only the gaze that flicked aside to greet her was too sardonic and deep for a child's.

'Uncommon fine weather for sailing,' Dhirken opened in tea-room courtesy. She fielded a fractional nod from her mate, her sharkish smile for the foreign upstart who had dared to give orders on her ship. While her challenge fixed his attention, crewmen armed with knives and cudgels grappled over the rail at his back. Arrived from a circuitous route through the bilges, they scaled the sterncastle by way of her cabin window, masked by the industrious scrape of holystones.

'Ah, Lady,' the foreigner said in his lyrical, singer's chagrin. 'Would you meet me with a threat?' Timed to a masterful fine point, he loosed the helm, whirled face about, and confronted the stalkers poised to jump him.

A following crest slammed the rudder. The unattended wheel spun like a ratchet and veered the brig off her heading. Aloft, heavy canvas sucked flat, then backwinded with a bang and a rattling thrash of slack blocks. *Drake*'s crewmen were hurled back a halfstep as the deck lurched in violent response. Seasoned sailors, they recovered by reflex.

'I haven't said whether I wanted you taken alive,' Dhirken remarked in joyous spite.

'Should that concern me?' As her men lunged, and the brig slewed and shuddered broadside against the swells, Arithon smiled.

The darkness blasted away.

Sunlight ripped down, its glare at full noon like the blistering stab of sheared iron.

'Sorcery!' someone screamed, while the attackers fell back in sharp terror. 'It's truth! He's the Master of Shadow!'

Arithon stood still and denied nothing.

Above other shouts of fear and dismay, and the dashing rush of shot spray, Dhirken's pealed order stopped panic. Her sun-blind mate found the wheel by touch, flung the helm down, and slewed the brig head to wind. Reviled by their captain's razor-edged tongue, the assault party firmed sweaty grip on their cudgels and regrouped.

Unruffled, unarmed, the man now revealed as the prince whose powers had leashed the Mistwraith let them close to surround him. 'Do as you please,' he invited through the hammering thunder as gear thrashed aloft. 'I have no wish to start a fight.'

'I'd say it's a bit late for such niceties,' Dhirken snapped. To her men, she added, 'Take him, fools. Hold onto him tight! Sorcerer or not, he's all mine.'

For a heartbeat, no movement crossed the deck beyond the whipping snake of slack sheet lines. Then, needled on by their quarry's bold amusement, the sailors obeyed orders in a sudden, vindictive surge. Grasped and yanked spread-eagled by men who outmatched his strength and weight, Arithon tossed his head to clear fallen hair from his eyes.

Through wrenching discomfort, he gasped, 'Dakar. I presume he's saved trouble and already told you my name?'

No one answered. The men glanced about and shuffled uneasy feet. Dhirken stood stripped of her bluster. Tintless as fine porcelain, her freckles stippled dark across the bridge of her nose, she spun on her heel and stared for searching minutes under her visored fingers. Quandary met her, unpleasant and real; for as the fat man had threatened, the sea lay empty on all quarters.

Water scribed a landless, flat line to the farthest rim of the horizon.

For a heartbeat only, Dhirken stayed at a loss. Then the flog of loose canvas displaced her shaken nerves and the scope of the *Drake*'s problem overshadowed all else. She whirled to face her mate, who now gripped the wheel with the desperate, whipped dog absorption of a man who wished himself elsewhere.

'Where's the log?' She had to shriek like a harpy to be heard over the wind-pummelled fury of thrashed tackle. 'What's our heading? Speed? What course? How long have we been underway, and where do you place our position?'

The huge man blew rolling sweat from his moustache. 'Your bargain,' he stammered. Too large a man to cringe neatly, he darted a glance to his shipmates. When no one stepped forward to back him, he swallowed and spoke out alone. 'The foreign cap'n was to navigate.'

'Fiends alive!' Dhirken made a whistling jab and stopped her cutlass just shy of taking flesh. 'We could be anywhere in Eltair Bay by now!'

The mate feared to look at the weapon that trembled at his heart. He thumbed his slit earlobe, plumbed dry of words, while the sun glinted off his bald crown.

At length, his captain lunged away, her gaudy scarlet shirt moulded to small breasts by the riffling pressure of the breeze. In a reviling cascade of filthy epithets, she dispatched the gawkers on the sidelines to stow their buckets and holystones, then scramble aloft and furl sail. 'Move lively, you louses! For every thread thrashed off my staysails, I'll have me a patch of flayed arse!'

Freed at last to vent her spleen upon the primary offender, Dhirken braced against the brig's wallowing roll. Light scalded off her studded bracers as she raised her cutlass and caught the tip through the ties at her prisoner's shirt front. 'Don't think to bluff your way through this. I was never drunk in the Kittiwake last night. You heard me plainly when I said the terms of your contract were fool's play.'

'Ah,' grunted Arithon, a hitch to his breath as a seaman bent his arm a notch higher. 'Since you didn't give me an answer, it's fair that I'm offering again.'

Dhirken twisted her weapon. A lacing sheared through with a thin rasp of sound and exposed a soft triangle of skin. 'What makes you think you've got aught beside your bollocks left to bargain with?'

'For one thing, I know where we are.' Under his chin, another lacing parted. Arithon held steady, even as Dhirken's blade dipped, snagged white linen, and nicked in a vicious downward tear. The sea plunged the brig through a bucketing roll and smacked her down in a trough. Spray pattered over decking and sail-hands, and Dhirken's jarred blade stencilled a scratch in new blood.

The sting provoked Arithon to scalding impatience. 'Go on and cut a bit lower,' he challenged. 'You'll find a parchment from Sethvir tucked into my waistband that states to the copper what I'm worth.'

'Sethvir?' Dhirken reached out, grabbed, and dragged cloth across steel in a howling rip that left him stripped to the waist. 'Sethvir of *Althain*? What is he but a legend told to snivelling little babes by their mothers?'

'Look and see,' said Arithon, the gleam to his eyes no less dangerous for the fact he was weaponless and trapped.

Aloft, the sail-hands' teamed efforts gradually reduced the *Drake*'s canvas. While the deck crew minded belaying pins and tackle, loosened sheets and whipped blocks subsided to a tidier thrum as the wind skeined over taut cable. Speech could be heard with less effort now, but Arithon volunteered nothing else.

Beneath the fluttering shreds of his shirt, he did in fact carry a scroll, several sheaves thick, fastened with ribbon and bearing a cracked seal that looked very elegant and old.

Dhirken used her cutlass to hook the ties and fish it out.

'You're welcome,' its owner said equably. 'The seal, which is genuine, belongs to s'Gannley. The line ruled as princes in Camris. Go on. Read. I invited you.'

The captain snatched the parchment off her weapon tip. Cut ribbons fluttered overboard on the breeze as she flattened the sheet and scanned the lines.

'Lady?' Arithon offered in grave diffidence. 'May I suggest you fetch someone who can read?' Subject to the captain's venomous glower, he gave a hampered, apologetic shrug. 'You're holding the sheet upside down.'

'Fiends alive!' Dhirken grinned in icy enjoyment, despite herself pleased by his boldness. 'You're going to die very slowly. Maybe one finger at a time, until we've attracted enough sharks for the rest of you.' The gold loops in her ears spat hard glints as she flipped the parchment into the startled grasp of her slit-eared first mate.

'What does it say?' she commanded.

The brig's helm was hastily passed off to a sail-hand.

Embarrassed to be handed a scribe's chore in public, the mate snarled at his smirking crewmates. 'Anybody laughs, I'll gut him later.' He cracked the scroll straight, puckered up in a squint, and in hesitant, strangled diction, ploughed his way through the first page, with its lists of gold in coinweight, its itemized inventory of Falgaire crystal, fine silk, and Narms carpet. Wealth beyond the wickedest dream of avarice drew every deckhand within earshot to crowd his elbows in excitement.

'Keep alert!' Dhirken snapped. 'If there's riches, we haven't seen one whit more than some straggly marks on a parchment!' As the mate fumbled through the next page, she cut off his recitation and regarded her prisoner, who, despite the agility of a weasel, had not managed to ease the suspended posture her men maintained to force him passive.

'These goods of yours.' She laughed. 'You're telling me you came by them honestly?'

'Now that *would* be prying.' Arithon stretched to extreme limits and managed to claw a toe-hold on the deck. Perhaps annoyed that the sailors who pinioned his finely-made wrists seemed determined to strangle his circulation, he added, 'I didn't ask how you acquired the lading list in your hold.'

'And you didn't seek to hire a smuggler's ship without particular reason, I see that.' Left the predicament that her brig was adrift beyond sight of bearings or shoreline, Dhirken fingered her cutlass.

Before she could render final judgement, Arithon cut in, sweetly reasonable. 'You have nothing to lose by listening. For the trouble I've caused, why not hear what you stand to gain?'

Shadows like cabled cobweb crawled across sanded wood and the leached white grain of drying planks. The slit-eared mate worried the corners of the parchments, while the deckhands watched their captain, stone-still. The squeal of the steerage gear, and the creak of the yards to *Drake*'s wallowing assaulted the unsettled silence.

Locked eye to eye with a prisoner no taller than she was, Dhirken sensed his taunting irony: as though death itself were a gambit tossed out to serve some feckless need. Since the habit of command made her cautious of allowing any miscreant to have his way, she hesitated; and the moment ceded a dangerous awareness that her crewmen sized her up like a wolf pack.

She had been challenged before them, by a man. Pitched to grasp at the first hint of weakness, they waited to see if she was afraid of him.

That fact alone saved his life.

'You've caused no trouble,' Dhirken pronounced at careful length. 'Inconvenience, perhaps. *Drake*'s still in Eltair Bay, and not lost. If I steer to any heading but east, we're bound to recover the shoreline.'

'Ah, but where?' Arithon matched her play like a card-sharp. 'The constables at Whitehold have a price on your head. Jaelot would imprison you and confiscate your ship if you can't meet their fines for unpaid tolls on strait passage. What if your landfall's at Tharidor? I don't know the *Drake*'s transgression, but the harbourmaster there said he'd retire for the pleasure of hanging you without a court of law.'

'Enough!' Determined not to seem flattered by the scope of his ability to sort gossip, Dhirken reached out left-handed, peeled a raised splinter from the wheel mount, and proceeded to pick her front teeth. 'My history and problems won't matter one whit if you're dead,' she said around her clenched bit of wood. 'Right now I see no reason not to silence your singing and throw off your bones for the fish.'

'You could do that,' Arithon agreed. 'Or, better, we could wager. Choose any city, any place in the bay or on the continent where you prefer to make landfall. By the forgotten arts of navigation, I'll steer the *Drake* to that harbour.'

'Sorcery!' Dhirken spat out a small shred of spruce. 'I've no use for such.'

'Knowledge,' Arithon countered. 'Imagine if you could sail straight out to sea, lose the merchant's patrols over the horizon, then carve a straight course for whatever haven your fortune should favour?'

'I don't bet.' Dhirken flung away her sliver, prepared to reacquaint him with her cutlass.

'You don't read, either,' Arithon shot back. 'Change just those two habits, and no contraband runner in these waters could match you.'

'Captain,' the seaman at the wheel volunteered in tremulous diffidence. 'Listen to the man. We could kill him any time. But if he's not lying, every one of us could be rich.'

'I will say, he has a sure hand on a ship,' the mate added.

'Ath, you puling puppies!' Dhirken sneered. 'Would you plead for him, then, liar that he is, and shadow-bending sorcerer as well?'

When none of her crewmen dared to meet her eyes, the captain weighed her own counsel. In the yards overhead, sail-hands faltered in their furling to eavesdrop; aware they were idle by their motionless shadows on the deck, Dhirken snapped off a brusque warning. To her prisoner, she said, 'If what you say is true, if this navigation isn't sorcery, then anybody here could learn it?'

'Anybody,' Arithon assured. 'My hands could be tied. Given proper instruments and my instruction, you could make and plot the sightings by yourself.'

'Then your hands will be tied and your feet also.' Pleased to snatch triumph from opportunity, Dhirken dispatched a sail-hand to scrounge in a locker for spare cord. 'The landfall I choose is the harbour at Farsee. Get us there. Or I'll see the crabs feed on your carcass.'

A busy interval later, bent over the contents of Arithon's satchel, *Drake*'s captain completed her amazed inspection of gleaming, strange instruments and charts. Wakened to the fact she was hungry, she drew breath to call Lad, then recalled the seasick accomplice, left gagged and trussed like a turkey below decks. She stood in disgust. Unless the fat landlubber had tossed up his guts and suffocated in her quarters, she was going to have to cut him loose.

Blade drawn in hand, Dhirken descended the companionway.

The shadowed dark of her cabin seemed much too quiet. She swore as her eyes adjusted, and swore again as she saw Lad, fallen dead asleep on her berth. The cook's best knife had fallen clear of slack fingers. An edge of reflected blue in the light through the opened stern window, the blade had impaled itself spare inches from the prisoner's boots.

But Dakar was too far gone in misery to grasp the advantage of the moment. His complexion was green and his hair lay screwed in sweaty snarls. Dhirken noted in amazement he had managed to gnaw through the gag. Of the galley sponge, she found no sign, even when she bent to recover the dropped knife.

Above her, between moans likely due to colic from ingested shreds of sponge, the prisoner gasped, 'Where's Arithon?'

'Tied to the mizzenmast pinrail, damned unpleasantly tight, if you please.' A moment's forethought, and Dhirken sheathed her cutlass, the cook's steel being handier to hack through knotted twine. 'There your man stays till *Black Drake* makes port where he's promised.'

As his bonds gave way, the Mad Prophet chafed scored wrists. 'How many seamen did he kill before you trussed him?'

Knelt down to free Dakar's ankles, Dhirken looked up sharply. 'None,' she said in irritation. 'Why ask? He gave himself freely.'

'Ah, lady.' Dakar heaved a soulful sigh. 'You don't know him at all. That's trouble. Whatever you think, whatever Arithon led you to believe, be certain of this. If he didn't kill, then you dance to his design.'

Dhirken stood, her eyes like sheared rivets in the gloom, and her dagger hand thoughtfully steady. 'You don't like him one bit. I don't find that reassuring.'

Dakar shook his head, then snapped his palms to his mouth to dam back another seizure. As he groaned an apology and stumbled through the companionway to be sick, Dhirken looked after him, her arms folded in tight trepidation across her breast.

'Well, by Ath, I don't trust either one of you,' she confided to her cabin's creaking bulkhead. 'Whatever the outcome, until I see a motive, I'm going to use my own judgement.'

Attrition

Along the coast of Eltair Bay, late summer hazed the jumbled, steep-sided valleys in their mantle of hardwood and evergreen. The oaks hung gemmed with acorns. Larks ceased singing to mark off territory, their fledged young gone from their nests. But in the mountains to the west of Jaelot where Luhaine fared on the errand deferred to him by Asandir, cruel cold ruled the upper altitudes with small regard for changing seasons. On cloudless mornings, the loftiest peak in the Skyshiels pricked the sky like a knife upthrust for a sacrifice. Ice-clad, glistening white, or else scoured of cover like a hammered scrap of unforgiving black iron, it shadowed even the deepest gorge glazed by snow melt through the clefts of Rockfell Vale. Under mist or in storm, its edged northern scarp split the winds. On days when the gusts raged the hardest, the wail of sheared air keened like a haunt through the glens and broken foothills beneath.

Foresters from Daenfal who worked traps in these wilds never tarried over their snares. They claimed the mountain's brooding could be felt in the sough of the breeze; a solitary man could go mad here, listening too long or too carefully.

In the hour the Fellowship envoy arrived to resurvey the Mistwraith's prison, the rain that drenched the green lowlands rampaged in blizzards across the heights. Gusts whirled over cliff wall and ice face, shrill as war steel dragged sharp across a whetstone. Driven snow scoured the incongruous stone stair cut into the scarp at the whim of Davien the Betrayer. The baroque scrolls of newel posts and chiselled, glowering gargoyles poked through blank drifts, sheeted like age-rotted dust covers over frivolously abandoned furniture.

To Luhaine's mage-tuned perception, the eyes of the carvings were not dead. Spells of guard wakened by his passage flared to coronas of energy just past the range of natural sight. Wild rocks would have shown indifference to his trespassing; the obsidian-flecked bones of Rockfell Peak were not dumb, but aware and watchful of encroachment.

Yet where an intruder who lacked Fellowship guidance might press upward unheeding, misguided to believe that this sky-framed, wind-burnished pinnacle would permit an unsanctioned presence, Luhaine paused. An unseen vortex more chill than frost, around which the gusts sucked and skirted like a current rechannelled by obstruction, he unreeled a tendril of awareness downward, touched the mountain, and tacitly requested a permission.

A vibration answered from the deep, a bell-stroke chord reminiscent of earthquakes, mournfully slow and drawn out. Too subtle to stir mortal senses, the language of stone held a grandeur so vast that time seemed dwindled and meaningless. To Luhaine, whose fussy penchant for austerity counted music a scatter-brained dalliance, the enduring character imbedded in primal rock made the quickened lives of plants and animals seem chaotic and shrill by comparison.

Rockfell's bleak depths lay cloaked by a dignity that humbled; its consent had extended through long-suffering centuries, to house and imprison those myriad entities bent in malice against the Law of the Major Balance. The latest of these was the Mistwraith, and there, even Luhaine's obstinate patience must bow in salute to the mountain's steadfast endurance.

Granted leave to resurvey the ward-spells that bound Desh-thiere's warped spirits captive, Luhaine diffused his presence. No longer a contained vortex of fine energies, he settled and sank downward into the heartrock of the mountain. Snow, ice and surface cliffs gave way to striated black mineral never harried by air or sunlight. The hidden depths whispered of earthsong and ores, and buried trickles of subterranean springs stitched a darkness interlaced with magecraft. Luhaine's perception could discern each gossamer strand, laid down in resonance and spun to shining harmony by his disparate Fellowship associates.

Davien the Betrayer had cut the original shaft, and also the five-sided chamber at its base that shaped the stone bounds of Rockfell's prison. Seamlessly pragmatic on first encounter, a blunt-cut statement of purpose that Luhaine knew well not to trust, the fibre of grand conjury that underpinned Davien's works held twists like kinked cord, and eddies like current under trout pools. Stealthy forces moved and moiled, outside of sound and beyond the pale of visible light. When enfleshed, Luhaine recalled such vibrations had pressured him to headaches. As spirit, he felt as if the spiked legs of insects prickled nerves he no longer possessed.

He deepened his search, skeined past the remnants of spells used to drill through the fastness of rock; beyond flickers, like sparks sieved through velvet, of older Paravian magecraft. Beneath the settled striations of the earth, shafts of unmined crystal rang still to the horn-calls of vanished centaur guardians. Here, like a glimmer of drowned starlight, rang the blessing of a unicorn's dance; there the captured echo of a sun-child's song. Had Luhaine retained the means to show physical emotion, the remembrance of faded beauty preserved in Rockfell's roots might have moved him to weep.

The only recourse left to him as spirit was to pour his balked pain into methodical labour. The mist-based entities that had driven off the Paravians remained here, alive, unquiet and too dangerous in malice to be entrusted to the mischance of fate.

Desh-thiere lay incarcerated behind three seals of stone, inside inter-locked sigils, each one structured to impound by the most ruthless deployment of energies. These shackles were not mazed like the defences set over Althain Tower, that a trained master could slip through and leave undisturbed. The bindings closed over the Mistwraith would admit nothing living, whether encased in quick flesh, or unclothed as pure spirit.

To sound the integrity of the completed ward, Luhaine could only settle into absolute quiet and take painstaking stock of the vibrations where anchor points fixed the spells to Rockfell's immutable granite. He must listen, unwind and verify each signature telltale fashioned by his Fellowship colleagues. Every mite of worked power must be inspected and mapped, the resonance instilled in each seal rune swept through exhaustive cross-checks for anomaly.

The construct itself shed a perilous corona, unquiet emanations whose very strength could spread an ache fierce enough to ravage bones and flesh. Its dire presence sieved through Luhaine's being as unkindly, muddling his aura into dissonance like a flame played along a bared nerve.

Asandir's intricate discipline had coerced cold stone to part and change shape and encompass; his handling rang forthright as the arced flight of swallows, or the trail of a falling meteor. Kharadmon's capricious energies cajoled order from raw chaos, then jagged spindles of white light across time and dimension, to stabilize the ward-glyphs into balance.

Were that flamboyant spirit not absent from Athera, he would no doubt have dropped in unannounced to crack some scathing comment.

Luhaine dismissed a stab of loss. Annoyed that the antagonistic rivalry he shared with Kharadmon could invade on stray thought and distract him, he realigned his lapsed concentration. The interfering ghost had scarcely been missed, and the risk did not brook a second thought, that his search beyond Athera for the Mistwraith's origin should end in tragedy and silence. A sorcerer who affected such caustic lack of manners would scarcely go astray through the course of a crossing between worlds. Any peril grave enough to leave Kharadmon compromised would be of far-reaching proportion.

Luhaine distanced his distress by immersing himself in the onerous tedium of work.

The energy coils fused in imprisoning resonance still sang in flawless balance. Piqued afresh by the masterful powers woven into the irreverent cartouche that finished one of Kharadmon's ward seals, Luhaine, in sheer irritation, repeated his last step. A crawling, half-sensed movement slipped through the slow probe of his awareness.

As if hooked by a thorn in clean grass, he stopped, backtracked, and re-sounded the passage just traced.

The magic's structure gleamed whole, its symmetry unsullied.

Luhaine paused. While the energies that bound Rockfell's mass into matter danced to the Creator's vast design, he combed through the seals once again. Nothing seemed amiss. And yet, elusive as a slivered bit of glass, the anxiety persisted. He distrusted the integrity of his own findings.

Possessed by the soul of a counting-house clerk, Luhaine pondered a whorled loop of spellcraft at random. In the laborious, jaundiced suspicion that Kharadmon could never resist baiting, he retested its anchor to the living stone.

Perfection rang back, every dying sigh of echo in predictable, harmonious register.

Luhaine could bore a mastiff for sheer, lockjawed tenacity. He could worry a conundrum for an hour, or a century, until he had tried every one of his colleagues to exasperated fits of frustration.

He set up wards to shield the emanations of his presence. Then he threaded his damped probe through the energy coils. Inside them, wrapped under spidery nets of illusion foiled at last by his masked approach, he discovered an infinitesimally small rip through the barrier of Asandir's wards.

He poised himself, examined the rent, then the tinselled veil of shields that hid its presence. The fact that Kharadmon's work still rang sound was significant. Grand conjury worked by a spirit-form naturally differed from the binding of a mage tied to breathing flesh. If one colleague's work showed no flaw, and the other bore sign of attrition, the change would be no anomaly.

A day and a night passed. The storm over Rockfell cleared to a crystal dome of stars, while Luhaine hounded every facet of this nuance to its frightening, unequivocal conclusion: the peril presented by the Mistwraith had widened.

Withdrawn from the deeps of Rockfell Pit, the sorcerer dispatched prompt warning to the Warden at Althain Tower.

'The wards that guard Desh-thiere have deteriorated, and the work is the Mistwraith's own. It pains me to say this, but no outside party can be faulted: the stolen knowledge the fell creature used to work its mischief bears the stamp of Arithon's training. Our dread is quite real, that the schooling he received from the masters at Rauven might one day key the power to set the captive wraiths free.'

Sethvir gave harried reply. '*This curse that binds our princes confounds itself more by the hour. Our hope lies in Kharadmon's charge.*'

Embroiled in the irrefutable aftermath, that the wards over Rockfell would require swift intervention and the help of a corporate colleague to mend, Luhaine dared not ask what else galled Sethvir to rare temper. Since an unpartnered spirit could not penetrate Rockfell's bindings, he must perforce stand guard at the pit until Asandir could journey north from Shand.

'*I regret to vex you further,*' Luhaine added, '*But this problem of black powder at Alestron is going to have to bide a while longer.*'

'It can't.' Like a whipcrack through still air, Sethvir's irritation spanned the distance to Rockfell Peak. '*The duke's foundry has been casting in secret again. I can't send Traithe to look in on this. He's busy curbing a plague of iyats that have set a string of house fires in Ghent.*'

'*Well have Dakar address Alestron's bit of mischief,*' Luhaine cracked back in a flayed up whirlwind of snowflakes. '*That's the least the useless drunkard could do, and just compensation, for his ruinous caper in Jaelot.*'

The notion was absurd, if not dangerous. But the straits exposed by the Mistwraith's activity posed too grave a threat. The Fellowship's affairs were strained to the point where Alestron's dilemma became secondary.

Precedents

Under Westwood's summer foliage, a company of Alestron's field-army dispatched to test its new-fledged might against the barbarians who plague the trade route reaps reward on its threshing bloodied swords; and twenty-eight clanborn men taken captive are marched to receive sentence under the mayor's justice in Karfael . . .

In a sunbaked glen within Alestron's domain, a man in dusty scholar's robes sets a touch match to a tube of bronze, and a spark flies, to unleash a booming roar and a belch of thick smoke; and a whining ball of stoneshot hammers into an oak grove, splintering green boughs like burst bone . . .

Far off in Atainia, jolted from reverie by the scream of rent greenery the width of a continent away, Sethvir of Althain raises a care-lined face and traces an eddy of wind, laden still with the acid pall of burnt brimstone; a pledge centuries old leaves him no choice but to send Dakar with all haste to plumb the ducal armoury at Alestron for its secrets . . .

VIII. *RENEWAL*

Old Avenor had been a small city. Abandoned through the centuries since the uprising, a line of weather-stripped, crumbled foundations marked the inner, Paravian-built citadel, where an elegant cluster of round keeps and a curtainwall had rested like a jewel's bezel on a knoll above the west seacoast. The setting commanded a broad, lowland valley, crowned still with stately oak and alive with game and deer. Through the reign of Tysan's past high kings, merchant trade and shipping had fared further south, from the generous cove harbour at Hanshire.

Since the current ruling mayor remained adamantly opposed to any form of royal alliance, the s'Ilessid prince who came to restore his ancestral seat could not resume the tradition of mooring rights. The diminished elegance of the Paravian ruin was too narrow for Lysaer's plans. He would build something larger, grander, a city like no other on the continent to stand as a monument for change.

The summer began with vetch lacing green runners over the tumbled walls that overlooked the Westland Sea, and ended in mud, noise and the rich, humid reek of slashed earth. Under blazing, dust-silted sunlight, through drizzling rain that hazed the hills like greyed muslin, the Prince of the West ordered the old, carved megaliths undermined and torn from their settings. If Paravians had once danced their blessing on this site, if the glimmering spirits of horned Riathan mourned the present desecration, Lysaer lacked mage-sight to perceive them. In past company of a Fellowship sorcerer, he had walked other Second Age ruins; the experience had impressed full awareness that such structures preserved a channel to renew the mysteries of the earth. If the prince was saddened by the fears of his citybred following, who looked unkindly upon the old ways, he must not let sentiment rule him.

What stones could be broken and dressed square for new use were unemotionally salvaged. Others too frost-cracked, too hard, or too stubbornly incised with old carvings, were dragged aside and piled on a hillock where bitterroot vine laced them over. There, when he craved solitude, Lysaer retired to think, or to practise his hand at refining the powers inherent in his given gift of light.

If an uncanny disharmony seemed to linger in that graveyard of riven blue granite, its disquiet only charged him to reaffirm his commitment. Once the Master of Shadow lay dead, new peace could reunite the rifts between factions. Then the old knowledge set aside for expedience could be the more splendidly restored.

While the late day sun slanted long, barred rays above the leaden heave of the breakers, Lysaer raised his chin from his fists and swept back hair tarnished with perspiration.

The voice that broke his sanctuary came again, pitched in exasperation from beyond the jumbled rim of the stone pile. 'His Grace is up there. Nowhere else. My Lord Diegan insisted, and he knows the prince's moods like a brother.'

A lull in the breeze framed someone's dubious reply. Resigned to untimely interruption, Lysaer stood. Ambient light snagged in the bullion on his sleeves as he flicked crumbled lichen from his hose and waved to disclose his location.

'Your Grace?' A sergeant at arms in a byrnie and the muted tan surcoat of Karfael's garrison spun and looked up in surprise. 'Who'd have guessed! What's in this place but creepy old carvings that even the gulls won't make nests in?'

As the visitor hitched his shoulders to even the weight of his mailshirt for the climb, Lysaer shouted, 'Don't trouble yourself! I'll come down.'

Though no state visitors were expected, his informal dress dependably never compromised his charge of sovereign responsibility. His doublet was cut of summer-weight silk, with gold trim and a discreet badge of rank. Close up, he needed no circlet or trapping to command the respect of his stature. By blue eyes unflinching in candour, and a majesty impressed since birth that no costly show of finery might replicate, the eye of the least discerning stranger must know him at once for a prince.

Disarmed by unwonted admiration, Karfael's road-dusty sergeant at arms was moved to offer him a bow.

'Please rise.' Lysaer offered his hand in courtly concern. 'The day's too hot for formalities. Forgive my impatience, but did your mayor allow me that company of archers whose service I begged leave to borrow?'

'The bowmen, certainly, your Grace.' Caught out, still coated in grime from his march, the man at arms received the prince's direct touch with embarrassment. 'Your quartermaster assigns them a barracks as we speak. My captain awaits you with news from the north, and a gift with my Lord Mayor's compliments.'

'Something that wouldn't keep, I trust.' Lysaer let Diegan's equerry fall in step behind as he strode through the sun-seared stalks of goldenrod, left mangled from the grind of the sledges used to drag the recalcitrant old stones. Beyond the forlorn hill with its discard mound, the site of Avenor's rebirth spread ochre and sable, the muddy wounds of gashed earth peopled by work crews like ants. The snap of ox goads and the ring of chisels peppered through the shouts of the stonemasons who directed the layout of new footings.

Lysaer paused to savour the sight. Immaculate in his trimmed doublet, his hair spun by wind to tangled filigree, he seemed a figure stamped out of legend, the blue of his eyes enriched to satisfaction for the vista of his dreams spread before him. Over these ragged beginnings he pictured the high, square towers he would erect in sandy, gold brick; from staked chalk strings, his mind raised curtainwalls and battlements, a fortified and defended city tranquil under banners and slate roofs.

Progress was already evident. Across acres of ploughed soil, past the riding school and its fixed rows of picket lines, above the meadows fenced aside for growing fodder, and the mowed greens where his troops drilled, he drank in the tang of coal fires. His heart thrilled to the clamour of the smiths' hammers that forged steel strapping for Avenor's future gates.

In this valley bequeathed by his s'Ilessid forbears, he laid down the marrow and the sinew for the army to become his honed weapon to defeat the Master of Shadow.

Inside the orderly works of his new demesne, the company in Karfael's colours stood out like a jerked strand through knit. Straggled through their midst was a double file of men, half-naked and pressed by armed riders into the parade yard behind the tent barracks.

'That's no troop of archers,' Lysaer said in brisk surprise. The glance he cast toward Karfael's sergeant was less an inquiry than a royal demand.

'No, your Grace.' In proud eagerness, the officer qualified. 'The reserve troop you dispatched to patrol the north road against clansmen met with good fortune in Westwood. A barbarian encampment was surrounded and ambushed, with twenty-eight prisoners taken. Our mayor in Karfael stayed their execution, in your name. He felt the wretched brutes would be better used as labour on Avenor's new walls.'

Lysaer launched off in long strides, his informal mien of the moment before banished to grim-faced reserve.

The guard sergeant had to stretch to stay abreast. 'Your Grace? What's amiss?'

His concern was regally ignored.

'Here.' The prince clawed off his belt and spun back toward the equerry. 'Take this.' In sharp disregard of manners or ceremony, he proceeded to remove his doublet, then bundled it into the attendant's arms. Stripped down to tinselled silk hose and the wind-snapped lawn of his shirt, he bolted downhill at a run.

Caught at a flat-footed standstill, the sergeant punished road-weary sinews to give chase. 'What's happened?' His breath snatched short over the rough ground, he pumped to keep pace with the prince.

'Your mayor meant well, certainly,' Lysaer flung back. 'But he acted beyond his authority when he thought to send prisoners as a gift.'

Battered by sticks through a brush brake, coughing dust from a shortcut across a meadow of cut hay, then hampered to slow agony by the additional drag of helm and surcoat and byrnie, the sergeant laboured to right a painful disadvantage in diplomacy. 'How may I help?'

'Your blade,' Lysaer gasped. 'Let me borrow it.'

The sergeant unsheathed his short sword. The instant the weapon was given over, the prince redoubled his pace.

Outstripped in a plunge down the earthworks for the moat, the hapless man at arms yielded before punishment and slackened back to a walk.

The dignified royal who had greeted him showed no qualms about scrambling through ditches. Whether the spring-fed muck at the bottom contained sewage or stagnant water, Lysaer plunged in to the waist to wade across. The sheen of his gold-striped silk doused in filth, he climbed the berm, vaulted the raw, chiselled edges of the wall's new foundation, and vanished to the cries of masons startled from their labour.

Practical in his abandonment, Karfael's rumpled sergeant at arms trudged off to find the road back to the barracks. Over-heated and set out of sorts, he concluded the contrary foibles of old blood princes were better off left to his captain's more experienced discretion.

At that moment, the ranking officer in command of the borrowed company sat his horse in a state of astounded inattention. Professional enough to be engrossed by the activities which occupied Avenor's new recruits, he rubbed his bristled chin with the back of a scaled gauntlet, and gaped at the volleys of arrows that rattled and smacked in even flights to the marks. Few missed. Such accuracy by itself was unnerving.

Across the practice field, other men rode armed with lances. Their agility in the saddle was breathtaking, despite the chaos that wove through their midst, as another team of foot, ambushed in drill, collapsed a field camp, complete with armoury tents and kitchen, and massed into bristling defence.

For a captain who had resigned from mercenary service to settle in a garrison command, the sight was one to strike awe, and then envy, and then a profound and weak-kneed relief that such superbly-trained cohorts would never face his troops as enemies across a drawn line of battle.

'Merciful Ath, will you look at that,' murmured the staffer who waited at his stirrup. 'They're using bulwarks of soaked hides to douse fire arrows.'

Karfael's captain twisted in his saddle and paused, as someone he did not recognize plunged headlong into his idle ranks of guardsmen. A shout followed, and a roil of sudden turbulence. Then the runner burst through, streaming water and spattered with black mud. The sweat-limp shirt on his heaving shoulders billowed at the waist like a peasant's smock. Dishevelled from head to foot, the young man charged on, straight into the roped knot of captives.

He held an unsheathed blade in his fist.

Caught lounging with dropped stirrups, Karfael's heavyset captain unhooked the knee draped on his pommel. With townbred, fashionably bland interest, he held his immediate order to intervene. Every veteran knew how it felt to suffer the wiles of forest barbarians. If a steel-bearing maniac was bent on private vengeance, the escorting men at arms would be decidedly inclined to enjoy a bit of fun before they took action in restraint.

But the intruder turned his blade to whistling use, not to maim prisoners, but to sever the cordage that yoked them.

The captain's bull-throated bellow sheared above the nerve-racking beat of the masons' mallets. He would sooner see barbarians dead in cold blood than suffer even one to go free. 'Who is that upstart? By Ath, pull him off!'

Four guards in his troop snapped to and dismounted. As they jostled to enter the milling knot of captives, the perpetrator leapt at them, shouting. 'By Ath Creator, this is an offence!' The sword spun, whining. Startled guards and half-naked clansmen shrank back to escape getting slashed. 'I'll not have slaves here! *No* man serves Avenor in shackles!'

The commotion turned heads on the wall-works. Masons and mule drovers left off their labour, while the mounted lancers at the edge of the practice field coalesced from their war-drills to stare.

Unmindful of outside observation, deaf to someone's rising call of inquiry, more guardsmen from Karfael elbowed into the fray to defend their assigned responsibility. Their captain screamed his indignation. 'What are these worthless wretches to you? Who cares if they perish where they stand? Ropes are too kind for their sort. Let the prince who receives them bind shackles on them all, that no soft-hearted dolt is like to cut!'

The fair rescuer flung back a wild fall of hair. Hedged in by bared weapons that licked in on all sides through the dusty, dazed bodies of the captives, he rammed his sword in dry earth, then clawed loose his cuff ties, peeled back filthy cloth, and raised his wrists before him. 'Well, chain me first, then!' he raged. A shocking, glacial blue against his flushed summer tan, his eyes held a warning to freeze thought. 'No man born in this realm shall be lashed like an animal before I should suffer the same!'

'Fiends plague my mother, a philanthropist!' The guard captain rolled his gaze skyward, pleased to deliver the order. He stretched his toes and recovered his stirrups, unmoved through the commotion as his men swooped to spread-eagle the rash idiot amid his coffle of clansmen.

The deed was accomplished with small resistance. Half the barbarians were wounded; the rest were too dazed and exhausted from the march to try more than token trouble. The tall scout they jabbed to make room for the newcomer was swollen nearly blind from a bruise. In touching and deferent courtesy, that one stepped aside, while a lieutenant volunteered the pole off his mace. The blond dissident found his wrists tied immobile and his elbows threaded through behind his back in less time than he had taken to speak out.

'What's going on here?' cried an authoritative voice from the sidelines. 'Your Grace?'

Made aware that his position was now hedged in by onlookers, Karfael's captain knew his job well enough to keep his eyes fixed on his guardsmen. As they straightened to attention after securing the new prisoner, he bellowed without turning around, 'Where's Avenor's vaunted prince? We've brought him a gift, and with it, a problem in discipline.'

Closing pressure from behind began to upset the stance of his destrier. The guard captain fought the animal steady in skilled play at the reins. Since he would make a shameful impression as an envoy if it turned to war training and kicked a bystander, he flung back an irritable shout. 'If your prince is not present, then send for him!'

A ripple stirred through the prisoners; the bound, blond insurgent strode to the limit of his noose and tipped up his mud-splashed face. Tugged a half-step as the added strain dragged the ropes, the lanky, one-eyed barbarian inclined his head in jeering satire. 'If you wish the attendance of Prince Lysaer s'Ilessid, unless my sight lies, you behold him.'

The captain from Karfael blinked in horrified astonishment at the scruffy personage he had issued crisp orders to abuse. 'You?' he said. 'The Prince of the West?'

Lysaer gave back a glare that could have raised curds on new milk. 'Tell your Lord Mayor,' he said in furious, regal arrogance, 'he may fight clansmen who rob caravans and kill them in battle. He may take them alive and try them on criminal charges. If they are guilty, he may exercise his lawful right to execute them. But I will suffer no enemy of civilized society to be set in chains as slave labour.'

The burly captain swung his leg over his high cantle and dismounted. 'Your Grace, forgive my ignorance.' Not waiting for his squire to take his horse, he gave mollified apology and drew his dagger. 'Let me cut you loose, and quickly.'

'Not yet.' Mantled in self-possession that should have been beyond a man strapped erect in dirty clothing, Lysaer issued correction. 'Every clansman here shall be restored to liberty first. For your presumption, to mete out Avenor's justice without my leave, they will stay free, to depart or join my cause as they choose.'

'That's rank insult!' The angle of his blade no longer civil, Karfael's guard captain gave the nearest rope a vicious jerk. 'These men are my Lord Mayor's convicts!'

'Not when they stand in Avenor,' Lysaer said on a yielded step to avert a stumble. His magisterial presence never wavered. 'Back down. Their fate is in my hands, not yours. Or else claim my sovereignty and my pledge to fight the Shadow Master, and plunge your damned knife through my heart.'

A madman might make such a statement, except the blue eyes clear lit in summer glare showed only steel-clad resolve.

The guard captain hesitated, his jaw set and every sinew primed for a thrust he could not in decency complete. Barbarian eyes watched him, mocking through their misery. Then the unfriendly presence that harried his back broke through. His cordon of guardsmen broke their line and gave ground, cowed to unequivocal surrender. Surrounding his men and the unfortunate coffle were the glittering lancers from the practice field. Hard as nails, poised on their hair-trigger leash of fine discipline, they were led by the jewelled and magnificent person of Avenor's dark-haired Lord Commander.

'You will do his Grace's bidding,' Lord Diegan demanded from the back of his tall, bay courser. Beyond the sun-struck dazzle that laced his naked longsword, his brown eyes stayed fixed and inimical on Karfael's cornered envoy. 'If you're minded to argue the matter further, you'll be offered an audience after the prince has withdrawn for the chance to be properly clothed and refreshed.'

As a competent but unrefined veteran who had risen to his post through the ranks, the captain dispatched as his Lord Mayor's emissary much preferred to argue out his differences in the sweat of a spar over weapons. Given the luxury of an attended bath, eased by servants who fussed over his old injuries and clothed him in lace and court velvets, he struggled to throw off embarrassment. When assigned this tour of duty, he had given little thought to the prerogatives of royal hospitality.

Hot in his layers of borrowed finery, nakedly vulnerable without his arms, he pitched himself to weather his formal meeting with temperamental blooded royalty. His mistake had been accidental; a prince who ran about half-clothed and dirty ought not to cavil at insults from town-raised strangers who, at best, were distrustful of his station.

If the jewels, the candles, and the splendours of the court were not beyond his scant learning to recount, the captain resolved to salvage the more pleasant memories of his experience to delight his wife and small children.

But Avenor's grand hall was as yet a foundation, roofed over with summer haze and stars. Torn between disappointment and jittered nerves, Karfael's envoy was escorted to the shingled shack used by turns for tactical meetings between the ranking officers, and by Avenor's shrewd old seneschal to manage the city's diverse finances. The interior with its rough plank floor was scantily furnished. It held no carpeted dais. The trestle at its centre, draped in white damask and arrayed with glittering crystal, could have been a jewel fallen out of its setting into the hovel of a thief.

Attended only by the pedigreed elegance of his Lord Commander at Arms, Lysaer pushed back his chair. 'I owe you my royal apology, Captain.' His tabard of indigo velvet flashed as he rose, spattered with reflections thrown off gold braid and seed pearls and sapphires. A captured sheen of lamplight played over his tinselled sleeves, and fair hair, now clean, bound under a gold wire fillet. The shoulders that filled out the doublet were not broadened by padding; the face, in planes like master-worked sculpture, needed no crown to heighten its nobly wide brow.

Thrust unschooled into refinements outside his experience, professionally shamed before the military excellence displayed unabashed on the practice ground, the guard captain squared his jaw.

Lysaer met his unease with a self-effacing smile. 'The strictures of my upbringing got the better of my temper, this afternoon. A sorry lapse, since, as you see, I have no hall yet, and no proper state for guesting visitors. Come, be welcome and sit. The wine won't be rough, or the food.'

A servant stepped from the shadows and pulled out a padded leather chair. The guard captain sank into the place he was offered, startled to scarlet embarrassment by the squeak of the horsehair upholstery.

'Your Grace, how was I to know you?' he burst out. 'The clan captives were not sent to offend. My Lord Mayor wished to be helpful.'

'No harm done.' Lysaer arranged his wrists on his chair arms, while the servant went on to serve wine from a cut-crystal decanter. 'But you must understand, far more lies at stake than a matter of idealistic principle. To chain hostile clansmen within a loyal enclave is letting the viper into our midst. Such men could become a ready tool for our downfall, should an enemy steal in and cut their chains. As oppressors, our ranks would stand weakened. I'll sanction no such liability in the heart of my city, to risk the security of my following.'

His goblet now filled with red claret, Lysaer turned the glass in jewelled fingers. 'So you see, the offence was not yours, but against my own royal trust, a private integrity I am oath-sworn as sovereign never to bend or to break.' Arrows of stained light bloodied his rings as he looked across in earnest entreaty. 'Best to kill cleanly, or else let any who oppose our new order stay at liberty to amend their reiving ways.'

'A worthy thought.' The guard captain raised his glass and swallowed, ill at ease, but at least lent fair grounds on which to argue. 'But what of my Lord Mayor's prisoners? Karfael restored your charter to these lands. His city's confidence has been breached, since he entrusted men into your hands who have done injury to his merchants. In setting them free, you have spurned him.'

Swift to resume an ongoing point of contention, Lord Diegan agreed. 'My liege, there's been an insult. You can't just let the issue rest.'

No glazing graced the crude casements. Summer moths pattered into the pool of the lamplight, to dance in crazed circles and die wing-charred. The damask table-cloth held a litter of tiny corpses, fluttering and maimed, or fallen limp. As if they were human, and bloody, Lysaer sighed, pained as few ever saw him. 'I understand the mayor's cause for outrage. But the sordid outcome of this case should be obvious.'

When the look on the captain's shaved features remained blank, the prince gripped his goblet and dashed off a neat swallow, as though to erase the sharp taste of bitterness. 'The clansmen I released were weary enough to drop where they stood. Most were wounded. Where can they run? They are weaponless. When darkness fell, a discreet troop of head-hunters with tracking dogs were set after them. This far removed from their bolt-holes in Westwood, I doubt if a man of them survives.'

'They could be lucky,' Lord Diegan interrupted. 'The drifters who raise horses in the meadows of Pasyvier could offer them shelter.'

'That's a long-shot.' Lysaer flicked a dying insect from his sleeve in sudden, nerve-fired impatience. 'If there are survivors, my point isn't lost. Word will be carried to the clans, and our troops here will learn a painless lesson. This is Avenor, where all men are entitled to the terms of royal justice. Any who disrupt trade or prey upon the roads will be handled according to their deserts.' He settled on his elbows, his blue eyes spiked with reflections thrown off by the lamp. 'Diegan, this is one thread in a weave of whole cloth. We must start thinking for the future. When my garrison marches to war against the Master of Shadow, they mustn't be divided in purpose. We can't maintain the burden, then, of guarding the roads in friendly territory. How can we ever clear the wilds of clan pests if we continue to fan the old hatreds?'

Impressed enough to shed his self-consciousness, Karfael's captain gave a grainy laugh. 'Wise tactics, if any clanborn barbarian can ever be made to know his place. But why ask for archers? I watched your bowmen at the butts. They are marksmen. Why borrow ours?'

Lysaer's formal sovereignty broke before a grin of boyish merriness. 'My own troops balked at their orders.'

Pained, Lord Diegan drained his goblet, then waved back the servant who bent to replenish his wine. 'No. Drink won't help. I need my head clear instead.' But a suspect brightness to his glance showed him already sunk in his cups. To the Karfael man, he said in stabbing sarcasm, 'His Grace could scarcely order floggings for men who objected to –'

'Lord Diegan,' Lysaer cut in firmly. 'Not now. We've been through this. I won't change my stance.'

Still nettled by the terrifying fervour Lysaer's lancers had turned against his veterans that afternoon, the captain coughed as the wine stung his throat in the course of his clumsy swallow. 'What's this?'

'A topic we'll save for tomorrow morning.' Still rueful, Lysaer motioned to the pages piled up on the sidelines, burdened down with trays and steaming platters. 'Spare me from the temper of my cook, instead. If we don't make an effort with his sauces and meats, he's going to be out here with the knives he uses to joint beef. Slow-spoken as he is, he moves like a weasel. If we let him think his efforts at the spit have been slighted, he'll skewer us faster than anybody's company of crack archers.'

All night, the burly captain from Karfael dreamed of the deadly, precise turn of teamwork displayed by Avenor's foot troops and mounted lancers. At sunrise, awakened in twisted blankets and running cold sweat, he wondered afresh why Lysaer s'Ilessid should require his troop of lack-lustre bowmen to muster and march inland to a secluded defile.

The haze of morning mists had yet to burn off and disperse. His beard and eyebrows grizzled with condensation, his mailshirt a grinding weight that hampered every effort to slap off the insects that whined in the absence of a breeze, the captain nursed a foul mood.

To judge by reddened eyes and a dishevelled state of grooming, Diegan beside him suffered the same fierce headache, courtesy of Lysaer's expensive brandies. At least, the fine skin around his eyes tightened each time his bay horse stamped and jingled its bridle. Whatever service Karfael's archers were to bestow on behalf of Avenor, the city's Lord Commander remained opposed.

'How much longer do we stand idle on the hilltops?' The captain could all but feel his gear rusting in the damp.

Lord Diegan turned his head, the expression mirrored in the rim of his gilded visor tightly drawn and cynical. 'Not long. Only until the mist lifts enough to signal your bowmen on the ridgetops. Blond hair should stand out in early sunlight. They won't find it hard to see their target.'

'You want *my men* to shoot arrows at *his Grace*? Ath Creator!' The guard captain's horse jibbed sidewards in response to his stiffened fists. Playing at the reins to resettle it, he said in pale outrage, 'The rumour's true then? The Prince of the West would test his gift of light? If this trial goes wrong, you know what will happen! Dharkaron's Black Spear and Chariot! We'll have a massacre. Your elite garrison at Avenor will run riot in misplayed loyalty and butcher my field troop like crowbait!'

'My liege insists it won't go wrong,' Diegan said in disparaging boredom. 'He's practised for months. He claims he's mastered a refinement of his talent. Said he'd burn the shafts to white cinders long before they fall and endanger him.'

'Why?' cried the captain. 'Why should he risk his royal person?'

'Well, *I* couldn't talk him out of it,' Diegan snapped. 'My men wouldn't take the order. If yours won't either, his royal Grace spoke his intention to march without escort and invite Hanshire's garrison to indulge him. Since Lord Mayor Garde would likely send heavy infantry with orders to provoke open war, and Lysaer won't harm any soldier he considers his ally, here we are happily slapping midges.'

In some unseen, mist-mantled glen, a wood thrush sang in falling triplets. A hare grazed under a gorse bush that had been invisible the moment before. Weak sun melted through, flooding the valley with mellow warmth. Lord Diegan straightened his chased helm, flicked beaded dewdrops from the crest feathers, and gave way to the misery that chewed him. In the arrogance he once used to provoke Etarra's dandies to rash escapades, he said, 'His Grace won't see reason. He made a fool of you yesterday. Are you townsman enough to dare to use his princely hide for a target shoot? Or did his manners at dinner overawe you enough to trade in your bollocks as a royalist?'

Karfael's captain returned a low laugh at the jibe. 'There's still bounty offered for royal scalps.' He gathered his reins, prepared to ride personally to his sergeants. 'Why not make this a sporting event? Eighty royals says your prince winds up bloody and dead.'

'Done,' said Diegan with quick recklessness. But his face stayed averted, as though his expression might betray him. 'If you win, let's hope the coin buys me peace. I'm tired of being heart-torn and angry.'

The captain paused, no fool in his reading of men. 'You love him that much. I can't fathom it.'

'Don't stay here, then,' Lord Diegan flung back, still adamant in his need to look elsewhere. 'Prince Lysaer has a way about him no man can resist. Every night I thank Ath that the Master of Shadow wasn't born with the same natural gift.'

Day brightened. The mist shredded in drifts above a landscape patched with swatches of summer foliage. With an agony that pinned him breathless, Lord Diegan heard cadenced hoofbeats as the captain's destrier cantered off; in dull misery he marked the shouted orders to the sergeants, followed by Lysaer's assent, absorbed without echo by the slopes.

Avenor's Lord Commander looped his reins in his elbow and masked his face in gloved hands.

Then a whining flight of arrows split the air, their sound as evil, as deadly, as any fallen on another summer's day, ones that had wreaked a bloody slaughter on the flood-trampled banks of Tal Quorin.

Pierced through by past horrors and present dread, Lord Diegan listened in suspension. But the moment gave back no crack of broadheads, nor the rattle as fletched shafts sliced and flickered deflected paths through snatched leaves. He heard no strike of steel into flesh, no screaming. Just a whispered shriek of air, and a heat that swept his skin in a fleeting, flash-fire burn of wind.

Over the settled silence left by the departed wood thrush, Karfael's captain bellowed in astonished incredulity, 'Ath! Almighty Ath, here's a miracle!'

Eyes scalded blind behind a screen of soaked leather, Diegan heard Lysaer's peal of gladdened laugher. 'No miracle, good man. But now, at last, I can answer to Maenalle's barbarians. I have means to defend my army from her ambush on the day they must cross the passes of Orlan to challenge the Master of Shadow.'

Unnerved and unmanned, Lord Diegan slumped weak-kneed in his saddle. His horse had dropped its neck to crop greenery; he understood he would have to dismount to recapture his reins, slithered down the beast's crest to loop behind its gold-trimmed headstall.

By the time Karfael's envoy cantered back to rejoin him, Lord Diegan stood in the grass. Dry eyed, at least lent the semblance of dignity by his veneer of Etarran cynicism, he looked up into the face of a veteran captain enraptured as if touched by light, as indeed, he likely had been.

Lysaer's presence did that to a man.

Crisp in his surcoat cut of silk, Lord Diegan regarded the town delegate in shaken, heartsore humility. He could not have given the order to fire; not even to test whether Lysaer's gift of light could be raised as shield and defence. The ache in his chest finally loosened enough to release its hold on his tongue.

'You owe me eighty royals,' he said to the captain. Then he smiled in elation that pierced him more sweetly than his fiercest climax with a woman. 'My prince isn't bloody and dead.'

'*Did you see that!*' cried the captain, too bemused still to acknowledge the outcome of the bet. 'His Grace of Tysan raised light and not an arrow in a thousand could touch him. He is invincible, and the army at his back cannot fail.'

Sacrifice

Hard by the trade road that wound northward to the city of Etarra, the old ford that once channelled the River Severnir spread dust-dry in the gloaming, a weed-choked bed of naked rocks and bent grasses, loud with the strident clicks of summer insects. The clansmen who hastened like shadows through the gloom made little noise. They had the last prisoner from the caravan bound and gagged before twilight darkened the west-facing rimrocks; and a stillness too uneasy to be mistaken for peace settled over the jumbled ravines etched through the Skyshiel foothills.

The ox teams used to draw the laden wagons sprawled where their drovers had last reined them, collapsed in dead, folded heaps amid the slackened leather of their traces. Throat wounds inflicted in practised slaughter were spared the sucking predation of flies only by the advent of night. The drays themselves had not been rifled. The tarps still secured their trade wares and goods since this raid had not been made for plunder.

Sickened by the coppery reek of fresh blood more than pride would admit, Caolle, war captain of Strakewood's last clansmen, stood with his foot propped on a rock. He cleaned his blades on a courier's black felt saddlecloth, careful to avoid the bullion fringe that might scrape and cause stray noise. Small difference that the deaths were of beasts, and not human. To any who followed the old ways, all wasteful killing was offence.

But in Caolle's experience, any milksop too squeamish to take life was a fool unlikely to survive. Etarra's northern league of headhunters saw to that, all the more since Lysaer's fresh alliances, which drove the clans' current need to waylay any caravan travelling in the company of a message rider.

Quiet footsteps approached to Caolle's right. Since just one man alive dared creep up on him while he held unsheathed steel, the war captain jerked up his bristled chin. 'Did you find that courier's dispatches yet?' The dagger in his hand moved a querulous fraction. 'If you haven't, I'm minded to squeeze his throat a bit. Get him dizzy, he'll sing out his answer that much faster.'

Lanky, tall, as self-possessed as cool marble, Jieret Red-beard stopped a careful, clear sword's length away. 'That won't be necessary.'

Caolle studied the lion crest on the cloth in his hand one last time, then straightened, his obstreperous nature focused to an assassin's piercing interest. 'You've read the satchel's contents already, I see.' Gold fringe shed a sullen sparkle as he tossed the felt where it would not mire his feet. 'If the news is bad, let me hear it.' War steel chimed in the gloom as he sheathed his dagger and tucked a blade that matched him for wear in the crook of one elbow.

The parchment in Jieret's fingers crackled as it passed into Caolle's ruthless grip. 'Our liege lord finally made his presence known.'

'And about time, isn't it?' Caolle squinted at the pages, snapped them straight to net the last, failing light, then coughed in surprise as he picked out the same lion crest in the seal. 'Jaelot? You're saying Prince Arithon was *there*?'

The Earl of the North had tact enough to know when his war captain's questions were best ignored. While Caolle read, he surveyed the unkind fruits of a raid most rapaciously executed: the huddle of bound survivors; their disjointed muddle of wagons, with hulks of felled draught animals in unbreathing, splay-legged heaps; and beyond, bunched movement in the gloom, the restless, milling mass of the outrider's horses strung together by scouts who worked in expedient silence.

Every extra mount would be needed to leave this place quickly despite the added risk of leaving tracks. While the weather favoured enemy patrols, clansmen in Rathain did not travel burdened; nor did they camp in one place for more than a snatched night's rest.

'Apprenticed to Halliron Masterbard?' Always a deliberate reader, Caolle paused between paragraphs to ruminate. 'A typical s'Ffalenn bit of cleverness: why didn't we guess his Grace might try that?'

'I doubt our liege acted for a ploy.' The boyhood memory remained all too clear, of the night Jieret had lain awake to overhear the old Masterbard berate a prince for squandered talents. Stung to reminder of a past when his family had been alive, the earl clenched his jaw. He waited with held breath through the moment of profound shock, as his war captain deciphered the last lines, which listed the damage Arithon s'Ffalenn had inflicted through his music on the night of the mayor's solstice feast.

'Dharkaron Avenger!' Caolle cranked the parchment into a tight roll, and metal scraped, dissonant, as the movement fretted his studded brigandine against the hilt of his broadsword. 'We have to presume that dispatch rider knows the content of this.'

The young Earl of the North stared into the gathering night, while breeze feathered the grass heads against boot cuffs spattered with the drying tang of blood. He could not watch as Caolle retraced the pitiless course of logic: that if the courier knew the name behind the desecration of Jaelot, he would have talked. Every drover in the caravan might already be primed to repeat his gossip, facts that at all costs must be kept from reaching the Mayor of Etarra.

'Ath's mercy, the damned prisoners outnumber us.' Caolle's blunt fingers closed, crushing the report with its black and gold ribbons and cracked seal. 'I wiped my steel clean too soon, I see.' The implied death warrant for two dozen lives sounded level and matter of fact.

But Jieret knew his captain better than the father he had lost, and no gruff bluster might fool him. 'We can't take the risk.' Behind his tortured acceptance lay a grief no years might tame, for the last time Etarra's army had found cause to march against Arithon s'Ffalenn, his people had nearly been exterminated. 'The others can move out ahead of us. No need to say what we've found.'

The parchment fluttered to the ground as Caolle's stocky hand closed over his chieftain's wrist. 'No, boy,' he said, though the earl at his side was anything but a child. 'They'll have to know. We can silence this caravan, and maybe the next, before Pesquil's patrols infest these hills with trackers. But word must leak out eventually. Just count ourselves lucky we've had warning.'

Yards off in the gathering darkness, a clansman cracked a joke to a burst of stifled laughter. Through a breeze-snatched hoot of rejoinder, Caolle said, 'You ride out with the others. Leave me to deal with what's here. I'll see it's done fast and clean, while the townsmen are sleeping and unaware.'

Jieret's expelled breath shuddered through the touch shared between them. 'You can't spare me!'

'No.' Caolle scraped his stubbled chin with the back of a gore-flecked wrist. 'We can't spare our liege lord, either. That doesn't mean we won't try. Now go. The longer we tarry in this place, the greater the danger. Another caravan's outriders could find the ruts where the wagons left the road. We daren't be tracked and found here.'

Sound advice, Jieret knew. At such moments, he understood his father's past silences all too well. No townsman could be faulted for paying bounty to headhunters when the horror of tonight's work came to light. But worse, far more lasting, were the consequences if Etarra's army found Arithon, and Avenor's new forces joined with them, as must happen, in time, despite this most ruthless precaution. Maenalle's reports out of Tysan were unremitting and grim. The army Lysaer shaped to hunt the Shadow Master promised a ruthless opposition that would suffer no clan ally to live.

'We'll need to pick a site to make rendezvous,' Jieret said at last.

As always, Caolle's thoughts ran ahead of him. 'At the Farl Rocks, deep in the Barrens.' No merchant would follow them there, and a headhunter tracking team, with great reluctance: the site had once been Paravian, and the old, carved markers that crowned its hills were firmly believed to be haunted.

Faced by the prospect of a hard, dusty ride on horses of uncertain quality, Jieret clasped wrists with his war captain in hurried salute. 'Make it quick,' he begged in an agonized whisper.

Then he strode off, uncannily quiet for a man of his loose-limbed build. His father had moved that way, too, Caolle remembered; no surprise. Both had learned their scoutcraft at his knee, to his own exacting standards. The grief at times stabbed through him, that despite every forced lesson in survival, his efforts could still fall short. Every advantage he could wring out of blood and experience might not keep this last scion of the earl's line alive long enough to marry and raise a grown heir.

Once Etarra's army marched, their life's hope could be wasted, to see the clans restored to rule under a s'Ffalenn high king at Ithamon.

A breeze flicked the offending twist of parchment into tumbling flight across the grass. Caolle bent with an angry chink of steel and speared the dispatch with his blade. He would burn the writ, then grind his dagger sharp on a whetstone. That his liege lord would never sanction the blood about to be spilled for his sake made no difference. Arithon of Rathain was not here to gainsay. Still, Caolle shrugged off a lingering, unpleasant recollection of green eyes that saw far too much, and a burden of conscience too deep for most men to sustain his Grace's locked glance.

'Be damned to you, prince,' the war captain muttered into the bristles of his beard. 'If niceties counted for everything, you'd have left us to die in your absence along the banks of Tal Quorin.'

While Jieret called the muster through the velvety night, and the chink of bit rings and stirrups stabbed through furtive movement as the scouts tightened girths to ride out, Caolle pried the official writ clear of his sword with a shrieking, dry scrape. For himself, he never imagined any life beyond the bloody heritage the fugitive clanborn had lived since the uprising. Yet the unwilling lesson learned in the teeth of Etarra's army had forced a view his dead lord, Steiven, could never in life make him see: some crimes against nature existed which no force of arms could put right.

That Arithon of Rathain should be placed in sovereign responsibility while set under a curse of violence was one of them. The very least a liegeman of Caolle's disposition could do was to slit a few townborn throats.

The war captain did not revel in murder; but as one who had buried too many bodies left spitted and scalped by marauding headhunters, the act carried little of Arithon's lacerating burden of remorse.

*   *   *

224

The sun threw a harsh, orange pall over hills that unfolded in hazed ranks to the horizon. Rain-thirsty soil crumbled, dusty, between shrivelled heads of yellow grass that in a past age had spread a waist-high, rippling green carpet over the fells. Once a meadow that rustled to the light dance of unicorns, the dry ground of Daon Ramon Barrens now thundered to the beat of an approaching rider.

Caolle had reached the Farl Rocks. His late arrival did nothing to alleviate Jieret Red-beard's taxed mood.

Informed where he stood on the flat-topped megalith he had climbed to use as a vantage point, he swore at the cloudless sky. 'By Dharkaron, he has salt, to presume we'd still be camped here.'

Powdered lichens fanned away on the breeze as the Earl of the North leaped down to face his informer, a Companion, one of fourteen young boys who had survived the slaughter at Strakewood to grow with him to manhood.

'We left him a horse,' Jieret ranted, angry now he was relieved of cause to worry. 'Mounted, he should have reached here three days ago.'

'Well, he isn't alone.' Blond and easy-tempered, the Companion who ventured this tidbit stretched, the flat iron studs on his brigandine too dull to catch the day's brassy light, and sword steel too polished glancing bright as if dipped in acid.

Jieret shut his teeth in a silent snarl. Spoiling for a fight, he strode off the grassy hillock and into the shadow of the defile where his company had slept on small stones through three long and fireless nights. If no man had seen a Paravian ghost, the site held a presence that somehow pierced the heart and left a man maudlin and sorrowful.

The horse just ridden in stood apart from the others. Through a lattice of drought-stunted alders, Jieret could see it, bridle fixed to a leading rein, and bearing a rider too narrow in the shoulders to be Caolle.

'Fiends plague us all, I thought so!' he cried, and exploded a finch to arrowed flight. Aware trouble would compound if he lingered, he threaded apace through the saplings, not snapping sticks despite his rage.

His war captain heard his approach anyway. Tired enough that his shoulders hunched, Caolle sucked a mouthful from his waterskin and spat in a hurry to free his tongue. 'She has two brats.'

Jieret stopped, knee-deep in blighted grass, and surrounded by a disgorged flurry of leafhoppers.

One look at Caolle's tortured stiffness, and the last of his anger drained away. 'I thought only males drove that caravan.'

The war captain grunted, lifted the waterskin and slopped the dregs over his head. A spill of droplets darkened hair the colour of filed iron, and channelled through seams that just now looked quarried into the crags of his face.

His eyes, bleak as charcoal, locked with Jieret's. Through the years since the tragedy at Strakewood, no Companion had ever confronted him over the past, when his insistence had overruled Arithon's plea to withhold the clan's children from the battle on Tal Quorin's fateful banks. Since the slaughter that had drenched summer moss in the next generation's young blood, Caolle was least likely to forget the cost of his personal misjudgement. 'These were hidden in the carpet rolls. Don't worry. I got them out before they saw the bodies.'

Jieret shut his eyes and somehow found the grace to hold his tongue, while more insects disturbed by Caolle's ablutions blundered in flight over his leathers and boots.

'Some things I can do well enough,' Caolle finished in a tone stripped bare of any insolence. 'But not even for the life of my liege could I draw steel on a woman or a child.'

The Earl of the North allowed himself an exasperated look at the unwanted prisoner who sat, bound astride the tired gelding. She was brown-haired, neatly made, and no doubt comely when she was not dirty and shaking tired. The reddened eyes that glared above the twist of rag which silenced her were frightened and fierce with defiance. She clutched a child of perhaps three years against her shoulder; a second infant slept in a saddlebag, a filthy thumb tucked in his mouth.

'Don't tell me,' Jieret prodded, antagonized by the prick of her regard. 'She screams if you take off the gag, and she's tried to knife you in the back?'

'Well, I did kill her brother,' Caolle allowed. He shook out his hair, drops flying off him like an ill-mannered dog after a swim. 'Our cause was sound enough. Every drover in that caravan knew about Jaelot. The news can't be kept close for long.'

But Jieret had expected that much. To the woman, he said, 'You'll go free, but only if you don't disrupt my men.'

She tossed her chin and looked daggers, most likely convinced she would be forced regardless, or abandoned in the wilds unprotected. Both prospects were tempting enough to a company who had seen every woman in Strakewood cut down without mercy by townsmen. Clan numbers were pared back to the point at which children would be a blessing to foster, whether stolen or begotten by violence. Only the helpless anguish of knowing the brutalities suffered by his mother and sisters kept Jieret on the side of moral decency. He reached out, caught Caolle's soggy sleeve, and drew him away down the defile.

Once out of the prisoner's earshot, he said, 'One of us needs to find Arithon.'

'Just how do you plan to do that?' Caolle rubbed a trickle of moisture off his chin and winced at the sting of small scabs. To judge by the state of his wrist, the woman not only scratched, but could land a bite like a champion. Seldom caught out in embarrassment, Caolle hunched like a bear with a thorn and gruffly pursued his objection. 'After the disaster our liege unleashed in Jaelot, the mayor's guard sent out a sweep of armed patrols. Neither they nor their packs of headhunters with beaters and twenty-three couples of hounds could track a royal hair of him.'

Too hardened not to guess the vivid means by which Caolle had extracted this information, Jieret bypassed the point without questions. 'Lady Maenalle, Steward of Tysan, asked for a rendezvous in a cove in the Gulf of Stormwell. Since Sethvir of Althain saw fit to pass on her request, we can presume that someone sent by Arithon will answer.'

'Well let me go,' Caolle said, much too eager for a man just in from hard travel.

Jieret returned an evil grin. 'Not a chance. Since you've brought us three extra mouths to feed, you can stay here and suffer the consequences. That poor chit's virtue is yours to guard as of now. I'll have to travel fast and light. Even with luck and good weather, I'll scarcely reach the north coast before winter.'

'Ath, boy,' protested Caolle. 'I'm your more expendable resource.'

'No.' Every inch as forceful as his father, Jieret would not be swayed. 'Arithon's life is worth both of ours. He is all the clans' hope for the future. You'll stay, and raid the roads, and hold that woman captive until what facts she knows become common knowledge. If fortune runs against us, the wait will be short. Too soon, my captain, you'll have that chance you burn for, to balance our feud with Etarra.'

Duplicity

When notice was served from Althain Tower appointing Dakar to search Alestron's guarded armoury for the presence of black powder weaponry, Sethvir's contact caught him in his usual shipboard posture, folded double over *Black Drake*'s lee rail. Even half-paralysed by nausea, the Mad Prophet cursed the wretched complications the assignment was bound to entail.

The ruling Teir's'Brydion had a temper like a viper, and three younger brothers whose manner toward strangers ran to bloodletting distrust. Any fool who approached their citadel with intent to meddle in their weapon stores was likely to find himself spitted before he could pick the first lock. Denied breath to denounce his fate by the piteous heave of his stomach, Dakar wished a pox on the Warden of Althain, until opportunity dawned like an epiphany, that every one of his miserable predicaments might be solved at a single stroke.

The Mad Prophet coughed, his beard split in crocodilian malice. 'Oh, perfect,' he confided to the lisping slap of *Black Drake*'s foamy wake. How convenient, if the Master of Shadow should suffer mishap in the course of the Fellowship's benighted service. Asandir could scarcely hold anyone to blame if the brothers s'Brydion came to slice Rathain's prince into mincemeat; and since Sethvir's gift of charts and navigational tools, Arithon, with his tender s'Ffalenn conscience, would be hard pressed to refuse any favour in return.

Dakar habitually sang while he plotted. Hoarse from days of gut-heaving sickness, light-headed in euphoric anticipation, he hummed off-key ditties in tones like ground gravel, until the cook set Lad to shy peas at him to drive him away from the galley.

The *Black Drake* bowled on through her offshore passage to Farsee with Arithon fastened to the spooled posts of her stern rail. Since the cook's flat refusal to hand-feed a prisoner, the captain had grudgingly allowed him the use of his hands. Where another man's pride should have rankled when twine lashings were replaced with the leg shackle kept to restrain malcontents, Arithon's humour stayed intact. His patience seemed unforced, even through Dhirken's irritable progress in learning the arts of navigation.

On calm days, he made copies of the nautical charts sent for his use by Sethvir. Sailhands who lounged between duties cheerfully called jibes and stared, while the nervous, hamfisted purser passed him charcoal and inks, and badgered him with endless questions. Arithon's amiable answers needled Dakar to fits of suspicion.

'Trust me, he wants something badly,' the Mad Prophet insisted to anyone he could snag into listening. When cornered on the subject, Dhirken picked her teeth with a shim of carved ivory, her thoughts veiled behind watchful eyes.

The focus of wagers and conjecture in the forecastle, Arithon stayed unperturbed, except once, when constant exposure to spray threatened him with saltwater sores. He had no choice then but to yield before need and shed his tattered shirt. The rope burns on his limbs had already faded, leaving an older, uglier set of scars he deeply preferred to keep hidden. As the speculative comments of the crewmen turned goading, he met them, word for word, in a striking, vicious satire that forced their grudging respect.

Days passed. Sun bronzed the prince's torso like a Shandian fisherman's, and since his lady captor withheld the kindness of comb or razor, he gained a piratical growth of stubble. The constant draw of wind off the spanker snagged his black hair into elf-locks. The fact he was clean the favour of a squall that had drenched him in passing that morning, he sat engrossed over a contrivance of wood being fashioned by the ship's laconic joiner.

His absorption proved deceptive; or else confinement served to sharpen his mage-taught, cantankerous alertness, since his head snapped around at the barest scrape of a boot-heel behind his back. Met by a slim-hipped outline against the morning's acid glare, his frown smoothed over at once. 'You seem just a touch impatient. Don't be. The channel to Farsee's harbour shall hale into view before sundown.'

Clad with the dash and flair expected of captains who ran contraband, Dhirken hooked her thumbs through the bronze-studded crossbelts slung over her calfskin doublet. 'We do, or you die. The stakes haven't eased in the slightest.'

The joiner cast a doubtful glance at the unbroken swells that bounded the forward horizon. Then he sighed, licked a scuffed knuckle, and resumed his nasal carping. 'I'm nobody's jeweller, to do brass with those bitty fine marks of engraving.'

Arithon turned over the half-complete copy of Leinthal Anithael's cross staff. 'There has to be a hand in the forecastle with some sort of talent for scrimshaw. The scale could be notched on the shinbone of a cow, then blackened in with ink.'

'Didn't think,' the joiner admitted in mournful respect. He reclaimed the original tool and tucked its superlative craftsmanship into his pitch-stained apron. 'I'm off to try, then.' Still shaking his head over imagined inadequacies, he sauntered off the quarterdeck, grousing. 'But mind you don't blather to me if the marks, when they're done, don't match yon beauty for perfection.'

Inimical silence remained like welded air between the *Drake*'s master and her captive. Uneasy to be trapped between them, the helmsman looked everywhere else but at his captain, while the thrum of taut rigging and the work of the steerage tackle pitched the tension ever higher. Dhirken did not worry her cutlass hilt. Controlled to the tips of her newly-pared nails, her very stillness crackled with brazen intent to pick a fight. Deferent to her mood, or else inspired by insolence, Arithon lounged at ease against the quarterdeck rail. His eyes stayed closed, as if he might snatch a nap in the sun; only his lips showed a faint, ironic smile until the lookout cried from the masthead.

'Land! Land sighted off our bow and three points to starboard!'

The shout brought every hand abovedecks to share in a gush of fast talk.

Unmoved to stir more than an eyelash, the Shadow Master ventured, 'The key to the shackle would be a kindness.'

Dhirken laughed. 'You speak too soon. No key and no freedom until we've sighted the beacon fires to tell where we've made landfall. How do I know you've not set us off course to Varens?' But her voice betrayed wild excitement.

'As you wish, Lady.' Arithon looked up, guileless, the grate of steel damped between his palms as he tucked his bound ankle beneath his thigh. 'But we're not set downcoast. You know it, since you made today's sightings and corrected *Drake*'s course for yourself. Shall we deal? You must decide very soon. Our further relationship depends on how well you keep your word, because my own plans have undergone a change.'

'Have they now?' Dhirken's hostility gave way to sarcasm. 'I'm defeated by curiosity. Do you always get your way through glib bargaining?' The key had been palmed in her hand all along. She tossed it hard, intrigued to test whether his reflexes were sharp enough to intercept its arc toward the sea.

Forced to snatch like a starved wolf, Arithon just managed the catch. 'This was easy?' He settled back, released the lock, and in studied offence rubbed the ankle the shackle had chafed raw. 'Ath forfend, don't let me hear about hard. Particularly since I need the *Drake* to sail north to recover my treasure without me.'

Dhirken flushed. Caught speechless before her gawking crew, she clapped both palms to her cheeks. When Arithon had the grace not to laugh, she spun on her heel to hide uncertainties she would have died before sharing. 'That's trust. Far more than I merit, maybe.'

Arithon arose to his feet. 'I'll be the judge of that.'

The awareness of his freedom vivid as a brand against her back, Dhirken kept her face turned away. Only locked limbs and will masked her trembling as he stepped close, trapped her hand in light fingers, and slipped the key back in her palm. The fact she was ice-cold and sweating in the heat could not possibly escape him. Cornered by old fears he must never gain leverage to pry at, she strove to regain her frosty distance. 'You could lose everything.'

'I've lost everything twice over already,' Arithon said. His past recklessness stood as living proof.

The deck seemed abruptly too small; or his presence beside her loomed too large. She whirled to go, the fist with the key clenched in white-knuckled tension, and her other arm raised to fend off inquiries.

Arithon's touch checked her rush, a feathery brush against her cheek made in thoughtless response to blind sympathy.

She recoiled an involuntary half-step, and the wakened understanding behind his close glance shocked them both. 'Ah, fiends take your damned bardic gifts,' Dhirken snapped, her fear of his sex molten fire in her blood, and her words a strained, metallic whisper.

Rumour named her a killer who had gutted the rogue who tried to steal her legacy in the *Black Drake*; but the sordid truth was more desperate. As a victim dealt an annihilating lesson in survival, she had use for no man's pity.

If the secret shame now threatened by clean empathy held pain enough to shatter her, neither was Arithon scatheless. Blindsided by a masterbard's power too freshly gained to be governed, he lost grip on his careful layers of subterfuge. For just a split-second, she saw through to his core, and recognized more than he wished.

Whatever his part in the massacre at Strakewood, he bore the scars of a loss more crippling. He had survived what could not be reconciled. For that, he would not belittle her weakness; he had too great a heart to seize advantage.

Eyes too bright, her throat closed against the invective she needed to drive off her avid crewmen, Dhirken cursed his selfless silence, that left her independence unbreached. Undone by the depth of his sympathy, she could not do less than his bidding. Before he ever asked, she accepted: *Drake* would sail north and recover his contraband, and deliver every coin-weight and bale anywhere on the continent he desired.

'I leave you Leinthal Anithael's dividers and cross-staff, and with them, all the broad leagues of the ocean. The bounds of your command shall be limitless.' Arithon's fleeting smile masked regret, that for him, simple flight held no refuge. 'My gift will grant you freedom from the shoreline and the space to seek your release.'

Dhirken jerked her chin up, stunned to an embarrassment perilously close to tears. But the quarterdeck was empty except for the staid presence of her quartermaster; in an uncanny turn of sensitivity, the slit-eared first mate had rousted every sailor back to duty.

Gloating over how easily Arithon had been inveigled to share the Fellowship's emergency appeal to investigate Alestron's armoury, Dakar raised no objection to crossing the East Halla peninsula. The route was heavily travelled, with hospices, inns and posthouses built between towns along the way. If they begged rides in merchant's wagons, or rented the use of a hack, the journey could be made inside a fortnight.

Dakar chewed on a corner of his beard to forestall his satisfied smile. While fishermen in cod-stained oilskins cursed the *Drake*'s gig for obstructing the landing, he scrambled onto the rickety wharves of Farsee at the heels of the prince he swore to ruin.

Arithon took his leave of Dhirken's sailhands, unwarrantedly cheerful for a man who had not seen a bed for five days. If the dockside miasma of tide wrack and fish, and the shuttling flight of screaming gulls wakened memories of his native shores, where he had been mage and heir to a pirate king, he displayed no trace of sentiment. In need of a bath and a grooming as any penniless seafarer, he possessed only the rolled bundle of Sethvir's charts, slung with his lyranthe across his shoulder. His scarred wrists were masked under sailor's bracelets braided from the rags of his shirt, and the fingers of both hands were swollen from overexposure to saltwater.

To Dakar's dubious glance, he replied in pained honesty, 'No, I can't play for our keep just yet. But there's no damage done that won't mend in three days. While we wait, I'll find a tailor with an eye for quality linen.'

Backed by a citrine dawn sky, forced to duck the sliding mesh of fishnets that a sloop's crew hauled down the docks, Dakar planted his fists on his hips and balked. 'That's a grand idea. Except you don't have any coin.'

Arithon flashed a sly grin. 'Well, your pockets jingle enough to tell me Dhirken's deckhands had rotten luck at dice. Since you've sworn off beer, why not stake me to a new shirt? The silver points cut off my old one will pay for modest lodging as long as you don't start any bar riots.'

Careful not to seem too agreeable, Dakar expelled an epithet. The journey to Alestron would be made in close quarters. Although Arithon had blinded his mage-sight, his unflagging penchant for observation must not be given cause for suspicion.

A fortnight and four days passed.

Dakar found the need for constant subterfuge as wearing as any despised rigour of travel. The posthorse he straddled to finish the journey was not the plug-lazy nag he had paid for. Possessed by a devil, determined to fray any tender patch of flesh that disagreed with a saddle, the creature jibbed, snorted and crabstepped in its ongoing effort to bolt. Dakar sawed its mouth and tried not to fall off in the scythed-down stubble of the hayfield where, masked from view by a hedge, Arithon had pulled off the thoroughfare to study the grim holdfast fastened like a barnacle to the crest of the hilltop ahead.

'Alestron,' Dakar said in a note of bothered smugness. 'The brothers s'Brydion keep their secrets like oysters, and their gates like a farmer's virgin daughters. Have you a plan yet?'

'What, before I've set foot in the city?' Reduced to an outline against the fog which still pocketed the lowlands, Arithon leaned forward and settled on crossed wrists against his grey gelding's crest. Having milked every roadside taproom since Farsee, he came primed with hearsay about Alestron's ruling family. Their citadel at a glance looked formidably impregnable against a brightening corona of daylight, an eyrie clutched with bristling keeps that overhung the notch of the valley.

The brothers s'Brydion held aversion to sieges, any man could tell at a glance.

The vale had been razed of timber to afford untrammelled visibility. Beyond the meshed fields with their late-season haystacks, walls and stone crenellations knitted like the clamped, mossy jaws of a trap around clusters of whitewashed outbuildings, craft compounds, and a limited common for grazing livestock. A steep, switched-back causeway led up to the stronghold itself. Mortar set with jagged ends of glass offered cruel reception to scaling ladders. A sapping team would need to bore through solid rock to undermine the high battlements, prinked now in light like sequins sewn onto a lady's veil, or ruled by hard shadows thrown off the barbazons, riddled like wormholes with arrowslits.

Alone among cities on the continent, Alestron had not fallen in the uprising that dethroned the old high kings. Five centuries past, the merchant guilds' bid to overturn clan rule had been crushed by force of arms inside the rammed splinters of the south postern. The tenacious s'Brydion dukes had maintained their ancestral power ever since. They suckled their heirs on the rough arts of war, and skirmished with rapacious ingenuity when the rival cities that flanked the narrow inlet to the sea set blockades to jam their trade at the harbour mouth.

In those rare intervals between wars, Alestron's ruling family nursed a maniacal distrust of their neighbours, then salved their fixated nerves by stockpiling weapons of every shape and description.

Framed as casual conversation, Dakar said, 'You know we can't set foot through the upper city gate without proof of legitimate business.'

'Well, I do have a plan for that.' Clever hands firm on his reins as a flock of blackbirds startled raucously from gleaning, Arithon stole a glance slantwise. 'You won't like the first part. I'll need you to squeeze into that dandy's pair of hose and fancy doublet.'

Dakar rolled his eyes. 'Ath's pity! Whatever for?'

The awful, ribbonned garments had been the insistent gift of an inn matron enraptured by Arithon's playing. The plain fact the clothing was tailored for the ox frame of a mercenary had given rise to ribald jokes since Tirans.

Broad where the fit was cut slimmest, the Mad Prophet saw no humour in the prospect of being squeezed into slow suffocation. In case the idea was a crack at his expense, he added, 'You can't be serious.'

Arithon nudged his gelding into stride back toward the road.

'I don't see what choking to death in red velvet has to do with spying out a heavily-guarded keep.' Dakar wrestled through a pause as his mount jabbed its head down to buck. 'A man could turn grey while waiting for you to answer a simple question.'

'I need you to pass for a merchant,' Arithon replied, oblique enough to fray a stone's patience. 'You didn't hear the rumour? Parrien s'Brydion needs a courting present to win a lady to the prospect of marrying into a war camp.'

Dakar blinked, digested this, then sensed like the wave of pressed air that preceded a hit in the gut, intimations of a wider design. 'Ah, no!' He sneezed out the dusty smell of hay in distress. 'Not your kingdom's crown jewels. You can't mean to sell the duke's brother the emeralds of Rathain.'

'Well, I hardly think the s'Brydion would waste their day over fakes,' Arithon said reasonably. 'Since we haven't the time for any better overture, the gems will have to suffice.'

Now was scarcely the moment to lend credence to a notion Arithon more than likely angled to disclose: that to Fellowship concerns, Rathain's crown jewels held far more than sentimental value. The emeralds in fact formed a matched set of focus stones whose arcane properties were held in trust for future generations. Wary of the power and training already at Arithon's disposal, the sorcerers had set painstaking wards to preserve the gems' secrets from the prince.

Dakar cursed afresh for the touchy complication to his plans while the sweat rolled in drops down his spine. 'You have no appreciation for the legacy your ploy could set at risk. Not one of those stones can be replaced.'

'Then you'd better charge for them dearly.' Arithon set off at a brisk canter.

While Dakar stewed in silenced dread and wrestled with rein and heel to curb his headstrong mount, the Master of Shadow met the morning with mettlesome insouciance, whistling a set of jaunty jigs.

Warp and Weft

In autumn, within the city of Etarra, a headhunter endures in fretful stillness, the velvets required for state audience an uneasy substitute for his weapons and mail; while, trampling like a bull over sumptuous carpets, his lace collar crumpled beneath double chins, the Lord Governor Supreme takes issue with his complaint: 'How should I know why the couriers from the east are delayed? It could be the weather. It could be the air. More likely, it's the marauding of barbarians, and isn't that your captain's vaunted duty to determine . . . ?'

Evening darkens Rockfell Vale, and though frost rims the oak leaves as it would on any other autumn night, the fox, the lynx, and the night-grazing hare do not stir from their lairs; for the summit of the peak looming over the valley is drenched in an uncanny glare of power, as the sorcerers Asandir and Luhaine labour to restore the wards which confine Desh-thiere . . .

In the citadel of Alestron, a sandy-haired captain appoints the day's sentries to guard the keep that houses the duke's armoury; while in the grand hall, the burly lord himself pushes the muzzle of his favourite mastiff off his knee, then calls for his brothers to admit the fat merchant who had arrived to peddle emeralds the day before . . .

IX. *SECOND INFAMY*

The chamber the s'Brydion heirs used for close business was situated like an eyrie in a drumtower deep within Alestron's inner citadel. In keeping with most things undertaken by the family, all three siblings attended Parrien's decision to examine the rare emeralds for his bridegift.

Ascending four storeys of narrow, turnpike stairwells made the Mad Prophet sweat and gasp. His round cheeks purpled to beet from the squeeze of his beribboned red doublet. By the time he staggered through the upper doorway the manservant swung open to admit him, he was snatching each breath in jerks like a gill-netted fish. To an impostor afflicted with swimming senses, the sumptuous, gold-fringed Narms carpet on the floor felt deep and treacherous as a mire. No better haven, the vast oaken table offered an unaccommodating surface upon which to drop due to faintness. Dakar glanced from side to side, desperate. But in poses that ranged from straight attention to slouched ease, the brothers s'Brydion occupied all the available chairs.

Committed irrevocably to Arithon's demise, Dakar plonked his strongbox down, unlatched the lid, and smiled through clamped teeth as the bearded giant who sat nearest raised battle-scarred fingers to rifle through its priceless contents.

Despite the neat stool and desk framed with square cupboards for parchments, and library walls lined with a scholar's collection of books, the chamber was misleading in its air of harmless gentility. Stabbed through the mild scents of papers and ink, a miasma of metal and oil gave warning that weapons were scoured clean of rust in this place more often than scribes penned new manuscript.

Across the wide table, the tawny-maned earl expelled a whistle through his teeth. 'Sithaer's damned, will you look at these!' He tipped the little coffer. The chilly patch of sky through an arrowloop raised glints of live fire in the heart of Rathain's crown jewels. Tinged biliously viridian, four heads bent to closer inspection.

His complexion no less green, Dakar wrung dampened palms on limp sleeves a handspan too long. 'I'm sorry.'

'Sorry?' Lord Bransian s'Brydion, Duke of Alestron, straightened up, by a head the largest man present. He wore his barbarous, wheatshock hair hacked short to accommodate a mail coif. The beard underneath grew untamed as bristled wire, and the surcoat that mantled his massive breadth of shoulder would have engulfed a lesser frame like a tent. Except for a linked chain of office as old and weighty as his title, he looked every inch the hard-bitten mercenary. His two brows met, scraped iron over eyes flecked like grit stuck in ice. 'No need to apologize, merchant. Your wares are as true as your promise. Never have I seen emeralds of such quality, even through the traders out of Shand.'

Dakar cleared his throat and eyed the other heads still huddled over the jewel cache. Each had the same mink-brown hair, two tied alike with worn leather, and braided in the antiquated style the old clans once wore for battle. The last crown was cropped as a shearling, except for the lovelock curled in solitary splendour between neat and tapered shoulderblades. If young Mearn looked least imposing in the bull-muscled company of his brothers, his volatile, jumpy reflexes made his presence no whit less dangerous.

Parrien and Keldmar, who could have passed for twins, tossed the priceless gemstones between them like play-dice, engrossed in irreverent bickering over which of them should break an intractable colt they both fancied. They insulted each other's horsemanship. With cheerful bad grace, they elbowed Mearn, but failed to convince him to arbitrate. Aligned cheek by jowl, their faces were alike as a matched set of carpenter's mauls; the knuckles, chisel-cut from one mould.

Dakar mustered ebbing courage. As if he reached into a nest full of asps, he clapped down the lid of the strongbox. 'Regretfully, these emeralds aren't for sale.'

Like puppets entangled in the same jerked string, the four brothers rounded to face him.

Parrien's broad knuckles bunched bloodlessly white, while Mearn shot off his stool in a fiery, incredulous burst of temper. 'What's this? Some jape?'

Above the commotion as Bransian crashed erect to slam and lock the chamber door, Keldmar said, 'Did you take us for imbeciles?'

Dakar braced his nerve and owned up. 'The gems were my ploy to gain a private audience, and for an urgent reason. I came to give warning. At this very moment, a spy has breached the security of your secret armoury.'

There followed the barest clash of locked glances. Then the family s'Brydion reacted in voiceless concert.

Parrien seized the coffer with the emeralds. 'Surety,' he insisted as Dakar howled in dismay. 'You've lied to us once. We'll just impound these until we've made certain you're not an impostor, too.'

Caught unarmed in the crisis, Keldmar flicked back his battle-braid, vaulted his chairback, and wrenched open a gryphon-bossed chest. A taint of oiled metal arose from the linen he ripped away to reach the longswords stored inside.

Fluid as fanned flame, Mearn skirted the table. Before Dakar could retreat to a defensive position against the wall, the point of a stiletto pricked his back between the looped and braided ribbons of his doublet.

Parrien whipped off his studded belt. Berating his weaponless brother's lack of foresight, he plunged in and strapped the erstwhile gem dealer's fat wrists.

'Ath,' Dakar gasped as his captor jerked the leather tight. 'Is this how you treat guests who volunteer friendly advice?'

Mearn twitched his dagger tip into the nap of the over-tight scarlet velvet. 'A breach in security's not friendly.'

Across the chamber, stripped of his state collar and muffled under the half-shucked folds of the alizarin and gold ducal surcoat, Bransian launched into interrogation. 'A spy? Which city sent him?' He yanked his head clear of fine cloth and tossed the wadded mass across a chair seat. 'Was it Tirans this time? Kalesh? Or that interfering Mayor of Dirn?'

Justly afraid of getting skewered, Dakar hedged, 'Does it matter?'

'Not really.' Keldmar straightened, a sword in each hand, his laugh slick as snow-melt chilled to ice. 'Whoever he is, he'll tell us before he dies.'

'I'll wait here in the meantime.' Dakar edged a hopeful step sideways and stopped, stung first by the knife point, and then by two blades at his breast.

'No.' Mearn leaned close, keyed to the fervour of a starved acetic. 'I say you'll come.'

Bransian flung wide the chamber door. Parrien bowed, extravagant as a gallant giving way before a rival. His look-alike brother put up his swords, curled his lip, and pushed by. Then Parrien shed his mummery for main strength and dragged Dakar toward the throat of the stairwell.

The Mad Prophet dug in his heels, to no avail. Towed like a spaniel on a leash, he had no chance to see where Rathain's emeralds had been stashed. No one answered when he pleaded. Instead, he found himself manhandled into a pounding descent of steep stairs by four wrathful brothers who cared not a whit for his safety. Between cursing the fancy hose that slithered down his ankles, Dakar prayed in frantic entreaty. If Mearn with his diligent stiletto chanced to trip, one innocent prisoner was going to die skewered like a sausage on a turnspit.

Keldmar redoubled that concern. Around the first landing, down the spiralling turn of the next storey, he launched into a series of energetic flourishes to test which blade was better balanced. Steel whickered and whined to his cuts, while Parrien offered unhelpful criticism.

'If you reach the spy first, be my guest.' Braid flying behind and foot extended, Keldmar sallied into a classic stop-thrust across the breadth of a landing. 'Dissect his guts with all the pretty style you like. But should I find the wretch, he'll just get butchered.'

'Not before we've pried out who's sent him,' Duke Bransian interjected through a flurried torrent of echoes. To Dakar, he added, 'Better tell us how you came to know of this spy.'

They reached the base of the keep. About to keel over from dizziness, jabbed in prevention by Mearn's knife, Dakar grasped to find a creditable reply. 'I'm a craftsman. Quite often great men neglect to guard their tongues in my presence.'

'Great fools, more like.' Bransian lowered a mailed shoulder and bashed through the outside door. 'Why warn us? You could as easily have kept silent.'

'Money,' Dakar managed between his piteous, whistling effort to suck breath. 'Wars play havoc with honest trade. Armourers demand pay, and jewels get requisitioned as taxes.'

Keldmar bared his teeth. His partial emergence into sunshine kissed his restless steel like the flash of strayed lightning against the deeper shade in the bailey. 'Won't be spit for peace now.' He sounded cheerful. 'Whichever mayor sent this spy has bought himself a thumping bloody fight.'

Mearn worried the knife against the small of Dakar's back. 'By Ath, you'd better run instead of chatter. Or we won't catch the slinking rat at all.'

The prisoner had yet to recover his wind. Unable to match the s'Brydion brothers' long-strided sprint, he bobbed against his bonds like a flounder dragged on a trawl-line, while a dairymaid burdened with pails and settling pans dashed clear of their path in dismay. Bransian kicked through a flock of loose hens and scattered them into squawking flight. Feathers flew like torn leaves in a scirocco. Dakar, flushed purple, inhaled one and sneezed. The damnable red doublet throttled him, armpits to groin, until his guts felt crimped in a barrelhoop. Had Mearn owned a shred of natural pity, he could have used his nasty dagger to slit the back seam and relieve an undue share of human suffering.

But the s'Brydion would slacken pace for no man while the secret in their armoury stood in jeopardy.

The keep set aside for their weapon-stores loomed above a spiked ring of battlements, its lichened crenellations notched into sky. Panting, limp as sloshed cream in a bowl, Dakar expected to expire of exertion long before his captors could herd him to the top. Even Bransian's ox thews would suffer from the strain to haul him up stairwells like deadweight.

Firm in his plan to faint and gain a rest, then slip off the moment he was abandoned, Dakar groaned and lurched to his knees.

Two pairs of hands latched his armpits like meat-hooks and slung him wrenchingly onward; apparently Parrien and Keldmar could ignore their bickering differences when presented with sufficient provocation.

While a muleteer freighting beer kegs to the lower district market jerked his team short of collision, Mearn's chilling chuckle pierced through the clatter of sliding hooves. 'Now, why should I have a strange feeling this pigeon we've caught isn't quite pleased to come along?'

Nobody answered. Teeth latched tight in winded misery, propelled in a headlong dash across the noisome runoff from the butcher's alley, hoisted over loose bricks to whacked shins and the howls of the infuriated mason left ankle-deep in the mortar upset from his handcart, Dakar wished the worst of s'Brydion ill temper upon the head of Arithon s'Ffalenn.

Ahead, in a bellow fit to split rock, Duke Bransian questioned the sentries posted by the arched upper postern. Dakar scarcely followed their round of emphatic denial. 'We've seen nothing, my lord Duke. No intruders have passed in our watch.'

Four stares accusatory enough to scald skin, and a knife on the trembling edge of murder impelled Dakar clear of his muddle. 'The spy's mage-trained,' he managed between gasps. 'He'll have ways to slip past unseen.'

'Through six guards and *twelve locked posterns?*' Bransian's brows knotted in fierce disbelief. His pale eyes fastened on Keldmar, who responded and jammed the sword he liked least through his belt.

Bransian hooked the ring that jangled at his hip, twisted off a key and tossed it into his brother's freed hand. 'The captain on duty is Tharrick. Let him into the keep through the guardroom and take a dozen men armed for skirmish. If the rest of us sally by way of the lower passage, we can flank this spy in the dungeon.'

'Do you suppose Tharrick forgot his sword, too?' Parrien murmured. He twitched at the belt that secured Dakar. 'If so, I'll just flay the intruder at my leisure.'

'You say,' Keldmar shot back. The leather tails of his fighter's braid snapped to his vehemently turned head, his shout dwindling behind as he left to skirt the base of the keep. 'What prissy bits of swordplay you practise are much better suited to helping the scullions shell peas.'

'Hah! So we'll see!' Parrien flung back in challenge. Left no other outlet for his spirited temper, he gave another jerk at Dakar's bonds.

Keys still in hand, the Duke of Alestron elbowed past his sentries and disappeared. The Mad Prophet blinked stinging sweat from his eyes. Snapped through a splay-legged stagger by the belt, he managed to make out a dank, narrow doorway under the shadow of the postern.

Within that maw of gloom, at the base of a shallow stairwell, Bransian's lips split in unholy delight through his unkempt bristle of amber beard. Then he turned the oiled lock and tripped up the latch. 'Come on. Or else Captain Tharrick and our brother are going to snatch all the fun.'

'Over one spy's dead body.' Parrien dealt Dakar a neck-cracking push that plunged him down through the darkened doorway and into the throat of an underground shaft.

There followed more flights of stairs, ranged downward or up in patterns that seemed random; they crossed over landings discoloured from the slow seep of springs, or ones caked in dry-rotted fungus. The tunnel reeked of mould and stagnant water. Oil from the cressets that flamed in iron sconces threw off a murk of fine soot. Bransian helped himself from the casks filled with unlighted spares. Burning brands clamped upright in both fists, a dozen more thrust cold through his belt, he looked like a warder from Sithaer itself, primed for mayhem from his hobnailed boots to the crimped frizz that haloed his crown. Like demons, his two brothers pressed at his heels. They hauled their stout-bodied prisoner in his flamboyant clothes over the streaked, black water that flashed molten bronze and crimson agate; past the whickering flames dragged flat and torn dim by their hasty passage down the corridor.

They stopped at short intervals to question the guards posted along the way. Men armed with daggers, crossbows, and swords who stood their turns of duty, locked in. An enemy who sought entry could kill them or try torture; their watch-captain alone held the keys to the doors they defended. Bransian's inquiries were hasty and rough. His impatience hammered echoes above the clang of locks and bars, while the sentries answered back in fearful care.

The last one to be pressured was emphatic. 'My Lord, there's been nothing alive in this passage. Not even a cockroach or a rat.'

'Well that may be,' snapped the duke. 'But we've been told there's a spy in the armoury. You'd better think well before you speak.'

The guard stared back in straight courage. 'A spy? Dharkaron strike me dead, my Lord, I've seen nothing!'

'Nothing is it? Blind and deaf, both, are you?' Parrien launched forward, Dakar still in tow. He snatched the guard's surcoat with his free fist and twisted until the man's mail cowl crushed painful links into his throat. 'Were you bribed, man? We'll have the truth.'

'Let up, brother,' Bransian boomed in complaint. 'How can he talk if you choke him?'

Parrien released fast and kicked the man sprawling on a floor slimed with silt from past flooding. 'No bribe, Lord,' the guard gasped. 'No spy. On my life, I swear this.'

'Your life *will* be asked, if you've lied,' muttered Mearn, his blade withdrawn from Dakar's back as he thrust past to tongue-lash the guardsman.

In a rushed and grating jangle of iron, Bransian unlocked the next portal.

The steel-bound grille swung wide to admit sucking draughts. These flagged the torch-flames to sullen embers, and split shadows danced like cavorting gargoyles. Shaking with sick fear, Dakar flexed numbed muscles against the pressure of Keldmar's belt. While still another lock, latch and bar were unfastened, and a braced oaken panel yielded to Bransian's heave with a pealing rasp of stiff hinges, the Mad Prophet fretted that his spurious plot had placed him in more than dire straits.

For a man to slip past this keep's defences defied the sane bounds of credibility.

Arithon was blinded to mage-sight; that left his masterbard's gift to raise the pitch which Named steel. But any sound ventured in this underground warren would have stirred echoes to roust up a corpse. And even if such heavy defences *could* be jostled open by resonance; even given the vicious scope of s'Ffalenn cleverness, the last stretch of passage lay blocked by a massive, geared iron gate. This ground tortuously upward on tracks, assisted by mechanical counterweights and a windlass worked by brute strength that made Bransian's sinews bulge like corded meat.

If the promised spy had not gained his entry, Dakar would be treated to the nasty sort of death he had angled to gain for Arithon s'Ffalenn.

Over the ratcheting din of rusted chains, Mearn ventured, 'Will you look? I see no footprints in the moss.' He shot a scathing glare at Dakar.

The portal screeched to rest with a reverberating clank. Bransian jabbed a chewed wedge of wood through the gears to lock the windlass, then stooped unperturbed to fetch his torches. 'You want to take chances? That herb witch we hired made less sound than a spider. Likely sorcerers don't leave any tracks.'

A more distant groan of steel and a crash through the upper bowels of the keep evinced Keldmar's progress abovestairs. Parrien sidled, impatient. 'You're blocking the passage, Mearn. If you don't step aside to let this fat man squeeze past, I swear I'll use your knife to end the problem.'

'You may need to slit his throat anyway,' Mearn said tartly. 'If the armoury's secure, the odds would suggest that perhaps this wretch *is* the spy.'

'Stop talking.' Bransian planted himself, bearded chin thrust forward. 'I want to listen.'

No sound met his stillness. A catspaw of draught teased the torches, then passed. The weave of the flames crawled upright and held, sparkless and steady and hot. Crowded by his brothers with Dakar leashed in tow, Bransian plunged into the pit black cavern of the dungeon.

There followed another long pause, filled by the burning hiss of oil-soaked rags and half-suspended breathing. No other light or sound stirred the dust-laden air. The nearest racks of shelving loomed dark as catacombs, twelve feet high, and picked out in the teased play of light. Floor to ceiling, the velvet darkness lay stamped with dull gleams where steel, riveted, hammered, and forged in the myriad shapes used for war, chipped back intermittent reflections.

'Nobody's in here,' Parrien said in cracking, incredulous fury.

Bransian slapped him in the chest to make him quiet. To the prisoner who wheezed at his elbow, he said, 'How long do you guess your spy's had access?'

'An hour or less,' Dakar answered.

'That's if he exists at all!' Mearn's stiletto flashed a hot line in the dimness as he snared one of Bransian's torches.

'Oh, but he does,' the Mad Prophet insisted in grim desperation. 'Be careful, he's clever as a fiend.'

Then, with a vindication that both maddened and humbled, a bright voice called answer from behind a wedged pile of barrels. 'Why Dakar, how wonderfully imaginative!'

Like windvanes in a stiff change of breeze, the brothers s'Brydion spun about.

Just beyond sight, the speaker was blithe. 'What did you trade for my emeralds, my friend? Arbalests? Lances? Shall we count?'

Dakar gulped air to retort. Before he found words, a twist at his wrists bent him to his knees on the floor. A heartbeat later, he struggled to accommodate as Bransian thrust all three smoking torches between his nerve-dead fingers and rattled low orders to his brothers.

Their chase would be hampered: the low shelves were too tightly packed to step through; and the intruder could be armed with whatever style weapon he might find amid the stores to strike his fancy.

While the brothers fanned out in a stalking pattern, Arithon resumed his ripping satire. 'A high king's crown jewels for a load of tempered steel, or *Dakar!* Could my life be the stakes that you bargained for?'

A stitch of reflection in stygian dark revealed Mearn in position to pounce. The voice paused in its monologue. A barrel canted to a rasp of shifted contents. A slight hesitation, like a held-back breath; then the cask toppled, upsetting its contents in a cascading, ear-stunning crash. Steel helms bounced from straw nesting. Numerous as the sins of the damned, they rolled on in a burst of winnowed chaff, to scatter across the stone floor.

Parrien shied clear, swearing. Bransian's path toward a lashed stock of spears was rudely disclosed as a nasal hooked on his instep. While the intruder's dancer-light footsteps pattered back out of range, Mearn brandished his stiletto and pranced to keep his footing amid a glorious, belling clamour of raw noise.

'Over there,' Dakar yelled as a shadow crossed his sight. 'He went right.'

'What? No honour among spies?' Nimble as a sailor, Arithon swarmed up the nearest rack to hand. 'Well, look, what have we here?' Poised near the ceiling, first his shoulders, then his feet vanished through a crack into gloom.

A spear bit the wood he had clung to. A second shaft cocked back to throw, Bransian skidded to a stop beneath the shelving, braced his stance, and took better aim. A sack of spare fletching ripped above. His cast went wild as a blizzard of feathers frothed down over his head. Spitting sour dust, snagged with small quills like a fox run amok in a goose pen, he roared out a blasphemy, while his airborne lance rapped jagged splinters off a post, and glanced off a hanging cuirass.

Metal screamed on metal, with Parrien forced to dive flat to escape the plunging fall of his brother's weapon.

Furtive rustles sounded the length of the shelf. The fugitive was moving again. Mearn elected to try climbing, while over the cuirass's diminished vibration, his brothers traded curses in tandem. Their imprecations were defeated as a banshee shriek creased the air. Arithon had discovered the sheaf of signal arrows. A short recurve bow designed for mounted archers strung and poised in his hand, he watched his first missile silence itself with a vengeful crack a fraction shy of Dakar's posterior.

'There's one from behind, for treachery,' he chided. The bowstring creaked into another draw. 'And a second for predictable obsessions.'

The next screamer knifed across the dark, sliced a dry thong, and cut loose a suit of old chain mail. The mass descended, jingling, and snagged Mearn like a cod in a lead-weighted net. Ripped off his perch, he went down. A thump, a grand puff of dust, and a screech of rude words through the byrnie marked his landing across the furled canvas of his grandfather's mouldered field pavilion.

'Slings, two dozen, for small stoneshot,' the intruder listed cheerfully. He slithered on and read another label. 'Leather bracers with brass studs, six score.' A faint sniff pocked the recitation. 'Dryrotted, for shame. Someone neglected their goose-grease.' A box sailed down from the heights, struck another barrel of helmets, and the subsequent grinding avalanche of metal cut Parrien off at the ankles. He staggered, measured his length, and slammed himself dizzy on the strut of a handcart packed with sand-bags.

The racket masked the grind of a bar from the stairhead. Across the fifty foot chamber, the upper level postern crashed back. Light cracked the dark, and soldiers poured through, Keldmar in the lead. Captain Tharrick raced a half-step behind, the spill of his torch a gleam on pale hair like blood on a sheaf of hackled flax.

'Our enemy's up in the shelving,' warned Mearn.

Another box flew and burst, this time against the wall above the stairway. Objects rattled and pinged down the risers. Peppered by ricochet, the soldiers lost impetus, windmilled, and yelled as their boots turned on footing made treacherous by a deluge of small stoneshot. Swords flashed helter-skelter. The scrape of blades and armour struck sparks against the wall as men collided and crashed on their buttocks.

Unscathed on the landing, Keldmar embarked in cold fury to light torches. Cloaking darkness burned away in the blaze. Too dazzled by glare to make use of his bow, the instigator became a backlit target.

Bransian hurled another javelin.

The sheaf of whistle arrows toppled over the shelf rim as Arithon shed the recurve and dropped flat. The weapon skimmed over his head, nicked a ceiling beam, and clattered end over end into the aisle adjacent.

Battered into retreat yet again by the shower of jettisoned signal arrows, Bransian shouted to his brothers. 'Axes! Hack through the braces to the shelving and let the whole tier collapse.' To the soldiers who sorted themselves to rights on the staircase, he ordered, 'Find bows. Set up a crossfire. I want that spy pinned down.'

Parrien reappeared from a side aisle, his braid leaking blood, and fists locked around the haft of a double-edged war-axe. Mearn, more resourceful, had raided the field pavilion's gear for the woodcutter's hatchet in the cooking kit. In paired force, their first crashing strokes hewed at the braces, to a sullen, clanking chime of jarred contents; while in a stirred blaze of cressets by the landing, Keldmar and Tharrick regrouped the soldiers in teams and dispersed them on course to fetch longbows.

That moment all the torches flicked out.

A few ragged shouts, cut off by Tharrick's order; then no sound beyond the echoing thunder of axe blows, and a low-voiced, insolent remonstration. 'Mind your feet.'

Keldmar became noosed in a snarl of flung bowstrings. Then a crash of wood and metal set the soldiers into howling disarray. 'Crossbows, ten dozen, and be careful the cocking latches don't get bent to perdition by the hobnails you wear in your boots.'

The laughing voice issued from the right, no longer in the swaying mass of shelves. Mearn stopped hewing, too late. A rope had been strung from the top tier. Hemp gave a wasp-thrum in warning; the unstable mass teetered, then cracked and heeled over to bash into the next row of racks. A sandpaper rasp of slipped contents continued, and a spill of boxed, baled, tied and crated contents rocked airborne in a cataract that thudded burst wire and litter across the flooring.

The soldiers sent off to string longbows were blocked or hammered flat by a matchwood bristle of splintered wreckage.

Keldmar gave fast orders to seal the upper doors, while Dakar was kicked and half-trampled by Parrien's sprint to block return access through the passageway.

Too encumbered to nurse his bruised shin, assured by the blistering fan of heat across his knuckles that the torches in his hands remained alight, if blackened by Arithon's weave of shadow, Dakar said, 'I warned you, this spy is a sorcerer. Whatever's in this armoury to attract the eyes of enemies, he'll go there before he tries escape.'

'The culverin,' muttered Parrien, and trailed off with a guttural curse.

A furtive scrape, a muffled sneeze, and a muted jink of metal betrayed the forecast's astuteness: the intruder was one shelf over, and moving fast in the opposite direction from the doorway. Mearn's lunge to flank his progress down the aisle immediately fouled in a crash, as meshed crossbows dropped minutes earlier to foil soldiers mired his ankles in turn.

'Entanglements, snares, and misfortune,' the spy chided in unabashed hilarity; well aware the phrase was borrowed from a ribald ballad about an adulterer's mistimed assignation, Bransian aligned his gaze to match the sound. A whoosh combed through the air above, knitted through by a soprano clink of curb chain. Caught flat-footed and staring upward, the duke was clobbered by a snaking mess of harness. Half-throttled by the drag of the horsecollar, laced head to foot in oiled strap-goods, he ripped out his dagger and began in frantic bursts to dice leather.

Having clattered through the last of the crossbows, his woodcutter's hatchet cocked to slash, Mearn poised in the darkness, listening. The armoury threw back a sullen stew of echoes. Bransian's quick and murderous breaths timed to the chink of dropped buckles, offset by Keldmar's exhortations to Tharrick's soldiers, engaged in grumbling effort to regroup and string longbows, to refrains of smacked shins and stubbed toes.

A finger of breeze brushed Mearn's skin. Then his ears caught a telltale creak of wood. A whispered brush of cloth chafed over metal; the spy had alighted from the shelving but a half-pace away from his position.

Mearn dropped his arms in a powerful down-swing. The torches burst back to a dazzle of full flame, and a lithe, compact body folded to one knee under the descent of the hatchet. Black-haired, green-eyed, and merrily sardonic, the spy met the stroke, a sword upraised in each hand. Steel screamed as the hatchet sheared and grabbed on crossed blades braced to guard.

'Bad luck,' said the spy on a grunt as the shock knocked him breathless. He let go of his weapons.

Mearn's backstep, and his jerk to clear the helve from his opponent's entangling parry met no resistance.

The hooked blades obliged and flew airborne. Inherent fine balance lent their trajectory vengeful life as they arced toward shocked and widened grey eyes and a mouth etched with grim determination. Mearn jumped, cat-quick in avoidance, while his quarry tucked, rolled, and disappeared through the space beneath the shelf. Mearn's thrown weapon hissed a half-beat behind, nailed wood, and bit off an appalling gouge.

Still meshed in looped harness, Bransian lost patience and charged. Helmets pealed, thrashed back to belling life as his progress raked the scattered debris in a snaking wrack of traces and hames. Bit-rings and buckles snagged on bowstocks and flanges, and the racket drowned all hope of tracking.

'Dharkaron's Black Spear!' Parrien screeched. 'Will you shut those things up?' Irate enough to abandon his post by the tunnel, he rolled onto his toes, then stopped his rush as the armoury went dark a second time.

Bransian ground to a halt amid a petulant chime of dragged steel. Captain Tharrick and Keldmar had used the brief respite to regroup the soldiers. The intermittent rattle of strayed slingshot betrayed their closing move to quarter the one aisle left untrammelled.

While over the stealthy brush of footsteps, the muted grate of weapons and mail, a soft voice pattered in monologue: 'Halberds, four score, admirably polished. Daggers for swordplay, eight dozen, boxed. Longswords, less quillons and pommels, two chests' worth.'

'By Ath, he's taking an *inventory!*' cried Keldmar in hoarse incredulity.

'Very good,' the spy remarked. 'Only a lunatic would come here to count your nice sharp swords for his health.' A distinctive, ratcheting clank issued from the bowels of the dark.

Always quickest with details, Mearn remarked, 'That's the large arbalest he's cocking!'

Keldmar yelled orders, and Captain Tharrick's men deployed in a two-pronged assault intended to sweep the third corridor. Running feet slapped stone, punctuated by the ping of a trigger latch, a creak of laminated wood, and a whine of taut-strung wire.

'"*Peppermint, rosemary, thyme, and mace*",' the spy chanted. '"*Beware evil weeds that grow apace*".' His weapon clicked and discharged.

The bolt hissed through the darkness and struck, its target a packed store of breastplates. Their shelf disgorged them in thunderous, skull-splitting noise. The three leading soldiers were scythed down outright, while plate armour spun and clattered on to unmercifully whack heads and batter elbows. The disarrayed ranks carried forward undaunted. The arbalest ripped out a second shot. Stacks of targes swayed and upended; their leather covered frames were spiked and studded with bronze, a punishing hindrance as they rolled every which way, and pared the soldiers' ranks even further. Survivors dispatched to complete the advance tripped a pace later and crashed flat. The spy, while he counted, had strategically jammed halberd poles in the bracing. Spurred on by white fury and Keldmar's imprecations, the soldiers scrambled upright, charged three steps, and blundered through a musty string of signal flags. Mould dust billowed up. The assailants staggered on, folded in virulent sneezes, while the spy clambered up a pike rack and slung himself sideways into the farthest tier of shelving.

Bolstered by Bransian and Mearn, his pursuers recovered their impetus and converged like a wolf pack down the aisles on either side. The frustration scalded, that sixteen men could be quartering the finest collection of weaponry in East Halla, and still find no target to skewer.

'"*Cailcallow tea, for easing the cough*",' the spy resumed in mad recitation. ' "*Groundsel and willow, for fever*".'

A flurried agitation in darkness, the soldiers manoeuvred to flank his lofty perch.

The recipes for herb potions and tisanes suffered a jagged break in metre. 'For threats, we'll just have to improvise.' Unseen hands heaved something. A hamper of buckles upset; then a cask of tempered steel broadheads hissed down and burst, followed fast by two crates of crossbow bolts. Men swore and leaped and pussyfooted through another jangling impediment, while their luckless lieutenant howled and fell to his knees to find an arrowhead jammed through his sole. His wounding was unlikely to be received as an accident.

Dakar alone guessed differently as a coffer of loose rivets showered earthward: Arithon seeded the floor with anything at hand to contrive noise. Master of Shadow he might be; but with his mage-sight blinded, the dark of his own making must slow him. He strove to compensate through his masterbard's ear, to wrest every nuance he could wring out of sound and to map the proximity of his enemies.

Dakar's thwarted spite allowed no admiration, that despite an unpardonable betrayal and a rude disadvantage in numbers, the Prince of Rathain seemed determined to finish the review asked by the Fellowship sorcerers.

'Spears, maces, morningstars.' A heavy something plummeted and struck off a burst of red sparks. The soldier poised halfway up the shelving grunted and dropped, a fist-sized dent in his helm. His demise ripped down two companions while darkness flowed back, and Keldmar, poised like an owl on a bracing, flexed his knife-wielding forearm and stabbed.

His blade met a belling parry. His next stroke gutted a field hammock. He lunged again, nicked flesh that bled, and snatched. His knuckles barked into a tossed sack of flints. 'Curse you! Your accent's not townbred. Who sent you?'

A rattle of seasoned yew issued from the blackness in reply.

'He's into the new stock for longbows!' Keldmar shouted. 'Close in from the west. We'll have him boxed against the stairs.' A stealthy touch at his shoulder made him flinch and curse: his younger brother had joined him on the scaffolding.

'Better kill before you ask questions,' Mearn advised. 'Another blunder, and Parrien's sure to lose his reason and abandon his guard by the passages.'

Keldmar gave a noncommittal grunt. The boards beneath his knees began to shake; Captain Tharrick had set more men to climbing.

Someone more agile dropped, slithered, swung onto the lower tier, and doubled back. 'He's under us,' Mearn whispered.

Keldmar peered outward, knife cocked above his head. A sour reek of leather flared his nostrils, then a piquant bouquet, chokingly laced with ammonia.

'Rats have been nesting in your hide stores,' the ruffian remarked.

Keldmar curled his lip and threw. His dagger smacked into something soft; leather, or maybe, human flesh; the angle was awkward to be certain. He leaned out to check. A supply net lashed up, caught, and whipped around his waist. Laced like a whore in a corset, he struggled and clawed at twining hemp, thumped an elbow into Mearn, and got himself tackled from behind by an overzealous soldier just arrived.

'He's ours, you fool!' Enraged as a singed cat, Mearn seized a mace and clubbed the blunderer unconscious.

Keldmar sat back up in a slither of slackened mesh. Dazed and rubbing a skinned shoulder, he chuckled. 'That was a bit harsh, brother.'

'Don't go soft on me just because you feel faint.' Mearn gave his brother's wrist an insistent jerk. 'If that spy breaks through Tharrick's cordon, he's going to run over our culverin.'

'You think we should drop at the north end and cut him off?' Keldmar was a large man who hated to move in a hurry. Opponents tended to forget that he could, which made for lucrative bets on his wrestling; and Mearn disliked being still.

The pair hit the floor running. Two steps, and Keldmar's toe struck an object that launched off a stunning, bell-tone clash of steel.

'Damned helmets.' Mearn cursed again, much louder, as Captain Tharrick mistook his presence for the spy's, and barely reneged his order to attack.

The shadows lifted without warning.

Torchlight surged back to flood shelving and stone walls; a limp fringe of signal banners; the jerked sparks of reflection off jumbled up swathes of spilled metal. Soldiers clung to the scaffolding, fish-eyed and blinking, while Bransian waved a fresh cresset toward the cranny that lay dimmest and farthest from the stairshaft. 'He ran that way.'

Mearn whirled in tandem with Keldmar; and the fleeing spy charged straight into them.

'Demon!' Keldmar side-stepped, snatched a quarterstaff from a barrel, and laced into a whistling attack pattern that blocked all escape down the aisle.

Mearn drew his belt knife and threw.

The spy dropped, tucked head over heels. He struck the floor rolling, a blur of packaged motion, while the knife flew high and stuck quivering in a ballista. Keldmar spun his stave upright, vengeance-bent as a farm-wife harrying a cockroach with a poker. One steel-shod tip rapped a near-miss against flagstone and snagged out a twist of black hair. Shouts and a clatter of running footsteps converged. Tharrick's least flustered soldiers lined up and fired off arrows. The barrage battered stone and rebounded. A better shot by Bransian snatched a rip in a sleeve already ragged.

Cracked a glancing blow by the stave, the spy shot out both hands and grabbed.

Over a hotly contested length of wood, stance braced to wrench free his quarterstaff, Keldmar caught a wide, green-eyed glance that blistered in joyful irony. Then the torches blinked out again. Caught blind in the instant the miscreant released his grip, the yank he achieved sat him down hard on his buttocks.

Mearn yelled, leaped his brother's crashed bulk and pounced. His knuckles skinned through the ballista's crossbrace. The intruder had gone under, but Mearn was as fast, and very nearly as slight. Undaunted, he wormed through the streamered silk of cobwebs in pursuit. His brother Keldmar's quarterstaff banged his heel with a sting that half-lamed him, and a second blow caromed off a strut. Deafened by the impact, Mearn yelled, 'You'll break the wrong skull, you oaf!'

Keldmar's disgruntled rejoinder entangled with the tardy arrival of Tharrick's benighted soldiers. 'Ath! Why not get out of my way, then?'

Mearn snatched a breath, lost wind to a maniacal burst of laughter, and scrabbled on after his quarry.

He re-emerged at the end of the aisle, panting hard enough to spoil his hearing. A pole racked with war gear tipped up. Mearn caught a faint, hissed scrape and a dusky whiff of old leather. Reflex turned his head, and sliding, a dozen studded saddles hammered straight into his face. Bowled over backwards and pummelled half-senseless, he heard through the creak of abused leather what he thought was a breathless apology.

Rage turned him berserk. He heaved up, shucking girths. A field lance jabbed his gut, butt first. He sat. Bereft of wind, close to paralysed, he could do nothing but gasp like a trout. The dropped weapon clanged next to him, followed hard by a fusty quilt of barding, which flapped down from above and battened him in wool and old horsehair.

'Sweet dreams,' wished a faint, merry voice.

Mearn punched at the fabric, coughed out the salty taste of scurf, and yelled as a running soldier rammed him flat over backwards. A scuffle erupted, and ended, with Tharrick's man moaning in agony; the stray lance had turned and stuck in his thigh, which to s'Brydion sense of justice served him right.

On his feet spitting venom and blood, Mearn blinked. The torches were burning again; or one was. Past the bare frames of the war chariots, limned in a gush of yellow light, the spy held a filched brand aloft in a scuffed and dirty hand. He was staring at the most dearly held secret in Alestron, the great weapon painstakingly created from the proscribed writings left by Magyre.

The culverin was not much to look upon: a mere tube of cast bronze, strapped to a wooden frame conveyed by a harness of pull ropes. Stacked to one side were its missiles: round spheres of stone at a crude weight of thirty pounds; and slung in a barrel, the accoutrements of its firing, assorted wands and hooks whose use was not obviously apparent. Ramming tools, touch matches, and a half-dozen hundred-weight casks that wore a faint reek of brimstone, lay stacked alongside some sewn canvas bundles the size of a man's doubled fists.

The spy was too clever not to guess the strange contrivance held a purpose connected with warfare. 'Behold, Sethvir, your rare siege weapon,' he murmured.

Then, in stunning ignorance, he tossed his torch in a hard throw over his shoulder. His intent was to divert the guards who secured the aisleway behind him; then he spun, the conflagration as his cover, to bolt and make good his escape.

Fire spat through a long, burning arc. It landed, malicious in accuracy, in the maw of an upset cask, rolled the full length of the armoury and wisped with the loose straw that had bedded the garrison's spare helmets.

Mearn screamed, snatched the barding from his legs, and plunged to stifle the flames.

The spy ducked from his path with faintly raised eyebrows, and an expression of madcap surprise. He had expected to divide his pursuit to fight the blaze, but the panic that ensued seemed disproportionate as Bransian converged from another aisle, Alestron's red bull banner ripped from its standard and flapping like an apron at his knees. In single-minded effort, the duke smothered his offering over Mearn's smouldering horse-cloths, unconcerned if he blistered his flesh.

The air recoiled in smoke and a reek of singed wool and silk. Low and urgent, Tharrick set his soldiers running to converge and cut off access to the underground passage. A barrel of oil upset in their path. The flooded stonework shimmered black and gold in spreading ripples. Their quarry took to the scaffolding, unsullied. While the skirmishers skidded and splashed and collided, and went down in a thrashing tangle, his chin pocked a triangle in the gloom above the leaned shelf where the recurve still swung on a nail. His quick hands snatched the bow. A wisp of lint floated down; the sort a besieger would wind overtop of a broadhead to make fire arrows.

'No,' Keldmar croaked. The fumes clogged his voice. He raised blackened hands and gestured to flag down the brother still posted by the passage doorway.

Parrien saw. Galvanized to instantaneous fear, his flesh prickled by the proximity of a danger unimagined by the fugitive in the bracing, he ripped out a pealing yell. 'Ath's grace, man! Don't be setting off sparks in this place.'

'For my pains and your trials, a gift,' said the spy, a catch to his tone that at last revealed his cornered desperation.

A touch match hissed. The first arrow arched down in a sizzling line,

252

traced by a fluffed trailer of smoke. Then the shaft struck, and splashed roiling flame on the upset staves of another barrel. Red, gold, and yellow flowered up in a welling spree of wild light.

The armoury had no ready source of water, little cloth beyond dust-dry canvas, and horse barding too eaten with moth holes to smother the air from greedy flame. Of least concern, now, was the enemy who launched the disaster. To prevent an explosion that would decimate their keep now preoccupied the s'Brydion to the exclusion of everything else.

'Get the chariots,' Bransian shouted. 'We'll use them to wheel the powder kegs clear!'

Parrien charged in, still gripping his war axe. A glance showed the duke's plan would be hampered. 'The shafts won't clear the turn around the shelving.'

'Hack them off.' Mearn snatched back blistered fingers and yelled over his shoulder. 'Tharrick, set your men to help!'

But the soldiers, under Keldmar, were already busy throwing field tents, camp stools, and infantry banners in frenzied effort to dam the oil from its downhill trickle toward the stone shot. A wafted bit of fletching snagged in an updraught, flared alight, and disintegrated into a falling rain of sparks. Flame sprouted, stinking of singed hide, and an oil-soaked chest of woollen gambesons whooshed up in the hellish, crackling tongues of a bonfire.

Charged with innocent intent, Arithon seized his chance and scuttled like a thief from the shelving. 'You'll want to leave while the bully boys are busy,' he said to Dakar, who had jettisoned the spent stubs of three torches, and now laboured to rise, no easy feat for a fat man with his wrists lashed in leather.

The Mad Prophet flopped through another frantic heave. 'Help me up,' he gasped.

'There's some urgent reason why I should?' Arithon looked on in staid inquiry over a cheek scuffed with dust and grazed bloody. 'You seemed cosy enough with the duke just a bit ago.'

Dakar glanced up in piercing focus. 'This fire you've started's going to kill us. We need to run, very fast, right away. Those casks by the wall will explode.'

Mage-taught to interpret small details, Arithon saw past Dakar's theatrics, grasped his genuine, sweating terror, and blessedly dropped further questions. 'Raise your hands.'

He held a knife clenched in skinned knuckles.

Dakar shut his eyes in blind relief. A kiss of chill metal, a swift tug, and the belt was slashed off his pinched wrists. He poised for the arm-wrenching yank that would haul him headlong to his feet, but none came.

The Master of Shadow had left him to fate, in an armoury stockpiled with black powder.

Smoke rolled in billows off the burning oil. The lowest tiers of shelving straddled spread lakes of fire and flung off a confused weave of shadows. Running silhouettes flitted across the glow. Tharrick's soldiers dragged off their wounded without any pause to fashion litters. Every other hale man bolted toward the stair, while the s'Brydion brothers in heart-wrung desperation gave ground before necessity. Engulfed in flaming wreckage and debris, they charged headlong toward the tunnel.

Before them fled the flittering forms of the dungeon's resident rats.

Dakar heaved stumbling to his feet. He lumbered to chase after Arithon, until hands snatched his collar and snagged him short.

'You're ours,' said Parrien, soot-blackened and furious.

The doorway darkened as Duke Bransian plunged through, closely followed by Keldmar and Mearn, the latter one limping. One of them ripped out the wedge from the windlass. Chain squealed. A rat blundered over Dakar's foot, and another one collided with his ankle. Then Parrien slammed him in the small of the back, and he pitched forward, running for his life.

The steel portal clashed down behind. The brothers sprinted, hazing Dakar ahead like a bear at a baiting. Another door slammed. The Mad Prophet stubbed his toes in a crack, caromed off a wall, and staggered down a flight of shallow steps.

Beyond this, a crook in the corridor; wheezing fit to burst, he pounded up some steep, uneven stairs.

Then an awesome, booming roar shook the earth.

Flying debris of splinters and steel showered and clanged and scattered against the corner wall as if raked by the thrust of a tornado.

A fist of hot air struck Dakar's back from behind and flattened his escort like ninepins.

Deafened, blistered, coughing bitter smoke and gritted cinders, the Mad Prophet snatched an instant to wonder if Bransian's huge frame had him pinned belly-down on any rats. Wits failed him. His head ached in reverberated pain like the stew of a mallet-struck pudding.

Too undone to finesse the spells he might have tried as a restorative, Dakar offered up a muzzy prayer to Ath for a speedy, smooth pass beneath the Wheel.

The alternatives did not amuse. Rat bites made ghastly infections; the s'Brydion would slowly disembowel him; and by far worst of all, Arithon was away, scot-free.

Cringing in mortified failure for the stunning misdirection of his plot, the spellbinder knew death itself might not save him. His irate Fellowship master would commandeer Dharkaron's own Chariot for first crack at his disembodied spirit.

Interrogation

When the brothers s'Brydion resolved to interrogate a miscreant, niceties fell by the wayside. Since the deepest and dimmest of Alestron's dungeons lay explosively gutted, the work crews who extinguished the fires now laboured to shovel away wet ashes and wipe the carbon from salvageable steel. The only other keep not jammed to capacity with weapons held a ring of glass traders incarcerated for fraud. Rather than suffer the delay while they were moved, Lord Bransian chose to weigh the blame for his ruined armoury in the sanctum of his private study.

Collared and dragged by the mailed fists of guardsmen back up the same tiresome tower staircases, then heaved with humourless force through the doorway, Dakar staggered into candlelight. The chamber where he had shown Rathain's emeralds was lit now by massive candelabra on stands at the four points of the compass. Grazed with patched blood and bruises, whooping in starved gulps of air, he sagged to his knees against the wall chest, left open since morning, when Keldmar had snatched his paired swords. The brothers were nothing if not thorough. Dakar's hands were trussed afresh in stout cord, beyond liberty to grope to see if other weapons remained swaddled in the oiled rags that lined the bottom.

If the Mad Prophet held out hopes to ease his plight through fast talk, the speed of events soured his opening. When Guard-captain Tharrick had no ready explanation for a spy who had slipped through his posted watch, the brothers s'Brydion lost patience. They ordered him stripped and flogged with supreme unconcern for bloodstains on their rich carpets.

Quaking and sick, Dakar shut his eyes against the poor wretch's screams as the lash fell. Tharrick was innocent of accepting any bribe, and zealous as any man might be in adherence to loyal duty; against the wily Master of Shadow, no sentry in Alestron had a chance.

Unaware he had spoken his opinion out loud, Dakar started as a bandaged hand clamped his nape.

'What was that you just said?' Mearn's unquiet pacing had carried him within earshot. Changed out of his dandy's velvets, he now wore scarlet riding leathers scaled across the shoulders with brass plates. His lovelock had singed to a frizzle. He had a marked cheek, a heel too tender to bear weight, and both hands poulticed for burns. The sting inflamed his already volatile temperament like the inexorable blaze of a slow match.

Dakar tried a noncommittal mumble.

'Say again!' shouted Bransian with a curt gesture to his left.

The mottled, ugly henchman who wielded the whip stopped his stroke, and Dakar's reply rang incensed across silence. 'I warned you before. You dealt with a sorcerer. And I said, you punish the wrong man.'

'Indeed?' The duke leaned out and snatched the dangling tail of the lash. Still in his scuffed and carbon-filmed armour, he twined the bloodied leather between skinned fingers, snapped hard, and jerked the stock from the grip of his lackey. 'If Captain Tharrick is guiltless, you are not.' A flourish of the swinging handle saw two hyper-alert guardsmen jump to cut the luckless officer down. 'Get him out,' Bransian ordered. 'But don't set him free just yet.'

With one eye puffed to a meaty, purple slit, the other half-lidded and speculative, he raked a sharp gaze over Dakar. 'Indeed, you haven't told us much of your connection in this. Who was this Shadow Master who has made such a wreck of our interests? How did he come to know you, and most of all, why did you betray him?'

'You have some fancy explaining to do if you're going to leave here alive,' Mearn added.

Fixated on Bransian's square, crimsoned knuckles, clenched and working through wet leather, Dakar licked his lips. 'Of course, I'll tell you everything. Where should I start?'

But no display of obsequious eagerness could deflect four s'Brydion primed to exact painful vengeance. Keldmar and Parrien arrived back from their baths. Each had a gingerly hitch to their stride, suggestive of stiffening bruises. Other tender patches were soothed in silks and ribbon-laced velvets in place of leather brigandines and studs. Still enraged, scuffed with nicks still oozing from scabs, they were quick to point out that the oaken table was sturdy enough to use to strap a victim down. If the inquisition grew prolonged, and torture was needful, chairs were at hand, and servants could be called to supply drink and a tray of cold lamb.

The guardsmen who had lately manhandled their luckless captain knew better than to risk their duke's displeasure by lounging in wait for direct orders. Before Dakar could draw breath to confess his first word, they hefted him upright, sliced his bonds, and stretched him flat on his back. This time, the men at arms shed their belts to restrain him. Dakar winced as buckles and studs bit through his thin hose to gouge at the bones of his wrists and ankles. Fear of greater pain set him talking.

Belaboured by stark disadvantage, that knotting a clever screen of half-truths and lies was no laughing matter in distress, Dakar lapsed into long pauses. To augment his miseries, any brilliant fabrication he could spin out of words would scarcely save him from unpleasant handling. Quite the contrary: Duke Bransian had already made clear his intent to serve his prisoner's gizzard up raw, then toss his twitching carcass to the not-so-tender pleasures of Alestron's public executioner.

Dakar licked dry lips and seized on the obvious inspiration. An explosion, a fire, then the vociferous, bloodletting trial of a guard captain should leave most men naturally thirsty. Any novice versed in granny simples knew the darker runes and seals that could compound the urge to drink into a driving obsession.

Though the setting of any geas lay in breach of the Major Balance, Dakar held the infraction as insignificant beside the certainty of being drawn and quartered as the cohort of Arithon s'Ffalenn.

To engage even the most rudimentary spell of ill while crimped in an over-tight doublet posed a problem; after several botched tries, Dakar had to settle for tracing the symbols with his toe. As adverse to concentration were skinned knees, the blisters raised by cinder burns, and the horrid pull of leather straps that threatened to dislocate both his arms at the shoulders. The s'Brydion flung him questions in a rapid-fire barrage, often shouting each other down to be first to make their point. Parched enough by himself to be susceptible to his own arcane blandishments, Dakar scarcely managed the presence to maintain his string of lies, far less to mouth cantrips to activate his construct and fan the desires of four bellicose brothers to encompass a craving for spirits.

Not least, his dire worry: that the s'Brydion style of viciousness might turn the more sullen when drunk.

When the cold supper demanded by Keldmar arrived in the care of a servant, Dakar rolled his eyes until they threatened to twist from their sockets. At the cost of an unholy crick in his neck, he managed a cursory inventory: the tray held a carafe of wine, five brimming flasks of dark ale, and a tally that fell short at three mugs.

In obstinate disdain of his older siblings' appetites, thin, nervous Mearn did not drink. While the candleflames sank in pooled craters of wax, and his brothers wolfed down strong cheese and meat pies, he regarded the fat prisoner in narrow-eyed, acid incredulity. 'You expect me to believe one such as yourself consorts with Fellowship sorcerers? That's not even plausible, it's foolish!'

Since his connection with Asandir was the single incontrovertible truth in the unlikely course of his confession, Dakar showed justifiable injury. 'Fiends and Dharkaron's vengeance! If you'd met my master just once, you'd realize such a tie is the *last* thing a man would dare to lie about.'

Bransian stretched to snatch the last ale flask from the tray before Parrien drained it dry himself. 'Wretch, I don't care if you sprang fully formed from the dungeon in Althain Tower.' Through a grand, steady pause, Alestron's dishevelled duke poured dark ale down his throat. In words not the least bit encouragingly slurred, he finished, 'Never mind your non-existent master. Just tell us where this Master of Shadow has taken himself to ground.'

'I don't know that. I said so before.' Had Dakar's hands not been dragged white by cruel straps, he would have torn his beard in frustration.

'You've said a great deal that adds up to nothing,' Keldmar grumbled. He shook the dregs of the wine carafe, then bellowed to a guardsman to collar the lazy steward and fetch up more food and drink. 'A man calls for a meal, and just on account of a pitiful few stairs, he gets a spread that's scarcely suited for a ladies' tea.'

'You ought to leave off the wine,' Mearn snapped. He sprang up again and paced the carpet, sulky as a falcon mewed up for moult.

Keldmar bared his teeth in a smile. 'The day I wish my little brother's advice on my pleasures, I'll certainly lie flat in my coffin.'

'Fiends and death, stop your bickering!' Bransian crashed the drained flask on the table with force enough to dent oak, and redouble the headache that slammed in reverberation through Dakar's skull and sinuses.

'Such temper,' murmured Parrien. 'If you're minded to thump something, my Lord brother the Duke, why not use the prisoner for the purpose? If he's going to keep prattling nonsense, I'd much rather listen to him howl.'

Alarmed lest his straits should deteriorate further, Dakar unlocked his tongue and embroidered on his woeful tale of subterfuge.

Two hours passed. The guard on the wall walk outside had changed twice. At ground level, Alestron's streets lay wrapped in fog and night silence, but for the distant clank of sheep's bells and the intermittent tramp of the night sentries. In the tower, the candles flickered and dipped, their frayed flames half-drowned in hot wax. At least six wine bottles stood emptied to the lees. Dakar ached too much to maintain strict count on the ale. His extremities had gone numb where the straps pinched, no improvement: extended hours with his limbs stretched immobile had knitted his back in screaming knots. The wearing necessity of renewing the sordid energies inherent in his geas of compulsion left him sapped to gut-sick prostration.

For all his expenditure of effort, the results were appallingly scant.

Parrien alone had succumbed. He lay sprawled gently snoring on the tabletop, his slack wrists folded underneath his velvet collar, and his cheek pillowed on Dakar's ankle. To one side, Keldmar nodded, looking owlish. Except for combative glares between statements, Duke Bransian seemed little changed.

Mearn was still upright despite his pronounced limp. Restless as a draught-teased spill of water, he quartered the chamber in unabated agitation. He fidgeted, impervious to every seal of suggestion, that nervous movement should strain body and spirit. Long since, Dakar felt, the man should have given way to a spell-turned, insatiable need for sleep.

Awake and cold-nerved as a fish, Mearn stabbed a finger into his oldest brother's shoulder. 'The fat wretch is feeding us a hotchpotch of lies. It makes me ill, that you let him keep it up.'

Bransian blinked like a tiger at the jostling, wiped beer foam from his whiskers and pontificated. 'Undoubtedly he lies. What I want to know is why he set himself up for the fall?' Another long swallow, a belch heaved up behind a massive, cupped hand; the duke gave his ale-soaked conclusion. 'That slinking little spy never struck me as a fool. You did notice, he caused damage, but never once struck to kill.'

'Well, seven of our garrison were lost in that explosion. I'm tired of games.' Mearn stalked toward the table. The scales on his shoulders sparked gold fire as his bandaged fingers clawed at the knife hilt in his belt. 'You and Parrien and Keldmar can drink 'til you're witless. I'm going to hear some truthful answers.'

The blade sheared from its scabbard with a sour, cold ring, and the sweat already beaded on the prisoner's face trickled in copious runnels. Dakar's frantic squirm creaked a protest from the straps. He desperately wet ashen lips. 'I've told you. The man is the Master of Shadow! No locked and guarded door in all the five kingdoms could stand against his fell wiles.'

As though tripped on cue, the latch clicked. The door spun open with decisive, oiled speed, and a dark-cloaked figure strode through. Tall, silver-haired, commanding in movement, the arrival flicked a cold gaze across the prostrate figure on the tabletop. 'Pray, don't let me interrupt,' he said.

'Asandir!' Dakar forgot himself, gave a frantic heave, and yelped as his bonds all but dislocated every joint in his limbs.

Knife in hand, Mearn started full circle, then fell back before the sorcerer's first glance. Keldmar more simply succumbed to the wine. He swayed, eyes squeezed shut, then crumpled beneath the table with an aristocratic ease cut off by a thud as his head came to rest against the carpet.

Lord Bransian rubbed his black eye and said solemnly, 'Ath, it's another uninvited guest. If you're selling anything, I hope it isn't emeralds.'

The sorcerer gave no reply. Beaten haggard, he stood cloakless in his travel-stained leathers, while draught from the door left ajar at his back flared and harried the stubs of the candles. He smelled of horse sweat and the crushed stalks of meadow grass, the last likely place he had snatched a nap. His demeanour showed every sign of having burned reckless power to keep a horse from flagging underneath him, through a journey of untold leagues.

No Fellowship sorcerer ever spent such reserves, or drove a dumb beast without cause.

Pressed by fatigue to a hardness like fired enamel; fixed in cold temper with no spark available for pity, he opened as though the duke and his brothers were not present. 'I came here at speed from Rockfell.'

A dreadful, uncontrolled shudder raked Dakar from head to foot. If the threat of Mearn's knife no longer held impetus, the fate he would suffer for his plot to harm Arithon defied imagination.

Asandir came straight to the point. 'Why should I trouble to punish you?' He took a step, the look he trained on his apprentice as depthless as glazed winter sleet. 'Arithon can handle his own slights.'

He raised a hand still grimed from lathered horse, sketched a rune upon the air above the spellbinder's body, and murmured a lyric phrase in Paravian. As if plucked to life, the air shivered through a cry like struck crystal. Its peal of layered harmonics felt very like another set of notes, set off by Arithon's whistle on the scaffold in the feast hall in Jaelot. The straps that bound the Mad Prophet ripped asunder; no less a constraint, every last brass button on his doublet flew off and pinged off the ceiling. Showered in their back-falling numbers, Dakar grasped after the fast-fading edges of an unbinding spell he would trade his right leg to remember.

But fear rinsed his will to stark blankness as Asandir resumed speech. 'Get up. Go. Luhaine's safe-conduct will see you past the guard and through Alestron's outer gates.'

In slinking humility, Dakar forced hurting sinews to move, to rise. No s'Brydion voice protested his freedom; none dared. Asandir's forbidding presence charged the room like new frost. Dakar tripped and reeled in his haste. Aware of Duke Bransian's glare like a coal dropped on his bare flesh, harried on by Mearn's thwarted bloodlust, he stumbled through the open doorway in a running plunge for the stair.

Behind him, the half-sotted Duke of Alestron ventured in an acid show of courage, 'Apparently the fat man didn't lie about his ties with Fellowship sorcerers. Is he your lackey or that of the Master of Shadow?'

Then Asandir's reply, never loud, but emphatic enough to pierce through the iron-bound portal as it shut. 'As soon as you and your brothers sober up, we need to have a serious discussion.'

When midnight came, Arithon still waited in the hayrick alongside the oak grove. The neat linen shirt tailor-made for him in Farsee hung torn at the elbows, grimed with oil and sooty dust. His left cuff was scorched, legacy of a fire arrow. The laces of the right were sliced and blood-soaked, courtesy of a s'Brydion knife throw; another shallow gash scored his ribs.

A jagged, clotting scab marred one steep, s'Ffalenn cheekbone, and the soft, cloudy drizzle that had dampened him since sunset wicked up the sulphurous reek of smoke that hung about his person.

Absorbed in the act of digging splinters from his palm, he looked up as something clumsy thrashed through the brush beneath the trees. A muffled curse followed, then the sound of cloth tearing, and a thud as a body collided with a low-slung branch.

A sharper oath issued through the rustle of the bough, and a dewed fall of droplets pattered into deadening leaves; apparently Luhaine's escort to Alestron's city gates had included no pause for the purchase of a four-penny lantern.

Without moving, Arithon said, 'Prophet of Madness. Lost your mage-sight, I see, to fatigue?' He sheathed his stolen dagger and carolled a line of balladry in lyrical, lilting satire. *'"And whither went thy trust, that thee abandoned?"'*

Dakar clawed his way into the open. Adorned like a springtide celebrant with sticks and sprigs of plucked oak leaves, he took a planted stance above his nemesis. 'Ath, what possessed you to start a fire?'

Arithon looked up, stilled as old rock in the darkness. 'And what did you expect, since you sent me in unwarned? Those casks contained a firespell, or some other seal of unbinding destruction, and *I'm mageblind!* People died. I was made the instrument. If you chose me as your proxy to fulfil some promised duty to Sethvir, I'd say you got far less than you deserved.'

A dangerous fury sparked within the green eyes.

Chastened to fear, wary with the knowledge that affairs had gone beyond a simple baiting, Dakar shrugged off a raking chill. Then, struck by the leashed temper in Arithon's regard, his own hot rage rose and shattered into stunned recognition. 'Fiends! *You guessed I would betray you!*'

'Guessed?' Arithon stood. Robbed by bruises of his usual easy grace, he caught up his lyranthe and belongings. 'More than that, my blind-sided seer. My strategy hinged upon that single fact. But don't be asking my gratitude.'

The damning train of past events stitched together, of an endless narrow corridor; of locked and barred doors; and of guard captain Tharrick, weeping broken on his knees, pleading still as the whip fell and fell, that no sentry posted under his command had done any less than maintain Alestron's security. Now, through abrasions and dirt and a racking, sharp ache of stiffened muscles, Arithon regarded the agent whose predictable betrayal had unkeyed those inviolably guarded posterns. His face showed contempt, and a brittle impatience as he slung satchel and lyranthe across his shoulders.

Dakar felt kicked breathless as a man just bludgeoned in the belly. 'May Daelion speed your spirit to the darkest pit in Sithaer. You've been using me all along! *What have I been but a living tool to further your unsavoury wiles!'*

'By all means, place the blame where it's properly due,' said Arithon in ringing, hard warning. 'I don't require self-indulgence. I never asked you for loyalty. But step softly. This time innocents have suffered. Cross me again at your peril.'

Dakar swung a fist to smash those fine-boned, impervious royal features. His blow deflected off a stinging parry. Then hated hands gripped and spun him, hurled him off-balance into the wet, wooded darkness.

Words equally scathing pursued him. 'Just like my half-brother, you'd give all in your power to kill me.' Arithon laughed in glass-edged malice that Halliron would have known for a foil to mask underlying anguish. 'You'll have to do that in cold blood if you can, my injured prophet. But wait for tomorrow. Unless you like the company of the brothers s'Brydion, we had best flee to Kalesh and catch a fast ship at slack tide.'

Trust

Lord Bransian, Duke of Alestron, awakened to the bother of wrapped, insistent hands pestering his shoulder until his teeth rattled. His gummed eyelids cracked open. Early light bit through his lashes like a raw stab of needles to the brain. Last night's drizzle had cleared off to clean sunshine, a change he would rejoice to do without. He groaned and tucked his face into the crook of one arm, while Mearn resumed worrying at his elbow with the brainless tenacity of a rat terrier. The ducal head felt thick as a melon. His temples throbbed like the stretched skin of a wardrum pounded by sticks furred in felt.

'Begone.' Bransian flailed a clumsy, thick fist to fend off his disruptive brother.

His aim flew wide by a yard. The physical half of Mearn's torment let up without dampening his wild spate of chatter. Since peace could only be recovered through an answer, Bransian moaned, pushed erect, and groped to recoup his bludgeoned wits.

Minutes passed before he attached any meaning to Mearn's invective. His first response was outright laughter. Absurd to believe, that he and his three siblings should be confined to their own keep by the whim of some Fellowship sorcerer.

'Mearn, if I didn't know better, I'd suspect that you tried beer and hallucinated.' Alestron's reigning duke pushed stiff fingers through the short hair at his temples, his swollen face reddened with affront.

A shadow fell cold across the sunlight.

Too peevish to notice, Lord Bransian snorted through another chuckle. 'By Ath, this is my city, after all. No sorcerer can usurp my authority.'

'Which point could be struck flat in a law court,' injected a pointed, level voice that scarcely troubled to appreciate the humour. 'Read your city's charter, as granted by Melhalla's twelfth High King.'

Bransian stubbed grit from the one eye that worked with knuckles puffed red from scrapes and scabs. He blinked, peered, forced gritty vision into focus, and felt reality return with a thud. Before his very chair stood a lean, tall personage, wrapped in silver-bordered wool, and watching him in thin-lipped acerbity. The manner of his presence was stark peril swathed in velvet, and his regard could unpick a man's thoughts. This was nothing if not a Fellowship sorcerer, solidly arrived in displeasure.

In keeping with his bloodline, no s'Brydion heir would forgo bristled pride to apologize. 'Pox and Daelion's fury,' Bransian groused. 'I wish you were a nightmare brought on by fatigue and bad wine. Since you're not, you can lighten my headache by leaving.'

Asandir laughed and sat down. 'We've a lengthy bit of business to attend, first. Do you want breakfast before we start?'

'No breakfast.' His flush tinged green at the edges, the Duke scraped back his chair. 'You're forgetting – I rule here.' He thrust to his feet in magisterial arrogance, then spoiled all dignity by shambling from the chamber on an unsteady quest for the privy.

The brothers left behind were scarcely more amenable. Keldmar and Parrien nursed the same furred tongues and evil hangovers, and Mearn's thin nostrils were pinched white at the corners, sure sign he was mad enough to murder. Too distrustful to sleep in a stranger's presence, far less one announced as a sorcerer, he had paced away the night in fuming idleness. The friends he habitually met for cards had gambled the week's stake without him. Some rival he should have beaten easily would be smirking over a winning cache. For that, Mearn sat and drummed his poulticed fingers on the tabletop. The pucker between his eyebrows suggested he preferred to be flaying mage hide in strips with a knacker's knife.

Bransian barged back through the doorway. He stretched until his knuckles brushed the ceiling beams and all of his joints popped and cracked. Then he spun a chair backwards and alighted. Disturbed air fanned by his movement bore a miasma of carbon and ash and singed hair. While the sturdy oak beneath him settled creaking to his weight, he treated his Fellowship visitor to a flat-eyed, inimical regard. 'You didn't answer my question, last night.'

Straight and ageworn as antique steel, Asandir smiled. 'I came as no man's lackey, but as the keeper of a trust sworn two ages before you were born.'

Pained by the prospect of a lecture, Parrien clapped his palms over tousled hair and wishfully muffled his ears. A planted, stubborn pace beyond his shoulder, Mearn looked primed to interrupt.

Keldmar seemed too fuddled to try speech, his stubbled chin propped on listless fists, and his bleary eyes half-lidded; yet it was he who spoke out of turn. 'By the Fellowship's presence alone, I presume the weapon we developed is proscribed?' At his eldest brother's snarling glare, he added crossly, 'Well, you can scarcely pretend our damnfool culverin's still a secret. Not when the armoury went up in black smoke and a bang to dunt the siege bells in their cradles.'

'No such secret could stay masked from Sethvir at Althain Tower in any case,' Asandir cut in.

'Why should your Warden stick his sniping nose in Alestron's private business?' Too fastidious to endure the chamber's frowsty tavern reek, Mearn crossed the carpet to avail himself of the cleaner breeze through an arrowslit.

'How plain must I be?' Asandir no longer looked either tolerant or amused. 'You've discovered that saltpetre, potash and brimstone can be mixed and ignited to cause a mighty explosion. You have turned this to destructive purpose, and fashioned a weapon more lethal than blade or crossbow. This culverin you've developed has small art to its usage. As yesterday most ably demonstrated, any ignorant fool with a torch can precipitate broadscale harm.'

An accusatory burst from the Duke s'Brydion, *'Then that was your spy!'* entangled with Mearn's declaiming shout, 'But the weapon was made for our defence!'

While sore heads alone stayed Parrien and Keldmar from compounding the altercation, the sorcerer raised a hand to stay outcry. 'Power by itself has no morals. What is to prevent the greedy man from turning this new force on his fellows with intent to exploit and force dominance?'

'We certainly don't plan on sharing our discovery,' Keldmar snapped, then regretted his vehemence and winced. 'Sithaer! Why else keep the weapon and shot locked away, under guard day and night by crack sentries?'

'Who will your heirs be?' Asandir arose. 'Can you guarantee their self-restraint?' Too tactful to pursue the contradiction implied by a captain's flecked blood on the carpet, he jerked out an empty chair and on the strength of a glance, recalled Mearn across the chamber to settle down.

'You built this culverin from a treatise written by Magyre,' the sorcerer resumed like struck iron. 'Had you met him, you'd know he was a frail old scholar whose conscience balked at swatting flies. He discovered black powder by accident, then pursued his study to make displays of fire and noise to amuse his grandchildren on feastdays. The Fellowship set our case before him, as I shall for you this morning. Under guidance of our counsel, Magyre set aside his experiments. Later, we learned he had cached several copies of his papers. For vanity, he could not bear to burn all his records, since his works had brought the young so much pleasure. Here we sit, scarcely one generation later. Already you have turned these pretty flames and loud bangs into a weapon to make widows and orphans. Magyre would weep, were he alive to know, but the damage is done. Your armoury is ashes, your citizens are terrified, and no secret can be harboured past a lifetime.'

Too rankled by the wreckage in their dungeon to listen to reason with equanimity, the brothers set squared jaws and exchanged a round of glances underlain by bedrock resistance.

Bransian thumped a mallet-sized fist on the table edge. 'If you're asking us never again to fire a culverin, you waste your time. We're not timid scholars to be cowed by what might shape the future, but a city surrounded by enemies. We'll yield up none of our advantage.'

'You will cast no more such weapons,' Asandir contradicted. A change touched his aspect, potent and frightening, as a storm charge might gather before lightning. 'This was never a choice. A different decision will confront you before I leave. When I have finished, you'll know why.'

Brash as they were, and fierce in contempt, not one of four brothers could muster a whimper of protest. The sorcerer gathered himself a moment in preparation, head bowed over the knuckles left folded on the golden, oak grain of the table. Far below, cheerful voices floated up from the courtyard as a guardsman cracked a coarse joke. Thin smoke from the brick yard furnaces laced the first stir of breeze as labourers began the day's firing. Such commonplace details fell strangely on the senses, distanced like a dimmed, surreal dream.

By contrast, in the study within the drum tower, details seemed cased in clear glass. Littered trays and emptied goblets and the gold-leafed spines of books assumed a transcendent sense of being. Sun through an arrowloop smote Asandir's crown and gouged the shadows from his creased face. For an instant, limned in light that burned away the stains of travel and the marks and bitter trials of past ages, he assumed the very image of a fair, untried mortal youth.

And then he spoke, his timbre as compelling as a masterbard's that no man within earshot could deny. 'From such weapons will grow others that cause ruin and death to a scope beyond your imagining, and on the power and tyranny enforced by such horrors, you will build a civilization driven by fear.'

'How can you know?' demanded Bransian.

The sturdy, capable fingers, tucked one inside of another, spasmed tight as Asandir looked up. 'I know because I was one of seven who caused such a thing to happen, on a scale this land will never see.' The merciless flood through the arrowloop touched eyes gone limitlessly bleak. The humanity in them was a fearful thing, paired to a burden more desolate and weary than any charge borne by a mortal.

'It scarcely matters to you here,' Asandir said. 'The horrors I helped to create were inflicted on another world, far distant, and inconceivable centuries in the past. They are the reason for the Seven's sworn Fellowship, as Athera became our choice to protect.'

Duke Bransian loosed a wordless grunt. Parrien, thoughtful, drew a wicked little dirk, and in silent, balked fits of annoyance, tested its edges by slicing off ribbons from his cuff.

266

'There's a fugitive spy on the run while you blather,' Mearn complained. When Asandir's regard encompassed him directly, he dug at an exposed cuticle, ripped skin to the quick, and fisted his fingers to damp the sting.

'The plight of that man is the least of your worries,' the sorcerer declared. The leashed power in him devoured the very air and leached off inclination for more argument.

Lent what passed for patience by his tender head, Keldmar stirred out of silence. 'You say he's not yours. Why protect him? He broke into our armoury and inflicted untold damage.'

'It is the culverin that brought me,' Asandir corrected. 'My Fellowship has a sworn covenant with the Paravian races, and by its law, that sort of weapon is forbidden. I am going to allow you to understand why before your final choice is presented.'

He went on to speak of the First Age legends, that preceded the time when Paravians or men came to settle the five kingdoms. Before them had lived the greater drakes, creatures of a vast and wild beauty, but ancient in clever intelligence. From the riddle of Ath's deepest mysteries, they spun dreams that Named, their unbridled ambition to expand the living fabric of the cosmos. Theirs was a deeply mistaken belief that higher mastery could be theirs for the taking. But they forgot, in their pride, that the Creator founded the birth of the world in compassion. In the end, the fruits of the drakes' making escaped their control altogether.

'Let me be plain,' Asandir said. 'The dragons did not originate evil, they spun energies that embodied senseless destruction. Their meddling with the mysteries spawned fearsome predators called Seardluin that lived for the dark thrill of killing. These creatures are not fables. Our Fellowship saw the last of them die at the close of the Second Age, and we count ourselves favoured to be alive. Athera still harbours drake-spawn that survive from that era: the lesser iyats are among them. Wyverns and Khadrim still fly and mate, but if any of the greater worms yet lie deep in volcanic caverns, they are diminished, and have abjured the temptations of true-dreams. Since the Paravians vanished from the continent, Sethvir keeps continual watch.'

The sun mote slanted with the day's progression; Asandir's seated frame slipped gradually into shadow. Not one of the s'Brydion brothers held mesmerized and listening ever noticed the change as his speech took on the soft, rolling cadence of the Paravian tongue. Whether his voice wove a seer's spell, or whether power enspelled the words themselves, only the sorcerer could have said. His meaning formed in direct imprint upon the mind, beyond definition of sound and symbol; the brothers experienced the past through Asandir's recounting, as sharply as though they stood witness.

*   *   *

A herd of deer grazing in a misted vale suddenly raised their heads, listening. There came no warning, no sound, not even the shower of dew from disturbed grass; just a sudden, explosive burst of motion as something massive and dark erupted from the brush beside the dell. A ripple of muscle under black, maned hide; a blurred feline shape and a lightning swipe of claws; then the scream of a dying animal. The herd bolted, spun, and bolted again, but the predator circled them, faster. A snap of a scaled tail, the gore of a horn, and another deer went down, tawny legs threshing; then another, neck-broken in the clash of fanged jaws. Too swift to flee, with a sinister, blurred grace, the Seardluin killed and killed again, until the dell lay bathed in steaming carnage, and the last doe lay gutted and still.

Threaded underneath the immediacy of vision, Asandir's account wove in sorrow. 'The Seardluin killed for sheer rapture, as a weasel may, drunk on the thrill of its senses. Perhaps, like the dragons, they could sense forces of animal magnetism loosed in fresh-spilled blood, and such power fed their excitement. Whatever warped inclination drove their nature, they would slay until the soil itself was sodden muddy red. The great drakes themselves lost young to their predation.'

The rest, written in scripture preserved at Althain tower, told how such depths of misguided ignorance came to be offered enlightenment through the brightest of power and knowledge. The Creator sent a gift to heal the ruin the dragons in their arrogance had set loose. Alone of all worlds, Athera became blessed with new children of Ath's making. The Paravians became the affirmation that order bound all structure into balance. Their kind embodied the divine example, that the quickened life misbegotten through the drake's feckless dreaming might in time be redeemed.

'And so came the three blessed races to Athera,' Asandir explained. 'Centaurs, Ilitharis, whose strength was to nurture the growing earth, and defend it with their blood if need be. Ath sent the small ones, the Sunchildren, to celebrate life's undying joy. Lastly, the Creator gave the Riathan, the unicorns, who formed the living bridge, the linked connection to all that is and will be. To stand in their presence is to know, unsullied, the unconditional love that embraces all things that exist.'

The histories preserved in Althain Tower catalogued the course of two ages of tragic confrontation. The world was both bright and desolate, since even the shining grace of the Paravians failed to turn the Seardluin's ungovernable viciousness from the heat and passion of the kill. The creatures organized into armies, and bound the drake-spawn into fell service. Wars were fought, and tragedy abounded, and Paravians lost their lives until their numbers dwindled nearly past hope of recovery; in those days, even the greatest and oldest of drakes mourned and repented for the suffering unleashed by their tampering.

'Our Fellowship was drawn here by drake-dream,' Asandir confided at last. 'The power of old dragons has a very long reach, and it chose us because we were deemed masters without parallel in the terrible arts of destruction. The engine we had taken to flee the horrors of our past was plucked from its transit across the deeps between stars. Crater Lake in Araethura marks the site where the forces arisen from the drake's desperate need hurled it earthward. We were given our deliverance there from the guilt and the agony that harrowed us since our acts. And though bloodshed by then was abhorrent to us, we fought to ensure Paravian survival until the last of the Seardluin lay dead.'

For the Fellowship, responsibility had not ended with the Second Age. Men came to Athera, refugees cast loose by the very cataclysm their earlier works had engendered. The home worlds left decimated were cinders, now, and elsewhere, survivors suffered wretched, ugly lives, doomed always to repeat the terror and the tragedy of their past, for they sprang from a society ruled by want and senseless fear, and they knew of no other way to live.

The Paravian races had fulfilled Ath's directive by ending the strife arisen through the dreams of the dragons. Since a peace bought through war was never their Creator's intent, to ease their sorrows and their losses, Athera's rich lands were ceded to their inheritance. Theirs also, the decision whether mankind should have leave to settle in cohabitation. At the council where humanity's fate was debated, the Fellowship interceded.

'A covenant was sworn,' Asandir said, gruff with the wear of a service that spanned inconceivable centuries of strife. 'We Seven undertook responsibility for ensuring the steps were never taken that could engender the means for mass destruction. For the sake of the Paravians, this world is protected, and shall be for as long as men endure.'

Around the oaken table, the s'Brydion brothers sat, dazed sober by the aftershock of visions. Parrien's knife lay abandoned to one side, its point impaled amid a creped litter of ribbons. Mearn regarded a chewed nail, this once in his life wholly still, and Keldmar's keen rivalry with his next oldest brother was displaced by unwonted respect. Mollified by visions of unicorns dancing, or stately, tall centaurs with stag-horned crowns and dripping, battle-red weapons, Bransian scrubbed his scabbed knuckles through his beard. 'Our culverin, then, is to be forbidden.'

'I will say plainly that black powder is a first step on that path that led your forbears to destruction.' Asandir straightened, as if flicked by a creeping small frisson of chill. 'A first step, and a tiny one, of seeming insignificance. But the insidious progression of change its use will bring is well known to us. The result over time would spoil the green earth, then breed an enslavement of the mind beyond your most dire imagining.'

The time had come to broach the subject of choice. Asandir clamped his hands on his forearms, his expression gone desolate as a man eaten hollow by old pain. 'Your family is not the first. Once, we sent men with inclinations such as yours to dwell in the splinter worlds through South Gate. They, in their turn, built a civilization based upon the machines that are proscribed here. The misguided, self-blinding madness inherent in such ways created the scourge you have known as the Mistwraith, and our greatest grief. The Paravians were driven from the continent by its dominance, and the restoration of clean sunlight has not recalled them.'

'Then the Fellowship's covenant failed after all,' Duke Bransian observed, surprised by the poignancy of his sorrow.

Asandir sighed before that painful truth. 'Desh-thiere's ills are ours to put right if we can. The choice you face is no less cruel a quandary.' He drew a fast breath, backlit now by the beat of noon sun against the stone beyond the arrow slits. 'You may allow Fellowship intervention to excise all memory of your culverin and the powder that kills.'

He encompassed the brothers in a glance sheared to purpose that perfectly disallowed pity. 'Or else you shall not leave this chamber for the rest of the days of your lives.'

'That's no choice!' cried Mearn, spiked to his feet by raw outrage.

Asandir looked at him, desolate. 'That's the sole option in the Fellowship's power to offer while our active numbers are diminished.' He surveyed each brother in turn. 'Think carefully. I can't stay here beyond sundown.'

Minded to raise protest, Mearn gave way before Bransian's right to speak first. 'No need to dally here quibbling. The culverin will be forgotten, as you wish.' The Duke of Alestron raised his chin in a concession that held bravado and the rags of mulish dignity. 'You have my consent. Do what you must and be done with us.'

'The others must choose their course separately,' Asandir said. In what seemed idle habit, he extended a forefinger to configure a pattern on the tabletop. If to direct eyesight, no design appeared evident, the far fringes of peripheral vision sometimes tagged his tracery in hair-fine trailers of phosphor. Upon closer study, the effect would be mistaken for the glister of reflection touched across lines of puddled water.

Too earthy to dwell on any puzzle wrought of magecraft, Parrien pressed his back against his chair, lips curled in a tomcat's grin. 'I don't much fancy being held here while my betrothed ups and marries some beardless rival. It would be a chill bed with only memories of a culverin to lie with. Do as you wish with me, Sorcerer.'

Keldmar snapped off a nod. 'Me also, though I won't pretend I like it. We earned that culverin through five years of hard work, not counting for injuries and the powder burns.'

Last to capitulate, Mearn said, 'We'd be free to pursue yon muckle clever spy?'

Asandir spared no second thought. 'Pursue all you wish. He's a difficult man to catch.'

Mearn gave his scowling, ungracious acquiescence, and for a second the room seemed to blur. The books, the varnished secretary, the bronze stands of the candelabra with their wax-dribbled sockets all rippled as if marred by a wash of pressed air. The smells of baked stone and sheared steel and musty parchment acquired a transcendent edge of clarity. Then darkness crossed sight like a footprint.

Restored to cleared senses, the brothers sat alone around their table. A space lately occupied by a sorcerer lay vacant, the memory of his presence gone with him. Sunlight angled in yellow bars from the arrow slits, shot through a haze of stirred dust motes.

First to move, Parrien rubbed thick fingers at his temples. 'Ath,' he said, bewildered. 'What possessed me to drink myself stupid on wine?'

Keldmar's bleared gaze fixed and focused on the dangling remains of burst straps. 'Which of you oafs turned soft and released the fat prisoner?'

Through the vociferous, insult-slinging quarrel that followed, not one of the s'Brydion could agree on any culprit, nor could they recall what had immured them in close conference through a night and half the next day.

'There's a spy running free while we scrap over nothing!' Mearn interrupted in withering disgust.

Duke Bransian shoved to his feet in a jangle of displaced armour, shouldered his youngest brother from the arrowloop, and bellowed down to the sentry on duty to roust out his best troop of lancers. Beneath his enthusiasm like sand in a blister rubbed a queer and infuriating hunch: that the fugitive sorcerer who had ruined his armoury was by now beyond reach of reprisal.

'The double-crossing criminals can't hide themselves forever,' said Keldmar, still glaring at a span of empty oak.

Parrien knuckled bloodshot eyes and ground out a derisive snort of laughter. 'They will if you don't stir off your arse. Are you coming?'

Ignited to a madcap race to muster weapons, four brothers pounded shouting down the stairwell to launch their belated hue and cry.

Resolves

'We've found where to send Elaira on her assignment to compromise Arithon s'Ffalenn,' the Koriani First Senior announces to Morriel Prime; in hand she holds the day's report from the sixth lane watch: *The smuggler's brig* Black Drake *has sailed to recover the riches held for the Shadow Master's use by Lady Maenalle; and the cove specified for final delivery will be south, at Merior by the Sea* . . .

In Althain Tower, on the verge of twilight, Sethvir pauses between penned lines of manuscript to receive Asandir's news from Alestron: 'The brothers s'Brydion hold no more memory of black powder or culverin; Rathain's crown jewels are recovered for return to storage at Althain Tower. Luhaine has destroyed the drawings and dismantled the moulds at the bronze founders'. Since the explosion in the armoury was too widely witnessed to recontain, sadly, Arithon must stand as our scapegoat . . .'

In a cell beneath Alestron Castle, an imprisoned guardsman languishes with a whip-torn back; and through each hour of his agony, he renews his cold vow of vengeance, to take down the Master of Shadow whose tricks had undone a lifetime of honest service . . .

X. MERIOR BY THE SEA

Immersed in sulky bouts of brooding since the disaster in Alestron's armoury, the Mad Prophet evolved his own brand of consolation. Since the Shadow Master's wiles could turn even the acts of an adversary to abet his most secretive design, Dakar would ease his stung pride and blunt the horrid quandary by drinking himself senseless as dead-weight.

Through the four-week voyage down the continent's east coastline, while Rathain's prince acquired the crazed instincts of a packrat and a variety of seasoned lumber from the millwright's in Telzen, Dakar sucked down beer, and rum when he could supply himself, with the joyless abandon of a fish. No brand of liquor could obviate the unpleasant truth: the prince whose affairs he was geas-bound to share was accursed by Desh-thiere. Over time, the destructive drive which had seen thousands slaughtered in Strakewood must re-emerge with intent to kill Lysaer, who once had been Dakar's best friend.

Primed to denounce the first sign of geas-bent aggression, the Mad Prophet kept beady-eyed vigilance in those maudlin moments between binges.

But the Master of Shadow could maintain seamless subterfuge, as his disguise as Medlir had well established.

Since patience was never Dakar's strength, his wits were well sodden on the day the patched sloop engaged to ship the new planks reached the southernmost call on her route. Jostled semi-conscious by a lurch, disturbed further by the muttered creak of towlines rigged to warp the weedy hull hard aground for her yearly refit and careening, Dakar fumbled to discover his flask lay empty. Too bone-lazy to regret the oversight, he lapsed back, eyes closed, and eavesdropped on the conversation currently in progress on the main deck.

Clear above the cries of gulls, and the thump of sailors' feet over the pawl of the turning capstan, he heard the Master of Shadow announce his intent to disembark in the tiny cove at Merior.

Too bored to examine s'Ffalenn motives; fuddled beyond recall that Merior was a sleepy, tropical backwater comprised of little but fishermen's shacks, the Mad Prophet crawled from his shadowy lair between decks. He wove past piled cargo crates, Arithon's lashed spruce from the sawmiller's, and smacked both shins and one elbow in ascent of the companionway ladder. Undeterred by bruises, or by the scathing oaths of sailhands who sprang to untangle the lines left befouled in his wake, Dakar blundered onward, while at safe remove from the rigging above, other seamen called cheerful encouragement.

'Hold your grief! If the fat lubber's going ashore, let him take his sandy boots, and good riddance!'

Dakar swayed on in a reeling cloud of whisky down the newly-set gangway to the beachhead.

The whitewashed cottages of Merior nestled in a little crescent cove, fringed with sea oats and palms, and notched into the narrow peninsula that bent like a hook to enclose the aquamarine basin of Sickle Bay. Here, the great combers that rolled in off the Cildein's vast deeps burst white and unravelled against a landspit scarcely three leagues across. Shadowed day and night by their thunder, this village offered the last, lonely settlement. Beyond, a wind-raked ribbon of barrier sands dwindled into bars and scattered coral reefs, where surf churned and creamed at Scimlade Tip. The neat, seaside anchorage was too cramped for trader ships. It boasted no breakwater and dock. The slatted wooden tower burned a beacon light for fishing craft, which moored in bad weather to battered cork buoys scattered like beads amid the chop.

The instant Dakar's step met immovable dry strand, he staggered, tripped backward, and sat. A grunt of forced air entangled in his throat, and a hiccup squealed through his larynx.

The only folk at hand to marvel were two barefoot, tow-haired urchins who sat on a barrel and smirked, then burst into shrieking gales of laughter.

Dakar blinked at them owlishly. Peevish before ridicule from children scarcely eight years of age, he unhooked a trailer of seawrack from one ankle and clasped his head to ease its gruesome pounding. The sky was blue and cloudless enough to hurt. Against a serried mesh of palm fronds spread a smelly, drying hatch of fishnets, jewel-strung with glass floats and stamped clay seals to repel iyats. A dog's distant yaps pocked the bawl of a lighterman who ferried another line from the ship. Fierce southern sunlight glared off sugar sands, and other things suspect and glistening strewn amid the jetsam at the tidemark. Too fordone to care if he sat in something noisome, the Mad Prophet flopped back on his elbows. To the sniggering towheads, he said, 'I don't see what's so funny.'

A shadow darkened his face, cast by Arithon, just come ashore with an unwieldy beam braced across his shoulders.

'Are you cap'n?' shouted the nearer child. The pair looked alike as halved oysters, all brown legs and grey eyes and simmering curiosity. Their unbleached trousers were grimy and ragged, and each wore a smock shirt, clumsily cut down from a man's size. The coltish angles of forearms and shins were sequinned in iridescent cod scales, and the narrow feet with their sturdy, splayed toes had likely never seen shoes.

'I'm not this ship's captain,' Arithon declaimed. He sounded as though he was smiling.

'Then you're captain of a bigger one, surely,' the other chimed in, while the first interrupted in shrill-voiced, point-blank demand. 'Who are you?'

'"*He's master of all things bleak and dangerous*",' the Mad Prophet misquoted, inspired by faulty memory of a gate arch inscription on an initiate's hostel that attrition had degraded to a brothel.

'The master, the master, the master,' chattered one child in monotone. The other sprang up and awarded Dakar a petulant frown. 'He's *not* Daelion Fatemaster!'

While fingers slim and dirty as a thief's entangled in a wisped, sun-bleached curl, the first child intoned in changed rhythm, 'The fat man's a liar, the fat man's a liar.'

Dakar tucked in his chin, the better to glare down his nose. 'Boy, you know little. In a contest of falsehood, I would certainly lose to this black-haired mountebank you champion.' His attempt to defend his impugned character met with indignant failure.

'I'm no boy!' The urchin shot erect beside her sibling. 'My name's Feylind.'

Dakar raised his brows. 'Well brat, I'm sorry.' A scuffed-up shower of grit pattered over the holed knees of his hose. 'Tell your sister to stop flicking sand on me.'

'He's not a girl, he's my brother!' Feylind shrieked, to her twin's renewed peals of glee. 'Are you stupid? You must be, to lie in the sun like a sausage.' This pearl of wisdom delivered, she turned her inquiry elsewhere.

Arithon had lowered his burden. Braced upright against hip and shoulder, the beam threw his angled features into shadow. Too pert for shyness, the child addressed him. 'Will you go back on the sloop?'

'I thought I was taking wood off her.' Apparently not in a hurry, he added, 'Your brother must have a name, too.'

'Fiark,' that small person supplied. 'Would you take us aboard?'

'The fat man can carry the board instead of you.' Feylind elbowed a place at her brother's side. 'Anybody can see he's a layabout. The work should do him good.'

'I'm no man's servant,' Dakar pronounced, dropped bonelessly prone with his eyes closed.

For answer, the monstrous beam walloped flat on the strand a handspan from his right ear. Riled to a leap of shocked nerves, Dakar unwisely scrambled upright. A ticklish flood of sand grains trickled down his collar and clung to his sweat-dampened skin. 'Damn you! I won't fetch and haul as your labourer!'

Alone with a vacant barrel and a gouged smattering of footprints, the Mad Prophet spun around to find the Master of Shadow halfway back up the gangway. On his heels, irrepressible, Feylind capered, with Fiark behind, stamping on the planks to make them bounce.

Dakar cupped his temples to contain his throbbing agony and shouted, 'You can't take those youngsters on board! The captain will never allow it.'

Arithon ignored him. Feylind twirled about and stuck out her tongue, while Fiark screamed back an obscenity, then taunted, 'He's master. He'll do as he pleases!'

Dakar shrugged in a last, fruitless effort to jog the grit out of his clothing. Through the pounding in his skull and the reeling assault of strong sunshine, a chill stabbed over his skin. For just an instant, the salt breeze in his nostrils hung tainted with fire-caught smoke.

Too cross to sort whether his distress was due to overindulgence, or some stillborn pang of gifted prophecy, he slapped his forehead and hauled off in pursuit.

The tide had turned. Sluiced by receding waters, the sloop's keel grounded and wedged fast. Her sails were inelegantly stripped. Agleam in a coat of wet varnish, her bare gaffs creaked and swung as her decks laid over and canted. Her waist was a cat's-cradle of lines and topping lifts, unstowed since her spars were unshackled. Progress for the inebriated became a trial of slipped steps and hooked ankles, overseen by jeering, half-naked sailors. Wise enough not to assay the slope of afterdeck companionway, the Mad Prophet latched his hands to the ladder's top rung and fastened himself upright to eavesdrop.

The vessel's grizzled captain braced against the dazzle of white decking, one brawny arm crooked through the backstay. 'The lighterman will ferry your dowels of locust wood,' he was saying to Arithon s'Ffalenn. 'The heavier planks will be delivered by a fisherman who hires himself out as stevedore. That covers the last of your lading list. I saw your plans. She'll be a pert little craft.'

'Thank you.' Attended by the twins, Arithon fished out a small pouch. 'The arrangements are sufficient.' Fiark admired the clever fingers as they dealt out smart payment in royals. 'If you're willing, I need another service.'

The coin changed hands and vanished into a greasy leather purse. Politely attentive, the captain said, 'Name your wants.'

'Shipwrights.' Bored by the talk, the twins began to tag each other's toes around the pinrail, while Dakar strained his ears over their rowdy noise to catch the last of Arithon's request. '. . . and one master craftsmen if he brings journeymen versed in his trade.'

The captain's leathery forehead furrowed. 'Whatever for? You've got only one set of tools.'

'They're prototypes.' Arithon sidestepped to avoid getting clobbered as the twins fell reeling into giggles and tussled like puppies at his feet. 'The smith here at Merior will be skilled enough to make more.'

'If not, there's a chandler's downcoast in Shaddorn. That harbour's more sheltered, if you want my opinion, and the southcoast trade galleys call there.' The captain chewed his moustache, distracted from inquisitive speculation by a shout and a lurch as the ship keeled another three degrees and a loose object banged belowdecks. He leaned sidewards to bellow down a hatch grating. 'I thought you had everything stowed!'

The cabin steward's invective spiralled up.

'Well blight take your excuses! Get a line and lash the forsaken thing down!' He turned back to his client with scarcely-veiled interest and no measurable improvement in temper. 'When do you want these craftsmen?'

'Spring will do.' Jostled by eight-year-old exuberance, Arithon knelt, flung out an arm, and rescued Fiark or Feylind from a skidding slide through the cordage. Blond curls mingled with black as he arose with the child pinned in his embrace.

The captain scratched his ear. 'Autumn would be easier. Skilled men without ties are tough to come by.'

Arithon swayed as the other twin fastened like a lamprey to his thigh. 'I can offer rich pay, for everybody.' The coins he produced with the finesse of a spell arched through the air, light licking gold faces as they fell.

The captain fielded the bribe and bared his sly teeth in a smile. 'Your shipwrights shall arrive with the violets.'

'What are violets?' shrieked the twin who pounded on Arithon's hipbone.

Feylind, presumably, answered. 'They're flowers, fishhead. The ground here's too salty to grow them.'

'You don't know everything,' Fiark retorted.

'No, she doesn't,' Arithon agreed, and silenced the fracas by prying the sister off his neck. 'Don't bicker, or you won't get your tour belowdecks.' To the captain, laughing, he added, 'Would you mind?'

Drawn grinning into conspiracy, the hard-bitten waterman relented. 'Take them yourself, but go lively. In another half hour, this bitch'll be aground hard as Sithaer, and ornery as a half-skint wyvern for the pinch o' the sand in her planks. Keep clear of the hold lest the ballast shifts.'

Slithered in a heap at the base of the companionway to evade notice as the conference ended, Dakar hugged his knees in stark misery. 'I knew it,' he mused in private conclusion. 'I just knew it! He's brought planks to build a damned war fleet.'

Immediately above, Arithon's face eclipsed the light. 'Right now, just one small sloop. You needn't fret. We haven't the coin left to arm her.' Under pressure from Feylind's impatience, a malicious glint stirred the green eyes. 'You're not in the mood to get stepped on, I trust.'

'The fat man's in the way again!' the insufferable Fiark proclaimed. Forced to give ground in a cloud of ill grace, Dakar heaved up his tipsy bulk and moved.

From the stern, his weathered face crinkled in calculation, the sloop captain tracked Arithon's answers to the children's eager questions. 'Knows his lines and halyards like a man born to blue water.' The old salt cast his moody gaze at the horizon as though stalked by invisible foul weather. 'Why in the name of mayhem would anyone found a shipyard in a site that grows not a stick of native timber?'

But the fat drunkard who might have lent insight now snored in an oblivious sprawl by the gangway. The captain spat downwind in disgust, then dispatched a sailhand to heave the sot ashore before he tumbled overboard and drowned underfoot in the shallows.

In obstinate refusal to permit the earlier, unsettled stir through his senses to give rise to his spurious talent for prescience, Dakar slept off his binge. Wakened to an aftertaste of dread, as if the visions jammed irresponsibly beyond recall had scalded their imprint in dreams, he sat hunched over dinner at a split-plank trestle in Merior's only boarding house.

The tea grounds in his mug streaked the landlady's white porcelain in ominous, unlucky patterns, and his brooding bought no peace of mind. While southern moths like antique lace battered the smoke-hazed tin lantern overhead, Arithon plied thread and needle to patch his second-best shirt.

'Shipwrights!' Fired by long-delayed pique, Dakar curled his cup in a rocketing slide that scattered through knives, chinked the honey pot, and caromed off a platter littered with fish bones.

Arithon shed his mending on hair-trigger reflex and rescued the mug before it shot off the table rim.

Balked of even that destructive satisfaction, the Mad Prophet raged, 'Who's going to finance your fool's notion, anyway? There's not enough coin in this whole village for you to sing for your upkeep.'

'Then you might be more gentle with the landlady's crockery. Or tomorrow we'll eat baitfish served raw on a cutting block.' Green eyes regarded him, thoughtful; and in the same tone as the banter came the answer Dakar least expected. 'I thought the crown of Rathain should bear the expense.'

'Your emeralds are safe back at Althain.' Had the tea mug remained in his hands, Dakar would have thrown to draw blood.

The knife-edged start of a smile compressed the line of Arithon's mouth. 'A pity, since you're hot to lay into me for something.'

Too tender to provoke s'Ffalenn temper head-on, Dakar attacked on a tangent. 'Well where will we live in the meantime? You can't want to stay until spring.' He dared not spell out the obvious: that the upheavals in Jaelot and Alestron were going to stir trouble. Elsewhere, two armies amassed to kill off the s'Ffalenn bloodline could scarcely stand idle at the news.

As though content to do nothing in response, Arithon watched the moths flare up and die in fitful spits of flame. A milk-warm, tropical breeze played through latched-back, diamond-paned casements, textured with salt and the taint of tidewrack and fish.

'Winter is coming everywhere else,' Dakar prodded. 'The Scimlade peninsula doesn't get frost, but in case no one told you, it rains buckets here.'

'I've leased the shell flats by the abalone cutter's.' Arithon spun the mug in a curling slide that missed soup bowls and plates by narrow margins, then thumped in an accurate jab to the nerve in the Mad Prophet's dimpled elbow. 'If you want to try carpentry, we've plenty of wood for a shack.'

'I can scarcely drive nails when I'm sober.' The Mad Prophet lapsed into offended silence.

By morning, he was once again comatose, and Arithon had to borrow a handcart to remove him to the site where his lumber lay. Dakar snored on through the ride, his arms and knees dangling, and his bearded chin tipped to the sky. Arithon dumped him in the shade to sleep off his poisoned stupor, then took stock of his future boat, stacked now in neat piles that beckoned to be shaped with adze and saw and plane.

The twins found him in less than an hour. Every minute after that, they infested the shell flats like a hopping plague of locusts, until every step a man took seemed encumbered. The Mad Prophet was slowest to differentiate between them. When he misnamed Feylind, she screamed at him until his ears rang; her brother preferred to throw stones. Arithon never minded their boisterous noise. Obstructive whenever the future was mentioned, he tousled the twins' hair like young puppies and stopped Fiark's arguments by letting him hold the ends of his chalk strings.

'They just lost their father to the sea,' the Shadow Master explained on the day Dakar woke to find his bootlaces kinked into knots. Lately discharged of a vociferous lecture on the topic of children who should be home in strict charge of their family, he was in no mood to listen as Arithon added, 'The mother has forbidden them to sail since he drowned, and in case you hadn't noticed, in Merior, only infants and the sick stay ashore.'

One boot half off, the other ingeniously entangled, Dakar looked up into green eyes untrustworthy for their mildness. 'So why do *you* stay ashore?'

'For my amusement,' the Shadow Master said.

Rankled again by the queer, warning ripple of impending prophecy, Dakar bit his lip, hard. The coppery taste of blood killed the vision's deployment fast enough. But peace of mind did not return. Eaten by nameless foreboding in the face of Arithon's complaisance, the Mad Prophet found no comfort in his vices. Every girl he pinched was somebody's wife, and twice he got pummelled by packs of brothers led by a wronged and vengeful husband. Merior's villagers were closemouthed and reserved, and their town, a dull backwater that made the bigoted stews of Jaelot seem a wistfully remembered time of paradise.

The days shortened; the fishing luggers sailed reefed to stronger winds, and the sandspit south of Scimlade Tip abided in its customary idyllic isolation. Arithon made no clandestine effort to stay abreast of events in the north. His easy-going humour under needling was just another sham, the sort of masterful, guileless fabrication his s'Ffalenn wiles employed to mask havoc. His work might seem unhurried, as he measured his fine wood in whistling patience. But the little sloop's keel was laid and her stem post set in the sort of studied, sustained effort that admitted no loophole for setback.

Like the baitfish before the barracuda, Dakar discovered he was unable to bury himself in detachment. Complaints became excuse to provoke arguments. 'A man could get permanently griped on a diet of saltfish,' he broke in after a laboured visit to the privy. 'And sleeping under sail canvas has me rotten with sores like the pox.'

'That might not be the case had you bought black beans and figs instead of that beer keg from the market.' Arithon bent to shape a raw plank, shirtless, the shiny lines of old scars browned by the sun.

'Curse you!' Dakar dug his fingers behind his waistband to scratch. 'They haven't sold figs or beans since the last cart returned from Shaddorn, and that's been better than a week.'

The adze sheared off a pallid scroll of wood. 'Six days.'

'Curse you!' Tired of the ocean, the heat, and the unending, brain-stabbing headaches brought on by the dastardly hours of banging required for maritime construction, Dakar jettisoned tact. 'All so that you can wreak vengeance in ships crammed to the gunwales with arbalests.'

Arithon paused, his tool stilled in warning between strokes. 'You speak like a master taleteller,' he said in pleasant deceit. 'Halliron would have applauded. I've only got enough wood for one vessel. A sloop. Thirty feet to the inch, and if I use sword steel or stone shot for ballast, the quarries in Elssine will have run out of honest grey stone.'

Half-inebriated, his tunic undone to the waist, Dakar lashed back in cornered fury. 'Who are you fooling? You know you are cursed. Lysaer is amassing armies while you dawdle, and –'

'What am I supposed to do?' The adze scythed down in a vicious, white flare of reflection and sheared off a sliver of spruce. 'Agree? Make you promises? *Confide?*' In the sudden stabbing sarcasm he used when a nerve had been struck, Arithon smiled. 'Much better to leave you dangling, Prophet. You're far less bother to me, drunk. Failing that, you might consider washing your underclothes. They're stiff enough to stand by themselves. If they rot from neglect, we'll all watch you greet Etarra's armies bare-arsed.'

'Oh, but you're careful, and nasty in your arrogance.' Dakar narrowed foxy eyes, suffused to a high, purple flush. 'You daren't mention your nemesis by name, do you? What about this town? It is innocent. You'll draw the danger to your web, sure enough. Do you tell me, will the children once again pay the cost?'

He had gone too far.

Blood drained on a breath out of Arithon's face. His green eyes watched, flat and fixed as a cat's. Lanced in the grip of raw fear, Dakar scrambled back, hands upraised to discharge a spell-ward of guard at the first twitch of movement from his enemy, for one twist of muscled hands could hurl the adze in a stroke pitched to murder.

'Ath forfend!' said Arithon s'Ffalenn. He raised a wrist and stifled back a belly whoop of laughter. 'Dakar, what are you thinking? This is a pleasure sloop, and when she's launched, *I'm sailing her to Innish!*'

A matter of a song and a widow denied reunion with her husband; the promise sworn at Halliron's deathbed that Arithon now claimed his full intent to honour.

Caught aback inside a spitting crackle of sparks thrown off by the collapse of an inept conjury, lent no grounds to attack unimpeachable decency, Dakar broke off his challenge, unsatisfied. The sop he had been tossed to force his silence assuredly did not include the truth.

A month passed, and the graceful frame of Arithon's sloop took shape on her ways on the shell flats. Fishermen returned from their dories began to stop and share news, or sometimes a fish from their catch. The reek of cod or halibut toasting over an open fire pervaded Dakar's whisky-soaked dreams. The autumn equinox brought in the feast days, and the twins brought yarn strung with folded paper talismans. Through the lattice of the palm groves, candles burned on every cottage windowsill. Amid the bonfires and the dances to celebrate the summer's harvest came the inevitable change to the wind patterns, and the driving, seasonal rains.

The deluge caught Dakar in a desperate, furious bout of hammering.

Indignant when the villagers dared to appreciate his discomfort too much, he retorted, 'Well how can I see to bang a nail with Ath-forsaken water in my eyes?'

'Wait till the rain stops,' Arithon suggested.

Dakar missed stroke and mashed himself a black thumbnail. His subsequent explosion exhausted filthy epithets acquired through five centuries of debauchery. Every curse and full blame for the weather attached to the Master of Shadow, and the twins, apt mimics, filched the best phrases to malign Dakar.

Arithon gripped his ribs, a suspect expression on his face, while white runnels streamed off his hair. Since the downpour doused the coal fire that fuelled his steambox, he used the chance to wash his clothes in a nail keg.

The children were kept home the next day.

'In bed with coughs, their mother said,' offered a fisherman in a syrup-slow, southshore dialect. Close with his words as a pinch-fist doling coins, he trudged with his fellows to launch the dories. But the wink he tossed over his shoulder gave fair warning: the widow whose household had been outraged by an influx of rough language might be along later to scold.

A moment of forethought, and Arithon sent Dakar on an errand.

The woman came between showers, a thin, stoop-shouldered figure swathed in the black skirts of mourning, her wisped hair muffled under an enormous oilskin. She carried sprigs of sage to ease her passage through the fishmarkets. Against the white sands and the wheeling gulls, and the silver-banked, cloud-silted sky, the storm harried her like an omen in beggar's rags.

Lent a shore bird's gait in her pattens, she picked her way past the puddles in the workyard as if apologetic for the crunch of her tread on the shavings. Met by sour smells of pine and wet oak, her swift, darting glance took in Dakar's crude shack, the gapped, miscut boards and bent nails a flute for the tireless sea winds. The rough-sawn windows boasted no shutters, nor candles in honour of equinox. The little paper talismans brought by her twins hung tacked to the eaves, soggy and entangled in their tethers. Austere as fine muslin, she rounded the building and stopped with caught breath at the absolute shock of discrepancy: before her, in grace that bespoke patience and a loving touch with raw wood, rose the clean curves of a sloop's frames. Neat, tight pegs fastened the stempost to her keel, under damp like a patina of new varnish.

A glance told the widow why the fishermen of Merior gave this outsider their respect.

The yard at first sight seemed deserted. Then the rhythmic tap at first mistaken for a woodpecker fell silent. A man crouched half under the unfinished hull stood up, compact, well-made, a mallet and chisel in his hands. Sawdust and shavings twined through his dark hair. He wore canvas knee breeches tied with fish twine, the cut ends whipped deftly in round splices. Too well-raised to stay shirtless in her presence, he snatched a soaked smock from a saw trestle and wrung out the water. She caught a disturbing glimpse of scars as the cloth dropped over his head. Too reserved to make comment, she strove not to stare as he flicked off scrolled shavings, then moved with his hand out to meet her.

His approach jarred her to an inadvertent step back. His build was small and light-boned as a hawk's, where the twins had painted a giant. 'You're the one called the Master?' She knew of no other address for him; even when maudlin and drunk, the stout companion never spoke his surname.

'Friends call me Arithon.' Eyes of a piercing summer green flickered over her. Then he smiled. Thwarted from shyness by warm fingers that touched and then steadied her elbow, the widow averted her eyes. Her reason for coming was not going to please him, and his manners left no excuse for brevity.

'You must be Jinesse,' he said. 'Here, come and sit.' He steered her the necessary steps across ground littered with angles of scrap wood, the sort the twins had often dragged home to whittle by the hob in the kitchen. A tarpaulin was whisked aside. Arithon set her down on the fine-grained teak stacked aside to become his sloop's brightwork, then melted back out of contact. 'These boards are dry, and more tidy than Dakar's lair indoors.'

Jinesse stared at her feet, and then, less comfortably, to one side, where she saw in mute shock that he had outflanked her. Adjacent to her perch rested the finished hulls of two dories the tarpaulin had also masked from view. Gripped fast to the greens, her hands clamped together in paralysed dread, for the sloop now in progress on the shell flats was too small to tow any more than one boat as tender. By Arithon's intent look of pleasure, she guessed: the craft had been made for her children.

Alarm tensed her shoulders and made her look achingly brittle. 'You don't make this easy.'

The Master upended an empty nail keg and seated himself, his wrists clasped loose at his knees. 'I know very well you've come to say the twins are best off without my company.'

Jinesse flinched. To stop the wild tremble transmitted through her posy, she opened bird-boned fingers and flung away the wilted sprigs. No matter how difficult, the dory perforce must come first. 'You should know they are destined to be apprenticed to a craftsman.'

His vantage below her defeated her armour of oilskins. Intimate as touch, his study mapped her dry-skinned, ageing fairness, then the pale hair wisped at her temples.

Annoyed by her nervous leap of reaction, Jinesse understood he was not going to grace her with an opening. 'My children lost their father to the sea. I would not see them drowned offshore in a lugger, and their acquaintance with you makes that hard.' She stopped, wrung mute by the sound of her own rough-sawn fear.

Arithon was first to break their locked gaze. Through fallen dark hair,

283

his expression stayed masked as the beauty of his voice leached the iron from her determination. 'I agree.'

'You'll sell the second dory, then.' Her business concluded, she stirred to arise and encountered an immediate obstacle. Unless she wished to hike up her skirts and step over him, the loom of the woodpile trapped her.

The smile that bent the near corner of his mouth revealed the disadvantage was intentional. 'The dory will not drown your little ones. Nor will the sea of itself bring them harm. Lack of knowledge will certainly do both.'

Nettled past diffidence at last, Jinesse exclaimed, 'Trust a man to make a simple thing impossible.'

'This is not simple,' Arithon said.

'I won't have their future tied to fishing, can't you understand?' He had been in Merior long enough to have seen the crippled old men while away their afternoons on the guest house porch; the horribly-swollen arthritic hands, or ones maimed and scarred, that could no longer draw nets from the sea.

But Arithon did see, Jinesse realized as he faced her directly. The compassion in his challenge, and the stillness of his patience made her wonder if he, too, had weathered losses. He said, 'The twins' father has died. Would you give them your fear as their legacy? Will you force them to ignorance, where now there is laughter, when the sea is born into their very blood?'

Against a terrible, ripping urge to break down and weep, Jinesse whispered, 'Don't argue. Let us go, build your sloop, and leave this village.'

'I will do all of that,' Arithon promised. A less sensitive man might have tried to reassure her by touch. This one did nothing but speak, in that voice which relentlessly stripped the protections she had patched over raw and stinging grief. 'But first I would leave you a gift. Let me teach your twins a mariner's skills, as my father taught me. I will give them the sea, and a freedom beyond fishing boats, and you can face your heart and learn to abide without terror.'

He moved. Before she could frame any protest, he had risen. As he pressed a warm weight into her chilled fingers, she almost missed the welted scars that disfigured one palm and both wrists. 'Here. Take my pledge. Your children shall be given all they need to stay safe, and you will find joy in their accomplishment.'

Jinesse turned over the token he offered in trade for her personal weakness: a scratched signet of white gold set with an emerald and incised with a rampant leopard seal. The ring was an heirloom, and with it, he granted a trust. Merior was too small for a man of his presence; all the village wondered why he needed refuge, and what sort of trouble he was fleeing. The sigil offered means to unriddle his surname and his origin, hers to pursue if she wished.

The gravity in Arithon's manner suggested power in that knowledge, and key to his deepest reserve. 'Jinesse, if after six months you still wish your children to stay ashore and apprentice in a craft shop, I shall help underwrite your decision. But let them have the dory until then. Give me that time to win your faith.'

'Let the craft be launched on the bay side,' she begged, the more wretched for the tremor in her plea.

He laughed, a chime of relief like bright music. 'I'd actually planned on Garth's pond. You don't have to watch. I'll look after their lessons myself.'

The sky darkened. A stiff, sudden wind flagged the palms by the harbour, and rattled the shack's ill-hung door. Chipped wood scudded like autumn-tossed leaves, to scrape and catch in her mourning skirts. A fresh downpour spun sudden silver over the dories strung out on cork moorings, empty in wait for the fishing fleet's return. Aching still for one left unpartnered, Jinesse clenched chapped hands beneath the humid chill of her oilskins.

Afraid of the secrets that surrounded this outsider, of what else he might soften if she lingered, she allowed him to escort her across the shell flats to the wicket gate by the market.

And then the bleak rain fell and swallowed him.

By the time she reached her tiny cottage with its roof of moss-draped cedar, and its front door painted with talismans which had done nothing to spare her goodman from the waves, the storm pounded in torrents across the spit. Arithon's ring was an icy lump in her palm. For days she left it untouched in the bottom of her wicker sewing basket. She was no gossip, with naught else to do but pry into an outsider's past.

Yet in the dark of the night when the twins were abed, and the sea boomed relentlessly against the headland to remind of its cruel theft, the toll of grief and loneliness chiselled away her resolve. She took down the basket, scrounged the dark emerald from its nest of thimbles and thread, and made an impression in candle wax. She used chalk to copy the leopard seal, then marked out the slanting, graceful runes that inscribed the inside of the band.

With the drawings wrapped in a packet the next morning, she hopped a ride on an old, creaking tinker's cart bound downcoast to Shaddorn. An enclave of Ath's initiates still kept a hostel in a remote cove by Sickle Bay, and there she stopped to make inquiry.

Rumour held the disappearance of the Paravians had set the old order into decline. Certainly the long, winding lane that led to the hostel was hedged on both sides by rank woods. Its buildings were stone, dressed out in moss-flecked sigils that were uncanny to the eye, and which touched Jinesse's skin to odd starts of gooseflesh. The grounds themselves looked unkempt, waist-deep in dog fennel and exuberant runners of wild vine. Unaware that initiates revered all growing things for their place, like most unversed visitors, the widow mistook their way of blessing for neglect.

Afraid to shout lest she find the silence one of desertion, she startled at movement, and was greeted by a white-robed old woman who answered her request before she spoke.

'Claithen's the brother who could help. Bide a bit. He will come for you.'

Jinesse was offered a bench beneath the knees of a hoary, crowned cypress. She cooled her feet in the trickle of a spring and worried her packet in fretful hands. The peace of moss-bearded hardwoods and an unpruned riot of citrus was broken by blackbirds who flapped and shrieked like viragos over seed grain that a wizened little cook tossed out of the door from the scullery. Unseen in a thicket, a quail called.

'You have a seal you need identified?' questioned a peppery voice.

Jinesse started, spun, and confronted a squat man with leaf-dark eyes, a bald crown, and a book clutched tight to his chest.

He gave her a jolly, wrinkled smile. 'I thought we should look for it here, that Ath's blessed sun shed his light on the knowledge you seek.'

The bench was wide enough for two, if tall for the brother's bandy legs. He sat, feet swinging like a child's, and balanced his fat tome on his knees. The serenity he commanded seemed to stare her through and finger every trouble in her heart. 'You've brought a drawing,' he prompted to crack her shyness.

She picked the string off her packet. Ath's blessed sun made the leopard seem ineptly drawn, a sad and unexpected embarrassment. The original had been like the man, elegant in grace, with a captivating fierceness noticed too late for the safety of hapless small prey.

Claithen regarded her chalked copy in silence. Then he smoothed open flocked pages and bared the selfsame blazon, except this one was beautiful, painted in silver gilt and black, on a field as deep green as fine emerald.

Jinesse need not know letters to interpret the crown above the sepia ink of the house name.

'The royal arms of s'Ffalenn,' Claithen murmured. Hands as age-flecked as the pages eased the book's boards closed. He reached out, touched a forefinger to the chalk-marked leaf in her lap, and traced an intricate pattern.

Whether the sign stood for blessing or curse, Jinesse had no way to know. But power translated across the touch; even through paper, she felt a flashpoint tingle of mystery cross her flesh. Her fabricated tale to explain her curiosity died unspoken. Never mind that the story was plausible: curious bits of jetsam were brought up all the time, oddments from the past, sea-crusted and strange, nested with the fish in the nets.

Yet with a tact that pierced, Claithen's quiet made a lie too wretched to contemplate.

'Who would wear such a seal?' Jinesse asked finally.

The initiate pushed back his ivory linen cuff and threaded a knobby finger along her unpolished scrawl of runes. 'It says here: "*To my sons, from their forebears, back to Torbrand*". Your man is the scion of Rathain. There's a prince of that line returned, by Ath's grace. His shadows helped return the true sunlight.'

Jinesse shut her eyes and swallowed hard. The outsider who sheltered in Merior by the Sea owned powers more dangerous than silver-tongued persuasion, skills more dire than any simple love of ships. She wished no involvement with his sorcerous secrets. Appalled fear for her children left her sick.

'You look tired,' said Claithen. 'In the buttery, we have herb tea in stone jars and new biscuits.'

'No thank you.' Jinesse stood up quickly, the paper crumpled in hands now smudged in damning, scarlet smears of chalk. 'I have to walk back to Merior. You've been helpful. I'll send down a basket of jam the next time a wagon comes by.'

Claithen peered up in gentle censure. 'No need. The world in its wisdom provides.' He freed a hand from his book and gestured toward the sprawl of the citrus grove. 'If it is Arithon of Rathain you have met, believe this. He shall do you no harm. The heritage of his bloodline will permit him no cruelty, and Ath's greater mercy walks beside you.'

Jinesse jerked back a step, breathless. Her children must never know the breadth of this quandary: their friend was the Master of *Shadow*, and if he stayed, his enemies would be visited upon Merior. He required refuge from the whole of the north, and their village offered too small a haven.

'I know very little of mercy,' Jinesse whispered; her husband had died of Ath's storms.

'Then life and Prince Arithon will teach you.' No longer placid, the initiate brother bobbed to his sandalled feet. He gave her a last, searching glance that, like the bitter taste of aloes, seemed to curdle the dread in her breast. 'In time, we shall come to meet again in this place. For now, I will see you to the gate since, sadly, my library holds no more help for you.'

Every step of the way back to Merior, Jinesse thrashed through agonized doubts. She weighed her children's recent triumph over grief, and the fragile, trusting gift of their happiness against the dark rumours that surrounded the revealed name of their benefactor. The truth behind Arithon's reticence burdened her, and chafed with the memory of his kindness. If he harboured deceits, their depth lay outside her grasp.

Timid in the end, loath as she was to confront him, she let the days pass one into another, and did nothing to forbid the twin's friendship.

*   *   *

Another outsider came to Merior, a woman who rented a cottage and set up a small custom selling simples. The convenience was appreciated. Before, the only apothecary was south in Shaddorn, and when a babe sickened or a fisherman suffered injury, the hostel of Ath's Brotherhood was a long, rough cart ride away. Goodwives gossiped with the village's two shopkeepers, and wondered if the woman's arrival might be connected to the other outsiders who currently inhabited the shell flats. Only Jinesse knew their questions were well founded, and she kept her own wary counsel.

Tiny as Merior was, folk there kept distance from strangers. Word of the woman's presence never reached the pair most likely to be interested, and despite the villagers' keen curiosity, her visit to the shell flats was unannounced.

She went, her cloak of grey wool snapped by harsh gusts off the sea, and her way directed by an elderly tosspot who informed in slurred gravity, 'You'll find the man, lady. Just follow the footpath toward Scimlade Tip and listen for the sound of the hammers.'

The autumn season had been fortunate; no deadly storms had whipped in off the Cildein to savage the exposed eastern shoreline. The mangroves that fringed the sheltered inlet dripped and tossed branches mantled in glossy foliage. Sheared stems of deadwood past gales had ripped down lay masked in weed-bound shadow. The cedar-shingled shack on the shell flats shook to the thrum of the winds, as the half-decked little sloop cradled on braces did not.

The sky hung streamered and low as drenched wool, and the hammers, that morning, lay mute.

Skirts lifted clear of runoff from the fishmarket, the visitor picked her way through damp-rotted oat grass and crossed through a wicket gate festooned with Dakar's holed stockings, left out for the weather to launder. The hesitant crunch of her footsteps stopped as a voice, light with a humour few ever overheard, raised clearly across the yard's stacked lengths of lumber.

'Bless you, no, that isn't elegant. You need to go with the grain of the wood, not across.' Framed by the lyre curves of the unfinished hull, the speaker bent over two intent tow heads, set lean fingers over a child's stubby, dirty ones, and redirected the stroke of the plane.

Under sure guidance, the blade sang across new spruce and scrolled up a ribbon-thin shaving. The child with the tool shouted in pleasure, while the other tugged at the man's idle arm and begged vociferously for a replay.

At that moment, Arithon of Rathain looked up.

The enchantress who intruded upon his privacy was relentlessly trained to interpret every nuance through detail. She took in the sailor's tunic, decently clean, but rumpled in emphatic rebuttal of royal birthright; the dark, uncut hair that cast an air of benevolent untidiness over a perception still mage-trained, and keen as a razor; the sea tan and shirt style that minimized old scars, and beyond these, surprise, masked behind the polite lift of black eyebrows.

The rasp of the plane died away. Two twins turned pitch-sticky faces and stared. The one to whom persistence had ceded the tool blew chips from the blade and demanded, 'Who's she?'

'Is that how your mother greets strangers?' the lady admonished, smiling.

'Are you a stranger?' Arithon countered, his guard nearly good enough to mask an underlying alarm.

Unprepared for the lurch of her heart as he regarded her, the visitor traced the end of the spar with her finger. The loving care that had guided its shaping sang through every fibre of the wood; as immediate, to her, the awareness of the hands that enacted the labour. Her shield of banality crumpled. 'I don't know.'

'But who *is* she?' persisted the twin who was female, her grip on Arithon's arm grown possessive out of blind instinct.

'The lady's called Elaira,' Arithon said. His bard's tongue made music of the name, and offered back skilled reassurance as he readdressed his visitor directly. 'Were you bidden to see me, or Dakar?'

Cautious of his empathy, now schooled to sharp strength by his study under Halliron, the enchantress defended, 'I came as a friend.'

'But your kind go nowhere without purpose.' Arithon's sudden, flat expression set a sting to that truth as he gestured toward the crooked lintel of the shack. 'You may as well come in.' A corner of his mouth crawled up. 'Or is it a Koriani preference, to address their affairs while standing ankle-deep in a mud puddle?'

Aware in that moment of the seeping, wet rings that darkened the hem of her skirts, Elaira stepped back. Her laugh of embarrassment was graciously passed over as Arithon dismissed his small admirers.

'Over there,' he said to the children, 'see that plank? You can prop it on the trestles and practise with the plane. If your work is very neat, I'll let you help finish with the gaff.'

This suggestion greeted with a whoop, the twins moved off, chattering. 'She has pretty hair. Red and brown all at once. Is he going to kiss her, do you think?'

The reply drifted back, rife with scorn. 'Feylind! You ninny! Why should he want to do that?'

Finished wringing out her damp hemline, Elaira straightened up to find Arithon beside her. His grip as he took her elbow was more firm than she recalled, and each steely, flexible finger seemed to sear through her sleeve like a brand. His sailor's dress and dishevelled grooming made him exotic and strange, too immediate a presence to bridge a prolonged gap of years and separation.

Then he drew her past the rude doorway into close gloom. By the feeble light threaded through chinks in the artless board walls, Elaira glimpsed coils of new hemp, a box jammed with cleats and oak blocks bought used from the local fisherfolk, and incongruous in the clutter, a level set of pegs that hung the Masterbard's lyranthe, his sword, and a new woollen cloak and an oilskin. Then Arithon closed the leather-hinged door. The shrill talk of the twins, and the hesitant, rasping first strokes of the plane came through muffled, while something amorphous slouched in the corner choked through a stertorous snore.

Elaira's small start transmitted to Arithon's hand.

Moved to amused exasperation, he called, 'Dakar!'

The mass gave a moan, unfurled, and dug plaintive fingers into a thatch of screwed hair. An epithet emerged. Then the fat hands groped blindly and closed on a whisky crock as though the contents offered sustenance and life. To a belch and a fanfare of rank language, the Mad Prophet cracked open bleared eyes.

'A woman!' He shot erect too quickly, slopped an astringent spill of spirits, and yanked down his shirt to cover the pink dome of his belly. The pleased smile he began froze and died as the female in Arithon's company crossed the unshuttered window.

'Dharkaron's Spear and Black Chariot!' Dakar battered to his feet in alarm. 'What are *you* doing here?' To Arithon, he cried in agitation, 'Send her out! Now. She's Koriani, and worse than a plague-storm of fiends.' Hazed by raw nerves, he hefted his crock. The draught he slugged down left his eyes squeezed tight shut. As if respite from sight lent him patience, he finished in forced enunciation, 'If Asandir knew you'd let her kind in, he'd bring down the roof on your head.'

Arithon steered Elaira past a brimming bucket. 'If you continue to shout, you'll achieve as much by yourself.'

'Damn you,' Dakar swore. 'This isn't funny. Mark me, if you don't send that witch packing, the one secret you can't afford to share will be in Morriel's ear by evening.'

Elaira's breath caught. The nuance of Koriani observation inferred the entreaty was genuine; that despite a master's training at magecraft and every informed and formidable defence, Dakar believed Arithon to be vulnerable.

Desperate that the order's plans for her should not yield any unexpected windfalls, Elaira wished herself blind and deaf as Dakar resumed his invective. 'Don't claim I didn't warn you.' Despite a tipsy sway that undermined his will to stay upright, he lurched in determination for the doorway. 'When Asandir makes his inquiry, tell him I had no part in this.'

The glare he shot Arithon held a beacon flare of hatred. Elaira sensed its passion like the flung-off, sudden sting of static, nothing like the disgruntled irritation the Mad Prophet had shown while intoxicated in the past. Unsettled by the profound depth of change in him, she watched him trip on unsteady feet and bang headlong into the doorpanel. A hinge burst from the abuse. Then the cobbled-together raft of planks gave way. Ejected amid a spill of razed boards, Dakar measured his length upon his belly.

The filtered rasp of the plane faltered and stopped, replaced by shrill laughter from the twins.

Dakar snarled a curse, ripped his doublet off the claws of bent nails, and rescued his dropped crock just as the dregs escaped the neck. 'Ah, Ath,' he grumbled. 'Should I be surprised there's no luck in the presence of a witch?' After a last scathing glower through the doorway, he heaved himself off to console his unhappiness elsewhere.

The renewed scrape of the plane over wood kept time to a peaceful stillness. In gloom scarcely mitigated by the additional influx of light, Elaira picked out a fungus colony of pans and rusted buckets scattered across the shell floor.

'You have to credit our spellbinder for originality.' Arithon pulled out the only available stool for her, then settled himself on an emptied beer keg. 'Dakar set all the windows in the roof.'

Elaira sat. Her fine linen skirt rasped on the saw-grained wood of the bracing, and her foot bumped an ill-fitted peg. The room's split personality haunted: ramshackle joinery at silent war with the lone, level trestle, spread with parchments lined with fine chalk. Sketched in a hand unmistakably Arithon's lay the plans of his thirty-foot sloop.

'Best keep your prophet's hands off the shipbuilding,' Elaira remarked with a dry smile.

Arithon laughed. 'The twins won't let him come near. "Keep your fat hands off, y'old drunk!"' His incisive imitation of childish scorn cut off in sudden sobriety. 'Enchantress. Koriani. How did you find me?'

Denied the easy, instinctive rapport of their first meeting, Elaira stayed still enough to mark the moisture that ticked off her soaked hem. She matched his gaze and gauged his reserve through her arts; and deduction implied the question pertained more to Lysaer s'Ilessid and his massed armies than to her, or any meddling of her order. 'I think,' she said, husky, 'you could guess.'

'Jaelot,' he surmised. Green eyes that threatened to dissect her heart like sharp knives turned down and fixed on the hands which had wrought a great and joyous miracle on the solstice: an artist's unfettered celebration of beauty that a fate cursed by geas had recast to invite his downfall.

His guilt filled an unpleasant interval, that his passion for music had led him to careless betrayal of the very foundation of his principles. Then he said, 'Are you here to help or to hinder?'

Elaira swallowed, set back by his directness. 'You don't know?'

That made him look up, pitched taut with an anger so virulent, she lost any footing to fathom its origin. 'What should I know?' His sarcasm raked her. 'Hasn't your order's prying interest in my affairs unearthed enough sorry facts?'

'I couldn't guess, not being privy to the secrets of the Senior Circle,' Elaira said, too wise to give ground to his temper. Her trained eye had caught the minute change in tension as he braced for her condemnation.

When she gave no reaction, he drew breath to say something less forgivable.

But the wry, patient tilt to her eyebrows set him back, and the malice he used to defend his deepest feelings bled away. His attention combed over all of her then, from the heavy auburn hair spilled loose from the braid that constrained its unruly fall, to the three coins for luck a thief's superstition made her sew to the turned-back lining of her cuff, to the silly wet drape of her hem. Her eyes in the gloom were soft opal and mystery, and firmly determined in kindness.

Disarmed, he laughed with the warmth she remembered. 'You won't be put off through ill manners, I see.' The compassion that kept his fate hurtful rasped through. 'I'm still in your debt for past service, but Dakar is forced company enough. Can you respect my flawed intentions and leave Merior?'

'That's what you want?' Elaira asked, amazed to find herself steady. Let him answer, and she would have excuse to evade the entrapment set by Sethvir's prophecy and Morriel's invidious plots.

'What I want hasn't merited much priority.' Arithon pushed to his feet. A gust raked the shed; the mirrored liquid in the pans shattered into rings touched off by fallen droplets. Outside, the plane lay silent, the twins fled off home as a barrage of fresh rain pocked the gapped shakes of the roof. 'Stay if you wish. I can't stop you. Once the sloop's fitted out, I will sail.'

Fretted by currents too dreadful to fathom, he paced, his quick energy a challenge: should her Koriani arts attempt to finger the changes Desh-thiere's works and a masterbard's gifts had stamped in him, the insight was not offered freely.

Elaira arose. On parting she gave him the two truths she had unentangled in her oathbound obligations: 'Merior has no one trained in herbals and healing. And the prophet you keep in your company would as soon put a knife in your ribs as offer you comfort or friendship.'

That evening, tied by Morriel's immutable will, she unpacked her jars and her remedies and arranged room and rent for an extended stay.

Dakar passed out senseless on the boarding house porch, while the fishermen who crossed the shell flats on return from their dories were arrested by a cascade of lyranthe notes. The melodies burned like sparks through the dusk, by turns exalted to a tingling joy, or else plangent with a sorrow to uproot the heartstrings and make the very stars seem to shimmer through the clouds like strewn tears.

Dispatch

Captain Mayor Pesquil, commander of the northern league of headhunters, straightened up from his examination, knee-deep in grass rimed with frost. His expression stayed as closed as a steel trap as he surveyed the site of the latest massacre. The dead did not reek any less in the cold, nor for having been chewed on by predators. Neither was Pesquil inclined to waste effort in fits of useless swearing. 'This was barbarian work, for a surety,' he announced. Bland as a bust in a tea room, he regarded the hands left befouled from close-up study of corrupt flesh.

The green-faced officer at his side swallowed noisily. 'But the wagons weren't robbed! Why should clan reivers slaughter bound men, then leave fine southland silks behind to moulder?'

Pesquil's thin lips curled, dimpling the scars left gouged in his cheeks from a childhood infection of the pox. 'I recognize the knife work. You would as well, were you seasoned enough to have seen the barbarian brats under Arithon's command slitting the throats of our wounded beside the Tal Quorin.'

Folded over by involuntary reaction, the city garrison officer crouched beneath the turned leaves of a hazel bush to retch.

The headhunter captain's dry scorn pursued him. 'Better puke fast and be done. You're riding at once for Etarra.' A leathery, thin figure in a dust-drab surcoat, Pesquil moved off to mete out a round of brisk orders.

His personal troop would remain and mount a stiff guard on the road, while the division of city garrison split off from patrol and returned at speed to the Mayor of the Northern Reaches.

Propped back erect, blanched and shaking, the officer wiped his chin and waved toward the corpses rowed in bound bundles beyond the angular, rib-splayed skeletons of oxen still yoked in the mould-furred leather of rotting harness. 'My Lord, before we ride out, surely we should spare an hour and see the fallen are decently burned.'

Paused beside his stocky, brush-scarred gelding, Pesquil reached for his saddlepack and freed a waterskin from its hide lacing. He yanked out the stopper with his teeth. While the officer attended him, diffident, he used the last, warm dregs to sluice the corruption from his fingers. At length, around the plug of moist cork, his thin lips pulled back in conclusion. 'Let the bodies stay as they lie.'

Not too shaken to show outrage, the officer gathered himself. 'But –'

Pesquil spun about, killed refutation with a glare like sheared iron, then ejected the cork into a horny palm. 'I said let them lie.' Unhurried, but efficient, he recapped the flask, gouged a shred of gristle from a thumbnail, then reached beneath his mail to blot his damp knuckles on his gambeson. 'Tactics before sentiment, always. I don't wish Red-beard's Companions warned off by any smoke. Let his barbarians stay encamped in this region, unaware. And when they raid again, we'll be prepared for them. My men will gain the bounties they merit. Better than last rites that yon murdered bones have no use for, your victims will be granted due vengeance.'

Through narrowed, joyless eyes, Pesquil watched the shaken officer hasten to rejoin his troop. Then he set his boot in the stirrup, mounted, and dug in spurs and bit to rein his mount around and ride out. The time had come to act on his gnawing suspicion, that these late bloody raids were not done for spite, nor for revenge. In the unerring instinct that had won him his commission, the headhunter commander sensed this slaughtered caravan lay connected with the Shadow Master.

A fortnight later, the stench of corrupt flesh a memory that rankled no less, Captain Mayor Pesquil cast his jaundiced regard on the gold-bordered curtains, the ebony and ivory inlaid footstools, and a sumptuous tasselled carpet which silenced his predatory tread, and clashed in evil virulence against green and purple tiles of fired enamel. The tastes of the city seneschal were typically Etarran. The embers in the hearth discharged enough heat to wilt a hothouse flower.

Snake-still in his formal black and white surcoat and silver gauntlets, Pesquil parked his lean length before a massive, carved desk. He worked his jaw muscles in irritation as the bootlicking little secretary scurried to fetch the mayor's seneschal from his nap.

The courtesy expected as that personage appeared, yawning and straightening his furred brocades and gold chains, was no custom Pesquil subscribed to. No bow did he give, no preamble in flowery language; he scorned men of pedigree and privilege as naturally as he hated barbarians.

He presented his case with the ripping flat brusqueness of a slap dealt to shame an incompetent. 'When was the last time this city received any courier or message from the southcoast?'

The city's chubby seneschal crumpled into his upholstered chair. A florid man with watery eyes, he rearranged his feathered hat, turned his knuckles to admire the sparkle of his rings, and raised his pencilled black eyebrows. He took his time answering; men arrived without appointment to make demands with crude manners well deserved to wait upon his pleasure. 'Summer, I should think. Why care?'

Pesquil clamped his fists in forbearance. 'Lord Commander Harridene's still out on campaign?' A drawn pause; a languid nod; Pesquil's next question rapped back fast as a ricochet. 'Who's acting captain of the garrison?'

Etarra's seneschal stiffened his spine, disdainful. 'You scarcely needed to disturb me to ask what any servant could tell you.'

A moment of locked wills, while bleak, cold black eyes stared down the pompous official. At length the seneschal blotted moisture from his fashionably-powdered cheeks and gave in. 'Gharmag's sick with the cough. His senior staff sergeant holds the temporary command.'

Another pale-cheeked puppy with pedigree whose father deemed he needed hardening, Pesquil remembered. No twitch of disgust crossed the raised bones of his features. Etarra's army had lost more than a skilled captain with Gnudsog's death in Strakewood; a strategist of unrefined tastes and no pretensions, he had at least kept a finger on the pulse of rumour in the drover's dives and taverns.

'Let me tell you what I learned in one hour from four caravan guards just in from North Ward,' Pesquil said.

The seneschal bristled. 'But this is outrageous! To barge in and berate me for not consorting with riff-raff in the streets. For your insolence, I should demand a review of your competence.'

'Try.' Pesquil bared yellowed teeth, his mailed fist at ease on the sword responsible for harvesting more clan scalps than any other blade in the northern reaches. 'This city's ignorant riff-raff, as you name them, have word of the Master of Shadow. They bandy tales in our taverns that every misbegotten sailor's told his grandmother since the traders' galleys berthed in winter dry dock!'

The overbred smirk on the seneschal's face dissolved like wax left near a fire. '*What?*'

'On the night of summer solstice, the city of Jaelot was half torn to wreckage by a sorcerer who lived there for months in disguise, but left with black hair and green eyes.' Unmoved by the seneschal's pasty-faced shock, Pesquil inflected his next lines like the cut and riposte of lethal steel. 'Alestron, downcoast, suffered an explosion inside a locked armoury that killed seven men. Although the s'Brydion duke is no fool, and his best troops combed the countryside for a fugitive who bore the selfsame description, no culprit was found. Arithon s'Ffalenn has come out of hiding in Melhalla. If the guild minister's council has not paused to wonder, or take steps to see why no messengers came through from that region, *somebody* had better act now. Or I'll personally roust Lord Mayor Morfett away from counting jewels for his daughter's trousseau over this.'

'Right away, right away!' The seneschal flurried a hand to dispatch his limp secretary on the errand.

Pesquil watched the agitated hurry raised by his news in stone-faced, scalding ill-humour. Braced for days of political manoeuvring while Etarra's beribboned city governance primed in agitation to act, he decided, cold-nerved, that he would arrange to carry the dispatches sent to Avenor himself. A hand-picked contingent of his headhunters would ensure information reached Prince Lysaer with all speed.

Shakedown

On the morn that Pesquil's company embarked from Etarra under dismal, sleeting skies for their arduous winter journey to Avenor, balmy southern winds flapped the pennons of a newly-launched sloop, moored amid a damascened circle of reflection in the distant, turquoise waters of Merior. The Shadow Master whose misdeeds were named in Mayor Morfett's sealed dispatches scarcely looked the mage-trained minion of evil. Clad in a plain linen shirt and loose trousers, he carried no weapon beyond a rigging knife. The tanned hands that drove the sweeping stroke of his oars as he rowed the sloop's tender ashore were innocent of spells or subterfuge.

Certainly no villager knew him for the author of uncivil deeds as he leapt barefoot into the shallows, beached his dory, and strode through the dunes and shoulder-high oat grass to call at the whitewashed cottage of Mistress Jinesse. Two fishermen who idled on shore leave grinned in lewd interest, for the widow's battened windows gave clear indication that she wished no truck with any visitor.

Arithon s'Ffalenn stood braced in the sun-washed sand of her yard, a crooked grin on his lips. Then he drew his rigging knife, pried the blade between the shutters, and slit the loop of cord that hooked the inside fastening pegs. As the loosened panels creaked wide, he laid a hand flat on the sill, saluted the watchers, and neatly vaulted through.

A dauntless shriek and a fishwife's imprecations drifted through the cracked boards. A mockingbird settled on the rooftree startled in a flash of barred wings. Then the bolt grated back and the widow's painted door crashed open, not to eject an impecunious male caller, but to liberate her towheaded twins, who bounded through, yelling their excitement, an overstuffed duffel slung between them. The panel flapped agape in the sea breeze. Something suspiciously like crockery crashed and broke against an inside wall. Moments later, Arithon emerged, the widow held in tow by her wrists.

'Really!' She tried to plant her feet, overbalanced, and stumbled into him.

Not about to waste the opportunity, Arithon grinned and snaked an arm around her waist. She pounded his shoulder with the fist just freed, and fingers pulled untimely from the mixing of bread dough shed small puffs of blown flour.

Jinesse shrieked, 'It's the woman who brews simples you should be dragging to your lair, not I, and certainly not my two children!'

'I do have nicer manners than to haul you unwilling to the shell flats,' Arithon admonished. His smile only widened, and she realized: they were bound due east for the beach. She turned her red face, and through disarranged hair, saw the little sloop perched like a gull on jewelled waters.

Her cheeks drained to ghastly white. 'Fiends and devils take your interfering spirit. I don't like boats. Let me be.'

'Quite the contrary,' Arithon demurred, his smooth voice jarred by her struggles, 'I've decided the first lady to board *Talliarthe* should be one afraid of the sea.'

Jinesse howled. 'You named your blighted vessel *Talliarthe*!' Her terror now spurred by indignation, she emphasized with a chop that glanced scatheless off the hard-knit muscles of his chest. 'How fitting!'

'Well, yes,' said Arithon, agreeably pleased; his sloop's namesake was the legendary sea sprite reputed to spirit off maidens who wandered inside the tidemark. 'Don't be angry. Your girl Feylind made the suggestion.' Staggered as a woman two fingers taller than his height thrashed and battered at his composure, he tucked his chin, changed grip, and hoisted.

Jinesse gave a pealing yell that all but deafened his right ear, then found herself tossed belly-down over his shoulder. A flock of feeding rails scattered and took wing like thrown birch chips. The twins ignored her cries and launched the dory, while Arithon made a gallant's apology and waded undaunted through the surf.

'You know I don't swim!' The widow's plea cut off on a racked jolt of breath as he ducked. The horizon spun through a sickening circle. Through the dishevelled locks ripped loose from lost pins, Jinesse saw herself deposited with the duffel on the stern seat. Panic overwhelmed her. She grabbed an oar and slashed to beat off her kidnapper, now waist-deep in green water with both hands clamped on the thwart to hold the dory against an onrushing comber.

Arithon dodged the whistling attack. The oar blade smacked short in necklaced foam. Gouged spray sheeted skyward and left him drenched and still laughing. 'Don't say,' he gasped, breathless, 'if you could swim, you'd jump ship. It's Ath's own blessing you don't.'

Jinesse spat out the taste of brine. She mopped a plastered swathe of hair from her neck, her glare fully spoiled by the trickling sting of saltwater. Then his firm push shot the dory ahead through the froth, and fright ripped a scream from her throat.

Arithon breasted the crest. Sleeked in wet clothes and lean as an otter, he vaulted the gunwale. Diamond streams of runoff spattered from his hair, no impediment as he twisted his purloined loom out of the widow's locked grasp. While shrieks that would credit a wild harpy shredded the mid-morning quiet, he proceeded with his abduction. Watching from shore, Merior's idle villagers absorbed every nuance and chuckled themselves into stitches.

'Well, it's fitting!' declared the boarding house landlady, drawn to her porch with her broom still in hand to oversee the outcome of the fracas. 'That Jinesse has been too straitlaced for health since the sea took her husband. Yon's a comely enough young man, for an outsider. His company just might lend a bloom to her cheeks. Mayhap then she'll stop fussing. To hear her carry on, you'd swear those poor twins were like to drown in Garth's pond!'

A kindly neighbour volunteered to douse the widow's fire and close up her vacated cottage. Over their laundry and their baking, Merior's gossips warmed to loquacious speculation. Lulled under mild southern sunlight, they remained unaware that larger threads of happenstance tied their favoured visitor to an imminent muster of armies.

The prophet whose gift of sight might have warned them held himself oblivious by acrimonious design.

Having twice stifled the onset of his talent for prescience, Dakar sprawled in a drunken stupor in the berth he had inhabited since the hour of the little sloop's launching. He moaned green-faced in his blankets, while the waters broke into chop and shoaled with the tide off Scimlade Tip, and the neat, painted dory bobbed to her destination. The vituperative outrage of the widow mingled with gull's calls and the delighted shouts of children. *Talliarthe*'s insolent, black-haired master boarded his passengers and cleated his tender to a towline. Then he slipped the pretty sloop's mooring and spread smart, tanbark sails to the wind.

Five days of fair-weather winds coaxed Jinesse from the grip of pale nerves. The sloop sailed through her shakedown like a pert, saucy lady, the slack as the breeze stretched new stays drawn in daily, and the promise of her design proven through in a smooth dance of passage. Jinesse emerged from clenched fear to final, exhausted recognition that her dread of blue waters gnawed her hollow and sick to no purpose. The twins thrived on clean sun and hours spent fishing from the stern rail. Arithon's company proved polite but evasive. His assiduous good manners at last reassured her that his plans matched his stated intent: to wean away her visceral distrust of the sea.

At dusk, with the black, notched forests of the southcoast a lacework border to a cobalt sky strung with stars, the little sloop's decks offered peace. While the moon spilled a path of molten light on dark waters, *Talliarthe* sailed lightly west. Soothed by the whisper of the wake against the crocheted caps on the wave crests, the widow perched on the cabintop with her knees tucked up in clasped arms. The strung tension she had suffered since her husband's loss had eased with the days. She could breathe the sea air, content, while the breeze off the sail combed her loose hair and spun the ends into tangles.

A lithe shadow against the frame of the cockpit, the Prince of Rathain stood in his loose linen shirt and plain jerkin, the tiller braced in hands that other nights, in quiet anchorage, had woven wizardly magic on his lyranthe. The twins slept below, entangled like kittens in a berth; Dakar lay wedged in the forepeak, his bilious temper stilled by the ale provisioned in casks at Shaddorn.

Enspelled by the moment's tranquillity, enervated by the unaccustomed freedom of having no household and no cares, Jinesse gave timid rein to curiosity. 'Why did you come to Merior?'

Arithon's face turned, his steep, angled features inscrutable against stars and sky. His answer came back unhurried, in the form of a chorus from a sailor's chantey. '"*Where sands lie like sugar, heave, me bully boys, ho! Where flowers bloom red, and the lily fair maids, boys, the maidens never say no."*'

When his light lines met with prying silence, he did not again shy from the subject. 'Why ask?'

'Somebody must.' A film of moisture cemented her palms to her shins. 'Nobody harmless has scars such as yours, and you made a free gift of your blazon.'

The sloop rocked over a swell, cupped a gust in taut gear, and thrummed into a complacent heel. Arithon braced a foot against the leeside locker and nursed his weight against the helm as water chuckled past the rudder. 'No secret there. Dakar will spill anything, drunk.'

Jinesse matched his evasion with flat truth. 'He hasn't, you know. He's wary of you as the man who burned his tongue once too often at the feast.'

Arithon flashed her a smile. 'Well he should be. Did you dare ask him why?'

Warned by a note like the slick draw of steel from its scabbard, Jinesse raised thin fingers to hook wind-ruffled hair from her lashes. 'The cobbler's wife tried. She said afterwards she'd take the simpler challenge and pry open an oyster barehanded.'

Arithon gave a musical, soft laugh. 'You know who I am. You'll have heard the dire rumours. Since you never exposed me, I prefer the belief that my conduct has lent foothold for trust.' A headsail whispered into a luff. He stretched, flicked a line off a cleat, and with the strength that was his most understated attribute, hardened a line with deft precision. The sloop quickened and sheared ahead to a clipped lisp of foam. Disturbed phosphorescence scattered like dropped sparks in the ploughed black waters of her wake.

Jinesse bit her lip, uncertain. If the prince who had knitted a torn thread in her destiny seemed content to leave matters there, she owned no such depths of self-assurance. 'If your purpose in bringing me is served,' she pressed, 'then why not put about and sail back?'

That annoyed him; the line of his shoulders stiffened under the rippling play of his shirt. 'It is night. There is quiet. Why pick at intangibles like a harridan?'

Hers, now, the power of reticence. Her children were belowdecks, all their safety given into his hands. If he was not a criminal, she wished him to explain why the talk of the traders should malign him.

An impatient moment later, Arithon answered, inflectionless and curt. 'I have not deceived. I have business to attend in Southshire, and a personal pledge to meet at Innish.'

A puff of wind dashed the sloop forward. The challenge Jinesse barely dared to utter fell eclipsed in the leap of white spray from the bow. 'Why not return me to Merior first?'

He heard anyway; over the work of the tiller, she met his blunt exasperation. 'Because I am not free, lady. Time is the hunting pack set at my heels, and the future, the thorn in my conscience. Your dread of seafaring is assuaged. Your children are able to develop their given gifts as they mature. At Southshire, you need not go ashore.'

'And at Innish?'

A queer catch of grief half-strangled itself in his throat. He said in forced lightness that had everything to do with shedding defences he had no wish to lower, 'Did you never think that I might need comfort or reassurance in return? What awaits me at Innish is a bereaved wife, and a grown daughter who never knew her father. Their loss is not beyond pity to encompass. But as a man raised in the absence of close family, I find myself disadvantaged. The ways of women's hearts are written in no chart. I go as a dead friend's emissary into a hostile home. Forgive my presumption, for asking the kindness of a stranger for my guide.'

Shamed, Jinesse averted her face. But the damage was done, his veneer of contentment peeled away. Her questions had distressed his faith in her trust beyond her small powers to mend.

'You wish a swift end to this passage, lady?' Arithon prodded.

With scarcely a pause, he bent, caught a line and lashed his tiller. Needled to sharp, restless energy, he leapt onto the foredeck to end a conversation she had no more heart to pursue. The topsail and flying jib were broken out and trimmed in merciless hard curves to slice the wind.

301

Talliarthe responded. The heel of her deck became animated, then violent, in concert with her master's mood. Arithon returned, soaking wet, to shoulder the pull of her tiller. He forced her painted bow three points nearer to the wind; and halyards and rigging thrummed to the plaintive keen of forced speed.

To remain above deck was to become showered with spindrift raked up like blown ice off the bow.

Stung by cruel salt and whipped by a dank lash of hair, Jinesse retired to her berth. A last glimpse through the hatchway before she fell asleep showed Arithon's profile notched in silhouette against a frost-point backdrop of white spray. Withdrawn and determined, he pitched his sloop before the brute winds as though the triumph of his handiwork against the elements could vindicate her rejection of his integrity.

Even had Jinesse been inclined to resume her appraisal of his conscience and character, Arithon s'Ffalenn gave her no chance. He drove his little sloop in a wreath of white wake to Southshire, made landfall in the dead of night, and rowed himself ashore before his passengers wakened at dawn.

Left no tender at an anchorage outside the moorings used by the traders' galleys, too distant to hail a shoreside lighterman, Dakar paced the decks and fumed. Like Jinesse, unless he wished to swim the broad mouth of the channel, he could do naught else but wait.

Arithon returned before nightfall in a dory laden with fresh provisions. The sacks of flour and the casks could not account for the telltale scent of tarred rope and sawdust, or the madcap glint in his eyes. If he refused to confide in the joy of his success, neither did he keep overt secrets. The papers he cached in the sloop's tiny chartlocker were contracts, ribboned with the seals of the shipwrights' guild. His commerce had been with craftsmen and ropemakers; a blind half-wit could deduce his intent to found a shipyard. What use he would make of that asset, Jinesse balked to contemplate. She shared, where she could, the blooming, self-sufficient contentment of her children and left Dakar to muddle his wits with beer.

As plainly as she might, she let the Prince of Rathain keep his peace with the secrets of his past. Her tolerance did little to win back his easy company; no ploy she tried stayed his drive to pitch himself and his sloop to the bleak, wilful limit of performance.

Talliarthe made landfall at Innish a fortnight past the winter solstice.

To her dying day, Jinesse would recall her first sight of the city; the spindled, coral towers meshed into sky, a gilt-edged silhouette that turned slowly rose against a fringe of dawn clouds. While Feylind and Fiark curled at her sides, she marvelled at the long, lean lighters that ferried the ships' crews ashore, black shapes like cut paper, with talisman scrolls or carved heads of beasts snarling at bow and stern. The cries of fish sellers drifted over lavender water, then the riffling stir of wind, with its mud-soaked scent of green river delta skeined with incense from the balcony braziers lit in brothels and rich ladies' boudoirs. Jinesse watched the light brighten the lace-roofed, pennoned towers; the scalloped merlons of the curtainwalls where Shand's old-blood royalty had walked; the pastel drumtowers with their odd, paned windows where the high king's council once held its yearly court; and in her ears rang sweet showers of harmonics as the living prince of quite another kingdom tuned a new set of strings on his lyranthe.

Innish was famed as the jewel of the Shand. As though spell-wrought, the moment held nothing mundane: no blackening smoke from a chimney fire, no wind-borne taint of rot from the tanneries. Even the catcalls the sailors flung at the whores who plied the dockside sounded lyric, slurred as they were in the broad-vowelled southcoast dialect.

Then Arithon damped his last, ringing chord and arose, a groomed stranger in a black doublet corded with silver. He wore hose and boots with embroidery and buckles, and a silk shirt with points tipped with pearls. Jinesse slipped her grip on the twins, kissed them both, and, unasked, remained in position at the sloop's rail.

'If you desire my presence, I'm ready,' she said.

That won his most fleeting smile. 'Dakar has been bludgeoned into sobriety. If he falls overboard, do you trust your twins to fish him out of the harbour?'

Arithon waited until her nerves softened, then lashed the fleeces to protect the lyranthe, slipped thin, grey gloves over his fingers, and handed her down into the bobbing dory. He climbed in himself and settled to his rowing with wordless, defined concentration.

Seen up close, the wharfside of Innish wore her decor like a tawdry, overdressed granddame fallen from wealth on hard times. The pilings were shagged green with weed, like harbour landings anywhere else. The air reeked of grease, decayed fish, and blood sausage, and the pretty pastel arches that reared above the crowd wore a pox of grey mildew and mould. The whores by city edict were required to wear bells. Their jingle chimed in sour descant over the oaths of the longshoremen bent under loads of boxes and bales. The gutters lay pooled with sewage dammed from egress down the culverts by thrown offal from the vendors, who cleaned hares for roasting over ramshackle portable braziers.

'I'm sorry,' Arithon said as Jinesse shrank from the stench. He peeled off a glove. 'Here, cover your nose. The streets will be cleaner past the waterfront.' He left the dory in the paid care of a street-child, took her arm, and drew her into turmoil like a carnival.

Brushed and buffeted, harried by stall keepers who pressed her to buy pins and ribbons and braided loaves of sesame bread, Jinesse longed for sleepy Merior, with its palm-shaded beaches and its huckstering squabbles between the gulls that flocked and dipped above the women who sat salting the fish barrels.

By the time they had crossed the dockside market and climbed the low, graded streets that led into the affluent upper town, Jinesse looked overset. Arithon sat her down beside the lip of a public spring, shaded by the stooped branches of a damson tree. A girl with a goose switch and three honking charges loaned her a jug for a drink. Inside a grilled mansion window, a caged bird trilled. A fat gander chuckled its bill in the water that ran, metallic with iron, over the jaws of a gryphon's-head fitting.

'The house isn't far,' Arithon said presently. While her head had been spinning, he must have asked for directions.

Jinesse gave back his glove and looked up as he helped her to rise. She found his face shuttered like quartz. 'You dread this.'

His step stayed deliberate on the cobbles. The polished buckles on his boot cuffs reflected trapped bits of sky as the leaf-filtered light flicked across them. 'No,' he said finally. 'But I do feel inadequate for the burden my master laid upon me.' His hand tightened, unthinking, on the cover of his lyranthe, and she realized he had reached his destination.

The painted little town cottage had once been a milking parlour, though the narrow, high windows were now graced with shutters, and the doubled door fastened with wrought brass. Nestled in a border of carob trees, walls of baked clay kept out the heat, and moss caked the barrel-tiled roof. Poised on the grained marble doorstep, Arithon gripped the knocker and tapped.

The door snapped open, as if the raw-boned woman inside had been watching the street through a spy hole. She wore straw-coloured hair swept back in combs, and despite a cherry-round nose and full lips, her expression was pinched and unfriendly.

'The sorcerer said we might expect you,' said Halliron's daughter in clipped greeting. Her gaze swept the bard and the woman in his company as if she hoped to find something to lend her the excuse to send them packing.

Only Jinesse knew the man well enough to discern the tension in his shoulders; his voice as he spoke was civil. 'My name is Arithon s'Ffalenn. As you have surmised, I was your father's last apprentice.'

'We were told. You've taken your time, have you not, to deliver his final bequest?' The woman jerked the door wide. 'By all means, come in and get this over with. I can't imagine the experience will mean very much, though my mother may feel differently. I could ask that you not make her cry. She hasn't been well, and further suffering will scarcely be a boon to her.'

Arithon entered the gloom of a pretty, tiled foyer. Potted flowers in enamelled crockery mantled the air in perfumes that failed to cut the underlying astringency of herbal pastes dispensed for sore joints. The woman gave a self-conscious sniff, fingered a crock as she passed in an unconscious check for dust, then led onward, over floors of fired tiles that made civilized replacement for rows of wooden stanchions for cattle. In a quiet parlour, she bade her visitors to wait.

'Let me see whether mother's awake.' She did not look back as she spoke, but bustled in prim hurry through a door sleek with old copal varnish.

Arithon glanced about, at the tasselled, stuffed hassocks, scattered foot-stools and cushioned chairs with their painstaking squares of embroidery; at walls tiered with shelves and glass cabinets jammed with alabaster ornaments, figurines twined out of jeweller's wire, and cloisonné flasks too small to be other than bric-a-brac. He turned once, full circle. Small as he was, the room begrudged even his neat grace. The seats set waiting at every quarter were a bastion, a wall, that had failed to repel boredom and solitude. Pressed on all sides by collected clutter, mute evidence of empty lives crying out to be filled, Arithon bent his head, hands folded on the cord that hung his lyranthe.

Jinesse bit her lip, half-suffocated. In this house, she recognized a trace of herself, and a fate but narrowly escaped; widowed, embittered, she had nearly done as this mother had, and hemmed in her children between tidy walls and old grief. *Talliarthe* had delivered her from far worse than fear, but she had no chance to share gratitude.

The closed door whisked open and Halliron's daughter beckoned the pair of them on.

Arithon stepped through into a bedroom alcove deep and musty with shadows. Jinesse entered on his heels, into air that smelled of age and sickness and lye soap. An armoire held a clutter of creams and jars, prinked with hard glints off cut glass. The bed, made up in ivory linen, cradled a narrow-eyed crone, propped board-straight amid a froth of lace-edged pillows.

'We know how he died,' the former Masterbard's goodwife opened in quavering, vitriolic rudeness. 'We heard he lived like a wastrel, travelling between towns in a cart.'

Arithon managed a smile with his bow. 'Dame Deartha,' he said in formal greeting. 'I am sent at Halliron's bequest. Have I leave?'

The hag jerked a clawed wrist. 'It was the music, he insisted. That's what took him from us.' Her mouth tucked into colourless pleats. 'I much doubt his blankets stayed empty, all those years.'

Discomfited by the beldame's evil glance, Jinesse looked in vain for a place to sit down. The bedchamber's single chair was already occupied by the daughter's angular bulk, which left only a footstool for Arithon. He took it, uncomplaining. His ringless hands wasted no motion as he unstrung the cord and slipped the lyranthe from her wrappings.

Jinesse found an unobtrusive corner by the clothes chest. The daughter tapped an impatient foot. The old lady jerked out a handkerchief and honked her nose while, nerveless in patience, the musician corrected the pitch of his strings.

'We have no use for songs, you know,' the daughter said in jaundiced scorn.

A last harmonic speared the gloom, cut in mid-flight as Arithon stopped off the string. His regard swept the invalid in the bed, measured the uptilted chin of the daughter. Their insults seemed to prick him like a challenge as he said, 'Ladies, let us see if you also have no use for pity.' His study lingered on them through a moment of trying quiet. Then he set fingers to fret and string and tore the locked stillness into melody.

One measure, two; the passion of his fingering arrested the air, and then remelted it into a cry. Notes winnowed free like leaves ripped on storm winds, blended into cascades that transfixed the heart with regret. The music wrung out under Arithon's hands begged no forgiveness for an abandonment of home and ties, but appealed for understanding through an offering of a beauty too wild, too forcefully inspired to be held or shackled in promises.

Arithon sat rapt, head bent to his playing. When he raised his voice in song, he did not see the elderly lady raise crabbed hands to her cheeks to brush off tears. Only Jinesse, herself half-paralysed by his spell, saw the mask of aggressive indifference crack from the face of the daughter. The woman hunched, still and dumb, while the denial and resentment known throughout life unravelled to bare the unanswered pain of a father-less child's yearning.

The unsubtle, searching scald of verses gave back husband and father, not as his family wished him to be, but as he had lived, delineated in imperfections and grand strengths. This was not the eulogy Arithon had delivered for Halliron in Jaelot, but in fierce words and harmony the bard's own statement, that given a mortal's years to live and to love, the mastery of his calling had demanded to be shared in lands far removed from his hearthstone.

By the time the last stanza was sung to its close, and the final chord rang thin and faded, the old lady sat dry-eyed. Her hands rested composed on the counterpane, while the young musician sent as emissary damped his lyranthe and looked up. Arithon waited, suspended in stillness, until she was ready for speech.

'My husband taught you.' Her desiccated voice had softened from cen-sure. 'Did he mention that he played that selfsame song on the very day he departed? But he did not style it your way.'

Steady under interrogation, Arithon laced his lean fingers over the lyranthe's silenced strings. 'The notes and the lyrics were Halliron's, as written. But by his straight bequest, the arrangement was to be my own.'

The daughter in her corner all but ceased to breathe. Too suddenly confronted by a Masterbard's empathy that owned power to bind her into change, the beldame looked away. 'My husband taught you,' she murmured. 'You, not his family, were his legacy.'

As though pressed to sorrow, Arithon said, 'I was his choice for the next link in a chain that extends back to Elshian's time. I chose to reveal what Halliron bequeathed me. In truth, that is all I can answer for.' His gaze on the crone's averted face did not waver, though the room had grown close, its tied muslin curtains sealing in the reek of strong remedies.

In an atmosphere thick enough to suffocate, Arithon gathered himself to finish. 'You should know. Your goodman was on his way south to be with you both for his retirement. An obligation of mine caused his delay. Blame me, not him, for the untimely manner of his death.'

'The Fellowship sorcerer who returned my husband's ashes claimed most emphatically otherwise.' The old lady raised a crippled hand from the tight-laced breast of her bedrobe. 'He said, prince, that you were not to be faulted. But my heart won't heal for a sorcerer's excuses. I ask a boon to discharge your debt. Since my husband died far from home, I would have you remain in this city through the rest of the season to play. It is fitting. Once Halliron earned mastery, he never returned. The people of Innish should be given their chance to share the fruits he has reaped through your talent.'

'Mother, that's hardly fair,' the daughter broke in, but Arithon waved her silent.

Suspended in silence, Jinesse watched the bard, and inwardly begged him to refuse. The tranquil retreat he had chosen at Merior held a purpose, perhaps key to his survival against the threat from the armies in the north. He was Teir's'Ffalenn, and royal, and answerable to no soul in Shand.

Never had the Master of Shadow revealed more of himself than at this moment, when he arose in compassion and bowed. In words unflawed by impatience, he answered the lonely, vengeful request of Halliron's abandoned widow.

'I will play the taverns of Innish, and gladly. But on condition that you and your daughter will agree to be present at every performance.'

The irony dogged Jinesse, over and over, as a return trip was made to the harbour to engage a reliable merchant galley to carry herself and her twins home to Merior: that had Arithon's playing been one whit less brilliant, the old crone would surely have refused him.

Visions and Voyages

A winter gale threads uneasy draughts through a taproom in Narms, while Captain Mayor Pesquil spills a moneybag over a tabletop and shouts down the balky argument of a merchant captain: 'You will rig your damned vessel for a northern passage. The message I bear is urgent and I won't stand idle for half measures. Better to risk delay iced into some benighted cove than be waylaid in the Thaldein passes by Maenalle's barbarians. I'll sail to north Camris and arrive in Avenor by springtide, whatever the price for your service . . .'

In a dockside bordello, abovestairs from the taproom where a Masterbard plies his lyranthe, the Mad Prophet stirs from replete stupor, wrung sick by the tingle of impending prophecy; while the doxy who shares his bed giggles through his fit, he cries words of warning concerning a discorporate spirit away on a desperate errand that stirs Sethvir at Althain Tower to alarm . . .

Sped by the last winter storms, the smuggler's brig *Black Drake* ploughs bold passage between the grey whitecaps of Minderl Straits, and beside her lady captain on the quarterdeck, Jieret, Earl of the North, chafes in restlessness, bearing news of grave import for a sovereign prince he has not seen for seven years . . .

XI. *DISCLOSURE*

The trader brig Captain Mayor Pesquil engaged from Narms by main force made safe port at Miralt Head with her cargo of crystal and iron ore, her fine southern wines and dyed fabric, and her rigging rimed with dirty ice. She would shelter through the season and refit gale-torn sails, then return on the milder airs of spring, laden with furs and seal oil, to rich profits at each destination.

For the headhunter captain and his hardened troop of scouts, the prospects ahead were less rosy. To cross the Plain of Karmak at midwinter meant a journey of commensurate discomfort. The island roads had few inns. What farmsteads and village hostels would cater to travellers kept their custom for seasonal caravans. In the cold months, their guest beds were stripped bare behind locked shutters, their mattress ticking haven for mice. Once the roads lay hardened under drifts and white ice, and the trade traffic waned, fare for travellers sold at a premium. Fuel and supplies could not be replenished before spring, and since storms off the gulf made each year's thaws chancy and difficult to predict, proprietors were sparse with provender.

The mobile, armed company en route from Etarra grew to hate the whine of the winds, and the slash of driven ice that clung in each fold of their cloaks. Helms lined with fleeces sang to the rattle of sleet. Nights were bitter and long, the ones spent unsheltered frosty with stars, while the howls of wolf packs rang through the frozen glens and made the horses drag, snorting, at their picket lines.

The first thing Captain Mayor Pesquil desired upon his arrival at the crossroads town of Erdane was the bath he had done without since the night of his landfall in Miralt. As an officer of the headhunters' league, he was entitled to take lodging at half-price; as an ally of Lysaer's, and an accredited affiliate of Etarra's armed garrison, the Mayor of Erdane extended due courtesy and offered him a minor guest suite in the palace.

The scouts were given cots in the barracks, and silver to seek their pleasures in the wall district.

Sunk in a brass tub of suds and hot water, his bristled face wreathed in white steam, Pesquil laced a sinewy, hard-knuckled hand over the knob of one knee; with the other, he sloughed off the flaked grey skin gnawed by frostbite between his splayed toes. His silt-coloured eyes were shut when the soft tap came at his door. Since he expected a servant with a razor, he raised a voice gruff as a cutler's rasp and granted permission to enter.

Instead of a liveried attendant, he received a rustle of damascened silk, a wafted assault of perfumed air, and a stifled explosion of giggles.

A train of ladies invaded his chamber, not the painted, brazen hussies he frequented after hard campaigns, but ones of impeccable pedigree. These had fine skin and tiny ankles threaded with pearls, and kidskin slippers. Their hair lay piled in pinned loops, or dangled down in pert ringlets, and jewels winked from the ribbons of their gossamer gowns like fruit rind baked in a solstice cake.

The two with dark hair and cheeks like new apricots were in fact the mayor's cosseted daughters. But seen alongside the tawny-haired one in the lead, the pair might as well have been servants. Collared in ermine and lace-worked gold, swathed below in pearled silk and gold tissue spangled with a sea-foam glitter of aquamarines, the third lady had a complexion translucent as alabaster and lashes like the nadir of night. Even without the magnificent cut of her clothes, her presence seemed designed by Ath Creator to arrest a man's breath in his throat.

Flushed to the dewlap folds of his neck, Pesquil jammed his shanks straight. The wet-leather scrape of his buttocks made the brass tub give tongue like a horn, and soap suds and water slopped over the rim, to ring him, glistening, his naked flesh cupped like an embryo amid a flood of smashed egg.

Proprietary as a hunting tigress, his visitor's glance raked over the stringy, scarred muscles of his torso. Her coral-pale lips bent before an amusement whose withering sting left no impact, sheer force of beauty having long since anaesthetized reason. Galled on by reflex, Pesquil plunged his hands beneath the scummed water.

An ugly man possessed of an iron dedication, the headhunter captain held his ground as a wolf might, nipped at by mastiffs.

'Captain Mayor Pesquil,' addressed Lady Talith, the affianced bride of Prince Lysaer s'Ilessid. 'I much doubt you would travel the breadth of the continent just to sample Erdane's hospitality. Since barbarian scalps are not in season until spring, I trust you carry news of the Shadow Master?'

Outside the window, grey clouds sheeted the sky. A sentry called, and a polearm clanged to signal the change of the watch. Beyond the open and violated inside doorway, a woman's voice raised down the corridor, scolding a child for wet feet.

Talith skirted the rim of the puddle, selected a bulky brocade chair, and slid it squarely in front of the wardrobe that contained the captain's fresh clothes. There she settled herself, while the elder of the mayor's tittering daughters produced a chatelaine's keyring, spun about and locked the door. Her younger sister moved to the hearth, peered askance with a girlish blush, and snatched up the towels left out to warm.

'I did not ask for bath attendants,' Pesquil said with a grate like the rough scrape of chain mail.

Talith laced slender fingers in her lap, her eyes direct and her smile, honey spread over poison. 'You shall have two, if they can break the latch and escape from the linen closet where we impounded them. I suppose some drudge will eventually hear their noise and set them free. The gossip should be lively, once the mayor's house steward finds we're all here, quite cosy with his lowborn guest. Is your silence worth the displeasure of your host?'

A sinew jumped in Pesquil's lantern jaw. He had few illusions; his most guarded point of pride was his station, won through achievement and competence rather than the accident of pedigree. Lady Talith was Etarran, no stranger to sordid jokes played for intrigue. The Mayor of Erdane's flighty daughters were scarcely in her league, though their nervous, darting glances showed them thoroughly intrigued with an escapade.

Although Pesquil scorned the confined standards of morality the westland cities imposed on their women, the mayor's hospitality implied a trust he misliked the principle of spurning. Uncomfortably aware of the youngest girl's fascination with the cock's comb whorls of hair that seamed the midline of his chest, forced on display before Talith's dizzying charms, the headhunter willed his hard limbs to relax. A rebellious ache beneath the waterline, another bodily part of him cheerfully rejected self-control.

He was male, after all, and not bloodless.

An absurd pull of laughter twitched Pesquil's mouth. If he shot up, streaming sour water to stride naked across the tiles and eject his unsuitable company, Talith would fairly scream with laughter. The daughters' too-avid curiosity was unlikely to cause them to faint.

The situation should have been uproarious, had he not been so roundly outflanked.

He cleared his throat, reached up and tugged off his last stitch, a greasy lace of leather, then shook hair like iron filings from its battle braid. 'You want something from me. The least you can do is pass the soap.'

Talith found the small cake in a tray the upset water had skidded near her feet. She bent in a rustle of scent and fine cloth, and obliged his whim with a vengeance.

The soap cake hurtled across the room.

'Temper!' Pesquil had reflexes like a striking snake; the suds scarcely rippled around his loins as he stretched and fielded the catch. 'I gather you don't like Erdane?'

'Is your bath too hot?' Talith's lashes dropped and halfway veiled her sultry glance. 'If the attentions of the servants are inadequate, you should be in prime position to judge.'

Too aware of his high flush, and while sweat nicked over his pock-scarred brow, Pesquil lathered his chest. Highborn chatter and double entendre never excited him to empty games of wit. Silence was more efficient, by his creed, and despite the leap and race of his pulse, he was cold-nerved enough to hold his tongue.

The ladies could blasted well wait until he had washed himself down to the last puckered scar. They would discover soon enough he was just a coarse soldier, prepared to call their bluff. Were he thrown out of Erdane, the mayor's lasses would be punished for their silliness. The vital news he bore would reach Lysaer that much sooner.

If the pretty dark daughters standing guard upon the doorway showed unease at his balky character, Talith's fresh poise only heightened under challenge. 'I am no ornament to be left waiting on a shelf.' She stood, jerked open a drawer, and plucked out the clean holland shirt scarcely wrinkled from its storage in a saddle pack. 'You have news of Arithon s'Ffalenn. That will mean war. I don't intend to sit here while you rouse my betrothed to muster his armies and quarter the continent to fight him.' A back-step carried her to the casement. She flicked the catch, pressed open the leaded panes, and tossed the shirt upward onto the snow-covered slates of the dormer peak.

Thin through cold air, a whistle spiralled up from the sentry who stood duty on the wall walk.

'You bloodsucking minx!' Pesquil snapped soapy fingers to the sides of the tub, while the water sucked and splashed, and the draught raked his leathered skin to gooseflesh.

Talith smiled. She would toss out his clothes, and be damned to his dignity. His scars would be the talk of every barracks in Erdane, as well as the boudoirs of the ladies.

There were limits. 'I don't know where the Master of Shadow is laired up. But he's disrupted the peace and caused havoc in one city, and killed seven men in another through an explosion of fire and sorcery. His movement has been traced southward, along the eastern coastline.' Pesquil's lips quirked like wire in his bristle of black beard. Eyes as flat as marsh mud glared upward at Talith, who weighed options as she might select a ballgown, a pair of hose and breeches in each hand.

'Lady,' Pesquil snapped, 'that's hardly enough to set armies marching, and it happens to be the sum of my news.'

'You come personally as courier,' Talith contradicted. The hose fluttered in the swirl of the wind, then snapped up to join the shirt in its icy eyrie. The girls smothered giggles; Talith inspected the trousers for inspiration, hooked the breech points in playful fingers, and began to unlace them, strand for strand. No pity in her, Pesquil judged, that she would neglect the least detail and fail to fling the towels, and even the benighted sheets off the bed.

'Why?' Talith pressured.

'Because your fussy pack of Etarran dignitaries was too soft for a winter passage.' Fuming through risen veils of steam, Pesquil gave a barked, ruthless laugh. 'By myself, I'll make sure the message gets through without barbarian interference. Prince Lysaer will receive this news before spring. I leave on the morrow, and if the Great West Road through Tornir Peaks is closed due to storms, I'll fare on by way of Teal's Gap.'

'That's a fool's errand!' broke in the mayor's older daughter, her hands clenched white on the door key. She darted a worried glance at Talith. 'Lady, the pass this madman proposes to cross lies in the Sorcerers' Preserve.'

Every child in the westlands knew tales of that place, where fire-breathing creatures once the scourge of past ages flew on pinioned wings sixty spans long. Whenever the wards at its boundaries weakened or failed, caravan drovers brought back nightmare accounts of draught stock slaughtered wholesale, or charred in their traces to bones and papered carbon.

'If the Khadrim don't flame you to a cinder, or tear you limb from limb with their jaws, there are hot springs, and mud pots, and lava wells, and no guide to choose a safe trail.' The girl cautioned, 'Better to stay neglected here in Erdane than to find yourself boiled alive.'

'Wise advice,' Pesquil said, eyes slitted. 'If you think my headhunters will serve as your escort to Avenor, Lady Talith, I'll skid my bare arse over every roof tree in this city just to prove you wrong.'

'You will take me,' Talith said. The breeches hooked on her fingertips fluttered out the window, snagged on a flagstaff above the rampart, and streamed, displaying frayed seams to the wind. Etarran to her devious core, she spared not a glance for her nervous accomplices.

Pesquil confronted her tawny magnificence, the water that embraced his hips chill enough to dampen the dregs of any man's ardour, and the soap squeezed to pulp in his fists. 'I won't.'

Talith held his gaze, locked eye to eye. But her lip trembled ever so slightly.

Like a kick in the belly, Pesquil recognized that the motive which drove her was love. He would not shake that, not if he killed her.

That moment a knock sounded at the locked door.

'The serving lad, arrived to mow off your stubble,' Talith said on a wicked note of triumph. 'We shall both be denounced and thrown out of Etarra, since I'm the indisputable bad influence.'

A truth, Pesquil allowed, as her fluttery accomplices froze short of the last, outrageous act.

Lysaer's future wife left the gutted armoire and pried the key out of the one girl's pinched grasp. She turned the lock, flung the door wide, and watched like a cat with a mouse in its paws as the page on the far side gasped and stumbled back in surprise.

'Do you see, I left the bedclothes untouched,' she said, and pealed into a last, merry laugh.

'Lady Talith!' her male victim ground out on a note of teeth-gnashing fury. 'I'll wear you a set of saddle blisters such as you'll pray for death to escape!'

Then, as the page dropped his basin and razor and fled, and the daughters embraced their conspirator in girlish bravado and wished her safe journey and good health, Pesquil shied the pulped soap out the window in the wake of his purloined apparel. Girt in the tepid discomfort of his bath, he concluded that any prince mad enough to marry a pedigree Etarran lady deserved to suffer merry hell and intrigue on the home front. Just as well the Master of Shadow would afford a sound reason for a husband to stay absent in the cause of bloody war.

Lysaer would need the violence just to stay sane with that brazen-mouthed vixen in his bed and ever busy, stitching steel claws through his vitals.

The first sound heard by visitors to the prince's new city of Avenor was the sweet, high ring of the armourer's mallets shivering the air between the stripped branches of the oak groves. Worn by a long and arduous journey, weary of the suck and splash of her mount's hooves through the rime of late-season snow, Lady Talith pushed back her fur-lined hood, the better to take in the view as Pesquil's cavalcade of headhunters crested the last rise and passed the gap in the hills.

Ahead, the clear, cold line of the sea slashed a sky like dirty ice. Flocks of gulls settled like caught twists of paper against the dunes, crusted with salt-eaten drifts. The city's unfinished walls commanded a high knoll, smirched with smoke from the brickmaker's kilns, and alive as an ants' nest with activity.

Windburned to a high flush, her silken hair silted in the collar of her cloak, Talith sorted through the jumbled supply sheds, the cruck built officer's hall, then squinted against sunlight torn through a broken cloud layer to pick out the ravelled outline of keeps and revetments and gate turrets. Inside the honeycomb shapes of partial structures, a single tower arose, near complete, the spoked beams of its roof line as yet bare of slate. The distant snaps of the ox drovers' whips, the limpid stream of banners, and the squeals of a hog bound for slaughter strained through the white rush of surf and the trumpet calls of an officer.

Even through inclement weather, the practice field lay in use. Directed by a mounted officer, a field kitchen spread half-dismantled in churned mud. A tent billowed flat to shouts and a timed release of guy ropes, while mule teams jostled supply wagons into position for loading. Marksmen fired crossbows at the butts; grooms with buckets swarmed up and down the horse lines to tend steaming charges led in hot from heavy exercise, while the men just dismounted shed empty quivers and short, compound bows, to take up pikes and renew their drill in the disciplined formation of foot companies.

When Lysaer's army marched against the Shadow Master, every soldier in the ranks would be hard trained and multiply skilled in the arts of warfare.

'I warned you, Lady.' Pesquil reined his horse into step beside hers, engrossed in professional survey. 'This place is more barracks than city. Your comforts are left back in Erdane.'

Talith said nothing, nor moved. But her horse tossed its head to a shivering jingle of belled bridle reins before she stabbed in her heels and sent it downhill at a canter.

'She must have hide like a crocodile,' the headhunter lieutenant complained. 'It's unnatural she should feel so fresh after six ugly weeks in the saddle.'

The journey from Erdane had been trying beyond endurance, even without the unwanted presence of the lady. Harried by blizzards, all but frozen to starvation in the Tornir passes, delayed a fortnight in wait for safe crossing over the ripping torrents of the Melor River ford, the headhunter party was fortunate to have reached Avenor before the first thaws.

'Well,' said Pesquil in dry humour, 'if her nibs strains her mount's tendons by miring its legs in a ditch, the problem at least will be Lysaer's.'

'Well give her credit, she's anxious for her prince,' the lieutenant grumbled. 'At least she didn't whine about the hardship.' He reined his horse carefully over patched ice and into the rutted mud where lately the mounted archers had fired volleys into straw sacking. Servants moved, drab against the mire, recovering those few shafts that strayed and scoring their markings on a tally.

Pesquil turned his head to eye the bristled targets, then raised eyebrows spiked like frizzed wire through the fur that lined his conical helm. He faced forward, shrugged off a rare thrill of admiration, and recovered the lapsed thread of his thought. 'You didn't look at her eyes, man. That minx isn't eager. She's vexed. I'll lay you three royals against your chased silver spurs: the pair'll meet and have a row like a thunderclap.'

Minutes later, unmindful of the sensation she had created in her ride across the tilt yard, the lady pried herself out of the suffocating hug her brother had clapped over her on sight. 'Talith, Talith!' His welcome came tempered with consternation. 'What in Sithaer are you doing here?'

Lightly mussed, her furs left ruffled to bent hair and the taint of lathered war horse, she tipped up her chin to view the brother parted from her for a year.

Diegan had grown harder, leaner. His elegant jewels were replaced by thick mail and leather that showed the rubbed shine of hard wear. The dark, handsome features were knit taut to the bone, rugged now with new angles where the flesh of languid living had burned away.

'By the look of you, I shall have to learn tactics if I'm to share in the dinner conversation,' Talith said. 'You seem a proper commander of armies. Though you have busy fellows doing more than one job like cuckoos packed into a hawk's nest, I didn't count many troops. Did you set all your soldiers to laying bricks?'

'Yes, in fact.' Diegan swept his fair sister into the buffeting activity that clogged the invisible division between the armed camp, and the domain of the masons and labourers. Over the creak of a dray laden down with hewn beams, the Lord Commander qualified. 'His Grace insisted the experience would teach our soldiers some fine points that might help with future sieges. You should have seen the mercenaries' expressions when they heard they'd serve a turn at taking orders from the master mason.'

'And did they?' asked Talith in sidelong malice.

Diegan laughed, strangely bitter. 'Under Lysaer? He has a gift.' He dodged a loose goat, a handcart crusted with dried mortar, and ducked the invitation of a blowsy woman festooned in scarlet ribbons. 'For our prince, they would do a groom's chores and whistle. I could use your tongue, sister, to scale the rust from my mail.' While a pack of recruits stopped, staring and silly, directly in the midst of the causeway, he cupped her elbow in his gauntleted hand and gave a firm steer toward the largest of the camp's timbered buildings. 'Don't mind the tenderfeet. Our most seasoned field troops are on campaign.'

At Talith's stark glance of surprise, Diegan warmed further to his subject. 'Our southshore trade routes don't close in winter, and the Caithwood road is rife with marauding barbarians. We hire out our finished companies as caravan guards. They gain hardening, our treasury takes a share of the merchants' profits when the goods are sold on destination, and the guilds pay the troops' daily upkeep.'

'How perfectly sensible and dull.' Talith raised the mud-splashed hem of her habit and mounted the gritty, planked steps to the hall. 'And naturally, Prince Lysaer fights beside them?'

'In fact, no. I thought I was taking you to him.' Suave before her blighted scorn, Diegan hurled back in piquant challenge, 'Perhaps I should pack you straight back to Erdane without a meeting.'

Talith bristled against his hand.

'Why are you here, sister?' Direct in a manner she had never seen before, Diegan searched her face as he might measure an enemy. 'Have you come to cast off his Grace?'

Behind her smile, Talith was furious. 'You'll have to wait and see.' In Etarra, the gallants would have eaten her alive, were her thoughts to appear so transparent.

For a second, Diegan poised, mailed fingers spread flat on the unvarnished door panel. Then he bashed the portal open, drew her inside, and the slanting light cut off at his back flashed obliquely over his teeth. Caught somewhere between oaths and laughter, he said, 'Lady sister, leave him if you can.'

Thrown into uncertainty by a reaction too difficult to interpret, Talith resisted her brother's pressure on her back as he traversed the unlighted hallway. 'Diegan, wait. We should talk first.'

Obstinate, he quickened stride. 'If you are here to break off your handfasting, by all means, do so. I shall not stand in your path.'

The smells of wax and wet horse rode the shadows; the wool runner was swept, if continually damp from the traffic of men who shed snow off of muddy boots. The boards underneath had been pegged while still green; seasoned now by the warmth of the hearth peats, they squeaked even to Talith's light tread.

Conscious of a closed door ahead, and of a heart that beat much too fast, Talith sidestepped, but could not evade her brother's grip. Puzzled by the odd, tormented tension that hardened him, she pushed back in diamond-cool clarity. 'Diegan, the man who led my escort is Etarra's best headhunter, your old friend Captain Mayor Pesquil.'

That halted him. With a freezing jingle of disturbed mail, Diegan shot out a fist and gripped his sister's shoulder. Hair the glossy black of new ribbon ruffled in the nap of his gambeson as he pulled her a stiff step closer and searched her face in the dimness. 'Pesquil? Here? I saw no banner. Ath Creator, what has happened?'

Unspoken between them in a corridor too narrow for comfort hung the name of the Master of Shadow.

In calculated, smiling obstruction, Talith knew just how to twist. 'Why not go ask the Lord Mayor and find out?'

Once, her brother would have shot back some barb to blunt the fresh thrill of her victory. Now, determination rode like a stranger on features she had known all her life. The Lord Commander who managed Lysaer's armies simply left her, the swept hilt of his sword dragged in a screaming scrape across the board wall as he jostled past.

A breath of sudden cold, and the door banged. Ceded her privacy in the pent, dreary gloom of the corridor, Talith chewed her lip in hesitation. She had come here to break off her promise to Lysaer s'Ilessid. Love by itself was not enough to ease the ache of his prolonged absence; her brother's queer challenge was not rational. She was Etarran, and beautiful, and knew her own mind; she never failed to get what she wanted.

From within the closed chamber ahead, she heard the rise and fall of someone speaking. Too proud to eavesdrop like a servant, she shook out the habit her brother had left wrinkled, stepped forward, and raised the crude door latch.

The hinges gave without a sound.

She stepped into a late spill of sun, flared through diamond-paned windows. Lozenged in thin, patterned light, a carpet woven in the exquisite taste of Narms' master guildsmen brightened the rough plank floor. The walls were panelled, and muted further in tapestries. A pearl-inlaid secretaire sat at right angles to a desk, and two cushioned benches carved in ebony. The rich, leather smell of books and parchment and a lingering trace of heated wax combined to frame an air of power and wealth. A page's velvet cap lay on a footstool by the hearth. Hedged between a pair of massive candle stands and a table half-buried under charts, the crown of a golden fair head bent close to that of an earnest little boy.

'We don't yet have a scribe, that's not civilized, I know,' said Lysaer s'Ilessid to the child. 'But that doesn't matter. A page should know how to fold and seal a document for the day he grows up to be a lord.'

The boy said something in dulcet, shy tones.

'The job is only boring before you learn how it's done.' A sculptured hand reached up, snagged a ribbon in Tysan's royal colours from a cache between quills and inkwell, and resumed patient instruction. 'Here, and here,' Lysaer said, a smile on his lips to tear the heart. 'Now the knot. Use two hands this time, and try not to smear the royal star.'

A striker changed hands, then the heavy brass seal with the star and crown sigil of Tysan. Undone by the page's worshipful concentration as he backed up with his burden to try afresh, Talith held her fingertips pressed to her lips as Lysaer s'Ilessid straightened up.

The light fringed his hair to a leafed blaze of gold. Unsoftened by the coarser glow of candles, his austere face showed an unearthly beauty no memory could preserve with due justice. The impact of cobalt-blue eyes stunned like a physical shock. The frozen moment, while Prince Lysaer sized up her waiting presence, spun the last shred of breath from Talith's throat.

His Grace of Tysan was not in rough attire, as she had expected, but ablaze with gold studs and a chain worked in pearls and small sapphires. His cuffs and collar were damascened silk, and his tabard, of trimmed velvet, looked cut from the shadow of a snowdrift. Every inch of him lordly, he poised for the space of a heartbeat.

Then a sudden, blinding smile enlivened his face with affection. 'Lady Talith!' In one fluid movement he vaulted the table. His rush set the candle flames streaming. Sooner than she wished, he reached out and touched, and enveloped her in welcoming arms.

The firm, muscled strength underneath his soft clothes lifted her, spun her, set her down. Talith was consumed, then ignited by his flame of vital heat. She sensed the sped pace of his heart as his knuckles sank in her damp ermine, and his lips seared a kiss on her forehead. 'You are just the person I wished to see, beloved. My writ was to reach you in the hands of the next messenger. Yesterday, our wedding date was set.'

Her anger in trembling ruins, Talith recovered her breath with a gasp. 'What?'

'We shall marry when the orchards are in blossom.' Lysaer consumed her with his gaze, then took swift advantage of her open-mouthed, speechless surprise.

'*Leave him if you can,*' her brother had mocked.

Wrapped in the prince's embrace, sealed to his lips in a branding flush of passion, that challenge rang sadly diminished. As though drugged, or enspelled, Talith felt her resolve sublimate like wax set in flame.

The kiss ended and left her bereft.

'By Ath, you crossed the passes. No wonder you're peaked. The journey had to be terrible.' Still talking, Lysaer set her down on one of the cushioned benches. With the same seamless charm, his page was dispatched to fetch mulled wine and scones from the bakehouse. Then, while she was still heady with his presence, Lysaer, Prince of Tysan, raised both her hands and savoured them, captive in his grip.

Only now did she notice the calluses inscribed by sword and lance and bridle rein, the telltale smudges of fatigue in the hollows of his face. The stamp of cold purpose lay on his good looks like the blued gleam of steel from the forge.

And like the first ice to trammel clear waters, reason caught up and flawed his joy. 'My dear, you are magnificent. No doubt my best officers are all stumbling into walls at the sight of you, but what possessed you to leave Erdane at this season?'

Talith had no more will to frame answer; then, as Pesquil's nasal tones intruded from the outside corridor, she lost all need to use words.

Lysaer stepped away. His jewels spat indigo sparks in the gloom, and candles winnowed by spurts of disturbed air threw wavering, ominous shadows. His pleasure erased before a turbulent frown, the prince flung wide the door to his private study.

Left, but not forgotten on her bench, decimated beyond reprieve by Lysaer's magnetic charm, Lady Talith sat in dumb misery while her brother and the Captain Mayor of Etarra's league of headhunters made free and entered, and dispatched the news that the Master of Shadow had sown havoc through two cities in the east.

Throughout, Lysaer listened, not rigid with outrage, but distilled instead to a leashed back, frightening fury. The glow from the casement etched his rapt profile and splintered through the gold ribbon on his sleeves.

'I have no verified facts from either government,' Pesquil hastened to add. 'But the rumours are spread through more than one source. Jaelot and Alestron are unlikely places for spurious tales of fancy to arise.'

A glint of sharp distress charged the depths of Lysaer's eyes as he reeled off a string of fast conclusions. 'They are port towns. It is s'Ffalenn design, and wantonly inflicted on innocents.' Passion frayed through as he added, 'The instant the weather lets the trade galleys sail, we'll send for documented evidence. At last I'll gain the leverage I need to turn Tysan's guildsmen. The threat this man presents is dire, but until now, only cities in Rathain saw the proof.'

Pesquil tapped the worn steel in his scabbard, his sidelong glance whittled shrewd. 'Erdane's offered you three hundred reserves already, upon presentation of hard evidence.'

Lysaer dealt the headhunter captain a spirited slap on the shoulder. 'Well done!' He surged behind his desk, seized pen and paper, and scribbled a rushed line of notes. 'We have much to accomplish in a matter of days. As you must be aware, you've earned a reward. I had a thousand royals posted for the man who brought the first word of the Shadow Master.'

'Use the gold to pay soldiers,' Pesquil said in a sudden red flush of embarrassment. 'Your army, they're prepared?'

Lord Commander Diegan broke in, 'The men are more than ready. On command, they would march against Dharkaron himself.'

'Weather won't delay us overlong,' Lysaer added. 'A third of our forces already lie south in Caithwood, on hired campaign against barbarians. Word can be sped by fast courier. Those divisions can be marched east directly.' Rapidly, he outlined his intent to gather Avenor's high officials and every ranking officer from the barracks. Then he spun and met the irate glare of Talith, who believed herself set aside and forgotten.

'You may wish the chance to freshen up from your journey,' the prince suggested.

Entrapped like a netted songbird, swept over by the eerie, concentrated focus still engaged by the impact of Pesquil's news, Talith endured as Lysaer's regard encompassed her closed features and after, every soiled nuance of her dress. He grasped her loose hands, found them cold, and his urgency gentled to concern. 'You'll want a lady's maid, of course. Wait in the anteroom. My page will deliver you refreshment there and my equerry will build up the fire. At least you'll be warm until I can arrange for a suitable attendant.'

Talith snapped back from his touch in offended fury. 'No thank you, my Lord Prince. If you're going to draw up plans to slay your nemesis, I shall stay exactly where I am.'

'But of course.' Lysaer stroked a fallen curl from her cheekbone, his tenderness too sincere to be patronizing. 'I expect you back once you've changed. This is no mayor's realm, to keep women at home uninformed.' He smiled, sternly royal, and admonished, 'You shall be Avenor's princess on the equinox feast. Could you doubt for a minute? The responsibility to defend Athera's cities must be shared. Your place through this war council is nowhere if not by my side.'

Outflanked and speechless, Talith inclined her head. She gathered mud-splashed skirts and swept headlong from the study.

Just past the door, she lost composure. Weakened and shaking, she braced against the saw-cut boards of the corridor while Pesquil's rapid consonants rang through the panel at her back. 'Provisioning's your worst obstacle. How many veterans can you send at first thaw to earn their passage as caravan guards?'

The Captain Mayor's point was too obvious: if Lysaer chose Etarra as the site to muster troops, the long march must be sustained across Tysan, through cities not yet won to his cause. To support an armed force across the continent before the harvest would require extensive planning and diplomacy. Any shortfalls created by logistics and supply must not disrupt the chance for alliance in the future.

'Much care is needed,' Lysaer agreed. 'At least until we reach Rathain.'

Most of the army had no choice but to hold back until the grass greened enough to graze for fodder. The roads would have dried, and ox carts would not mire in mud left softened by the thaws.

'Diegan claims your men are ready,' Pesquil interjected. 'I would ask, are they good?'

Lysaer answered in guarded excitement. 'We have four thousand, enlisted. An hour remains before sundown. Let us go and observe them, and see if their achievements can impress you.'

As Talith overheard, her bitterness deepened, that once again her love must make way before the great quest to stalk down the Shadow Master. Her autonomy could not be sustained against Lysaer, and her anger fell powerless before yearning. She moved off, beaten humble by misery, to seek refuge in the quiet of the anteroom.

Pesquil's last question pursued her. 'You can move armies from here to Sithaer and back, Prince. There's little to stop you. Except how will you know, once your muster is accomplished, where to corner the Master of Shadow?'

'Trust my foresight,' Lysaer replied in iron-clad surety. 'When the time comes to march, I possess a sure means to find out.'

Rendezvous

Like a vulture cramped in a roost sized for finches, the brig *Black Drake* dominated the tiny, cove harbour of Merior. Crowded by the swing of her cable, the moored dories of each absent fishing lugger wallowed in her hulking shadow. Jieret Red-beard lounged at her rail, peeling across his hawk nose from the burn of the strong southland sun, the quilloned knife just used to pare his nails still unsheathed in his hand. Relaxed though he seemed, the sailhands who had shared winter passage from the Gulf of Stormwell maintained their distance. The lad had cold eyes and no patience for the fool who dared cross him while he simmered with impatience.

A raucous flock of gulls arrowed up, disturbed by the sight Jieret waited for: rapacious under timed oarsmen, *Drake's* tender sheared through a wind-caught slash of spray to pull under the brig's leeward side.

The only black head on board was Captain Dhirken's.

'He isn't here,' Jieret said, nettled. The thunk as his weapon struck upright in the rail rang across a closing gap of water.

'Not,' Dhirken cracked, her jet braid dangled down her back as she aimed a poisonous glower upward. 'And damn you for scarring my bright-work in pique for your prince's bad promise. There's ale enough in my hold to nurse yer male temper till ye're witless, flat out, or paralysed.' Poised in the bow to snatch the line tossed down by a deckhand, she made the boat fast to a cleat. To the jinking swing of her cutlass, she scaled the side battens in scorching irritation.

Regaled in a man's velvet knee breeches, red shirt, and a flamboyant vest with pearl buttons, the event of her presence had raised a storm of wild gossip in the sleepy fishers' village where Arithon s'Ffalenn had signally failed to keep his rendezvous.

The settlement was pitilessly remote, its quiet less idyllic than a calm that threatened stagnation, with its rows of shuttered cottages and a near-deserted market stacked with fish barrels, rancid and reeking in the turgid noon heat. Impatient with the soporific rustle of palm fronds, and the chink of clay charms to keep iyats from unravelling tired fish nets, Jieret wondered why his liege had chosen the site in the first place.

The longboat rocked as the rowers shipped oars. Arrived at the rail, their captain talked still with inspired venom. 'May the whore's pox plague your vaunted prince. If he's light with his word as all that, I'm sore tempted to act in kind. Myself and my mates, we could live like fat mayors on his contraband.'

Jieret freed his blade and stepped back as Dhirken vaulted aboard. 'You know where to look for Prince Arithon?'

Dhirken's lips split into a nasty grin. 'Aye. He's at Innish. So said a wee, pale snip of a woman. It's to do with a promise he chose to honour.'

'You'll sail there?' Jieret pressed.

Poised on braced legs, her back stiff as nail stock, Dhirken shrugged. 'If I don't, you'll walk, is that so? With all his blighted treasure on your back? You've got lint between your ears to think he's worth it.'

A pause ensued, while the busy wind flicked through the laces on Jieret's jerkin and ruffled his raw-spun copper beard. The tropical sky scored glints in hazel eyes that seemed to view a sight very different.

When Dhirken snapped her rings against her cutlass hilt to recoup his attention, the Earl of the North stated baldly, 'If not for my liege, I wouldn't stand here alive.'

'Well at least sheath that dirk before you stick somewhat else with it.' Brazen in distaste for loyal sentiment, Dhirken spun away to chastise the longboat's oarsmen, now crowding the rail at her shoulder. 'Do I pay you my silver to gawk? Smarten up and haul in that tender!'

'We're sailing for Innish.' Jieret grinned unrepentant over his knife blade. 'And don't say for the sake of sparing my dastardly back.'

'The whore's pox on you, also!' Dhirken's sidelong glance in malice scored somewhere in the middle of the earl's chest. 'Your royal friend left no charts for the southcoast. If you don't want to dance on the equinox as shreds for some crab on a reef, you'd better pray there's a merchant's galley laid in at Shaddorn willing to sell her spare rutter.'

Baleful enough to scald air, the lady captain turned her raunchy invective to send her hands flying to make sail.

Burdened under full canvas, *Black Drake* ran hull-down, driven by the hard, pranking winds that partnered the shift in the season. The coast slipped past, green and gilt, the land breeze a pomade of citrus blossom spiked through with the resin of slash pine.

At Shaddorn, a fickle squall and a running, high swell had the traders' galleys battened down in sheltered waters like boiled crabs salted in a barrel.

'Damned merchant captains!' Incensed and soaked from a rain shower,

Dhirken peeled off her oilskins in the musty gloom below decks. 'Stupid down to their toenails. My *Drake* tries on an honest charter forbye, and look at them! All huddled together like sheep gone spooked by a wyvern.'

She stalled her tirade long enough to accept a mug of soup from the cook. 'No charts for sale, they say.' Broth sloshed the rim as she gestured in sulky frustration. 'It's all spite. Just because I tail-whipped their tubs in the Eltair ports and undercut their prices, they'll nurse useless grudges and obstruct us every way they can.'

Days were lost as sails were reefed to slow their passage. *Drake* nosed her way forward, a leadsman in her chains to call the mark, and a lookout posted aloft to spy out reefs lest shoaling waters set her aground. Forced to find anchorage each night by dark, Dhirken stalked her brig's quarter-deck like a panther, while Jieret cursed the tropical airs that mouldered his leathers and patched rust on his daggers and sword. He refused to think of his clansmen. By now, the news out of Jaelot had reached Etarra; in the lapsed months since he left to track Arithon, a storm of war would be brewing.

Weather at least showed him favour. The winds stayed fair through the *Drake*'s coast-hopping run down to Southshire. Tucked between the hill country and the oak hammocks of Selkwood, the seaport's shingled roofs pricked taut angles through the smoke from the rendering of resins and turpentine. A coin tossed to a lighterman across shining water bought Dhirken her assurance: the maze of the Harbour Street markets included a chartmaker's stall. Packing a minor arsenal of knives along with her favoured cutlass, *Drake*'s captain rowed herself ashore. While her crewmen grumbled on shipboard mending sail, she quartered the city on foot.

The thoroughfare was packed. Gourd sellers burdened under poles and baskets plodded between rumbling drays from the stone quarries at Elssine, behind mules panniered in silk bales from Atchaz, and abalone shell from Telzen, bound for the furniture makers. Chipped wood littered the gutters by the shipyards, with the half-shaped hulls of galleys rowed like picked bones on their ways. Under wind-flapped awnings, Dhirken prowled the shaded alleys of the shoreside market, with its glass blowers and snake venom sellers, its fragrant crates of citrus and its stalls that reeked of strong cheese, where robed bands of Sanpashir nomads drove nimble goats.

Dhirken elbowed through a begging squad of urchins to reach the chart-maker's shop, slammed inside, and confronted a gnome-like old man enthroned amid pens and coloured inks.

His moist eyes regarded her in scholarly curiosity. Then a cheery smile stirred his drooping moustache. 'I expect you're after maps for the coast-line to Innish?'

At the captain's stiff glare, he waggled a moth-eaten goose quill. 'Ach, there'd scarcely be two of you, yes? The young master sent word in a letter last month, along with pay to see your needs met.' The cartographer bobbed beneath his counter, rattled aside rulers, tufts of string and worn nibs, and popped erect with a ribboned roll of parchment. 'Your chart, lady captain, with yon mannerly gentleman's compliments.'

'Dharkaron's hairy bollocks!' Dhirken advanced a nettled step. 'I'm nobody's bound lackey! It's naught but a stray slip of fortune that I bothered to visit here at all!'

'Aye, well, you needn't stay riled for my sake.' The little man's spirits stayed unshaken. 'Yon fellow made demands of the shipwrights that were fair preposterous. They howled just as loudly. He still got everything he wanted. Are you going to take this, or spit on it?'

Dhirken snatched up the offering as if it held poison. Back in the street, she fished out the notepaper nestled inside. The strong, concise hand that had first taught her letters requested her to offload two bullion chests at the shipwright's mansion near the harbourmaster's office.

'Smoke his Grace out for a louse!' Dhirken snapped through gritted teeth. 'Let the Prince of Rathain pay his own debts.'

But the shipwright had evidently received another letter, for when the captain reached her command, hot and distempered, a tender manned by a liveried lackey lay tied to the *Black Drake*'s anchor cable.

The first man she met after off-loading coin chests was Earl Jieret, slouched with his boots braced in bald-faced insolence on her chart desk. 'Daelion's two-eyed vigilance,' she swore. 'Is your liege lord always as conniving in his ways as a thief?'

Eyes underlit by jittered reflections as he whetted the blade of his longsword, Jieret shrugged.

Too aware the selfsame steel would be turned against her in challenge should she balk at resuming the brig's course, Dhirken gave a wicked, joyous laugh. 'Oh, I'll sail on to Innish, if only to deliver to Arithon's royal face my word on his bloody-handed arrogance.' She breathed deep and added in stringent offence, 'But damn you, earl or no, if your loutish feet stay parked on my chart locker, we'll not stir up sweat getting out of this port!'

Black Drake made Innish by the spring equinox. Anchored out of smuggler's habit in position for speedy departure, Dhirken needed no invective to see her sails stowed and longboats launched in a stream of seamless industry.

'What did you promise them?' Jieret asked from his armed stance by the portside companionway.

Hard by the mainmast pinrail, shredding a leg of roast lamb with neat teeth, Dhirken tipped him a guileless glance. 'What else but shore leave, to scour the taverns in search of yon mountebank prince?'

'Ath forfend!' Jieret threw back his bearded chin and laughed. 'I wish I could go along, just to watch your mate break town-born heads.'

'Just pray that's all he dunts.' Dhirken shut ale-dark eyes, mouthed a silent wish, and tossed her stripped bone landward in a sailor's habit that kept the harbours infested with glossy rats. 'My mate's in a fair rotten temper, let me warn you. The tropics give him itches in places he'd rather use to tup doxies.' Pitched to a sulky froth of tension herself, she licked grease off her fingers and grimaced. 'Your prince, when we find him, had better show something more than a whim for veering off his course. Southcoast ports are too lax to charge tariffs. As a contraband runner in these waters, we're wasting and useless as whore's bells strung on a corpse.'

'Don't have me speak for my liege,' Jieret said, too apprehensive himself to show sympathy. 'It's a likely guess his Grace won't welcome the tidings I bear from the north.'

'Don't think to weep on my shoulder,' Dhirken retorted. 'A thousand times, I've wished I'd never met the man.'

Packed with crewmen in ribald, high humour, the Drake's longboats raked shoreward across waters pooled molten brass under sunset.

Earl Jieret remained alone at the brig's rail, too proud to shelter in the stern cabin despite full awareness that by city law, his clipped clanbred accent was enough to arraign him for execution. He leaned on damp wood, his cold-cast patience a mask for wound nerves and anxiety. Once again, he waited, fingering the worn quillon dagger, looted seven years past off the corpse of a headhunter killed for the murder of his family. The touch of whetted steel made him wonder whether Arithon s'Ffalenn still cherished the boy's knife for whittling given that day for remembrance.

A breeze frisked ripples on the harbour. Up the river delta, a fitful flash like turned mica, a millwheel revolved in lowered light. A cormorant flew, pursued by squabbling gulls. Jieret breathed in the tang of cinnamon from a spicer's shed and watched the southern waters fade from rose to ice purple between the peaked rambades of the galleys. The daytime commerce of the dockfront wound down, chanting stevedores replaced by the fluting whistles used to summon lightermen. Dogs barked, and cliff swallows skimmed in the dying glow above shell-coloured towers. Vendors' carts and ale drays rumbled to the clatter of muleteams while the working crowd dispersed homeward, to reappear, thicker, clad in festival ribbons and bearing a weaving swarm of brands. The massive brass fire pans on their pilings were lit, each one twelve spans apart, and crackling hot sparks across the quay. Lamps burned in the brothel galleries, on the decks of ships at anchor, to skein on black waters a serried, fire-dance of reflections.

The towers blazed in necklaces of candles, and the cymbals of street singers chimed through the dusk. The feast of spring equinox, at Innish, was a mad, dizzy whirl of gaiety dressed out in lights.

Aboard the darkened Drake, jumpy as a caged wildcat for the fact he lay surrounded by enemies, Jieret listened to the shrieks of the doxies, and the deeper rasp of male rejoinder; the frenetic laughter from the puppet theatres, and the thumps on the water as boats collided to slurred apologies from handlers too drunken to trifle over chipped paint or marred brightwork. Haunted by distant memories of the spring bonfires from his childhood, Jieret tried not to wonder how the feast might be celebrated, had his clans not been hunted by townsmen, and were his prince not accursed by Desh-thiere.

An overloaded boat crammed with roisterers rocked under the stern. Screaming laughter, lit by a frenzy of lamps, the rowers banged their oars against the strakes at the load line and demanded feastday alms. 'Call down a blessing for the night, good master! Toss us a copper. Or we come aboard to bring you joy.'

Jieret jerked back from the rail, hand gripped to his dagger. He dared not reply, even to send the beggars packing; as a clanborn earl taken captive in a town, he would be publicly maimed before death.

While the pranksters thrashed oars to manoeuvre their boat alongside, he gripped his knife and weighed hopeless odds, that he could stay alive long enough to deliver the news of Lysaer's muster to his liege.

Amidships, something banged in the galley. 'Muckle plague o' fiends!' The heavyset cook came on deck, a kettle slung in meaty hands. He peered in harried temper at the straggle of dandies, who passed a wine skin as their fellows argued and drew lots to determine which man should lead the boarding party.

Jieret flourished his blade in grim salute, while below, to a tempo of mistimed oars and obscenities, the pair of gallants who picked the short straws swayed upright and clawed to locate the strakes.

'Look how they sparkle, the pansies. Mighty lot o' jewels on a bunch come whining for largesse.' The cook turned a soulful glance to Jieret. 'No need for that hog sticker, man. This is the *Drake* they're bothering, and our Dhirken, she don't like visitors.' His take on the matter neatly practical, he raised his pot and tipped out a scalding rain of broth.

A scream, a shout, a fat splash, followed by a tangle of shrill curses; the boat rocked off, the occupants who remained less merry and reeking of chicken stock. The drunk one thrown overboard yelled and thrashed, half-gagged by the weeds of his finery. The cook gazed down at the fracas, intrigued. 'Should we wager how long he tries to swim before he thinks to jettison that platter of a hat?'

Wound taut as wire in a half-crouch, Jieret said nothing as the prow of a lighter eclipsed the swimmer.

'Ah, pox! We'll change terms,' the cook coaxed, reasonable in the face of setback as the passing boatman offered the victim a grip on his thwart. 'Let's say five silvers on whether yon lighter makes the quay without fouling an anchor chain and capsizing.'

But again Jieret Red-beard did not answer. Over the receding clamour of scalded revellers, amid the warp through weft racket of voices that rebounded from the stews at the harbourside, his forest trained senses had picked out one whose singular timbre he recognized.

Neither was the cook as engrossed in amusement as he seemed. 'Look smart. Our captain's back.'

A longboat sliced across the weave of the lightermen's lamps, rowed to the reach of timed oars. Her crew reversed stroke and backwatered, and the craft glided into the shadow beneath the *Black Drake*'s hull. The cook stowed his soup pot and tossed out a line. Seconds later, seamen scrambled up the battens, cursing skinned knuckles and bruises in scarcely suppressed tones of triumph.

'Dear lady, a note sent ashore would have found me,' retorted a firm voice, but animated now, its inflection reschooled to sound townbred, and vastly more carefree than Jieret's past memories from his father's lodge in Strakewood Forest.

Dhirken cracked into ripe laughter. ' 'Twere fair reckoning, prince, after the Kittiwake. I gave my men full leave to roust you by any means they saw fit.'

'Yes, well,' said Arithon s'Ffalenn from a poised step on the side battens. Unaware of any listener above him, he added in laughing exuberance, 'My Innish patrons didn't fancy the *Black Drake*'s crew. I kept my bargain despite them and left not a second before midnight, but more than one tavern in the upper city will never again be the same for it.' He reached the rail, arranged neat, ringless hands to vault over, and light from the half-shuttered lantern on deck washed black hair, then the spare, foxy angles of a face seven years had changed not at all.

Jieret pressed through the crowding sailhands, knelt, and bent his head to the man he had last seen over the grave cairn of his slaughtered parents. 'My Liege of Rathain.'

Time stopped.

Arithon's fingers locked on grained wood. The breath spun out of him as if impelled by a suffocating weight. The young man on the ship's deck before him might have been a ghost restored to flesh, for the grief that marked his blanched features. For one numbed second, dread for returned obligations made Arithon recoil in pain.

Then his unbearable apprehension by itself forced the moment to snap.

The Shadow Master hurled himself over the rail in a welcome that burst all restraints. 'Jieret!' He caught the young man by the wrists and raised him, stunned all over again as the earl last seen as a twelve-year-old boy arose to full height and dwarfed him. Arithon fell back a step, his joy overwhelmed by amazement. 'By Ath, man! Caolle must be proud. You've grown into the very image of your father.'

Jieret blinked through a suspect brightness, flushed with pleasure and odd shock, that the neatly-made prince before him still fitted the mould of his memory. 'Your Grace, I'll come of age before winter. I ask your indulgence, that you accept my formal service now. The news that I carry won't wait.' In a doubled-hand grip, he offered the old quillon dagger carried off the bloody field in Strakewood.

Exposed before Dhirken's curiosity, jostled by the press of *Drake*'s crewmen, Arithon turned the blade over in recognition. Fine fingers still sensitized by the lyranthe string recorded the nicks of hard usage. As if the separate, belling vibrations of the blows the steel had staved off, and the life spilled from each opened wound stung his senses, he said, 'Mine the honour, Earl of the North.'

In complete disregard that the moment was not private, to the speechless amazement of hard-bitten sailhands who knew nothing of customs kept by old high kings, blooded royalty knelt before his prospective vassal. With a clarity wiped to acid by his singer's trained diction, Arithon swore the traditional oath of sovereign prince to liegeman that sealed a pact of guardianship, and ended with the lines, 'For the gift of feal duty, Earl Jieret s'Valerient, my charge of protection; for your loyalty, my spirit shall answer, unto my last drop of blood, and until my final living breath. Dharkaron witness. Take back this blade as token of my trust, and with your true steel, my royal blessing.'

Arithon arose, smiling and steady, unlike the past oath-taking to Jieret's father, that had taxed him beyond reach of all peace. Unknown to any present watcher, a bloodpact sworn under the full influence of his mage power had already forged a life tie to the grown boy before him, that bound their two fates more strongly still.

The Master of Shadow commandeered the chartroom for his meeting, and in words that asked only friendship, requested Dhirken to attend.

'What about the fat prophet?' the captain asked, cool as granite in the cramped companionway, despite her sharp desire to be away. 'My crew ran across him in a brothel. My mate could be sent to fetch him out.'

Seated before the stern window, featureless in outline against panes of glass starred by the glide of passing lanterns, Arithon gestured his refusal. 'Let Dakar bide. I was to leave the port of Innish in the morning, in any case. Dawn is soon enough to roust him out.'

Dhirken's steward trimmed the gimballed lamps, then departed without sound and shut the door.

His ambiguity banished with the shadows, Arithon looked not a whit older than in the hour he last left Strakewood. Haggard, then, beset as any of Deshir's clan survivors, he contained himself now in tight-reined calm that implied an unbreakable composure. Elegant in a bard's clothes trimmed in silver and onyx, his shirt of pale silk tailored close to narrow wrists, he folded hands that were callused only on the fingertips from an artistry confined to fret and string. The boy's knife accepted by the grave cairn in Deshir would have been used to trim lyranthe pegs, if the gift was remembered at all.

No detail of this masterbard's mien suggested the unconscionable, merciless strategy once spun out of magecraft and shadow to spare the clans from decimation on the weapons of Etarra's garrison.

Daunted by sudden uncertainty, that perhaps he did not know his prince at all, Earl Jieret assumed the seat opposite. By size and dress set apart, he wore his deerhide jerkin unadorned, laced with ties that would not catch stray sunlight, or betray him by chance-made noise. His flecked hazel eyes devoured the royal presence, while the red hair that matched his dead mother's spilled in wind-caught tangles over shoulders grown broad in new manhood.

Dhirken slouched against the bulkhead. Discomposed as a cat flicked by raindrops, prepared in her way to be obstructive, she watched in still malice as the earl launched his case to press his prince to reclaim an abandoned sovereignty.

'Lysaer gathers forces to march a war host against you, even as we speak. Despite Caolle's best effort, word of your doings in Jaelot broke through and reached Etarra's mayor.'

'No one could stop that,' Arithon said. His green eyes stayed wide, almost black in the lamplight, and his concentration harrowed as he said, 'Jieret, what price did you pay for those few months of silence? *How many died?*'

He did not refer to fallen clansmen.

Under that horrified, knife-point regard, Jieret remained as unflinching in the face of necessity as ever his father had before him. 'My war captain knows. I left before Jaelot's disaster became public, to seek your Grace and bring word. How many died is no issue, then or now. These armies mean death for my clans, and your liegemen. I would know whether to count on your help to see how many of our own we can save.' He paused, the large fists clenched beneath the table top half-braced for an explosion that never came.

Arithon said in stifled quiet, 'You've come a long way for this audience. *You have my attention.* Go on.'

Jieret swallowed, then forced a game shrug. 'By my father's memory, I should have guessed you wouldn't welcome this. Lady Maenalle sends warning. The force in training at Avenor is highly skilled and designed for swift expansion with mercenaries. Caolle has figured the muster from Rathain's allied cities could be thirty-five thousand strong.'

Pale as if spun out of glass, Arithon threw off his impulse to give way to fury. 'When the war host closes, Lord Jieret, you have my promise here and now. Your clansmen need stand no ground for my sake. What bloodshed cannot be avoided shall happen far from the soil of Rathain.'

'You would inflict your grand slaughter on the turf of uninvolved innocents?' Dhirken interrupted, despite herself drawn in. 'Merciful Ath, just to feed itself, a force of that size would strip the countryside like a howling plague of locusts!'

Arithon scarcely glanced aside at her. 'Can an army march upon the sea? Can a fleet pursue me while blinded with shadow? Lysaer's backing comes from merchant trade. How long will the guilds pay him to waste their profits trying to chase and trap a fugitive who can elude them at will? If I can possibly arrange things, there shall be no pitched battle at all.'

'You might escape, though not easily,' the captain admitted. 'The oceans can't hide you forever and I won't charter *Black Drake* to serve under Rathain's royal banner.'

'There even I draw the line,' Arithon countered, whipcrack fast. 'The vessels at risk shall be mine, built in a temporary shipyard at Merior.' A flick of amusement twitched his lips. 'I will need the *Drake* at the outset, but only to run messages and timber. And I offer an exceptional rate of pay.'

The grip of Dhirken's fingers on her forearms warned of argument, if not an outright rejection. Arithon plunged ahead before she could speak and asked Jieret to detail all he knew of Etarra's build-up in the north.

Laid out in detached recitation, the facts were unrelenting. Lysaer's skilled diplomacy had long since knit every city in Rathain into a unified alliance. The upset at Jaelot had renewed cause for fear and spurred old hatreds to a fresh fervour.

'My liege,' Earl Jieret ended in stripped candour, 'your loyal clans have been hard pressed. To escape the summer forays by headhunters, chieftains as far south as Halwythwood have been forced to seek refuge deep in Daon Ramon Barrens. For fear of the old ruins and Paravian haunting, companies hesitate to track there. But such sanctuary cannot last.'

A pause, while Jieret hooked his knuckles and waited. Dhirken used the interval to loosen the knots that tied her bracers, then pick out laced wires and draw them off. The uneasy spatter of lantern light traced long, shiny scars that marred the length of both wrists. As minutes marched by and Arithon s'Ffalenn withheld comment, the silence seemed to glaze the very air. The *Drake* swung at her anchorage, paired to the waltz of night winds, while the distant, happy roar of the festival crowds dinned in the background like a dream.

Earl Jieret looked up at last. Locked to his sovereign lord's patent, knowing gaze, capitulation jarred through him like crossed steel. 'Yes, there *is* more, your Grace. At Alestron, Duke Bransian s'Brydion would beggar his state treasury to have the head of the sorcerer who wrecked his armoury. The description on his writ for arrest fits your person so closely that Lysaer can play on the connection and gain armed support for the asking.'

'And Alestron, when pressed, can present a force of fifteen thousand on the field,' Arithon sliced back without humour. The beaded silver tips on his cuff ties flashed in strangled movement, then held as if nailed by a spell. 'There's no secret. S'Brydion gold has staked the upkeep of enough mercenaries to repopulate most of East Halla.'

Jieret coughed back the grin that arose despite his plucked nerves. 'I should have guessed yon by-play to be yours.' Intuitively bold as his mother before him, he challenged his liege's coiled patience. 'You have your royal reasons for close confidence, no doubt. But the s'Brydion line is clanblood. A canny prince in your predicament should have approached them as possible allies.'

'I don't want allies!' Arithon bit back. 'This time, I'll have no clan following stand their ground to bleed in my name. I need ships and two years in which to build them.'

'Your enemy's armies won't stall for that.' Dhirken weighed the razor-edged interplay, intrigued despite her better instincts. 'I've heard the talk in the seaports. Let me tell you, the s'Ffalenn name is anathema.'

Arithon's head snapped around, his eyebrows arched first in an acid surprise that expanded to venomous delight. 'What did you think? That I did nothing better since Jaelot than play ditties in taverns for small coin? You've delivered the cargo sent by Maenalle of Tysan for my use to deplete this vaunted war host. Let me say how I plan to spend the proceeds.'

The Master of Shadow began in measured phrases to speak. Long before he finished, Jieret's strained censure had dissolved into rapt attention. He did not ask, after all, what became of the signet ring with Rathain's blazon that he noticed its Teir's'Ffalenn no longer wore. Captain Dhirken seemed unable to tear her gaze from the clever, musician's hands, folded and quiet on her chart table. A coldness invaded the pit of her stomach, that she had ever dared to mishandle this man, or chain him like a miscreant to her taffrail.

His mind worked level upon level with a subtlety that nipped her skin into gooseflesh. On his travels, Arithon had quartered his kingdom. What he noticed, he remembered, and all things he put to a singular and ruthless analysis. He had studied every turn of Rathain's roads, traversed in Halliron's pony cart. He knew each hollow in which an army could be ambushed, and each hill crest where its scouts would be exposed. He knew his cities; had read them, mayor and council and guildhall, and reduced their strengths and weaknesses to one or two pared phrases. That his touch for subversion and strategy had plotted the ruin of Etarra's forces in Strakewood was confirmed beyond equivocal doubt. Whether, as Lysaer s'Ilessid insisted, his person should be hunted down and killed, Dhirken lacked the moral will to say. But every maudlin and drunken warning the Mad Prophet had tried to deliver through an ill-advised passage to Farsee had been nothing less than honest truth.

What the Shadow Master had done in his months as bard's apprentice was to arrange an information network of astonishing breadth and depth. The dispatches would collect in taverns and ports, to be picked up by an agent he would specify; and not a one of the contacts held the whole pattern, or knew to whom the letters would be passed.

'If Captain Dhirken would consider running message packets for me there's no move Lysaer's army can make that I won't hear in advance,' Arithon summed up. 'If they march before time, Jieret, your clans can disrupt their supply lines with very little exposure. I can build my ships and be gone from known shores, and this dangerous, misguided war host will melt away under the weight of its own unwieldy upkeep.'

Dhirken braced against the table, this once caught unbalanced by the drift of the ship underneath her. 'You bear no grudge toward these townsmen for this uprising raised in your name,' she forced out in gritty admiration. 'Ath forbid, and woe to us all, if that poor fact should ever alter.'

'I agree.' Arithon stood in fraught impatience. 'Will you undertake this one task? I would pay any price you demand.'

'I think I don't have much choice,' Dhirken said. 'The sooner you're off the continent, the better, I should say. Or everything afloat will be conscripted at the ports and forced into service for war transport.' She gave him a bargainer's grin. 'I'll have my fee in advance, though. If you fail, or get killed, or mishap fouls your rudder, I want to be rich enough to lay the *Drake* by until the bad times pass over.'

'By all means.' Arithon stepped back and unlatched the companionway with a debonair flourish. 'Let's retire to your hold and see what sort of wealth strikes your fancy.'

For the treasure was fully accounted for, the lading list accurate to the last crate and bale. Circled in musty lantern light, Arithon and Dhirken pressed between the packed cargo: the stacked crates of Falgaire crystal, wrapped and nested in straw; the iron-strapped bullion crates stamped with guild seals, and the carpets packed in lavender to discourage moths. Fine silks; exquisite tapestries; bronze lanterns paned with blown glass; the wine tuns and the rare brandies; the glazed pottery; to the last, breathtaking bolts of damascened silks and patterned linens.

Pleased by her settlement, Dhirken braced her hip on a wine barrel and flicked back the wisped end of her braid. 'What'll you do with the rest of this?'

'Sell it in the markets here at Innish. The proceeds will fund my small fleet.' Arithon trailed his fingers along a bullion chest, his madcap inventiveness struck into sudden sobriety. 'The seals on this chest are Etarran.'

'You didn't know?' Outside the glow of the lamp, Jieret stooped under the deck beams.

'Know what?' Arithon spun to face him, his elegant silks marred with grime and a sharpened frown on his face. 'Lady Maenalle's letter said she wished to stake a fortune to undermine Lysaer's armed strength. I wouldn't see her clans suffer undue persecution at the hands of Avenor's war host, but if I wasn't desperate not to play for killing stakes, the donation would have been refused.'

'Donation?' Earl Jieret elbowed past a bundled tier of carpets. 'Your Grace, when I saw Tysan's *caithdein*, she insisted she was returning what belonged to Rathain's crown in the first place.' A vindictive smile split his beard. 'Everything in this hold was hauled overland from Etarra by Lysaer s'Ilessid, then torn out of his hands in clan ambush atop the Pass of Orlan.'

'Oh, that's rich!' Dhirken folded into helpless laughter over the rim of her barrel. 'Dharkaron drag you to the devil, prince! You'll do all you say and take to blue water, underwritten by your foe's stolen fortune!' In admiration tinged with regret, she regarded the man etched against the hold's murky darkness. 'A pity for you. The time you need to complete your grand plan is one year too much to expect.'

Arithon's smile cut the gloom like edged lightning. 'That's scarcely a setback, lady captain. Lysaer can muster his force at Etarra. He can outfit and march them the breadth of the continent at vast and ruinous expense. But to engage and wreak my ruin, he first has to find me. That will cost him a long and merry search.'

The Shadow Master stretched, caught the lantern from its peg, and flung an expansive gesture toward the ladder that led to the hatch. 'What do you say? We could broach that cask you're perched on. Let's drink like old friends to the charter you've earned, and my most cherished hope of freedom.'

Bargain

The cherry trees in Tysan cast off their spring mantles, and flurries of pink and white blossoms gusted over the fringe of the war banners. Petals sprinkled the surcoats of the men in the cavalcades and strewed the lashed tarps on the supply wagons which furrowed black tracks in the mud beneath Avenor's north gate turrets. With the equinox feast and the prince's state wedding a month gone, his royal city rededicated its heart to the coming war against the Master of Shadow.

Lysaer's new bride had no choice but to endure through the massive upheaval involved with launching the campaign. Her husband was rarely at her side. Surrounded by advisors and officers, he could be glimpsed between trips to the armouries and stock sheds; or some days not at all, closeted as he was through lengthy meetings with his secretaries and his seneschal. The dispositions, the inventory lists, the arrangements for wagons and supplies seemed grindingly endless.

Nights in the fast quiet of their high tower chamber became a guarded time of solace for them both. Clenched in the passion of her husband's embrace, Talith unleashed every charm she possessed to kindle his ecstasy, then storm his keyed nerves until his ongoing worries became seared away by blind passion. She melted to Lysaer's skilled touch until her own starved response touched off his rapture in turn, to eclipse and scald out self-awareness. In his arms, she let nothing intrude; not the discipline of fractious young officers, nor frayed temper from the trials created by marching armed companies across leagues of bad roads; or allotments wrung from a dwindled treasury, to hire galleys for crossing Instrell bay to reach established supply lines in Rathain.

Talith had no hope to change fate. Prince Lysaer's peace of mind was inextricably linked to his drive to kill the Master of Shadow.

A third of Avenor's garrison had already marched in hired passage as caravan guards. The rest embraced a feverish schedule to set final polish on training already knit into close discipline. Talith lived in dread of the moment when the meadows burst into high flower. However sweet a nest she could weave with new love, once the season could provide for the draught teams, Avenor's last divisions would depart. Her splendid royal husband would be nowhere else but in the dust of the vanguard with his officers.

But this morning the war horns were still silent. The casement panes loomed blank as pearl inlay while the dawn slowly quenched the last stars. Birds outside roused and chirped in sleepy twitters against the tap of a wall sentry's step. Talith rolled over. Her hair a dragged spill of honey from her temples, she slid her flattened hand beneath quilted silk in a sensuous quest for warm flesh.

Strong arms enfolded her from behind. The embrace robbed the bite from chill air, even as the coverlet slipped off her creamy shoulders. Lysaer nestled his chin in her nape and murmured into her ear. 'I can't take time for you this morning, my love.'

She twisted to face him. The rasp of his suede doublet against her skin raised the disturbing discovery that he was already dressed. 'The sun isn't up. You aren't wearing silk.' Apprehension cranked her tone a pitch higher. 'Where are you going?'

Lysaer kissed her, languorous and light until she struggled to fling off the bedclothes that mired her hips and knees. His touch infallibly drove her to heat until she ached in surrender. Before she recovered from the storm to her senses, he melted back, lost in the shadows by the armoire.

A whispered flick of strap leather and a chink of dangled spurs disclosed his intent to pull on his boots without the service of his valet. Before her alarm could find voice, Lysaer spoke. 'In the land of my birth, by old custom, the king would ride into the wood and slay a spring boar to prove his prowess. Not to be shamed by tradition, beloved, I've set the day aside to go hunting.'

'You're mad!' Talith shot erect in a churned up calyx of silk sheets. 'Why rush off to bloody some hapless, mean creature?' Etarran enough to make her pique sting, she flared, 'Does the Master of Shadow not offer sport enough?'

A dangerous, brittle stillness claimed the space where Lysaer stood. Then the hiss of his expelled breath tore through his protracted quiet. 'Dare you question my love for you?'

Talith gasped. 'Ath show me mercy, how can it compete?' And the tears came, hot and stormy, for the way his honest hurt could devastate her defences. 'Is it so hard?' With sadly swallowed pride, she admitted, 'I dread the day you must leave me.'

A boot dropped with a thud against the carpet. Then the mattress gave to his knee. Cool fingers cradled Talith's chin, turned her stiff neck.

Lysaer's lips moulded to hers and shared the salt on her mouth. 'One old boar shouldn't keep me past nightfall if I'm quick and skilled. As for my regard, lady wife, how can that be measured against a commensurate evil? You've married a prince who is human flesh and blood.' Like the rip of cold iron, he added, 'If you, who are closest, think my heart isn't torn, then rejoice, for I have triumphed. Every man bound to follow me onto the field must never guess how this duty chafes my spirit. Did you forget?'

His grip tightened. *The criminal I go to ruin is my mother's bastard son.* I beg you, bear up and be brave. The killing of a half-brother is burden enough on my conscience.'

No touch from her could soothe his inner pain; no word existed to hold him: Lysaer slipped gently away.

By the time Talith's misery relented enough to meet his need for her smile, new sun bronzed the east casement. Long since, her prince had summoned his huntsman and gone.

His quest for the royal boar turned inland and wound through the glens, bedecked in new spring like worked lace. The cool shadows still pocketing the hill flanks gave way to tepid light. Lysaer went attended by three men at arms and his equerry. His sole badge of rank, the star and crown embroidered on his saddlecloth, stabbed a prick of unquiet reflection. His hounds ran collared in stitched leather; his horse's trappings were plain. The polished ash boar-spear socketed in his lance rest sported no ribbons or inlay. Its sharpened head snicked and fretted through the greenery as he rode, a flame of silvered steel wreathed in yellow puffs of disturbed pollen.

Beyond the tangled bittervines netted over the banks of a marsh, the huntsman encountered fresh boar's slots. The black, boggy earth lay hacked and churned where the creature had savaged the ground, perhaps rooting up fallen acorns, or else testing its own rank strength. The hounds were given the scent. A ridged moil of black and tan bodies, they surged baying down the glen to a whipped, pale turbulence of ferns.

The prince of Tysan set spurs to his mount, his hair like sun-caught flax and his gloved hands easy on the reins. Eager and restive beneath him, his blooded horse crashed through saplings and brush, and scattered winged tempests of finches.

'Fiends plague us!' groused the taciturn captain at arms as the royal escort mustered to follow. 'Your wives had better like sewing. Here's good clothes we're going to shred to rags.'

The hounds streamed through the underbrush in a primal, belling frenzy. In his sensible cross-gartered hose and leather jacket, the huntsman blew his horn to speed his pack, while riders ducked branches and splashed through the sky-printed mirrors of puddles in chase.

Through the course of that first, mad gallop, the party lost sight of their prince.

The pack was whipped off at the first check and a search begun for the man. Avenor's master huntsman proved a skilled tracker. He found the prince's horse inside the hour, grazing knee-deep in meadow grass and marsh mallow, its saddle flaps caught with pinched leaves. Both stirrups dangled. The boar-spear was gone from its socket and the reins rested looped, neither broken nor trailed on the ground.

Of Lysaer s'Ilessid, they found no sign.

While the hounds milled and snuffled and whined their frustration, then lolled panting on their bellies, the leathery old huntsman pursed bearded lips and fingered his coiled rawhide whip. 'I see no sign of any accident. If you'll hear my opinion, let be and go home. His Grace wanted time to himself.'

'You would take such a chance?' The burly captain flicked bruised leaves off his thighs and adjusted the sour leather of his gauntlets. 'His Grace holds our hope of deliverance. Enemies know it. This could be a barbarian trap.' His order sent the equerry back to summon Captain Mayor Pesquil and muster men for an organized search.

'You waste effort.' Too laconic to be rankled over doubts about his competence, the huntsman raked back streaked hair and snapped his fingers to break off a growling confrontation between a hound couple. 'I'd know, were barbarians about. The ground's too mired to hide footprints. If enemies lay waiting in ambush close by, no blackbirds would scold in the brush. Your prince will return when he's ready. If you trouble the headhunter captain to check, mark me, he'll tell you the same.'

Poised beyond view in dense brush on a knoll, the royal subject of the argument listened as the voices of his retinue grew heated. Lysaer grinned in smothered amusement, then crept away through the trees.

He turned south, determined to stay solitary. For the wise old huntsman had interpreted his wish like a brother: this day's work had little to do with a ceremonial hunt to kill a boar.

The season was too new for the trees to be leafed in full canopies. Patched, ephemeral shadows imprinted the ground like a cat-tangled skein of loose yarn. Black earth and rotted oak mould breathed through the burgeoning fragrance of greenery and undergrowth sprigged in yellow buds. Too warm in his suede jerkin, Lysaer slid damp hands along the grip of his boar-spear. In all ways, he dreaded this errand.

But a meddler in force who used magecraft to terrorize and kill; a reiver in whose name clan barbarians committed outright slaughter; such a one deserved no stay of mercy. While unwary cities were attacked out of hand, no upright sovereign dared waste the time to search through conventional trackers.

To ferret out the Master of Shadow's location, a prince sworn and dedicated to his people's defence must not cavil at a liaison that might yield results through arcane scrying.

But even for moral right and mercy, the prospect of sorcery left Lysaer deeply unsettled.

Truly alone for the first hour since the machinations of a sorcerer had banished him through a World Gate into exile, shouldered since with responsibility bequeathed by long-forgotten ancestors, Lysaer thought of the mother he had barely known. Lost when he was four into the arms of a s'Ffalenn lover, she had been the only daughter of a high mage. From her had come his given gift of light and Arithon's deadly touch at weaving shadow. Lysaer's last memories of her were indelibly twined with the scents of citrus and spices; of delicate jewels and silver chains, and a rippled fall of pale hair. The Lady Talera had made no spells in his presence that he could recall. More clearly he remembered his father's savage rages, the acrimony of the kingdom's prim seneschal, and the lengthy, hushed sessions of the kingdom council following her repudiated marriage vows.

Horror still revisited through his recollection of the trials, the miasma of late-burning oil lamps intermingled with the sweaty fear of the accused. Then the weeping agony of the families through the purges, as every man, woman and child suspected of sorcerous activity, or in sheltering the queen in her escape, was sent to the executioner's block for justice. The poisoned, vicious anger of his royal father still cut, at his request to ask his mother's family for the training to develop his born talents to full advantage.

Whatever cloaking spells and trickery Queen Talera had used to shame her lawful marriage and beget her bastard, her cuckolded husband never shed his passionate distrust of magecraft. Her legitimate firstborn had grown to manhood without so much as a herb witch to tell him whether he had inherited any further arcane potential from the distaff side of his bloodline.

Whereas Arithon had been raised by the high mage himself. His powers had been moulded by the arduous discipline demanded by a master's training.

Lysaer jabbed the butt of his spear into the loam of the deerpath. The breeze had died. Sun cloaked his shoulders in unpleasant heat as his track meandered through the bottomlands, crossed like sable braid with the trickles of spring-fed freshets. His uneasy mind spared no thought for the splash of startled frogs and the whirred wings of marsh wrens and blackbirds. Distaste for his charge warred with childhood jealousy, never quite silenced by the principles expounded by his father.

The words still haunted, burred with the memory of the wax-scented gloom of the privy chamber as the royal spate of rage finally cooled. *'My son, ideals and strengths and the foundation of sound rule are never so simply reconciled. A king who values his subjects will treat with them as a fellow man. Power to upset natural order goes ill with royal office, that by nature must wield influence over lives. The concepts of justice and fairness are not born through greater strength. They spring instead from sympathy with the lowliest weakness.'* The King of Amroth had looked upon his heir, the seams of a life-time's bitter decisions softened to entreaty on his face. *'The judgements you make for the crown when you inherit will be hard enough on the heart. You will need a mind undivided between the laws that must govern humanity and the uncanny secrets of the mysteries.'*

Experience lent vicious validation to such counsel.

Queen Talera had been moved to desert her family for something more than spiteful vengeance. She had gone, she insisted, to right a balance, then been lonely enough to bury the grief of her sacrifice in the comfort of illicit love.

Briefly beguiled into friendship with her bastard, Lysaer had seen the insidious way fine knowledge of power could corrupt mercy. The secret fear rode his heart: how the means to sway fate might corrode a man's spirit to forget his humanity and embrace an abstruse creed without pity. Wider knowledge could blind the eye to suffering; or why else should Athera's greatest arcane order give even indirect sanction to a prince who had turned the shining wisdom of his upbringing toward acts of unconscionable slaughter?

Shadows had been used to entrap an army; magecraft itself, to bind and kill.

And yet the Fellowship sorcerers who held the sure resource to forbid such offences stood back and did nothing at all.

Lysaer refused to resent the sorry fact that he stood alone in his resolve. He would act and risk perilous consequences to find whether the Koriathain were willing to lend their arts to help him track down a felon.

The enchantress's cottage lay deep in the glens. Upon Lysaer's arrival, late day spun cobwebbed shadows across vibrant green moss and tender grasses. Shoots of sprouting herbs and the whiskered leaves of coltsfoot grew in hoed rows by the snaggled sprawl of a withy fence. The dilapidated dwelling beyond sagged in the roof beams like a toadstool leaning to rot. But the shutters were whitewashed and the stone step swept clean of debris. Footsore, thirsty, his heartbeat rushed by apprehension, Lysaer strode up to knock.

The panel swung open to his touch. From a gloom flecked by the unsteady eye of one candle, a cracked porcelain voice bade him enter.

The boar-spear was too unwieldy to carry indoors. Lysaer rested its shaft against the outside lintel. The hasty breath he snatched to brace his nerve was ingrained with must, tallow grease and unwashed fleeces, and a fierce tang of aromatic herbs. Beneath lurked a taint of less pleasant things: of stale ash and husked insects trapped in cobwebs; of rust and dried blood and grated rootstock. A tingle kissed his nape as he stepped in to a shrill squeak of floorboards.

Something moved beyond the light like the smooth slide of bone against cloth. 'You do not come to hunt beasts, son of s'Ahelas.'

Startled to be named for his mother's kin, Lysaer sidestepped in failed effort to escape the glare of the candle. Stopped by the touch of something iron against his knee, he sensed the bundles of dried herbs in the rafters, and wool hooks draped with pallid skeins of yarn. 'I came to seek counsel.'

The tart voice snapped in correction. 'You came to ask to know the refuge of your half-brother, Arithon, your purpose to arrange for his death.' In flame-rimmed outline, a withered hand lifted. An unseen treadle creaked, and the starred spokes of a spinning-wheel squeaked to life in a sudden whir of air.

Rinsed in trickled sweat, Lysaer made out the crone's form. She sat, swathed in dull cloth, hair like spun glass and spider's thread an uncombed blur in the darkness. Hooded eyes fixed him, sunken pits in a skull. The cleft lips looked as if they were stitched the way paupers dressed corpses out for burial.

Lysaer raised his courage to open a distasteful negotiation. 'Do the Koriathain condone the wanton use of arcane power? Walls and buildings in Jaelot were unlaced, stone from stone, and none who suffered saw justice.'

The spinning wheel settled into rhythm. 'You speak of an event on a coastline far beyond the chartered boundaries of Tysan.' A sibilance of cloth, a scratch of dry fleeces and yarn turned off the spindle, teased between waxy, crabbed fingers.

'Rathain's own prince was the instigator.' Calm under questioning, Lysaer said, 'Do the powers of Athera permit such a prince to despoil the same cities bound under his sovereign protection?'

The crone's chin lifted. 'For this you set yourself to pluck a man's life from the hands of Daelion Fatemaster?'

Bored through by a gaze like struck flint, measured in every detail, even down to the trembling gold highlight on his hair, Lysaer forced a bold step. 'I would defend the weak and the innocent against any man whose misuse of grand conjury caused them harm.'

The whickered turn of the wheel held steady. Pinwheel shadows flared over a plank table, a leather chest, and a hamper of laced withies in one corner. 'If I grant you the scrying you desire, you will use it to violate the peace. Our Koriani creed cannot sanction bloody war.'

Lysaer advanced to preserve the initiative. 'I haven't come empty-handed.'

'A bribe? That's impertinence, to presume earthly wealth could sway any sister of my order.' The crone heaved up a coarse scratch of laughter. 'Prince, you waste time. Take up your spear and go hunt the boar. He would show you more sport for less danger.'

Hands clasped before him in cool censure, Lysaer said, 'I give the beggars in my court a better hearing.'

A creased palm slapped the whirling wheel to a stop. 'Would a beggar offer bloodprice to take his half-brother's life?'

'Would you let a point of kinship overset a whole kingdom's right to justice?' Across darkness, through eddyless air clogged with the rancid reek of tallow, Lysaer felt the probe of the enchantress's regard like subliminal pressure against his bones. Iron to his core, ruled every breath by royal dignity, he quelled the swift prick of affront, that this enchantress should dare to question his morals, or doubt his fitness to act on behalf of a jeopardized society. 'In allowance for mercy, I would say instead that I petition for help to mete out a swift act of cautery. Who else is qualified to outmatch this evil? Or should civilization be abandoned to suffer, and a people see ruin for a sentimental principle, hinged on an accident of birth? Do we shelter one life, regardless of ancestry, then sanction the act of mass murder? Answer me fairly: can the breach between townsman and clanborn ever hope to be healed for as long as Rathain's prince remains alive?'

The treadle squeaked again and revived the lagged spin of the wheel. 'You imply the Koriani Senior Circle is remiss? For Arithon s'Ffalenn, Morriel Prime has already made disposition.' A tuft of wool flitted free of the crone's grasp and drifted like an errant spirit across the candle's thin halo. 'You mistake us. We are not as the Fellowship, to turn blind eyes to events. I can lend your endeavour this much, Prince of Tysan: you shall suffer no interference. Should you find your quarry and run him to ground, force of arms shall be left to prevail.'

'You would dismiss me unheard?' Lysaer cried.

An invisible movement jerked the lint on a draught, and a snake hiss whisper lashed the gloom. 'How dare you!'

But the implied admission stood: *that the Koriani Prime already knew the Shadow Master's whereabouts.*

Lysaer outfaced the crone's ire. 'Before the Mistwraith invaded Athera, your order did not trifle with nursing the sick. They peddled no petty charms for iyat bane and let herb witches attend birthings and sick livestock. Koriani magecraft at one time was said to cure mortal wounds. Initiate sisters weren't culled from your orphanages, but sent to your hospices by parents, lest their talents languish without teaching. What of your hopes to restore such lost influence? Is your sisterhood content to remain overshadowed by events? As a prince pledged to mend this land's rifts and sad hatreds, I would suggest your Prime's goal and mine at heart aren't so terribly different.'

The crone's gaze devoured him now, sharply enough to raise a flush. Hazed by his own rapid heartbeat, Lysaer finished on a drawn note of acid. 'I beg to suggest this exchange is no tawdry bargain, but a just restoration of a moral balance. I once visited Althain Tower. Sethvir's storerooms hold treasures that perhaps should be brought into daylight.'

'You meddle beyond your depth, Prince!' But the enchantress faltered in her spinning. The wheel lost impetus. Slackened a bare instant from firm tension, the yarn snapped into spring-loops and tangles, unnoticed as her eyes pinned his face.

Riled by the disparate sense of being memorized for future study, Lysaer lifted his spread palm and raised the bright current of his gift.

Light bloomed from his fingertips. The sediment of gloom flowed away as though strained from murky water to unveil the cramped room in its poverty: the threadbare coverlet on the trucklebed, moth-nipped and fringed with ravelled seams; furnishings worn to a patina of hard use; and walls swagged in warped shelves, crammed with a herbalist's collection of flasks and packets of root stocks.

The enchantress proved an angular woman with sunken cheeks and puffed hands. Her shapeless brown twill hung speckled with wax and napped to frayed seams at the cuffs. Brown walnut eyes might have been warm, were they not touched to an impervious glitter that stabbed even the dead air for its secrets.

'Speak your bribe then, Prince.' Her face a leather mask, she added, 'If you seek to gain, you must abide by my judgement. Your case will be weighed on grounds of moral merit, but beware. You trespass in affairs beyond your depth.'

Lysaer drew breath and found himself trembling after all. Necessity impelled him to commit himself. 'I have seen in the store vaults at Althain a weighty sphere of cut amethyst. Traithe named that jewel the Waystone of the Koriathain.'

The crone gave a clipped cry. A candle-caught sparkle of tears rinsed her cheeks, quarried in seams and tired hollows. 'We never knew,' she said in a shattered whisper.

Misplaced since the time of the uprising, the Great Waystone held capacity to channel the trained awareness of one hundred and eighty enchantresses. The crystal had stood as the keystone of Koriani power. Since its disappearance, the sisterhood had been as a body blinded, reduced to crippling weakness.

If means could be found to restore its possession into the hands of the Prime, the order could rebuild its lost influence. The Koriathain might regain their former strength to steer events in mercy and compassion; to alleviate those trends of daily suffering the Fellowship in its arrogance deemed unworthy of attention. Through the Great Waystone, the medicinal virtues of herbals could be raised beyond individual treatment, plagues could be averted, the course of storms bent aside; earthquake and wildfire forced quiescent. Once more the order could act to spare the world from its imprint of senseless, natural disasters.

The crone sat bemused, her hands draped loose amid the carded wool in her lap. 'Ath bless your vision, Prince of Tysan.' Flushed to deep gratitude, she attended the matter of his asking price. 'Approach and stare into the candle flame. My art shall grant the augury you ask of us.'

Lysaer dispelled the blaze of his gift. While the shadows rushed back and veiled her in obscurity, he crossed the worn, creaking boards. The isolate flame glowed through his hair, the tips of each strand fired bright as spun wire. He aligned his sight as the crone had directed, and inhaled the fragrance of lavender and pennyroyal and mint, and the fox-musk scent of whatever had been used to cut the oil from raw fleeces.

The crone neither spoke nor moved. Her lashes stayed parted as her eyes glazed blindly into trance. The knuckles in her lap twitched once and stilled, chapped to cracks like the glaze on cheap crockery.

Tense, lightly sweating, Lysaer waited empty-handed for the magic to touch him. Seconds passed. The candle's fire bent and wavered and thrashed up its rippled, thready fumes. His eyes burned with the strain of fixed focus. The transition that plunged into prescient dream fell seamless and silent, outside his five senses to fathom.

One moment he stood in the enchantress's cramped cottage. The next breath he was nowhere at all, a disembodied presence shot through a swoop of uneasy distress. Then his awareness contracted into a sharp, focused vision that encompassed a vista far distant . . .

. . . *the azure harbour sparkled under mild, salt winds, creased by the satin splash of breakers. Against a fan of palm trees and the fluffy, low clouds of the tropics, a man in sailor's garb closed a bargain with an aproned craftsman. 'My shipyard will be settled at Merior by the Sea,' he informed. 'Your contract will extend for two years, through the course of building ten brigantines.' As he turned to depart, the fall of southern sunlight limned glossy black hair and a face of steep planes and narrow angles; eyes clear-cut as dark tourmaline revealed him as the scion of s'Ffalenn . . .*

The mirror-bright clarity of the scrying splintered, savaged by a claw-rip of hatred. Lysaer screamed in thwarted rage. The curse-driven impulse to draw steel, to dismember an enemy beyond reach unstrung his reasoned, royal bearing. He thrashed a step backward and spun, to seek the cottage doorway where his boar-spear waited ready to his hand.

But the walls, the blurred spice of herbs, the candle and crone: all were banished. His foot raised no squeak of waxed floor boards. Instead, he crashed through damp branches.

Lysaer jerked short in bewilderment. The unconsummated passion raised by the scrying sheared through his body in waves. Banished back to the wood by some twist of fey spells, he stood at the verge of a glen.

The air wore a diaphanous mantle of twilight; grass and fiddlehead ferns drooped to a tarnish of dew.

Lysaer shuddered in the cold air. His oak spear lay at his feet. He snatched up the weapon, still fired in every nerve by an untamed blaze of animosity.

Movement across the clearing caught his eye.

Embedded in shadow beneath the tree limbs, a boar waited, head down and bristling to challenge the disturbance in its territory. Failing light printed the curves of its tushes, varnished with spittle. The pits of mean eyes scanned the gloom to a twitch of pricked ears.

Lent a hunter's concentration by the riptide shock of Desh-thiere's curse, Lysaer had no space for fear. The scrying had shown him his enemy, and now the berserk need mauled through him, to tear living flesh and draw blood. He raised his weapon, levelled its barred cross-piece, and crouched to meet the boar's attack.

His move broke the beast's snuffling uncertainty. It gnashed razored ivory, lowered its coarse neck and charged.

Dew scattered before a snapping click of cloven hooves. The boar came on, a brute mass of churning sinew and foul, snorted breath.

But Lysaer saw no animal bearing down on the braced tip of his spear.

Imprinted against the vague darkness, he aimed instead at the black, glossy hair; the detested, trickster features of his half-brother.

Lysaer's lips peeled back in poisoned exultation as the boar pounded headlong toward his vitals. The spear graced his hands like a smoothed bar of light, nervelessly steady and sure.

Perhaps the crazed beast sensed its doom; or else the fickle wind cast the scent of oiled metal, poised ready to be sheathed in hot hide. At the crux of the last closing stride, the boar swerved. The spear jabbed its shoulder and ripped deep. Impetus drove the weapon home through its straining mass of muscle. Bone hammered and grated in vibration through the wood in Lysaer's grasp.

The wound he dealt was mortal, but not quick. The boar squealed its agony and thrashed. It tussled to gore, to a spray of gouged turf and bruised grasses. Its killer held fast to the spear shaft, partnered in a battering dance of death. Raised to sick thrill, Lysaer savoured fierce strength brought to helpless, thwarted rage; he gloried in his ascendance, and as his victim weakened, he revelled in its pain.

He twisted the spear, felt the blade slide past bone and bite deeper, to hack and ravage and bleed white. Through his curse-driven fervour of elation, he gloated in the knowledge that finally, his half-brother lay within reach.

Before the turn of the year, the unprincipled creature dying on his steel would be the Shadow Master, Arithon s'Ffalenn.

He hacked at the boar's carcass long past the final quiver of life. Then a last, savage shiver rocked through him. Chilled in running sweat, smeared with torn greens and the hot copper reek of spilled blood, Lysaer felt his obsessed fit of fury drain away.

Awakened to shamed honour, he discovered just how far from sanity the witch's filthy scrying had driven him.

The spear fell from his slackened fingers. Drained from the aftershock of magic, he bent, arms hugged to his breast. The stink of death and faeces revolted his civilized senses. He crouched, overcome, and was rackingly sick on the grass.

Captain Mayor Pesquil sighted him there, huddled in the muck beside the butchered boar, steaming in the cold air of twilight.

Prince Lysaer flinched at the swish of soft steps in the grass. He gathered himself and shoved erect. 'Don't touch me,' he said.

Pesquil looked him up and down, careful not to study the remains that lay mauled beyond salvage as a trophy. In damning, steely quiet, he noted, 'I see you took your beast without any contest at all.'

Untouched by remorse, Lysaer recovered the sticky shaft of his weapon and braced his bruised body to full height. 'Avenor's army will march to sure victory, now. I know where our enemy lies hidden. The main muster shall take place at Etarra. Then we'll need galleys, as fast as we can hire them, to sail our war host southward to Merior.'

'What are you talking about?' Pesquil snapped.

'Arithon s'Ffalenn.' Over bloodied fingers, Lysaer s'Ilessid smiled. 'We shall find him holed up in Merior, building ships to prey on merchant commerce. His pirate father did the same. If we can cross the continent and put our war host to sea, the Master of Shadow will lie in his grave by the winter.'

Feeling cleansed, Lysaer understood that the Koriani witch had been wise in her way to arrange his tryst with the boar. The catharsis of violence had restored his control. He could review her scrying now with equanimity. A detail slipped past in the first heat of vision pricked now to the forefront of his mind.

The bullion chest in the sand by his half-brother's foot, offered to bind honest craftsman, had carried an Etarran guild brand *as well as the wax seal of Tysan*. The Master of Shadow could never have acquired such a coffer, except through Lady Maenalle's collaboration.

Stiffened to sharp outrage, Lysaer said, 'Ath's mercy on her. We have beyond doubt been betrayed.' There and then in Pesquil's presence, he swore his royal oath to wreak vengeance upon the *caithdein* of Tysan. 'Mark my word, Lady Maenalle's life is forfeit. She has forsaken her realm and sent all my raided gold to serve the cause of Arithon s'Ffalenn.'

Interstices

In the glens beside Tysan's seacoast, a boar's blood clots in matted grass; a candle stub charged with energies from a dangerously significant scrying dusts trailers of failed smoke through an abandoned cottage; a prince rejoins his worried retinue; but unlike every other night, the Warden of Althain fails to track these events from his tower, immersed as he is in the deeps between stars in search of a colleague's lost spirit . . .

Within Alestron's state chamber, a dishonoured captain marked with raw whip scars stands straight to receive the sentence of his duke; but the words that condemn him to exile mean less than the knowledge that an envoy rides north to seek word of the war host being raised to hunt the Master of Shadow . . .

In Avenor, under low-bellied clouds and fine drizzle, the last companies gather under Tysan's royal banner, then form up in smart columns to march east; while before the arch of the gatehouse, Lady Talith sheds tears of farewell in her husband's embrace, saying, 'Kill the felon swiftly and return.'

XII. *ELAIRA*

Arithon's sloop *Talliarthe* slipped back into Merior's tiny anchorage after a late night passage. The fishermen abroad in the pearl grey of dawn simply saw her, returned without fanfare and tied off to an unused mooring. By sunup, Jinesse's young twins repeated the discovery. Their bout of ecstatic shouting rang shrill through the glassine air. Through the wheeling flocks of sea birds startled from the watch tower, the children rowed out in their dory and came back an hour later. Braced in the little boat's bow lay an exquisite bowl of Falgaire crystal crated in straw and a bolt of blue silk for their mother, sent with Arithon's compliments.

Disturbed at her washing by the widow's confounded dismay, the boarding house mistress offered counsel. 'Keep his gifts or sell them for silver, but don't be silly over nothing! Yon outsider's a man who knows his own mind.' The large woman thrust out the dripping end of a bedsheet. 'Hold this.' Her strong, collected hands wrung the cloth. 'You'll offend him, and deeply, if you slight him by sending them back.'

Returned to her cottage with her apron spattered with soap suds, and her hair tugged into a shag of wild ends by the sea breeze, Jinesse slammed her door and shot the bar. Then, unsettled to note how the shimmery, pastel silk heightened her thin-skinned, fair colouring, she locked the bolt away in her dower chest. The crystal bowl was too delicate for the kitchen. It lay unused behind glass in her dish cupboard, its luxury displaced as diamonds tossed in burlap. Even in gloom when the candles were cold, stray light struck the cut facets and woke a vibrant, rainbow shimmer, too rich to belong beside vessels of commonplace clay.

Then the gossip stormed through Merior like wildfire. In the front room of her herb shop, the Koriani enchantress still in residence received word from a young mother who stopped to collect an infusion for a convalescent child.

'The outsider's back, and no one knows why, except to use our village for a smuggler's haven.' In no hurry to leave, the goodwife offered a half copper, and tucked away the wrapped remedy in return. She fussed at the fringe on her shawl and added, 'You heard about that black brig which stopped here in his name? Well, she carried a cargo of gold and rare riches. The cobbler's wife says the whole cache was sailed west and buried in the sands of Sanpashir.'

When this comment raised nothing but silence, the woman tried a fresh angle. 'You know that rough woman captain and the outsider are in league. Both carry scars from past violence. Jinesse may well come to grief through her friendship. I should fear, were I in her place.'

'I don't believe Jinesse will suffer,' Elaira said firmly. Unbound hair mantled her shoulders, dimmed to brown smoke in the shadow as she stepped past the dormer. She dropped the coin into the milk crock that served her as strongbox, then returned.

If she knew more of the outsider's doings, she was unwilling to talk. Wide open and direct, eyes the fathomless, pale sheen of electrum stayed level and pinned on her client.

Disturbed by that close a scrutiny, or perhaps frozen out by the silence, the mother made haste and departed.

Elaira sighed and decided to brew tea to ease the starting, tight pangs of a headache. In place of relief, she felt deep unease, that intuition had served her correctly: Arithon s'Ffalenn had come back. Spared the painful indignity of chasing his shirt tails to Innish, as Morriel's orders would eventually have insisted, the enchantress shook off the unreasonable desire to throw down everything as the twins had, and run with skirts flying to the beach.

Temptation could mount to an insidious ache, to invent some excuse to call on Mistress Jinesse and ask if she had seen him, or talked, or knew how he had weathered the winter cooped up in the incense-soaked taverns of the southcoast.

An interval later, slouched on one elbow at her work table surrounded by stubs of chalk, snipped lengths of brown string, and twists of figured tin laid out to fashion sigils to repel iyats, Elaira stirred from troubled thought. She rubbed long-boned fingers at her temples, startled by the diced slant of sunlight through the casement; her hands had lain idle through the morning. In the sandy yard outside her window, the goat-bells had stilled, each animal tucked on folded knees under the patched shade of the scrub thorn.

Elaira grasped her oak stylus and selected a ribbon of metal. Resolute in concentration, she embossed the unquiet ciphers that fashioned a spell of go-hither into the wafer thin alloy. Arithon s'Ffalenn had returned to Merior. If he planned to stay, hearsay would inform her soon enough.

But the impact of the Shadow Master's intentions outpaced even the villagers' loose talk. *Black Drake* sheared into port by sundown. Hard in her wake came three merchant galleys crammed to their load lines with lumber from the Telzen mills. The fleet had brought its own lightermen and stevedores. The next day Merior's cramped quay seethed like a kicked ants' nest with oared boats, while cargoes of imported planking were offloaded and set down in stacks on the sandspit beyond the village. The arthritic old sailors left the boarding house porch to observe, and even the most clouded eye among them could not mistake seasoned oak; the sawn boards of spruce and fragrant cedar; the beech; the rare locust; the fine teak which rimmed the raked crests of the dunes like buttresses.

Delivered to the beaches above Merior to the last beam and billet came the marrow to fashion blue-water ships.

Speculative gossip led to spirited wagers, met by cheers from the winners when yet another galley bearing tools hove in from Southshire. Feylind took interest in *Black Drake*, then threw a swaggering tantrum when balked in her desire to have a red shirt like Captain Dhirken's. The trading sloop that used the Scimlade beaches for her yearly careening haled into port out of season. She delivered a master shipwright and seventeen journeyman craftsmen.

Onto the strand of Merior, seemingly overnight, came the sinew and skilled labour to begin the manufacture of hundred-ton keels. As suddenly, the load-bearing fleet raised anchor. To the beat of the drum and a white thrash of oars, or the crack and belly of filled canvas, the vessels made way and returned to their customary trade routes. Gusts from the north bore the tang of fresh timbers; then the rattling hail of hammer, saw and chisel, as crude shacks sprang up to house the influx of outsiders.

Merior's hardy villagers met over beer in jammed parlours, and lashed up a storm of troubled talk.

In plain words, Arithon told any who asked of his plans. He would build ten brigantines, dismantle his craftyard, and leave Merior unchanged by his tenancy.

Certainly his choice of location bore out the spirit of his promise. 'Not to fret,' said the gouty old fisherman who diced with his cronies beside the boarding house steps. 'Or why should yon outsider lay the bedlogs for his ways on the Scimlade sandspit? First heavy blow from the east, and Ath's seas'll scour his works away. Not being a landgrubbing fool, that's his stamp o' surety his roots aren't for keeping.'

'He's treated fair with Jinesse,' the wife who poured lager chimed in. 'Nobody's cheated. And he's said, for the noise and the bother, he'd fix any lugger's broken tackle and take no fee like a neighbour.'

But as the first timbers were sunk and fared smooth, men with comely young daughters found their worries less easily settled. The craftsmen who bunked in their ramshackle cabins earned silver with no place to spend it. Merior boasted no ready tavern or house of entertainment, as Dakar had gained bruises to determine. Approached in the sapphire twilight by a knot of fishermen off the luggers, Arithon heard through their complaint and made immediate contingency.

His warning was posted by dark, that any worker who caused trouble would be turned off without hearing; then that problem averted long before it arose, a boat was hired to bear the craftsmen in shifts for leavetime downcoast in Shaddorn.

Throughout the days of upheaval, the villagers' wild conjecture, the disorders of change adroitly smoothed over, Elaira kept to her shop. She cast no patterns of divination to mark the activity of the prince she had come to Merior for the unparalleled cold purpose of binding with ties of affection. Progress at the yard was on everyone's lips, through the week as the whipsaw pit was fashioned. Under Arithon's swarm of labourers, pole buildings for the joiner's shop, loft, and steam shed were raised and roofed. Summer winds off the ocean swept inland and raked up buttresses of thunderheads to lash squalls across Sickle Bay; in contrast, the peninsula's weather inclined to stay dry. The shakes for the walls were left stacked aside, while through the close, humid heat of afternoons, over the grumble of distant thunder, the first keel for an eighty foot brigantine was laid between stem and sternpost. Beset from sunrise to dark by the feverish clangour of hammers as the frames were set up and dubbed fair, Elaira employed no feminine artifice.

If the mores of the Koriani Order commanded her to offer herself as bait, for stubborn pride she would do no less and no more than maintain an obligatory residence. The village was too small, too close. If Arithon s'Ffalenn could avoid her throughout the two years ordained to build his fleet, his effort of itself framed a statement.

In the cool airs each dawn, she arose and lit her brazier to brew the day's decoctions and tisanes. In the wind-torn late afternoons, while storms flared and cracked across the bay, she walked the dunes to collect seaweed to distil into tincture of iodine. The weather might settle to its sultry summer pattern, but the days failed to pass unremarked. Teased by awareness of Arithon's presence, her thoughts stayed hooked to distraction, as though the boundaries of controlled quiet and trance were made unruly and permeable. The disciplined stillness required for her arts gave no surcease, but chafed and pressured her innermost nature to reclaim its desired alignment.

The small magecraft Elaira worked through her crystal, by which she enhanced the efficacy of her remedies, stroked her nerves to unwanted sensitivity until, on the wings of slipped thought, she could sense even Arithon's footfalls through the shared, sandy ground of Scimlade Tip.

Frustrated, irritable, she heaved a gusty sigh and battled her reluctance to face another morning fixing simples. Amid her bundles of dried goldenrod, tansy, and the skinned stems of aloe selected to mix a paste for lacerations, she cast a jaundiced glance over stoppered glass bottles in sorry need of her attention; her depleted stores of comfrey, gentian, and mint, perpetually in demand for babes who suffered from colic. A coil of hair slithered down her bare forearm, glinted with auburn like copper chipped through dark rust. She snapped the offending lock over her shoulder, and noticed the time lost to daydreams.

Brisk in self-reproach, Elaira rummaged behind her still for the poultice pot, dipped water from her pail, and chained it from the tripod to boil. The open doorway at her back let in the sea breeze, and the inventive notes of mocking birds who carolled to mark their spring nests. Cats from the fishmarket strolled in at will to rub through her ankles or sprawl in silken languor at her feet.

She resisted the temptation to rise and serve them the left-over cod from her breakfast. Ruled by iron will and the Koriani creed to ease what she could of mortal suffering, she murmured the litany to focus her innermind, and stopped, mid-phrase, as the light changed. A mild chill crossed her spine. Subtle as a wisp of cirrus might dampen the fall of a sun mote, the cool sensation between her shoulderblades resolved to clear warning that a presence observed her from the doorway.

Thrilled through by a ridiculous rush of joy, she broke off, considered; then bit her lip, quelled her smile, and turned around.

Arithon s'Ffalenn leaned like a waif against her lintel.

Restrained by the nuance of mages, he would not cross her threshold without an express invitation, though in sun-faded breeches, laced at the calf, and no shoes, he looked common as a journeyman carpenter. His shirt was full-sleeved and open. Ringless, loose hands were tucked in folded arms, and hair straight and glossy as a crow's spread primaries fanned the tanned wedge of his brow. His lips stayed chiselled and serious, an odd contradiction to the strung, wary poise behind his candour.

Just barely, Elaira quashed her impulse to speak first. Her eyes, pale slate, awaited his pleasure in bland inquiry.

Arithon averted his glance, tapped a finger too fine-jointed for a labourer's against his elbow, then smiled and gave back the ground he had stolen through surprise. 'The shipyard's master has learned how I like things done. Since the works can be left to themselves for the morning, I thought I might call.'

The pot over the brazier burbled to a boil. In pretence of seeming busy, Elaira bent to shorten its chain, then reached for the mint and the stone-bladed knife she preferred over steel for cutting herbs. In careful, measured increments she trimmed and crumbled the leaves on a clean square of linen. 'You don't suffer from contusions or colic? That's ill timing.'

She felt his attention flick over her, sharpened. Before his study could read her, she rocked him off-balance again. 'Come in, or go, or say what you want. I'm not going to fly out of the window.'

He laughed, but stepped no closer. 'You know herbals and remedies. I'd a mind to ask if you'd teach me.'

Jarred by his unexpected request, Elaira dropped her knife with a clatter. The tip struck an earthenware crock and snicked off a chip of enamel. 'Why?' she said, then instantly regretted it as she sensed through his fractional recoil an answer too painfully obvious.

Arithon s'Ffalenn had been mage-trained. The strictures of his discipline would insist on fair balance: spell paired with counter-ward; any application of force, no matter how small, matched in its kind by restraint. Hounded by a curse that might demand bloodshed on a field of unbridled violence, straight principle would drive him to seek a surgeon's knowledge to bind wounds and set bones and heal.

'Ath, I'm sorry,' Elaira blurted. 'Never mind. My tongue runs ahead of sound thought all the time, it's the monumental failure of my upbringing.'

Not quite disarmed, Arithon looked back in spare amusement as she faced him. 'I don't believe it.'

Elaira grinned. 'Well, it's true. Ask how many birch rods my seniors broke trying to retrain my attitude. They say I have a rotten, stubborn mind.'

'Is that a refusal?' His voice held a note she would have sold her crystal to decipher.

But the clamour of her feelings rang far too insistent to leave any space for intuition. Elaira dusted crumbled herbs from her fingers while the poultice pot steamed and spat at her elbow, its agitation as thick as her thoughts. Acutely attuned to just who this man was, of what he might come to mean to her, she balanced her own desperation against the spun thread of his control. Although he would leave without protest if she asked, Morriel had bidden her to solicit his interest, no matter the means or the cost.

'I might teach you herbs and their physical handling,' Elaira said at last, and hesitated.

He came to her immediate rescue. 'I'm certainly aware some constraints must be set.' How else to protect the arcane secrets she was sworn to keep within her order? But he left this unspoken in natural reticence, as any spirit must who had schooling in the subtleties of power; his background in all likelihood lent him access to such knowledge, since many of the plants used for medicines held magical properties as well.

He finished, 'Even with the connections to ritual left out, your recipes would be better founded than any I could get from a hedge witch.'

The moment hung, while Elaira fought through a turmoil of indecision.

Arithon could not know what he laid in her hands: the one opening her heart could not deny, hand in glove with the opportune chance Morriel Prime desired to bind him. The sculptured grace of his fingers stayed vulnerable and stilled, while his eyes watched, the same suspended green of a tide pool poised between flood and ebb. Then, as the interval grew prolonged, a sharp, marring change pricked him into dismay. 'Ath in his mercy, not you as well. *You can't be afraid of me also.*'

Impelled from uncertainty by a response too self-honest to deny, Elaira waved him inside. 'By all means, if you're worried, come in and terrify me further. The upset is frankly quite welcome.' The crease between her brows eased to pleasure. 'Won't grubbing for root stock spoil your hands?'

'I can hope I'll enjoy finding out.' Irrevocably then, Arithon crossed over her threshold, and through the one vital moment she needed to read him, the light interfered and hazed his form from behind.

Her cottage was small, two meagre rooms conjoined by a single doorway. Elaira felt each of his light, restless steps, while his busy mind surveyed her dwelling. She wondered what he saw, since meticulously little of her character lay exposed for prying eyes.

The rafters supported a storage loft, accessed by a narrow ladder. On pegs spiked into the beams, the roots she had foraged through the winter months hung in string bundles to dry. Glare through the salt-filmed dormers caught on the incised clay seals to fend off mould and stray iyats. Beyond her plank table, a mismatched rack of shed deer antlers hung her cloak. Straight boards in Merior became seats for dories, so her cottage boasted no shelves. Her jars of prepared remedies were stacked in willow hampers along the wall, sorted and labelled, and preserved by runes scribed in ink ground from minerals. A brick oven and the coiled glass tubes of an apothecary's still jammed the hearth, the overburdened mantle above crammed with jars of wooden spoons and mismatched kitchen crockery.

As impersonal as the room were the clothes Elaira wore, of grey twill and cambric edged with flax ribbon dyed with mulberry.

She disdained earrings; kept no jewellery beyond a braided silver bracelet dulled from careless wear. The quartz pendant strung on light chain at her neck was no ornament, but the working badge of her order. Her feet and her hands were brown and bare, hatched at wrists and ankles in tiny scabs and white scars from briar scratches taken while foraging.

Conscious of Arithon's regard like a play of pressed air across her skin, Elaira added comfrey and thyme to her mix. She talked to dispel her unease, while he quartered her workroom again, his caged-panther passage too deft to cause disturbance, and his clasped hands not touching anything. 'Do you know how to bless and cut oak? If so, you can start by building yourself a stool. I'd have you sit down. Is it some older habit, or piratical dishonesty, or did Halliron let you pace like a ghost?'

Poised alongside the thin paper spread with flowers too delicate to preserve by hanging, Arithon spun in wide surprise. 'You'd rather instruct a blunderer?'

'I don't know,' Elaira said, truthful. Aware as Jinesse had never been of his capacity to perceive nuance in others, but to be misunderstood himself, she added, 'You could say I've just undertaken to find out.'

Her unexpected barb let him laugh. 'Ath, you are forthright. After two weeks of bargaining with unctuous sawmillers, I find that a welcome relief.'

'Well it can't last.' Elaira grinned also. 'People aren't fond of ticks or midges that nip too close to the skin. Or so said the old thief who raised me. He was wise enough at least not to die on a felon's scaffold.' She raised the square of linen and tipped the crushed herbs in her pot. 'I'd planned to go foraging this afternoon. Unless you like watching poultices boil, we'll meet then? No study of herbals can start anywhere else but with the live plants in the field.'

'Lady, consider me enchanted to accept.' Arithon returned an unfettered smile, then bowed and as soundlessly left her.

So began an odd, suspended interval, fractured from connection to past or future like a jewel unencumbered by a setting.

Spring flowed across the Scimlade peninsula, ephemeral as reflections on glass, the seasonal cycles of trees, moon and tides more subtle in tropical latitude. Only the discerning observer could track the changes as vegetation quickened and renewed, to the flight of ocean birds in migration. Arithon had been well-taught by the mage who had raised him. He knew to walk barefoot in her medicinal garden, and to dig for roots with wooden implements. He had a sharp eye for detail. By day, they walked the marshes where blue heron stalked fish, he with his coarse, sailor's trousers rolled above the knee and a collecting bag slung at his shoulder, and Elaira with her skirts kirtled up.

The virtues of purslane, stargrass, and marsh mallows were partially familiar to him. He could lay hands on the trunks of red maples and willows, and in an odd, listening stillness, sense the quickened flow of spring sap. Her guidance was scarcely needed to show which bark to harvest, or how much to cut from one tree. The small herbs and mosses native only to Athera or partial to southern climate, Elaira pointed out and explained as they perused the sun-drenched glens and sandy scrub for tasselflower, poke, and boneset, or the deepest shade of the oak hammocks for galls. She was pleased to see he did not learn her lore by rote, but lingered on his knees in the hot, sandy soil to draw into himself the nuance of each plant, to seek the hidden, intuitive secrets inherent in leaves and flowers and roots.

As he knelt in clean earth, his hands cupped beneath the tiny, starred bell of a nightshade's flower, Elaira stole the moment for herself, to align the surface traits of the living man with the aura pattern revealed by her First Senior. The oddity struck her, that an uncharacteristic diffidence flawed his bearing as he bent a queerly desperate intensity over the plant under study.

A scarcely visible tremor flawed his touch, before he curled his fingers shut and knuckled his fist against his forehead.

Wary of a half-glimpsed gap in his defences, Elaira froze where she stood. Something had upset his mage-sight. Warned by deep instinct that incautious words would drive him to protect himself through temper, she scarcely dared to breathe.

The stricken depth of her silence translated through to him anyway.

After a second, Arithon glanced up at her, his gaze something more than shadowed, and his black hair whorled against his damp skin by the anguished pressure of his fingers. 'You know, don't you,' he accused in blunt defence.

Elaira lowered her basket to the ground. With the mild, slow moves a bee-keeper might use to steal honey from a smoked hive, she settled in the meadow beside him and arranged her mud-splashed skirt around her ankles. A killdeer ran piping to draw notice from its nest, while high overhead, a black vulture scribed spiralling circles.

'I've guessed something's wrong,' she admitted at length. 'Common nightshade is a poison and a narcotic. Used for healing, the extract can act on the eyes, and the heart, or ease a child with the colic. But it has no property to induce prying that I was ever aware of.'

The tiniest twitch of a smile turned his lips. 'Subtle lady,' he said, but chose not to share whatever pain had grazed so near the surface. The elbow she used to prop her shoulder rested scant inches from his thigh. As always, he made no move in avoidance; but as scrupulously, he also never touched. Even by chance, over the roughest of trails, he maintained a meticulous distance.

To pressure that barrier as Jinesse had done would be a grievous mistake. Through reticent silence, Elaira sensed recrimination. Unwittingly, he had relaxed too much. The ease of her company had laid siege to a reserve he had no inclination to slacken.

But before he found the courtesy to escape from her presence, Elaira shot him a sidewise grin. 'What was that ruckus at the yard the other morning?'

Green eyes widened through a second of surprise. Then, in an explosion impelled by relief, Arithon snorted into laughter. 'Dakar. What else? We've hired in a blind rope splicer with a tongue like a viper. The framers took bets on a contest of insults, the winner to mete out some prankish punishment.'

Elaira peeled the sticky hair from her nape, then flicked out the ends to rebraid them. 'And Dakar lost? What was the forfeit?'

His glance drawn to admire her dark locks, that sparked to bronze fire where the sun touched, Arithon set his chin on crossed wrists. 'Old Ivel bet the lads that our prophet was too fat to squeeze into an empty tar cask. Dakar managed, of course, as a point of sore pride. But when his elbows got jammed, and he asked for help to get out, an enterprising joiner clapped on the lid and nailed him in. He wound up adrift in Garth's pond.'

'Jinesse's twins fished him out?' Elaira asked between gasps.

'No.' Arithon wiped his eyes and snatched the breath to answer. 'Are you kidding? Feylind would as likely raise cheers while he drowned, and Fiark would sling rocks at his tombstone. Dakar shouted and pounded until the staves sprung and began to take in water. The old men who idle on the boarding house porch finally netted him to shore and broached the cask. But they filched his beer store as payment.'

Restored to companionable ease, Arithon gathered himself to his feet. Against custom, he offered his hand to assist Elaira up, and in gifted inspiration, she released his warm fingers a half instant before he did so on his own.

Their eyes met.

'Rare lady,' he said again. But the shadows were gone and he smiled.

After that, he relaxed in her presence as Halliron Masterbard must have known him, freed for a brief space in time from the burdens inflicted by Desh-thiere's curse and royal bloodline. The work at the shipyard drove him to relentless hard labour, while the frames were bevelled, then set erect and dubbed fair, to be followed under the harsh sunlight by keelson, side keelsons, and bilge stringers.

The hour after the knightheads were set, he reappeared at the cottage, his clothing pungent with a resinous sprinkle of spruce shavings. Every moment he could spare was spent in Elaira's company.

Foraging trips drew them further afield, into the deep, still bayous that fringed the shores of Sickle Bay, alive with cormorants that startled from their step with awkward cries, and the singing hum of summer insects. By noon, they found refuge in trackless glens of red cedar, alive with jewelled moths clinging wing-folded in the undergrowth. They carved footprints over the sand hills, amid the clacking, arrowed flit of dragonflies. In a silence removed from the shipyard's brisk clamour, Arithon allowed the salve of Elaira's companionship to ease his veneer of tight reserve. Time and again she resisted any foray into topics that leaned toward the personal. Unlike everyone else, she never once questioned his integrity. He began to laugh easily, and spoke more than once of the high mage who had raised him on the world beyond the West Gates.

'My grandfather was sparing in his praise of apprentices,' Arithon volunteered on a night outing. They had gone to gather herbs for talismans of ward best harvested under influence of the moon, and now rested side by side on a fallen log while a fox barked deep in the brush. Arithon toyed with a storm-broken branch, exploring by touch the tiny, green buds of a live oak's acorns, that ripened light tan and jet black. 'My grandfather insisted we think for ourselves and achieve for our own satisfaction. Deep study of the mysteries were their own tough path, he always said. To live for approval of others was a pitfall that begged a false turning.'

Cued by a queer little hole in her gut, that *now* was the moment she had angled for, Elaira refused to look at him as she said, 'And do you seek approval from others to know you did right in Etarra's attack on Deshir forest?'

Her reference to the children killed with the clans in his defence made him surge to his feet in recoil. The oak branch thudded earthward with a dropped thrash of leaves and his eyes bored down at her, anguished. 'Who else beside the clansmen who survived could be aware that the deaths of those children were beyond fate's grasp to prevent? Daelion Fatemaster show his mercy in fair judgement for their murders. There is no absolution, no redress. For I can never be reconciled with what happened in my name that day on the banks of Tal Quorin.'

'You swore an oath as Rathain's prince to protect your feal clans.' Elaira looked up, her features traced with silver light. If he wanted to flee or strike out at her presumption, he was stopped by the tears that sheened her eyes.

'What makes you take my troubles for your own?' The veined silk of the oak leaves shivered as he began and checked a step forward. A moonbeam cast through the boughs overhead played like a wisp of dropped floss over the edge of his cheekbone, then grazed insubstantial as spirit light across his full sleeve and the attenuated knuckles of one hand.

'I wasn't, in fact,' Elaira said in dry rebuke. 'It's an entrenched bad habit, like saving wing-broken birds and rescuing waterlogged spiders out of horse troughs.' She threw back a damp smile, unwilling to draw unfair advantage from the birth-gifted empathy that ran in him deep enough to lacerate. 'Did I ever tell you what I did as a penniless chit on the day I caught the Mayor of Morvain's son tormenting a mongrel in an alley?'

'Rare lady,' he said, softened at last to ease his guard. 'You did not.' A shadow limned against gauzy plumes of ground mist, he bent, twitched the oak branch aside, and resettled himself at her feet. While the small southland finches rustled in the treetops, he listened as she told of the exploit that left a young boy with injured fingers, and which set an end to her freedom of the streets, to place her in Koriani fosterage.

'The herb witch who sold simples to the prostitutes had always insisted I had talent,' she finished, her hands nested tight on her knees and her hair channelled into silky torrents by the bleached linen pleats of her blouse. 'If I also suspected the amethyst in the pin I'd just stolen had once been a mage's scrying crystal, the dog was terrified and about to end up hamstrung, and I was too angry to care. Right or wrong, I copied the symbol I had seen the poor-quarter herb witch use to ill-wish patrons who cheated her. I recall not being surprised, or even horrified, as the knife slipped in falling and stabbed the mayor's son through the wrist.'

Enfolded in the milky warm air of the night, steadied by Arithon's silence, Elaira eased knotted fingers and shrugged. 'I escaped sentence and burning because the Koriani undertook to heal the child in exchange for a claim to take me into permanent fosterage. They said if they hadn't intervened, the boy would never have recovered. His nerves had been severed. Not by the steel, but by an ill wish wrought of raw magic.' She looked aside at him, her eyes like flawed quartz, and the evanescent scent of her melded warp through weft with the heavier perfume of cedar. 'If I can presume, I may understand, just a little, how wretched you must feel.'

She ended with a clipped cough to mask a shiver. 'Do you know, it often still haunts me. I never knew if the mongrel was spared.'

Amid the rich, living fabric of the woodland, the man at her feet seemed a clamped knot of silence, turned in on himself in stark brooding. Alarmed, that perhaps she had dared too much, Elaira summoned full command of her art and looked at him; and what she read in every locked joint and in the raised tilt of his head was a longing of unbearable proportion. She ached to reach out, to test his emotion and see whether she could shape from one vulnerable moment a bond of immutable trust. She wished to touch him as she had never yearned for anything else in all of her proscribed life.

But instinct reared through desire and stopped her.

Without knowing why, she broke his mood, sharply, and led him off on a tangent. 'What words would your s'Ahelas grandfather have for me, to care more for a dog than a child?'

'He would have said, of such a child, that the dog was the more blameless spirit. In my case, he warned on no uncertain terms. The powers of mages and the burdens of a ruler make an incompatible legacy.' Arithon clasped his arms around drawn-up knees, his admission burred rough as he added, 'Once, I could have listened and been free.'

Over the rasp of spring crickets, a whippoorwill called its slurred triplets. While Arithon pursed his lips and whistled back like a mimic, Elaira reviewed his phrasing, for as a bard, he was wont to be precise; and swift as a prick through crowding thoughts, she grasped the implication to his statement: '*For I can never be reconciled with what happened in my name . . .*'

'You *knew*!' she exclaimed with a force that scared the bird silent. 'Before Etarra's armies ever marched, you understood the northern clans were going to be slaughtered.'

He regarded the sequinned edges of the leaves, his lashes widened as if by some force of concentrated focus, he could interpret the tracks of the wind as it brushed through the palms. Beyond these, across stands of saltmarsh dusted soot-grey in the moonlight, the stippled prints of stray gusts threw pewter sheets over the jet waters of the bay.

But the soft anonymity of the night had lost any power to calm.

'Their chieftain had Sight,' Arithon confessed on a struck note of anguish. 'Steiven's vision held truth, more's the pity. I backed up his claim with a tienelle scrying.'

In his royal presence or his absence, Deshir had been fated to suffer

Etarra's invasion. The pain of past dilemma sharpened every angle in the face of the Teir's'Ffalenn charged and tied to an unwanted royal heritage.

'*So, prince, are you guilty?*' Asandir had once asked of an event too entangled to separate a whole verdict with clean certainty.

Elaira mapped the surge of trapped feelings in a man seldom given to shared confidence, her fingertips touched to her spell-crystal to enhance her clarity of sight. But nothing of pity could stiffen her for the blow as Arithon turned toward her, and disclosed, 'The clans of Deshir should have died to a man, had I not stayed and used sorcery in defence. *That was all that held me to the letter of my sovereign oath.* So you see,' he ended in an agony he might never unburden, 'it might not matter, to know if the puppy was saved. More than two hundred clansmen survived the fight at Tal Quorin. But there is no settlement to be found in such a victory. I can't sort past the deaths and the bloodshed to say if their lives matched the cost.'

A slow breath unreeled from Elaira's throat. Eyes closed, her knuckles pressed to her lips to stem the fatal urge to cast off her vows and tell him the damaging intent of her Prime Senior's directive, she locked down a cry of pure misery.

Morriel Prime had been mistaken, and Lirenda dead wrong, to seek a binding to track this prince's movements. The Fellowship of Seven had judged well to insist that the s'Ffalenn compassion in Arithon's character had ruled his actions to a pernicious degree. Yet if mitigating circumstances argued his case for the butchery of Etarra's army in Deshir, the future offered no such remission.

Indeed, no sounder option existed than to choose as Arithon had, to build ships to escape in extended exile.

Elaira had not even realized she wept until droplets splashed hot on her knuckles. She sensed a rustle of movement, and then Arithon was standing, a bleak silhouette against the boughs with their netted sparkle of spring stars. Two hands pressed briefly on her shoulders, warm and something less than steady. 'I'm sorry, rare lady.' He sighed with a sibilance like pearls rubbed in velvet. 'I've done you no kindness tonight. If I grieve for any small thing, it is that.'

Then his touch melted back and left her desolate.

Cold and alone in the wine-rich anonymity of the forest, Elaira let the tears slip through her fingers. Time itself blurred until the emotion welled dry and burned out of her.

She faced one last bitter thought.

What the Master of Shadow needed from Merior was the release his proscribed fate would not allow: for Lysaer's armies were already moving west, to repeat and compound Strakewood's tragedy in the coils of Deshthiere's curse.

If the graceful brigantines mapped out in the sail-shed were not finished and launched by that hour, Arithon s'Ffalenn would never survive to be hounded by his conscience. He would instead become torn out of life, cornered like a rat on the beach.

Beacon

Summer sunset rinsed like a spill of scarlet dye over the spire of Althain Tower. Brassy heat fretted curls in the vine leaves latched over its age-gritted stone while the hour subsided into afterglow. Outlined by a window, and lined in sky clear as indigo-stained glass; diminished beneath his laden bookshelves, Sethvir listened to the squeak of a loose shutter and the dry, whispered winds off the desert. Beyond these, like a strand of silvered thread in common linen, he sensed the bright play of power that channelled through the third lane. Each facet of its grand mystery keyed into harmony with the wheeling stars. Scribed by the dance of sun, moon and tide, the strung, static matrix of harmonics plunged through a sliding shift in resonance: and the earth itself rang with the advent of solstice.

The Warden of Althain started erect. Touched by belated recollection of company about to arrive, he blotted his pen nib on his cuff.

His remedy for lapsed hospitality was to quarter the library like a fishing heron, snatching papers off his littered table. He raked his unshelved books into tipsy piles, grabbed bits of string and augury cards to use as stopgap markers, then gave up and left the last covers flopped open, stacked in alcoves and unswept corners.

Inkwells that lacked stoppers remained where they stood, since every cupboard and aumbrey lay crammed already with oddments.

Asandir arrived at the lower gate before Althain's Warden thought to rummage for a comb to clear the month's tangles from his beard. His neglected grooming scarcely mattered. No others would come this season. Traithe was at King Eldir's court in Ostermere to ease a dispute between the Elkforest clans and the merchants of Quaid; Luhaine remained entrenched at Meth Isle to assist its guardian spellbinder to quell a resurgence of karth-eels.

In Third Age Year fifty-six forty-five, the Fellowship's solstice convocation of necessity was reduced to a partnership of two.

Worn by more than long leagues in the saddle, Asandir dropped into the seat by the casement. With him came a sulphurous tang of brimstone. His sleeve cuffs were marred with black-rimmed perforations pricked by a fall of live sparks. The ends of his shoulder-length hair hung tarnished and raggedly singed.

'I'm fortunate not to have burns,' Asandir admitted, just back from renewing the bindings which confined the fire-breathing Khadrim to the Sorcerers' Preserve. The winged predators held an uncanny penchant for knowing when Fellowship reserves were taxed thinnest. Where they sensed weakness, they would harry like a wolf pack, inspired to a frenzy of bloodlust.

Too reticent for speech, the Warden of Althain roved a restless circuit of the table. He touched objects and book spines in aimless passing, his eyes not just distant, but glazed.

Asandir sharpened to attention.

His piercing, worried survey of Sethvir's jumbled caches showed him a scraggle of dried herbs, three nuggets of amber glass, and a wren's moulted flight feathers scattered like slate knives amid of a clutch of round stones from a stream bottom. These were netted in the gossamer windings of the usual visiting spider. Disturbed by the abandoned look to the clutter, and nary a tea mug in sight, Asandir pinned his colleague with imperious concern. 'What's happened?'

Sethvir started, blinked, then thumped down in the nearest windowseat to a riled, dusty puff from a cushion. 'What hasn't? I have too much news, and every bit of it grim.'

Since spoken words were a bother, Sethvir gave a haunted shrug, then shared, through a merciless, crystal-clear vision, an event scarcely ten hours old . . .

Cloudy dawn sheathed the peaks of the Thaldeins. The heavy air muffled the shod ring of hooves and flapped the fringed cloths of the banners: the crown and star of Tysan's royal blazon paired with a new-made sigil, a sunburst ablaze on a white field that Princess Talith had sewn to commemorate the alliance against the Shadow Master. Now, the trained war host from Avenor laboured up the switched-back curves that laced rocky promontories, the men on foot flushed from exertion and each winded mount patched in sweat.

Ahead lay the Pass of Orlan.

Nervous officers mustered their companies into tighter formation. Over the bunched columns, wary of ambush by barbarian archers, Lysaer s'Ilessid projected his gift in a magnificent blanket of hazed light. The ward glowed as starlight on snow, a gossamer shimmer sheeted through veilings of cloud.

The footsoldiers marched fully-armoured for battle. Ahead stretched the defile where their liege's proud company had once been reduced to a pauper's march to Erdane. A dire score remained to be settled from that raid, since Lysaer's stolen wealth had come to be transferred into the Shadow Master's cause. Restitution had been promised for the slight to the realm. Blood would be claimed for due justice.

Yet no barbarian ambush lurked at the height of the pass. Only the whine of the winds met the scouts sent to search, and white mist, and cruel scarps, and dark rock.

The cavalcade crawled on through the defiles. The challenge appeared first as a shadow sketched against darker grey: the *caithdein* herself, clad in no finery at all. Lady Maenalle's leathers had never been dyed, a significant slight, though perhaps only Lysaer understood. This time their meeting did not signify even the dignified colour of her office, the black traditionally worn in the presence of sovereign blood.

The badge of Tysan's regency was sewn at her breast, indigo and gold: the hues of sun and sky that shone through and framed her between precipice and vertical rock.

Straight as a sword, but weaponless, the *caithdein* of Tysan stood afoot in the path of the advance riders, the standard-bearers, the tall lancers three abreast that formed the block of the elite royal bodyguard. The officer in the vanguard drew rein before her and signalled his column to a halt.

The crack of hooves subsided. A horse snorted to a jingling chime of bit rings. Silence abided, shrill with the mewling cries of hawks. The gusts of high altitude moaned across stone, while the tight-meshed columns behind disarranged to make way for Lysaer s'Ilessid.

Caithdein, Lady Maenalle, offered the prince no obeisance. She stepped forward, her cropped hair wind-whipped and bare of even a circlet. She offered no royal address, but glanced in contempt at the golden bloom of light sheeted through the breaking clouds overhead. 'Does your Grace fear an ambush? Send out scouts. Search the rocks. They are empty.'

'Once before they were not.' Lysaer reined back his mount, who protested restraint and jibbed sideways. 'Your clans have earned little footing for trust. Do you presume and come asking my forbearance?'

'You have my word there are no archers in this pass,' Maenalle replied.

'If there were, they would be dead men.' Lysaer lifted a gloved fist. The ward he had raised as a shield against arrows flared white-hot, then burned away in a dazzling snarl of sparks. While the horses in his company shied and plunged at his back, and his officers steadied them, cursing, he added, 'Speak quickly. My mood isn't kindly or patient.'

Maenalle met his arrogance as she might treat with an importunate child. 'You've dared to claim Avenor and stand to arms by right of your bloodline, although you're unsanctioned for ruling power. As a man who would wrest advantage from this realm in pursuit of a personal feud, I make my formal protest. For the good of this kingdom, I demand you abandon your campaign to kill the last Prince of Rathain. Arithon s'Ffalenn is no threat to Tysan. The Fellowship of Seven has named your cause false, and my duty lies first to the land.'

Lysaer gave back cold contradiction. 'In that loyalty you are forsworn already.' Breeze ruffled his hair and the trappings on his mount in a running, pale fire of stirred gold. 'What are the Fellowship, if not in league with the Master of Shadow? You also have lent him your support. Against that specifically, I warned.'

Maenalle's hawk-yellow eyes never wavered. 'Coin and goods levied in Rathain were sent back to their sovereign prince, through the sorcerers' auspices. To what end the Teir's'Ffalenn disposes of what's his is no affair of mine, nor yours either, get of s'Ilessid. This I will say, before witnesses. If you are still the man you were born to become, a prince true to your heritage with Tysan's given charter as your law, you will turn about. Command your captains to retire your troops and leave Rathain's affairs in peace.'

Lysaer inclined his head in heavy sorrow. 'You ask too much. Arithon s'Ffalenn is a danger to us all. For the safety of innocents, no scion of my line worth his name could stand down.'

'Dare you be first then, to spill the blood of a *caithdein* of the realm?' Maenalle said.

'I'll do less.' Lysaer s'Ilessid uttered sentence. 'I will invoke town law and bid Isaer's executioner to end the life of a thief who plunders caravans.' He gestured to his officers, gloved fingers a raked blaze of jewels against a sudden lance of full sunlight. 'Take her.'

Two captains dismounted at his bidding. At need, they borrowed lead reins from their mounts' harness in readiness to bind a prisoner.

Lady Maenalle spared their approach not a glance. Bred to serve at the right hand of princes, her pride of bearing approached a near physical force, tempered well to stand royalty down. 'Think what you do! Appoint my death and you forswear guest oath, given in amity at my hearthstone.'

Over the heads of his hesitant officers, Lysaer snapped a rebuttal. 'Better I be forsworn as a man than the justice of this realm become debased. No affectation of courtesy will mitigate the punishment due for your act.' Implacable in regret, he added, 'Who am I, to uphold my personal honour before the protection of my townsfolk? They are untrained in magecraft, reliant upon my gift for their defence. Are Rathain's people any less helpless than they, to be abandoned to a sorcerer turned criminal?'

Unbending, Maenalle gave him back her freezing silence.

And still her captors vacillated. A sharp word from their sovereign was required to jolt them to resume their given duty.

The elderly woman did not flinch, even as they laid hands on her unadorned wrists, jerked them together and bound them in leather. Throughout the course of their handling, while the gold star blazon was torn from her jerkin, Lady Maenalle's wide eyes remained locked upon Lysaer's face.

Only when they finished and cast her trussed on her knees before the hooves of the royal charger did the *caithdein* deliver her last word. 'Beware, oathbreaker. The authority of my office shall pass through the Fellowship sorcerers to my grandson. Tysan's clans remain loyal to your line, false prince, but for you, our goodwill is forfeit. From this day forward, expect an arrow from the shadows, poison in your cup, and a knife at your throat, among my people. My life is offered, that they will know you for what you have become: no saviour, but the slave of the Mistwraith's design.'

Lysaer regarded the woman he had ordered broken through a moment of pitying quiet. Then he said, 'To your sorrow, brave lady, and to the waste of your life, you are misled. I ride to war as defender of peace against a man who was born with no conscience. The great of this land, of which you were one, diminish us all when they fall sway to endangering influence. If the crown of this kingdom was once under Fellowship province to bestow, for the good of all people, I claim it back.' He gathered his reins without triumph. 'Where lies the virtue in tradition and what good is law, when its use has been turned to threaten innocents? I give you my hope, that when the Master of Shadow has been thwarted, your clans may one day come to welcome me.'

'They may live to swear fealty to your sons,' Maenalle said. 'If my life should fall to the sword of Isaer's headsman, on my heart's blood, I promise, never you.'

The vision snapped apart like age-rotted tapestry scattered to dust in a gale. Sethvir hunched by the casement, his beard clasped in thin, ink-stained fists. He said in haggard grief, 'Lysaer was prince enough to keep his men in hand. They did not mishandle her beyond the indignity of shackles, but placed her under guard in a mule cart to bear her for formal arraignment.'

Asandir locked his fingers, knuckle on bone, in a white mesh of fury on the tabletop. Head bent, eyes shut, he scarcely felt the stroke of desert air across his skin. While the power in him shimmered in leashed stasis, and his flesh, a vessel too well-tempered to crack, stayed locked into stillness, he wept in straight sorrow, and lamented an event his Fellowship could not stay.

True sight must not be undone before emotion. Root and cause for Maenalle's downfall lay in the Mistwraith's curse. Even if the means lay at hand to sunder its hold upon the princes, for the lady who was the dedicated *caithdein* of Tysan, salvation must come too late.

Fifteen days would see her dead on a scaffold in Isaer, by town law and s'Ilessid command.

A *caithdein* with the courage of lions and an integrity more steadfast than diamond, struck down in dishonour by the hand of her own prince: the epitaph carried a venomous sting. For Maenalle, there could be no more ugly an ending, no more bitter a wreckage of cherished hopes.

'We are indeed come on ill times,' said Asandir, chastened by remembrance of the Mistwraith's first entry through South Gate, then the uprising that dethroned the high kings. Beset by such trials five centuries in the past, not a living member of his Fellowship had conceived how the tangle would breed tragic consequence.

Now, he dreaded to ponder what shape the future might take.

Huddled by the casement, Sethvir turned his old man's profile toward the first, scattered stars, his beard like hooked yarn in the pestering play of the wind. Better than any, he knew Maenalle's mind. His sighted talent had tracked the bitter hour as she had weighed her course of action, then made her choice to dispatch her messenger to Althain Tower. As if his train of thought had been spoken, the Warden of Althain concluded, 'She saw in the Teir's'Ffalenn a hope of protection for her clans, should the worst befall and Desh-thiere's curse lead to more cruel persecution. I could do no less then, but match her steel courage and see her missive passed on to Arithon.'

Given the burdens inherent in his post, Sethvir's pragmatic wisdom displayed daunting toughness. Pained to humility by the decisions borne alone by Althain's long-suffering warden, Asandir forced a change of subject. 'What do you know of Kharadmon?'

Sethvir shook his head in befuddled irritation and fired back visions in jumbled summary.

The hastily-vacated cottage of the Koriani Senior who inhabited a glen near Avenor; then the old enchantress herself, veiled and cloaked and swathed in sigils of secrecy, on foot to seek her Prime with a message of pressing importance; then the bones of a boar in a trampled dell, the skull laced still in the spent, pallid glimmer of the Koriani summoning spell that had goaded it onto the spear. Nearby, abandoned, lay the death weapon, imprinted by the geas-turned hatred that had driven the motive of its killer . . .

'The upshot?' Asandir prompted, as yet too perturbed by the news out of Camris to track his colleague's vaulting chains of logic.

Rare exasperation flared blue-green eyes to full focus. 'You didn't note the energy signature for exchange and consent, nor the tell-tale discharge invoked by Desh-thiere's curse?' Sethvir qualified. 'Lysaer s'Ilessid struck some bargain in exchange for a Koriani scrying. He's certain to know Arithon's in Merior.'

'At what price?' Asandir said.

Distempered enough to tug at the knots in his beard, Sethvir snapped back to the displaced thread of conversation. 'I don't know. At the time, I was too deep in trance in search of Kharadmon to track the event at its origin. Whatever mischief's afoot, the upshot will surface soon enough.'

That time, Asandir caught the infinitesimal hitch in the fabric of Sethvir's explanation. 'Kharadmon,' he blurted, a stab of alarm through his vitals. '*That's* what has you vexed! Ath's infinite pity, what worse disaster did you find?'

Sethvir shot out of his nook in a galvanic heave of distress. 'That's the problem,' he whispered from the shadows, his mind locked again on the limitless sky through the casement. '*I found no trace of Kharadmon at all.*'

Asandir braced spread hands against the table as if the very floor had rocked under him. 'Nothing,' he mused. The word faded without echo into the dust and trapped heat of the chamber, soured with must and parchment, and the peculiar, gritty reek of years upon years of used ink. No comfort could be drawn from the spin of clean breeze from the hills, nor even from the fast and warded stone that framed Althain Tower's protections.

If Kharadmon had suffered mishap, their hope to defeat the Mist-wraith's curse was rendered a lost cause at a stroke. The Black Rose Prophecy, which linked the Fellowship's return back to seven with the event of Arithon's willing kingship, became fully undone before time and fate could let it flower. Too fierce to believe the future had been lost on the day that set prince against prince in spelled enmity; too raw now to endure another grief in vanquished stillness, Asandir pushed erect and glared at his colleague's turned back.

'Let us set such a beacon that the sky will burn,' he announced in chiselled rage. 'Wherever Kharadmon has strayed, whatever ill keeps him captive, I would carve out power from the heart of this earth and configure a spell of white light to draw him homeward. Or all we have done to give mankind a home amid the grace of the Paravians has gone for naught but wrack and ruin!'

'We can set the first wards on the solstice tide, but it's certainly incon-venient.' Sethvir found an ant fallen trapped in a saucer and ushered it to safety with a feather touch. 'I hate to undertake such a difficult binding at a time when I've run out of tea.'

Asandir's mouth twitched. 'Ath. You know better. Have I ever shown up here without a fresh supply? This must be the first occasion in a thousand years of trials you've neglected to know in advance what simples I brought in my saddlebags.'

'I've been busy,' Sethvir said on a wistful, sad note of reproof. Long gone were the days when he had the leisure to grow strawberry leaves and chamomile and enspell them to flower out of season.

The dungeon chamber in Althain Tower had no windows cut through its white marble walls; and yet, on the eve of summer solstice, while the latent play of lane-force shimmered through the power focus set in its smoky onyx floor, the meadow-rich fragrance of catmint and sweetgrass twined through the storm-charge scent of ozone. As if the cut hay essence of the season itself partnered the forces that coursed through its ancient rune circles.

Barefoot, draped in an ankle-length robe abraded to threads at the hem, Sethvir set beeswax candles in the black gargoyle sconces arrayed at the points of the compass. Asandir stalked beside him in daunting silence. Stripped down to shirtsleeves and the scorch-marked leathers he had ridden in, he crossed corded forearms over his chest and spoke the incantation to call down a spark from the polestar. When the energy answered, as it must to a mage of his stature, and white starfire burned tame in his hand, he knelt in thanksgiving and homage and ignited the wick of the north taper.

Sethvir summoned flame to light the south one. East and west were set burning with sun ray and moonbeam, while over the tower's lofty battlement, the turning constellations spiked and danced the measured seconds before midnight.

To fashion a beacon-spell potent enough to recall a kindred spirit across the deeps between worlds, the Fellowship sorcerers laced bridles of pale energies through the rune-circles. To each interstice in the focus pattern, they fixed precise markers, attuned to a facet of the mysteries. Through their hands flowed the tides of distilled wisdom: secrets bought from centuries of knowledge and observation, from the filament of silence that enacted the stealth of an owl's flight, to the quickened burst of seed into sprout. They invoked the endurance of oak trees, singly by Name, until thousands of forest-tapped roots were called aware to volunteer their grounding as anchor. They braided the voices of sweet summer stars, and the staid pull of planets to their courses. Wild wind and grass were coaxed into coercion, and their million, partnered voices whispered measures in counterpoint and litany.

Mountains were asked to lend solidity, and the dark heart of stone gave back its sure self, to bell subvocal vibrations and waken the somnolent earth. The third lane shrilled now to a higher-pitched current. Waves of summoned energy dashed in succession into the construct formed amid the focus pattern. The Paravian runes glittered, then lashed to spitting life like the splash of molten metal over coals.

The interlaced mesh of static tore the ears, and the air bled a stinging wash of ozone.

Unlike a Koriani binding, amplified through crystal and fettered in raw domination, the layered weave of spells conjoined through Althain Tower held no constraint of forced mastery. Asandir and Sethvir worked in strict balance with the signature chord of the earth, reaffirmed in all its grand mystery, then exalted and wrapped through by the untamed exuberance that sourced the light-dance of life.

Midnight arrived.

The onyx floor tolled like struck bronze as the solstice charge surged down the lane. Gathered powers seared active with a scream of white light. Partnered in cold concentration, the paired sorcerers encompassed the mesh of their weaving, spoke a word, and on the strength of request, locked the whole into seamless stasis. The air stressed to recoil inside the tower, while the rune circles channelled the lane pulse into silken arrows of harmony.

Asandir and Sethvir rested for an hour, seated side by side at the foot of the stairwell with their backs pressed against warmed stone. Althain's Warden used the moment to unfold the clasp knife he used to sharpen pens and pare the yellow rims from his toenails. Asandir settled back against snow-grained marble and slept, his callused hands quiet in his lap. Two hours before solstice dawn, the keening of the setting stars roused him. Sethvir stared into space, his eyes misted over and vacant. Asandir touched his shoulder, arose, and stretched the cramps from his limbs.

Midsummer daybreak found them back on station at the focus. They repeated last night's binding in the scald of the sun surge, and again at noon; at sunset; at midnight.

By then the stone tower sang like a tuning fork to the powers leafed into stasis within. The burn of leashed energies coiled bright enough to blind, and sear unprotected flesh to carbon. The air itself seemed to glister with pent force, and the stone of the floor to breathe in counterpoint.

Heightened to peak activity, the focus could not be left unguarded for a minute. Asandir remained below to stand watch and steady the emergent flaws incited by the lane's random properties. Sethvir retired to his sanctum in the upper library. There, he brewed tea and pored over books on celestial mechanics, and filled page upon page with columns of mathematical figures in the minuscule, sharp-edged black script he used for his personal notations.

The navigational wards to guide the spell-beacon required fifteen days to formulate. Sethvir worked alone, ensconced within a subliminal spiral of linked strictures, light-scribed in air and in darkness. He gentled each layer in sigils stamped whole from the elements. Sun and storm lightning; wind and driven rain; fire and water and frost; he forged direction into spells like an arrowhead in flight, then bore the spitting, crackling mesh of sealed conjury down to the Asandir at the focus.

The coupling of raw power to the intricate spell of guidance required another day and a half.

'I can't recall feeling this tired since the hour the Mistwraith broke our barrier wards at Earle.' Asandir raked back hair wicked with sweat and gazed askance at the blaze of their parallel conjury. Only a fool, or an unschooled spirit would dare face the construct head-on. A beauty shuttled through its coils to beguile the unwary mind. To stare too long was to risk being drawn in by a harmony that gloved bitter peril, its currents too pure for mortal flesh. Direct exposure would bring blind, witless madness, for reasoned thought could not sustain the unshielded chord of world life-force.

In the shadow by the stairwell, poised between steps, Sethvir made a small, shocked sound. Asandir spun around, locked eyes with the Warden, and deduced the sure source of his distress. 'Don't speak. It's the Lady Maenalle, is it not?'

Sethvir said no word, but an image bled through, of a packed square in Isaer, where townsmen thronged before a scaffold hooted and called jibes at the condemned, lashed in cruel isolation to a post.

Neither sorcerer moved while a handful of seconds shredded themselves in suspension.

Then Asandir loosed a terrible cry that rocked echoes off close marble walls. 'Shall we not let her die unremarked?'

A hammered glint of temper simmered through the mist of Sethvir's tears. 'Indeed, let us not.'

He and Asandir whirled in unison. In flawless accord, they locked step, advanced to the heart of the pattern and joined hands. To the last, unfinished thread of their construct, they laced the signature of Kharadmon's signal Name.

Sethvir bowed his head. His consciousness divided into distance and held through his body's fine trembling; while on that far scaffold, a hooded executioner drew back a silvered blade of steel.

On the cusp of its fall, the Warden of Althain said, '*Now.*'

Asandir severed the spell's ground ties to the trees.

Power unfurled and howled. Light blossomed until the very air seemed to melt and burn and rage airborne. The beacon spell fashioned to summon back Kharadmon roared aloft toward the stars embedded in its homing. Its grand departure stabbed light across the sky like a portent of Ath's fury unleashed.

In Isaer, the scorching banner of its passage was the last sight Lady Maenalle beheld as the sword slammed home through her heart.

Healing

Attuned to an herbalist's sensitivity, Elaira tracked the near to invisible change in the light through the long days, while growing life on the Scimlade peninsula embraced the full bounty of summer. She watched, too, the subtle shifts in Arithon's mood through the weeks after the solstice. In him, like a breath held suspended against an influx of poisoned air, she sensed the pressure of outside events that passed tiny Merior by. Up coast, in cities plied by the trade galleys, news would be spoken of the muster in Rathain. Arithon sent no overt dispatch to inquire. Nor did he make any obvious effort to gain word of the enmity his acts had seeded in Alestron or Jaelot when the tinker's wagon visited from Shaddorn.

He spent his days in gruelling, sweaty labour alongside the joiners who steamed the planks to bend over the trued frames of his brigantine. If a night's deep talk by the bay shore had caused him to forgo their past hours of foraging, he came every eventide, his hair tousled wet from his bath, and his temper still brisk as sheared granite from managing his disparate teams of shipwrights. While darkness fell, and the gulls over Merior's fishmarket screamed and settled to roost, Elaira instructed him in the healing arts. He learned every nuance she knew to stop bleeding, to splint broken bones and tie sutures. She brewed tisanes and explained their banes and virtues, mixed poultice pastes to ease arthritic joints, and treated the myriad lacerations and small injuries that arose amid the fleet and at the shipyard.

Wherever possible, she gave him space and distance. If no caring contact could ease his unreconciled agony of conscience, her dry barbs of wit could make him laugh.

Whether her deepest suspicions were true, and Tal Quorin's past tragedy had damaged him further, she stifled her desire to pry. Some facts were better off left to bide beyond range of her order's covetous grasp.

'You aren't paying attention,' Elaira admonished on the night he asked what her life had been like as a Koriani novice. 'We spent a lot of time learning to draw sigils to drive out rats, and if you burn your fingers on that flask, there'll be no music for the wedding.'

'What wedding?' Arithon snatched up a linen rag to shield his grip on the hot container.

'Can't you take pity on the matchmaking goodwives in this village?' Elaira scolded in fond exasperation. 'You'll spoil their gloating over six months' hard work, then break their hearts since your calls at my cottage create their juiciest hours of gossip.'

'And you told them?' he said in stifled alarm.

Elaira returned a glare of owlish propriety. 'That with Dakar in tow, your new ships were going to need extremely potent talismans to avert incompetence, misfortune, and iyats.'

Rathain's prince grinned through the flame-rippled air off the brazier. 'Plain truth.'

The sorrow struck Elaira at sudden, odd moments, that such joy must become the first thing to wither when Arithon's cursed fate overtook him, and the contradictory ironies embedded in his nature came to exert their inevitable pressures. Bound to a course of inescapable violence as he was, she could not shake her dread that Morriel's belief would prevail, and his very strengths of character become the catalysts to drive his mind to destruction.

Whether the compassionate intelligence that sourced Elaira's fascination had engaged his deeper feelings in return, he lent her no chance to find out. To Jinesse, who maintained a tenuous, dutiful friendship, he seemed as he always had: willing enough to speak when addressed, but disinclined to volunteer his confidence.

Despite a reluctance too elusive to finger, he played to brighten the wedding of the cobbler's daughter and the freckled youngest son of the abalone cutter, who had no touch for his father's trade and sailed as hired crew with the fishing fleet. An adept from Ath's Brotherhood came to bless the ceremony, hooded in robes of stainless, white linen, threaded at the hems and collar with interlocked seals of gold and silver. The feast lasted long after the summer twilight faded. Dancers whirled in carefree circles around the bonfires, while smoke tanged the humid air, rich with the aromatic oils burned to repel swarming insects. Seen through the celebrants' capering shadows, the groom looked smart in his new broadcloth jacket, his bride flushed and radiant under curled lemon hair, wreathed in oak greens and scarlet ribbons. The bronze bells sewn on her slippers chimed merry time to her joy.

Seated by Jinesse, her hands filled with spiced bread and hot fish, Elaira mellowed to the fast-paced, seamless peal of lyranthe notes that stitched out the polished, brilliant rhythm.

But for the widow who recalled Arithon's performance on *Talliarthe's* deck and again, more forcefully, at Innish, the measures described by the bard's skilled fingers seemed as mere surface ripples thrown out to mask the grand depths. Where Elaira was drawn by curiosity to inquire, Jinesse chewed her lip and admitted, 'His mind is elsewhere, tonight. His heart is not in his music.'

The twins chose that moment to badger their mother for taffy. Through their engaging, boisterous noise, Elaira found no graceful way to reopen the lapsed conversation.

The next week a squall line raked in from the east and upset the run of fair weather. Battered fishing luggers beat under reefed sails for the shelter of Merior's harbour. In perennial mixed blessing, the fleet's safe return came accompanied by the indiscriminate misfortune that abounded among men who worked at sea.

Tinselled with falling rain that hissed through her firebrand, Elaira struggled up the exposed spit toward the shipyard. The night was a roaring black maelstrom around her. Freak winds battered wet skirts against her shins and shredded spindrift in bursting, white sheets off the breakers. Exposed to the storm's raw brunt, the pole sheds shook to the blasts, while a loosened plank banged a madman's tattoo, and dilute flares of lightning lit the anvilled clouds to stirred sulphur. Elaira picked an uncertain path between obsidian puddles and dune grass streamered like frayed ribbon. Against the heave of roiled surf, the looming frame of the half-complete brigantine combed the gusts to shrill vehemence. Nearer to hand bulked the mass of the chart loft, needles of candleflame pricked through its ill-fitted shakes. Inside the sole building to be graced with four walls, the yard's roisterous labourers gathered over trestles to eat supper, compare conquests and shoot dice.

Arithon's workers were unattached men. Given an hour of unsupervised freedom, they would drink to ease boredom, and become crapulous; divided by disparate origins and rivalries, not a few were wont to pick fights.

Resigned to plain fact, that every black eye and skinned knuckle would arrive on her doorstep for treatment come the morrow, and that Arithon's visits would lapse while the wrongfully battered sued for their rights to restitution, Elaira marched up to the chart loft and hammered a fist on the door.

Her torch spat sparks like thrown sequins. The rain laced a damascened fall off the drenched ends of her hair, her plain cuffs, and the layered hems of cloak and skirt. Her insistent rapping took a moment to be noticed. More seconds passed as voices declaimed inside, before a chair scraped and somebody moved to raise the latch. The portal creaked inward and faces peered out, sallow in the glow of cheap tallow dips, or brosy with drink and primed to proffer lewd comment.

Elaira spoke first, her voice a steel ribbon through the background clamour of banging tin flagons and a buffeting roar of conversation. 'Fetch your master.'

Movement heaved through packed bodies. Arithon appeared, dishevelled from the press, his attentiveness masked behind inquiry.

'There's been an accident to a fisherman!' Elaira shouted through the scream of the gust that flagged her torch flame. 'You're needed.'

Shadowed in the swoop of the draught, Arithon pulled in a careful breath. 'You're mistaken if you think I can help.'

Behind the arm he held braced against the door jamb, two burly craftsmen elbowed each other and exchanged ribald leers. Hampered by the total lack of privacy, Arithon stepped into the rain and let the storm slam the door shut behind him. He said nothing more. The hard wind flogged his black hair into tangles, before the wet slashed the strands and bared his expression to the fickle rags of torch light.

Presented with a wall, Elaira bent on him every power of observation she could wring from her Koriani arts. The gusts lagged for an instant. The recovered leap of the cresset showed him unmoving in the beat of the downpour; except the light dashed and flared across the abalone beads that weighted the ties of his shirt. His breathing was fast and unsteady. Through his hard-leashed control, the enchantress found no foothold to determine why he might meet her request for help with falsehood, or what hidden circumstance should fracture his mood in distress.

As always when his reticence thwarted her, she met him head-on with plain honesty. 'The boy who just married caught his wrist in a line during an attempt to strike sail. The damage is extensive. Broken bones, torn flesh and dislocation. Without arcane help, he'll stay crippled. The union you just helped to celebrate in such joy will come to be dissolved.'

Recoiled to astonishment, Arithon burst out, 'But why?'

'Local custom,' Elaira said, disgusted. Despite his sympathy, she dared not give in to her urgency and grasp his arm to hasten him away from the chart shack. 'Your masterbard's training at law can't cover every regional backwater. With regard to marriage, some places keep stubborn traditions. Shepherds' enclaves in Vastmark shun women for lack of fertility. Settlements above Waterfork in Lithmere demand a tax to be paid before nuptials. For Merior, a bride's father holds the right to nullify her contract at any time before her first childbirth if the match is ruled unfavourable. The law was first written to curb wife beating. Its practice has extended to include cases where a husband loses his livelihood. What chance does this boy have? And you saw the girl. She adores him.'

Arithon s'Ffalenn stood a second longer, his features veiled in the drowning thunder of rainfall. Then he said, 'Wait. I shall come.' He pushed back inside, to return a minute later with the leather-wrapped bundle of his lyranthe.

'Ath's mercy!' Elaira exclaimed, her patience torn through by his obstinacy. 'It's your mage-sight that boy requires, not any comfort drawn from music!'

'For that, I'm sorry, rare lady.' Arithon tucked her sodden fingers through his elbow and drew her into the darkness. 'But since the battle on the banks of Tal Quorin, my bard's gift is all I can offer.'

'Can't? Or won't?' Distraught and furious to believe he might obstruct her through some tangle of guilt-induced conscience, Elaira raised the flittering torch and let the light fall full on his face.

His contact with her hand jerked away as he twisted, muscle meshed to bone in an anger not quite savage enough to mask a grief of immeasurable proportion. Through the thrash of storm wind and water, amid harried black puddles that seemed utterly to swallow the tormented flame above her fist, Elaira felt Koriani talent and intuitive instinct noose disparate memories into painful focus: Dakar, haranguing a man he believed to be vulnerable; then like hammered echo, the unnerving study Arithon had once subjected to a growing stalk of wild nightshade.

More than blood had been sacrificed to Desh-thiere's curse in the massacre at Tal Quorin, Elaira perceived in horrified discovery. *Arithon s'Ffalenn had lost touch with his mage-born talent.* Transfixed by shared pity, she wrenched to a stop in her tracks.

Arithon paused also, aggrieved enough to have laid flat all his defences. '*Ei ciard'huinn,*' he said in lyric Paravian, which translated, *I am exposed.* 'I could wish that Morriel shouldn't know.'

Appalled to concede just what she had forced him to betray, Elaira swallowed. Words failed. Apologies were useless. Numbed and uncaring if the sluiced wet on her cheeks held some droplets that fell hotly salted, she ached, sieved through by mute misery.

His eyes brilliant green, his manner recaptured into calm that deferred all blame, Arithon pried the torch from her. He resettled the lyranthe's strap across his shoulder, reached again, and recovered her chilled hand. 'Rare lady, the grief is not yours. It's hardly worth the lad's future happiness.'

His touch soothed back the drowned mass of her sleeve, found her wrist, then warmly closed and drew her onward. Through a stumbling succession of steps, she was forced from shocked stupor to react.

'The gift of s'Ffalenn compassion will kill you,' she snapped. 'That's not worth any lad's happiness!'

Through the dark, limned in demonic, snatched shadows by the claw of wild wind through the cresset, Arithon s'Ffalenn shook his head. 'I'm not made up of divided parts, but a whole being flawed by Desh-thiere's curse. What use to mourn? The trained gifts I abused to spare clansmen have enforced their own measure of protection.'

Through their sodden, paired walk across the village, Elaira found nothing else to say.

Forced to hard practicality at last, she broached the necessary question as she reached for her door latch. 'Jinesse told me your bardic inspiration dissolved long-standing hatreds at Innish. But this healing will demand a weave far more powerful. I should never attempt it by myself. How good are you?'

'I don't know.' Still as cut shadow against the storm-rinsed shakes of her cottage, Arithon added, 'Halliron died soon after I won through to my mastery. If my limits have yet to be sounded, at least, after Jaelot, we can expect there are true strengths to draw on.'

'Tactfully put!' In a less worried moment, Elaira might have laughed. 'Though, Dharkaron's Spear and Chariot, if I'm to risk losing my walls to a whirlwind of unmanaged powers, I could wish the night was a mild one.'

She bashed open the door. Inside, under a draught-caught flutter of wax candles, the injured boy lay stretched on her worktable, clad still in his workaday oilskins. The floorboards beneath were streaked with rainwater and blood, the sandy prints of fishermen's boots not yet lent time to dry. A weather-worn woman huddled on a stool alongside, her greying hair pinned up with basket straws. Fingers chapped red by a lifetime gutting fish for the salt barrels lay clasped in sleeves bedecked in an iridescent glimmer of shed cod scales.

Elaira doused her torch in a bucket by the step, tossed off her drenched cloak and excused the relation directly. 'You were kind to wait. I'll send word the minute we have news.'

The woman arose, pulled her knot-worked shawl over tired shoulders and asked in diffidence, 'With your leave?' At Elaira's swift nod, she bent and kissed the boy on the cheek.

A scraped breath of pain escaped him at even so tender a touch. 'Go, mother,' he gasped through locked teeth. 'Sit with my Elie and comfort her.'

His lyranthe set aside, Arithon crossed to steady the woman as she stumbled, weeping, toward the threshold. He saw her safely out, latched the door, then peeled off his shirt in a flicked scatter of droplets.

'Use the towel on the hook by the basin.' Elaira clasped the boy's sound wrist to measure his pulse. Her clinical study took in his face, pallid as ambergris, then timed the thin rasp of his breathing.

A half-second later, Arithon arrived, the towel slung over his bare shoulder.

'I dare not dose him with soporifics,' Elaira explained, her speech in Paravian to spare the boy from disheartenment. 'Too dangerous, with the body thrown this deep in shock.'

Despite her involvement she could not escape the awareness of

Arithon's presence; of the warmth that radiated off his skin and his rock-steady calm. He moved after a moment. Warm hands gathered up her wet hair and blotted its drenched coils in the towel. Then, collected and firm, his fingers raked through and divided the wet strands, then plaited the rich mass into her usual neat braid.

'You'll need to see what you're doing,' he murmured in a musical, deep tone that stroked over wrought nerves like a tonic. He fished out a tie string from his cast-off cuff and knotted his work, then tossed the soaked towel on the stool.

Elaira quivered through a long, wretched spasm and discovered the space to unbend screaming tension and relax.

To the boy lying white-faced and bleeding, Arithon said, 'Lad, I shall need to hear your name.'

'The wedding,' the boy gasped. 'You played for me.'

Attentive to the ruined limb lying cradled in its slit shreds of sleeve, a mangled mess of wrecked meat and bone beyond help of splint or compress, Arithon replied, 'So I did. But knowing what you're called is scarcely the same as the way you would say it yourself.'

The boy heaved in another taxed breath and whispered his agonized answer. Arithon said something back in a murmur of syllables, too softly for Elaira to understand. Then he moved off a step, caught up his instrument and untied its storm-drenched wrapping.

In Paravian, he added, 'That's a very ugly injury. The bones are too shattered to set. I presume you plan to draw his spirit from his body and knit the torn sinews by surgery?'

'Surgery won't be enough,' Elaira gave terse reply. 'I'll have to set up a power field and sigils, to force a regeneration. The spells by their nature are cross-grained and difficult. We very well might lose him.'

'Don't even think that.' Arithon reappropriated the stool and couched his shining instrument on his knee.

A harmonic pealed through the rattle of freshened rain on the shingles. The wind's sour moan wove in ragged refrain, then a spill of notes like dropped crystal, sliced by a tingling play of chords. One by one, fourteen fine strings were adjusted to stinging, true pitch.

Then Arithon tested the mettle of his instrument as Elaira had never before heard him.

The whining complaint of the gale seemed immediately diminished into distance. Braced by a framework of ringing, clear measures, Elaira fetched kindling and lit the brazier. With hands that shook less, she set clean water to boil. From her hampers she selected her stoppered flasks of tinctures, then patterned a ritual blessing to enhance the virtues of a chosen mix of restoratives: wild thyme and tansy to ward against infection; goldenrod and black bryony for poultice; betony and devil's bit to speed healing; groundsel to slow bleeding and dittany to ease fever. In an unremarked moment between ordinary tasks, the trial flow of melodies

379

reached a consummate perfection, then slid through a figured change of key.

Heightened to preternatural focus by the sound, Elaira had no space to question the nature of the change that flowed through her. On a square of bleached linen, she shaped the sigils to deaden pain. Against the white cloth, in ordinary candlelight, the silver-weave mesh of the foundation spells took shape under her hands. The spiralled configuration of renewal grew in painstaking steps like linked chain. Each subsequent ward traced its own signature of energy, fine-drawn as silk from her fingertips. Where her own skills left off, the spell weave became snatched and quickened into resonance by the emergent, cascading harmonies that reeled from Arithon's strings.

Keyed by pure sound to primal potency, rune meshed to rune, the pale, phosphor glimmer of the set-seal at last joined complete and burned active in a fired surge of light. Through vision left fractured by welling, sudden tears, Elaira gasped, touched to awe. In perfected beauty to wound the imperfect mind, she saw the delicate interstice of her sigils bend into balance with the lyranthe chords, then lock against themselves and spark into flares of raised power.

Channelled into depth by bardic talent, the refigured mystery of wards she had handled half her life spiralled into coils of contained force. The very air seemed to vibrate, its essence shaved thin, as if chiselled by frost or high altitude. The life-force that flowed through her veins and her bones felt recast to silk and white diamond.

The impact on breathing flesh was too wild to sustain. Like a stress tear in tissue, her concentration wavered.

Elaira cried out to warn that her art had slipped her grasp. Her hold on tuned energies buckled. The next instant would see her share in the work crumple in a roaring flashburn of backlash.

Arithon murmured a Paravian encouragement. His limpid flow of music changed pitch.

A soaring progression of chords razed the dross from her mind, firmed her courage, then whirled her to rarefied clarity. Resteadied in a step, then launched still further, into resharpened vision akin to the scope of a tienelle trance, Elaira clamped aching fingers to her temples. Scarcely able to breathe, she battled to ground the intensified nexus of awareness cast into her hands by a channel carved out of clean sound. Whirled into trance, inspired to join the musician's lightning dance and pair her energies to a limitless flight of skeined song, she let go and rode the wave of her instincts.

She came back to herself on her knees, chalk in hand.

Where each patterning had started and finished, she held no clear memory. Yet the figured circles now blazed complete under her hands: of watch and protection, each safeguard to cradle a spirit drawn out of the flesh.

The alien, vital splendour of her handiwork and Arithon's shimmered in joined vibration, to etch weary sight and half-blind her.

Shaking, Elaira recouped scattered wits and arose. She lit beeswax candles to mark the major points of the compass. Peril stalked her. The cottage was a vessel aflood in roused power. Sharp currents nicked over her skin and jagged sparks from the lyranthe's silver strings. The four walls enclosed a space etched in vibrant, poised arrows of dire force. Now she dared not suffer misstep. The parameters she trod were unforgiving. Arithon also must not fail to be aware that his slightest slipped note might strike a dissonant tangent and lash up a lawless burst of ruin.

The gale outside seemed faded to insignificance, the drumroll of wind-driven downpour made deadened as if swathed under a caul. Lapped in thick shadow, the musician bent over his lyranthe, arched fingers a flying, deft dance over frets nicked gold in tepid flame light. Drawn on by his knife-edged harmonics, teased by rolling roulades of bright chords, the forces that gouged the wild limits of chaos were coaxed stable, then teased into balance.

Then the bard raised his head and locked eyes with the enchantress whose gifts interleaved with his music.

The contact set off a small shock, a prick like a needle through fire. Elaira sensed in advance the precise instant when Arithon flattened his hand and silenced the ringing call of his strings; melded in wordless awareness, she felt every barrier and bulwark of the mind shred between them.

No wall remained.

The art that his masterbard's skill had seized into resonance had been her own, made malleable like metal in a crucible, then recast to intensified vibration. The drawing force of the music had fused their two spirits into a single current.

Afraid to move, hurled beyond the tears that ached to be shed, Elaira stood transfixed, his touch softly still in her mind. The unveiled compassion in the contact stopped her breath; would through sheer force have felled her, had the lyranthe not spoken again.

The measures woven now shaped a clear affirmation, notes layered into patterns that invoked Name. Compounded through remembered strictures from his mage training, and the deepest gift of bardic empathy, Arithon recaptured in song the essence of the boy's self-perception.

This he framed into a mirror turned inward against itself.

To theme, he added slow, tolling chords to lull the mind. Coaxed past reach of worldly pain, the injured boy on the table eased into sleep. The lyranthe cajoled, then beckoned, each progression of chords netted into beguiling illusion that lured the tranced spirit and enfolded it in a clarion blanket of ecstasy.

Led to stunned awe by the sensitivity of Arithon's perception, shown wonders through the vision of trance state, Elaira *saw* tight-laced bundles of notes strike and winnow the uncertain air. The forged lines of power called forth from bare elements unreeled into ribbons of refined light. Blind to his own gifts, the bard perceived none of the form wrought by his genius. He played on by instinct to fashion a spell as unerring as any construct brought to focus by a master of magecraft.

Arms hugged to her chest, Elaira endured the precise, tearing force as vibrations pealed out like fine wire to halter the boy's stunned consciousness. She watched the musician draw, like thorns from bleeding flesh, the life essence out of breathing tissue.

A snap cracked the room.

Her spell circle flared like wind-fanned coals. Each painstaking sigil blazed and closed fast, to contain the unmoored spirit of the boy.

The bard's line of melody trod one last measure, then dwindled away into silence. A fearful weight of leashed force charged the cottage. All that tied the boy to the vacant housing of his body was a filament spanned over oblivion, less tangible than a spun thread of thought.

'Merciful Ath,' Elaira cried on a scraped whisper.

She had witnessed spells cast by senior enchantresses, through crystal resonance and amplified alignment; she had studied under healers in the greatest hospice in Athera, but nothing in her grasp of the mysteries prepared her for the frightful turn of mastery Arithon had shaped and then strung to binding ties through an intuitive rendition of pure melody.

'Rare lady,' he answered in response to shocked thought. 'Have you not guessed? Your vision itself was my sounding board.'

Through a ripped hitch of breath, meaning reached her: his mind was with her still, a bright, steely line sheathed deep inside her awareness. Hand in glove with that presence, she saw beyond the veil, past the privacy he kept before every man living.

Shattered in reaction, then answered warp through weft by response like a peal of wild harmony, Elaira felt the tuned chord inside her arise to accept its perfect match.

She understood unequivocally and finally, that the conduit forming the bridge to the man was emotion: affection of equal depth and breadth to the regard she already held for him. She saw the love he had systematically, even ruthlessly stifled before the damning assumption that her interest was no more than a ploy arranged by Morriel Prime to track his personal affairs.

Elaira had no chance to savour the exultation of their mutual rapport.

All wonderment became reft from the moment by need: the injured boy's condition was too critical to suffer even the smallest delay.

Years in the healer's wards had shown how the diurnal shift in the mysteries could blur all boundaries. The bindings between spirit and flesh lay the weakest while the balance between dark and dawn hung poised on the axial turn of the earth. Through the nadir of night, the mortally ill were most wont to strike fleshly ties and pass beneath Daelion's Wheel.

If the boy on her table was to survive, her work must be prompt and precise.

Elaira bludgeoned stunned wits back to sharpness. With her spell crystal cupped between her damp palms, she bent once again to her invalid. The damage looked all the more daunting for the boy's scarce-breathing flesh. From Arithon she borrowed the courage to ignore the clamour of better sense, that for prudence and safety, such a mass of mangled tissue should be dressed out for a clean amputation.

Nothing if not stubborn, whipped on by the cry of her heart for the waste of a life at the threshold of uselessness, Elaira hurled her will through the core of her crystal's white focus. For whatever end, she shouldered the supreme risk and began the arduous course to align sigils with seals, then pair their arcane forces with the properties of herbs to rebuild the boy's mangled wrist.

Bone, blood, muscle and cartilage, each required separate sets of spells. The delicate flux of forces brought to bear must align to match the body's own magnetism.

Elaira scarcely marked the moment when music first partnered her efforts.

But when her hand trembled in closing a difficult sigil, a chord rang out to steady her. If her heart sped in fear, if strain threatened to crack her for the complex flux she must guide by trance through her spell crystal, reassurance pealed back and enfolded her in a shower of calming notes. Again and again her disciplined suspension was annealed through the focus of Arithon's playing.

The miracle shimmered through air and through flesh. As slivered bits of bone were slotted one into another like puzzle pieces, then stapled in place with fine magic, perfection ruled every move. Like a construct of engineered geometry, Elaira held her grasp on the multi-layered balance of spells. The bard's gift sustained her hands and her mind as she reconstructed ripped cartilage and restored the ligaments to rebind each disarranged wrist bone. Her sight did not blur through meticulous removal of flayed bits of rope fibre, any one of which might seed a lethal infection.

Then each vein and capillary had to be refigured; riven sinew repaved in light-tracks to reconnect the ends of sheared nerves. Tendons must be sewn whole, and frayed muscles drawn together in painstaking rows of gut stitches. Elaira toiled on in agonized concentration. Sweat dewed her temples and rolled down her jaw. Yet the needle in her fingers did not slip that a dancing, merry measure did not shepherd her back to dexterity.

Sweet melody braced her still as she slathered the closed wounds in poultice paste and bound on splints and clean bandages.

The candles by then had burned low. In shadows that flickered to each breath of draught, Elaira pushed herself unsteadily erect. She snuffed the wax lights on the spell circles. Tired beyond grace, strained past clear thought, she fumbled and found her reed broom and dusted away the grand axis that sealed the power in the ritual chalk lines.

Still tranced through the lattice of her spell crystal, her consciousness moved in mage-sight. As pent forces and stay-spells gave way, a sound like rent fabric sheared across the throb of blood in her ears. The wards burst asunder and the spirit bound captive reeled free.

Seconds passed, measured in uncertain terror, that flesh might cease effort, unquickened. Then the boy on the table stirred and moaned.

Elaira felt the breath reel out of her. She slid to her knees, lost to dizziness. This time, no music leaped to ease her. She found herself too drained to rise, too spent to insist that the invalid stay quiet while she mixed the necessary draught to bring sleep. The enchantress buried her face in laced hands, unstrung by a running fit of trembling.

The boy could die yet. She wept for frustration as exhaustion yawned an impossible gulf between what was needed, and a vacuum that sucked away energy.

Too late, too faintly, a gilded play of lyranthe notes rocked through the span of stilled air. Elaira struggled to rise and recover the willpower to match them.

Failure dragged her down. The grand nets of harmony seemed frayed beyond reach, diminished and tinny with distance.

Pressed by the fogs of unconsciousness, she grasped after the bard's measures and understood: his melody was not tuned for her after all. The irresistible call of each fretted chord was pitched to settle suffering and smooth her patient into sleep.

Elaira thrashed against the honeyed compulsion to surrender all ties to awareness. Arithon must not be abandoned with the burden of securing the boy's weakened life signs. Hours would pass before his body stabilized from the fluxes of a major, forced healing. But thought bled away in a fierce, sucking rush. Thrashed by the demands of channelled power, bruised by the after-tides of a backlash too savage to grapple, the enchantress collapsed against the grain of cold floorboards, beaten down into darkest oblivion.

The febrile flutter of a single candle became the first harbinger of an awareness that returned in slow stages. Her lashes cracked open. Still set adrift in a welter of confusion, Elaira clung to that pinpoint of light. She sensed like an odd and unwonted peal of sorrow the silent absence of a melody.

As stunned senses rearranged to sustain reason, she pieced together bits from her surroundings: the storm had abated to a fitful splash of droplets off the shingled cedar of the eaves. The shutters of her bed-chamber, swung and latched open, let in the raw thunder of the breakers churned up by strong winds. Each contrary draught came freighted with smells of salt and tidewrack and soaked foliage.

A solitary cricket rasped from the cranny behind her clothes chest. Its song sounded wracked out of true, a coarse intrusion after the masterful play on fret and string that had beguiled her spellcraft in sweet-ringing waves to new heights.

Best not to recall that partnership too clearly; Elaira squeezed her eyes closed. The sting of loss lanced her, regardless.

The grinding, dull throb of taxed nerves released her one limb at a time. She noticed she lay half-supine on her pallet. A warmth beneath her cheek held a scent of clean skin and the muffled rhythm of another heartbeat. Snapped back on a breath to full consciousness, Elaira came aware that she rested in the circle of Arithon's arms.

He had not taken time to retrieve his damp shirt. The same hands that had commanded the lyranthe to high art cradled her cheek and her waist. The disfiguring scars on his wrists were left unabashed in plain view. His hips were twisted underneath her, his bare feet still braced on the floorboards; as if he had sat, her weight borne in his arms, with intent to settle her to rest.

And a phrase, *not her own*, rose and burst across her thoughts: some temptations could be too sweet.

Languid in the throes of exhaustion, Elaira absorbed the possibility an empathic link might still be in place between herself and the Shadow Master. The spells they had handled in paired resonance had been strong ones. The aftershocks to the mind could hitch and start in a thousand unpredictable directions.

Content with inclinations left in harmony with his, she melted to the pleasure he drew from this brief, stolen moment: the comfort of her body secure within his care, her narrow, lean limbs folded neatly.

Man and prince and musician knew peace. Arithon held in the tender awareness that this happiness might never come again.

Elaira cherished each detail along with him. The rich, auburn hair he had braided while wet now spread, combed and shining, to mantle her shoulders. No drag of wet skirts weighted her ankles, only the nap of a blanket. Underneath, she wore very little beyond the linen of her shift.

A kinetic sense of her wakening must have reached him.

'Elaira?' Arithon inquired, softer than a sigh. 'The lad rests quietly. Forgive me, but for you, I had to stay to be certain. Someone had to watch over your recovery.'

A frown marred Elaira's forehead, for his need to excuse what was obvious: had she failed to awaken from this backlash on her own, he alone held the masterbard's talents required to revitalize spirit with flesh. The initiates of Ath's Brotherhood owned the knowledge to help, but her collapse was immediate and their hostel lay leagues down the road.

Arithon had ignored no contingency. His lyranthe lay as he had left her, leaned against the wall by the headboard and ready to his hand if need required. The filaments of fourteen silvered strings scribed lines in reflection, captured intact from the candleflame.

Delivered into warmth from the haze of oblivion, Elaira realized another thing. Arithon s'Ffalenn had never before spoken her name while alone in her presence. That belated recognition shot a prickle of reaction clear through her.

Attuned to the uneven catch to her breathing, Arithon lifted his hand from her waist. As he had many times through the hours of the night, he trailed reverent fingers through her hair to smooth an unruly wisp from her temple.

The barest taut frisson knit the length of her back in response. A sound of dismay escaped him; as though he willed her to stay peaceful in her daze, and felt deprived by the speed of her recovery.

Elaira could have laughed in that moment for sheer joy. His presence of itself had called her back, as no other living spirit ever could.

Then event caught up with reality. Imprinted against the sounding board of his body, she felt him gather himself tense, to disengage and rise at once. Her plea escaped before thought. 'Please stay.'

His words viced to indifference, Arithon said, 'Lady, I'm relieved to see you waken. On my way, I'll send Jinesse to attend you.'

The desperate force of will in his effort to pull free shuddered through the contact between them. An awful, uglier truth arched across their tuned empathy: that what feeling he had would be denied out of self-preservation. He still believed her interest was false, created on command by Koriani aim to manipulate him.

And anger shocked through Elaira like white fire, that her attraction had been genuine long and long before Morriel's hideous plotting had seized on her love as a gambit. This she determined to let him see, before the consequences ruined them both.

Strong, sun-browned from her long days of foraging, Elaira stirred against his move to rise. She pressed him back and looked up, and locked his gaze with her own. 'Before Ath, before life, I love you. That's been true, I think, since a rash escapade led to a hayloft in an inn yard.'

She had just one moment to realize how weary he was himself, and how ill-prepared. No defence did he have, no ready barrier, as she moved in his arms, then closed the embrace and laid her lips against his in surrender.

An immediate quiver lanced through him. The hands at her back closed hard and locked. His kiss met hers in a riptide of unleashed passion. Scalded, consumed, uplifted, exalted, for the unforgettable space of a heartbeat they were one flesh and one mind. The harmony between them stopped thought and waived every limiting fear for the future.

Then Arithon s'Ffalenn made a sound like a man lashed to torture.

His head turned, broke her hold and snapped aside. He jerked upright in a wildcat recoil, as a creature roped down for the knife might escape its deathblow in a slaughter pen.

'Ath, oh Ath!' he gasped, his voice broken.

Elaira sought his expression, and saw the face of a man betrayed.

Her own pain re-echoed in devastated imprint, she saw his eyes, stretched wide and bleak in the candlelight as he forced his breath back into stopped lungs. 'What have I *done?* Dharkaron show us both mercy, *your feelings are as mine, and I thought Morriel had sent you!'*

Pinned on the prongs of that ugly, dual truth, Elaira lost words. She had spirit in her only to endorse the more truthful obligation. Spurred by the overriding cry of her heart, she raised a hand in comfort to cup the side of his face.

Her touch never connected.

A whirlwind of motion heaved her up, flung her back. Arithon's hands turned wholly ruthless as he twisted out from underneath her. Discarded in a shivering heap upon the bed, Elaira clawed back tumbled hair and blinked to clear her vision from a ruinous, blinding fall of tears.

She never heard his step cross the room. But his pose said all his speech could not: back turned, head bent, his expressive fingers fanned in white outline against the board wall, while his shirtless body was raked and raked over in wretched, quivering spasms.

'Don't come,' he forced out as he sensed her intent to arise.

The slithering fall of the blanket turned informer, or maybe the shift of air across his skin: she would disregard his plea. This time, he would be pressured too far. Integrity, joy, the bright, tragic fabric of the miracle shared between them would unstring all of his control. 'Don't come. I beg you, for your life's sake, don't.'

'For *my life?'* Elaira gasped. Her surprise yawned as wide as the night that pressed inward, to drown the failing candle on its stand. 'Beloved, what is there of me that is not yours before anything?' She advanced a step toward him, and the creak of a loose floorboard seemed to peel his raw nerves and wring out a drawn, silent scream.

The next second, her raised hand would touch him.

He sucked an agonized breath, then in scalpel sharp diction, launched into flat recitation: '*All states of fleshly desire to renounce, this I vow. All ties of the heart, of family, of husband and lover to put aside, this I vow.'*

Elaira stopped, stunned, between steps.

The words fell and chilled her, unflinching as steel sliced through a fall of running water, and familiar: hatefully abhorrent to the last, most damning consonant. Arithon gave her, line by line from a masterbard's knowledge of law, the binding oath sworn by a Koriani initiate over the Prime's master crystal.

The phrases continued, implacable. '*And should I weaken or falter and come to forswear my commitment, all that I am shall be forfeit, body and mind. This I vow, no witness beyond the Prime Circle, no arbiter beyond the crystal matrix into which I surrender my Name and my imprint as surety through all my living days.'*

There came a space, rasped to dissonance by the chirp of the cricket.

Elaira masked her face and muffled her ears, helpless. She could not escape fate. No move forward was possible, now, even to unman him, even to defeat the unassailable integrity that acted in sacrifice to spare her: not without admitting that her Prime Matriarch had a hand in this design. To say that leave had been granted to break her order's primary vow was to gut an inviolable trust.

What Elaira felt for this man was real, untarnished. Yet she could not wrench hope back into her hands, nor cross the gulf, nor complete the desire between them. Not without sullying forever the shining truth of her love, that Morriel's manipulation had no part of.

No word existed under earth or sky to explain that her presence here was less due to Koriani intrigue than to the burden of Sethvir's warning prophecy.

She must have made a sound in her torment.

For Arithon gathered himself again and forced speech. 'Lady, for the love that I bear you, let me leave. Your order's vows cannot tolerate my claim. Give me torture and loss, give me death, before I become the instrument that seals your utter destruction. Of all the atrocities I have done in the past, or may commit in the future, that one I could never survive.'

There was nothing to do, nothing at all, but stand aside, mute, and let him pass.

Convergence

While the craftsmen at Merior's shipyard whisper among themselves that the night at the healer's has brought their master back changed, his tolerance thin-drawn as wire, the brig *Black Drake* makes port bringing word that city garrisons in Rathain have been called to muster at Etarra; and the news causes Arithon to send his request, asking rendezvous with a clan lord who dwells in the forest of Selkwood . . .

Since the portent which slashed the night sky in the hour of Lady Maenalle's execution raised the city of Isaer into panic, and while Lysaer's officers labour to dispel fraught dread among the troops, Asandir rides out from Althain Tower to seek the clan encampment along the Valenford River and invest the *caithdein*'s grandson with Fellowship sanction to inherit her powers of office . . .

When word from the watcher on the seventh lane reaches the Koriani Council that Elaira's attempt to bind the Shadow Master through affection has been met with flat failure, Morriel Prime issues sharp rebuke as her First Senior questions the outcome: 'Our initiate did not fail to gain Arithon's trust. On the contrary, rather her prince has outmanoeuvred us, and through flaws in our own design . . .'

XIII. *WAR HOST*

High summer cast blistering light over the anvilled stone summits and knife-edged cornices of the Mathorn Mountains. Under their frowning rims, the taint of pine resin filled the copses, huddled in their tangles of black shade. Witch hazel grew riot in the defiles, floored in moss and speared sedges, and hazed silver in clouds of midges where springs trickled down from the heights.

But where the garrisons from Rathain's allied cities mustered on campaign to destroy the Shadow Master, the land bore a seamed, brown scar.

Sunset glared over Etarra's brick walls, a dull, red eye through the dust churned up by its war camp. Lysaer s'Ilessid and his force from Avenor were a fortnight overdue. Under crowding and the added strain of delay, the masses of idle troops and their uneasy convocation of commanders strained loyalties and stressed the ties of diplomacy.

Men grew to hate the scrape of crickets in the scrub as they quartered the stripped hillsides to meet the insatiable need for wood to fuel their cookfires. Outside the high walls, the heat at day's end hung over the stubble of grasses, sucked brown by the rainless season or else milled to chaff by the hooves of foraging livestock. The breezes settled at nightfall, to leave a rank, unhealthy morass: the reek of urine-soaked muck from the picket lines; of unburied garbage and open latrines; and the meadow scent of hayfields flattened under the burden of field pavilions and provision tents. Each day brought more arrivals, with yoked teams of thin-flanked oxen hauling their groaning supply wagons past the knots of beasts and the stalled carts of the trade caravans displaced by right of war.

Last to arrive, Avenor's companies marched in to the snap of blazoned flags and the horn calls of officers. Wilted as any other troop in their sweat-dampened surcoats, the discipline on them sparkled. In deadly, polished order, they raised their camp in a landscape powdered ghostly monochrome by the endless haze of gritted dust.

The Prince of the West made his entry through the city gates at twilight to a thunderous welcome from the populace. Under the cut-brass light of a dozen torches, his jewels sparked like fallen stars amid his attendant guard of riders. At his side, Lord Commander Diegan cut a proud figure, resplendent in his silk and white diamonds and his hair ruffled sable under the bullion fringe of the royal standard. Poor folk and craftsmen thronged the wayside to throw rose petals and call appreciation. The wealthy, the guild merchants and their families, cheered and waved scarves from the balconies, which made the horses curvette and shy. The brick-trapped heat arose off the cobbles. Even the scent of the flowers crushed under the hooves of the destriers became clogged with the alkaline tang of parched earth.

Diegan regarded his sovereign lord with critical care. Fear had blunted support from the cities in Tysan after the sorcerous portent that crossed the sky during the barbarian chieftain's execution. Lysaer had exhausted himself in diplomacy to ease the guilds' entrenched suspicion of wizardry. Only Pesquil's iron-clad handling had kept the troops in discipline through the confines of a near windless crossing to reach port at Narms.

Now, strain and weariness masked in gay decorum, Prince Lysaer caught a posy thrown by a blushing young girl in a window. He inclined his head to a row of clapping merchants, and through teeth clamped in a fixed smile, said to Diegan, 'These were your people, once. You could show them a bit of gracious interest.'

Straight in his saddle despite the suffocating heat, Diegan stayed stiff-lipped and obstinate. The laughing, light-hearted gallants who called his name were as strangers to him, changed as he was from the man who had ridden from these same streets two years ago. Now, chiselled lean by rough training, in fact more than title the hard commander of troops, no change in physical prowess could blunt the instinct for politics bred into his bones since childhood.

'You're stepping into a snakepit!' he snapped to his prince. 'Sithaer's devils and furies! You've left the garrison captains of sixteen cities alone for hours to fret and wait upon your pleasure. Don't be astonished when their arguments rip your plans to useless shreds. They'll never let your officers have charge of their commands. They'd cut their own throats or see you dead, first.'

'To the everlasting victory of our enemy,' Lysaer replied in that honeyed tone which dealt reprimand like a slap. Eyes the heavy blue of his sapphire studs stayed trained on the throngs in the street. Still smiling, he tossed the posy in his hand to a grinning, toothless grandmother, then curbed his mount hard to forestall a shy as a sprig of dried lavender winnowed down from the dormer of a perfumer's shop. 'If the prospect of bearding a few snakes leaves you squeamish, I don't need you at my side.'

'I wouldn't miss this.' Reckless in challenge, Diegan countered, 'Etarra's guilds have a nasty, short memory for favours, and for years your sweet war camp at Avenor's been a bottomless drain on their treasury. If you're offering yourself for political sacrifice, be very sure I want to stay and watch.'

A double-edged pride backed Diegan's stab of mockery, as much for the masses of craftsmen and brown-clad apprentices who made deferent way for their cavalcade, as for the wedge of officers, turned out in glittering and lethal perfection at their backs. This city had been his turf. The pedigree birthright he had forsaken to serve Avenor and Lysaer s'Ilessid brought a swell of tightness to his chest. As they rounded the last corner of the thoroughfare, by perverse urge, he wished the whiplash instability of Etarran intrigue to unstring this prince's self-assurance: to have just one unanticipated setback carve his insufferable royal confidence to proportions more malleably human.

None but a fool would refuse to fight beside Lysaer s'Ilessid against the Shadow Master. But on the advent of new war, against the ugly, blood-soaked memories still carried from the past campaign in Strakewood, Lord Commander Diegan desperately wished back his lost equilibrium. He needed the cat-cool independence of the dandy he had been that gave no man leave to lead his heart.

Heat rode the air like a blanket, thick with the reek of packed humanity. Oily fumes drifted from the great bronze pans of the braziers, lit to commemorate the arrival of s'Ilessid royalty. Above the swept marble stair, the copper-leafed doors of the council hall stood closed and latched behind guards in red and gold livery who held back the crowding, raucous throng which loitered to stare and speculate.

Inured to the flare and temper of Etarran street mobs, secure amid the ring of Lysaer's captains, Lord Commander Diegan dismounted. He left his horse with the prince's equerry. Humidity bogged the night like liquid glass, freighted with the calm of pending storm. Lysaer should have looked hot in his mantling layers of state finery. For this meeting, no symbol of dress had been spared: the fingers of both hands flashed jewels; his full-sleeved, damascened shirt was hemmed with bullion braid; and bracelets cuffed the bones of his wrists. Over a tabard of indigo silk, he wore Avenor's linked chain of office. Dusky red against the purer gleam of his hair lay the gemmed circlet of his royal rank.

Every move he made embroidered by the flash of costly tailoring, he mounted the shallow stair. The duty guardsmen made way to admit him with servile humility.

The royal escort entered the foyer, with Lord Diegan tense enough to suffocate. The knit weight of his mail bore him down beneath his surcoat, and the hair at his temples clung with sweat. To affirm his unease, the clash of the officers' weapons and the grate of their tread across the tiles became overwhelmed at once by the clamorous argument that raged inside the great hall.

Amid a shouted uproar and the crash of someone's banging, vain efforts to restore order, Etarra's minister of city finances mounted to a pitch of hysterical fury. 'Would you beggar the treasury? To move thirty-five thousand to sea before winter cannot be done without ruinous use of borrowed funds.'

'Cost be damned!' cut in Lord Commander Harradene in his grinding, martial bellow. 'You want this Shadow Master dead? Then use the two eyes Ath gave you and take a long look at the map!'

'Listen to Harradene,' a garrison captain interrupted in the clipped style of Rathain's northern coast. 'It's a dead simple case of wise tactics! Merior's the Fatemaster's very nightmare of a place to mount a large scale attack. The coast road through Shand is no option. Did your counting clerks think of supply costs over a thousand league march? Never mind we'd have no morale left to fight with. Yon sorcerer would've flown his little coop before we could hack our way down the peninsula.'

'Ath!' In the hallway, Lord Diegan spun in alarm to his prince. *Who told them Arithon's location!* I'll have the head of the fool who spilled the secret!'

'That could be awkward,' Lysaer said with a maddening, mild glance. 'Since the fool, as you call him, was myself.'

Diegan's attempted rejoinder was lost as Commander Harradene's declaiming bellow rattled the glass in the sconces.

'To Sithaer with your whining trade ministers! The *only* chance we have is to surround and attack in force by sea. Harry the sorcerer against a lee shore. Once he's dead, you can natter over debts and owed interest 'til you kill yourselves with sheer worry. At least our people will be safe!'

While captains representing a dozen city garrisons raised a storm of yelping objections, and the thumping for order on the tabletops gave way to a clangorous bell of steel, the steward on duty by the entry took notice of the movement behind him: the quiet guard of officers, advancing, then the bejewelled presence they escorted. Obsequious in relief, he hurried to offer obeisance. 'Your Grace, my Lord, they are frantic. Let me announce your arrival.'

Lysaer advanced a sharp step and touched the man's wrist in restraint. 'If you please, just open the door without fanfare.' To Avenor's Lord Commander, straight-lipped and furious at his side, he flipped an insouciant shrug. 'What became of your Etarran taste for bloodsport and nasty politics?'

Diegan returned a tiger's smile. 'Allow our sworn allies to argue themselves to paralysis? Well if you fail to master the pack this time, and Pesquil doesn't murder you for indecent lack of priorities, I'll personally remedy the lapse.'

He trailed his prince through the archway to accost Etarra's grand war council.

Under the musty fringe of trade guild banners, mewed in by dagged drapes of red velvet pulled over the hall's lancet windows, the war commanders in their blazoned surcoats, dyed leathers and mail, and the trade ministers in ribbons and creased sarcenets locked horns in belligerent contention. The hall rocked with echoes. Marble friezework and groined arches resounded to a hell-bent boil of high temper. Secretaries scribbled notes and ran messages. Every man a seasoned master of dissent, the trade ministers connived in stifled whispers, faces masked beneath the deep brims of their exotic feathered hats. Atop the high dais, crammed into a conspicuous gilt chair, the Lord Mayor Supreme of Etarra dabbed sweat off his quivering double chin. Flushed in his overtight layers of brocades, he flailed like an agitated puppet, and failed at each turn to make himself heard through the clash of raised voices.

Cryptic good sense drove one visiting foreign dignitary to avoid the crush on the benches. Keldmar s'Brydion of Alestron leaned on a square gilt pillar, an arras at his back and one negligent shoulder turned toward the gathering. His other hand masked beneath his cloaked elbow, he kept gripped fast to his dagger. Appointed by his brother to represent Alestron's case against the Shadow Master, he had to display the earl's blazon everywhere he went, lest his accent get him skewered for a forest barbarian each time he opened his mouth.

After seven days of insults stopped just shy of bloodshed, and apologies from fools invariably attached to commiseration over the political misfortune of his speech, Keldmar's countenance was slit-eyed, his mood jumpy, and his contempt for the doings of pompous officials explosive as live eels in a cask.

When the seneschal's harebrained assistant had the temerity to leap into the face of the black-bearded veteran, Commander Harradene, then pulled his eating knife to batter the table to seize attention, Keldmar stifled a burst of laughter behind upturned, sardonic lips. Etarra's vaunted alliance was about to erupt and run riot. The ranking officers of Rathain's city garrisons were inflamed enough to draw steel and gut the trade ministers and their secretaries, to say nothing of the other nattering windbags in stuffed velvet who objected to the costs of campaign warfare.

Keldmar cheerfully prepared to field whatever mayhem swirled his way. He weighed the prospect of pinking a few lame-brains who had dared mistake him for the get of the fugitive clanborn, while the spat between war captains and the hatted ranks of ministers climaxed in screaming crescendo.

A crack of whipped air rocked the chamber, to an actinic burst of white light over the central dais. Shouted invective died as if slammed by a thunderclap into stunned and terrified silence.

'Ath have mercy on you all!' pealed an acrid, carrying voice. 'For believe it, the Master of Shadow will show none when his ships are built and he takes up the piracy of his ancestors!'

Blinking through flash-blinded vision, Keldmar saw a vivid, fair-haired figure stride through the press from the doorway. Laced in a dazzle of gold and the ice-point sparkle of royal sapphire, the newcomer's advance was attended by a dark man muscled lean from hard training, then a compact knot of officers in a smart polish of accoutrements.

'What a perfect, meek target we offer, bent one against another, and over a matter as transient, *as petty* as expense.' Lysaer s'Ilessid, Prince of Tysan, mounted the dais with quick grace. Every eye in the chamber fastened on his person. Sizzling silence met the outraged fury which charged him from head to heel. The royal presence of him towered. Before the chair of Etarra's Lord Mayor Supreme, he spun and glared over at the gathering. 'Arithon s'Ffalenn is indeed ensconced at Merior. His location has been chosen most carefully, and I warn, to trap him there won't be simple. War against any scion of s'Ffalenn has never been bloodless. This campaign will cost more than gold, more than lives, more than heartbreak, if we bicker ourselves into failure. Give anything less than total effort, and I promise: no city in the land will stay scatheless. No innocent life will escape suffering.'

The alderman of Etarra's south quarter swiped his bonnet off his bald head, inflated for passionate rebuttal.

Lysaer rounded fast and cut him off. *'Seven thousand lives were lost against the Master of Shadow in Deshir*. Would you make that ten thousand more? Twenty? This encounter against a criminal sorcerer must be fought on his own chosen ground – a deadly proposition. We must overcome any odds set against us, else give this man time to complete the fleet of ships the barbarians of Camris have funded. Let that happen and you'll see a scourge upon your sea trading galleys such as you have never imagined.'

Splendid in rage, Prince Lysaer played his words like shot arrows, straight enough to flatten pride, kill objection, shame petty and divisive rivalries that would undermine his sworn cause. Keldmar s'Brydion curled his lip at the deference shown by the cowed city ministers. The garrison captains, too, were mollified, dressed down like children caught brawling. They might not relinquish their commands outright. But as they gave this prince full attention, their allegiance would be pulled in and knotted like so much wound string. Gold would be given for ships at Werpoint to transport the war host downcoast.

The Duke of Alestron had dispatched two brothers to attend his complaint against the Shadow Master. Mearn had carried formal protest in appeal for kingdom justice to the clanborn regent of Melhalla. As envoy to Etarra to gather news, Keldmar had neither authority nor desire to tie s'Brydion interests into alliance. The family quarrel lay with Arithon Teir's'Ffalenn, a claim of bloodprice for seven guardsmen and the wanton ruin of their armoury. Keldmar need only return to tell his brother's captains to engage a blockade, then smoke the slinking sorcerer out of Merior by the Sea.

On the dais, impassioned in his tirade, Lysaer glimpsed movement at the edge of the grand hall. Attuned to every small shift in the ranks, he turned his head and caught a flash of scarlet on gold: the too-prominent blazon of Alestron's grand duke, that signalled an untimely departure. His discreet and timely signal wakened an answering deployment from the royal officers beneath the dais stair.

Once Keldmar s'Brydion worked clear of the press and slipped through the pillared arch to the foyer, four of Avenor's glittering captains barred his way to the street.

Tall enough to intimidate, his clansman's plait as haughty a statement of his bloodline as the tabard that clothed his straight back, Keldmar measured each officer with narrowed, stone-coloured eyes. 'Am I a prisoner?' he asked, his challenge flung into their very teeth.

Yet the discipline instilled at Avenor would not rankle at words. 'You are the prince's invited guest,' said the senior man among them. 'His royal Grace would not have you leave without extending his hospitality.'

No use to argue the points clan custom held in difference with merchant city law; that to bow to sovereign power from another kingdom's prince denounced Melhalla's founding charter. Avenor's officers closed about their quarry, gracious, but unsmiling. Since the sincerity of the s'Ilessid intent could only be tested through steel, Keldmar s'Brydion held his temper and went along.

Permitted to go mounted, his escort saw him from the posthouse where his horse was stabled to a field camp wedged between the rising ridge of the Mathorn mountains on Etarra's northern quarter. The site commanded a view across the Plain of Araithe, with its broad roads branching east and north. In glittering disarray, like opals spilled by haphazard hands into folded sable velvet, the campfires of the Rathain's city war host flickered and burned across the lowlands. Black as an ink spill to the east spread the marshes that fed the headwaters of the River Valsteyn, the croaking tempo of night-singing frogs scared mute by the shouts of men dicing away hours in idleness, or quarrelling for the favours of camp followers.

A sullen wind prowled the hills, stirring through layers of muggy heat and the louring pall off the cookfires. Churned dust hazed the moonbeams, shot through broken clouds above an earth that wore its burden of armed troops like a beggar's rags of motley. Keldmar awaited his appointment on a cushioned stool, a goblet of good wine in his hand, while the tap of bullion fringes edging velvet hangings whispered of pending storm. Lysaer's equerry, a liveried manservant, and two pages hovered in the shadows to serve his slightest want.

The pavilion's rich appointment masked no softness; its doorway boasted two outside sentries, and beyond them, the competent deployment of a first-class field troop at rest. Keldmar knew war. No fault could be found with the force Lysaer s'Ilessid had mustered and trained at Avenor.

Three thousand four hundred eighty-three men; the captain who lingered from the escort expressed his regrets for another seven hundred, forced to remain behind at Isaer.

'Why were they left?' Keldmar asked to carry the conversation.

He heard then of the execution that had ended in chaos when a terrible, sorcerous portent crossed the sky.

'Our liege could ill spare the men,' the captain finished. 'But Avenor couldn't shirk its due part in suppressing the unrest expected from Tysan's clansmen. The condemned was Lady Maenalle s'Gannley, descended, they say, of the old Camris princes.'

Keldmar sipped his dry wine and scarcely marvelled. Townborn upstarts dared to describe the honourless act of a *caithdein*'s murder to his very face because competence such as this camp possessed required no excuse for effrontery.

His own brother was an old-blood duke; that Alestron remained governed under the charter granted at the hand of a duly crowned high king was no pittance. Without prior cause against Arithon s'Ffalenn, for the lady's ill usage, Keldmar would have spurned the cup for his dagger.

Only for the sake of shared enmity would the Prince of the West receive his hearing.

The hour grew late. Pages set out fresh candles, while campfires in the valleys dulled to a glaze of red embers. The coming and going of wakeful men gave way to the tramp of posted sentries. Clear above the camp's settled quiet came the sound of jingling harness. Then a man called in challenge and was answered. A ripple of awareness like a biting snap of frost passed over those field tents still lighted.

Warned by the signs that stamped brisk command, Keldmar arose as the horsemen drew rein beyond the tent flap. The equerry hastened through to grasp the reins of a gold-stitched bridle.

Then a stuttering flicker of torch light licked over a tabard flecked in jewels and bullion, and Lysaer s'Ilessid strode in from the dark. He peeled off his fine gloves and circlet, tossed both with a smile to the younger of his pages. The elder one handed him a goblet and flask. Hands burdened, the prince crossed the thick carpet, replenished Keldmar's empty cup unasked, then poured for himself and sat down. The camp chair cupped his frame in easy grace despite the encumbrance of state clothing.

'I'm sorry for the inconvenience of your wait, my lord.' Up close, his eyes were unflawed as a zenith sky, direct and sharp under brows the stretched arc of a hawk's wings. Burnished in candle glow, his straight cut hair gleamed a pale, fallow gold as he added, 'I envied your escape from the tedium. Etarra's minister of the treasury is slow as old frost when it comes to sealing writs for supply draughts.'

'Then you won your gold to hire a fleet,' Keldmar surmised, the curl to his lips very much an amusement, and his hand on his goblet pinched white. 'Did you also gain consent for your officers from Avenor to displace the captains of your allied garrisons?'

Lysaer sipped his wine, sparked to a lucent thread of laughter. 'My designs are so obvious?'

Keldmar's false levity tore away. 'I judge what I see. Your camp is professional. Has resentment on the part of Rathain's city captains indeed tied your vaunted royal hands?'

Unmoved, unstung by the sudden probe, Lysaer looked down; the charged, ruler's presence about him lent a stillness akin to sorrow. 'If our disparate commanders can't pull themselves together, I'd have them mend that weakness early. For against Arithon s'Ffalenn, the rank and file who follow their orders shall have no second chance at all.'

'They rejected your officers, the green fools.' Keldmar did not mock. The untouched wine in his goblet hung like pooled ruby against the brighter scarlet of the ducal tabard.

'A folly to be cauterized in bloodshed. It stands to reason,' Lysaer said. The late meeting had fretted away his serenity, and yet he was proud; he refused to give rein to restless pain and pace in the private comfort of his pavilion. 'Our late crossing through Halwythwood passed without incident, but my headhunter captain, Mayor Pesquil and I, share agreement. Rathain's clansmen only wait upon our weakness, our disorder, and our sorry, unwieldy lack of unity. They'll strike between here and the coast. We can't take the easy route to East Ward. That road crosses low country where our supply carts could bog down at each rain. Nor can we risk the trade galleys to an unsheltered northcoast harbour. Our march is for Werpoint, and harder. It's a cruel step to suffer, but the trials ahead will force our war host to its temper. The army that sails from Minderl Bay will be my honed weapon by then.'

Keldmar regarded the royal person, his admiration silent before challenge. Let Lysaer be first to broach what lay between them, intangibly thick as the storm now brewing in the dust-flat, sultry night.

Like the sword tempered to welcome hard blows, the Prince of the West opened the match. 'The Master of Shadow despoiled your armoury by sorcery and killed good men in your service. For that, you would fly south and raise your garrison at Alestron, and attack him in his haven at Merior. Why should your duke wait, you will say, upon a balky alliance of town garrisons? Why bide, while we argue among ourselves and leave the enemy at large to slip away?'

'You left one thing out,' Keldmar said, and slammed his filled goblet on a side table. 'You have Daelion's own bollocks, for expecting my brother to swear you s'Brydion loyalty.'

Lysaer looked up then, degrees colder than the frost-point gleam in his sapphires. 'I know clanborn pride, none better,' he said. 'I put Lady Maenalle to death.'

A moment passed in glaring silence while, royal to the bone, the prince in his majesty refused outright to explain or excuse his summary act.

Blistered by that courage, then forced to unwilling respect, Keldmar was first to look away.

Lysaer's smile warmed then like a sudden fall of new sunlight. 'I don't ask your duke's word in vassalage. How could I dare? You've lost an armoury and seven worthy lives to the wiles of Arithon s'Ffalenn. Over wine, for an evening, let me tell you what my father and grandfather suffered. At the end, I will ask, and you will answer as your brother's interest requires: to wait, and time Alestron's attack in concert with mine, or to risk your loyal following alone in unsupported action.'

When Keldmar drew breath to retort, Lysaer forestalled him. 'No, listen. Let me tell you why your fifteen thousand, no matter how trained, will never seal your success.' And in the sultry dark, across veiling candleflame and above the growl of distant thunder from the ridges, he spoke of the sea raids on the world of his birth that had brought his father's kingdom to its knees.

The storm broke over the Mathorns at dawn, smacking the oiled canvas tents like sails and upsetting the horses on the picket lines. Lightning flared across clouds churned like dirtied fleeces, until the rains fell and rinsed the air grey. Lord Commander Diegan found his royal liege still curled in his chair, his head cradled in forearms clothed yet in the sparkle of last night's crumpled finery.

A virulent slam of thunder shocked the earth. Lysaer's recoil from the overwhelming bang scribed in the arc and flare of every unmerciful band of braidwork.

Lord Diegan grinned over the litter of emptied wine flasks at the prince's dishevelled state of grooming. 'Well,' he said, cheerful, 'did you win him?'

'If I survive the hangover, I think so.' Lysaer pitched his words in precarious care through the shuttering rungs of ringed fingers. 'Is it raining?'

'Ath,' Diegan said, appalled to an evil grin. 'The vintage must have been excellent. The sky is gushing floods to swamp the frogs. Are you going to move? Or shall we call off that tactical meeting you scheduled for first thing this morning?'

'I hadn't forgotten.' Lysaer stirred and settled tenderly erect. 'Mind you remember when we meet the Duke of Alestron, in case the trait runs in the family. Keldmar s'Brydion has a demon's own tolerance for drink.'

The war host gathered to rout out the Shadow Master organized itself, and arranged its vast lists and supply lines, and coalesced in a seething morass of steel helms and spears and ox drays. The last march began to cross one hundred and twenty leagues of road between Etarra and the port on Minderl Bay. On departure, the banners snapped in fresh wind and horn calls wailed salutes from the city battlements.

Within an hour, the panoply paled. The columns laboured east in a soup of sucking mud, while supply carts stuck and foundered to curses from the men, stripped bare to the waist, who levered the mired axles from greedy earth. Horses lost shoes, and wet leathers chafed sores that stung to the run of salt sweat. Through the final, sweltering grip of late summer, the ground baked hard, and the dust rose, choking, to sting nose and throat and rim the eyes red to a punishing sting of raw glare.

Garrison banners and the surcoats of the officers lost their colours to a settled layer of grime. Man and beast and ox dray groaned under a brassy arch of sky. Like toiling ants, the army crawled across the dry plain toward the city of Perlorn. Supply wagons gouged the way into ruts, their teams harried on by the flat snap of ox goads. By night, the provisions were sheltered in palisades built by the vanguard as drop points, each one defended by its allotment of bored guards.

If barbarians watched from the thickets and the dank, rocky seams of the gullies, the most vigilant outrider never saw them. That clansmen lurked there, Captain Mayor Pesquil never for one instant ceased to doubt. He ran his squads of headhunters to the bone on scouting forays, and engineered foxy diversions to catch lapsed sentries and roust laggard companies back to discipline. He bullied and exhorted and had hard cases whipped where he caught standards slackened more than once.

But his officers could not be everywhere. The garrison companies were unused to the wilds, resentful of the hard ground, and sour, smoked meat, and nights spent slapping off insects. When the first leagues passed without incident, the young and the untried, the old and complacent, were first to let down their guard.

The morning dawned when eighteen divisions discovered the bungs prised out of their water barrels. The casks in neat stacks were drained to the dregs, and their draught teams and oxen dropped dead of slit throats at the picket lines. Other tales of woe travelled up the lines, of cart axles broken and food supplies fouled beyond salvage.

Over the cooling carcasses of dead beasts, Pesquil dispatched his trackers. They rode out with dogs in tight, guarded teams, and ran circles over false trails.

'Barbarians dragged the ground with a fresh deer hide, or a fox pelt,' he reported, dry as the parched rocks that bristled the landscape, and wholly unsurprised. 'This is the work of Red-beard's scouts.' He hawked phlegm from a corner of his mouth. 'No use to hunt them. They know how to choose easy targets.'

His hair a gilt beacon against hills feathered with browned grasses, and his hands at ease on his destrier's reins, Prince Lysaer listened without censure, even as Pesquil spat again.

'My headhunters are better spent staging false raids to keep our own sentries alert!' His eyes like jet beads in crimped leather and his jawline grizzled in pepper and salt stubble, the headhunter captain finished in disgust. 'These raids aren't staged to kill, but to delay us. They could succeed. Storms and cold won't wait while we flounder.'

Between prince and captain, the frustration crackled, that the officers from Avenor had been trained to counter just such petty harassment.

'The garrison commanders must come to us, asking,' Lysaer replied in the steel calm he wielded these days like a weapon. 'Their captains must be willing, or their people won't give their heart for us. Later, you know that could get them well killed.'

Pesquil returned a sour grunt. 'You won't let me rattle their nerves into line, well, they're going to have to get bloodied. Nothing for it. Pedigree pride hates to bend.' He shook his head, raked a lank fall of hair from his temples, then crammed on his conical helm. 'Fools. It's their greenest young boys will get buried for their blunders.'

Forced on short rations, men learned to set a sharper edge on their vigilance. The change earned small respite, too late. In one chilling move, the barbarian raiders adjusted their tactics to compensate. Through the heavy dawn mist, leather-clad figures were sighted while stealing away from the picket lines. Men rousted half-clothed from their blankets seized horses and swords, and gave chase to find themselves lured into the deep brush and surrounded, then picked off at whim by hidden archers.

A day was lost to rage and panic, and a second to rites for the fallen.

The fact that the town garrisons had been singled out confirmed Pesquil's theory of planned and leisurely scoutwork.

'No mistake, the ground and the victims were chosen.' The headhunter captain's tactless summary assigned heavy blame on the pedigree captains packed into Lysaer's field tent. 'We've rid the ranks of some useless brash fools. Maybe now your high-bred officers won't howl so loudly if my men ride under cover with their patrols.'

'They'll be welcome, but the lesson's understood,' assured the captain from Narms who had suffered the most humiliating losses. 'Next time, no man of mine will rush to react in hot haste.'

'No, they won't,' Pesquil answered, inimical. 'Red-beard's Earl Steiven's own son, and clansmen don't replay their tricks twice.'

His words were borne out before noontide when the next ranks to die tumbled into a pit trap sunk into the clay of the roadbed. The snare had been dug through the night, over a span where wagons had rolled scatheless at sundown. The location had been selected for exhaustive inconvenience, on a banked causeway over a gully. The ditches were too steep for wagons, laced with cracks and sharp shale to lame even unburdened horses. Where the terrain offered safe crossing, if a head-hunter scout was not at hand to warn of spring-traps and nooses, men died. The lucky were cut down choking, but still alive. The less fortunate broke their necks, or thrashed in screaming agony, ripped on stakes and disembowelled. A courier sent from the head of the column drew rein in a sliding sting of gravel to inform that more snares had been sprung up the road. The way to Perlorn was cut off, supply wagons stopped until work crews could fill in the pits.

Scouts were doubled; then doubled again, and the empty road itself set under watch. The barbarians struck like wraiths and vanished into the summer broom. Outriders who were careless died beyond sight of their fellows, or were killed when their dart-shot mounts spooked and bolted, jerked neck-broken from their saddles by thin cords left strung through the scrub. The raids came at random. Ox teams were shot down with arrows, or men, taken as they sought some thicket to relieve themselves. Harried like an elephant by hornet stings, the war host lumbered onward. The weather broke into rain again as the road wound and steepened and scrolled through the slab-faced hills that framed the upper range of the Skyshiels.

'Ath, this can't go on,' wept a young recruit whose sergeant had died in his arms on a desolate, rocky stretch of road.

'It can. It will. Damned clans'll show you worse before Werpoint,' cracked Pesquil, paused to water his brush-scarred gelding at a mountain spring between patrols. 'A smart soldier toughens up and survives.'

But hungry men managed setbacks less smoothly. Rations were short-ened again, as supplies became hard to replenish. Anger built as losses mounted. Time could ill be spared to mount a task force to scour the brush to rout out elusive bands of barbarians. To fire the grass and haze them off was no option in dry weather. A wrong change in the wind could as easily turn the conflagration and smoke back upon them to the ruin of the crawling ox wagons.

'Remember, they're Arithon's allies,' Lysaer said on night visits to bolster morale around the campfires. 'If our war force fails to make Werpoint before the storms, we have lost good men for no cause. To lose heart and falter now will just abet the Shadow Master's design.'

The prince's exhortations might bind the men to fresh purpose, but no effort might cool the biting frustration as the war host lumbered into the high country, a month behind its set schedule.

Then the last summer heatwave shattered before a driving line of storms. Rain lashed and fell in wave upon wave of fierce cloudbursts. Water splashed in rungs off the uplands rock to pool in murky torrents and flood the low ground. The ravines swelled and boiled into white water fanged with grey rock, treacherous to ford, and at times impossible for the draught teams. The wagons were lightened, the food, the tents, the supplies drawn across on strung ropes, then the carts laboriously lashed together and planked over as makeshift bridges. More days were lost, while armour and weapons rusted and the spirits of the men corroded to depression and gloom.

Then the storms cleared before a sweeping wave of cold. Huddled in the frost stiffened folds of their blankets, men slept as they could, or shivered on watch under silverpoint, glittering starlight. Winds off the Skyshiels were the cause of early frost, but here fell the first warning, in the breath of fickle gusts that would build and brew up the winter storms.

'The howl of wolf packs would be more welcome,' Lord Commander Diegan said to Lysaer when a wayward blast through their pavilion extinguished the lamps yet again. 'Fiends plague the hindmost, we're scarcely past halfway to Perlorn!'

The worst of the route lay ahead, in Pesquil's relentless opinion.

Midmorning showed them the ravine through Valleygap, and a road traced with thin ruts over scattered rock and moraine, between stony embankments grizzled with stunted stands of trees. Higher, the escarpments broke into crags littered about the knees with trunks like slivered bone where tapestried stands of black fir lay rent through by debris from past slides.

Under the gliding sail of hawks, Pesquil regarded the saw-toothed rimwalls, holed by black caves and peppered with crannies for ambush. 'Calves to the slaughter,' he murmured to his prince. 'You want to be quit of your dandybred captains? Let them all pass this gap decked out in their pretty blazoned surcoats.' His bearded lips split into a cough, contempt choked just short of laughter.

Lysaer looked aside, his eyes flat enamel while his horse pawed the gravel underneath him. 'They will not dress plainly. My advice was ignored. Our troops from Avenor, and Harradene's veterans, and your headhunters had best jump to compensate. My charge to all divisions who are wise to clan ways is to shoulder responsibili*t* / for this war host and get them through Valleygap safely.'

'As well hand young Red-beard your royal life on a salver,' Pesquil said, and spat, while cold gusts tapped the lacing against the scratched steel of his bracers.

'My life rests in your hands, first, Captain Mayor.' Lysaer s'Ilessid straightened before his officer's surly mockery. Whetted to an icy, royal tone of command, he added, 'If Jieret Red-beard would lay traps to ruin good men, your designated task is to forestall him. For I shall ride with our weakest link, the garrison companies out of Narms.'

Pesquil uttered a volley of bitten oaths. While rude words slapped back in echoes off the forbidding ramparts of the rock, he glowered down the swale, mindful that his prince was no fool. All the same, the task ahead made his nerves crawl. A made haven for barbarians, perfect eyrie for spring-traps and stone falls, the scarps that notched the way promised dire trouble and murder. Irked to his bones, Pesquil reined round his scarred gelding and spurred off to issue harsh orders.

Grouped into tight, defensive phalanxes, the war host paused in its tracks. Neither man nor beast would enter the defile until Valleygap's heights were made safe. For that, Captain Mayor Pesquil dispatched his best trackers and scouts to scour the rimrocks on either side. The paired groups of two hundred advanced up the slope in fanned formation, three to lead each foray team, then a back-up band of six to a dozen trailing, to move in support if enemies were flushed, or point men ran into snares.

The footing across the Skyshiel ridges was a fiendish mix of slate and black shale that splintered under boot soles and shot spinning, chinking fragments downslope. These sliced through the greenery and caused furtive rustles. Men would spin, hands gripped to their weapons, while the rattle of every descending ricochet slapped taut nerves to razor response. Stealth of any sort was impossible. The scout who eased his vigilance on presumption such disturbances were harmless would be the one downed first by covert archers.

The sun blazed down like a scourge, bit glare off the rock faces and dazzled from every sluiced spring and puddle. Assaulted at each turn by the surfeit of light, the eyes struggled and ached to compensate; to unriddle the deep shadows blanketing the defiles and fir groves. Anything motionless could hide there, unseen. The summit ridges were exposed to the rake of the wind, scoured clean by the snow and weather, then chiselled to split edges by frost. To stand upright was to offer a target outlined in sky; to crawl or worm forward became torturous misery, over shale points that shredded the hands and the knees bloody, or through the low furze that stabbed prickles through mail and clothing.

The terrain was of a stamp to make a man's spine crawl in constant, uneasy shivers. Against a savage beauty that presented an unrelenting danger, the veteran teams searched through the caves and the crannies to smoke out any clansmen poised for ambush, or to disarm death traps set above the road. They advanced with their teeth clamped in silent prayer and fretted their nerves into knots.

Barbarians would be ensconced and waiting to kill, not a scout among them ever questioned. The unnatural creatures were fiends at covert murder and Valleygap's vicious, untrustworthy gullies presented opportunities too perfect to pass up.

Hours passed. Sweating out wary impatience on the road at the horns of the gap, Pesquil received his reports. Nothing, and nothing; the rocks stayed empty of sign. He paced. He loosened his gelding's girth, then tightened his bracers and swore. Perched on the tarps of a wagon nearby, a long-faced captain from Anglefen twisted his mustachio and questioned the Captain Mayor's agitation.

The headhunter commander spun on his heel, his face a contorted, black scowl. 'Ath! Those rocks are rotten with bolt-holes. Clansmen lurk up there bent purely on massacre. I'll stake my life on the certainty.'

'Obsession, more like,' groused a drover, but softly; the Captain Mayor's temper was respected.

Another hour passed, uneventful. Troops made to wait in formation under the blasting noon heat became irritable, then restless. Their sergeants sent increasing requests down the line, urging the decision to resume march.

'Nobody moves!' Pesquil cracked to Lord Diegan. 'Are they deaf? When the road's safe, I told them. Only then. Let them fret and rejoice to stay breathing!' To the paired scouts who hovered at his elbow for fresh orders, he said, 'You, take the north ridge; you, the south. Go topside and slow the teams down. I don't want anybody getting slack and complacent.'

A derisive hoot erupted from the garrison columns. Another voice carped on the Captain Mayor's dwindling courage, to stall and delay, when Valleygap's crags were so obviously untenanted.

Pesquil stood his ground and ignored all the remarks, his black eyes stark as bog water and the sinews in his jaw cable-tight.

Minutes later, the prince drew rein at his shoulder.

From astride, dewed with sweat beneath the shadow of his visor, Lysaer regarded the headhunter captain's corked back, fiery unease. 'You're worried,' he said in careful inquiry.

Pesquil snapped off a nod. 'I don't like this. Not one bit. I'd sleep better under rockfalls and log traps. My trackers say they have yet to find so much as a wretched bent fern.'

'What do your hunches suggest?' Lysaer tipped off his helm and shut his eyes as a breath of fir-scented wind ruffled the stuck ends of his hair.

'My hunches? They're screaming.' Pesquil scanned the slow circle of a carrion bird above the cliffs, then cracked the knuckles of his sword hand in deliberate succession. 'We're not the cats in this game, your royal Grace. Count on my instinct, we're the mice.'

Lent no sign upon which to hang reason, after the next hour, he relented. His trackers could descend from the summits in stages, to quarter the slopes to the valley floor. Hard on the heels of his directive came report of twenty-six fatalities from the north face.

'Missteps and falls,' said the scout, breathing in jerks from his run. 'The men standing said nothing looked amiss. The casualties just stepped on solid rock that gave under them.'

Pesquil threw the reins of his gelding to the staff sergeant at his elbow. 'Go back up,' he told the scout. 'And get another man to run relay to the south ridge. All teams are to stop where they are. These were no accidents, nor just bad luck. Let no one advance any farther until I've unearthed the reason.' To Prince Lysaer, he added, 'Tell your garrisons to make camp. We won't be moving before sunset, that's certainty. Warn the captains. Their divisions must be kept on a very tight leash. It could take days to clear this pass.'

Squat, and staid in his stride as quarried rock, Lord Commander Harradene of Etarra arrived in a sour chink of mail. Eyes of china-doll blue seemed at odds with his grizzled black eyebrows, pulled now into the scowl that his recruits nicknamed 'the bear's lair'. 'Pesquil, your runner from the south face is down with a broken leg. Seventeen falls off the slope, from his side. He wished you to hear his report before the bone-setters numb his wits with a posset.'

'Tell him the matter's already in hand.' Pesquil rolled his shoulders, bent, and let the heavy mail shirt he preferred for mounted use slither off by its own weight. He heaved the limp mass over his saddlebow, unlashed a light brigandine from the roll behind the cantle, then dragged that over the rust-streaked leather of his gambeson. The sergeant led his gelding off unasked.

Corded like a grizzled old predator, Pesquil checked his weapons before Commander Harradene's florid presence. 'Hold the garrisons to order with an iron fist,' he said in crisp haste. 'No man leaves camp. Not even to forage for firewood. Believe this, I dread what I'll find up there. The traps to welcome our army through this defile have been long months in the planning.'

Shadows painted the deep vale of Valleygap in virid, umber and purple. The cart ruts snaked between the louring slabs of slate, cut against a sky like lucent silk. Here and there setting sunlight licked a pinnacle to a lingering flame of red gold. On his knees in a thicket beneath the dank jut of an overhang, Pesquil jammed his knife into its sheath and crouched back on his heels. Always when his blood ran hottest, the curses stuck cold on his tongue.

'The Ath-forsaken rock's been trapped,' he said. 'I expected as much, but here's proof.' He sifted his fingers through a litter of stone crushed into the moss by his knee. 'Litter left by a chisel. Steiven was bad, but Dharkaron avenge, Red-beard his son is a demon.'

A moan cut the gloom from a man sprawled downslope, pinned in place by the agony of broken bones. Whether his hurts included fatal bleeding, no one dared reach him to check. The hale scouts poised at their Captain Mayor's shoulder were too bitterly experienced to give way to the concern that tore at their hearts.

Pesquil stood up, his iron-grey hair at one with the gloaming in the fir thickets. 'Pass my orders. Have teams make their way down to the wounded, but on ropes where the rock is laid bare. Check your footing. This ravine's a natural death trap, a rock slide just screaming to happen. Let's not be the fools to set one off.'

The scouts organized to depart.

'One more thing,' Pesquil called after them. 'Any man not rescued by nightfall stays where he lies. All territory we've covered that's clean stays guarded. I want no barbarian foray skulking in to foul our backtrail in the dark.'

Hand signals answered; his men were efficient, those few inclined to argue long since broken to sharp discipline. The scouts who served in the headhunter's league knew very well: the ones who followed orders stayed alive.

Yet even for scouts grown crafty through experience, Valleygap offered no respite. The spring-traps set waiting in the path of the teams who laboured to help the wounded were not set to kill, but to cripple.

'The scrub is full riddled,' a shaking veteran reported, arrived with the litters into the safety of the camp. Behind him, borne gasping in a stupor of pain, came the fallen, the arms which had attempted to help their fallen comrades staked through with sharpened slivers of wood; or their legs, gashed white to the bone, if the bones themselves were not snapped.

Under full night, the moon scored the ridges like polish on ivory above the black swale of Valleygap. Hunched in a hellish flare of torch light, Pesquil counted the best of his scouts among this first round of casualties. Gripped by brittle patience, he regarded each one's suffering, then cracked orders that made men leap to fetch garrison healers to attend them. 'Let every town-coddled lancer see the cost of fighting Red-beard's barbarians. Then let them hear 'til they shake in their boots, for when they face the Master of Shadow on the field, they will suffer a thousand times worse!'

Anger brewed like live current around the campfires. Wood was too scarce for the cooks to bake bread; the brick ovens stayed dismantled, while men choked down dry chunks of biscuit and chewed leathery slabs of sour cheese. Over talk and the measured tread of sentries, above the soft snorts of horses who pawed in complaint for scant fodder and the low of disgruntled oxen, they heard the brisk concern of their officers. Then chilling as nightmare came the shattering screams as a deep gash was cauterized, or a bone set straight for the splint. The cliff scarps shredded every cry into echoes. Clean wood smoke laced through the sickening stink of charred flesh. The men mustered to bring war to the southern spit at Merior lay that night in their blankets, unsleeping and stifled by raw dread.

Caithdein of Shand

Two days prior to autumn equinox, the workers in the shipyard at Merior cut seasoned lengths of pitch pine to start the new brigantine's decking. Arithon was not on hand to mark the occasion, nor would he be present as the keel was laid down to begin the construction of the second. Withdrawn from the company of his workers, he ferried the comatose person of Dakar aboard his painted little sloop. He had not returned to the Koriani herbalist's cottage even for the hour when the last splints were removed from the boy's wrist to show bone and muscle healed straight and smooth beneath a spider-laced mesh of pink scars. The same morning, remarked by the fishwives, *Talliarthe* slipped her mooring and set sail.

The course she steered through fair-weather swells was due northwest off the reefs; the passage she accomplished was brief. She made port in the harbour at Telzen to place orders at the mills for new lumber and to pick up a packet of dispatches. Bent to dark brooding by ill news from the north, and a recount of unmentionable tragedy, Arithon pressed on upcoast and dropped anchor in a forested cove twenty leagues distant from Elssine. Alone in the blaze of a cloudless, calm morning, he rowed his dory to the beach.

At a time and place most carefully appointed, he grounded the boat in an exploding flock of terns and dragged her up beyond the tidemark. Wrapped in air that smelled of scrub pine and sea wrack, surrounded by the plaintive calls of fishing birds, he whistled a clear major triplet.

Then he perched on the trunk of a storm-toppled palm and waited, hopeful that his past request for a rendezvous had been received in good grace. In time, a lanky clansman clad in deerhide emerged from the brush to meet him.

No rustled foliage betrayed the presence of others, though such scouts were certainly there, crouched in concealment amid the vine-choked thickets and oat grass, and alert behind their strung bows. Well versed in his dealings with clansmen, Arithon understood the wrong move would see him skewered with a hail of broadheads at short range. Unprepossessing, a target limned in full sunlight, he showed no sign that he cared.

The clansman spoke, and was answered by prearranged words in Paravian. A carved wooden token changed hands.

His other lean fist never far from his knives, the scout fingered the incised falcon set against a shaved crescent moon, device of Shand's past high kings. 'Ath!' He pulled a vexed frown. Beneath mottled streaks of stain to mask the line of his profile, he looked little older than Jieret. 'It's his Grace of Rathain? Our chieftain's going to lose silver. He wagered on a galley flying banners and a retinue prinked with large emeralds. Is your vaunted prince still on board?'

A smile flicked Arithon's lips as he rose. 'My sloop holds a fat prophet with a belly ache. He was much too sick to come ashore.'

A pause ensued. When the visitor listed no further passengers, the young scout recovered slack manners with a flush that left him dusky to the hairline. The unassuming figure before him was given a second, piercing study, though prior assessment had been accurate: the black-haired arrival carried no visible badge of rank. Small and neatly made, he wore the loose, shabby dress of a fisherman and carried no weapon beyond a longsword in black metal, the sleek line of its swept-back quillons half-buried in a fold of linen shirt. 'Arithon Teir's'Ffalenn? Your Grace?'

'Just Arithon, if you please. As well, you can call off your hunting pack.'

The clan scout jerked up his chin. 'Not so fast. Any man could carve out an old high king's device or parrot a phrase in the old tongue. Show me proof. I'd be certain of your bloodline.'

'None but a fool would lay claim to my name, with half of the north roused to arms.' Turned brisk in distaste, Arithon yanked loose his right cuff tie. He peeled back the sleeve and bared for inspection the deep, welted scar seared into the length of his forearm. The brand had been left by the light bolt cast against him by his half-brother that had doomed him to Desh-thiere's curse.

'That will satisfy.' Relieved to be spared a proving wrought of magecraft or shadows, the scout pursed his lips and shrilled the piping call of a plover into the thicket behind him.

A movement behind the pine branches revealed the form of a man, who unfolded from a crouch and emerged on a cat's stride onto the sandy verge. He topped the seed tufts of the oat grass by a head. A black and tan laminate bow made of horn hung from his immensely broad shoulder. He had a beard like rooted wire, clipped short. A fat black pearl strung on a braided cord nested in the tanned hollow of his throat. His hair capped his skull, glossy as a sable's pelt licked through with silver, and salted pure white at the temples. The bones of his face were like fitted, stamped bronze, and imposing, coupled with straight brows and eyes of lucent turquoise.

'As your Grace may see, the hunting party consisted of one,' he addressed in a baritone flawed in the grain like burred oak.

He side-stepped to display the arrows in his shoulder quiver, fletched with grey heron quills and pointed for small game. The sword he carried was a masterwork of arms, figured with interlace that made its great size appear deceptively delicate.

Arithon tilted his head to measure the frame that towered over him. He did not repeat the error of the scout. 'Lord Erlien s'Taleyn, High Earl of Alland?'

'To a prince who wears rags, plain Erlien will do.' Frost-crystal eyes swept the scion of Rathain and dismissed the whole man in fierce challenge. 'Your mother descended from our own s'Ahelas royalty, it's said. Well, I set no truth to the claim. The blood of the kings my forebears served was substantial, and you but a mouse with scarcely the growth to do more than bloody my kneecap.'

Arithon shrugged, grave-faced. 'Be warned then, my lord. Since I favour my father, that should charge you to keep careful guard on your kneecap. What's more, if you've lost any silver over galleys and flags, I shall pay off the debt myself.'

Erlien burst into deep-chested laughter, while the pearl at his neck danced on its tether of thong. 'Dharkaron himself! I'll admit we tested your presumptions. Since in fact you have none, you're most welcome to the Kingdom of Shand.' He drew a black-handled dirk from the back of his belt, kissed the reversed blade, then intoned in overdone courtesy, 'As *caithdein* and this realm's steward, my life's pledge as surety for visiting princes. I beg for the sake of tradition that you leave my poor shanks intact.'

'Dharkaron witness, I might.' Arithon stretched his stride to fall in step as the chieftain and his scout led off through the undergrowth. Not about to seem cowed by the massive man looming beside him, he added, 'Should my sloop be left anchored in plain sight?'

'Don't trouble.' Erlien flashed back a bear's lazy grin, hands flexed in a disquieting, powerful contrast as he sheathed his enormous knife. 'Your boat's a fine morsel of bait. Should a galley put in to investigate, we'll lighten her cargo as forfeit. City captains well know to steer clear of these coves. We've sunk the keels from under the rash ones, or any who played cocky and forgot.'

Affable, even easy, as the chieftain's manner seemed, the stalking grace of his tread reflected resounding unease. He carried paired dirks in the cuffs of his boots, and he skirted his native thickets like quarry.

411

Vexed to quick chills by his bardic intuition, Arithon offered, 'I'll surrender my sword, if that would reassure you.'

Erlien slammed to a stop. Spattered with sun through the chinks in high pine trees, his shoulders stayed unrelaxed. The eyes turned to Arithon were narrowed and sullen amid a wind-lined mesh of crow's feet. 'And that would do me good with your full command of shadows at my back?'

'It might.' Arithon sustained that burning, light gaze, though his palms broke into a fine sweat. 'The blade is the same one carried by my ancestors. She bears the name Alithiel.'

'Paravian-wrought. I'd heard of her.' As a thrush took wing in a whir of drab feathers, Erlien smothered a hair-trigger start. 'Then the legend is true, that your sword is enspelled to dazzle an attacker into blindness?'

'Only if the defending cause is just,' amended Arithon. 'We'll both keep our sight. I didn't come here to force any favours through sorcery.'

'Yet you're a peril in our midst all the same.' Erlien tapped his weapon hilt, the fringes on his buckskins the only ripple in resinous air. Cut off from the sea breeze, the scrub forest was stifling, the sky through green and bronze needles cerulean as fired enamel. 'If you'd give up your arms, what would you balk at? Being tied, or blindfolded, or dragged through the salt bogs at knife point? To put the issue baldly, does any means exist to disarm the dire powers of your birthright?'

The scout drawn in as witness of a sudden looked jaggedly unsettled.

Very still, his eyes wide open under spiked, dark lashes, Arithon forced his stance to stay easy despite the prickles that stabbed down his spine. 'Dharkaron as my witness,' he said at length. 'If when you're finished I can stop Lysaer's headhunters from reiving through Shand after scalps, no paltry indignity you might name lies outside the reach of my patience.'

'And if I prevented you leaving?' Erlien pressed. 'There's a price on your head, in Alestron.'

The scout momentarily forgot to breathe, as the bristling tension between the two men strained thinner and tighter and more deadly.

'For that cause, I would certainly fight.' In a blinding, smooth move, Arithon unsheathed his longsword. Paravian steel sang faintly at the kiss of the air to its edge. The black metal shimmered flint-sharp with highlights: scribed along its length, the interlaced angles of silver runes gleamed, rainbowed like chipped crystal, but raised to no pulse of ancient magic. Only the commonplace reflections of green pine and bright sunlight grazed its polish as Arithon held the tip at guard point.

'Why fence with manners?' invited the Prince of Rathain to Shand's top-ranking chieftain. 'Let's settle this now, then talk like sane men afterward.'

'To first blood, then,' Erlien agreed in fierce pleasure. He shrugged off his bow and quiver and cleared his own steel to do battle.

With no appointed arbiter and not a second's breath of warning, he attacked with all the force of his muscular height and stature.

Arithon matched that killing thrust with a parry that staggered him backward. Small, compact, he moved like wind itself. But no feat of quick footwork could counter Erlien's greater reach. The high earl pressed his advantage of size to the fullest. His weapon slapped back in riposte with a skill that whistled air; clanged into Arithon's guard like a forge hammer.

The dismayed scout jumped back in avoidance, while paired blades whined and clashed, flat ground to flat in a nerve-painful scream of separation.

Whatever Erlien's claim at the outset, the offensive he waged against a man not an enemy implied no possibility of quarter.

Caged in caught sunlight, the whickered beat of steel was unsparing of life and limb. Before the clan lord's bracing, fast offensive, Arithon was driven hither and yon like a wasp at the whim of a gale. The shocking clash of each parry left him no space for recovery. He required full strength to turn the battering blows, to deflect the chieftain's larger blade away from a crippling strike.

The ground itself offered hazard. Rotted trunks lay matted in creepers and thicket, any open space between laced with roots and littered in sticks and fallen pine cones. Too beset to mind his footing, unable to glance behind to secure a clean path for retreat, Arithon ducked and twisted by cat's reflex. Only the catch of greenbriars against a calf, or a poke of stemmed scrub, warned when his way lay impeded. Sand and matted needles offered dismal purchase, a sore disadvantage. He must meet each of Erlien's strikes in perfect form, or risk a slipped step. To be jostled off-balance would bring disaster. He would be run through or cut before he fell, and time and again, the treacherous soil gave and parted under his light tread. Too hard pressed for speech, he pitched his body to the limits of speed and reflex in a stripped labour of self-defence.

Inevitably, the strain told on Arithon first. Blade locked to blade in a screaming bind, his hands ran hot sweat, and his lips peeled back from his teeth as wrist and sinew resisted the twisting pressure that sought to disarm him. The spiked limbs of a deadfall hedged his back. He could not spring clear, but had to muscle his sword against Erlien's, for agonized seconds bearing up under the levering brunt of the chieftain's remorseless weight. A twist of his body unlimbered his sword from Erlien's. He jumped left, the only way open to him.

And ready for that saving step yet again was a whistling blue fence of steel.

Taxed sinews this time could not respond soon enough. Arithon had his blade up, but not positioned. The blow whined into black steel and slid through, diverted from a chest strike, but not clear of his left upper arm. A line of scarlet opened through Arithon's sleeve.

'First blood!' the scout cried in close to hysterical relief. 'My lord, the match is yours.'

But the same hair-trigger instinct that had saved Arithon from being mired in a thicket warned him now not to lower his guard.

Erlien's next riposte clanged into a solid parry, and the next and the next, the very same. Driven into a hollow bristled with saplings, the Shadow Master thrashed a near-fatal step into the grabbing twigs of the brush. Then, inspired perhaps by extremity, he leaped backward into the deep undergrowth. To reach him, Erlien must follow. Swords pinged and sheared through green sticks. Pruned bits of foliage took scything flight. Arithon burrowed backwards like a rabbit and emerged on clear ground, while Erlien smashed blundering after him. For the first time since the duel started, they were parted by more than a sword's length.

Arithon stood, desperate for respite, heaving painful, fast breaths, his sleeves plastered to lean limbs by running sweat and blood. He did not look like a mage or a prince. Beaten to graceless exhaustion, he had no breath for words, no vitality left to frame expression. The sword still raised over an arched mesh of briars trembled in the struck fall of sunlight through the high crowns of the trees.

No less tired, his buckskins patched dark on his shoulders and his fringes flecked in hacked leaves, Erlien lowered his blade, braced the pommel against his hip, and deliberately stripped to the waist. Then, without speech, he discarded his shed leathers, caught up his weapon and resumed.

Every rule of mercy was abrogated. To the scout, watching agonized as blade met blade in a screech of choked-off vibration, disaster seemed unavoidable. The odds had been pushed too far. Cornered beyond recourse against an opponent who outmatched him, Arithon was going to be forced to use sorcery or shadows just to avoid getting butchered.

The driving brilliance had gone from his speed. His steps in retreat were clumsy. Snatched off his rhythm by roots and dense brush, time and again he had to grasp his blade two-handed to stave off Erlien's assault. Blood flew in shocked droplets from the marked arm that, even bracing, quivered from sapped strength.

Fatigue had blunted the edge from Erlien's style also. Pared to a bare framework of training, he was solid and methodically sure. The force of his body behind each attack wore and worried and hammered his slighter opponent past telling. Blade sheared on blade through a harried retreat that strained the nerves in suspension. Each riposte that threatened ending became snatched back and sustained by Arithon's beleaguered guard, enjoined in dogged effort to defy his inevitable fate. He took a cut on the elbow, shallow, but distracting for the sting; then, in short succession, two more marks on his shoulder.

Sawn to a tortured pitch of tension, the scout scrubbed sweat from his eyes. He watched Arithon crash into another thicket. Twigs whipped. Steel snicked through leaves and clanged in indignant embrace. Tattered greens fluttered down to the whistling grunt of effort through locked teeth as Arithon smashed sidewards through sticks to evade a lethal cut to the head.

There came a screeling cry of steel on steel, blade raking blade from tip to crossguard. Borne backwards into a whippy mass of saplings, Arithon dropped, twisting, to one knee. The sword in his hand sang protest, locked still to Erlien's crossguard.

The chieftain found himself hampered in the narrowed press of the branches. Smaller, slighter, better able to move in close quarters, Arithon snatched his sole chance.

In a flying, sun-caught arc, he wrested his blade clear and hooked the point. Metal bound to metal. The chieftain lost grasp on his weapon to a stinging clamour of stressed sound. Through a short, hampered flight through close brush, the sword tangled and sliced down, point first, to impale itself in dark earth.

Erlien backstepped to recover, hooked a leg, and crashed onto his rump. Head flung back, blue eyes of feral intensity wide open, he sprawled with his chin upturned to meet the black blade that descended in fine, ringing temper to lick the bared cords of his throat.

Running blood, scuffed and nicked by briar and brush, Arithon glared through a soaked fall of hair. Sweat glued his hands to a sword that quivered in unsteady, light-caught spasms. 'Why?' he gasped, his voice husked out of true by his wracking tremors of exhaustion.

Erlien glared up that bared ribbon of steel and said nothing; and silence itself spoke as signal.

A ring of clan archers rose from hiding. They gripped bows with nocked arrows and their aim was trained at short range upon Arithon s'Ffalenn.

He greeted their presence with a wordless cry, spun on his heel, and cast his sword away. The black blade tumbled through the briar with a sharp, outraged ring, then thudded to rest at the feet of the scout, who dared make no move to recover it. Back turned, his arms braced between the trunks of two trees as though he begged help to stay upright, Arithon waited.

The expression on his face was not relief, not fear, not impatience: it was anger, naked and hot enough to wrench through his body in spasms. When the command to loose was not given to the archers, he pulled in a screaming breath. With all of his masterbard's diction, he demanded, imperious, 'Why?'

Erlien's first word was to his bowmen, a curt command to stand down. His answer to Arithon came inflectionless and short. 'As the clan chief responsible for this realm, I found it needful to test your mettle.'

'With your very life?' Fury overlaid with incredulity, his fine hands clamped into fists, the Shadow Master spun again to face the clan chief.

'Did your man Steiven leave you in ignorance? That's how it's given to *caithdeinen* to test princes, if need provides no other way.' Erlien mustered his will and arose, brush-scraped and weary, but unscorched by the royal ire bent upon him. 'You heard how Lady Maenalle of Tysan came to die?'

A wretched, prolonged shiver wrung Arithon from head to foot. 'I heard two days ago, about Maenalle.' Then he shut his lips, aggrieved and grim, not only for the fate the Lady s'Gannley had suffered at the hand of her prince, but for the goods which funded his shipworks, that laid guilt for her death at his feet. Erlien's statement also forced him to reassess a past the more painful, for indeed, it had been with his life that Earl Jieret's father, Lord Steiven, had compelled his prince to swear crown oath before the bloody battle at Strakewood.

To this living steward who sought to try him to the bitter limits of integrity, Arithon said, 'Your reason hasn't answered my question.'

'Because it's obvious.' Erlien brushed off the leaf mould that clung to his sweat-damp knuckles. 'You're living bait for a war host thirty-five thousand strong. If you come here to involve my clansmen, I would measure firsthand what took place on the banks of Tal Quorin. Did your sorcery and your shadows defend your feal following, or in fact, merely shield your own life? I was duty-bound to find out.'

As Arithon stiffened, Erlien raised a swift hand. 'I wished to know, too, if you could fight. Before Ath, I've sworn! I'll not offer my people as a shield for a weakling prince who lacks courage. And if you proved true to honour and seized no advantage through fell powers, though you died on my sword here and now, there's a balance met. Shand would be spared from your nasty coil of contention.'

'With my body sent off to Alestron for bounty?' Arithon unbent his fists to peel back the hair slicked to his forehead and temples. The anger had gone out of him as water might spill from a sieve. He looked and moved as if his wounds stung, though his sarcasm bit as he added, 'You made just one bitter mistake. I didn't come here to ask any clansmen to stand in my defence.'

Lord Erlien looked chagrined as a bear caught by bees while licking a muzzle glued with honey. 'Fiends plague! Then why are you here?'

Arithon gave a sour laugh. Touched to distaste by the widening stains on his shirt, surrounded by the avid band of scouts, he said, 'When I've finished being the subject of a bleeding exhibition, I'll recover my manners and tell you.'

The council arranged by Lord Erlien at Arithon's request had been called under open sky. Present were clan chiefs from Atwood in East Halla, and others from Orvandir's hill country. Not a few had travelled an inconvenient distance to be present. Given the nature of the *caithdein* who ruled Shand, the smell of tired horseflesh, the dry rounds of whispers, and the poisonous curiosity that pervaded the encampment scarcely came as a surprise.

Few of the elders called into attendance were inclined to share counsel with a stranger.

Lent the afternoon to apply his insight into the character of Alland's high earl, Arithon reviewed his conclusions. Erlien's authority was trade-marked by a quick, inquisitive mind. In love with talk, jocular in dis-missal of his guarding ranks of archers, his strength was quirky humour and an unfailing eye for detail. He liked surprises, encouraged combative rivalries among his captains, and seemed to thrive on keeping light guid-ance on disordered, freewheeling enterprise.

Gathered without ceremony at twilight beneath the sandstone ledges of an abandoned quarry, the inner circle of Shand's old-blood clansmen waited around a communal fire.

The introduction Lord Erlien offered his guest came typically pointed in acid. 'On my honour, I've determined this prince is not here to claim loyalty for the distaff side of his pedigree.'

'Did he try, he would die here,' a hook-nosed granddame in a snowy battle braid cracked through the gathering dusk.

'My clan elders,' Erlien presented. He jostled Arithon forward with an expansive, bold gesture toward the tight-gathered band who owed the realm of Shand feal allegiance. 'As you see, your welcome won't be tender.' His broad, tanned palm clapped the slighter man's shoulder in yet another boisterous round of challenge.

Braced like still iron as the blow fell, his unbound scabs crusted to discomfort, Arithon gave way but one step.

In vicious approval, Alland's earl finished, 'Master them, mage, if you can. For by Ath, they're a bloodthirsty bunch. All week they've been vying for the chance to be first to stake out your carcass for the ravens.'

'Despite your pledged life as my surety?' Arithon's bow answered cold as a slicked glint of steel. The rent and bloodied edges of his shirt flut-tered, plucked by the pine-scented breeze which flowed over the quarry's far rim. Above jumbled stones clothed over in creepers, the sky paled to lavender, stippled by faint early stars.

Erlien assumed the high seat, a flat-topped boulder set apart by a woven red throw rug. Replete as a sun-warmed adder, he surveyed his disgruntled pack of clan chiefs and chuckled. ''Ware Torbrand's temper. I've tasted its sting. Rathain's royal line might breed runt-sized, but there's mettle enough for all that. His Grace has come here to bring warning. By right of arms, he's earned his chance to speak.'

Arithon did not sit, but strode into the cleared ground by the fire. His footfall made scarcely any sound, even over washed gravel tailings. Splashed in the copper play of firelight, he was a form rendered in planes and shadow, the hawk-sharp angles of cheekbone and chin seared into profile against the gloom. His glance raked over the hard-bitten company who waited to hear him bearing weapons and bows, and no small measure of distrust. Arrogance bracketed one elder's mouth; hard patience stiffened another's back. A flaxen-haired woman near the sidelines stared in frank curiosity, while others projected unsettled hostility on faces lined like worn leather from lifelong exposure to southern sunlight.

Exposed on all quarters to unfriendly stares, Arithon would not be hurried. He measured them all, to the last, most inimical granddame, until not a clan chief among them could mistake the stamp of his presence.

This prince was s'Ffalenn, and touched bitter by his past, and above any other thing, dangerous.

Run short of patience since his trial at swordpoint, Arithon plunged straight to the crux. 'A war host thirty-five thousand strong is on the march to the coast of Minderl Bay. Although the feal clans of Rathain have been given my leave to cause their companies delay as they can, without additional intervention, the army could put to sea before winter. A fleet of galleys for transport is already mustering at Werpoint.'

He let no shred of sorrow show for the fact that Lord Jieret and his war captain were belike to use his royal sanction to spill townborn blood in punishing revenge for past losses.

Focused at need on necessities, Arithon let the chisel-cut buttresses of sandstone throw back the temper in his voice. 'If any portion of this army wins through, they'll eventually sail here to Alland. I've undertaken to escape, self-sufficient to sea by that hour. My departure should draw any threat away with me. But the best laid plans are not enough. The curse Desh-thiere has woven over me is remorseless, a compulsion inflicted without quarter. I would have you understand what that means.'

Evoked to a masterbard's command over language, he described the fearful loss of control he had suffered, when, on the banks of Tal Quorin, he had come to face his half-brother. The moment, wrenched out of harrowing memory, when nothing and no one had mattered; when the last of his integrity had been torn away and undone, consumed by a storm of blank hatred. Terror remained. The truth could not be glossed over or evaded. He would have sacrificed all without compunction, from the green growing land to the life of his last feal clansman to meet the curse's insatiable demand for the life of Lysaer s'Ilessid. While the geas held sway, all his love and conscience and humanity could be twisted to count for nothing at all.

In the bleak depths of nightmares, Arithon still tasted the poisoned ecstasy which had gripped him through that past second in time. Once, his half-brother's life had lain in his hand to crush without mercy, without thought.

Only young Jieret's intervention had averted irremediable disaster.

'The compulsion I bear lies beyond sane control,' the Master of Shadow said in summary. His forced, iron stillness lent a civilized mask over scouring humiliation. Through every day that he woke and breathed, he fought to withstand the vicious irony: despite his most diligent effort, the horror might happen again.

'If I chance to be cornered,' Arithon finished. 'If I should once encounter my half-brother on the field, my actions will brook no conscience. Shadows, sorcery, or human lives, whatever lies to hand will be seized as a means to wreak destruction. Lysaer's obsession with my death will stop at nothing, and I am mindful this is your land. The scope of the peril I may draw here is without precedence, and I've come to entreat your clans to withdraw to safety until this pass is finished. I've made plans as I may to distance myself from my enemy, but there can be no guarantees. Before the drive of the Mistwraith's curse, my best-laid strategy could run afoul.'

The stunned and thinking silence that gripped the council circle lasted for scarcely a heartbeat.

'You can't expect us to turn tail!' snapped a frost-haired scout on the fringes. 'The false prince murdered his *caithdein*. Before we see his annexed war host run riot through our territory, we'd sooner quash their effort at the start.'

Shouts haled back in agreement. 'Who needs foreign headhunters riding for scalps here in Alland! Even without their interference, an army that size would strip the land as it passes.'

Braced for the wrong sort of argument, Arithon rounded on Lord Erlien in incredulous, exasperated dismay. 'Are your elders all deaf? Have none of them heeded a single word I've said?'

The regent of the realm twitched his huge shoulders the way a wolf might shrug away flies. 'For Shand, we judge as we see fit.'

'If you're offering help to fan the fires of this war, I refuse you.' Scalded to impatience, Arithon flung back an ultimatum. 'This time, I'll give townsmen no cause at all to link my name with clan defenders.'

Erlien stretched, unbiddably tempered in mischief. 'In that case, my friend, you should've lost a certain sword fight.'

There was more; a depthless black malice gleamed in the clan chief's eyes, even through the shifting play of firelight.

'You've cause to oppose Lysaer already, I see,' Arithon probed in hedged caution.

'Prince Lysaer's no clansman's friend,' Alland's high earl allowed. 'Not since he proclaimed and enforced the execution of Tysan's sworn *caithdein*.' Sharp enough to note the Shadow Master's catch of grief, he added, 'You're no uninvolved bystander. Clan news passes more swiftly than before. The affray by Tal Quorin saw to that.'

A locked moment passed while Shand's chieftains looked on. Then Erlien grinned like a shark and confessed to Arithon, 'I drew steel in addition to address a complaint on behalf of the *caithdein* of Melhalla.

Your attack on Duke Bransian's armoury at Alestron was unprovoked, and against one of her feal vassals. Since you crossed into Shand, by kingdom law, form demanded her claim should pass to me.'

'Oh Ath,' said Arithon, suddenly laughing. 'I *thought* that's why you tried to take my head.' He pressed a forearm to his stinging ribs, rueful enough to be honest. 'Your ally should get her facts straight, though. That wasn't an attack. I had a charge that turned awry to lend help with Fellowship business.'

Erlien's smile stretched wider. 'Well, Prince, for my part, by right of arms, you're acquitted. I found out well enough. You don't use your sorcery for spite. The s'Brydion line always did have a nose for foolish trouble. When Duke Bransian's liege lady asks, I shall say you disarmed me, yet mind well: Lysaer s'Ilessid may have revoked his right to safe conduct, but the s'Brydion of Alestron are clanblood. Should that hawk come to roost in a nest outside your favour, the duke's within his rights to claim your life.'

'Should he come to me for due reckoning,' Arithon said dryly, 'I will answer him fairly on my own.'

Satisfied at last to dispense with past grudges, Lord Erlien stretched the kinks from his shoulders. His slant-eyed glance of appreciation encompassed Arithon's too-straight stance. The prince looked more than ever like a boy who had suffered a beating, each tender move considered in advance to minimize stiffness and discomfort. 'Well, be advised to give Alestron wide berth until your scabs heal.' Enjoying Arithon's glare of black rancour he added, 'Where are you bound in that toy of a sloop, after you leave our forest?'

A log fell. The sullen leap of sparks flicked a dancing, hot gleam in the depths of Arithon's eyes. 'North.' A corner of his mouth crawled up. 'Why rely on the fickle course of storms? I'd a mind instead to try to turn Lysaer's fleet before he can sail from Werpoint harbour.'

Erlien sank his knuckles in black beard and gave his chin a vigorous scratch. 'Well you're not my sworn prince. That being beyond your power to change, you lack any grounds to deny my clansmen their due share of the fun should the Fatemaster turn your plots astray. If you've got a mind to stir a hornet's nest through sabotage, let me tell you, in Shand, we're crack experts at cattle raids.'

Indeed, armies could not move, even by galley, without sustenance in the form of beasts. A whoop erupted from a clan lord. Someone else shouted for a cask to be broached. With a burgeoning flare of enthusiasm, leather jacks were fetched out, and someone unrolled a dog-eared set of charts from a saddle pack. Played across by moving shadows as the chiefs he commanded plunged headlong into plans for their most cherished pastime, Erlien summed up in complacence, 'Yon false prince from Tysan can recruit his fine army as he pleases. He may find it tough to invade foreign country if his men have nothing to eat.'

420

Arithon's scathing rebuttal was forestalled as a scout in a braided leather vest dug his sore ribs in laughing sympathy. 'Accept your lot and be merry. Anyone who bests our clan chief at swords, Lord Erlien adopts as a brother.'

Once started, the idea of resistance gained momentum with wild enthusiasm. While the fire collapsed to red embers, the celebration grew rowdy to cement shared friendship and genius. A half-drunken contest at archery commenced with a torch on a pole as a target. The air gained a taint of singed fletching, and silver changed hands in spirited wagers as contestants compared bows and cracked disparaging remarks. Erlien's clan lords drew lots and shot against a vicious and inventive interference to spoil the aim of close rivals.

No one noticed until the cask reached the lees that Arithon s'Ffalenn had left their company.

The band of scouts dispatched to the shore in haste brought back their belated report: *Talliarthe* had sailed, most surely under cover of shadow. Despite four men set as sentries, the cove where she had anchored lay black and empty under the moon.

Erlien s'Taleyn, High Earl of Alland, received the news with a head-shaking, throaty spill of laughter. 'Dharkaron himself! Should yon Shadow Master think we are quits after he's fairly disarmed me in a fight, he shall in due time be shown better. If this false prince, Lysaer, and his war host plies south, we shall give him sharp welcome, with or without s'Ffalenn sanction!'

Tidings

As near as Koriani scrying could determine, the Fellowship of Seven met the imminent collapse of the peace with indifference, despite the fact that Athera's royal lines were their own irresponsible creation. While war against the Shadow Master mounted to a certainty, the sorcerers kept close in their own affairs, as reticent as they had ever been at the time Etarra was abandoned to the destruction unleashed by Desh-thiere's curse.

Whatever crisis had shaken them to mount an earth-shaking conjury from Althain Tower on the force of the past summer's solstice, the cause continued to elude the most diligent Koriani seers.

The mood of their Prime Enchantress grew brittle under the pressure as events outpaced the scope of her informants.

Where once the Great Waystone had enabled her Senior Circle to track the Fellowship's intent, now, they could only hurl probes and futile auguries against impenetrable wards. When Sethvir of Althain chose secrecy, he could circle his tower in guard spells as opaque as Paravian ironwork.

Tenaciously unwilling to leave to the passions of geas-cursed princes to run their fell course unremarked, at the head of an order founded on principles of merciful intervention, Morriel Prime settled in for autumn equinox at the orphan's hostel maintained in the coastal fortress at Whitehold. Situated where the flats of a lowland peninsula jutted north into Eltair Bay, the high, pale buttresses of the citadel's inner ward shaded a cobbled courtyard that rang to the shouts of parentless children by day. By night, the high, mortised walls contained the chalked circles and candles laid out for spell rites performed in seasonal rhythms under starlight. If the sentries posted over the gatehouse were troubled by the uncanny vibrations of sealed ritual, they were bound to withhold their complaint.

Since history held that a former Senior Circle had once saved the city from flooding under a tidal surge through the might of a winter storm, Whitehold's welcome toward the enchantresses remained an entrenched tradition. The orphanage over the years had pre-empted the brick mansions on both sides of the narrow street.

The Prime commandeered a high, pillared chamber, once the solar of a rich shipping merchant. Rows of paned casements aflood with east sunlight warmed the damp air on clear mornings. The view overlooked the strand. Beyond the workaday clutter of lighters beached like seined fish on the sands, the bearded combers hurled themselves in ranks of filigreed foam and exploding spray. Vacant mooring buoys beaded the heave of leaden waters. Every galley available for charter had sailed north to Werpoint to serve Lysaer s'Ilessid as troop transport.

Morriel basked in the windowseat to ease the cruel ache in her joints. Gone were the days when she could meditate without the distracting, soft comfort of cushions. Intolerant of cold, less patient with setbacks, she forbade the attendance of her First Senior since Elaira's failure to establish herself as Arithon's mistress. On the night the younger initiate had unmasked the man's defences and roused him to passion, the direct force of his character coupled with s'Ffalenn compassion had shocked a signal the clear length of the seventh lane.

A grave enough obstacle to the transfer of prime power, First Senior Lirenda's fascination with the Shadow Master must be shielded from added temptation through the polishing phase of her training.

Morriel assumed the knotty burden of tracking the s'Ffalenn prince's movements since his recent departure from Merior. For this purpose, a coffer filled with blown-glass spheres lay open to her inspection. Embedded inside each fragile globe, suspended in miniature reflection by an initiate whose talents were manifest through air, morsels of live event had been captured by the dawn's lane watchers.

The Koriani Prime bent in focused intent over each detailed imprint. Hooded in shawls like a fortune teller, she prodded the orbs to and fro and arranged them in patterns by subject. Throughout the past month, the disparate collection of happenstance gleaned from the continent's east coast narrowed steadily toward a convergence.

Only those subjects charged and weighted with emotion would impress themselves into the lane flow: in Merior only that morning, a tow-headed set of twins had badgered a blind splicer who worked rope for a brigantine's ratlines. Morriel cradled the glass with their image, sharp in analysis of the spirit and loyalty to Arithon impressed in those paired young faces. Her clawed nail rolled that sphere aside.

Another, captured from close council within the walls of Alestron, showed Duke Bransian s'Brydion and his brothers immersed in fierce discourse over maps. By the patterns of the marker pins under their hands, Morriel gleaned their intent to join their armies with Lysaer's war host in the campaign to trap Arithon on the sands of the Scimlade hook. Associated, but contained in a smaller glass, a dishonoured guard captain clad in beggar's rags hunkered over a stolen bread crust. No less fervent in dedication, this one ached for the chance to claim vengeance. His hatred burned hot against the Shadow Master who had undone his claim to pride and credibility.

Northward, under octagonal towers at Jaelot, merchant guildsmen grumbled over the edict from their mayor's council that conscripted their fastest galleys and dispatched the fleet northward to serve the allied muster at Werpoint.

Transactions abounded up and down Eltair Bay, where vessels of load-bearing capacity changed hands, or were chartered out for Etarran gold.

Morriel marked one image orb aside for its oddity: a flotilla of derelict fishing luggers moored in a hidden cove off Crescent Isle that should have passed unnoticed but for the curiosity of a passing school of dolphins. Since Lysaer's affairs were infallibly couched in ceremonious, forthright candour, the Prime tapped the glass that failed to fit in irritable speculation, then moved on with her methodical review.

While affairs on the waterfront transpired apace, the war host itself remained bogged down in Valleygap, low on supplies, and harried by outbreaks of clan raids. The latest trap had sprung a rockfall across the narrow roadway. Reduced under glass like black ants, soldiers laboured with shovels and ox teams, shifting boulders to clear the choked pass.

Of Jieret Red-beard and his clan Companions, the lane watchers had traced no sign. Either their scouts had abandoned the site since the ambush, or they slept by day and no man among them dreamed with sufficient intensity to deflect the lane's magnetic flux.

Morriel curled crabbed fingers in yet another spasm of stray pain. Eyes bead-bright in concentration, she considered the last three spheres in the coffer whose meaning lay provocatively obscured.

In the first, *Black Drake*'s wily captain scoured the sailors' dives at Highscarp, recruiting a disreputable stamp of crewmen even her smuggler's brig should hesitate to sign for passage.

In the next, a graceful, painted sloop lay tucked in a secluded anchorage by the fir groves of Ithilt. The Mad Prophet curled like a leaf against her headstay, croaking drunken ditties, his pudgy hands clasped around the whiskey crock he had nursed since his mishap with the vat in Garth's pond. The Master of Shadow was not on board. The image trapped under glass replayed its maddening, repetitive cascade of surf; the cove's crescent beach showed no tracks.

Another sphere garnered a league to the northeast showed a herd of deer fleeing some disturbance. Twinged by impatience, Morriel traced the slick, cold surface of the glass. Tonight's lane watch, perhaps, could pursue these disparate threads to their origins. The order's most gifted scriers had been advised to sift events in *Talliarthe*'s vicinity.

Dakar's presence offered proof: the Prince of Rathain had returned to his kingdom, sure sign he angled for conflict. Outside Elaira's influence, Arithon's mind was a maze of subtle intrigues a mere image could scarcely hope to track. Whatever he plotted, incessant lane watch offered tantalizing glimpses, but seldom enough insight to back a forecast. Though Elaira had affirmed that the s'Ffalenn prince had impaired his mage-sight, he had not lost the disciplines of his mastery. A trained awareness and a masterbard's instincts yet enabled him to batten his emotions in stilled silence. The lane flow picked him up rarely, and almost never when his movements displayed intent.

Balked to a hissed sigh of anger, the Koriani Prime snagged hands as fleshless as bird's claws in the dark purple silk of the quilts. How many hours of her life had slipped past in such futile analysis of circumstance? When her order had wielded a grand power focus, events had been drawn direct, causes joined sequentially to consequence by their links of energy resonance. Knowledge had reigned in place of these hours of sifting and guesswork. Dhirken's unlikely recruiting; the mass of wilted, cut pine boughs in Ithilt that disrupted the foraging deer; perhaps even the derelict fishing luggers would have shown indisputable connection to Arithon's designs; or they would not.

Perhaps no such ties existed.

Morriel pinched colourless lips. The doubts, the error, the wearisome differences of opinion that evolved as her Senior Council argued out points of probability made a pitiable grasp of world affairs.

Stymied by circling thoughts, harassed by the hyper-acute hearing inflicted by the seals to stall death, Morriel longed for the luxury of thick wool tapestries, that just for this hour, might ease the barrage of distractions. A colicky baby wailed through the voice of a house matron, scolding. In the courtyard beneath the arched casements, a boy ward chopped wood for the kitchens. A door groaned open on a lower floor to admit a chattering group of girls sent off to draw water from the well. A servant thumped through the shelves in the scullery, while the cook banged down a tin bucket to catch the wax peelings off a new wheel of cheese.

Morriel wrenched strayed attention from the disparate clamour, stitched by the winds off the bay that thrummed sullen notes through the shutters, and the clear, high peal of an officer's horn that signalled a galley weighing anchor. Eyelids thin as blue eggshells twitched closed as she sought refuge in the calm of meditation.

The gnawing pain in her body pursued, even through the veils of iron discipline. Stillness brought no peace, but cased her thinned bones in aches that never for a second relented. Deep sleep in these hours lay beyond reach, and the frail, shallow whisper of each arrhythmic breath seemed to span the very width of eternity.

The day must inevitably come when she would fail to attain the peace of higher consciousness. Between herself and her long-sought release, at every turn of fateful event, hung the spectre of Arithon s'Ffalenn. Elaira's love had captured his heart well enough, but had failed to win through to his bed; far better for First Senior Lirenda if the cursed prince had succumbed to plain lust.

A knock at the door snapped the threads of conjecture. The Koriani Prime roused like an unhooded falcon, blinked through a quick stab of pain, and in a scraped whisper of signal displeasure, demanded the reason for disruption.

The latch snicked up and the portal cracked to admit an oval face netted in coils of black hair. Lirenda, First Senior, did not step inside, but swept down in an arrowed mass of skirts until her forehead pressed her bent knee.

The contrast struck at odd moments, between this grown woman and a vain young initiate from a pedigree family who had begged to be taken in for training. Even humbled by desire, Lirenda had been too haughty for obeisance. Prodigious talent had burned in her like live coals, almost too wild to contain.

Blooded pride was still there, but tempered now by ambition. The driving desire to win, and the lonely heart that had prompted the girl to affect conceit now lay buttressed by ironshod discipline. Morriel pondered the change, satisfied that the precepts of mercy could be taught. Heartfelt emotion was less biddable, a fearful point of vulnerability in a candidate appointed for prime succession. Against the highest of stakes, Lirenda must be moulded to survive.

Ever testing to expose any trait that might admit loophole for failure, Morriel's censure cut the fused moment of silence. 'You dare much.'

Abased in the confines of the doorway, Lirenda did not flinch at the omission of her title. 'I dare nothing. News has arrived for your ears alone.'

'What under Ath's sky cannot be made to wait?' Morriel Prime contradicted. 'If you came to say something important, let me hear.'

Lirenda's frosty poise never wavered. 'I beg you, reconsider. The subject is too weighty to broach without due precautions.'

Too subtle a creature to show disdain or approval, the Koriani Prime snapped fingers like dry sticks. 'Rise, then. Admit the one who awaits in the corridor behind you as well.'

At Lirenda's rebellious catch of breath, Morriel gave a cracked exhalation. 'Do you think to gainsay my wishes? That's unwise. I already know the source of your news. Another senior has travelled from Tysan to see me, yes? She was ordered to keep watch on events at Avenor. She would scarcely leave her post for a pittance.'

'Matriarch, beldame Haltha is here,' Lirenda admitted through a rustled hitch of skirts. 'Shall I lay down a ward to preserve privacy?'

'No. Fetch the news bearer. I shall attend what protections are needed myself.' While Lirenda withdrew to obey, Morriel Prime veiled the glass image spheres in a shawl. Then she shrugged off her quilts with laborious care and stood upright.

Her lavender robes dragged at her skeletal form like the wings of an exotic moth as she opened a wall chest and drew out the silk bag that wrapped one of the order's lesser focus jewels. Unveiled, the white quartz burned with caught light, a spike of cold flame cased in crystal. Morriel paid no heed to the movements of her underlings in the doorway. She cupped the gem's faceted weight in palms like dead leaves, then cast her stilled thoughts into its lattice to enhance her tuned reservoir of power.

Heightened awareness flooded through her.

Brick and mortar, she sensed the framing presence of the mansion, board floors infused like ghost dreams with the tap of women's steps and the tears of growing children and the trace glow left by past conjuries. Spent fragments of ward seals clung like grit in old plaster. Layered underneath in shadowy lacings of hallucination, Morriel could nearly detect the subliminal groan of over-stressed natural energies. More than ever as her years advanced, their febrile ring teased her consciousness, as though the grain of painted moulding and sea-damp stone walls struck and vibrated, spun into contrary currents by the strictures of time-faded sigils.

Morriel gave such fancy short shrift. To pity the heart of inanimate substance while breathing humanity still suffered was a Fellowship affectation, as ruthless to life as their bloodless, isolate meddling.

She raged alone in bitter knowledge that since the Waystone's loss, the sorcerers perused her sisterhood's affairs at their whim. The most potent ward at Koriani command never stopped Sethvir's prying, or Luhaine's lugubrious surveillance. At best, Morriel could impose a construct upon the air to lend warning of Fellowship presence. Sealed through the principles of elemental domination, every sound to occur within her chamber could be tracked and confined by scribed runes. The resonance she knotted through her crystal recorded the expanding signature of each event in a shimmer of subliminal blue light.

Should any outside power seek to bleed off a trace pattern, Morriel Prime would know at once, with First Senior Lirenda little the wiser. The old Prime had learned when pursuit of perfection could become a wasting mistake. Serpent-sly, she preferred to discover which facts the sorcerers came to monitor, then tailor her precautions to suit.

Lirenda was dedicated, but she had much to learn of the strengths to be gained through abstinence. She stood now in a simmer of prim impatience while her Prime rearranged fragile limbs in their closest approximation of comfort amid the quilts.

By contrast, the senior enchantress just in from Tysan presented herself for audience in humbled quiet, her fustian clothes still wrinkled from the road, and her seamed features chalky with weariness.

427

'Your will, Matriarch,' she murmured. Beneath the probing regard of the Koriani Prime, she sank to the floor in obeisance.

'You have my leave to speak.' Morriel nested her hands in her robes, her porcelain hair strained through by cold fire in the shimmer of spell-tempered air.

'My Prime,' the beldame opened, while the grimy hem of her skirt fluttered to her terrified trembling. 'A decision of grave moment was given into my hands and I was forced to a choice. For an act of unconscionable independence, I throw myself on your mercy. I closed a bargain with Prince Lysaer s'Ilessid. In exchange for the secret of his half-brother's interests at Merior, I have his witnessed assurance that the Waystone of our order was never lost.' In rising, uncontainable excitement, she finished, 'The jewel is whole still, and held in close care by the Fellowship sorcerers at Althain Tower.'

Morriel raised clawed fingers to stifle a warbling cry. This news was momentous, their vanished grand crystal revealed at long last! Thrilled by a tingling, expansive rush of joy after tedious years of proscribed power, the Prime reached out a shaken hand and traced her seal of blessing above the prostrate senior's hood. 'You are forgiven your presumption. Indeed, well done!'

These tidings afforded great hope. If the stone were recovered, not only could the disarranged humours of her body be drawn back into balance until the trials of her succession were surmounted, but means might be restored to quell damaging storms and banish disease, and even to throw off the suffocating constraint imposed by the Fellowship of Seven.

In heady elation, Morriel locked eyes with her First Senior.

Lirenda's flush in the heat of stunning news showed more than exhilarated eagerness: under her varnished layer of poise flashed a spasm of unguarded anger.

Morriel seized upon that oddity. Barbed with searching power, sped to sharp force by the spell crystal still meshed with her mind, her scrutiny lanced through the First Senior's reserve to wrest out that sand grain of dissidence. Understanding followed like a hammer blow to rock. Lirenda's displeasure stemmed from personal betrayal, that the Waystone's location had been bought at a cost of endangering the royal fugitive at Merior.

Proof stung, that the prime candidate's recurrent fascination for Arithon s'Ffalenn had indeed threaded deep enough to unbalance her grasp of affairs.

Pricked spiteful in displeasure, Morriel narrowed eyes like black pebbles and snapped an immediate order.

'First Senior, I charge you to take the Skyron focus stone. Leave for Atainia and muster a grand circle of one hundred and eight seniors. You have one task: confront Sethvir and wrest back our Great Waystone.

Fail in this, come back empty-handed, and you may consider yourself unworthy of your post.'

Expressionless as sculpted alabaster before the evident censure of her Prime, Lirenda returned a polished curtsey. Her back unbent, braided hair like chiselled jet under the flicker of spelled air, she said, 'Your will is my pleasure. I shall not disappoint you.'

Morriel watched, arranged in brittle stillness as her appointed heir arose in fervent grace and departed.

To the elder still prostrate at her feet, the Prime cast a less jaundiced eye. 'Put aside your fear, Haltha. Arise. You acted at great risk for an end you judged to be worth any sacrifice. Your service deserves due reward, but necessity drives me. I lay on you my request for a small, additional service.'

The beldame straightened before her mistress, head bent in submission. 'Matriarch, I am yours to command.'

Morriel lifted an arm reduced to bone wrapped in paper-thin tissue, twitched aside her shawl, and selected an orb from the array beside the opened coffer. She set its glass weight into Haltha's hand and said, 'Repeat the scrying you made for Lysaer s'Ilessid, which exposed Arithon's ship-yards at Merior. Let the man whose likeness you hold be given the self-same knowledge.'

Permitted no leave to question, the senior enchantress cupped the sphere, which held the tormented reflection of the dishonoured captain from Alestron. 'Your will,' she intoned.

Outside the close chamber, like a sudden, clouding omen, a child in the courtyard started wailing. Worn beyond care for any infant's painful trials, Morriel granted the weary senior her permission to retire. Alone in the chamber as the morning's last sunlight retreated into chill shadow, she closed her eyes to resume meditation. Her ancient heart beat unburdened by remorse for the mischief she had loosed to hound the last heir of s'Ffalenn.

Should one rancorous, whip-scarred guardsman pursue his cherished vengeance and bring the Shadow Master's death, or if his passion for murder simply fouled s'Ffalenn machinations and caused a fatal delay for Lysaer's war host to exploit, the difference would be moot.

Arithon dead or maimed at second hand would disentangle Lirenda from the flaw that endangered her succession to Prime power. One last detail remained.

The instant Morriel felt restored enough to resume the burdens of her office, she demanded the attendance of her errand page.

'I have a message for the duty watch to be sent immediately by lane current,' she commanded. 'Initiate Elaira is to be found and informed that my sanction for congress with the Prince of Rathain is as of this moment withdrawn.'

Indeed, against the prospect of a restored Great Waystone, the woman's assignation was no longer vital. Of far weightier import, First Senior Lirenda must succeed in her contest against Sethvir. Then stronger means would lie at hand to curb her ill-founded infatuation, if through brute luck, or thrice-damnable s'Ffalenn cleverness, the subject of her weakness mastered the odds against him and survived.

Sunset, Midnight and Noon

Informed on the lane surge at sundown that Morriel Prime has released her charge to seek liaison with Arithon s'Ffalenn, a bronze-haired enchantress in Merior weeps in gratitude for restored honesty, and in loss for shared love that must languish unpartnered; through the quiet, resolved hour as she packs to depart, she prays for the man, that he might stay free to refound his happiness with another . . .

In the deeps of the night, ripped awake by an uncanny, clear dream that tells where to find the sorcerer who had fired his duke's armoury, a bearded blond outcast scratches old whip scars, arises, and begins a journey to Merior by the Sea to enact his sworn blood vow of vengeance . . .

On a rocky slope above Valleygap, on the day of his twentieth year that clan custom reckons full manhood, a red-bearded chieftain called Earl of the North bends back his black bow, sets his aim on one figure above the crews who shift rocks in hot sunlight, and lets fly an arrow inscribed with the name of the killer who brought untimely death to a father, a mother, and four sisters . . .

XIV. *VALLEYGAP TO WERPOINT*

The arrow launched. The arc of its flight was vengeance, ripping down from the heart of the sun, a hissing, humming resonance of parted air no experienced man of war could mistake.

Captain Mayor Pesquil of the northern league of headhunters pitched himself down and sideways into cover one fatal instant too late. Before he struck ground, the four-bladed steel broadhead aimed to take him slapped into the small of his back.

He landed hard enough to slam the wind from his lungs and trip a frost-rimed hail of stones into rattling descent down the slope. Their noisy, bouncing fall through stunted brush and cracked saplings caused men to glance up from their labour with wagons and shovels amidst the boulders which jammed the road below. Pesquil snatched air to shout warning of attack, then gasped, wrung mute. A spasm clamped his muscles. He could not breathe, could not speak, but only hug the flinty soil, pain-white and clammy with weakness.

Felled in a helpless, curled bundle, his hands jammed into cold earth as if by main force he could wrest back his grip on self-command, Pesquil shuddered in the gravel. If his scouts posted on the ridge line had not seen him go down, or if the others on watch on the low ground ignored the warning set off by disturbed pebbles, they deserved to be cut down for negligence in the raid about to sweep down the defile.

Pesquil strained to hear past the hammered beat of blood in his ears. Yet no more arrows hailed down. He picked out no shouts of alarm from his carefully-posted guard of scouts.

The unbroken quiet spurred him to a rage of colossal proportion.

He had always understood the snares at Valleygap had been fashioned to take down headhunters. Now, lying agonized in the scald of his own blood, Captain Mayor Pesquil cursed with ferocity: fool that he was, he had not understood until the endplay. Jieret Red-beard had blindsided him. Pressured too hard keeping others alive, he had never once thought to imagine himself as the ultimate, targeted prey.

Ring within ring, by spring-trap and rockfall, then the suspect boredom of two quiet weeks without incident, the last ambush in these inhospitable vales had been staged to deprive Lysaer of his most effective commander.

The patrol arrived. With breathless worry, they dispatched a runner to fetch help and bring in a litter. Pesquil lay slit-eyed and gasping, cut at each shallow breath as the sawing bite of the arrow lacerated more vital tissue. Throughout the ordeal as they raised his limp weight and arranged him face-down to be carried, he mouthed silent curses against the clan name of s'Valerient.

Twilight settled early in the pit between the hills. Pesquil became aware of a dimness thick with mildewed canvas, musty wool, and the hated, dank smell of crumbled shale that pervaded the gap's deep ravines. The hospital reek of medicinal herbs and an uglier stink of charred flesh lifted a curl to his lips. A mauling throb in his back and the virulent sting left by cautery played over every ugly bit of trauma imposed upon his body to remove the barbarian arrow. The injury was bad. He needed no doom-saying healer to tell him.

Prone on a camp cot, hating the jelly-limbed lassitude that kept him there, Pesquil held no care at all that the coverlets cast over him were woven silk, emblazoned with the star of s'Ilessid.

The first he knew of Lysaer's presence was a stir of movement at his bedside, inflected with a gleam of gold hair.

'Dharkaron's divine vengeance, Prince,' he ground out. 'You must have better to do.'

'If that's true, you're not fit to give orders.' Lysaer made an imperious gesture. Across the field tent, a servant shovelled out from beneath a chinking pile of horse trappings, tossed his oil rag into the lap of a hovering page, then hastened to bear his lamp to the bedside. The prince took the light, excused the man, and hung the carry ring from a chain on the ridge pole.

He seated himself again beside the cot, in no apparent hurry to depart. 'The day brought no more attacks. Harradene's division cleared the last debris under cover of canvas and shields. You can rest easy. The war host is intact and still in high heart, and the way through Valleygap lies open.'

His stubbled cheek rough against the sheen of silk pillows, Pesquil tracked Lysaer's presence with slitted eyes. He fastened unerringly on the single fact left out. 'So my patrols found no sign of the archer. Tell Skannt to triple his sentries. When the supply train arrives, don't trust the stores. Test the biscuit and cheese on my tracking dogs.'

'I should have expected you'd not shirk for sick leave.' Lysaer smiled with that grave arrogance that seemed inborn into old-blood princes. 'Before you get wrapped up in duties that can wait, I thought you'd like the chance to study this.' He bent, raised the limp, dry hand that trailed outside the bedclothes, and pressed a sharp object into the captain mayor's palm.

'The broadhead removed from your back,' the prince said.

'I see that.' Pesquil turned the razor-sharp edges of the steel, nicked here and there from the healer's probe that had grazed and slipped through the effort to draw it out. The lamplight skittered and flared across the flanges, which were not smooth, but gouged with lettering gummed black.

'If that's an inscription, I can't focus just now.' His flame of nervous energy quenched by lethargy and pain, Pesquil's disgust emerged as a querulous snarl. 'Too many drugs. I recall asking not to be dosed.'

'The healer would never have held himself steady through your screaming,' Lysaer said in gentle censure. 'He had to dissect half your backside. If you hadn't worn silk beneath your gambeson, he'd never have cleaned the wound at all.' The prince did not share the cold truth, that no soporific posset troubled Pesquil's concentration. Despite every effort and a brutal round of cautery, Pesquil's sunken flesh and fevered skin affirmed the healer's prognosis: the wound was still bleeding inside. 'Do you wish to know what that says?'

'I can guess, sure enough.' But Pesquil stirred in fretful effort to pass the broadhead back.

Lysaer turned the steel blades. 'The letters on the first blade say, *"from the son of the Earl of the North"*.'

'Jieret s'Valerient, I thought so.' Pesquil shut his eyes, his sallow complexion paled to rubbed ivory, but without the grace of patina. His skin hung paper dry under the flutter of the lantern. 'Go on.'

'The next says, *"for my lady mother, and four sisters"*, and the next, *"for the slaughtered innocents by Tal Quorin"*.' Lysaer trailed off into silence, his eyes, cold blue, on his injured officer, and his hands prepared to mete out a bracing restraint in case rage turned the wounded man distraught.

Pesquil stirred, impatient, a hissed breath caught through his teeth as the agony in his back snapped him short. 'The last engraving would show my name. You've never seen a clan vengeance arrow? Stay lucky, my liege. Few men survive them.'

The hesitation which followed affirmed Pesquil's suspicion, that the sucking black weakness which raked him boded no good: the prince's long-faced healer had surely pronounced him to be dying.

'A barbarous custom,' Lysaer said in what seemed a disjointed interval later.

Had Pesquil been hale, he would have laughed. 'The clans weren't first

435

with that practice. Townsmen during the uprising assassinated the High King of Havish with a sword engraved with his lineage.' Too close to his pass beneath the Wheel for tact, he ended on a wisp of scorching irony, 'You should know well, Prince – since you carry a blade specially forged to kill a sorcerer.'

The prick struck home: the sword in Lysaer's scabbard since the hour of his march on Tal Quorin bore his enemy's name in reverse runes.

Whatever Lysaer replied, Pesquil did not hear. The throttling pull of dizziness had dragged him too deep to unriddle spoken conversation. Like a spark whirled in downdraught toward the nadir of night, the bullish, stubborn thread of his thoughts spiralled off into emptiness. He was too tired, too thirsty, too cold. A siren song of lassitude sapped away his will to wrench the world back to clear cognizance.

And yet, one thing remained. Today's arrow had proven that a lifelong antagonist had sired a worthy son to succeed himself; Pesquil pushed back against his shroud of fogged wits. He gathered breath against the dreadful gnaw of pain and said, 'Lysaer s'Ilessid, fetch your scribe.'

A horrid, fraught interval passed, while he clung to awareness and waited. Patchy vision showed him movement and a voice nearby said something urgent. A cup pressed his lips, filled with cold water and a bracing unpleasant sting of herbs.

Pesquil sucked down a greedy swallow. 'Is the man here?' he gasped. 'Tell him, get out his pens and his ink.'

'He's here,' Lysaer answered from somewhere very close. 'Say your peace, man. The words will be written as you wish.'

But the surly old veteran wanted no letter to a loved one. Captain Mayor Pesquil pushed restlessly at his pillow. He poured the last breath in his body and the dregs of plundered strength into instructions to ensure Jieret Red-beard and his fourteen Companions would not be left an opening to obstruct the army's passage on to Werpoint.

The headhunter commander who despised rank and privilege delivered his last bequest with a prince in attendance at his bedside; the hour had been left too late for a scribe. His dark eyes unseeing in the spill of the lamplight, Pesquil never knew the hand that transcribed his wracked lines was royal, and steady in its office. His last words came widely spaced, fought out with the same fanatical dedication that had enacted the bitter slaughter at Tal Quorin, and that even the act of dying could not unhinge.

Captain Mayor Pesquil of the northern league of headhunters passed the Wheel bound still to his duty.

Whether he dreaded his reckoning with Daelion Fatemaster, or felt remorse at the last for the clan lives he had claimed for paid bounty, no living man ever knew. Prince Lysaer laid aside his lapdesk and pen, closed the fixed eyes with their joyless fervour extinguished, then shrouded the gaunt, sunken architecture of the face in the colours of his own royal blazon.

Shaken into a closer knit by the loss of their wiliest headhunter, the war host pressed eastward in the hands of Lord Commander Diegan. Lysaer s'Ilessid swore his intent to make Pesquil's monument their safe arrival in Perlorn. To that end, he implored every garrison commander to allow a staff officer from Avenor to ride at their sides to lend advice.

'The late captain mayor set the finishing edge on the training given to these men.' The prince ended in earnest entreaty, 'I offer their expertise to you in Pesquil's late memory, to avoid another loss like the last.'

The irony followed, that the dour captain's death became the catalyst to end petty adversity. Since the absence of his abrasive bullying revealed how they had come to rely on his experience, the royal request was accepted. The officers from Avenor were supremely well-versed in their handling of men. From the moment their influence touched the garrison troops, the war host began to cohere from an unwieldy amalgamation of divisions and wagons into an order to surmount any odds.

In a victory over shared hunger and uncertainty, the last companies cleared the pass of Valleygap under a cold, cloud-raked sky. Adversity met them, cruel enough to test their newfound unity. The wagons sent west to resupply their stores nestled amid grass salted grey under the season's first killing frost. No one attended the packtrain. The beasts which had drawn the drays wandered loose, wild-eyed and skittish before the outriders who angled in to catch them. A sweeping patrol of the surrounding hills unearthed no traps and no sign. Barbarian marauders were not in evidence, nor the hired drovers, nor any of the men at arms appointed to safeguard the provisions.

Of three tracking dogs culled from the pack to test the jerked beef, two died in snarling convulsions.

'Fire the stores,' Lord Diegan ordered in compliance with Pesquil's last testament. The hounds were too valuable to waste trying to separate which casks were tainted, and which not. Despite the devastating hardship, the last forty leagues to Perlorn must be crossed by men with empty bellies.

'They'll get there thin, but living,' Lord Harradene cracked, braced to forestall any dissidence. But his order raised no dispute; after Valleygap, the garrison divisions had learned when not to argue with experience.

The vanguard completed the last leg to the walled city of Perlorn, a ten-day march that ended in cheerless disorder after dark. Camp was pitched under stone ramparts, while torches streamed in the gusts. The wind also hummed through the tent guy lines, and bit the skin red on men's faces, and whirled the steam off supperpots filled for the first time since Valleygap. Its whine came interspersed with fitful, veering blasts from the east.

'Weather's changing, do you feel it?' announced the captain mayor's successor as he barged into the royal command tent. A middle-aged, vigorous stick of a man with a boisterous sense of humour, blond whiskers and a squint, Captain Skannt sniffed air burdened with the smoke from filled ovens. 'Autumn rains will soak us any time now. Best to shake up the sentries on the perimeter, your Grace. Tonight, mark my word, you'll see the first wave of deserters.'

By morning, Lord Harradene had twelve men arraigned and stripped for public whipping. The garrison divisions with less vigilant guards simply had gaps in their ranks.

Clouds like layered slate masked the hills at the horizon when, reprovisioned at punishing expense by a city hoarding its harvest against the onset of winter, the columns reformed to continue their march eastward. They wound through hills and vales half-erased by a grey smoke of drizzle, then slogged beside laden carts, bespattered with mud thrown off mired wheels. The teams slipped and laboured over roads transformed to soaked ruts, or washed out by freshets swollen from the silvered rungs of water shed off the stone shoulders of the Skyshiels.

Yet even as the wagons groaned and stuck fast in muck, or an axle broke, or someone sat to wad his boots with lint to ease the nip of raw blisters, Prince Lysaer was there on his caparisoned destrier to call encouragement, or share in rough jokes and commiseration.

Tired men straightened their spines as he passed. Drovers took to polishing their harness buckles in sure pride that the prince would happen by.

As the road steepened through the north-facing spurs of the foothills, the rain changed to sleet. The hollows lay scabbed with grey ice. Cartwheels and oxen crunched through puddles snap-frozen, then ploughed by their passage to shards like white cullet, salted in heaps at a glassworks.

Their forward progress was impeded just as cruelly without the added trials of clan raids. Hard cold already shackled the mountains. The peaks that fanged the southern horizon wore caps of new snow, and over the chink of bit rings and harness, the outriders heard the hunting song of wolf packs, moved down from the heights as the grazing game sought shelter in lower country. Advance scouts breasted the hills to the stoop of northland falcons, plumed now in their winter white. Thrashed by falling sleet, stung by the astringent, damp winds that howled off the wave-battered coast, men marched wrapped in blankets and slept bundled together for warmth. The stock grew thin on frost-killed fodder, and the crossing of each bouldered streamlet became a fresh ordeal, with leggings and boots slow to dry. Captains oversaw their troops, head-down in frozen misery, and yet morale did not flag. When the rank and file from the garrisons seemed too chilblained and dispirited to oil their weapons, the elite troops from Avenor shamed them to reach for new standards. A rivalry arose and flourished on that comfortless, hard road, until no company wished to appear less polished than the prince's personal troops.

After weeks in tenantless wilds, the last forty leagues became a trial of discipline and endurance. Across the flats, with their spindled stands of salt-scoured trees and weathered rocks painted with lichens, horses cast shoes. Officers' tempers frayed to epithets. The proud columns that had marched from Etarra in splendour straggled at last into Werpoint three months later, ragged, bone-weary, but fused at last into seamless dedication.

The divisions who formed up for camp assignment beneath the tall, limestone battlements might be trail-worn and hungry, but their spirits remained undaunted. Amid the petulant snap of banners and shouted directions from their officers, they crawled into tents to sleep, or hunkered down before the fanned flames of campfires and spoke of southern lands and warm doxies.

The Master of Shadow was but one man before their armed thousands, and Merior was a village on a sandspit.

'We'll be home with our families for spring planting,' men said, and made jokes, warmed to the belief that they were invincible under the steady blaze of Lysaer's confidence. Against all adversity they had made the port of Werpoint before the winter storms closed the harbour. While the white crash of waves plumed and subsided against the shingle, the lanterns of the anchored vessels commissioned to transport them clustered and tossed on black waters, awaiting only full daylight to begin the process of loading.

For the war host's ranking officers, the outlook was less rosy. Inside city walls, dogged by strings of equerries sent with supply lists, and accosted by pedigree garrison captains who demanded to be billeted indoors, Lord Commander Diegan met harassed city ministers and strove to placate upset tempers. More a supply stop and a fishing port than a bustling centre for trade, Werpoint languished in a state of seething chaos, ill-prepared to offer succour to the encampment spread at its gates. Already burdened beyond capacity by the mixed fleet of merchant brigs, galleys, and fishing sloops packed into each south-facing cove, the harbour inlet was a crosshatched forest of spars and tar-blacked rigging. The narrow gaps of open water between hulls seethed, busy as canals with lighters and oared boats bearing captains, crews, and supplies to and from the congested wharfside.

No matter that Rathain's garrisons had arrived to eradicate the dreaded Master of Shadow; everywhere Lord Diegan presented his requisition orders, he was met with testy exasperation.

'The supply trains are late, what else?' snapped the beribboned city seneschal, cornered at last in a cramped office behind a granary guarded by pikemen. He raked nail-chewed fingers through the kinked hair at his temples. Eyes pouched and bloodshot from sleepless fretting swivelled sidewards as he talked. 'Your troops want fresh bread and meat, well, that's damned inconvenient. Yon thrice-damned fleet in the harbour has made itself felt like an infestation of rats. For each day your troops were delayed, their crews had to be fed and housed. Every captain and his purser thinks to bully our merchants for provisions they frankly haven't got. Have you checked the taverns?'

Unbathed, unshaven, heartily in need of mulled wine to cut the inhospitable northcoast chill, Lord Diegan drummed his gloved fingers on the hilts of his weapons and allowed that he had not.

'There's neither room nor lodging to be had,' the testy little seneschal ranted on. 'Every taproom's crammed to bursting with sailors, most of them passed out drunk. Our chief councilman's daughter walked outside her garden gate two days ago and got solicited like a dockside bawd!'

Lord Diegan uttered a showy apology, then finished with his nastiest smile. 'Now get me an empty council chamber with a fire and a staff servant, and a board with hot food for my twenty officers. After that, I don't care if you throw your mayor out of his personal bed suite! The Prince of the West will have quarters befitting his station.'

The seneschal paused like a terrier outfaced by a mastiff, measured the threat in the Lord Commander's stance, then dispatched a cringing underling to roust up the mayor's house steward.

Other setbacks could not be so easily bullied into correction. Lysaer returned from his waterfront consultation with the fleet captains in a towering, restless state of angst. 'The wind's blowing in from the wrong quarter,' he announced, ripping a glove off with his teeth.

Justifiably smug since his success at commandeering a room that overlooked the harbour, Lord Commander Diegan glanced up in startlement. Perched astride the settle, and relaxed in sanguine comfort for the chance to shed his onerous shirt of mail, he watched his liege's signs of temper with bland humour. 'Be careful. You'll swallow forty carats out of pique. Are you saying we can't start the loading tomorrow?' When the prince's taut expression failed to ease, Diegan tossed his surcoat aside, the holes that wanted mending forgotten. 'Better put off the staff meeting, then. The garrison here will rend your royal hide. Werpoint can't support thirty thousand mouths. They've sold their stores from the harvest, and news just came in. Clansmen fired the standing grain in East Ward. Surplus can be bought to carry the city through, but only if we've freed up the trade galleys before the harbour closes for the winter.'

Prince Lysaer tossed his gloves and his silk-lined storm cloak to his hovering equerry, then gestured the servant's dismissal. A vexed stride brought him to the table, where he ripped off the end of the bread loaf pried away from the kitchen staff with threats. He stared at the steam that arose off the morsel, shot a glare at the darkened casement, then spun in barely-held fury. 'This can't happen. I didn't raise and train a grand war host only to be stopped by a run of poor luck and the ridiculous misfortune that the winds choose to blow southeast!'

'Oh?' Lord Diegan lounged back against the stone beside the settle and crossed his ankles on a footstool. His rowelled spurs snagged cuts in the embroidery, a fact to provide a spurt of sour pleasure, since the mayor's house steward had been niggardly about supplying clean towels, and no servant had come to replenish the wood in the firebox. While his prince paced the carpet, too distressed to eat, Avenor's Lord Commander said in gentle satire, 'You'd think the better of setbacks if we were frozen alive by some fell mix of sorcery and shadows?'

Lysaer stabbed the air in a sign to avert malfortune. 'Hold your tongue! It's a fool's move to invite an ill fate.' Suspicion rode his thoughts, every hour, that the Master of Shadow must have some hand at play. Although the delays at Valleygap seemed exclusively targeted in revenge against Pesquil and his headhunters, Rathain's clansmen were Arithon's feal allies. No man acquainted with s'Ffalenn wiles could rule out the chance their strikes had been timed as one thread in some wider design.

Unease ate at Lysaer like acid on a burn, until even waking reason felt like nightmare.

'The wind will shift,' Diegan insisted. Helpless in his need to ease his liege lord's distress, he scrounged a goblet and shared his mulled wine. 'We've overcome our due share of setbacks.'

Exhausted and thin as any one of his officers, the Prince of the West accepted the glass in distraction. He had no heart to add the point just argued in force by his fleet captains: that when the wind veered, the winter storms would rake the east coast with the change. If the blue-water ships could batten their hatches and ride out such gales in fair safety, the galleys could withstand no such punishment. Their lower freeboard and oar ports would take on water in high seas. Heavily loaded, rough conditions would force them to seek sheltered harbours, or run the high risk foundering.

'The supply shortage here is already critical. If our troops aren't to starve, we must move them south with all speed.' Lysaer swirled the dregs in his wine glass, driven in determination as Lord Diegan had never heard him. 'This is our most critical hour. If we don't put to sea within the next few days, the war host we have gathered against the Master of Shadow is a wasted cause, and every loss sustained at Valleygap gone for nothing. I've arranged to start loading tomorrow. The fleet captains aren't happy, but I've forced their consent. The galleys will sail with the evening tide, whether we have to row against headwinds every league down the length of Minderl Bay.'

Strike at Minderl Bay

While unfavourable weather and supply shortage preoccupied the war host's ranking officers, in the wind-torn darkness of Werpoint's outer harbour, a returning longboat's crew shipped oars beneath the rolling hull of a merchant brig named the *Savrid*. The deck lantern swung cold on its ring. From a point halfway up the side battens, her captain cursed the duty watch in dangerous, soft words, his breath a ghostly plume in the raw and salt-laden air. He vaulted over the rail, prepared to roust miscreants, then gasped, caught short by the prick of a knife.

'Don't shout,' murmured a stranger from a point just behind his right ear. 'Just step forward, quietly.' The accent was crisp, vowels lilted in the dialect spoken by Rathain's forest clansmen.

Hooded against the wind, a packet of sealed dispatches snugged into his breast from the officers' council with Prince Lysaer, the brig's captain bristled.

The knife prodded harder and sliced clear through his best woollen cloak.

'Move on,' the barbarian said, unreliably agreeable. 'Or don't. I can bleed you like a pig right here, and my archers in your crosstrees won't even twinge against firing on unarmed oarsmen. You wish your bully boys to live? My liege would prefer they don't suffer, but I'd as soon run them beneath the Wheel if you balk.'

The captain shut his eyes, his clean-shaven jaw clamped in outrage. Mistakes could not be unmade. Likely his watch officer had been huddled by the galley stove sharing tales with the cook, instead of on patrol as he should have been. As a merchant's command, *Savrid*'s hands were ill-suited to the rigorous demands of a war fleet. Three weeks standing dull rounds at anchor watch had undermined the best effort to maintain vigilance.

Sorry, now, for his choice to secure his ship on the fringes to stay clear of tangled anchor lines and crowding, the brig captain gave clipped surrender.

At once he was blinded under the stifling wool of his own cloak. Since his barbarian captor disliked foolish chances, his hands were expertly bound. Through muffling cloth, he scarcely noticed the scuffles while his oarsmen were captured and silenced one after another as they clambered over the rail.

Common sea hands all, they were no match for raids and practised violence.

Pricked by the knife, guided on by a shove, the captain could only let himself be bundled aft, through the companionway into his stern cabin. Against the squeal of the door hinge and the snick of the latch, he heard short words exchanged with someone else of uninflected speech. Then unfriendly hands spun him backwards. He toppled into an ignominious sprawl in the blankets of his own berth.

His blindfold was whipped off with enough force to scuff his fair-skinned cheeks to a flush. Light-haired, blue-eyed, and burly enough to have worked his way up from a mate's berth, the captain raised his square chin and glowered into a flare of lamplight fierce enough to make him squint. 'Sure's ebb tide, whoever you are, you're going to be made to pay for this.'

'How much is your dignity worth?' quipped a voice with stinging, cool clarity. The speaker was small, compactly made, and mantled in plain-cut wool. The brassy spill of the oil flame played over black hair and eyes like summer leaves. A thin, chiselled mouth bent in dry irony at the flustered state of his captive.

Whatever the shanghaied captain expected, that opening set him at a loss. 'Who are you?'

The stranger gave an elegant smile, reached out a limber hand and snatched the dispatch packet out of his prisoner's tunic. 'I'm the one wretch this lively war host has convened at Werpoint to eradicate.' The beautiful fingers snapped through the wax seal, flicked open folded papers and tipped them in unbreathing steadiness toward the light.

Savrid's captain gave a galvanic heave in protest, then bellowed, his body slammed backward by the clansman's reflexive restraint. Silenced by pain, he fought to sort meaning from insouciance. 'The Master of Shadow? *You!*'

His outburst was ignored. Allowed space to grapple his blind, staring fear, the brig captain gasped, 'Ath have mercy, you're here to close with the army at Werpoint!'

Green eyes glanced in displeasure over the lit rim of parchment. 'You're nothing if not misled. War is exactly what I'm here to forestall.'

'Lies!' The captain spat at the feet of the sorcerer his ship had volunteered to help destroy.

The broad-shouldered clansman returned the insult with a low burst of laughter and swiped his knife toward the harbour. 'Did you see an attack fleet? No? Well, you wouldn't. Because all we have with us are eight quick men, a cockleshell of a dory, and Arithon's dinky pleasure sloop.'

The companionway door creaked open to an icy flood of fresh air. Another rogue crammed into the stern cabin, planted as a wrestler beside the man self-proclaimed to be the fugitive Prince of Rathain. The deck lantern picked out details as the shadows slewed to the swell: a hooked nose and shifty eyes, then the shelf of a tattooed cheek, sliced by tangled, mud-brick hair.

'Crew's all stowed.' The newcomer's darted glance sheared over his sorcerer master with respect, then brushed off all else in contempt. A brass hoop glinted in one ear, and scratched gold rings looped over fingers toughly sinewed as grappling hooks. With his flat thumbs laced through his belt, the seaman had the same sleek grace as an unsheathed scimitar left propped to rest against the bulkhead. 'When are you wanting to weigh anchor?'

'Inside the hour.' The Shadow Master tapped the dispatch. 'As we hoped, *Savrid*'s assigned on patrol.'

Resentful, the captain broke in, 'What have you done with my men?'

'They're unharmed.' The sorcerer scarcely paused in his reading, at ease with the brig's rocking dance against her cable, except for a tension that suggested an attentive ear to the wind. Through the fitful, thumped footfalls as the prize crew on deck made thorough acquaintance with the brig, he added, 'I doubt they're pleased, trussed as they are in the forecastle. Short of taking their lives, that was the best I could do.'

'Don't expect me to thank you,' the captain snapped. 'Why else are you here, but to kill?'

Again, he was ignored. The black-haired prince cracked the dispatch into folds and perused the parchment chart beneath. 'Jieret, your war captain's gloomy hunch is justified. The Prince of the West knows all about my shipyard at Merior. I wonder who betrayed my happy plans?'

As if that shuttered, flat tone signalled danger, the bearded clansman shifted stance. His knife hand started to a flash of sheared light.

The other swarthy scoundrel sidled straight from his slouch as the Shadow Master closed his edged musing. 'Unless we want a war host down our throats and in our blankets, there's no room left for half measures. Some risks will have to be shouldered.'

'Ath's Black Avenger! Haven't we done that already?' The clansman stared uneasily at the shifty-looking seaman, then swore afresh as the creature glared back like a felon. 'My liege, you're mad just to be here.'

Unsettled enough to forget himself, he straightened, cracked his head on a deck beam, and ripped out in rife exasperation, 'Takes an underfed stripling to love seafaring!'

Then, as the captive on the berth dared a move, he spun like a wolf, his knife poised to throw. 'What do you wish done with this one? Jam him in up forward with the rest?'

Disturbed beyond caution by the dispassionate gaze that swung from the dispatch and pinned him, the brig captain wrenched at his bonds. 'Don't think to get rid of me so easily.'

A spark of vicious humour lit the Shadow Master's mood. 'Stay then. You'll do just as well. Lysaer might fare better with a witness.' To his clansman's repressive dearth of comment, he added, 'Jieret, your moping isn't going to change my mind. If the prisoner's complaints drive you to distraction, you've got my permission. Bind his mouth.'

The brig captain tried an immediate protest.

'No,' rebuked the red-bearded clansman. 'It's quiet you'll stay as my liege lord requires, or a good bit worse will befall you.'

Trussed in his cloak, riled like a fighting cock bagged for the pit, the brig captain fumed while the Master of Shadow gave over his command to the mountebank.

The slant-eyed seaman displayed an evil grin throughout his crisp orders to make sail. As wary as though he hazed a coiled snake, the Shadow Master clarified his wishes. 'See that this vessel takes timely station in the channel. The lanterns you'll need for running lights and signals are listed with the passwords for handing off the watch.'

The dispatch changed ownership in bristling tension, as if the pair made uneasy allies.

'Remember our bargain.' The scruffy seaman gave a sly, parting chuckle. 'If your move goes wrong, no loyalty. I'll be sailing as I see fit.'

Far and long after the brigand departed, the displaced captain worked and tugged at his bonds. He failed to loosen the rope or the wool by a hair's-breadth; clan raiders were experts at knots. Yet as the rush of busy sailors swept across the deck topside, and commands rang out to haul anchor, the dread prince that Lysaer had raised armies to destroy did nothing more than to embark on a virulent round of pacing. Through the clack of the capstan's pawls, the bearded barbarian watched his master cross and recross the tiny cabin, his restless touch roving from chart locker, to table, to blanket chest through a crisp and disquieting silence.

Little else about the sorcerer seemed remarkable. The tunic he wore was patched at the hem, and a sailmaker's stitch laced his scabbard. At each fresh change, while canvas was unbrailed and braced full, he held a tigerish pause as he measured the activity abovedecks. When the brig shouldered forward and heeled to the wind, he eased back into soft, balanced steps.

Time passed. The lantern flame fluttered and failed. As if the clansman's peace of mind frayed out with the light, he stirred in the shadows and rummaged through lockers until he found the striker and spare lamp. By touch, he filled the oil well, lit the fresh wick, then hunched in gloomy restraint at the table until the hot frame of the doused one cooled.

Over the uneven jink of metal as he used his knife to dismantle the workings for cleaning, he offered in deep-voiced hesitation, 'There isn't a damned thing I can say to talk you out of this.'

'Merciful Ath!' The smaller man whirled in an explosive ferocity that threw the bound captain to inadvert recoil. Crammed in confinement, his backbone knuckled against the side ribs, he beheld an unalloyed agony stamped into the Shadow Master's face.

'Jieret,' the criminal rebuked. 'What choice do I have? If this war host isn't stopped right here, right now, we're going to see another bloodbath. Well, whoever comes to die for the wrong cause this time, I won't sit back and let it happen. Not in my name, and not on Lysaer's chosen battlefield!'

The knife blade flashed. A crumble of carbon nicked off a tin screw and dulled the varnished surface of the table. Absorbed by blackened fingers and the fussy concentration required for threading a new wick against the jostling toss of the ship, Jieret set his jaw. No man to contest what could not be governed, he scrounged a rag to clean the lamp's sooty glass, while canvas cracked and bellied above decks, and the brig changed to a northerly heading.

'Steady as she goes,' cried the helmsman; the screeling wail of gusts through the rigging subsided to eerie quiet as the vessel veered and lumbered downwind. Left the squeal of the yards in their trucks and the creak of burdened stays in place of conversation, Jieret Red-beard closed and latched the tidied lantern. Past the stern windows, distanced behind the roiled wake, the harbour of Werpoint spread like a whore's gold-shot silk, the scalloped shores of the coves beaded with the lights of a thousand closely-anchored ships. The headland glittered also, limned from above by torches set streaming on the battlements; and from landlocked, sheltered hollows, a widespread glow of fires sowed the fields where the war host camped.

The clansman's bearded profile loomed a notch in the view like the anvil silhouette of a squall line. 'Well if it's possible to provoke a behemoth and survive, the least I can do, my prince, is back you with all of my heart.' The assurance came measured and steady; and yet when Jieret arose to hang the lantern, the changed flare of light showed a face tinged chalky with fear.

Hours crept by like slow torture, fretted out in nerves and apprehension. Minute to minute, the brig's trussed captain suffered in sweating dread. His vessel sailed large, the breeze on her quarter, then hauled her wind, the enemy crewmen given orders to brace sharp up. *Savrid* swept the channel on the east leg of her patrol in faultless trim, the slit-eyed mate an able enough master despite his disreputable looks. Before the black shoals that fanged Crescent Isle, a leadsman was set in the chains. His precise, timed shouts as he called off the mark offered a morsel of reprieve. Whatever the Shadow Master's intentions, the luckless brig would not be scuttled on the rocks.

Gritty-eyed and aching, the captain jerked awake from an unquiet cat-nap. The swells beyond the stern counter heaved dull pewter under the advent of dawn. The wind still freshened. Stiff southeast gusts had the sailhands aloft to tie in a reef. In snatched bits of invective they maligned numb fingers and canvas turned unwieldy in the cold.

If the lamp had been left to burn out, the aft cabin was not empty.

Before the stern window, poised at the sill on propped forearms, the Master of Shadow waited against the foam raked off the brig's rudder. He said gently, 'It's nearly time.'

An oath lilted back from the gloom. Jieret Red-beard shouldered into view, a pair of fleece bracers in his hands. At Arithon's swift query, he said, 'They're mine. And yes, before you ask, they'll fit you. I trimmed them down with my knife.' Hardened against any protest, he added, 'If you stay bull-stubborn and go through with this, I won't have you tear yourself raw.'

Arithon managed a smile, slicked with the grimness a condemned man might carry through his last march to the scaffold. Then he drew a sword of spectacular artistry from his scabbard and laid its black blade on the chart table. Disarmed, his expression of humility at odds with his killer's reputation, he freed his laced cuffs and bared slender wrists to his liegeman.

The barbarian showed no surprise at the marring white tracery of scars he tucked underneath the leather cuffs. He drew the ties firm then went on to lash his sovereign's wrists with braided leather.

'Jieret,' Arithon said. 'Thongs can break. I saw wire in the starboard locker. Forget about pity and use it.'

The clansman drew a fast breath to argue; stopped. The corners of his mouth flexed down until his moustache bristled into his beard. He accepted the bidding in dumb misery, drawing the wire tight in forceful jerks that had everything to do with a duty he found abhorrent.

His prince endured in distanced stillness, his averted gaze turned to the brightening sky outside. On deck, orders passed to counterbrace the yards. The imprisoned captain shifted against the bulkhead, puzzled why his vessel should heave to in the middle of the channel.

The barbarian finished trussing his prince, then positioned himself on the chart locker. 'I'm ready,' he announced in distaste.

Arithon squared his shoulders. He made a last survey of the coves, cluttered with mismatched hulls, masts and spars and crosstrees packed in layered ranks like a forest denuded of foliage. Angles of tarred ratlines jagged scribbled ink above waters tinged silver and rose under daybreak. His stance stayed in balance despite the pull of tied wrists, while the brig bucked the crests and lost way under him, shuddered by the whitecaps that slapped her broadside from the south. 'Make sure this ship keeps her station,' he insisted, then added in cutting entreaty, 'Jieret, by your oath as my liegeman, I charge you. Don't let me give way, no matter how horribly I scream.'

The clansman looked as hag-ridden as though he stared down the throat of a waking nightmare. 'Ath's mercy on us both! My liege, you don't have to do this. Can sparing one seaside village be worth the price of such a risk?'

A slim form limned against salted glass, the Master of Shadow gave stinging correction. 'Merior's folk aren't my birthright. But a woman there holds my signet ring as pledge that her children shall stay safe.'

'Forgive me,' Jieret whispered, for eight years in the past, on Tal Quorin's greening banks, the decision had been no whit different. 'Don't hold me to blame in my fear for you.'

'Wasted effort.' Above the laboured creak of ship's timbers, Arithon's voice sounded easy. 'Save your pity instead for the captains lured here in the misled belief they were threatened.'

One moment the city of Werpoint rested in stilled peace, the anchorage thatched with masts and hazed soft gold by daybreak. Menace seemed absent; unreal. No inhabitant expected the Shadow Master's presence. Unremarked, he gave no bodily sign in warning, no showman's flourish designed to awe or terrify his audience. Arithon s'Ffalenn simply poised with a dancer's concentration and spun the shadow he had ruled since his birth.

The snare he designed was for Werpoint.

A giant black leopard bounded over the rim of the southern horizon. The apparition swelled to monstrous proportion, then snarled in a silent, silhouetted show of fangs and swallowed the risen disc of the sun. For an instant, two diminished slits of sky glared through its eyes; then it blinked.

Darkness clapped down, soundless, complete, unnatural as if the air compressed to felt.

No star burned, no light. Werpoint's broad headland seemed snuffed from existence, its harbour and ships swallowed up as completely as if Daelion Fatemaster had gone berserk and unravelled the thread of creation. Banished into fell darkness, a city in its entirety lay erased.

Terror undid the brig's captain. He screamed in muffled panic behind his gag. Across the water, unseen through that featureless dark, the fog bells of Werpoint pealed the alarm. Trumpets shrilled on the anchored galleys, their clarion distress borne downwind.

Low and urgent, Jieret spoke through the clamour. 'My liege, at least leave the flame in the lantern. I can't guard your reason if I'm unable to see.'

Arithon perhaps failed to hear him; or else words themselves became meaningless noise as he braced in the dark for a retaliation now beyond any power to revoke.

The bang of a thunderclap ripped the sky into light. From Werpoint, in strong defence, Lysaer s'Ilessid hurled his gift full-force into counter thrust against his sworn enemy. Bolts split the darkness like craze lines dashed through obsidian.

In a wilful, cold-blooded dance with disaster, Arithon of Rathain had wakened the curse of the Mistwraith. The need bloomed and burned, to hammer force against force, until one or both of them lay dead.

People, causes, Werpoint's naked vulnerability the next instant came to mean nothing. His body limned in actinic bursts of glare, Arithon surged toward the stern window. His lips peeled back from bared teeth in a mask that abjured his claim to humanity. Empowered but weaponless, he sought to raise his hands. The bonds on his wrists caught him short. The jerk he tried to free them doubled his frame and an animal snarl rasped his throat.

Worried, perhaps, that the force of his fury might come to dislocate his joints, Jieret clenched his sovereign's elbow and dealt him a violent shake. 'Arithon! For your very life, don't give in to this now.'

The Master of Shadow gave a scraped cry that violated mercy to witness. The fury that knotted his limbs let go. He staggered and all but fell.

Jieret caught him, while the veil of shadows that prisoned the daylight flared and flickered, weakened under Lysaer's strike from Werpoint.

Steady as tide, Jieret murmured while the man in his hands hissed in a shuddering breath. 'Easy my liege. Easy. The effect of the curse can be tempered. If I didn't believe it, I'd never have let you attempt this.'

The sounds of wind and waves acting on hull and canvas marked time amid flickering hell. Then Arithon s'Ffalenn seemed to master himself. 'I can bide,' he said. In the edged blue flare of Lysaer's lightnings he looked bloodless and drawn, flesh wracked to bone by sourceless agony.

A heartbeat's hesitation, and Jieret s'Valerient released him.

Arithon turned back toward the stern window. Now, the work of the brig in the channel swell jostled his stance as he recovered his footing and gazed outward. His screen of darkness showed moth-eaten gaps, where knives of fierce light had torn through. Softly as rainfall, determined as flint, he took patent charge of his handiwork.

Timed on the next flare of sheet light that rocketed from Werpoint's battlements, he played with the tattered edges of his veil and let its stressed fabric dissolve. To an onlooker's eye, the shadow cloak over Minderl Bay seemed to falter, then fray, then sear off like a flame-scalded web. Sunlight and Lysaer's blaze in riposte sheared a swathe of glare across the waves.

The respite proved false: for across the cleared waters to the south loomed the tanbark sails of an inbound fleet of black ships. They were brigantine rigged. Over hulls lean-lined as greyhounds, the bellied swell of headsail and spanker cupped the gusts and trampled up spray. The yards were squared to the wind. Running a relentless, downwind course, the fleet sheared in formation toward Werpoint. As a scythe set to raze through a stand of ripe grain, they spelled doom for the vessels packed at anchorage.

The bugle calls from the galleys shrilled in treble urgency. Captains screamed desperate orders and frightened crews rousted from their berths. Lines were cast off, or cut, and moorings splashed free. The chattering plink of a capstan's pawls carried in strings on the gusts.

In Werpoint the alarm bells pealed out their call to arms; the war camps seethed black, distressed as kicked ant-hills with the distanced forms of running men. From his unseen vantage on the wall walks, Lysaer s'Ilessid would recognize the oncoming fleet. He would see in their lines and the trim of red sails a memory resurfaced from childhood: brigantines fashioned by the hand of s'Ffalenn, built in the shipyards at Merior at sorcerous speed, and now, attacking for pillage and piracy.

Provoked as a cold point of strategy, his rage would burst all bounds.

The light bolt he launched in defence of his own slashed the dawn like a scimitar. Air shrieked. The sky flashed blinding white, then rebounded into fumes and smoke, lit to churned orange by a firestorm of raw, ignited power. The holocaust scalded across wave crests rent to steam, until the bay seemed a cauldron brewed by demons.

'Now,' urged Jieret Red-beard. 'Now!'

Against the stern window, a silhouette etched into what seemed the infernos of Sithaer, Arithon quivered like a string cranked taut and then plucked, a quarter note shy of its breaking point. Perspiration gilded ribbons down his temples and jaw, and his soaked collar clung to sinews like taut cable. He seemed a man racked, or a victim tormented by a course of untenable stress.

On the berth, forgotten, the brig captain heard him snatch in a short, sobbed breath. A snarling tic twitched his cheek. He controlled it. The hands behind his back dripped clammy sweat, each finger clenched until his short-cut nails stabbed a rash of red crescents in his palms. In a brutal, contained courage, despite nerves peeled raw by the scourge of Desh-thiere's curse, Arithon kept grip on his reason. He danced his shadows like catspaws across the water, by turns masking his oncoming ships. In and out of the light, through glare that waxed and fled before countering darkness, his brigantines came and went like smoke. They sailed substanceless, ghostly, all the more threatening for the fact they seemed an apparition.

A clap and a boom volleyed over Werpoint. Against the massed fleet and his sworn mortal enemy, Lysaer retorted in pure light. The sky above the battlements split with the blast. Arithon's teasing play of shadows became snuffed in one towering burst of raw force.

The bolt jagged on and struck the bay, a hammer on an anvil of waves. The inrunning fleet of brigantines exploded into crackling fire. The throaty report slammed a shock through the wind as timbers, canvas, sails and spars ignited, touched off like a torch to inferno.

Struck by the backlash of that virulent, unbridled violence, Arithon lost his last, harried hold on self-awareness. Before Jieret could react, he screamed primal rage and rammed the mullioned casement with his shoulder. The panes shrilled and burst to flying fragments. Then the hands in restraint drove him mad. Arithon twisted like an eel, eyes wide open and wild. Glass slivers stabbed through his shirt linen and reddened his clansman's clenched fingers.

Jieret swore, shifted grip, and gasped in retching pain from a hit to the belly. 'No you won't,' he ground past a stopped hitch of breath.

Arithon thrashed free in a reeling charge that carried him toward the companionway.

Jieret rammed after in pursuit. 'Show your face outside and you know what will happen. By your very orders, that criminal of a mate will slit your throat and claim this brig as his prize.'

The Master of Shadow flung back a mocking laugh not a man of his friends would have recognized. 'Not if I freeze the living flesh off his bones with bindings wrought out of shadow.'

'Dharkaron's vengeance on your twisted bargains,' Jieret swore. He crashed past the table and tackled his prince from behind.

From the vantage of the berth where the captain lay bound, the progression of the fight seemed unnatural. A man so much slighter should never be able to wrestle with success, hampered as he was by bound hands. The disparity in weight by itself should have forced a surrender. Paired in an insane violence, clansman and prince rolled and battered across the deck, then struggled, still locked, to their feet.

'Arithon! My liege!' Jieret's cry wrung off as a kick staggered him into the gimballed lantern. Shadows flared and jumped to the swing of tipped flame. Arithon thrashed in possessed fury. Backward and forward he raged, Jieret's efforts to contain him marked in flittering lamplight, each curse cut to grunts by the quick, starved breaths of exertion.

Jieret clamped both arms around his prince but failed again to pin him down; as well stay magma with silk thread.

A booted heel spiked his instep and rocked him backward. Fast reflex spared him a bitten wrist. In a blistering show of heart, he kept both fists clamped in rucked shirt. Bloodied from the glass, he resisted with the tenacity of a fiend through the punishment, while the pandemonium set loose against the city of Werpoint raged on unheeded outside.

Across a bay serried in restless waves, the snarled, dark tints of spent shadows stained the air, sliced through by light and fanned flame. For the fleet of fired brigantines bore downwind still, chivvied onward by the gusts into a spark-torn, twisted chain of wreckage. Every hapless, trapped captain in Werpoint's harbour saw them come as they screamed frantic orders to crewmen half-stupid with terror. The brigantines now were unmanned, a mindless, deadly, threat against the galleys and merchant brigs striving to pull up anchor and make way. Shouts and horn blasts entangled on the gusts, overwhelmed at ragged intervals by booming blasts of light as Lysaer sought to rout his enemy's unnatural cloak of darkness. Sails cracked out, loosed from their gaskets by sailors whipped aloft to act by main fear and urgency.

Through the dross of patched dark, through rank bad judgement and confusion as hull ground into hull, the imprisoned captain on the *Savrid* deciphered a shattering truth: the straggle of fired hulls had lost their clean lines. The raked masts and spars glazed in outline by fire no longer wore the shapes of the brigantines Lysaer had spent his powers to destroy.

No fleet of deadly warcraft out of Merior, this ragtag chain of hulls: the hostile vessels which closed upon Werpoint were unarmed old hulks, a derelict gaggle of fishing boats and rafts, packed with dried fir boughs and floss, which exploded in fanned sparks and flurried in the breeze, to touch alight whatever lay before them. The illusion of shadows that once masked their shapes had winnowed away to reveal the cunning trap beneath.

Anguished witness to the fate of the east-shore trade fleet, the brig's captain wept in beaten grief. A hand's reach away, or one thrust of a knife, the enemy responsible had his back turned. Still locked hand to hand with his clansman ally, the sorcerer showed no care for the ruin his ploy swept through Werpoint's harbor. His deranged fit raged on unabating. While the stern cabin's furnishings were trampled over, upset, or smashed wholesale, the brig's captain hoped with a vindictive turn of spite that the combatants would pummel themselves to mortal injury.

Even bound, Arithon used his head, his knees, and his feet to bruise and strike. Jieret Red-beard vented pain in choked oaths. The only grip his prince could not break was the hand he held latched in black hair, and that insufficient to stay him. The clansman came aware in clear dread that Arithon manoeuvred toward the uncanny blade still left unsheathed on the chart table.

'Ah no, my prince. Never that.' Jieret at last resorted to blows in return. His merciless fist bashed his liege lord in the jaw. While his adversary reeled, half-stunned, he snatched up the black sword himself.

The evil in Desh-thiere's curse roused the Paravian guardspells ingrained since its forging to defend in the cause of just conflict. Steel clove through air with a terrible, belltone keen of overlaid harmonics. Silvered runes set into its smoky length lit and blazed, sheened like mercury transformed to white light.

'Arithon, hear me!' Jieret screamed.

His anguished appeal went unheeded. Tortured by pity, all but unmanned, he grasped the quickened blade and in a tight, controlled cut, slashed his sovereign's exposed shoulder.

Contact wrung a cry from the man and the elements. A flare of white sheeted through the cabin. Nothing like any weaving of Lysaer's, the clean blast of brilliance came twined with a peal of struck sound. The resonance climbed in unbearable sweetness. Its harmony unstrung the mind. The passions of hatred and sorrow alike were dashed out in a celebration of life that made of all strife a desecration.

Smote by a longing that ached through his bones, the brig captain groaned for the sorrows of the world. Fired to unalloyed grief, stripped in a heartbeat to the dross and clay that cased the naked sum of his mortality, he heard Arithon s'Ffalenn cry aloud as if his heart had been torn from his body.

Still screaming, the Shadow Master folded to his knees. Blood streaked from the gash traced in flesh by Jieret's cut. The enchanted scald of light nicked over the white bone, laid bare beneath his slashed shirt. A marring edge of scarlet flowed down the black blade, then sublimated away in the heatless burn of magics laced through immutable metal.

Jieret stood frozen. Unaware of his sticky hand on the grip, or the grazed pain of his knuckles, he shook with running tremors and wept unabashed, tear for tear in shared anguish with his prince.

'Ath,' Arithon moaned, crumpled finally to lean in sobbing weakness against his liegeman. He hid his face. 'Spare me. I beg you. Desh-thiere's works are too strong, too much for any born man to fight sanely.'

Earl Jieret showed him no quarter. 'You have no choice. Stand up!' He raised the sword, the singing flare of spellcraft now diminished to a fast-fading whisper.

Even the memory of its sustained chord made Arithon's voice grate like gravel. 'Had my hands been free, you know very well I'd have killed you.'

'But they weren't,' Jieret said, unequivocal. 'You made most sure that wouldn't happen.' As his sovereign still shrank in avoidance, he added, 'Shame on you, for cowardice! Did you think you suffer anything I don't feel also?'

Already pale, Arithon went colourless to the lips. He tipped up his head. 'The bloodpact. Ath's mercy, *you feel this?*'

'My liege,' Jieret begged, appalled too late for the inadvertent cost of his admission. 'Don't spurn my part. You charged me to safeguard your integrity. Whatever you say now, as *caithdein*, I am bound. I shall hold you to the letter of that promise.'

'You feel this?' Arithon repeated, his tone skinned into shrill horror.

Merciless, Jieret cut him off. 'That can't be permitted to matter! No one alive can shoulder the burden you carry. You have a job to finish, or blameless people here and in Shand will start dying.' Brutal by necessity, he seized his prince's forearm, hurled him upright and around to face the stern window. When Arithon recoiled and tried to flinch aside, Jieret wrestled him immobile in a shackling grip that spared nothing.

Pinned still and gasping, Arithon had no choice but to behold the unalloyed impact of his handiwork.

The conflagration touched off by Lysaer's defence still raged in coruscating flares of torched sails. Sparks and flying debris flew windborne. Passed from vessel to vessel in Werpoint's jammed harbour, the fire was having its fell feast.

'So end what you've started,' snarled Jieret, 'and bedamned to your whining.' Then he touched the dire sword like Dharkaron's black Spear against his sovereign's quivering nape.

Wrung, wretched, dragged back from the precipice by Jieret's edged scorn and the lacerating beauty of the wardspell instilled within his weapon, Arithon s'Ffalenn bent his head. He drew a breath. His bound hands flexed and tightened. Shamed to reclaim the scattered threads of his design, he raised his chin at last, and measured what remained to press advantage from the destruction his ruse had created.

Turmoil reigned in Werpoint harbour. In the crush of frenzied flight and confusion, vessel collided with vessel. Bowsprits rammed broadside into galleys mired in anchor chains; luggers swept downwind and battered into ships struggling with sails caught aback as crews hauled to check their yards and claw free of the eye of the wind.

To rack and utter ruin, Arithon added shadow spun to a fiendish edge of subtlety. He dimmed the shores of Crescent Isle to make the shoals appear more distant. He cast masking flares of darkness in the eyes of harried helmsmen through critical moments of judgement. Those few vessels brought safely underway were lured astray from the channel. Some lurched aground, to be struck in a scream of broken timbers by following ships unable to veer off. Other captains tacked in misled timing and found themselves against a lee shore, or else turned about, once again in the path of the ruinous maelstrom that stewed in Werpoint's harbour.

The fire, wind-driven, showed mercy to none.

Where Lysaer's opposing talents were hampered by the need to spare allies, Arithon stiffened shadow at will. Even without access to the wellspring of his mage talent, training lent advantage and finesse. He could play his gift to gossamer illusion, or snap wave crests to ice in a swift, freezing absence of light. Where the fleet fled the fire, he used cold as a weapon, to jam sails, and ice rudders in their pintles. Many a stricken quartermaster fought to clear his fouled steering, while the smaller slower luggers in their path were overtaken and mulched to wreckage beneath the trampling bows of crippled ships.

Thin as the cries of flocking gulls, the screams of the injured carried on the breeze to Arithon's vantage at the stern window. For all his clever strategy and wilful bleak purpose, he was not unscathed by the suffering. Taxed to visible, shivering pain, he sought to spin aside again; to abjure his killing touch on those fell tides of shadow and give way at last to despair.

454

Like rock behind him, Jieret forced him back with a prod of spelled steel, and never one shred of human mercy.

Denied leave to turn away, Arithon could not know that Jieret was weeping. Locked against the force of a grief stifled ruthlessly silent, the clansman's knuckles on the sword's grip were rigid, marble-white, and his eyes showed the anguish of a spirit torn up piecemeal. He held unbending to his given service, the black blade ever steadfast, even as the inevitable few vessels tore free of the harbour's morass of fire and billowed ash to run the straits toward the open sea.

By then, Arithon had recovered self-command. Every raw nerve clamped back under control, he called his own crisp order to the mate and crew above decks. Men jumped to lay the *Savrid*'s yards until her canvas came alive to the wind. Greyed to an outline against a pall of blown smoke, she sheared off on port tack, her course laid east across the channel. She no longer sailed unaccompanied. Off her bow, arisen like phantoms, rode more ships spun out of shadow. From his pirate father on Dascen Elur, Arithon held brutal knowledge of the nautical tactics needed to execute raids in close quarters. The shadow fleet he designed to blockade the channel was formidably arrayed, bristling with weapons and archers, and flying full sail braced sharp up.

Harried like minnows before shark's teeth, the vessels in flight wore ship, their choice to run the gauntlet between a wedge of armed vessels, or to turn behind *Savrid*, sailing free, and flying friendly colours from her masthead. They closed in brash confidence, their crews beaten limp from perils but narrowly averted.

Too soon, their captains' guards were lowered; the shadows swirled and thickened, and the fire arrows, shot by clan enemies in *Savrid*'s own crosstrees, hissed from the darkness to claim them.

A pall of choking cinders interleaved with the gloom. The cries of sailors who leaped overboard to escape being burned alive shrilled over the crack of stressed timbers. In Werpoint the bronze bells still tolled in distress. Here and there, amid planks that flamed and hissed in the barrage of cold waves, those galleys left whole manoeuvred to spare survivors who thrashed at the mercy of the sea.

Against maritime misfortune, Lysaer s'Ilessid had no recourse. His vast armies ashore were helpless to do aught but brandish their weapons and curse.

The disaster to the merchant fleet played itself out, while under cover of blown smoke and shadow, the pirate crew manning the *Savrid* launched a longboat and slipped away. They would seize a fatter prize, the reward plucked from chaos that the Shadow Master left them for their service. Under a helmsman carefully chosen for loyalty and two crewmen hired on for risk pay, the brig rounded the headland and turned south-east, to sail close-hauled down the coast. Werpoint slipped astern, eclipsed by the forested shores of Crescent Isle.

In time, the taint cleared from the air.

Sunlight poured untrammelled through the shattered stern window and sketched the man there in glancing light. Slowly he turned his head. In a voice grained hoarse from the aftermath of stress, he said, 'Jieret. It's safe, I think, to free my hands.'

The ebony sword flashed, moved; the gleaming tip dropped from fixed guard. The red-haired clansman whose age, in the daylight, was not a day more than twenty, sawed through the bonds tied with cord. Then he cast down the blade as though its mere touch burned his skin. The clanging reverberation of tempered steel against the deck caused him to shiver and shrink. His hands trembled. Minutes passed as he fumbled with torn fingers to untwist the crimps in the wire.

When the last bond gave way, he dropped to his knees, hands clasped to the ripped bracers that had scarcely spared the royal flesh beneath from the rigours of curse-bound directive. He could not bear to look up, nor confront what awaited in the face of the sovereign he had obeyed to the ruin of all pride.

'My liege lord,' he entreated. 'I beg your forgiveness.' In agonized remorse, he convulsed his fingers in torn fleeces. 'Rathain's justice and Dharkaron hear my case, I had no way else to keep your orders.'

Arithon s'Ffalenn pried loose his chafed wrists. He turned around, careful in movement as if his bones were spun glass and his being might shatter at the jar of a wrongly-drawn breath. A moment passed while he stood with closed eyes. The running blood from his shoulder seeped through his torn shirt and tapped the white spruce of the deck. Then he stirred. He laced narrow fingers over the damp, copper crown of the *caithdein* who had abused him; who had broken his royal will on the point of a sword to force a cruel round of strategy to its finish.

'Jieret,' he whispered. The tracks of his tears had dried on his face. Rucked hair flicked his cheek in the play of the breeze through the shattered panes of the stern window. 'Arise, man, I beg you. We share a brother's trust. What pride or integrity do I have left that this curse hasn't thoroughly undone?' His wounding note of compassion snapped all at once to bare a core of acid bitterness. 'If ruin and despair are any cause for satisfaction, take back your heart and stand tall. By strict count of burned planks and wrecked ships, we have rather brilliantly succeeded.'

Indeed, no army would sail upon Merior to take down the Master of Shadow.

Reckoning

On the smoke-hazed battlements of Werpoint, Lysaer s'Ilessid stood in freezing wind and tainted sunlight and regarded a vista of wrecked hopes. The enormity of fate seemed unreal, years of careful planning reduced to ruin within hours by one strike of diabolical cunning. Longboats plied the bay to rescue what remained to be salvaged after the Shadow Master's surprise attack on the harbour.

Lent the outlines of embossed paper under blown drifts of smoke and cinder, tired oarsmen jagged tortured courses through clots of half-submerged timbers and steaming wreckage. They dipped skinned knuckles into raw brine and hauled in survivors who were stunned, half-dead from immersion in cold waters, or worse. Too many were brought in screaming from the hideous agony of burns, the jostling passage back to safety and shore too much for seared flesh to endure.

Their cries cut Lysaer to the marrow and the heart. The disaster spread before him in wreckage and in suffering was no one's fault but his own. He resisted the urge to knuckle his eyes to ease the raw sting of wind-borne ash. Nor would he bend to craven need and retire from view to nurse his despair in private.

He felt a fool.

Cold, bitter fury consumed him for the lapse that had cost him his fleet. Despite the heat of conflict, a ruler's steady reason should have prevailed: *he ought to have known at once that the attacking fleet of brigantines could be no more than illusion*. Even under direction of a sorcerer, human craftsmen at Merior could never complete so many hulls since the shipyard's founding the past spring.

Alone among his war officers and ship captains, Lysaer had held fore-knowledge to unriddle this ruse in its fiendish turn of simplicity.

Eight years past, in a grimy back alley in Etarra, he had watched his

457

half-brother spin a toy-sized ship out of shadow for the delight of a ragged pack of children. Small as that vessel had been, a creation of whimsical fancy, her execution and design had been perfect to the last detail. On the banks of Tal Quorin, Arithon had criminally proven his regard for the young was no more than a charade to lull suspicion and buy trust.

On Minderl Bay, for stakes unconscionably higher, he had repeated his game of illusion. Except now his ploy with ships had been cast in life size to enact a bloody toll in human lives.

Lysaer let the winds snarl his hair and dam back the tears he refused to shed in remorse. Shamed beyond self-forgiveness for the towering temper that had pressured him out of control, he ached in guilt-fed silence. How well his enemy had judged him. Teased into anger, baited to a rage as mad as his father's in Dascen Elur, he had savaged the very sky with his gifted powers to ignite that chain of fire ships, and enact the very letter of the Shadow Master's design.

How Arithon must be laughing, the poisoned depths of his adversary's dishonour a personal and private triumph. Lysaer slammed a fist on cold stone until his knuckles split.

At his shoulder, Lord Diegan had to speak twice before his sovereign prince heard him. 'Your Grace, if you insist on staying out here, at least allow your valet to clothe you in warmer attire.'

Lysaer succumbed to a violent shiver. He choked back the burst of undignified laughter that clawed for escape from his throat. In fact, he wore nothing beyond a holland shirt snatched in haste from his bedside. The tails flapped like flags about his naked buttocks; before the world, he offered a ludicrous sight, standing in plain view, chapping his muscular royal thighs.

'I shall dress.' His words fell remote through the clamour of bells from the quayside. As a war prince, he was remiss. His people had suffered a shocking setback. Whatever the enormity of his shortcomings, their morale must become his immediate care. His sorry error in judgement and his disastrous, misled defence lent no excuse to deny them support through his presence.

The garments he donned were cut from blue velvet and gold tissue, and his jewels, the best ones he owned. Arrived at the quayside in every trapping of state rank, Prince Lysaer met the oared boats with their pitiful cargoes and dirtied, ringed hands steadying their gunwales at the wharf. From the unremitting, ugly task of dealing with the losses left by his ill-turned defence, he spared himself no hardship. Nor would he acknowledge the whispers of adulation offered by Werpoint's populace, who insisted his gift of light had spared their city from total ruin.

If word on the streets cast the Prince of the West as a hero who had beaten back the Shadow Master, many a stranded ship's captain had cause to curse the fires spawned by his powers of salvation.

Grim-faced and diligent, his fine clothes marred with sea water, blood, and smeared tar, Lysaer faced down every ship's master and sailhand to confront him with incoherent rage. To their faces, he rebuked them in bracing, selfless dignity. 'Do you think you're the first to suffer for the wiles of s'Ffalenn? Did I never say his shadow-bending sorcery presents an unspeakable danger? If one glancing encounter makes you quiver and turn tail, leave now and count yourselves lucky to go living. My ranks have no place for faint hearts.'

In brisk, snatched moments between assignment of shelter and arranging care for the injured, Lysaer dispersed patrols of headhunters with tracking dogs. These scoured the southern coastline for sign of the fugitive crews who must have manned the enemy fleet of fire ships.

To the wounded who cried aloud for vengeance, he bent his bright head. 'Stay alive,' he entreated. 'Any man hale enough to fight shall claim his due right to justice.' The maimed were promised a haven for themselves and their families at Avenor. For the dying, the prince gave solace: on his knees in the blood-rinsed bilges of open boats, and on the docks, beneath the shadows of soldiers set to work hefting litters.

Premature twilight dimmed the sullied, ash-silted air. Relaunched under torch light, the longboats rowed now to recover a freight of cold corpses. Officers laboured under lamplight to tally the full count of casualties and to list any ship that repairs could restore and make seaworthy.

Then the headhunter patrols returned on lathered horses from their southbound sweep of the countryside, exhausted and worn at their failure.

'Sorcery,' the heavyset rider appointed as spokesman insisted to Captain Mayor Skannt. He cast uneasy glances at the shadows to each side of him, while his tired horse blew and dripped sweat. 'We found no track, no sign. Not so much as the cinders from a campfire. If those fire ships were crewed by living men and not demons, then some trick of fell sorcery built them a bridge to escape across the face of the sea. Had they trodden the honest earth, we'd have scared up some sign of them.'

Inclined to treat such fear as hare-brained fancy, Skannt gave the prince and the town council his report in the dockside warehouse set up as headquarters, his rapid-fire speech at odds with his slouched posture against the door lintel. 'Had to have hidden a few dories under shadow, and a fishing smack to pick up swimmers,' he summed up, succinct. 'Your fugitives escaped by sail. Had they once come ashore, there's no living way they'd have slipped past the noses of my tracking dogs.'

Lysaer silenced Diegan's intrusive comment with a placating touch of one hand. 'I didn't expect the patrols to take prisoners. Arithon's by far too clever to provide us loose ends and mistakes. But our sea captains needed the belief that we tried. The ones left unsatisfied with the result of your search will become the more diligent to pursue the criminals back to Merior.'

Skannt took his leave with a disdainful smile, the spark of the fanatic masked under lazy, half-lidded lashes.

The interrupted council resumed the grinding long list of its agenda. 'What use to give chase?' cried Werpoint's withered harbourmaster. 'The winter's upon us.' Crumpled on his chair like a heap of mouldered rags, he held onto manners through biting contempt, and managed not to spit while in the royal presence. 'We've nary a handful of vessels not holed, and hulls with charred masts won't sail anywhere. What armies you move must now go on by land, and the bay road's a rough march as the weather turns.'

The grim knot of men in charge of supply lines exchanged glances in freezing lack of comment. The decision was going to have to be given within hours to disband the proud war host from Etarra. Ath's storms would hold for no man's just cause, and soldiers brought to starving could not fight. Stockpiles in Werpoint were already drained from the prior demands of the fleet. No righteous need could change fact. The city had no more resource to spare the muster against Arithon s'Ffalenn.

As the mayor's council heated into chin-jutting argument, and officers shouted and banged tables, Lysaer jumped erect and burst apart declaiming factions in a bristling show of royal outrage. 'Will you not stop? Our men at arms are living! That's reason enough to give thanks to Ath, that we'll have them to fight again at need. We are reduced to sad choices, but all is not lost. Let us act well and use reason, and salvage whatever we may. Unless we wish to cede the Master of Shadow an easy victory, we must review what resource we have left and seek the one alternative that might make the next campaign unnecessary!'

And so began the sober process of remapping the assault over the wreckage of old plans.

Aid might be garnered from Jaelot and Alestron; a fast courier was dispatched southward through the post relay to Minderl, where petition could be sped on by galley.

'How much of an army must we have to strike at Merior?' Lysaer said in forceful conclusion. His trimmed blond hair feathered shadows over his ringed and tired eyes, yet weariness stole nothing from his character. No trace of his gnawing anguish flawed his voice or his bearing as he added, 'The village there has no resources, no garrison, nor any natural advantage of landscape beyond its troublesome access. My troops from Avenor are hardened. They'll survive a winter march. The core of our veterans from Etarra have the heart to weather setbacks. Let's look to patch together a reduced fleet, and find captains stung to rage enough to sail them.'

Impelled by royal influence, the dignitaries of Werpoint and the factions of disgruntled officers plunged into a night of rapt planning. By first light, to a marvel of swift decisions, the process of reorganization had been detailed and begun. Lysaer scarcely ate or slept. Every moment he could spare from arbitration and the thankless, unending task of smoothing the ruffled tempers of the merchants, he spent at the bedsides of the wounded or scribing letters to the widows of the dead. No detail was too small for his attention, no diplomacy too petty to express.

Men came into his presence worn, or frustrated, or enraged to the point of violence. Without exception, they left inspired to fresh purpose.

Sundown of the following day saw the bedchambers requisitioned for the royal suite cluttered under layers of nautical charts, discarded stacks of dispatches marked urgent, and plates of gnawed fish bones couched upon crusts of stale bread. The carpets were gritted with sand and soil from the tramp of petitioning officers. Red-eyed, hoarse from talking, chapped from prolonged exposure to the whipping winds off the harbour, Prince Lysaer s'Ilessid cast himself with irked force into the depths of a cushioned chair.

He looked pale enough to be ill. The speech just delivered to the garrison captains of Rathain had been a masterwork of hard statecraft. Thwarted in purpose, cast down in defeat, the prince had shown not a flicker of despair. While in the public eye of his troop captains, he had been the unbent picture of royal pride.

Only Lord Diegan could imagine the cost and the heartache such care for his following had cost. Every promise Lysaer had made had been ruined; every hope built over the course of eight years crumbled down in one hour of fire and trickery.

The main force would begin the laborious process of disbanding on the morrow, lest they starve where they camped in the onset of winter. The order should have caused mayhem, when trail-worn, hardened captains were told to turn back, and retrace the steps of every brutal league they had crossed since departure from Etarra. No one spoke of the fatalities they would suffer from weather and sickness throughout the arduous march home. Brought to fighting pitch, forged into a magnificent weapon, they were to turn tail with their steel unblooded. The tight-knit purpose, the hard work, the tremendous expenditure of effort and gold: all had gone for naught.

Captain Mayor Pesquil lay under a stone cairn in Valleygap, his death reduced now to a sacrifice without purpose, another name on a list awaiting vengeance.

For Lysaer s'Ilessid, who had dedicated himself to the cause of Arithon's defeat, there could be no more bitter a debasement.

From his place by the emptied command table, Lord Diegan waited for the officers, petitioners, and city councilmen who clustered in knots in the corners to clear themselves from the room. As the glitter of the last jewelled pourpoint disappeared in the shadow beyond the doorway, he knuckled his eyes, crusted and stinging from the documents and tactical maps perused for hours by candlelight. 'Your Grace, you must rest. To recoup from this setback will be daunting enough. You'll never stay fit if you drive yourself harder to ease what cannot be changed.'

Insurmountable problems would grow no less. What steps had been taken in salvage had been completed at whirlwind expediency. The markets were emptied of food. Those ships still fit to restock them had sailed for Jaelot, crammed with Avenor's best troops; the rest were a loss, sad snarls of burned spars on the beachheads.

The tap at the chamber door was unwelcome, another needless, petty worry the s'Ilessid prince could do without, since every visitor came bearing his burden of complaints. Lord Diegan straightened sore shoulders as the mayor's chamberlain poked in his head, his sorry, hound's face a pale blur against the wilted lace of his collar. 'Your Lordship? Your Grace?' He hurried to stave off rebuttal. 'A sea captain's here. He demands to be granted admittance.'

Lord Diegan lost his temper. 'By Ath! Send him on with the others.'

'I tried. He wouldn't go.' The chancellor's flurried excuses cut off as Lord Diegan shot straight, hands mired to the wrists in the litter on the tabletop.

'What ever it takes, throw him out!' A quill pen tossed awry by the Lord Commander's agitation sliced in arced flight to the floor. 'He can present his requisitions until the roof falls in and get no more joy from the effort. No stores remain to be issued.'

'Your pardon, my lord.' The chancellor coughed in forbearance. 'This man bears no supply writ. He's from the brig *Savrid*, and he claims on some authority to bear a message from the Master of Shadow.'

'He has a whole ship?' Lord Diegan cut in, astonished enough to relent. His query entangled with Lysaer's clipped gesture to hasten *Savrid*'s master in for audience.

The seaman wore a merchant's broadcloth. Fair haired, his sturdy frame fleshed on the spare side of corpulent, he had honest blue eyes and a wary stance on the carpet. The cap in his hands showed crushed prints in the velvet from the fretted grip of thick fingers. Too independent to bow before royalty, he bestowed a curt nod of respect. 'My Lord Prince.'

Lysaer regarded him in the unblinking, even quiet he kept while hearing out arbitrations. 'You may sit,' he said first, then waited in regal patience while the man found a chair by the chart table. 'You say you've met with the Master of Shadow. I would know in your own words exactly how that came about. No one will question until you've finished. Take your time and be careful to tell everything.'

The brig captain draped his mangled cap on his knee. The same clear-eyed squint he used to trim his sails measured the stately prince by the casement. The weariness on the royal features did not escape him, nor the glacial, forced control behind the facade of poised patience. The captain spoke at length, a mulish set to his chin. 'The man told me you were cursed by the Mistwraith to fight.'

462

'Arithon s'Ffalenn is a sorcerer,' Lysaer replied. 'He would say anything to undermine your moral faith.'

The royal sincerity moved the seaman to visible distress. His boot scraped the carpet, and his troubled glance flicked aside. 'In this case, I don't think so.'

Lysaer's regard turned hard as chipped aquamarine. An imperious sidewards gesture stilled his Lord Commander's affront as he urged, 'Say why, and plainly. You need not fear for what you believe to be the truth.'

The story of *Savrid*'s part in the raid upon Werpoint harbour unfolded in slow, precise phrases, from the efficient act of piracy that had requisitioned her use, to the neat manner she had been abandoned at an anchorage on the north side of Crescent Isle.

In devilish ingenuity, every one of her yards had been unshackled from the masts, with the halyards of headsail and spanker left flaked in cut coils over her pinrails. Her gear was left whole, but unable to carry sail. Nor was her captain entirely certain he would have pursued the small sloop that Arithon had used for his escape, even had the option existed. Whatever Lysaer claimed, however he framed his grand cause, the prince he called enemy was not the born killer he was named.

Until his last breath, *Savrid*'s captain would recall the black sword in the hands of the clan liegeman who had slaughtered pride, even broken the man's will to hold him to a desperate act of prevention.

'We knew of the ship stolen from the fringes of the straits,' Lysaer said. 'You have the audacity to claim the theft was not done under Arithon's auspices?'

'I said, not by Arithon's hand,' the brig captain corrected. 'His reason was plain, when I asked him. He said he'd rather a liaison with a shiftless seaman for the risks he undertook to stop your fleet. He wished no honest man to suffer in the backlash, if his intentions chanced to go awry. He worried. Any ally of his might be tortured, if caught. He seemed anxious to keep that from happening. If the captain he paid met a felon's death, at least such an end would serve justice.'

Cocked on the edge of explosive movement, Lysaer gripped his hands to the arms of his chair, his chiselled features turned wry. 'An admirable and plausible excuse. The s'Ffalenn were born clever to a man. You say you bring me a message?'

The captain wrung out a breath in trepidation, his blunt fists clamped on his knees. He closed his eyes and spoke, haunted by the stark event as the Prince of Rathain had knelt at his side to cut his bonds.

'*I'm going to set you free,*' Arithon had said. '*But in return, I ask for one service. Go as my messenger to Lysaer s'Ilessid. Tell him in my name that I chose to destroy his fleet and strand his war host at Werpoint. Bid him remember, should he make disposition to pursue me. The burning was provoked by my fullest intent while the vessels at anchorage were not loaded.*'

For the blood on his hands, Arithon s'Ffalenn had made no apology. Seamen would be dead in the wreckage and the flames, and some, from drowning and exposure. But the stabbing, awful facts lent him credence through hard truth: the death toll by design could effortlessly have been five times that of the losses inflicted by Tal Quorin. Not only the fleet, but the war host raised against him might have been decimated in the selfsame stroke.

Thirty-five thousand lives had been spared an untimely pass beneath the Wheel.

The stillness in the royal chamber as the captain finished speaking was absolute. Outside the latched casements, the whistle of a lampsman drifted up from the street. The jingle of harness bells on a rich lady's carriage overlaid distant shouts from the waterfront. Sailhands from wrecked vessels packed the taverns and the brothels, most of them penniless and stranded. The town watch spent increasing hours stopping brawls, and theft was a mounting problem.

Lysaer s'Ilessid surveyed the ship captain whose message skirted very near to treason. Whether the man would ever have lent his unstinting service was now moot. His part at Werpoint had compromised his trust through delusion that the Master of Shadow was no murderer. Rather than pressure the issue outright in judgement, Lysaer clasped his fingers in a flaring sparkle of sapphire rings.

He used a short interval to balance his thoughts, and to damp back the sting of private shortcomings. Once he, too, had been beguiled into trust by his half-brother's disingenuous, glib tongue. 'If I ask,' he said gently to the captain, 'would you lend your *Savrid* to my cause? She is needed more sorely than ever in the past to bear me south as an envoy to Alestron.'

Still shaken by the memory of the clear, harmonic tone roused from a spelled edge of swordsteel; pierced in conscience by recollection of Arithon s'Ffalenn on his knees, unmanned by horror and begging release from the trials laid on him by his oath to a widow in Merior, *Savrid*'s captain sighed and shook his head. 'I'm sorry, your Grace.' A scar on his heart he lacked words to express forced his reluctant decision. 'Your cause is not mine. If you insist on pursuing Rathain's prince in the south, you must do so with no help from me.'

'The Shadow Master compromised your ship!' Lord Diegan protested. 'Are your crewmen complacent at his handling?'

'My crewmen are alive and untouched by the fires.' The captain snapped his cap off his thigh, jammed it over his hair, and without awaiting royal leave, shoved in spare haste to his feet. 'Prince Arithon did not a man of them harm. I would have things remain as they are.'

Stolid as seasoned oak, he spun on his heel to depart.

'You can't just let him go,' Lord Diegan bristled to his sovereign, while *Savrid*'s master excused himself and closed the door. Cat-touchy in his annoyance, the Lord Commander ploughed through the stacked charts and papers, located the wine flask, and scrounged for cloth to wipe two goblets clean. 'Ath knows, we can't spare the use of that ship.'

'No,' said Lysaer, his gaze like chipped flint as his closest confidante served him. 'But this is not Avenor. I have no rights of royal requisition here.'

Deceptively bland, absorbed in the thinking speculation he engaged to solve his knottiest problems of state, the prince spun the warm wine in his glass, the fingers of his left hand laced through the hair at his temple. Dying light from the casement picked glints in the rings entwined through blond locks. His eyes looked bruised and wounded tired, at odds with his reflexively proud bearing as he wrestled with harsh thoughts and conscience.

In this hour, the flicker of the candleflames lit no prince, but a man, punished by event and embittered by a cruel blow to pride.

The sight stopped his Lord Commander's tirade.

Honoured to humility, Diegan saw his prince had let down his lofty public majesty before him in trust as a friend. He felt his heart twist in response. Anguished by every thoughtless past moment, when he had wished the royal self-esteem to falter, he now felt diminished in shame.

In the mortifying sting of defeat at Werpoint, he came at last to know that the humanity had been there all along. Beneath the lordly ruler, the bright poise, the unshakeable, inspirational confidence, Lysaer had the same flaws and needs as any other. The sacrifice he made to become an example to his people reduced his Lord Commander to disgrace.

In a voice choked to gentleness, Diegan said to his liege, 'All too well, we both know, the Master of Shadow knows how to strike to manipulate.'

Lysaer said nothing, but only tossed off the wine to its dregs. 'The wiles of s'Ffalenn drove my father to mad acts of grief. Given my stance against him, I should be foolish to expect the bastard would not seek to try the same with me. My given gift of light offers strength, but no wisdom. I am no better man, no less prone to frailty than my sire. But to bring justice to the Shadow Master's victims, and for the protection of this land, I must find a way to stand strong. Restraint must be arranged to guide me to act more responsibly.'

Diegan refilled his prince's goblet and stood mute, the decanter clutched in his hands. He felt like the world's own tormentor to broach the dangerous loose end which remained. 'My prince, you have a deep heart, and a morality this s'Ffalenn sorcerer knows well how to twist into shackles. He has you torn through with pity, exactly as he wished, and I refuse to let you weaken in remorse. You are our strength and inspiration. If you are susceptible to the Shadow Master's subversive handling of events, what of the people on the streets? I am Etarran enough to lend warning. I dread greatly what *Savrid*'s captain might say to undermine the staunch fibre of society.'

'Let the man go.' Lysaer shook back bright hair and sighed. 'His fellow captains who lost ships will scarcely applaud his choice of loyalty.' Distanced by exhaustion and a wrenching thread of melancholy, Lysaer resumed in dogged force. 'Have you been to the infirmaries, Diegan, where seamen lie dying of burns? Or the taverns? At every street corner, there are stranded sailhands left destitute and begging for copper. Werpoint has been dealt a harsh lesson. I wouldn't care to be caught in the quayside taverns alone with opinions in sympathy with Arithon. That could easily get a man killed.'

So it might, Lord Diegan agreed in silent irony. His prince's deep pain could as well have been his own, for the error in judgement he had suffered. As Lord Commander of Avenor, with a war host at his disposal, he should have set up some support plan to protect the Prince of the West from this insidious attack on his honour. Too much responsibility lay on Lysaer's shoulders. For the future, Diegan resolved that his liege must never again be abandoned to bear the brunt of every happenstance alone.

When the wine was drained to the lees, and Lysaer finally asked for his valet, he gave his Lord Commander the last, most poignant observation. 'We shall weather this. Never undervalue your part, my Lord Diegan. At Etarra, you'll recall, it was you and your lady sister who reminded me of Arithon's wicked nature. Whether or not the Mistwraith had a part in any curse, whether or not my ungovernable temper was rooted in an aberrant geas, two facts still cannot be argued. I am the only spirit alive with the gifts to battle Arithon's shadows; and the destructive acts against Jaelot and Alestron remain proof positive of my half-brother's criminal nature. To go on and see him dead will serve justice and restore this land to final peace.'

After Thoughts

Far offshore, under starlight on the deeps of the Cildein, Arithon rouses aboard his sloop, *Talliarthe*, to find his swollen wrists wrapped up in poultices, and his berth watched over by his *caithdein*; the thought crosses his mind, with no small humiliation, that he will not again risk the s'Valerient line in the course of his feud against Lysaer. 'Jieret,' he whispers, 'by my royal command, you must marry and get an heir, and look to your clansmen's survival . . .'

Leagues to the south, in the shipyard at Merior by the Sea, two joiners dicing through a drunken turn of watch are interrupted by the windborne smell of smoke; in belated alarm, they stagger outside, to discover the one finished hull ablaze on her ways, and the ropewalk set alight and well burning . . .

Entangled in sleep in the Mayor of Werpoint's guest suite, Prince Lysaer cries out in the throes of a nightmare; while outside his chamber door-way, in a loyalty sprung from the heart, Lord Commander Diegan arises, Etarran enough to shoulder for political expedience what his prince is too merciful to condone – the assassination of the ship's captain sympa-thetic to Arithon, that word of Desh-thiere's curse not become common gossip in the streets . . .

Glossary

AL'DUIN – father of Halliron Masterbard.
    pronounced: al-dwin
    root meaning: *al* – over; *duinne* – hand

ALESTRON – city located in Midhalla, Melhalla. Ruled by the Duke Bransian, Teir's'Brydion, and his three brothers. This city did not fall to merchant townsmen in the Third Age uprising that threw down the high kings, but is still ruled by its clanblood heirs.
    pronounced: ah-less-tron
    root meaning: *alesstair* – stubborn; *an* – one

ALITHIEL – one of twelve Blades of Isaer, forged by centaur Ffereton s'Darian in the First Age from metal taken from a meteorite. Passed through Paravian possession, acquired the secondary name Dael-Farenn, or Kingmaker, since its owners tended to succeed the end of a royal line. Eventually was awarded to Kamridian s'Ffalenn for his valour in defence of the princess Taliennse, early Second Age. Currently in possession of Arithon.
    pronounced: ah-lith-ee-el
    root meaning: *alith* – star; *iel* – light/ray

ALLAND – principality located in south-eastern Shand. Ruled by the High Earl Teir's'Taleyn, *caithdein* of Shand by appointment. Current heir to the title is Erlien.
    pronounced: all-and
    root meaning: *a'lind* – pine glen

ALTHAIN TOWER – spire built at the edge of the Bittern Desert, beginning of the Second Age, to house records of Paravian histories. Third Age, became respository for the archives of all five royal houses of men after rebellion, overseen by Sethvir, Warden of Althain and Fellowship sorcerer.

pronounced: al, like 'all,' thain, to rhyme with 'main'

root meaning: *alt* – last; *thein* – tower, sanctuary

original Paravian pronunciation: alt-thein (thein as in 'the end')

AMROTH – kingdom on West Gate splinter world, Dascen Elur, ruled by s'Ilessid descendants of the prince exiled through the Worldsend Gate at the time of the rebellion, Third Age just after the Mistwraith's conquest.

pronounced: am-roth (rhymes with 'sloth')

root meaning: *am* – state of being; *roth* – brother 'brotherhood'

ANGLEFEN – swampland located in Deshir, Rathain. Town of same name at the river mouth with port to Stormwell Gulf. One of the six port towns that link sea trade-routes with Etarra.

pronounced: angle-fen

root meaning is not Paravian

ARAETHURA – grass plains in south-west Rathain; principality of the same name in that location. Largely inhabited by Riathan Paravians in the Second Age. Third Age, used as pastureland by widely-scattered nomadic shepherds.

pronounced: ar-eye-thoo-rah

root meaning: *araeth* – grass; *era*–place, land

ARAITHE – plain to the north of the trade city of Etarra, principality of Fallowmere, Rathain. First Age, among the sites used by the Paravians to renew the mysteries and channel fifth lane energies. The standing stones erected are linked to the power focus at Ithamon and Meth Isle keep.

pronounced: araithe, sounds like 'a wraith'

root meaning: *araithe* – to disperse, to send; refers to the properties of the standing stones with relationship to the fifth lane forces.

ARITHON – son of Avar, Prince of Rathain, 1,504th Teir's'Ffalenn after founder of the line, Torbrand in Third Age Year One. Also Master of Shadow, the Bane of Desh-thiere, and Halliron Masterbard's successor.

pronounced: ar-i-thon – almost rhymes with 'marathon'

root meaning: *arithon* – fate-forger; one who is visionary

ASANDIR – Fellowship sorcerer. Secondary name, Kingmaker, since his hand crowned every High King of Men to rule in the Age of Men (Third Age). After the Mistwraith's conquest, he acted as field agent for the Fellowship's doings across the continent. Also called Fiend-quencher, for his reputation for quelling iyats; Storm-breaker, and Change-bringer for past actions in late Second Age, when Men first arrived upon Athera.

pronounced: ah-san-deer

root meaning: *asan* – heart; *dir* – stone 'heartrock'

ATAINIA – northeastern principality of Tysan.

pronounced: ah-tay-nee-ah

root meaning: *itain* – the third; ia suffix for 'third domain' original Paravian, *itainia*

ATCHAZ – city located in Alland, Shand. Famed for its silk.
pronounced: at-chas
root meaning: *atchias* – silk

ATH CREATOR – prime vibration, force behind all life.
pronounced: ath to rhyme with 'math'
root meaning: *ath* – prime, first (as opposed to an, one)

ATHIR – Second Age ruin of a Paravian stronghold, located in Ithilt, Rathain. Site of a seventh lane power focus.
pronounced: ath-ear
root meaning: *ath* – prime; *i'er* – the line/edge

ATHERA – name for the continent which holds the Five High Kingdoms; one of two major landmasses on the planet.
pronounced: ath-air-ah
root meaning: *ath* – prime force; *era*–place 'Ath's world'

ATHLIEN PARAVIANS – sunchildren. Small race of semi-mortals, pixie-like, but possessed of great wisdom/keepers of the grand mystery.
pronounced: ath-lee-en
root meaning: *ath* – prime force; lien – to love/Ath-beloved

ATHLIERIA – equivalent of heaven/actually a dimension removed from physical life, inhabited by spirit after death.
pronounced: ath-lee-air-ee-ah
root meaning: *ath* – prime force; *li'era* – exalted place, or land in harmony; *li* – exalted in harmony

ATWOOD – forest located in East Halla, Melhalla.
pronounced: at-wood
root meaning: *ath* – prime vibration/Ath's wood

AVAR s'FFALENN – Pirate King of Karthan, isle on splinter world Dascen Elur, through West Gate. Father of Arithon; also Teir's'Ffalenn 1,503rd in descent from Torbrand who founded the s'Ffalenn royal line in Third Age Year One.
pronounced: ah-var, to rhyme with 'far'
root meaning: *avar* – past thought/memory

AVENOR – Second Age ruin of a Paravian stronghold. Traditional seat of the s'Ilessid High Kings. Restored to habitation in Third Age Year 5644. Located in Korias, Tysan.
pronounced: ah-ven-or
root meaning: *avie* – stag; *norh* – grove

BECKBURN – market in the city of Jaelot, on the coast of Eltair Bay at the southern border of Rathain.
pronounced: beck-burn
meaning not from the Paravian

BLACK DRAKE – a brig often hired to run contraband, captained by a woman named Dhirken.

BLACK ROSE PROPHECY – made by Dakar the Mad Prophet in Third Age Year 5637 at Althain Tower. Forecasts Davien the Betrayer's repentance, and the reunity of the Fellowship of Seven as tied to Arithon s'Ffalenn's voluntary resumption of Rathain's crown rule.

BRANSIAN s'BRYDION – Teir's'Brydion, ruling Duke of Alestron.
    pronounced: bran-see-an
    root meaning: *brand-* temper; *s'i'an* – suffix denoting 'of the one'/the one with temper

BWIN EVOC s'LORNMEIN – founder of the line that became High Kings of Havish since Third Age Year One. The attribute he passed on by means of the Fellowship's geas was temperance.
    pronounced: bwin, to rhyme with 'twin', ee-vahk, as in 'evocative,' lorn, as in English equivalent, mein rhymes with 'main'
    root meaning: *bwin* – firm; *evoc* – choice

CAILCALLOW – herb that grows in Athera's marshes, used to ease fevers.
    pronounced: rhymes with 'kale-tallow'
    root meaning: *cail* – leaf; *calliew* – balm

CAITH-AL-CAEN – vale where Riathan Paravians (unicorns) celebrated equinox and solstice to renew the *athael*, or life-destiny of the world. Also the place where the Ilitharis Paravians first Named the winter stars – or encompassed their vibrational essence into language. Corrupted by the end of the Third Age to Castlecain.
    pronounced: cay-ith-al-cay-en, musical lilt, emphasis on second and last syllables; rising note on first two, falling note on last two.
    root meaning: *caith* – shadow; *al* – over; *caen* – vale/'vale of shadow'

CAITHDEIN – Paravian name for a high king's first counsellor; also, the one who would stand as regent, or steward, in the absence of the crowned ruler.
    pronounced: kay-ith-day-in
    root meaning: *caith* – shadow; *d'ein* – behind the chair 'shadow behind the throne'

CAITHWOOD – forest located in Taerlin, south-east principality of Tysan.
    pronounced: kay-ith-wood
    root meaning: *caith* – shadow – 'shadowed wood'

CASTLE POINT – port city at the western terminus of the Great West Road, located in the principality of Atainia, Tysan.

CAMRIS – north-central principality of Tysan. Original ruling seat was city of Erdane.

pronounced: kam-ris, the 'i' as in 'chris'

root meaning: *caim* – cross; *ris* – way 'crossroad'

CAOLLE – war captain of the clans of Deshir, Rathain. First raised, and then served under Lord Steiven, Earl of the North and caithdein of Rathain. Currently in Jieret Red-beard's service.

pronounced: kay-all-e, with the 'e' nearly subliminal

root meaning: *caille* – stubborn

CILADIS THE LOST – Fellowship sorcerer who left the continent in Third Age 3462 in search of the Paravian races after their disappearance after the rebellion.

pronounced: kill-ah-dis

root meaning: *cael* – leaf; *adeis* – whisper, compound; cael'adeis
colloquialism for 'gentleness that abides'

CILDEIN OCEAN – body of water lying off Athera's east coastline.

pronounced: kill-dine

root meaning: *cailde* – salty; *an* – one

CILDORN – city famed for carpets and weaving, located in Deshir Rathain. Originally a Paravian holdfast, situated on a node of the third lane.

pronounced: kill-dorn

root meaning: *cieal* – thread; *dorn* – net 'tapestry'

CLAITHEN – an adept of of Ath's Brotherhood in the hostel south of Merior.

pronounced: clay-then

root meaning: *claithen* – garden; earth/soil

CORITH – island west of Havish coast, in Westland Sea. First site to see sunlight upon Desh-thiere's defeat.

pronounced: kor-ith

root meaning: *cori* – ships, vessels; *itha* – five for the five harbours
which the old city overlooked

CRESCENT ISLE – large island located east of Minderl Bay in Ithilt, Rathain.

DAEL-FARENN – Kingmaker, name for sword Alithiel; also, one of many Paravian names for the Fellowship sorcerer, Asandir.

pronounced: day-el-far-an

root meaning: *dael* – king; *feron* – maker

DAELION FATEMASTER – 'entity' formed by set of mortal beliefs, which determine the fate of the spirit after death. If Ath is the prime vibration, or life-force, Daelion is what governs the manifestation of free will.

pronounced: day-el-ee-on

root meaning: *dael* – king, or lord; *i'on* – of fate

DAELION's WHEEL – cycle of life and the crossing point which is the transition into death.

    pronounced: day-el-ee-on

    root meaning: *dael* – king or lord; *i'on* – of fate

DAENFAL – city located on the northern lake shore that bounds the southern edge of Daon Ramon Barrens in Rathain.

    pronounced: dye-en-fall

    root meaning: *daen* – clay; *fal* – red

DAGRIEN COURT – market in the city of Jaelot, on the coast at the southern border of Rathain.

    pronounced: dag-ree-en

    root meaning: *dagrien* – variety

DAKAR THE MAD PROPHET – apprentice to Fellowship sorcerer, Asandir, during the Third Age following the Conquest of the Mistwraith. Given to spurious prophecies, it was Dakar who forecast the fall of the Kings of Havish in time for the Fellowship to save the heir. He made the Prophecy of West Gate which forecast the Mistwraith's bane, and also, the Black Rose Prophecy, which called for reunification of the Fellowship. At this time, assigned to defense of Arithon, Prince of Rathain.

    pronounced: dah-kar

    root meaning: *dakiar* – clumsy

DANIA – wife of Rathain's Regent, Steiven s'Valerient. Died by the hand of Pesquil's headhunters in the Battle of Strakewood. Jieret Redbeard's mother.

    pronounced: dan-ee-ah

    root meaning: *deinia* – sparrow

DAON RAMON BARRENS – central principality of Rathain. Site where Riathan Paravians (unicorns) bred and raised their young. Barrens was not appended to the name until the years following the Mistwraith's conquest, when the River Severnir was diverted at the source by a task force under Etarran jurisdiction.

    pronounced: day-on-rah-mon

    root meaning: *daon* – gold; *ramon* – hills/downs

DASCEN ELUR – splinter world off West Gate; primarily ocean with isolated archipelagos. Includes kingdoms of Rauven, Amroth, and Karthan. Where three exiled high kings' heirs took refuge in the years following the great uprising. Birthplace of Lysaer and Arithon.

    pronounced: das-en el-ur

    root meaning: *dascen* – ocean; *e'lier* – small land

DAVIEN THE BETRAYER – Fellowship sorcerer responsible for provoking the great uprising that resulted in the fall of the high kings after Desh-thiere's conquest. Rendered discorporate by the Fellowship's judgement in Third Age 5129. Exiled since, by personal choice. Davien's works included the Five Centuries Fountain near Mearth on the splinter world of the Red Desert through West Gate; the shaft at Rockfell Pit, used by the sorcerers to imprison harmful entities; the Stair on Rockfell Peak; and also, Kewar Tunnel in the Mathorn Mountains.

pronounced: dah-vee-en

root meaning: *dahvi* – fool, mistake; *an* – one 'mistaken one'

DEARTHA – wife of Halliron, Masterbard of Athera; resident in Innish.

pronounced: dee-ar-the

root meaning: *deorethan* – sour tempered

DESHANS – barbarian clans who inhabit Strakewood Forest, principality of Deshir, Rathian.

pronounced: desh-ee-ans

root meaning: *deshir* – misty

DESHIR – northwestern principality of Rathain.

pronounced: desh-eer

root meaning: *deshir* – misty

DESH-THIERE – Mistwraith that invaded Athera from the splinter worlds through South Gate in Third Age Year 4993. Access cut off by Fellowship sorcerer, Traithe. Battled and contained in West Shand for twenty-five years, until the rebellion splintered the peace, and the high kings were forced to withdraw from the defence lines to attend their disrupted kingdoms.

pronounced: desh-thee-air-e (last 'e' mostly subliminal)

root meaning: *desh* – mist; *thiere* – ghost or wraith

DHARKARON AVENGER – called Ath's Avenging Angel in legend. Drives a chariot drawn by five horses to convey the guilty to Sithaer. Dharkaron as defined by the adepts of Ath's Brotherhood is that dark thread mortal men weave with Ath, the prime vibration, that creates self-punishment, or the root of guilt.

pronounced: dark-air-on

root meaning: *dhar* – evil; *khiaron* – one who stands in judgement

DHIRKEN – lady captain of the contraband runner, *Black Drake*. Reputed to have taken over the brig's command by right of arms following her father's death at sea.

pronounced: dur-kin

root meaning: *dierk* – tough; *an* – one

DIEGAN – once Lord Commander of Etarra's garrison; given over by his mayor to serve as Lysaer s'Ilessid's Lord Commander at Avenor. Titular commander of the war host sent against the Deshans to defeat the Master of Shadow at Tal Quorin; high commander of the war host mustered at Werpoint. Also brother of Lady Talith.

pronounced: dee-gan

root meaning: *diegan* – trinket a dandy might wear/ornament

DURN – city located in Orvandir, Shand.

pronounced: dern

root meaning: *diern* – plain/flat

DYSHENT – city on the coast of Instrell Bay in Tysan; renowned for timber.
>   pronounced: die-shent
>   root meaning: *dyshient* – cedar

EARLE – Second Age ruin, once a Paravian stronghold, located on the southern tip of the peninsula in West Shand. Site of the defences that contained the Mistwraith's invasion prior to the uprising incited by Davien the Betrayer.
>   pronounced: earl
>   root meaning: *erli* – long light

EAST HALLA – principality located in the Kingdom of Melhalla
>   pronounced: hall-ah
>   root meaning: *hal'lia* – white light

EAST WARD – city in Fallowmere, Rathain, renowned as a port that served the trade-route to Etarra from the Cildein Ocean.
>   pronounced: ward
>   no Paravian root meaning as this city was man's creation

ELAIRA – initiate enchantress of the Koriathain. Originally a street child, taken on in Morvain for Koriani rearing.
>   pronounced: ee-layer-ah
>   root meaning: *e* – prefix, diminutive for small; *laere* – grace

ELDIR s'LORNMEIN – King of Havish and last surviving scion of s'Lornmein royal line. Raised as a wool-dyer until the Fellowship sorcerers crowned him at Ostermere in Third Age Year 5643 following the defeat of the Mistwraith.
>   pronounced: el-deer
>   root meaning: *eldir* – to ponder, to consider, to weigh

ELIE – name of a newlywed woman in Merior. Short for Elidie, which is a common southcoast girl's name.
>   pronounced: ellie (longform, el-ed-ee)
>   root meaning: *eledie* – night-singing bird

ELKFOREST – wood located in Ghent, Havish; home of Machiel, steward and *caithdein* of the realm.

ELSHIAN – Athlien Paravian bard and instrument maker. Crafted the lyranthe that is held in trust by Athera's Masterbard.
>   pronounced: el-shee-an
>   root meaning: *e'alshian* – small wonder, or miracle

ELSSINE – city located on the coast of Alland, Shand, famed for stone quarries used for ship's ballast.
>   pronounced: el-seen
>   root meaning: *elssien* – small pit

ELTAIR BAY – large bay off Cildein Ocean and east coast of Rathain; where River Severnir was diverted following the Mistwraith's conquest.

pronounced: el-tay-er

root meaning: *al'tieri* – of steel/a shortening of original Paravian name; *dascen al'tieri* – which meant 'ocean of steel' which referred to the colour of the waves.

ERDANE – old Paravian city, later taken over by Men. Seat of old princes of Camris until Desh-thiere's conquest and rebellion.

pronounced: er-day-na with the last syllable almost subliminal

root meaning: *er'deinia* – long walls

ERLIEN s'TALEYN – High Earl of Alland; *caithdein* of Shand, chieftain of the forest clansmen of Selkwood.

pronounced: er-lee-an stall-ay-en

root meaning: *aierlyan* – bear; *tal* – branch; *an* – one/first 'of first one branch'

ETARRA – trade city built across the Mathorn Pass by townsfolk after the revolt that cast down Ithamon and the High Kings of Rathain. Nest of corruption and intrigue, and policy maker for the North.

pronounced: ee-tar-ah

root meaning: *e* – prefix for small; *taria* – knots

FAERY-TOES – a brown gelding Dakar won dicing with mercenaries.

FALGAIRE – coastal city on Instrell Bay, located in Araethura, Rathain, famed for its crystal and glassworks.

pronounced: fall-gair, to rhyme with 'air'

root meaning: *fal'mier* – to sparkle or glitter

FALLOWMERE – north-eastern principality of Rathain.

pronounced: fal-oh-meer

root meaning: *fal'ei'miere* – literally, tree self-reflection, colloquialism for 'place of perfect trees'

FARL ROCKS – standing stones located in Daon Ramon Barrens, Rathain; site of a rendezvous between Jieret Red-beard and Caolle. These markers once channelled the earth forces for the Paravian dances at solstice and equinox.

pronounced: far(l)

root meaning: *ffael* – dark

FARSEE – coastal harbour on the Bay of Eltair, located in East Halla, Melhalla.

pronounced: far-see

root meaning: *faersi* – sheltered/muffled

FATE'S WHEEL – see Daelion's Wheel.

FELLOWSHIP OF SEVEN – sorcerers sworn to uphold the Law of the Major Balance, and to foster enlightened thought in Athera. Originators of the compact with the Paravian races that allowed men to settle in Athera.

FEYLIND – twin daughter of Jinesse; sister of Fiark; inhabitant of Merior.

    pronounced: fay-lind

    root meaning: *faelind'an* – outspoken one/noisy one

FIARK – twin son of Jinesse; brother of Feylind; inhabitant of Merior.

    pronounced: fee-ark

    root meaning: *fyerk* – to throw or toss

FIRST AGE – marked by the arrival of the Paravian Races as Ath's gift to heal the marring of creation by the great drakes.

FORTHMARK – city in Vastmark, Shand. Once the site of a hostel of Ath's Brotherhood. By Third Age Year 5320, the site was abandoned and taken over by the Koriani Order as a healer's hospice.

    meaning not from the Paravian

GARTH's POND – small brackish pond in Merior by the Sea, on the Scimlade peninsula off Alland, Shand.

    pronounced: garth, to rhyme with 'hearth'

    meaning not from the Paravian

GHARMAG – one of the senior captains in Etarra's garrison

    pronounced: gar-mag

    meaning not from the Paravian

GHENT – mountainous principality in Kingdom of Havish; where Prince Eldir was raised in hiding.

    pronounced: gent, hard 'g'

    root meaning: *ghent* – harsh

GNUDSOG – Etarra's field-captain of the garrison under Lord Commander Diegan; acting first officer in the battle of Strakewood Forest; died in the flooding at the River Tal Quorin.

    pronounced: nud-sug, to rhyme with 'wood log'

    root meaning: *gianud* – tough; *sog* – ugly

GREAT WAYSTONE – amethyst crystal, spherical in shape, once the grand power focus of the Koriani Order; reputed to be lost since the uprising.

GREAT WEST ROAD – trade-route which crosses Tysan from Karfael on the west coast, to Castle Point on Instrell Bay.

HALDUIN s'ILESSID – founder of the line that became High Kings of Tysan since Third Age Year One. The attribute he passed on, by means of the Fellowship's geas, was justice.

    pronounced: hal-dwin

    root meaning: *hal* – white; *duinne* – hand

HALLIRON MASTERBARD – native of Innish, Shand. Masterbard of Athera during the Third Age; inherited the accolade from his teacher

Murchiel in the year 5597. Son of Al'Duin. Husband of Deartha. Arithon's master and mentor.

    pronounced: hal-eer-on

    root meaning: *hal* – white; *lyron* – singer

HALTHA – Senior enchantress of the Koriani Order; assigned to keep watch on Avenor at the time of the city's restoration.

    pronounced: hal-the

    root meaning: *halthien* – white aged

HALWYTHWOOD – forest located in Araethura, Rathain.

    pronounced: hall-with-wood

    root meaning: *hal* – white; *wythe* – vista

HANSHIRE – port city on Westland Sea, coast of Korias, Tysan; reining mayor Lord Mayor Garde; opposed to royal rule at the time of Avenor's restoration.

    pronounced: han-sheer

    root meaning: *hansh* – sand; *era* – place

HARRADENE – Lord Commander of Etarra's army at the time of the muster at Werpoint.

    pronounced: har-a-deen

    root meaning: *harradien* – large mule

HAVISH – one of the Five High Kingdoms of Athera, as defined by the charters of the Fellowship of Seven. Ruled by Eldir s'Lornmein. Sigil: gold hawk on red field.

    pronounced: hav-ish

    root meaning: *havieshe* – hawk

HAVISTOCK – south-east principality of Kingdom of Havish.

    pronounced: hav-i-stock

    root meaning: *haviesha* – hawk; *tiok* – roost

HAVRITA – fashionable dressmaker in Jaelot.

    pronounced: have-reet-ah

    root meaning: *havierta* – tailor

HIGHSCARP – city on the coast of the Bay of Eltair, located in Daon Ramon, Rathain.

ILITHARIS PARAVIANS – centaurs, one of three semimortal old races; disappeared at the time of the Mistwraith's conquest. They were the guardians of the earth's mysteries.

    pronounced: i-li-thar-is

    root meaning: *i'lith'eans* – the keeper/preserver of mystery

IMARN ADAER – enclave of Paravian gem-cutters in the city of Mearth, who dispersed in the times of the Curse which destroyed the inhabitants. The secrets of their trade were lost with them. Surviving works include the crown jewels of the Five High Kingdoms of Athera, cut as focus stones which attune to the heir of the royal lines.

pronounced: i-marn-a-day-er

root meaning: *imarn* – crystal; *e'daer* – to cut smaller

INNISH – city located on the south-coast of Shand at the delta of the River Ippash. Birthplace of Halliron Masterbard. Formerly known as 'the Jewel of Shand' this was the site of the high king's winter court, prior to the time of the uprising.

pronounced: in-ish

root meaning: *inniesh* – a jewel with a pastel tint

INSTRELL BAY – body of water off the Gulf of Stormwell, that separates principality of Atainia, Tysan, from Deshir, Rathain.

pronounced: in-strell

root meaning: *arin'streal* – strong wind

ISAER – city located at the crossroads of the Great West Road in Atainia, Tysan. Also a power focus, built during the First Age, in Atainia, Tysan, to source the defence-works at the Paravian keep of the same name.

pronounced: i-say-er

root meaning: *i'saer* – the circle

ITHAMON – Second Age Paravian stronghold, and a Third Age ruin; built on a fifth lane power-node in Daon Ramon Barrens, Rathain, and inhabited until the year of the uprising. Site of the Compass Point Towers, or Sun Towers. Became the seat of the High Kings of Rathain during the Third Age and in year 5638 was the site where Princes Lysaer s'Ilessid and Arithon s'Ffalenn battled the Mistwraith to confinement.

pronounced: ith-a-mon

root meaning: *itha* – five; *mon* – needle, spire

ITHILT – peninsula bordering Minderl Bay, located in kingdom of Rathain.

pronounced: ith-ilt, to rhyme with 'with halt'

root meaning: *ith* – five; *ealt* – a narrows

IVEL – blind splicer hired by Arithon in his shipyard at Merior.

pronounced: ee-vell

root meaning: *iavel* – scathing

IYAT – energy sprite native to Athera, not visible to the eye, manifests in a poltergeist fashion by taking temporary possession of objects. Feeds upon natural energy sources: fire, breaking waves, lightning.

pronounced: ee-at

root meaning: *iyat* – to break

JAELOT – city located on the coast of Eltair Bay at the southern border of the Kingdom of Rathain. Once a Second Age power site, with a focus circle. Now a merchant city with a reputation for extreme snobbery and bad taste.

pronounced: jay-lot

root meaning: *jielot* – affectation

JIERET s'VALERIENT – Earl of the North, clan chief of Deshir; *caithdein* of Rathain, sworn liegeman of Prince Arithon s'Ffalenn. Also son and heir of Lord Steiven. Bloodpacted to Arithon by sorcerer's oath prior to battle of Strakewood Forest. Came to be known by headhunters as Jieret Red-beard.

    pronounced: jeer-et

    root meaning: *jieret* – thorn

JINESSE – widow of a fisherman, mother of the twins Fiark and Feylind, and an inhabitant of Merior by the Sea.

    pronounced: gin-ess

    root meaning: *jienesse* – to be washed out or pale; a wisp

KALESH – one of the towns at the head of the inlet to Alestron's harbour, located in East Halla, Melhalla, and traditionally the enemy of the reigning s'Brydion duke.

    pronounced: cal-esh

    root meaning: *caille'esh* – stubborn hold

KARFAEL – trader town on the coast of the Westland Sea, in Tysan. Built by townsmen as a trade port after the fall of the High Kings of Tysan. Prior to Desh-thiere's conquest, the site was kept clear of buildings to allow the second lane forces to flow untrammelled across the focus site at Avenor.

    pronounced: kar-fay-el

    root meaning: *kar'i'ffael* – literal translation 'twist the dark'/col-
                 loquialism for 'intrigue'

KARMAK – plain located in the northern portion of the principality of Camris, Tysan. Site of numerous First Age battles where Paravian forces opposed Khadrim packs that bred in volcanic sites in the northern Tornir Peaks.

    pronounced: kar-mack

    root meaning: *karmak* – wolf

KARTHAN – kingdom in splinter world Dascen Elur, through West Gate, ruled by the pirate kings, s'Ffalenn descendants of the prince sent into exile at the time of the Mistwraith's conquest.

    pronounced: karth-an

    root meaning: *kar eth'an* – one who raids/pirate

KARTH-EELS – creatures descended from stock aberrated by the *methurien*, or hate-wraiths, of Mirthlvain Swamp. Amphibious, fanged, venomed spines, webbed feet.

    pronounced: car-th eels

    root meaning: *kar'eth* – to raid

KELDMAR s'BRYDION – younger brother of Duke Bransian of Alestron; older brother of Parrien and Mearn.

    pronounced: keld-mar

root meaning: *kiel'd'maeran* – one without pity

KHADRIM – drake-spawned creatures, flying, fire-breathing reptiles that were the scourge of the Second Age. By the Third Age, they had been driven back and confined in the Sorcerers' Preserve in the volcanic peaks in north Tysan.

> pronounced: kaa-drim
>
> root meaning: *khadrim* – dragon

KHARADMON – Sorcerer of the Fellowship of Seven; discorporate since rise of Khadrim and Seardluin levelled Paravian city at Ithamon in Second Age 3651. It was by Kharadmon's intervention that the survivors of the attack were sent to safety by means of transfer from the fifth lane power focus. Currently sent to the worlds cut off beyond South Gate to explore the Mistwraith's origin.

> pronounced: kah-rad-mun
>
> root meaning: *kar'riad en mon* – phrase translates to mean 'twisted thread on the needle' or colloquialism for 'a knot in the works'

KIELING TOWER – one of the four Compass Points or Sun Towers standing at Ithamon, Daon Ramon Barrens, Rathain. The warding virtue that binds its stones is Compassion.

> pronounced: kee-el-ing
>
> root meaning: *kiel'ien* – root for pity, with suffix added translates to 'compassion'

KITTIWAKE TAVERN – sailors' dive located in the city of Ship's Port, Melhalla.

KORIANI – possessive form of the word 'Koriathain;' see entry.

> pronounced: kor-ee-ah-nee

KORIAS – south-western principality of Tysan.

> pronounced: kor-ee-as
>
> root meaning: *cor* – ship, vessel; *i'esh* – nest, haven

KORIATHAIN – order of enchantresses ruled by a circle of Seniors, under the power of one Prime Enchantress. They draw their talent from the orphaned children they raise, or from daughters dedicated to service by their parents. Initiation rite involves a vow of consent that ties the spirit to a power crystal keyed to the Prime's control.

> pronounced: kor-ee-ah-thain (thain rhymes with 'main')
>
> root meaning: *koriath* – order; *ain* – belonging to

LANSHIRE – north-western principality of Havish. Name taken from wastes at Scarpdale, site of First Age battles with Seardluin that seared the soil to a slag waste.

> pronounced: lahn-sheer-e (last 'e' is nearly subliminal)
>
> root meaning: *lan'hansh'era* – place of hot sands

LAW OF THE MAJOR BALANCE – founding order of the powers of

the Fellowship of Seven, as written by the Paravians. The primary tenet is that no force of nature should be used without consent, or against the will of another living being.

LEINTHAL ANITHAEL – great Paravian navigator who was first to circumnavigate Athera
    pronounced: lee-in-thall an-ith-ee-el
    root meaning: *lienthal* – direction; *anithael* – to seek

LIRENDA – First Senior Enchantress to the Prime, Koriani order; Morriel's intended successor.
    pronounced: leer-end-ah
    root meaning: *lyron* – singer; *di-ia* – a dissonance (the hyphen
        denotes a glottal stop)

LITHMERE – principality located in the Kingdom of Havish.
    pronounced: lith-mere, to rhyme with 'with here'
    root meaning: *lithmiere* – compound word with the sense 'to pre-
        serve intact or to keep whole', as in to maintain a
        state of perfection

LUHAINE – Sorcerer of the Fellowship of Seven – discorporate since the fall of Telmandir. Luhaine's body was pulled down by the mob while he was in ward trance, covering the escape of the royal heir to Havish.
    pronounced: loo-hay-ne
    root meaning: *luirhainon* – defender

LYRANTHE – instrument played by the bards of Athera. Strung with fourteen strings, tuned to seven tones (doubled). Two courses are 'drone strings' set to octaves. Five are melody strings, the lower three courses being octaves, the upper two, in unison.
    pronounced: leer-anth-e (last 'e' being nearly subliminal)
    root meaning: *lyr* – song, *anthe* – box

LYSAER s'ILESSID – prince of Tysan, 1497th in succession after Halduin, founder of the line in Third Age Year One. Gifted at birth with control of Light, and Bane of Desh-Thiere.
    pronounced: lie-say-er
    root meaning: *lia* – blond, yellow or light, *saer* – circle

MACHIEL – steward and *caithdein* of the realm of Havish. In service under King Eldir.
    pronounced: mak-ee-el
    root meaning: *mierkiel* – post, pillar

MAENELLE s'GANNLEY – steward and *caithdein* of Tysan.
    pronounced: may-nahl-e (last 'e' is near subliminal)
    root meaing: *maeni* – to fall, disrupt; *alli* – to save or preserve/col-
        loquial translation: 'to patch together'

MAENOL – heir, after Maenalle s'Gannley, Steward and *caithdein* of Tysan.

pronounced: may-nall

root meaning: *maeni'alli* – 'to patch together'

MAIEN – nickname for Maenalle's grandson, Maenol.

pronounced: my-en

root meaning: *maien* – mouse

MAGYRE – scholar who discovered the secret of black powder. In accordance with the Fellowship sorcerer's compact, he was forced to give up his studies, but a copy of his papers survived.

pronounced: mag-wire

root meaning: *magiare* – a chaotic force

MAINMERE – town at the head of the Valenford River, located in the principality of Taerlin, Tysan. Built by townsmen on a site originally kept clear to free the second land focus in the ruins further south.

pronounced: main-meer-e ('e' is subliminal)

root meaning: *maeni* – to fall, interrupt; *miere* – reflection, colloquial translation: 'disrupt continuity'

MARL – Earl of Fallowmere and clan chieftain at the time of the battle of Strakewood Forest.

pronounced: marl

root meaing: *marle* – quartz rock

MATHORN MOUNTAINS – range that bisects the Kingdom of Rathain east to west.

pronounced: math-orn

root meaning: *mathien* – massive

MATHORN ROAD – way passing to the south of the Mathorn Mountains, leading to the trade city of Etarra from the west.

pronounced: math-orn

root meaning: *mathien* – massive

MEARN s'BRYDION – youngest brother of Duke Bransian of Alestron.

pronounced: may-arn

root meaning: *mierne* – to flit

MEARTH – city through the West Gate in the Red Desert. Inhabitants all fell victim to the Shadows of Mearth, which were created by the Fellowship sorcerer Davien to protect the Five Centuries Fountain. The Shadows are a light-fueled geas that bind the mind to memory of an individual's most painful experience.

pronounced: me-arth

root meaning: *mearth* – empty

MEDLIR – name carried by Arithon s'Ffalenn while he travelled incognito as Halliron's apprentice.

pronounced: med-leer

root meaning: *midlyr* – phrase of melody

MELHALLA – High Kingdom of Athera once ruled by the line of s'Ellestrion. The last prince died in the crossing of the Red Desert.

pronounced: mel-hall-ah

root meaning: *maelhallia* – grand meadows/plain – also word for an open space of any sort.

MELOR RIVER – located in the principality of Korias, Tysan. Its mouth forms the harbour for the port town of West End.

pronounced: mel-or

root meaning: *maeliur* – fish

MERIOR BY THE SEA – small seaside fishing village on the Scimlade peninsula in Alland, Shand. Site of Arithon's shipyard.

pronounced: mare-ee-or

root meaning: *merioren* – cottages

METH ISLE KEEP – old Paravian fortress located on the isle in Methlas Lake in southern Melhalla. Kept by Verrain, Guardian of Mirthlvain. Contains a fifth lane power focus and dungeons where *methuri*, or hate wraiths, were held temporarily captive before transfer to Rockfell Pit.

pronounced: meth isle

root meaning: *meth* – hate

METHLAS LAKE – large body of fresh water located in the principality of Radmoor, Melhalla.

pronounced: meth-las

root meaning: *meth'ilass'an* – the drowned, or sunken ones.

METH-SNAKES – crossbred genetic mutations left over from a First Age drake-spawned creature called a *methuri* (hate-wraith). Related to iyats, these creatures possessed live hosts, which they infested and induced to produce mutated offspring to create weakened lines of stock to widen their choice of potential host animals.

pronounced: meth to rhyme with 'death'

root meaning: *meth* – hate

METHURI – drake spawned, and iyat-related parasite that infested live host animals. By the Third Age, they are extinct, but their mutated host stock continues to breed in Mirthlvain Swamp.

pronounced: meth-yoor-ee

root meaning: *meth* – hate; *thiere* – wraith, or spirit

MINDERL BAY – body of water behind Crescent Isle off the east coast of Rathain.

pronounced: mind-earl

root meaning: *minderl* – anvil

MIRALT – port city in northern Camris, Tysan.

pronounced: meer-alt

root meaning: *m'ier* – shore; *alt* – last

MIRTHLVAIN SWAMP – boglands filled with dangerous crossbreeds, located south of the Tiriac Mountains in principality of Midhalla, Melhalla. Never left unwatched. Since conquest of the Mistwraith, the appointed guardian was the spellbinder, Verrain.

pronounced: mirth-el-vain

root meaning: *myrthl* – noxious; *vain* – bog/mud

MORFETT – Lord Governor Supreme of Etarra at the time the Fellowship sought to restore Rathain's monarchy following the captivity of the Mistwraith, and during the muster for the war host against Arithon.
pronounced: more-fet
no root meaning from the Paravian

MORRIEL – Prime Enchantress of the Koriathain since the Third Age Year 4212.
pronounced: more-real
root meaning: *moar* – greed; *riel* – silver

MORVAIN – city located in the principality of Araethura, Rathain, on the coast of Instrell Bay. Elaira's birthplace.
pronounced: more-vain
root meaning: *morvain* – swindlers' market

NARMS – city on the coast of Instrell Bay, built as a craft centre by men in the early Third Age. Best known for dyeworks.
pronounced: narms, to rhyme with 'charms'
root meaning: *narms* – colour

ORLAN – pass through the Thaldein Mountains, also location of the Camris clans' west outpost, in Camris, Tysan. Known for barbarian raids.
pronounced: or-lan
root meaning: *irlan* – ledge

ORVANDIR – principality located in north-eastern Shand.
pronounced: or-van-deer
root meaning: *orvein* – crumbled; *dir* – stone

OSTERMERE – harbour and trade city, once smugglers' haven, located in Carythwyr, Havish; current seat of Eldir, King of Havish.
pronounced: os-tur-mere
root meaning: *ostier* – brick; *miere* – reflection

PARAVIAN – name for the three old races that inhabited Athera before Men. Including the centaurs, the sunchildren, and the unicorns, these races never die unless mishap befalls them; they are the world's channel, or direct connection to Ath Creator.
pronounced: par-ai-vee-ans
root meaning: *para* – great; *i'on* – fate or 'great mystery'

PARRIEN s'BRYDION – second youngest brother of Duke Bransian of Alestron; older brother of Mearn, younger brother of Keldmar.
pronounced: par-ee-en
root meaning: *para* – great; *ient* – dart

PASYVIER – meadows in Korias, Tysan, where clanblood drifters raise horses.
    pronounced: pass-ee-vee-er
    root meaning: *pas'e'vier* – hidden little vale
PERLORN – city in Fallowmere, Rathain on the trade road midway between Etarra and Werpoint.
    pronounced: pur-lorn
    root meaning: *perlorn* – midpoint
PESQUIL – Mayor of the Northern League of Headhunters, at the time of the battle of Strakewood Forest. His strategies cause the Deshir clans the most punishing losses.
    pronounced: pes-quil, like 'pest quill'
    root meaning not from the Paravian
PRANDEY – Shandian term for gelded pleasure boy.
    pronounced: pran-dee
    meaning not from the Paravian

QUAID – trade city in Carithwyr, Tysan; inland along the trade road from Losmar to Redburn. Famous for fired clay and brick.
    pronounced: quaid, to rhyme with 'staid'
    root meaning: *cruaid* – a specific form of clay used for brickmaking

RADMOORE DOWNS – meadowlands in Midhalla, Melhalla.
    pronounced: rad-more
    root meaning: *riad* – thread; *mour* – carpet, rug
RATHAIN – High Kingdom of Athera ruled by descendants of Torbrand s'Ffalenn since Third Age Year One. Sigil: black and silver leopard on green field.
    pronounced: rath-ayn
    root meaning: *roth* – brother; *thein* – tower, sanctuary
RAUVEN TOWER – home of the s'Ahelas mages who brought up Arithon s'Ffalenn and trained him to the ways of power. Located on the splinter world, Dascen Elur, through West Gate.
    pronounced: raw-ven
    root meaning: *rauven* – invocation
RENWORT – plant native to Athera. A poisonous mash can be brewed from the berries.
    pronounced: ren-wart
    root meaning: *renwarin* – poison
RIATHAN PARAVIANS – unicorns, the purest and most direct connection to Ath Creator; the prime vibration channels directly through the horn.
    pronounced: ree-ah-than

root meaning: *ria* – to touch; *ath* – prime life-force; *ri'athon* – one who touches divinity

ROCKFELL PIT – deep shaft cut into Rockfell Peak, used to imprison harmful entities throughout all three ages. Located in the principality of West Halla, Melhalla; became the warded prison for Desh-thiere.

    pronounced: rock-fell

    root meaning not from the Paravian

ROCKFELL VALE – valley below Rockfell Peak, located in principality of West Halla, Melhalla.

    pronounced: rockfell vale

    root meaning not from the Paravian

s'AHELAS – family name for the royal line appointed by the Fellowship sorcerers in Third Age Year One to rule the High Kingdom of Shand. Gifted geas: farsight.

    pronounced: s'ah-hell-as

    root meaning: *ahelas* – mage-gifted

SANPASHIR – desert waste on the southcoast of Shand.

    pronounced: sahn-pash-eer

    root meaning: *san* – black or dark; *pash'era* – place of grit or gravel

SAVRID – merchant brig chartered to transport armed men from Minderl Bay to Merior.

    pronounced: sahv-rid

    root meaning: *savrid* – thrifty

s'BRYDION – ruling line of the Dukes of Alestron. The only old blood clansmen to maintain rule of their city through the uprising that defeated the rule of the high kings.

    pronounced: s'bride-ee-on

    root meaning: *baridien* – tenacity

SCIMLADE TIP – peninsula at the south-east corner of Alland, Shand.

    pronounced: skim-laid

    root meaning: *scimlait* – curved knife or scythe

SEARDLUIN – drake-spawned, vicious, intelligent cat-like predators that roved in packs whose hierarchy was arranged for ruthless and efficient slaughter of other living things. By the middle of the Second Age, they had been battled to extinction.

    pronounced: seerd-lwin

    root meaning: *seard* – bearded; *luin* – feline

SECOND AGE – Marked by the arrival of the Fellowship of Seven at Crater Lake, their called purpose to fight the drake spawn.

SETHVIR – Sorcerer of the Fellowship of Seven, served as Warden of Althain since the disappearance of the Paravians in the Third Age after the Mistwraith's conquest.

    pronounced: seth-veer

root meaning: *seth* – fact; *vaer* – keep

SELKWOOD – forest located in Alland, Shand.

    pronounced: sellk-wood

    root meaning: *selk* – pattern

SEVERNIR – river that once ran across the central part of Daon Ramon Barrens, Rathain. Diverted at the source after the Mistwraith's conquest, to run east into Eltair Bay.

    pronounced: se-ver-neer

    root meaning: *sevaer* – to travel; *nir* – south

s'FFALENN – family name for the royal line appointed by the Fellowship sorcerers in Third Age Year One to rule the High Kingdom of Rathain. Gifted geas: compassion/empathy.

    pronounced: fal-en

    root meaning: *ffael* – dark, *an* – one

s'GANNLEY family name for the line of Earls of the West, who stood as *caithdein* and stewards for the Kings of Tysan.

    pronounced: gan-lee

    root meaning: *gaen* – to guide; *li* – exalted, or in harmony

SHADDORN – trade city located on the Scimlade peninsula in Alland, Shand.

    pronounced: shad-dorn

    root meaning: *shaddiern* – a type of sea turtle

SHAND – High Kingdom on the south-east corner of the Paravian continent, originally ruled by the line of s'Ahelas. Device is falcon on a crescent moon, backed by purple and gold chevrons.

    pronounced: shand, as in 'hand'

    root meaning: *shiand* – two/pair

SHANDIAN – refers to nationality, being of the Kingdom of Shand.

    pronounced: shand-ee-an

    root meaning: *shand* – two

SHIP'S PORT – town on the coast of Eltair Bay located in West Halla, Melhalla.

SICKLE BAY – body of water located inside the Scimlade Peninsula in Alland, Shand.

s'ILESSID – family name for the royal line appointed by the Fellowship sorcerers in Third Age Year One to rule the High Kingdom of Tysan. Gifted geas: justice.

    pronounced: s-ill-ess-id

    root meaning: *liessiad* – balance

SITHAER – mythological equivalent of hell, halls of Dharkaron Avenger's judgement; according to Ath's adepts, that state of being where the prime vibration is not recognized.

    pronounced: sith-air

    root meaning: *sid* – lost; *thiere* – wraith/spirit

SKYRON FOCUS – large aquamarine focus-stone, used by the Koriani

Senior Circle for their major magic after the loss of the Great Waystone during the rebellion.

    pronounced: sky-run

    root meaning: *skyron* – colloquialism for shackle; *s'kyr'i'on* – literally 'sorrowful fate'

SKYSHIEL – mountain range that runs north to south along the eastern coast of Rathain.

    pronounced: sky-shee-el

    root meaning: *skyshia* – to pierce through; *iel* – light/ray

s'LORNMEIN – family name for the royal line appointed by the Fellowship sorcerers in Third Age Year One to rule the High Kingdom of Havish. Gifted geas: temperance.

    pronounced: s-lorn-main

    root meaning: *liernmein* – to centre, or restrain, or bring into balance

SORCERERS' PRESERVE – warded territory located by Teal's Gap in Tornir Peaks in Tysan where the Khadrim are kept confined by Fellowship magic.

STEIVEN – Earl of the North, *caithdein* and regent to the Kingdom of Rathain at the time of Arithon Teir's'Ffalenn's return. Chieftain of the Deshans until his death in the battle of Strakewood Forest. Jieret Red-beard's father.

    pronounced: stay-vin

    root meaning: *steiven* – stag

STORMWELL – Gulf of Stormwell, body of water off the northcoast of Tysan.

STRAKEWOOD – forest in the principality of Deshir, Rathain; site of the battle of Strakewood Forest.

    pronounced: strayk-wood, similar to 'stray wood'

    root meaning: *streik* – to quicken, to seed

SUN CHILDREN – translated term for Athlien Paravians.

SUN TOWERS – translated term for the Paravian keeps still standing on the site of the ruins of Ithamon in Daon Ramon Barrens, Rathain. See Ithamon.

s'VALERIENT – family name for the Earls of the North, regents and *caithdein* for the High Kings of Rathain.

    pronounced: val-er-ee-ent

    root meaning: *val* – straight; *erient* – spear

TAERLIN – south-western principality of Kingdom of Tysan. Also a lake of that name, Taerlin Waters in the southern spur of Tornir Peaks. Halliron teaches Arithon a ballad of that name, which is of Paravian origin, and which commemorates the First Age slaughter of unicorn herd by Khadrim.

    pronounced: tay-er-lin

root meaning: *taer* – calm; *lien* – to love

TAERNOND – forest in Ithilt, Rathain.

pronounced: tear-nond

root meaning: *taer* – calm; *nond* – thicket, copse

TAL QUORIN – river formed by the confluence of watershed on the southern side of Strakewood, principality of Deshir, Rathain, where traps were laid for Etarra's army in the battle of Strakewood Forest.

pronounced: tal quar-in

root meaning: *tal* – branch; *quorin* – canyons

TAL'S CROSSING – town at the branch in the trade road that leads to Etarra and south, and north-eastward to North Ward.

pronounced: tal to rhyme with 'pal'

root meaning: *tal* – branch

TALERA s'AHELAS – princess wed to the King of Amroth on the splinter world of Dascen Elur. Mother of Lysaer s'Ilessid, by her husband; mother of Arithon, through her adulterous liaison with the Pirate King of Karthan, Avar s'Ffalenn.

pronounced: tal-er-a

root meaning: *talera* – branch or fork in a path

TALITH – Lord Diegan's sister; betrothed lady of Lysaer s'Ilessid.

pronounced: tal-ith to rhyme with 'gal with'

root meaning: *tal* – branch; *lith* – to keep/nurture

TALLIARTHE – name given to Arithon's pleasure sloop by Feylind; in Paravian myth, a sea sprite who spirits away maidens who stray too near to the tide mark at twilight.

pronounced: tal-ee-arth

root meaning: *tal* – branch; *li* – exalted, in harmony; *araithe* – to disperse or to send

TASHAN – Elder on Maenalle's clan council, present at the raid on the Pass of Orlan.

pronounced: tash-an

root meaning: *tash* – swift, quick; *an* – one

TEAL's GAP – pass in the northern spur of Tornir Peaks in Tysan, which passes through the Sorcerers' Preserve.

pronounced: teel's gap

root meaning: *tielle* – ravine

TEIR – title fixed to a name denoting heirship.

pronounced: tay-er

root meaning: *teir's* – 'successor to power'

TELMANDIR – ruined city that once was the seat of the High Kings of Havish. Located in the principality of Lithmere, Havish.

pronounced: tell-man-deer

root meaning: *telman'en* – leaning; *dir* – rock

TELZEN – city on the coast of Alland, Shand, renowned for its lumber and saw millworks.

pronounced: tell-zen

root meaning: *tielsen* – to saw wood

THALDEINS – mountain range that borders the principality of Camris, Tysan, to the east. Site of the Camris clans' west outpost. Site of the raid at the Pass of Orlan.

pronounced: thall-dayn

root meaning: *thal* – head; *dein* – bird

THARIDOR – trade city on the shores of Instrell Bay in Melhalla.

pronounced: thar-i-door

root meaning: *tier'i'dur* – keep of stone

THARRICK – captain of the guard in the city of Alestron assigned charge of the duke's secret armoury.

pronounced: thar-rick

root meaning: *thierik* – unkind twist of fate

THIRD AGE – marked by the Fellowship's sealing of the compact with the Paravian races, and the arrival of Men to Athera.

TIENELLE – high altitude herb valued by mages for its mind-expanding properties. Highly toxic. No antidote. The leaves, dried and smoked, are most potent. To weaken its powerful side effects and allow safer access to its vision, Koriani enchantresses boil the flowers then soak tobacco leaves with the brew.

pronounced: tee-an-ell-e ('e' mostly subliminal)

root meaning: *tien* – dream; *iel* – light/ray

TIRANS – trade city in East Halla, Melhalla.

pronounced: tee-rans

root meaning: *tier* – to hold fast, to keep, to covet

TIRIACS – mountain range to the north of Mirthlvain Swamp, located in the principality of Midhalla, Kingdom of Melhalla.

pronounced: tie-ree-axe

root meaning: *tieriach* – alloy of metals

TORBRAND s'FFALENN – founder of the s'Ffalenn line appointed by the Fellowship of Seven to rule the High Kingdom of Rathain in Third Age Year One.

pronounced: tor-brand

root meaning: *tor* – sharp, keen; *brand* – temper

TORNIR PEAKS – mountain range on western border of the principality of Camris, Tysan. Northern half is actively volcanic, and there the last surviving packs of Khadrim are kept under ward.

pronounced: tor-neer.

root meaning: *tor* – sharp, keen; *nier* – tooth

TRAITHE – Sorcerer of the Fellowship of Seven. Solely responsible for the closing of South Gate to deny further entry to the Mistwraith. Traithe lost most of his faculties in the process, and was left with a limp. Since it is not known whether he can make the transfer into discorporate existence with his powers impaired, he has retained his physical body.

pronounced: tray-the

root meaning: *traithe* – gentleness

TYSAN – one of the Five High Kingdoms of Athera, as defined by the charters of the Fellowship of Seven. Ruled by the s'Ilessid royal line. Sigil: gold star on blue field.

pronounced: tie-san

root meaning: *tiasen* – rich

VALENDALE – river arising in the Pass of Orlan in the Thaldein Mountains, in the principality of Atainia, Tysan.

pronounced: val-en-dale

root meaning: *valen* – braided; *dale* – foam

VALENFORD – a city located in Taerlin, Tysan.

pronounced: val-en-ford

root meaning: *valen* – braided

VALLEYGAP – pass on the trade road between Etarra and Perlorn in the Kingdom of Rathain known for shale slides and raids

VALSTEYN – river which springs from the Mathorn Mountains in Rathain, and which crosses the Plain of Araithe.

pronounced: val-stain

root meaning: *valsteyne* – to meander

VASTMARK – principality located in southwestern Shand. Highly mountainous and not served by trade roads. Its coasts are renowned for shipwrecks. Inhabited by nomadic shepherds and wyverns, non-firebreathing, smaller relatives of Khadrim.

pronounced: vast-mark

root meaning: *vhast* – bare; *mheark* – valley

VERRAIN – spellbinder, trained by Luhaine; stood as Guardian of Mirthlvain when the Fellowship of Seven was left shorthanded after the conquest of the Mistwraith.

pronounced: ver-rain

root meaning: *ver* – keep; *ria* – touch; *an* – one original Paravian: verria'an

WARD – a guarding spell.

pronounced: as in English

root meaning: not from the Paravian

WARDEN OF ALTHAIN – alternative title for the Fellowship sorcerer, Sethvir.

WATERFORK – city located in Lithmere, Havish

WERPOINT – fishing town and outpost on the north east coast of Fallowmere, Rathain. Musterpoint for Lysaer's war host.

pronounced: were-point

root meaning: *wyr* – all/sum

WEST END – small merchant town in Korias, Tysan. Once was a great port, before the Mistwraith's invasion, but the loss of navigational arts set the city into decline.

WEST GATE PROPHECY – prophecy made by Dakar the Mad Prophet in Third Age Year 5061, which forecast the return of royal talent through the West Gate, and the bane of Desh-thiere and a return to untramelled sunlight.

WESTLAND SEA – body of water located off the west shore of the continent of Paravia.

WESTWOOD – forest located in Camris, Tysan, north of the Great West Road.

WHITEHOLD – city located on the coast of Eltair Bay in East Halla, Melhalla. Once saved from storm surge and flooding by a circle of Koriani Seniors.

WORLDSEND GATES – set at the four compass points of the continent of Paravia. These were spelled portals constructed by the Fellowship of Seven at the dawn of the Third Age, and were done in connection with the obligations created by their compact with the Paravian races which allowed men to settle on Athera.

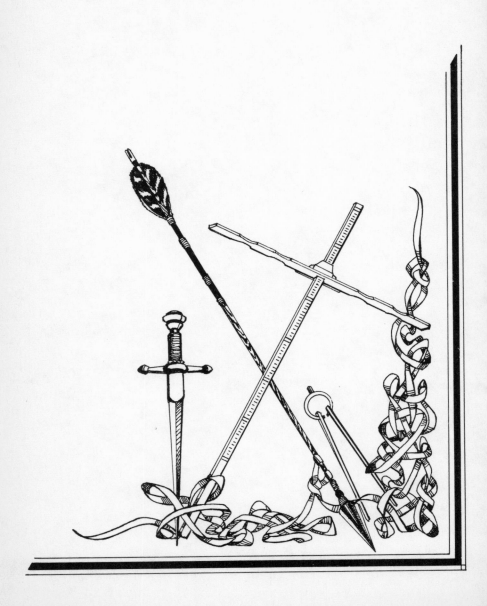